WHAT THE CRITICS SAY ABOUT *SINGLE*:-

'Succinct, authoritative dialogue is matched by an impressive narrative flair . . . I guarantee you'll be riveted all the way'
Cosmopolitan

'There's warmth . . . lustiness in encounters with lovers, and a pervasive sensuality throughout, all in a framework built by an accomplished storyteller. To be enjoyed'
Library Journal

'Follows in the tradition of Erica Jong's *Fear of Flying* and Lisa Alther's *Kinflicks* . . . crisp, witty and tightly written'
Newsagent and Bookshop

'Very real . . . She has written an entertaining novel about women who are not fighting for identity and sexual fulfilment, but who are surviving as mature and productive people'
Los Angeles Times

The author of this stunning book, Harriet Frank Jr., is an established figure on the Hollywood scene. As a screenwriter she has written, in collaboration with her husband, Irving Ravetch, starring roles for Paul Newman, Steve McQueen, John Wayne, Jon Voight, and Robert Mitchum in such films as *Hud*, *The Long Hot Summer*, *Conrack*, *Hombre* and *Home from the Hill*. The New York film critics gave *Hud* their Award for the Best Written Screenplay of 1963.

Also by Harriet Frank in Sphere Books:

SPECIAL EFFECTS

Single
HARRIET FRANK

SPHERE POPULAR CLASSICS

SPHERE BOOKS LIMITED

"I'll face the unknown.
I'll build a world of my own.
No one knows better than I myself
I'm by myself, alone."

from "By Myself," by Howard Dietz
and Arthur Schwartz

1

THE END of the affair seemed clearly in sight. It was plain when one's postcoital thoughts turned to hot buttered toast and strong black coffee. She longed for both, although the man asleep beside her had wonderful legs and beautiful muscles running down his back. Toast with jam. Thin toast. Strawberry jam with red perfect berries still tasting of the sun and sand they grew in. She yawned hugely and shifted away from Cass. He ground his teeth in some remote sleep-drenched confrontation. She sat up naked and chilled to study him. He did look charming, she gave him that. Dark hair, dark lashes, greedy face, stubborn mouth . . . boring, boringly young.

She slid from bed without waking him. She found her shoes and panties by the door and her dress draped over a chair. She smiled a little at the hasty carelessness of it all. She reached for her glasses on the bedside table and swore aloud as they eluded her blind groping.

"Where *are* the goddamn things?"

She found them, thrust them on and made for the bathroom, scratching absently.

She hated his taste in wallpaper. Some kind of an ethnic horror in black and brown. And the vanity of the little cub. She squinted at the vast array of lotions, the silk bathrobe, the English hairbrush, the water pick, the fistful of toothbrushes, the stationary bicycle, weapons clustered to defeat even the first feathery touch of age.

She was brutally indifferent to her own image in the glass. Large clear eyes, yes, woefully nearsighted. A long nose, straight, rather distinguished. A mouth hinting of appetite — men looked at it first and lingered on it. Too strong a chin, a jutting chin that warned of strong opinion strongly expressed. The body was nothing much, tall, flat, robust. She had warned lovers on occasion that sex for her was largely in the mind. She knew a hundred and fifty witty dirty limericks. She had read yards of erotic Japanese literature. She was curious, inventive, athletic, tireless. What they heard whispered in the dark often startled them.

She selected a toothbrush at random, scrubbed, spat. A fling of cold water, her fingers raked through her short hair, a cigarette butt plucked from an overflowing ashtray completed her morning ablutions. She lit the stub, her eyes narrowing against the sting of the smoke.

"Nell?"

"In here."

"It's five-thirty, for Christ's sake."

"Six."

His tone was hostile. "Aren't you even going to take a goddamn bath?"

"At home."

"Why do you always light out of here like you'd stolen the silver?"

She walked back into the bedroom, crossed it with rapid strides and hunkered by the bed.

"Go back to sleep. If you still feel lousy, if you're still coughing, come into the office and let me look at you. Drink some orange juice."

He raised himself on one arm and looked at her, smoothing his hair, devoted to his appearance, preening. "Where are you going?"

She was soothing and patient. "Where I go every day. To work." Her hand went out and touched his face. "A little fever, maybe. Take your temperature."

He pushed away from her fretfully. "I'm sick."

"Not very."

"I'm sick of this fucking affair."

"Ah," she said mildly, "that's something else again." She stabbed the cigarette out neatly.

"You're a crazy woman in the dark, and in the morning — cold haddock."

"Mmm." She was struggling into her jacket. "Well, at night I'm in heat, and in the morning clear-eyed and surfeited."

"Nell, come in here."

"Take some aspirin. Two. Three. Can't hurt."

"I don't want aspirin. I want a stud fee."

She was at the door. "I'm your doctor. You don't pay your bill. I'm taking it out in trade."

She was gone.

She drove too fast with the windows down. The smog already smudged the sky, dimming the California sun. She listened to the news briefly, switched to the delicate melancholy of a Schubert sonata. She was reminded again of the pleasures of being alone, of letting her thoughts spool lazily like threads unwinding. One had to be eccentric or old to respect that profound inner quiet she found so delicious. That was the joy of living with William. Her grandfather had a positive mania for stillness. Long, silent meals. Evenings washing over them as they sat side by side in the garden, the old stone wall tangled in grass and ivy, the final night call of a dove pulsating just before dark. Then when the conversation came it was heated, spiced, a fencing match.

Well, it was peace no longer. He had shattered it. She put the thought aside, vowing to deal with it later and to deal with it harshly.

It was then she saw the apartment. I hope it's bloody expensive, she thought. I'll make him pay for at least half.

It was a ridiculous building, all jutting corners and glaring glass, set in a contrived crush of trees and flowers, but there was the smell of the sea in the air and beyond a stingy strip of beach. She parked her car and approached it cautiously, peering into the huge courtyard. Three swimming pools steamed into the morning air, all shaped like kidneys and all a poisonous blue. And be damned if there weren't waterfalls spilling from hidden pipes into concrete troughs. It was an amusement park Eden, the hibiscus grossly enlarged, the fir trees pitifully stunted. Above her a banner waved in the breeze, promising nirvana: MARINA ONE. SAUNA, TENNIS, POOLS, HAWAIIAN WATERFALLS, PRIVATE PATIOS, THE GOOD LIFE, SINGLES ONLY.

He was sitting in a deck chair, a dog asleep on his chest. He was unshaven, his skin deeply tanned. She ticked him off instantly: lazy, likely to run to fat, lecherous. She deduced the last by the long, nimble look he gave her, stopping short of her face.

"You have an apartment for rent?"

"Yes, ma'am."

"I'd like to see it."

He unwound himself from the chair, hoisted the pup under his arm. "You ever live in a singles apartment before?"

"No. Never before."

She was already poised on the edge of displeasure, sniffing the insistence of next-door neighbors, the pressures of intimacy with no possibility of escape; life without the blessed dignity of the closed door.

"They're a mixed bunch. I've got 'em divorced, I've got 'em dumped, I've got 'em suicidal. The noise level is high, the turnover rapid and the atmosphere unbuttoned. You sure it's your dish?"

"We'll see." She shoved her glasses up into her hair. "Are you the owner?"

"Jake Cooley," he said.

"Do you live here yourself?"

Doubtless he did, in a welter of dirty shorts, dog-eared books, crushed beer cans and the faded scent of someone's perfume on the pillow slip. Would there be something singular? — a bust of Lord Byron, a collection of Baudelaire?

"Top floor," he was saying. "The rent's six hundred and twenty a month, first and last in advance."

"Fair enough," she said. "I'm Dr. Willis. Good morning." She held out her hand.

4

"Pleased to meet you, doctor. It's upstairs, next to mine."

The tiles of the kitchen were a shade of pink she particularly loathed, the insistent color of dime-store nail polish, English pastries, the nervous rose flush of menopause. She let him precede her through the apartment; he kept the little dog tucked under his arm and its tail thumped against his stained and worn chinos. He had not shaved. He had the look of a castaway prepared to be amiable to the natives and to survive at all costs.

She paused to rap on the wall. "Paper thin," she observed. She passed by him into the bathroom. One glance sufficed.

"The toilet bowl is unspeakable." she said pleasantly, "and the stain on the bedroom wall is unmistakably semen."

He shook his head. "He was an untidy fellow. People don't have much respect for the places they live in. They mostly rut and eat and relieve themselves and call it home."

"Apparently." She made for the window and strained at it, but it was jammed shut. She slammed her palm against it until it gave. "A little soap would help," she suggested.

"Never thought of it," he told her complaisantly.

She thrust her head out. There was only the merest wedge of blue visible from her vantage point, as if someone had torn a scrap of cloth and let it fly like blue silk into the wind. But the air was salubriously full of salt and foam, the landscape recalled Antibes and a large white sail suddenly floated by, a stately swan on a pond, its canvas flapping and cracking loudly, making her throat tighten with its spank and flair.

She turned back into the room. "It's not a generous view but I like it." She paused a moment and studied him. "Now about me, Mr. Cooley. I'm not convivial. I don't want to meet airline pilots. I'm neither predatory nor frustrated. If you'll paint this room white and put a dead bolt on the door, I'll take it."

"Well," he said, "you should lend a note of class to the place." He rocked on his heels in front of her. "Doctor, huh? What kind of a doctor would that be?"

"I'm a medical doctor. I practice internal medicine. My specialty is gastrointestinal problems. Gut aches and the like."

"My Aunt Fergus was a veterinarian. I guess that's as close as we come to medicine in my family. A very determined woman, my Aunt Fergus. Unmarried and hell on bores, deadbeats and mankind in general."

"She sounds very sensible to me," Nell said.

"When will you be moving in?"

"Tomorrow."

"I'll get right on it. White paint, you said."

"Pristine white."

"There's one other thing."

"And what's that?" she asked, jingling her car keys impatiently.

"I'm an insomniac. Every once in a while I'll be cooking myself ravioli at three in the morning or playing some Beethoven on the record player. If that doesn't work I do a couple of laps in the pool. It could be at any time of the night."

"I'm not easily bothered," she said, "and you might try some calcium for sleep."

She started down the stairs. He called after her, leaning over the balcony. "I have a poker game every Monday night. The boys drink a little beer. Sometimes they raise a ruckus if the cards aren't falling just right. Nothing mean, but they cuss and break up some of the furniture."

She stopped on the landing and looked back up at him. "I'll be out Monday nights."

He wasn't talked out. "My Uncle Tyler, that's my uncle on my mother's side, used to say look before you leap. It wasn't original with him but he sure as hell said it often enough."

She smiled. "And did he?"

"No, ma'am. He just put his head down and rammed on ahead."

"You have interesting relatives, Mr. Cooley. I'll see you tomorrow." She waved and went. He pulled his nose thoughtfully and watched her go until she was out of sight.

His house had a dry, sweet smell as if someone had crushed lavender in its dark hallways. Her room on the third floor was shabby and old-fashioned, the walls faded to the color of honey,

6

the bed narrow, lumpy and virginal. She had never tired of the delights of it, the sagging bookshelves, the painted furniture, the chair broken to suit her posture, the smell of ink drying in a pot beside a pen that scratched fiercely, the mirror dim and scored with age cracks, the bunch of pinks or geraniums she had jammed into an empty pickle jar.

Here she had lived, slept, studied, nearsighted, gnawing on her glasses. Here she had wept, raged. Here she had fantasized, stuporous, on long summer days: a man's mouth, a hand between her legs, her own mouth moving, roving.

He sat in a chair and watched her. She searched his face for any sign of regret and saw that it was as remote and composed as always.

She stripped the room methodically in her mind's eye, angrily removing every trace of her long stay there. What would it look like with the books, the Daumier drawings, the Chinese vase, the scrap of Oriental carpet, the tennis rackets all flung without care into boxes and cartons and hauled away? She fought down the annoying sting of tears and opted instead for anger.

"You're a bastard, throwing me out like this. You really are."

He folded his fine, delicate hands and remained silent, heavy, preoccupied.

"You're the only man I ever loved."

His voice when he spoke was dry. "You've been in a dozen beds, my girl."

"Two dozen. Anyway, where's your sense of responsibility?"

He remained silent. She emptied her drawers in an untidy flood, tangled the clothes and dumped them into a suitcase. "Besides," she fumed, "you *need* me. How are you going to live without me? You're chronically absent-minded. You don't balance your checkbook. You dribble cigar ashes on your shirt. You smell like a zoo unless I remind you to bathe. Ugh. You're disgusting."

"Not entirely."

She turned on him, studied his face with desperate intensity. "You'll fall down and break a hip," she threatened. "You'll become reclusive. You'll eat candy all day long and become diabetic."

"None of these things."

She floundered for a weapon. "You'll be lonely."

He closed his eyes to ward her off, a trick of his that maddened her.

"I warn you," she said, breathless for battle, "you'll turn to religion."

"Unlikely."

He rose then, a tall, spare figure, fine head, white hair. It seemed grotesque to her; he looked like a young man fresh from the hands of a make-up artist, made up to resemble an old one. For one moment she felt what it would be like to lay her head against his chest, to feel his hand heavy on her head.

"Turn loose, Nell," he said. "You're too long in the tooth to be sequestered with an old man. It's unnatural, it's regressive, and besides you wake me when you roll home, damp and still tumescent from your current lover."

"I'll give him up," she said promptly.

"Mama's girl — possibly, if she were still alive. Daddy's girl — absurd at your age. Grandpa's girl — totally neurotic, my dear."

"But you sweet old cock," she murmured, "I love you. I like talking to you or even being talked at by you. You're sensible. You're undemanding. You're witty — quite often. You're even handsome, in a desiccated kind of way."

"I want to live alone," he said stubbornly. "I want to prepare for what must be my imminent end. I want you to go forth."

She slammed a suitcase shut. "I'm deflowered. I'm independent. What more do you want from me?"

"I'm very old. You need to let go. Anyway, you're moody. Untidy. We have political arguments. You avenge yourself on me for every man who bores or annoys you."

"You'll take up with a Pasadena widow, damn it! You'll leave all your money to someone else." She bit her lip to stop a sudden childish tremor.

He picked up a silver-framed picture of himself she had thrown into a cardboard carton. "That was taken fifty years ago, at the peak of my virility. Leave the damn thing behind."

She snatched it back from him. "You have no family feeling. Your arteries are hard. *You're* hard."

She was being rancorous now. He disdained it. "This place you're moving to. You say it's by the sea?"

"It's one of those damn fool singles places where I'll undoubtedly drown in the tears of the divorced ladies wailing through the night."

"You're single," he said flatly. "You belong there."

"You don't draw blood that way. Better try something else."

"You're overbearing."

"Better. What else?"

Long afterward she would remember the concern in his voice. "You're incomplete, my love."

The barb landed. She gathered up her coat and glanced once more around the room. She made up her mind there would be no further outbursts.

"What final word of wisdom?"

"Come back Saturday night. We'll play chess."

She grabbed him in a crushing embrace. "Stay alive," she commanded, and ran before he could deny her.

Nell attracted strays. Ellen, her office nurse, was first among them, a thin frantic woman given to head colds and girlish crushes. She was a model of efficiency in the office and the lab, one of life's victims otherwise, defensive of Nell to the point of obsession. She knitted Nell scratchy afghans, put a comic valentine on her desk and presented sugary fudge at Christmas. She blushed deeply and frequently. She carried a wad of damp Kleenex clutched in her hand. She was a cross to bear.

"Dr. Steinberg's waiting for you. He's been on a rampage ever since he got in." Her voice was a wet whisper. "He's already fired the new lab girl and he called a collection agency — a *collection* agency — to handle this office. He said if the patients didn't start paying their bills he'd haul their . . . their . . ."

9

"Asses," Nell prompted gently.

". . . into court."

Nell put a comforting arm around the woman's shoulder. "I think that's dandy. Let's give him a list of my deadbeats, too."

"You wouldn't do a thing like that, Dr. Willis. Your patients adore you."

"Where is he?"

"In his office. With Mrs. Katz."

She walked toward Amos' office, led by the rancid smell of his cheap cigars. She heard his voice raised through the closed door.

"Take off the goddamn weight. Stop telling me it's your thyroid. Your thyroid is the only normal thing about you. You're fat because you eat like a pig. Go take those piss shots those phony Beverly Hills doctors give you. Pay through the snout. But don't come whining to me about palpitations. I've got really sick people to deal with."

She waited outside, lounging against the wall till the wave broke over Mrs. Katz.

"Stop crying, for Christ's sake. Minnie, stop, or I'll tweak your tit. Now, listen. Eight hundred calories. No strudel. No chicken fat. No little nosh during Johnny Carson. I want to see you in six weeks. If you haven't lost that lard by then I'm sending you to a shrink. He'll ask you how you and Marvin shtup, Minnie. He'll talk about oral sex. You won't like it, Minnie, so do what I tell you."

Mrs. Katz, a tremulous, tear-stained mountain, stumbled out. "Dr. Willis," she said, grasping at Nell, "your partner's crazy. He's a crazy man. If shouting and yelling were malpractice you'd be in plenty of trouble."

Nell clucked and soothed. "It's only his manner. Another visit or two and you'll be used to him. We've all had to go through it."

"My daughter's marrying a ballet dancer next week. A skinny nebbish with long yellow hair. A boy in tights with cotton padding you know where. Who wouldn't eat? Of course I eat. I'm nothing but nerves — *hungry* nerves."

"Get in here, Nell. I want to talk to you." Amos loomed upon them. "You still here?"

"I'm going, Dr. Steinberg. Maybe I'm going to another doctor."

"Go. In good health."

He grabbed Nell and pulled her through the door, slamming it in Mrs. Katz's astonished face.

Nell took out a cigarette and perched on the edge of the desk. "Don't smoke in my presence."

She lit it nonetheless and expelled a long stream in his direction, studying him.

He was a bear of a man, hairy, pugnacious, solid as a house. He had the dark, angry look of his parents, patrician Jewish refugees who lived in Oriental splendor in Bel Air. They took tea in the afternoon under the brooding gaze of a Rembrandt of dubious authenticity. They played chamber music together and grew monstrous mauve orchids and battened on their only son. He remained unmarried, dutiful, enraged.

He slammed into a chair, thrust his feet up on his desk and glared at her.

"You fucked your brains out last night, didn't you? I can tell. You only get that pinched look when you've gone down on somebody."

"You're charming this morning."

"Tell me about it." He put his fingertips together and bared his teeth.

"Amos, what's on your mind?"

"I've got a problem."

"Like what?"

He began to hook paper clips together. He stared at the ceiling. He got up and walked to the window.

"I got you through school. Right? I pushed you. I hammered facts into your head. I cut up your cadavers. I gave you beautiful lecture notes. I held your head when you puked on rounds. I fell in love with you."

"All of that and more."

She remembered him as he was then, hollow-eyed, brilliant, erratic. She remembered the long Sunday dinners, with his mother seated regally at the head of the table, his father docilely at the foot. She remembered the table gleaming with silver almost too heavy to lift, the room dark at noon with rose velvet drapes, the funereal bouquets hinting at death approaching. She remembered Amos carefully placing her in his life.

"My best friend, this clever little shiksa," he had told his parents. "Very smart for a goya. Top of her class. Behind me. But *just* behind."

"Not married?" That had been a little tug at the oedipal string from Mama.

"Not married."

"A lovely young woman like you."

"He only wants to sleep with me, Mrs. Steinberg," she had told her. "Not to worry."

His father had hidden a nervous laugh in his napkin.

He had never taken her there again. Later, when they'd opened their office together, his mother had come bringing an exquisite Georgian inkstand. She had even conferred a dry, powdery kiss on her cheek. It had been a gesture of alliance. Two practical women, one to nurture his work, one to bind him close with delicate, age-spotted hands.

His voice interrupted the reverie.

"Nell," he said suddenly, "I've been messing around. With a sixteen-year-old girl yet."

"As I recall," she told him, "you graduated cum laude. Messing around? Surely you can command the language with more accuracy than that."

"All right, I'm involved with a nubile, silken, rather vicious brat, a nymphet, if you will, a half-ripened peach. Daphne fleeing an overheated Apollo. A child of the times, avid, expert, oh, how expert, with just the merest touch of venereal disease."

"Are you telling me you have the clap?"

"Lower your voice," he said, "and be supportive for a change. I'm coming into your office for a shot."

"You're *not.*"

"Well — I can't reach my own left buttock — and I'm sure as hell not going to the Free Clinic."

She clucked censoriously. "Congress with minors? At your age?"

"It would never have happened if you'd let me into your bed."

"No excuse, Amos."

"Are you going to help or no?"

"Certainly. I'll paint your balls as blue as a Mediterranean sky."

He was suddenly meek. "I'll take your night calls for a month."

She regarded him thoughtfully for a moment. The fact was he could easily give himself the shot, attend to himself quietly and discreetly, with no fuss. But it was necessary for him to let her know that he had a life independent of the one they shared in the office, that he slept with young girls, allowed them to infect him. It was perverse, altogether like him.

She held out her hand. "Come on."

He yelped with pain at the needle. "Christ, woman, all that training and you haven't learned how to throw a shot without maiming a man?"

"Consider it penance."

He sat on her examining table with his pants drooping forlornly at his knees, piteous, Chaplin without comedy.

"What do you know about passion?" he accused her. "You're a cold cunt. I know how you live. You hunt the pack like a hound, cut one out, cut one up, and you're gone."

"Not so. My intimate friends remain my friends. Cry on my shoulder. Borrow my money."

"You want to know how it happened?"

"No."

"She looked like you must have at that age."

"She certainly didn't behave like I did at that age. At that age all I did was read Virginia Woolf and masturbate to Mozart. It's spoiled me for everything else since, too."

He pulled up his pants and marched to the door. "I want to be around when it happens to you."

"When what happens, Amos?"

"When someone hits a vital nerve. When someone melts the ice."

"I expect I'll make an absolute spectacle of myself. Witless, defenseless, depraved, despondent. Everything you could possibly hope for."

"Now you're sore." He came back and draped his arms around her in a brotherly hug.

She broke free of him and opened the door, waving him through it. "Kindly go to work," she told him.

She refused a heavy patient load for herself. She insisted on having enough time for each case. The speed with which most medical care was given offended her deeply. The most endearing thing about Amos was his total support.

"No factory medicine. No assembly line medicine. I don't have to drive a Jaguar and you don't need charge accounts at Saks. No unnecessary lab work, no thirty-dollar vitamin shots, no placebos. But keep up, Nell. Read the journals. Burn the midnight oil. I'm going to know if you goof because I'm a very hotshot doctor."

They had been in partnership for a month when they went a hundred thousand dollars into debt, sued successfully by a middle-aged woman with greasy yellow bangs and a mild case of anemia. Nell had administered a few iron shots which had caused some yellow splotches on her buttock and had, her attorney told the court passionately, repulsed the woman's husband, leaving her rejected, crying out in the night, pleading for sexual sustenance; vainly, vainly, for he, the husband, revolted to the very depths of his being by those rust-colored stains on that (already) wrinkled ass, refused ever again to perform his marital duty, could not, in point of fact, your honor, with the best will in the world, get it up anymore.

But Amos remained strong in those early days. "Never mind, we'll get 'em," he had told her with his arrogant German Jewish confidence. "Word'll get out that we make house calls. Where are they going to find medics like that, Nell?"

"On the soap operas," she told him.

They had located under the freeway near the old soldiers' hospital in Sawtelle. There are plenty of specialists in Los Angeles and Westwood and Beverly Hills, Amos told her; we're needed here. So they had settled in a low stucco building among the Japanese truck gardens and the Japanese nurseries and the Shinto temples north of Sepulveda Boulevard, and they drew students from U.C.L.A., pensioners from the large English colony in Santa Monica, beach people from Venice, the shy, elderly ones and the dazed hippies, the runaways, the junkies and winos. The nucleus of their practice remained the demanding, querulous friends of Mr. and Mrs. Steinberg, Senior, with their fading memories of Vienna and Berlin and Budapest, flickering out as the years passed in this new, barbarous, unlettered country.

She faced one of them across her desk.

"Pacemaker? I don't understand." Mrs. Lowenthal laced her fingers together tensely.

Nell came around and drew up a chair beside her. She untangled the old woman's hands and held one firmly in hers.

"Did you go to the Horowitz concert, Eda?"

The woman was diverted, her face glowing. "The man is a poet. Sublime."

"And you? You practice every day?"

"No more. I can't. These days I'm helpless. Exhausted. You know."

"That's why we're talking about a pacemaker. To give you back your music."

"Where does it go?"

"Into your chest. A wonderfully skilled team of doctors implants it. Your heart will beat normally again, you'll have your strength back, and you'll play beautiful afternoon concerts for me and everyone who loves you."

"A mechanical doll. I'll be a wound-up toy."

"You'll be a woman of sixty-five with a future. You won't be tired anymore. You'll buy me a very expensive present and tell everyone I'm a genius."

"I know a lawyer who is just forty and very well off. Come to tea. He's looking for a wife."

"I've already had a lawyer, dear Mrs. Lowenthal. I'm looking for a tinker now, a tailor, a cowboy, a sailor."

Mrs. Lowenthal was confused. Nell abandoned her slight joke.

"Bring George with you next Wednesday. I'll arrange with him about the surgery, about your care."

"George. George sits in the garden by the summerhouse, reading Balzac. If I die, he'll look up with his finger still on the page."

"We'll do it without him."

Mrs. Lowenthal bent a pale, probing gaze on Nell. "You stay alone. Unmarried. By your own choice. What is it like to live like that?"

"I hesitate to inflict," she told her, "and I don't want to be afflicted. There's some pride involved. Some regret. Some gloom. An occasional triumph. It's I who read in the garden without looking up."

Mrs. Lowenthal nodded. "The lawyer I was speaking of, he's not interesting enough for you. I'll look further."

Nell laughed. "If you do, I like the kind that come out from under the rocks."

"Pardon? Pardon? I don't understand."

"I don't either." Nell linked her arm through the woman's and guided her to the door.

"I was alone one summer in Paris," Mrs. Lowenthal mused. "I sat under the trees in the late afternoon. I drank wine. I let a very young boy take me home. I never saw him after that night. I didn't care. That one night was enough. They're afraid to let you know how nice that is — to do what you want, to surrender, without guilt, freely." She patted Nell's face. "I'm not afraid of that thing anymore, that pacemaker. Thank you." She was gone.

Nell went back to her desk, pushed the clutter of papers aside, swung her feet up and folded her hands behind her head. She felt agitated as she always did when confronted by the frailty of what she dealt with. A mechanical box in the chest, and if it didn't work a sudden stabbing pain, a dark murmuring somewhere in the body, and all that vibrated and defied would be stilled.

She decided to prescribe for herself. A long walk, a hot fudge sundae, the expensive Watteau drawing she coveted in a Rodeo Street gallery. She shrugged them off impatiently. Cass's head between her legs, a healthy smell of warm skin, her own mouth offering feverish service. That was better, better, best.

She gave in to caprice and reached for the phone.

He was slow to answer but she waited him out patiently.

"You were lying out by the pool, naked as a jaybird," she told him, "and now you have a warm groin from all that sun and a mind full of obscene conjectures."

"What the hell! — is that you, Nell?"

"If I were there right now," she breathed, "what could I do to you if I were there right now, my randy friend?"

"What you're doing *now* is a helluva thing to do to me. I've got an erection so big it's knocking this phone off the hook."

"My new address is Marina One. Apartment twenty-three. I'm moving in today after we close the office. Come over tonight. I'll have the pictures up and the bed made."

"We'll do something dirty," he said jauntily.

"I doubt it," she countered. "You have such a paucity of imagination."

"And what's that supposed to mean?"

"It's youth, mostly," she sighed. "Never mind. I'll think up something for both of us. Don't come before nine unless you want to line shelves." She hung up.

At the big house she was ruthless, a rampaging Genghis Khan. The moving men stood in awe as she prowled through the rooms ticking off what she wanted. Her grandfather's housekeeper, Mrs. Keitel, watched, her stern bony face wearing the look of a woman suffering rape. Nell had never liked her. She had the fussy possessive air of a nanny. She warred against dirt, disdained aesthetics (flowers shed petals, sunlight faded carpets) and she talked to herself and God in a harsh New England twang.

"Those things are your grandfather's," she snapped as Nell waved the George the Second table, the blue delft jar, the Victorian armchair into the brawny arms of the waiting men.

"All too good for him," Nell said. "All he requires is a narrow bed, a bowl for gruel, a Gregorian chant and your nasty cooking to be completely blissful. I'm going into the kitchen now." And she stalked past the hapless woman.

"I'll take the Crown Derby, too." She opened the china cabinet and scanned the delicious porcelain like a child at a candy counter. "Two plates from the Lowestoft. That heavenly blue. And all the Meissen dessert plates. And the Baccarat crystal, and the plates from Provence for breakfast and the Sabatier knives and the French copper pots and the Peking glass for roses. Now, linens!"

The woman pursued her, her face flushed and frantic. "You're not leaving us a thread!"

Nell paid no attention to her; she was now focused on the linens. "Let him sleep on nails. Porthault? No. Vulgar." She pushed a pile aside. "I'll take the Irish with the crochet edging. I like linen that crackles when you make love on it, don't you, Mrs. Keitel?"

She heard the little gasp and she grinned. "Clearly, you're repelled by talk of the flesh, but I'm moving out, Mrs. Keitel, so now it can be all New Testament and leftover lamb soup in this house."

"Running off and leaving him," the woman muttered darkly.

"*Thrown* out. But never mind. Now, listen. If anything troubles him, the slightest cough, the smallest pain, you call me. I'm leaving him in your care, but reluctantly, and only because he insists. But you *watch* him, do you hear?"

"Your voice is loud enough. Of course, I hear."

"And pray that nothing happens to him, because if it does, the first thing, the *very* first thing I'll do is throw you in the street, and your Bible and your wretched baggage after you."

Alone, she looked about the drawing room, the room that held so much of her history. She remembered being brought here long ago. Her grandfather had come to the funeral wearing a black suit and a look very far removed from melancholy. Surely he grieved for her departed parents, but he seemed instead like a man putting aside a fettering role.

"You'll like living with me," he had told her. "I'm extremely permissive, enlightened and modern and I will treat you like the adult I see you are."

"How soon can I smoke?" she had asked him promptly.

"Is that the only vice that occurs to you?"

"I bet you know about all of them." She had put an arm through his then and walked from the cemetery without a backward glance.

"I do know all the vices," he had told her over tea, "but I choose mine carefully." He hovered over a tray of pastries presented by the waitress. "Just as I choose a little cake. The one which pleases me. The one that will just suffice but not surfeit. Do you follow?"

"I'm glad they died," she had said suddenly.

"And why is that?" He was grave but not shocked.

"They only loved each other. Mama told me once that my father came first . . . and he said the same thing. Do you have anyone else who will come first?"

"Not a soul."

"Then *I'll* be first." She was positive and assured.

She had commanded him from that day to this but now, powers failing, he had begun to turn away. Damn him. After she had spent so many years beguiling and entertaining him.

Well, she had thoroughly looted the house, realizing all the while that she held a forlorn hope he would pursue his goods and chattels. Grasping at straws. Asinine waste of time.

"Be careful of that vase. I intend to put my own ashes in it one day."

The moving men stared at her in horror.

She fled the house.

Marina One in the late afternoon bustled in anticipation like a beehive, murmurous, swarming. Already some of the tenants leaned over their balconies, glasses in hand, shirts wrenched open, ties askew, as if they had all survived a peril-torn journey home. Smoke rose here and there from stoked barbecues; blood red meat and charcoal assaulted the air. Somewhere a wind chime evoked a gentler garden and in the pool a pretty girl swam, her hair spread around her like a golden flower.

Jake Cooley watched Nell direct the movers, a curt general with no time to waste.

"I see you got here all right. Give you a hand?"

"No, thank you, Mr. Cooley. I'm paying thirty dollars an hour for the brawn you see."

"Well, if you want a cup of coffee, the pot's always on the back of the stove. I polish off about twenty cups a day myself."

"That's nineteen too many. Think of your nervous system, Mr. Cooley."

"Steady as can be." He lingered for another moment. "I'm putting a steak on about seven-thirty, nicely marbled and weighing two pounds. Cut you off a slice if you care to stop by."

"I plan to be too tired to eat. Thanks just the same."

He was unoffended. "You don't have to be neighborly in a hurry," he said. "Or at all. Everybody can graze their own piece of range. But I'm getting tired of cropping the grass by myself, so I thought I'd ask."

He looked at her amiably. She found that she liked his lazy good humor. "Ask again," she said, and hurried up the stairs after the two lumbering men, warning them that anything they broke, they would have to pay for. They said something profane and she answered in kind. By five o'clock they were gone, leaving a cigarette butt ground into the carpet and a bill of startling proportions.

She dispersed her possessions as quickly as she could unpack them, with her easy flair for things in their proper places. The small sang de boeuf vase near the large Sung bowl, a drop of blood against the snow. The leather-bound books were stacked carelessly on the table, three drawings grouped beside them, another standing on the floor just because she liked it that way. Let the lamplight strike the worn upholstery of the Directoire chair. Worn things had a kind of grace that pleased her. She would wax the table tomorrow. None of those nasty quick polishes but a slow sensuous rubbing with English wax. She would buy flowers, white narcissus and white tulips and bugger the cost. She would buy everything for a finicky, fastidious dinner, trout, endive, Vouvray because Colette had mentioned it once in a favorite novel. And cleansing powder and ammonia and a stiff scrubbing brush for that elemental sense of order in her soul.

"Very elegant. Very tasteful."

She turned to see a man lounging in the door she had left ajar.

He was small and thin to the point of emaciation. He wore a waistcoat which immediately delighted her; it was Edwardian and flowered, a fantasy waistcoat with embroidery and gilt buttons. He had a long slim throat like a ballerina's and balanced on it a hatchet-sharp face and strange dog-brown eyes.

"Devon Scott," he said. "Peeping Tom and neighbor."

She wavered between good manners and a sense of outraged privacy. Crouching on the floor, surrounded by books, she was put at a disadvantage. It was difficult to stand on one's dignity kneeling.

"If you leave your door open around here it is taken as an invitation to drop in."

"Well, if those are the rules of the game — "

He advanced, ferreting out the best chair and settling in with a satisfied air. With a slight groan Nell rose to her feet and made a tidying pass at her disheveled hair.

"Am I intruding?"

"Not at all — but as I haven't been to the market yet, all I can offer you is a glass of reconstituted orange juice or an apple with one bite already taken out of it."

"I'll tell you what brought me. I saw the movers bring in all those beautiful things and I had to see who they belonged to. Childish curiosity but I always try to satisfy it. Are you nosy at all?"

"I sometimes read other people's mail if they're foolish enough to leave it lying around."

"The fact is we all huddle together in this place. We wander around like spirits any time of day or night, scratching on doors, making tribal circles around that barbecue pit out there, having intimacies over the washing machine, passion in the Jacuzzi, borrowing booze, sharing beds. Have you ever seen starlings perched on a telephone pole at dusk? No song, no flight, just a silent gathering? Well, welcome to the wire. Welcome to Marina One. We'll all move down one and make a place for you."

"I hope I don't frighten the flock," she said.

"You can always pound on a wall and someone will come running. We lend money to each other on demand, dry tears, remember birthdays."

"Mine's next month — but I don't celebrate them anymore."

"You needn't mingle if you don't care to. Instant friendship is like instant pudding, synthetic, tasteless, artifically flavored. But no one makes the real thing anymore."

He was obviously a nice little man, living on the fringe of things, needful, speaking to people at bus stops, at concerts, at monuments, holding doors ajar, assisting with packages, terrified at being anonymous — no need to fend him off.

"Come visit again," she said. "As soon as I'm settled. I'll make a great effort."

"You won't regret it," he beamed. "I'm amusing, a superior cook and as faithful as an old dog."

She called Cass and put him off, suddenly desperate for sleep and solitude. She was enclosed and lost in a dream of Roman streets and extravagant Italian glances with men in pink shirts floating after her with cries of "Bella, bella, Signora," when the pounding on the door awakened her. She put on the light, squinted at her watch, saw that it was approaching four and groaned aloud.

"Doc? Doc? You in there? You awake?"

"What is it? Who in hell is it?"

"Jake Cooley."

Crossly she stumbled out of bed, tangled hopelessly in a robe which seemed to have seven sleeves.

"What in God's green name?" She thrust a pugnacious face out into the dark.

"I got an emergency."

"My partner is taking my calls," she said fuzzy with sleep.

"I'm sorry to bust in but I've got a tenant in a little trouble."

"Do you know it isn't four yet?"

"Yep. It's early and it's cold, but this little gal is in some kind of a fix. Her roomie called me. She's doubled up and hurting."

"Why don't you roust out her own doctor at this ungodly hour?"

"She hasn't got one. Aren't you up to the Hippocratic oath this early?"

"Just barely. Let me get my bag."

She followed him out into the fog and chill of the dark morning. Lights still burned throughout the building. Unaccountably she noticed that Cooley's bathrobe had the legend "Swanson's Gym" across the back and that his legs, visible beneath it, were strong and hairy. She was conscious of her own utilitarian flannel and the messy flopping of her worn-out mules.

"I see you wash your face before you go to bed," he told her, as though reading her thoughts. "I like a clean face on the pillow, myself."

"You'll forgive me if I don't make small talk," she said. They cut across the tennis courts and past the kidney-shaped pool.

"It was just a passing observation," he said. "Doesn't require any comment if you don't care to make one."

They raced across the grass side by side. It was soaked with dew.

"These two women live together," he told her. "Hortense and Eunice. Black and white. Nothing complicated — they just split the rent. The black woman's head is where it ought to be. The other one lives in a tree."

He pounded along the walkway. She had to run to keep up. Somewhere a window was flung open and a complaining voice ordered them to "Button your lip out there, for Christ's sake, I'm trying to get some sleep!"

The woman who opened the door to them was all bone and angle and towering height. Close up, Nell saw that her face had the planes of a Congo Kinshasa tribal mask, strong vertical lines for brows, a downward slash for the mouth, skin the shade of dusky blue plums. Her voice was deep, sure, flat.

"Everything's coming unglued in here. She's sick as a dog."

Jack indicated Nell. "It's okay, Horty, I got an M.D. right here. She's going to patch things right up."

"You a doctor?" Hortense sounded doubtful

Nell nodded. "S.C. Medical School, class of sixty-nine."

The black girl shook her head in disbelief and gestured toward a bedroom inside. "She said something about a party. She ate some chili or something. That girl loves junk food."

"All right, I'll take a look at her. Her name's Eunice?"

"Eunice Forrester."

"How old is she?"

"She'd sooner cut her throat than tell you."

Jake waited outside. The room she was ushered into was a tangle of disorder. There was a jumble of plants on the windowsill, a horde of carefully collected rocks and stones, a Victorian porcelain doll with a staring countenance, a brooding black and white photograph of Garbo as Camille and a rainbow of dresses, dangling like soft scarfs from every piece of furniture. The cover on the bed was a network of cigarette burns, which had been whimsically embroidered around, as if they were the hearts of some unusual garden flowers.

They found Eunice hanging over the side of the bed, lifting a putty-colored, sweating face as they entered.

"God," she cried, "am I sick. If there *is* a God. It's coming out of every end of me!"

Despite her woes, Nell saw that she was a jaunty little blonde with a slightly out of date prettiness, like a calendar face from the thirties.

"Whoever you are — do something — or I'm going to ruin this rug right here and now." She gagged violently.

Nell stood by the bed, took her pulse, spoke quietly. "Chili, huh?"

"Oh, God, don't say the word. I'll whoops again!"

"Just breathe through your mouth. How long ago did you eat it?"

"At eight, at nine, who remembers? Oh, shit, you're like one of those damned nurses — you go in to have an abortion, they

24

want to know when you had measles. Give me something, any-thing, *every*thing!"

"Did you have any liquor tonight?"

"I don't drink. Lots of sex but no alcohol. Oh, Jesus."

Nell opened her bag, moving swiftly. "I'm going to give you a shot of Demerol for the pain, and a shot of Compazine for the nausea, and some Lomotil for the diarrhea."

"I don't like needles. Horty, tell her I don't like needles."

"Just shut up and do what she says!"

"There's nothing like a loving spade friend." Eunice gasped and groaned and flopped back on the pillows. "She's like a South-ern mammy, my Hortense. Horty, you're my mama."

Nell prepared the needles, swabbed the girl's arm, injected her. Eunice howled at the first one, howled again at the second, looked at her resentfully.

"Don't you leave me until this works. I feel terrible. I know I'm going to feel worse."

"You'll feel better in a minute. Just try to relax."

Eunice made a disbelieving face. "You sit down. You too, Horty. Nobody leaves this room. I'm so *dizzy.*"

"Are you ever," the black girl told her. "Shut your mouth now. Try and go to sleep." Hortense put her hand on Eunice's fore-head, brushing her damp hair back. "I told you not to go over to his house, didn't I? You ever going to listen when somebody smarter than you tells you what to do? Huh?"

"God," Eunice said woozily, "that was some little party. Not very big but very busy. Just the three of us. Do you know how many arms and legs there are in a bed when three people get in it? There were only two when I walked in on them but they moved over and made room for me. I don't know, I was just delivering him his birthday present, a super body shirt that cost me the moon, and there he was, the shit, in bed with her. I was so sore at him. But she was nice. Pretty, skinny and pretty. She said, 'Darling, he's a prick, but I'm not.' Hah. Never be taken in by a pretty face, my friends. What that lady did to me, I mean, Vaseline and a broom handle, honestly! It got crazier and crazier.

I'll tell you this, it's a good thing they didn't climb into the ark three by three." She gave them a pale, unfocused smile. "That's how we got to the chili. It was so damn athletic in that bed we all worked up an appetite, and he had chili sent over and we all put it in one big bowl and ate it with soup spoons. It was either spoiled chili or spoiled cock, I don't know which, but here I am. *Whoops.* Oh, my God."

Hortense looked grim. "It's that bastard director she works for. He's been fucking her over for months. I told her to quit him."

"She sounded right at home." Nell's comment was uncritically offered.

Eunice had closed her eyes. "I heard what you said," she said. "Well, it wasn't always like that. I'm a small-town girl, Kelso, Washington. I bet you never heard of Kelso, Washington. It's right next to Longview, which is fifty miles from Portland in the rain. Clean, open country. That's me, Eunice, the country girl. Some time back, of course, though it isn't all that goddamn innocent in the country either. I knew a boy, Kelly Frasier, he did things with sheep and his daddy's horse. So there you are. I mean, *I* stay with the human race. At least I think they're human to start with." She suddenly sat up. "Doctor, I've got to go to the bathroom again." Her eyes were wild, she dangled rubbery legs over the side of the bed.

Hortense and Nell supported her across the room. She pushed them away at the bathroom door.

"I'd like some privacy," she said loftily and shut them out.

"Privacy," Hortense snorted. "She's in the sack with two other people and she wants privacy."

Groans and curses sounded from Eunice through the closed door. Hortense sat on the edge of the bed and looked at Nell.

"I don't know about that one," she said. "She's had five abortions, and every time she comes home like a squeezed lemon and says to me, 'Horty, I'm going to join a modern dance class' or 'Horty, I may turn Catholic,' or 'Horty, lend me money for a shrink.' And I do, and she spends it on an Indian rug or fake pearls or megavitamins. It's all crap."

"She seems to depend on you."

"She puts those skinny arms around my neck and hangs there till one day I'm gonna turn black in the face — or at least blacker than I am." She sniffed. "She's a baby. If she wasn't around I'd probably get one of those shivery little hairless dogs and make a baby out of that." She dragged a blanket off the foot of the bed and wrapped herself in it.

"How long you going to be in there?" she shouted.

"I'm out." Eunice wavered in the doorway. "I want to be cremated and my ashes scattered on his breakfast food."

She fell across the bed. The two women settled her into it and covered her. She groaned once or twice and then she slept. Her breath came and went in little sighs, as if breathing at all were pointless.

"Want a cup of coffee?"

Nell nodded. The two women tiptoed into the kitchen.

They were silent while it was being made and sat silently a while over their cups.

"What do you do, besides look after her?"

"Me, I teach school. Before that I worked as a fry cook, with a book propped up above the stove, conjugating verbs while I fried bacon for cowhands. I come from Texas, forty miles from Lubbock. She's not going to die on us, is she?"

"No. She'll be all right. She's going to sleep right through tomorrow."

"She's crazy."

"Well, neither you nor I can cure that."

"Amen."

Nell got to her feet and yawned widely. "I'm off, then."

Hortense walked her to the door. "You going to send a big bill?"

"No bill. This one's for the sisterhood. But tell your friend not to make a habit of it."

"Thanks. Good night."

Nell paused at the top of the stairs to appreciate the drama of the thin moon hovering low over the sea. She was both weary and wakeful and began to regret Cass, when Jake came out of the shadows and stood beside her, an unlit pipe in his mouth.

"Everything tamped down?"

"All quiet."

"What's the tab for the house call? I'll take care of it."

"It's on the house. But in case you feel I'm your resident physician, disabuse yourself. Blood can flow into your heated, lighted, filtered swimming pool before I'll lose sleep again."

"Want a couple of eggs?" he asked easily.

"If you do them in butter."

He waved her into his apartment. It was antiseptically clean and in perfect order without the blank look which usually accompanied such meticulous care. It was like a room in a New England house where neatness is a part of tradition and things preserved are the marks of thrift and character. She watched him as he moved around his kitchen and tried to place him in the lexicon of the men she had known. Recounting the list to herself she was a trifle startled at its length and variety. Men, she realized, were an indulgence she allowed herself the way other women gave in to cravings for fine French furniture or chocolate creams or massage. That predilection for male company explained Cass. She amused herself with the thought that had she seen him in a shop window she would have tapped the glass and told the proprietor, "That one, please, the one with the sleepy eyes. No, I don't want a talking doll, just wind up all the essential parts and I'll take him home."

It hadn't happened that way, of course. She'd met him sleeping on the grass of his Bel Air house when she'd called to attend his father. Amory Belwright, relentlessly successful since the age of twenty, his letters already published, his wastebasket emptied for posterity, had been felled by a stroke which had pulled his handsome mouth awry and retired him from the movie business and the beds of a dozen famous ladies.

She was the last to see the expiring gleam in his eyes flare as he died in the vulgar grandeur of his plaster palace. She had been the one to seek out the son with the news of the death and offer a consoling embrace, which led in short order to another, and another, and still another on the very day the old man had given up the ghost. A particularly delicious bonbon in a particularly fancy box was Cass, but it appeared now that that craving had been satisfied.

Before him? An icy surgeon who had thawed to the extent of suggesting that he give up his Pasadena wife, his ancient Packard, his seat on the Board of Regents at Berkeley for her. He had lasted as long as his considerable bag of sexual tricks astonished her. When they came panting and exhausted to conversation, her interest lagged, and she sent him a book on abnormal psychology with the words "Thank you" emblazoned on its flyleaf for having so extended her repertoire. And then the silent poet who dabbled strangely with his toes, and the bitter politician who could only get it up while John Chancellor was intoning the evening news, and then memory balked and what difference did it make anyway? Her attention, her passion, her true grit belonged to her job. She thought it pompous to call it a career — it was a job that took her time, her temperament, her tears, her sweat, one in which failure caused lacerations of the mind that no man had ever elicited from her.

Jake was back with breakfast. The eggs were sunny-side up and parsleyed, the toast was hot, cut and buttered, coffee was in flowered Danish cups. He proffered a napkin of damask and sugar in a heavy silver pot.

"You do yourself nicely," she said, holding the cup aloft.

"I treat myself to the best I can get."

"I see that."

He sat opposite her, spread his napkin with a flourish and tucked into his food with gusto. "I built this place," he told her. "It's my own rabbit warren. I used to keep rabbits when I was a kid, rabbits and pigeons and a red ant colony, which didn't go down too well with my mama. I got a great kick out of seeing how they organized themselves, how they ran their lives. Now I'm doing the same thing with people. And here we all are, backing and filling, pushing and shoving for a spot at the trough. Enlightening and sobering. Yes, indeed, enlightening and sobering."

Nell studied him over the rim of her cup. "You make me uncomfortable, Mr. Cooley. I'm not sure I want to be under your watchful eye."

He shoved his plate aside and lit a large black cigar, puffing smoke in her direction. "Nothing to worry about. I'm an ordinary kind of fellow. I allow for other people's lapses and hope they do the same for me. It's to my credit, I think, that I read Emerson and change my underwear daily and make a full disclosure to the Internal Revenue Service. I share my dinner with anybody who comes to my door. If a woman passes through my life, I give her breakfast in bed and any other consideration I can think of. In matters sexual, I'm affectionate, leisurely and properly grateful to my partner; without undue immodesty, I think I can safely say that I'm experienced and innovative. I never argue religion or politics. I write my old mother once a week, although she has disowned me publicly for drinking, swearing, gambling and other offenses. I throw back undersized trout. I've never been known to cheat the phone company."

Nell said, "When can we embark on an affair?"

"At your convenience," he said promptly.

She laughed. "I'm going to enjoy your company, Mr. Cooley. I can see that."

"I'm always on the premises. Drop in any time." When she looked at him, he added, "There's no other lady around at present. That is to say, nobody has put a toothbrush in the glass next to mine. There's a nice little waitress who drops in some rainy nights, but she's got a husband in San Dimas and she's just sheltering, you might say." He paused. "Would anybody jump for his trousers if I knocked at your door?"

"It's not likely."

"Well, fine," he said. "We'll be running into each other."

2

THE WORDS appeared on the clapper board for the twenty-seventh time:

> The Right People
> Director . . . Alan Leonard
> Cameraman . . . Loren Mitlin
> Take . . . 27

Eunice, seated at the rear of the projection room, slipped out of her shoes and wriggled her toes like a child paddling in its bath. The figures looming large on the screen before her played out their dramatic pas de deux: close shot, medium-close shot, over the shoulder, her POV, his POV — the scene was repeated over and over. The exorbitantly paid actors found no nuance, no shading. At a million dollars apiece they went through their paces, a theme without variations, mechanical, plodding, low-key. Eunice yawned loudly, opening her jaws until they creaked.

Alan, blue-jeaned and Gucci shod, whirled in disbelief and scanned the dark room. "Who the fuck is making that noise!"

"It's me," Eunice said. "I'm the only one in here besides you and Roy."

He pounded up the aisle with search-and-destroy rage in his face. When he found her he hauled her upright. "Serious work is being done here," he said in a choking voice. "How dare you impede the serious work that's being done here?"

"It's boring, Alan," she said, pulling herself free from his grasp. "It's very, very boring. I think since I'm your personal secretary and friend that I ought to tell you the truth, that's all. And the truth is, it's boring."

"Putting aside your atrocious judgment," he snapped at her, "you are here to take notes and telephone messages, period. You are not here as a colleague, a critic or anything beyond the dumb cunt that you are."

There was an uneasy stirring in the dark and the cutter spoke with a perturbed Texas drawl. "Take it easy, Alan. Come on, now."

Alan's finger stabbed in the direction of the rebuke. "Watch it, my friend," he warned. "You're here on sufferance. There's a smart young twenty-year-old kid breathing down your neck right out of S.C. Cinema School who calls my office fifteen times a week."

The cutter got to his feet, a cigarette glowing in the dark. "Listen, pricko," he said. "I worked for Wyler and Minnelli and Ritt when you were jacking off in the mail room. I own a condominium in Bakersfield and my house is paid for, so simmer down or I'll walk and leave you sitting with this turd."

Alan grinned. "I love you, Roy," he said.

"Yeah, you love me. I don't love you."

"How many films have we done together?"

"Movies, not films. And the answer is too many."

"Roy, trim a little off the front for me. Use the second take, it's the only one in which she doesn't sound like she's stoned out of her mind, and let me see it after lunch." He snapped his fingers. "And you, Eunice, come on, we'll take a ride."

She followed him out into the bright sunlight, blinking owlishly. He walked ahead of her with his bantam cock strut, compensating for his being closer to five feet than six. She trotted after, her silver bracelets chattering. Two men in black suits and silk ties hailed him. When they were close enough they draped arms around him and stood in a conspiratorial huddle. Eunice leaned languidly against a tree, waiting. Alan's ready grin flashed, he ruffled one of the men's hair with impudent good humor, he patted a buttock close at hand. But in another moment the bodies stiffened, the arms dropped, the voices in the hastily convened meeting on the sidewalk under the spreading pine tree grew louder, Alan's loudest of all.

"I want you to realize that I'm not being willful or obstreperous. I've put eighteen months of my life on the line with this picture out of a deep conviction that it says something worth saying about the human condition. Now I'm not going to fuck that up, and with the utmost respect, gentlemen, I'm not going to let you fuck it up with haste born of sheer panic. I'll have an answer print for you as soon as I feel the picture is right. Not later, not sooner. It's in my contract, boys."

There was an angry hum as if a hive had been struck. Alan's voice rose above it.

"You'll have a festival picture, gentlemen, and without vanity, I suggest you might even have a prize picture. Let's all work toward that end." He closed his eyes as if some swelling chorus were chanting a sonorous Amen and then he walked back to Eunice and swept her toward his Jaguar.

"I want to be sucked from Laurel Canyon to the end of Mulholland Drive," he said, sliding under the wheel.

Her mind flashed to the time she had been strolling home from school and a car had pulled up, a smiling, handsome young man offering a ride, and though warned often enough, threatened with horror stories, murder, mutilation, white slavery, sexual perversions too terrible to recount, the day had been hot and she was tired, so she slid in beside him, grateful for the air conditioning, the soft leather seat, had sat up prim and proper, her schoolbooks and notebooks, triangle and ruler arranged neatly in her lap, her feet tapping to the music coming from the radio, such a big, luxurious car, the ride so smooth, gliding so effortlessly; when he had turned to her with that nice, crinkle-eyed smile and asked:

"Do you blow the bugle?"

"What?" she had said.

"Do you blow the bugle?" he had repeated.

She had no idea what he meant, was about to reply that she had no competence with any instrument, was on the gym team, not in the band at all, when her startled gaze was captured by the thing that grew from his lap, that stood up so suddenly and immensely from his open fly. She dimly began to perceive what he had in mind and she had begun to cry. He had pulled over hastily at that, brakes squealing, lunging past her, had almost fallen out of the car himself in his scramble to get the door open and deposit her safely on the sidewalk.

Did she blow the bugle?

Well, yes, she did, as a matter of fact, had learned how. You could hardly get through life, hardly go out on a date, without taking a man in your mouth.

What she didn't like was the necessity to assume the abject posture, to bow her head, bend her knees. The submitting thing bothered her. Something symbolic there.

Alan was finished and still panting. She glanced up at him, at his handsome, pouting face.

"I don't like blow jobs."

"That's an infantile, repressive attitude," he said smugly.

"I want to get into a nice bed with Lady Pepperell sheets and have somebody kiss me on the mouth and tell me he loves me. Then I want to lie on my back, not on my stomach with my fanny in the air like a dog, but on my back, so he can see my face and I can see his. Then I want him to come into me and not grunt or say anything mean but just melt into me and call me a sweet name and last and last so I get to come first for a change. I don't want to be tied to a bed, or peed on, or hit, or crawl around on all fours with a man on my back yelling giddy-up! or suck somebody off driving around the greater Los Angeles area."

"Find a fourteen-year-old high school kid with pimples and you've got it made," he said. He stopped the car, zipped his fly and lay back with his eyes closed. The sun beat through the windshield of the car. A meadowlark sang three liquid melodic notes.

"Are we just going to sit here?" she asked.

"Yep." He pushed his sunglasses up on his forehead. "You know what I want?" he said suddenly. "What I'd rather have than the biggest come since King Kong? A good picture. Just let John Simon compare me to Fellini and my cock will stand up like a soldier. I don't want cunt . . . I want Cannes. How do you like them apples, Eunice baby?"

"Then why did you do that rotten thing to me with that woman last night?" She looked at him with accusing eyes.

"Because I'm fucking impotent where it counts," he shouted. "Scorsese is a young pisher . . . Spielberg is still a kid . . . I'm forty-five, for Christ's sake. My bones are already bleaching on the goddamn beach. I've had three wives. I've given sixty thousand dollars to a shrink. I've read a hundred great books and slept with my tennis pro and I still have nothing to say. My father did a million dollars a year in the rag trade. My mother raised seven hundred thousand dollars for Hadassah. My brother's a brain surgeon. *I'm promising.*" He slammed his hand on the steering wheel and yelped in pain.

She leaned over and patted his cheek. "You can go down on me if you want to."

He groaned. "Big deal. A mercy fuck from a goyish basket case. Jesus, why didn't I go to Harvard like my father wanted me to?"

She slid back to her own side of the car and stared out the window, her eyes welling suddenly with tears. "That's the trouble," she said, "I don't ever make anyone feel good."

He whirled on her. "Make *yourself* feel good, dummy! Shit, you're hopeless. You've got no self-image! Stop seeing yourself as dog do-do for a change. Listen, I'll treat you to my shrink. No strings."

She sniffed disdainfully. "He's suing you for his fees. I've seen the lawyer's letter."

"Okay. I'll send you to *est.* On the picture."

"I don't want to go. A friend of mine went and they started off by calling her an asshole. I get enough hostility in this life."

He grinned. "Well, then, I'll eat you. But I'll say something nice first."

The birds sang again. Little did they know. Eunice lay back and closed her eyes and told *herself* all she wanted to hear.

Alan kept her working late. He snarled over a typing error, swore abusively when he learned he was overdrawn at the bank, smoked a joint in preparation for his return home to wife and family and left shortly after eight o'clock.

She sat at her desk, sunk with fatigue, feeling too inert to move. The cleaning woman came in, a pretty Mexican girl who smiled brightly and waved a greeting with a dirty dust mop.

"You stay late?"

"Hello, Maria. I'm going to water the plants and then put on my dancing shoes and dance out of here."

"He work you too hard, maybe."

"That's right. And how about your husband letting you work like a dog with five kids at home?"

"He very handsome. I like him. You married, Miss?"

"No," she said bitterly. "I have to fill in my silver pattern before I take the great step."

She got up, took the watering can and went into Alan's office. She had made a lush jungle bloom there. She talked to the plants as she misted them. The cleaning girl shook her head and clucked behind her back as if she were watching the antics of the insane.

"Turn out the lights before you leave, Maria. We've been getting hate mail from management about waste. And dust his desk. He checks to see if you do every morning, the prick."

She went down the echoing empty corridor. The studio was still. She paused for a drink at the water fountain. It ran dry. One day, she thought, it will all dry up and blow away.

At the far end of the corridor a lone writer emerged from his office, his face the gray color of the interned.

"Hiya, baby," he called. "Want to grab a drinkiepoo around the corner?"

"Hello, Mr. Stacy. No, I've got to get home and we both know your wife is waiting for you."

"Wrong, honey, she's in some motel somewhere with a lady masseuse. But never mind. I'll ask you again."

She walked down the stairs, beginning to feel the dull throb of a headache. Hortense was teaching late. She'd have to make her own dinner. The thought of a fried egg sandwich made her mouth sour with distaste.

Outside the night air blew cold and wet. The gate guard, shirt buttons straining over his girth, was the bearer of bad news.

"You've got a flat tire, girlie," he said sucking his tooth.

"Oh, no."

"Flat as a pancake. Got a spare?" He ambled toward her.

"Yes. Bernie, I know you're going to be a darling angel and change it for me, aren't you?"

He shook his head. His jowls trembled with the back and forth motion. "No, girlie, I can't do that. I've got a weak back." He laughed. "A weak back and a strong mind. You call the auto club."

"I don't belong."

"I've been a member for twenty years. Best money I ever spent."

"Well, I don't belong and I'm in trouble." Her voice slid high, went frantic. "What am I supposed to do?"

"Lift up your skirt and stick out your thumb. Somebody'll stop for you." He guffawed.

"Let me use the phone, you oaf." She squeezed into his glass cubicle. He gave no ground. She was aware of her backside being pressed by his protruding, billowing gut.

"Lissen," she said hotly, "no feeling up, you hear? I've had *enough* today!"

He heaved his bulk out into the driveway, his face aggrieved. She remembered that Devon Scott was working on the lot. He often stayed late, reluctant to face his empty apartment.

"Scotty, it's me, Eunice."

"You're working late, pet."

"I have a flat tire. I didn't get any lunch. Alan's been shitty all day and Hortense is out with her boyfriend and . . ."

". . . and the stock market fell and three urban guerrillas bombed a bank and Chicken Little says the sky is falling and I'm coming right away." He was soothing and fatherly. "Go sit in the car and wait for me."

She flounced past the guard and got into her car, huddled miserably in the corner. She was wearing a 1930s voile dress which she had bought with cries of joy in a thrift shop a week ago. In the penetrating chill of the California night it seemed symbolic of all the kitsch of her life. She slid down on her spine in the boneless adolescent slouch of her girlhood and raged at herself. Here she was, alley-cat miserable in fabled Hollywood watching an Exxon sign flicker on and off, tasting stale, smelling of faded Norell, hampered by the day that had passed, wretched at the prospect of tomorrow.

"Oh, Mama," she said aloud, imploring that faded weary woman long in her grave. "Oh, Mama, why'd you go and die on me?" She tried to sort out her sudden grief. It couldn't be for that bony silent woman whose only maternal gesture had been a dry kiss of farewell when she'd left home.

She thought about her mother sitting at the kitchen table with its dreadful oilcloth cover, its ketchup bottle oozing like clotted blood, the smell of cat pee which never left the room; her mother's pale myopic eyes looking ahead to her early death. Home. The frame house with the broken concrete steps and a dusty lilac tree making a brave seasonal show. Her father had promised to mend the step and died the Saturday after he rented the concrete mixer. She had always been secretly convinced that his death had been a purposeful avoidance of work. For years her mother had murmured "bad health" in explanation of his presence on the front porch, slumped, inert, overall clad, the cat resting eternally in his lap.

"He took a bad chill working over to Weyerhaeuser," her mother had said long ago. "He never threw it off, I guess." And there he had sat while her mother ironed for neighbors at fifty cents a basket and blushed as she produced food stamps at the grocery store. Eunice remembered how the minister had searched and floundered for a eulogy and produced, "He was a kind husband and father" as he had been laid to the perpetual rest he had not earned.

It had all been her mother. Her music lessons bought in exchange for housecleaning, her graduation dress purchased with saved pennies, the sugary pink cakes baked from mixes for her birthday. And finally, her benediction and sad blessing when she had decided to go.

"You ought to leave if you don't think there's anything here for you, Eunice." She heard again the sound of her tired voice like a dry stalk rustling. "I'll give you enough for the Greyhound. And my winter coat."

"It's sunny in California."

"Is that where you're going?"

"They have oranges growing on trees in the front yards."

"Is that right?"

"After I get a job you could come on down and stay with me. I'll get a place with a wall bed. Wouldn't you like that?"

"You'd be better off on your own, I guess."

"You don't have any spunk," Eunice had cried with youthful contempt. "Are you just going to live and die going to the A and P and those damn church meetings?"

"What would you do with me if I was to come?" Her mother smoothed the apron in her lap and sat with downcast eyes.

"Well, first I'd give you a home permanent. Then we'd go to Grauman's Chinese Theatre. We'd eat out in Mexican restaurants. We'd go to Disneyland. We'd paint our toenails red. We'd eat shrimp cocktails. We'd buy black underwear. We'd have our fortune told."

"You go along. You can send back postcards."

She had packed that very night with anger she did not understand. She had stuffed the worn Gladstone bag with her worn sandals and flowered jersey dresses. Her mother had helped, silently folding her slips and adding the torn nightgowns without comment.

"I went to Chehalis on my own once," her mother said.

"Chehalis. It's a *cow* town, like this one."

"I met a man there."

She had dropped the sweater she was flinging into the bag and regarded her mother with surprise.

"*You* met a man?"

She nodded. "I went up to get my teeth fixed. Your father said he couldn't stand my front teeth bucking out like they did. He said to go get them fixed so I went up to Chehalis to the credit dentist."

She sat down on the bed and leaned back, brooding, garnering scraps of the past.

"I remember I got off the bus and it was raining. I was supposed to go straight to the dentist but I didn't."

Eunice sat beside her. "What'd you do?"

"I went and had a vanilla ice cream soda in the drugstore. Then I went for a walk down the main street. I looked in the jewelry store window and saw a pair of little gold earrings for pierced ears. They were the prettiest things. I had the money for the dentist in my purse. I went into the jewelry store and asked to see the earrings. The man in the store was very nice. Polite. He asked me did I have pierced ears and I said no. And he said, 'Well, those are for pierced ears but we do that for you on the premises without charge and it doesn't hurt a bit.' I don't know what got into me. I said, 'Well, how much are they?' And he said, 'Thirty-two fifty.' I had fifty dollars for the dentist so I told him to go ahead and get them out of the window and fix my ears so I could wear them."

"Was he the man?" Eunice wrinkled her nose, already disappointed in the adventure.

Her mother went on, straying in a more pleasant place. "He took me in the back room and sat me down in the chair. I remember it started to rain very hard then. You could hear it come down cats and dogs. He asked me what my name was and I said, 'Mrs. George Wilson,' and he said, 'No, your first name,' and I said, 'Helen.' And he said, 'Helen, you have ears like little pink shells from the sea.'"

"You do, Mama."

"And he took my ear lobes in his hands and petted them like I do the cat. And then he pierced them and put in little studs and he wrapped the real earrings up like a present. Then he asked me to stay until the rain stopped. There weren't any customers. So I did."

She touched her mouth with a tentative finger. "We talked and talked just like we'd always known each other. He told me how he'd wanted to play the violin in a symphony orchestra but his father owned the shop and wanted it to stay in the family. He said he'd gotten married when he was seventeen to a girl his father picked out for him. She had chronic stomach trouble and couldn't eat anything but boiled food. He said he took violin lessons by mail. I told him I loved the violin and he asked me would I like to hear him play. I said yes and he got it out and played a piece. To tell you the truth, it sounded pretty scratchy to me but I said it was just lovely and I enjoyed it very much. Then he asked me was I a happily married woman and I said I had been married a long time and he said that isn't the same thing. Are you happy? I said I'd been very happy when I was a child. And he groaned right out loud. He did. He groaned. Then we just sat there and looked at each other. The rain stopped and he gave me my package and walked to the door with me. He just said one thing."

"What?"

" 'I'll never have another afternoon like this one.' "

"That's *all?*"

Her mother stood up. "If you'd like to take those earrings along with you, you can."

Scotty drove up alongside her in his 1935 Studebaker. It was burnished brown, waxed, the glove leather soft and redolent. He leaned out the window and called to her.

"Lock up your car. I'll get it fixed for you in the morning."

She grabbed her purse and slid in beside him, shivering in her thin dress. She pawed for a cigarette and matches, scattering coins, chewing-gum wrappers, a sprinkle of old tobacco.

"My house is in Mars," she said darkly, "so everything is shit."

"Your problem is not astrology, it's disorder." He tossed her his jacket. "Put that on." Then he glanced at her critically. "Eunice," he said sternly, "what are we to do with you? You're not a Southern deb, so there's really no point to this loony, demented way you carry on. Did you have dinner? Probably not. Did you have lunch? Have you been to the bathroom in the last twelve hours?"

"I'm a camel," she said.

He nodded. "Do you have money in your purse for muggers and such? I venture not a sou. If I hadn't been working late you would've probably stood on Ventura Boulevard and hitched a ride with Charles Manson."

"Scotty," she said, "you're so nice. You're always there when I need you. I wish you were my brother."

She snapped on the car radio, put on the heater and closed her eyes, fragile and submissive. She had a child's habit of surrendering to someone else's care; a door held ajar for her, a salesman's practiced smile, her hairdresser's caressing hands, even her dentist cupping her chin made her feel singled out and protected.

"I think I might lose my job," she said suddenly.

"I'm not surprised. Your typing is atrocious, your spelling is illiterate."

"I do other things."

He grimaced. "You fall to your knees on command. You can hardly put that in a job résumé."

"So do you," she said. "I've peeked through your window."

"I'm old and lonely. You're young and pretty."

"Fat lot of good it's done me." She shrugged, turning an offended back to him.

"If I were your brother," he said firmly, "I'd have a great deal to say to you."

"I have a brother," she said resentfully, "and he lives in Grand Rapids. I went there once after I had an abortion and got anemic. He put me in a back room on a lumpy old bed and gave me a Bible and five dollars a week to live on. He poured my perfume down the toilet and threw out my lipstick and told me to take cold showers. He's only thirty-eight but he has white hair and halitosis and I *hate* him."

"My mother," said Scotty, "wept when I was born and said she wanted a girl. She dressed me in a ballet tutu and never cut my hair. My father put me up on a table one evening and made me dance in front of his cronies who had come in for poker. As a result I bugger boys and you sleep with the world at large. And neither one of us has an adequate excuse."

"I'm twenty-five years old, do you know that?" she said angrily. "With my luck if I had a baby it would probably be a mongoloid. I've tried everything," she wailed. "I go on water diets to stay thin and enroll in charm schools and hang around in singles bars and go on Pacific liner cruises and sleep with waiters and say prayers in three different religions — and here I am, in nowhere city." She stabbed her cigarette out fiercely and jabbed an accusing finger at him. "You're no better off. I've heard you crying through the walls. I have, lots of nights."

"I weep easily," he said. "I was probably watching Bette Davis die."

"Why don't we take up with each other?" she said airily. "A friend of mine married a gay boy and she's happy as a lark. He picks out her clothes and decorates the house and buys her gorgeous antique jewelry."

He paused at a stoplight and shook his head in disbelief. "Eunice," he said, "I have never rolled a sailor in a hotel room, I've never chained anybody to a bedpost, I've never looked at a boy under eighteen or accosted anyone at the urinal in a men's room. What in God's name makes you think I'd fuck up your life by moving in with you?"

"At this stage I'd try anything."

"Not with me, you won't."

There, she thought, as they rode on in silence; that's what always happens. Little screen doors slide down between people. You can see through them and even press your lips against the wire mesh, but you are still separated.

"I'm tired of sex anyhow," she told him.

"Not a moment too soon," he retorted.

"Are you satisfied with your life? Do you want to get up in the morning?"

"Satisfied?" he sniffed. "When one is a vampire, my love, the diet is blood."

"I wish I'd taken a taxi home," she said. "You depress me."

"That may be a good thing. You need shaking up. Try getting off your back for once, Eunice. You might find that your feet will hold you up."

"I'm sorry I asked you. Maybe I'll have a thing with a girl. God knows men have been a big nothing."

"Try abstinence."

An old man crossed the street in front of the car, bent double, his face turned to mold by the green light washing over it. For a moment she saw her father lying in his cheap coffin, his features pinched by death. She blinked rapidly, but death was still there.

"I don't want to go home just yet. Hortense is out and the canary is at the vet. I know what will happen. I'll get into the refrigerator and gobble everything in sight. I'll gain pounds by the minute. I'll have to stick my finger down my throat. Couldn't we just ride around for a while?"

"No," he said. "There's an old Susan Hayward movie on. If you want I'll stop and get us a quart of ice cream and two spoons and you can come in and watch."

"Pistachio," she said and sat back, content.

3

THE WINDOW SHATTERED, hurling glass into the room. The kids slouching behind their desks like flowers wilting emitted an enthusiastic war whoop, suddenly free of the torpor that sun and lessons had produced. Yips, cries and catcalls rose in a chorus. Hortense was on her feet in one fluid motion and pounding the desk with her fist in another.

"Knock it off," she snapped. "And I mean right this minute, people!"

"Hey, it's war, man!"

"We gettin' hit from outer space."

"It's the Fourth of fuckin' July. Yeah, yeah."

She approached the window warily. In the playground below she saw belligerents, one huge and white, the other small, quick and very black, writhing and struggling, panting, sweating, swearing.

"You two," she yelled. "You down there, I'm talking to you!"

The struggle went on, unabated. She whirled back into the room.

"Not a peep," she commanded, "not a sound. Now I'm leaving this room and I want to hear the silence of a grave. *That's* so quiet I can hear the worms crawling, you understand?"

"We gotta *study* while you down there?" drawled the largest, the most insolent boy, lounging over his desk.

Hortense disdained an answer. She turned to the blackboard,

snatched up a dusty eraser and approached the rebel. With one decisive motion, she balanced the eraser on the top of his head. The other kids watched with curiosity.

"Now, big mouth," she said coolly, "this eraser better be just where I put it when I get back or it's going to be your tail in the principal's office. What I'm saying is, don't budge, don't fudge, don't even let wind or you're in big, big trouble. You listening, *mouth?*"

An awed silence fell over the room. The large boy began to sweat. He remained frozen, the eraser trembling, as Hortense stormed out without a backward glance.

She crossed the playground on a run and got between the antagonists just in time to take a fiercely knotted fist slammed into her ovary. She yelped and slapped in the same moment, swinging her hand back in a wide, emphatic arc. She was in the middle now, smelling sweat and blood and possibly even urine released in the hot anger of the moment.

"Stop! Stop! Damn you little pissants, I said quit it!" Panting and heaving, elbows out from remembered street fights of her youth, she pried them apart and held them squirming and squealing at arm's length.

"Just what the hell is going on out here? Just what the hell do you think you are doing? *Answer* me!"

The little black snuffled and blinked away tears. "He . . . he said my girlfren' got crabs. He said he been in her pants and *knew* — so I tromped him . . . and I'm gonna tromp him *some more.*"

Hortense waggled him back and forth in her fierce grasp. "Your *girl*friend, you little snot? You're *eleven* years old . . . *what* girlfriend?"

He groped for dignity. "I got one."

She shook the other boy till his head rolled. "Is that what happened?"

"Naw!"

"Then lemme hear right quick."

". . . it was nuthin'."

"You damaged school property and knocked each other cockeyed and you've got the brass to say it was nuthin'? I'll nuthin' you!"

"Lemme go."

She turned him around and booted him ahead of her with a shoe planted firmly against his backside. "March," she ordered. Bumping and colliding, kicking one and dragging the other, they made for the building.

The bigger boy assumed outrage. "You can't shove me around . . . you can't lay a hand on me, it's against the law."

She laughed, her grin splitting her face. "*I'm* the law right this minute, little boy, and I don't see any lawyer in your corner. March!" she repeated.

She herded them through the hall, past a group of giggling girls.

"Give it to 'em, Miz Washington."

"Lookit Mr. Big Shot, with his ass in a sling."

"Yoo-hoo, Fred Kolenkamp, you gonna eat shit, man . . ."

At the door of the office she let go and stood regarding them. "You got a comb in your pocket?" she demanded.

The little one looked at her sullenly and whipped one out.

"Use it."

He dragged it through his hair, his eyes never leaving her face.

"You got a hankie?" she said to the other.

"No."

She took one from her pocket and thrust it toward him. "Blow." He honked loudly into the handkerchief and started to hand it back.

"Nuthin' doin'. You get that washed and ironed and bring it back."

"Yes, ma'am."

"Miz."

"Yes, miz."

She shooed them through the door.

Harry Saul looked up from his desk in the principal's office. He had dark, sad eyes and an exhausted, hapless air.

"What have we here?"

"Muhammad Ali and Joe Frazier. We've also got a broken

47

window in my classroom, twenty minutes of my class time wasted and sexual precocity which will curl your hair. They'll tell you. Also, I may have sustained internal injuries but that's par for this course."

Harry's fingers snapped at the two cowed boys. "Get into that office and sit down, fifteen feet apart, and wait for me."

They slunk past him into the next room. Harry sighed and shrugged.

"Why didn't you let the little bastards kill each other, Horty?"

She grinned. "I love a fight. Seriously, Harry, come down tough. My kids are getting too big a kick out of this kind of thing. It's like having a ringside ticket at a heavyweight match every day of the week."

"I'll hang and quarter 'em."

She nodded and turned to go.

"Horty?"

"Yes?"

"Can I ask you something?"

"Make it short. I've got thirty-five monkeys loose up there."

"How do you cook a pot roast?"

She turned slowly to look at him. "What did you say?"

"I asked you how do you cook a pot roast?"

"Who the fuck do you think I am?" she said coldly. "Aunt Jemima?" She stared at him, her hands resting on her broad hips.

"What are you sore about?"

"I teach English. You want recipes, haul your ass to your home economics department." She turned again to leave.

He sagged against his desk and rubbed his hands over his eyes.

"Horty," he said, "my wife walked out on me two weeks ago. She left me with an eight-year-old boy and a six-year-old girl. She isn't coming back. She didn't leave a forwarding address, she didn't leave a phone number. She didn't say any goodbys. We've been eating tuna fish for fourteen nights. I'd like to try a pot roast."

"You've been dumped, huh?" Her tone changed, softened.

"I feel like I've been hit by a ten-ton truck." He looked at her with despairing eyes. "How could she do that, walk out cold like that, two kids . . . ?"

"A man does it every day," she said. "Hell, in my family there wasn't *anything* but leftover women. No, sir, there wasn't a man over ten in the whole cottonpickin' bunch of us."

In her mind she ran over the list again. Aunt Jody, hot-blooded and good-looking, left to wait table in a soul food joint. Aunt Essie, with six children and six dollars in a fruit juice can. Aunt Tacey, with cancer in the right breast who died alone in a charity ward. It was with something of an effort that she continued to listen.

"Fourteen years," he said. "I never missed a birthday or an anniversary. I bought her a new car every three years. I never looked at another woman."

She interrupted, holding up a staying hand. "I'm hearing you tell the story, Harry. She must have had something on her mind."

He was abrupt, harsh. "You girls stick together, don't you, no matter what?"

"Honey," she drawled with exaggerated sweetness, "we ain't had too much help from you guys. Look. Maybe you're kinky in bed. Maybe you're tight with a buck. Maybe you zig when you're supposed to zag. How do I know?"

He was stiff. "I'm sorry I brought it up." He began to arrange papers on his desk with fussy particularity.

She regarded him calmly, easing off.

". . . You take a bunch of carrots, a bay leaf and three onions," she began, and then broke off. "I'll type it up and stick it in your box."

He retreated into formality. "I'd appreciate it very much," he said.

She was at the door. "And, Harry," she crooned. "All that crap about not lookin' at another woman — you've been lookin' at me for six years and today was the first time you got to my *face*." She laughed and threw a farewell wave over her shoulder.

The showers were out of order, the gym was closed, so the teachers' washroom had to do. It smelled of pot. Hortense, standing by the dirty sink, a black hair curled like a snake in its grimy depths, the soap a jellied sliver, wondered who had sought the consolation of cannabis before her. She pulled her blouse over her head; naked to the waist, she began to wash like a field hand, scrubbing under her arms, lathering her strong neck, digging into her ears with soapy fingers. She worked up a real sweat after a day with the kids — bellowing, cajoling, exalted, fed up. But then labor was nothing new to her. She had swung a hoe down a corn patch with the same vigor. She had herded pigs at the top of her voice. She had pulled a foal from a mare, cleaned the shit from the outhouse in the backyard, awakened at dawn to milk cows, scrubbed the kitchen on her hands and knees, the water stinging with ammonia.

The door behind her opened as she scattered water off her body, shaking herself like a doused dog. A woman edged gingerly into the cubicle, giving her a critical look.

"I would have knocked if I'd known you were going to be nude in here."

Hortense's eyes were mischievous. "I've got tits, you've got tits, all God's chillun got tits. Don't be a damn fool, Mildred. I've got a date with my man. I don't want to go dirty, because he gets up close."

She put her shirt on again. "And you're teaching sex education to your kids." She shook her head; Mildred was hopeless. She sloshed cologne down her arms, between her breasts, behind her ears. The smell of jasmine filled the room.

The other woman stared at her, strong, glowing, fragrant. "That smells nice," she said slowly.

Hortense tossed her the little vial. "I buy it by the gallon."

"Well, thank you."

Hortense brushed past her. "Put it between your legs," she said brashly. "It'll change your whole life."

She came upon Booker asleep in his car, his face upturned to the sun. She paused to admire him, the blue black sheen of his skin, the big thighs, the large humorous mouth, a line scar left over from childhood which gave vulnerability to what would have

"Hello, Mr. Brown. They're down at the courts. They're expecting you." She regarded Hortense warily. Booker ushered her past the girl with his arm under her elbow.

The rooms they crossed were cool, polished, bland. The paintings were reproductions, the flowers artificial. There was no wit anywhere, no eccentricity; everything was costly, cumbersome, uncomfortable, controlled. The very temperature was regulated, there was no sense of spring light, of spring air. Nothing was communicated, no pleasure was expressed, no evidence of family life was to be extracted.

Booker waited for her reaction. She sniffed and muttered, "White bread." Then they were outside, walking down a mile of manicured grass to the courts. Two players were warming up lethargically. Two figures in pale dresses lay back in deck chairs, watching without interest. Booker approached them, the potency of his smile preceding him like the sun's rays. He held his racket aloft and waggled it in greeting.

The older woman rose from her chair. She had a deep tan, deep lines, narrow, intelligent eyes. Her voice was flat, crisp.

"Hello, Booker. He's been watching the clock for you all afternoon."

She turned and smiled at Hortense. She was a woman with large white teeth, an angular body, a springing, electric mane of hair. She thrust out a warm dry hand.

"Who's this handsome lady?"

"Mrs. Todson, Miss Washington. A friend of mine."

"Come sit with me," she said, "and we'll drink while they kill each other."

Hortense found herself relenting, her defenses ebbing. The woman had a kind of candid and unaffected air which pleased her.

They settled into chairs. Her hostess was all boneless grace, folding onto the cushions like a ribbon, loose and limp. Beside her, on a table milky with dust, stood a pitcher of lemonade. A bee circled it, settled on the rim, wobbled there a moment, fell. For a moment the women watched the battle, the sodden flutter of wings. On the courts the men called jocularly to one another, danced on the balls of their feet, contended. The bee thrashed feebly. Hortense plunged her hand into the pitcher, fished it out and held it on her open palm. It staggered drunkenly back and forth in a weaving trail, circling on itself.

"Fly off," Hortense commanded, "and remember who saved you."

It was a ritual of childhood for her. It had been spoken a hundred times to ladybugs and housespiders, to caterpillars inching sinuously up her brown arm, to red ants and even to black cockroaches found in her bed.

"I hope you were finished with that lemonade," she said blandly, "because I think you are now."

"No problem. I'm drinking vodka." Mrs. Todson lifted a bottle and squinted at it. "It would appear I've been drinking a *lot* of vodka." She seemed mildly surprised. "Can I fix one for you?"

Hortense shook her head and slumped down; the chair was too small for her. Her knees jammed against her chest.

"You're too big for that chair," said a high sweet voice. The girl was young and bruised-looking, like a peach a moment past its prime. Her eyes were intensely blue, her mouth bloodless.

"Try this one."

"My daughter." Mrs. Todson waved with a disinterested gesture. "Stacy."

"You Booker's friend?" The girl stood in front of her, peering like a curious five-year-old.

Hortense offered a slight nod in assent.

"Are you shacking up?"

Mrs. Todson's sigh was less dismay than disbelief. "Christ," she said, "you're sixteen years old. Hasn't that fancy-shmancy girls' school taught you *anything?* Next you'll be picking your nose. If I were Catholic I'd throw you to the nuns." She appealed to Hortense for tolerance. "There are no social graces left. If they think it, they say it."

"I teach school," said Hortense calmly. "I'm used to sassy kids."

The girl laughed. "Booker's been giving me tennis lessons. He's a tiger."

Hortense wiped the perspiration dewing her upper lip and snorted. "He's a tiger, is he?" She sat back in her chair and bent her stern gaze on the girl. The girl returned the look, meeting Hortense's black velvet stare with one of her own.

Mrs. Todson felt the constraint in the air. "Stacy still sleeps with a teddy bear," she said.

"Well," drawled Hortense, "I sleep with Booker, so now we got it all sorted out."

She lay back in her chair, looking up through the green filigree of the trees surrounding the court. She stretched her long legs out in front of her, raised her arms above her head in a good muscle-easing stretch. Somewhere in the grounds a power mower cut grass. Her nostrils widened, pleased with the scent. The two women preserved a respectful silence, as if some glossy exotic bird had come to perch among them.

On the court the action was fast and aggressive, both men ripping their shots. There was no slicing or cutting, no hanging back at the base line, instead clean, flat strokes, each of them hitting hard and all out, and the rhythm of the game was a satisfying metronomic thunking of the ball on the green asphalt surface. Nor was a point ever very long; the two men played the same kind of game, the big game, serve, return, volley, serve, return, smash. They seemed extremely well matched, with the swift, easy movements that only first-rate players have. Hortense sat up to watch. The men ranged from one side of the court to the other in what seemed to her two or three quick steps, bounding from the base line to the net in a blur of speed. She concentrated on Ted for a while. He was very good, his strokes flat, hit with pace every time, low over the net and deep in the corners. Then her attention went to Booker. She had watched him in dozens of matches and she knew how duplicitous he was being now, how cleverly and artistically he was throwing the game. He was missing just a bit too often, his key shots grazing the white lines, skidding just beyond them, the lobs, the cross-court volleys, the overhead smashes, missing the lines again and again by the merest fraction, by a hair. He didn't hit into the net — nothing that obvious — he simply hit the ball out. A little. It's a game of inches, he had told her; today everything seemed to be half an inch out of the court. If confronted, he could shrug it away, claim his timing had been off. But she was certain he was playing "client tennis."

Yet he made Ted work for his victory. The two sets ended with identical scores, 7–5, 7–5.

"Two points the other way," Ted said happily as they came toward the chairs, toweling off sweat, "and you'd have won."

"Timing's off today," Booker grumbled.

Ted, energized and ego-stroked, preened in front of the women. "Not bad for an old man," he said.

Mrs. Todson stuck out her tongue and dipped it delicately into her drink. "My darling," she said, "we have a five-thousand-dollar sauna, a thirty-five-thousand-dollar country club membership, a Norwegian masseur and two complete physicals a year to make you the man you are. But you were splendid." Her voice slurred slightly. "Perfectly splendid." She looked up at Booker, who was gathering up his can of balls and his racket.

"I think we're having roast beef for dinner. I never know, my cook's on the take, so it may be hamburger, but do stay."

"I'd love to, Mrs. Todson, but Hortense and I have a favorite place at the beach. The chef's gotten something special going for us tonight, and he's a friend, so we can't let him down."

Hortense felt a hand on her upper arm. Ted leaned over her. The ghost of his cologne still lingered on his wet torso. He had a finely shaped head, like the portrait busts of Alexander, and the eyes were just as blank and cold as the stone.

"I know he threw the game," he said in a tone too low for the others to hear, "and I know you don't like it. Stay for dinner."

She rose to her feet, brushing off his hand.

"He's on to you, Booker," she said. Then she turned to Mrs. Todson. "You've got a lovely garden. I enjoyed sitting in it."

Hortense started up the grass hill, her stride long and easy.

Stacy looked after her and whistled between her teeth. Booker wavered between fury and urbanity. After a long moment he found a smile.

"She spent a lotta time in Sunday school," he said. "It took."

Ted picked up his wife's drink and drained it. He had the certainty of a man never questioned. "I can take you without any edge, Booker. I'll demonstrate that next time." His voice was cool, kept its neutral tone. "I fancy-dance a lot in my business," he said. "I can give you lessons in that, too."

Booker rebounded with ease. "My mama always told me, 'Booker,' she said, 'if you put your finger in the jam pot, you're gonna get caught.' Next time I'll beat your ass."

"You got it."

They did not shake hands. Booker followed Hortense, swinging his racket and humming boldly off-key.

At the end of a cul-de-sac overlooking the freeway traffic snarling through the San Fernando Valley, Booker laid her on the back seat of his car. She had one leg out the open window, the other up under her chin. Her orgasms were quick and repeated — she hit like a slot machine paying off, spilling, flooding, profitable every time. Her hands clutched at his buttocks; they patted, they applauded, they approved.

As for Booker, he made love like a boy, ardent for pools and tides, jackknifing off a log into a stream and coming to the surface again, dripping and grinning, calling out raucously, weedy, drenched and joyous.

"Sweet Jesus Christ, God Almighty." He burrowed his face into her belly and nuzzled ferociously. "Gimme some of that every day and I'll live to be a hundred."

Hortense heaved him to one side and groped for her purse, abandoned on the front seat. "Well," she said, "you do that better than you do anything else, I'll say that for you."

He hugged her back to him, unwilling to be finished. "One more time."

"You didn't even have the ticket for this ride," she said tartly. "I'm sore at you."

He cupped her breast and gently traced the nipple with his mouth. "You didn't *act* sore."

"I've been balling with you since I was twelve years old," she said. "You know just what I like and how I like it but that's just being *used* to each other. We're not twelve anymore, Booker. At least I'm not." She dragged a comb through her tangled hair and found a candy mint, which she crunched ferociously between her strong white teeth.

Piqued, he clambered out of the car, adjusted his fly, picked up a rock and pelted it at a tree. He waited to be invited back. He waited on Hortense's pleasure.

"Now I want to talk to you." She stuck her head out the window. "Turn around and get back in here."

He glared at her. "The only way you're any fun at all, Hortense," he said thoroughly riled, "is when you've got your legs open and up on my shoulders and your big fat bossy mouth shut. If you think I'm gonna get in there and get chewed out by you, you got another think comin'. Anyhow, I know what you're gonna say."

"I'm waitin', Booker."

"Piss off, Hortense."

They were children again, cuffing and spitting at one another. It had always been that way between them. She remembered sitting next to him on a sanded wooden church bench, her hands twisting the thigh under his smelly cord pants, pinching and pinching while he fought not to cry out. She remembered the first time they'd made love, on the bank of a dried-out stream, she on her back among the cow pats and flies, he manfully mounting her, yelling, "Where, tell me *where*, I can't find the hole!" They had wrestled in a barn on rainy days with the calves watching them with round wet eyes. She had fought him like a virago, biting his ear, kneeing his groin, until she made him say girls were as good as boys any old time. And this was after they had been lovers, sleeping sweetly in the hay. Kiss or kill. Sometimes both at once.

Now he sat down on a rock and chewed a stalk of grass and showed her a stony profile. She got out, slammed the car door, shoved him over to make room and plopped down beside him, legs wide, her hands hanging between them. She nudged him with her shoulder.

"I've always been smarter than you," she said, "and you know it. Listen for your own good."

"Shit."

"My mama's dead. Your mama's dead. All we've got is each other. I've *always* told you what to do."

He shoved her off her perch. She thumped into the dirt and looked up at him disgusted. "That's pure childishness, Booker."

She stood over him. "You're gonna hear it because I'm gonna say it. If you keep on the way you're going, you're gonna end up wearing black and white shoes, a diamond pinkie ring and making phone calls for a nigger whore. You're hustling, Booker. That's what you were doing this afternoon and that's what you've been doing ever since we came up north."

He was on his feet and fairly hopping with rage.

"I'm the tenth-ranked tennis player in Southern California," he shouted. "I've played exhibitions with movie stars. *Movie stars!*" He thrust his face close to her. "Dinah Shore, Charlton Heston, Dino Martin, Efrem Fucking Zimbalist! Old Blue Eyes himself had me down to Palm Springs for two weeks. Whadaya mean, *hustling!* They wait in *line* for me!"

A small dog appeared on the rise before them yapping shrilly. Hortense whistled the dog to her side, ruffled its coat and murmured to it while Booker thrashed in front of her like a gaffed fish.

"I don't need no righteous Baptist to tell me how to cut it!"

She'd had enough. She rose, marched over to him and clapped a hand firmly across his mouth. "Shut up now. Hush," she said. "I've got more to say. You've got five more years and then you're going to be too old for what you're doin'. You can't figure to make it forever with that tennis racket or even with that bulge in your pants. I want you to go back to school. I'll help you. That don't mean silk shirts from Eric Ross or a fancy pad or a Mercedes-Benz Four Fifty SL. That means one room and a lot of grind and the fuck of your life once a week if you keep your grade average up." She let go.

He wiped his nose with the back of his sleeve and glared at her.

"You got to be kiddin'! One year from now you can call my secretary in Beverly Hills for an appointment." He snorted derisively. "I don't have no house key tied around my neck anymore. I don't have holes in my shoes. I got *charm*, honey."

"A black cock's no different than a white cock," she said flatly. "What're ya gonna do when they find that out?"

He grabbed her and snapped her head back and forth. "Whada *you* know about white cock?" She had lifted weights in the gym all summer and he felt the results as she shoved him. Flat on his keester in the dust, he was still wild. "You gettin' it off with whitey?" he demanded.

She grunted in disgust. "I should have left you in Texas," she said. "You could've stood with your back against an adobe wall and sucked your teeth for the rest of your life and dug the cooties out of you with a penknife."

She started for the car. He loped after her.

"Booker, come with me," he taunted. "Booker, I can't make it up north without you." He mimicked her voice with perfect accuracy.

"I was fifteen and foolish," she countered. "Now I'm twenty-eight and smart. You gonna drive me or do I have to hitch?"

4

STELLA CARVER could see in the dark. She could peer through her almost empty apartment and into the recesses of her soul. Of the two, she preferred the monastic simplicity of the apartment. It was a plaster box, nearly empty, containing not much more than a metal cot with an often-washed white coverlet, an oak rocking chair of surpassing ugliness, an enlarged snapshot of a man looking at her with a brooding worried stare, fading away now to the blur of an old daguerreotype. In the corner were three-dozen empty whiskey bottles lined up in neat rows. Beyond, in the kitchen, a carton of cottage cheese bloomed with mold, an apple shriveled and rotted, an empty birdcage swayed beside the open window, the bird long flown.

She appeared to be sitting idly in the chair, a large writing pad across her lap, but her face, in the dim light, had a ferocious and imperious air as if she were commanding something into being. After a moment she scrawled a word or two on the paper, crumpled it and consigned it to a growing pile beside her. She got to her feet and walked back and forth across the room through the welter of balled papers like fallen leaves at her feet.

She was a tall woman, formidable. Cadgers gave her a wide berth. Children withheld their smiles. She heard no small talk, she indulged in none. She was forgotten at Christmas, and other anniversaries went unmarked as well. Her whole persona warned the world to mind its own business. She went about hers as secretively as a closed clamshell, asking no quarter. Her work was sacred; she was a poet, the rest of life profane. She drank with monumental thirst but in a solitary way. A fraternal arm about her shoulders in a bar would have elicited a stream of vivid abuse couched in the language of a truck driver. There was no one to share her kind of loneliness. It was a force she bowed to alone.

Her large gray alley cat sat on her sweater and watched her with cautious gray eyes. They did not like each other, but he was a presence she felt she needed. Words addressed to another living being were a release for all the others dammed up inside her, obdurate and heavy like stones in her mind.

"Move, you great fat thing." She shoved the cat onto the floor. He arched his back and spat. "Give me back my sweater." She sniffed at it as she shook it out. "Cat hairs and randy." She struggled into it. It had a hole in the sleeve. The pockets sagged from her constant thrusting. It was an unflattering color. She hauled a squashed cigarette pack from its depths, thrust a broken cigarette into her mouth, lit it and let her gaze stray to the bottle-filled corner.

"Well," she said aloud, "the wellsprings are dried up and the booze is gone. Must see to that." The cat ignored her. She went to the closet and took down a floppy black hat which she clapped onto her springy gray hair. An old purse followed, turned upside-down and vigorously shaken to disgorge a candy wrapper and a fine linen hankie, beautifully embroidered.

"Not even a bus token. And me with sand in my mouth." The need to scavenge seemed to infuse her with life.

"Who haven't I put the bite on this week yet?"

There had been the airline stewardess in the laundry room, a silly sentimental girl who'd thrust a dollar in her hands with an embarrassed but virtuous smile; there had been that little butterfly of a man who lived above her, Scotty or Dotty or Potty, she couldn't remember his name, who had produced a lovely bottle of Scotch and a warning. "Watch the liver, Stella, when it's gone it's gone, love."

And the black girl with the striking eyes and the acerbic manner who had parted with a six-pack.

"But that's only for watching baseball games," she had objected. "I'm a serious drinker."

"Honey," the girl had said, "you been living next door to me for a year, I *know* what kind of a drinker you are. But that's all I've got and I probably shouldn't be giving it to you."

She had taken it. "It's an inelegant drink, but you're very kind."

There was, of course, always Jake. Jake. He created an unnatural anxiety in her. Doubtless because she was beholden to him. Jake, who gave her an apartment in this tacky, dry-wall Shangri-la rent-free because he had been one of the hundred and seventy-two people to buy her thin volume of poetry bound in green vellum the color of lettuce. "Cultivate and Harvest." He had even read it. He had even understood parts of it. Behind that doggedly male face was some hint of excellence. If she had friends she might have allowed him to be one. As it was he could be called a patron. Rich as bloody hell, too. A wad of bills like a boxer's fist stuffed into his pocket, bound around with a rubber band. Jake it would be.

She came out on the landing of her apartment. Below, Marina One pulsed with early evening life. It was the time of showers and pissing, shaving and primping, priming and hoping, that strummed through the compound like a throbbing pump. In the picture window across from her a man naked to the waist chopped onions with great tears rolling down his face.

"Hi." His greeting belied his swimming eyes. "How goes it?"

"Do I know you?"

"Benson. American Airlines. I'm in and out."

Jake was in the swimming pool. He swam till he was brute-tired, surfacing and submerging like a dolphin. As he hauled himself out on the coping he saw her ridiculous shoes planted close to his nose. They were brown, scuffed, disgraceful. One of them was untied.

She hunkered down until they were face to face.

"Five dollars would see me through the night very nicely," she said without preamble.

"For food or drink?"

"Drink, of course."

"I don't think so." He hoisted himself out, grabbed a towel, working over his dripping body with careful attention.

"Have you gotten tight all of a sudden?" she said rancorously.

"You can come up to my place. I've got a two-pound steak. Sirloin. Prime."

She shuddered. "Blood meat. Grain's the thing, my boy. Barley. Rye. Not slaughtered cow." She held out an insistent hand. "You can spare it. Come on." She was not wheedling. It was more like a command.

"I don't think so," he said again. He looked at her with distaste. "You haven't washed your hair in a week, Stella. You're beginning to get gamy. You'll give the place a bad name."

"This place? Steaming with fornication and frenzy. I don't see how I could. Consider the money a loan then."

"You don't pay back loans."

"I'll dedicate my next book to you. I'll make you immortal with a kiss." She grinned without mirth. "I'm going to the Dead Duck Bar with or without money. If they present the bill and I stiff them, they'll call the police. You'll have to come and get me out of jail. It'll cost you more. Surely, you can see that!"

"Hand me my pants."

"Ah, good."

"I'm not giving you the money. I just want my pants."

"Prick. Bastard. Asshole."

She gathered the dreadful sweater about her shoulders.

"I'll be up late," he said pleasantly. "You can drop in for a sandwich if you're still on your feet."

She stormed past him. "I am always upright in every way," she said, "looking down on the verminous world beneath me."

On the television set a row of dancers offered a view of crotch and smiles of dazzling whiteness to the watchers standing at the bar. It struck Stella as she elbowed a place for herself that the hand of the Creator was as unsteady and erratic as her own. Look at the odd shapes and sizes human beings assumed; two skinny girls exposing their jagged hipbones and rounded navels, a snout-nosed fellow with merry blue eyes, an old woman with the ruin of her life tracing its lines across her face. At the end of the bar was a tall young fellow with damp, slicked-down hair and a guile-less look. He had a cut scabbing from too close a shave, a sweet, full lower lip, the high color of a child. His hands were big and raw with grease making half-moons under his nails. He stood looking into his half-filled glass with infinite sadness, his bony Adam's apple bobbing in his throat as he belted down one drink and then another.

She made for him. Standing close, she caught a whiff of naph-tha soap and cheap bay rum. She knew his sort. He would wash his dog on Saturday morning, his car on Sunday. He would replace the toothpaste cap and hang his tools in neat patterns on a garage wall. He would know how to repair a watch, how to get a kite smoothly airborne. He would sail one in a public park on a windy day. His teeth were doubtless without cavities, his soul without stain. She watched him tossing his drinks back. He winced at the sting, coughed into his fist. She made a clucking noise of disap-proval.

"A pleasant drunkenness is achieved slowly, young man," she said. "The sun is going to come up tomorrow morning. You needn't rush to meet it."

He turned sea green eyes to her. "Ma'am?"

"That grain ripened slowly under a bountiful sun in Scotland. It gentled in beautiful handmade barrels. It recalls peat fires and bogs. And you're guzzling it like a hog."

"Well, I don't know anything about that. I just want it to hit me, is all."

"A thirst can be slaked at the water tap. A need has to be nurtured."

He squinted at her uncertainly. "Lady, you drink your way, I'll drink mine, if it's all the same to you."

She inched in beside him and pulled off her hat, stuffing it carelessly into her pocket. "I have a problem," she began.

"Ain't we all?"

"Mine is pressing. I haven't the price of a drink on me."

He turned back to his glass. He had been hustled before. But not by the like of her. She tried again.

"Well, then, could you spare a dime for the ladies' room?

They've put pay toilets in there for some barbaric reason. If you won't help me with one call of nature perhaps you'll help me with another." Her smile was bold; she had a pirate's audacity. The young man shook his head, bested, dug in his oily jeans and handed her a dime. She threaded her way through the tables with a purposeful stride, jabbing with an elbow to clear her way.

The ladies' room bore a sign reading "Little Girls." She snorted at that and passed into the candy-box pink cubicle. A torpid black woman, eyes closed, sat beside the dressing table. On it, in a saucer, were a handful of coins and a two-dollar bill. A small handwritten scrap of paper thanked one and all for gratuities. The woman groaned aloud, shifted into a deeper dream. The room stank of Lysol and face powder. Stella stood for a moment, then scooped the contents of the saucer into her hand. She hesitated over the bill, but not for long. She snatched that up too.

At the bar she scattered the money in front of her and rapped for the barman's attention.

"Glenlivet. No water. No ice. Full measure, please. Fill the glass till you wet your finger."

The gloomy young man was still there, nursing his drink.

"What'dya do, rob a piggy bank?"

She was serene. "I stole it," she said comfortably.

He swiveled around to give her his full attention. "You're kidding."

She saw that in his innocence he would leave his front door open, his car unlocked. He would point out mistakes to a bank manager, file an honest tax return, return a lost watch, give honest change to the penny.

"You must be far gone, lady."

"Very far indeed."

He was suddenly on to her. "Hey, I bet they got an attendant in the washroom. They keep a little plate out for tips. That's what you lifted. That's right, isn't it? Poor old lady's probably got five kids somewhere."

"Yes. It's dreadful to be driven to such behavior." The barman set a drink in front of her. She let it sit there. She was like a gambler turning away from the crap table while a stack rode on a bet with bad odds.

The young man appraised her a moment. "Hell, I ain't standing next to you. You'll probably lift my wallet off me." He took it out of his pocket to assure himself it was still there. As he flipped it open she saw the picture of a girl with pointed features and long hair. The sight of it seemed to agitate him.

"I've been tryin' for an hour to get drunk and I'm sure not there yet. When I was in the navy all it took was two three-point-two beers and I was pain-free. Yes, sir, two beers lying on Waikiki Beach in Hawaii was all I needed. Hell, you can get drunk on the air over there, on the frangipani blossoms. I wish I was back right now — I'd do another hitch in the goddamn navy to get there. I'd trade this whole state for Hawaii. They got everything we got, only better. The girls are better. They don't put their hands in your goddamn pockets. You don't have to buy 'em a nine-dollar steak. They just sit on the beach with you and rub Man-Tan oil on your back and treat you like you were a fucking king."

Stella began to sip her drink. "Be quiet now," she said.

He wouldn't have it. "Bars are for company," he said angrily. "Why don't you just get a bottle of wine and sit on a curb huggin' it between your legs. That way you can *roll* home when you're all finished."

"You're looking for a fight, aren't you? Well, there's a great beefy-looking clod down at the end there. I'm sure he'll oblige you."

She turned to the bartender, pointing to her change on the counter. "There's enough there for another, isn't there?"

"No, ma'am, there isn't. Even if you don't leave me a tip . . . which you don't."

"When my ship comes in," she said smoothly. "You're sure there isn't enough? Perhaps you miscounted."

"You're two cents short, lady."

"For want of a nail the shoe was lost." She sighed deeply.

The young man was still there. He stepped in. "Give it to her. I'll pay."

"I misjudged you," she said. "You're a prince of philanthropy."

He shifted back a little so he could study her. "You're something else," he said. "You don't even say thanks."

"I don't say please either." She was busy watching the glass being filled. "Short measure there, my friend."

The barman scowled at her. "If they were all like you I'd lose my job. The boss says *when* in here, lady."

She took the glass and made for a dark corner. The bar was for single patrons. She watched a deeply tanned man bite the ear of an underaged girl at the table next to her. She heard the buzz of conversation made cheerful by Old Grand-Dad and Miller High Life and bar Scotch. She found the young man standing beside her, drink carefully balanced in his hand.

"Can I sit down?"

She relinquished her privacy crossly. She was edging toward that moment when her mind moved swiftly from image to image, leaving a rush of words boiling in their wake. Damn. He persisted, his hand already grasping a chair.

"You have my attention until the glass is empty. That seems fair since you paid for it."

He scraped the chair and settled his thin frame onto it. She saw a button missing from his shirt cuff. She saw freckles trailing in a golden pattern up his arm.

"I gotta talk to somebody," he began abruptly.

"You can train yourself not to," she said flatly.

He paid no attention to the sarcasm. "My old lady took off tonight. Just like that. Took my navy skivvy bag, stuck her transistor and her hair dryer in it and took off."

"Your mother?" she queried. "Is that who you mean? Your mother left you?"

"Not my *mother*. She died in sixty-seven. My wife. Julie. I've only been married two years. Two years Valentine's Day. That was her bright idea. She even got herself some of those red bikini pants with hearts all over 'em, you know?"

"No. I'm afraid I don't know. Mine are plain white cotton."

"They said 'Happy Valentine' right across the ass."

She burrowed into her glass, gulping deeply. He seemed impelled to further intimacy. "By the way, my name's Ben D'Agostino. I'm of Italian descent."

"Molto bene."

"Yeah," he grinned, pleased. "That's it. Italian. You got a good accent."

"Those are the only two words I know." She paused. "I know two others in English. Good night."

He gestured to her drink. "You still got somethin' in there. Stick to what you said. I talk while you got somethin' in the glass."

She honored the bargain. "Very well. Did you beat your wife? Is that why she flew the coop?"

"Beat her?" He was indignant. "Listen. I painted the kitchen twice for that bitch, once green, once blue, because she changed her mind in the middle. I did all the cooking. Tortellini, spaghetti with clam sauce . . . nothin' bought, nothin' frozen. I washed the goddamn windows. I built her a doghouse for her little yappy dog and cleaned up the turds he left on the floor, too. Shit, I even rung up curtains on the Singer because I got taught to sew in the navy and she didn't know how. Six pairs. She didn't have to lift a fucking finger."

"You're a man among men, Mr. D'Agostino."

"Ben. You're fucking A." He jabbed a finger at her. "I been ten years on my present job. No sick days, no goofin' off. I got a triple A credit rating at my Security Pacific bank. Car's paid for. Television's paid for. Appendix which I had out four months ago . . . paid for. I made my service insurance over to her, I give her a solid gold heart for our second anniversary present plus three pairs of black pantyhose . . . I held her in my lap like she was a kid when she had bad dreams. And she ran off."

"You tell a sad story," Stella said, and drained her glass.

"That's all? That's all you gotta say? A sad story?" He was outraged.

"Not *Oedipus Rex* . . . not "All in the Family." Perhaps somewhere in between." She dragged out her hat and clapped it on her head, preparatory to rising from her chair.

"Boy, I don't know. You're tough as nails. I don't think I can talk to you, lady."

"I'm a realist," she said. "Plain-spoken. Harsh, perhaps. But bracing. It's lucky you ran into me instead of some great soft pillow of a woman you could blubber into."

"I don't know," he said again, shaking his head. "You're a real dingbat." He peered through the half-light at her. "How old are you, anyhow? I can't see with these twenty-five-watt bulbs they got in here."

She picked up a match, struck it and held it up to illuminate her face. "Take a good look."

He studied her, grasping her hand until the match burned her finger and she quickly shook it out.

"You're not bad looking. I had an English teacher once, looked like you. She flunked me. But you're salty. I like you."

"That's up to you."

"Why don't we take a walk on the beach, huh?"

"For a host of reasons," she said. "You're a stranger. The night air gives me asthma. My shoe has a hole in it."

"It's nice on the beach tonight. Hey, the grunion are running." He tilted back in his chair, suddenly buoyant and enthusiastic.

"The question is," she said carefully, "where are they running to?"

"Come on. You know what grunion are?"

"Little silvery fish. Slithery, slippery, slyly salaciously silver."

He stood up, pulled her up. "You talk too much. Let's take a walk."

She was too bemused and too drunk to be afraid. "All right. Lead away."

She awoke to the sound of the sea and the scratch of wet sand on her back. Somewhere, foggily, there was the recollection of an amorous tussle on the beach the night before. There was evidence of it in the beach fire dying away in the daylight, in the limp condom draped over a stick, in a denim jacket which did not belong to her hung over her shoulders. Yes, there had been some goatish revelry, of that she was quite certain. She recalled a cock as big as a hockey stick and waved around with the same reckless abandon. She'd been struck in a heap by the saucy redness of his pubic hair. Who could have guessed at a bush so flaming God himself might have spoken out of it in a stentorian voice. He'd been at her rump and at her front like a great friendly collie dog, all tongue and blister, and he had even, in his transport, cried out a cheer which sounded like a salute to his high school football team. Of that, she couldn't be sure. Perhaps it had only been, "God, Stella, I'm coming," but it had seemed to her that there was a "rah, rah, rah" in there somewhere. Seduced and abandoned? Neither? Both? Never mind. She hoisted herself on an elbow, hairpins springing from her disordered hair, and looked at the scene before her.

A city truck trundled along the sand, combing it like a fussy mother, digging tracks with its steel teeth. Up came pennies and wedding rings, bottle caps, fragments of sea-smooth glass and finally a woman's shoe. Had the woman fled? Had she drowned? Was she a limping Cinderella some-where in the city?

Out on the swells a boy rode his surfboard, seal black, seal slick, in his wet suit. When he saw her he saluted with a jaunty wave. On this morning she felt impatient with the young. He waved in vain. Damn foolishness, wandering off with that youngster from the bar. Could have gotten her throat slit for an encounter so brief she could not remember the taste of his kiss or the look of his backside.

She debated washing her face in the cold saltwater, shuddered, decided against it. A cruel rumbling in her gut reminded her of the many hours she had gone without eating. She thought about a glass of wine, darkly red, sweet Jewish wine perhaps, as break-fast. She was not likely to come by it. She hauled herself upright and massaged the small of her back.

On the boardwalk, a little man, swaddled in a huge prayer shawl and skullcap, opened the doors of a storefront synagogue. It was a lovely sweeping motion he made as he threw the doors wide to welcome the Sabbath and the presence of a God who did not disdain the Orange Julius stand abutting His shrine.

She turned away from him to see her hat and her bag lying on the scuffled sand.

My God, she thought, it looks like a rout, a thorough rout. She stooped, groaned, retrieved them. She took a cursory glance in her pocket mirror, searched for signs of lechery lingering in her face. None. A purple bruise on the neck was all. She grinned, knowing for certain he had a mark on him somewhere, too. Give as good as you get. She lived by that.

It was then she saw the woman running, a Diana jogging down the beach toward her. The figure hesitated, swerved, made toward her. It was that doctor from the Marina. She vaguely remembered her. Now she pounded toward her with vitality so forceful it made Stella recoil.

"Hello there." Nell stopped beside Stella.

Stella noted with some resentment that despite the run she breathed with ease. She would have been bent double herself.

"Yes, good morning," she said vaguely.

"You're out early."

"I am taking an early-morning constitutional," Stella said with elaborate dignity. She smoothed her hair by wetting her fingers in her mouth and patting it into place.

Nell pulled a towel from her neck and mopped her face. "Well," she said, "you've left your panties behind you, if that's the case." She indicated a rather scruffy pair of briefs blowing away in a sudden gust. "Are you all right?"

Stella watched the panties flapping across the sand with no discernible embarrassment. "My old mother always said, 'Air your private parts and you'll never have a sick day in your life.' She said other things just as foolish. Yes, I'm all right."

"I'm Nell Willis. We live in the same apartment building."

"Delighted to make your acquaintance." Stella sat down suddenly on a stump. "Whoopsie-daisy," she said. "All that roistering has taken the stuffing out of me."

Nell watched her, then made a casual offer. "I've run a mile and that's enough. I was going to have coffee on the boardwalk. Join me."

"If you pay. I haven't a red cent — or a blue one or a green for that matter."

"Be my guest."

Nell tucked into eggs and bacon and toast and cereal with gusto. The same food steamed untouched in front of Stella. She broke a roll into little pieces and made pellets of them, arranging them in a pretty pattern on the tablecloth.

"You appear to me," Nell began, "to be an intelligent woman. Is there any reason for you to be a suicidal one as well?"

Stella made more bread pellets.

Nell cleaned her glasses and adjusted them on the bridge of her nose. "You see, you'll get D.T.'s sooner or later. Probably sooner from the look of you. Not eating. Lying around in the night air. Lapping up liquor. You won't expire in a lovely swoon saying something epigrammatic, you know. You'll get pneumonia. Your lungs will fill with fluid. You'll drown. It takes a long time, dying like that. You struggle. You choke. You wouldn't like it."

"My God," said Stella, "but I'm sorry I ran into you. Who asked you to speak to me?" She put her elbows on the table and leaned toward Nell. "People have a way of taking me up. I don't really understand why."

Nell shrugged. "They adopt dogs from pounds. They help the blind across the street. Probably foolish, I agree."

"I'm a poet, you know."

"Yes, I've read you. You're quite good."

"Good!" Stella snorted. "Read me again. I'm far better than that, my girl."

"You don't write 'pretty' things . . . nothing lyrical . . . nothing very hopeful either."

"I choose the commonplace, the plain, the ordinary, even the ugly. Those are my subjects. That's my meat."

"Are you famous?"

"No. Not famous. Decidedly not. I've had very little attention from the professional and the academic critics. I've never been nominated for the National Book Award; the Bollingen committee, year in and year out, do a very consistent job of ignoring my existence. No matter. A prize from them is like a dog accepting a bone, up on its hind legs with its paws in the air, for doing a trick. I have no loyalty to any literary clique; any literary theory that tried to swallow me would have to disgorge me again in a hurry. I'm not an imagist or a cubist, an objectivist or a social realist, I don't belong to the Black Mountain or the San Francisco schools of poetry." She paused, shrugged. "I live a poet's life. They can take me, they can leave me — I move in my own orbit."

"That should make us great friends."

Stella shook her head. "I don't muck around looking for friends. I have other fish to fry. Are you rich?"

Nell beckoned for the bill. "Not very."

"Too bad. I'm writing a book of verse and I'm looking for a soft touch so I can keep mind and body together while I do this very important work."

"Look further." Nell rose to her feet. "Why don't you put that egg on that bread and eat it in the car while I drive you home? I think it's a crime to waste food. Also, if you don't eat you'll keel over on me and I'll have to give up my Saturday looking after you, which would be a nuisance."

"It looks like a cold yellow eye," said Stella, but she slapped the egg onto the bread and followed her benefactress.

Stella enjoyed riding in the taxicab. She enjoyed the darkly shaded streets with the heavy trees inclining toward one another to make a somber arch of green. She delighted in the jumble that had Tudor mansion jostle New England saltbox, stately Colonial abut a steel and glass box. Oh, how the rich played with their money. Here stood a small Versailles of potted orange trees, there sprawled an acre of grass untroubled by weed and as close cropped as if sheep had been at it; beyond was a cupid wrenched from its French garden, boxed and crated and hurled across the world to gaze into a smoggy California sky.

And there she was in front of Henry's house and it was best of all. It reproached its neighbors with its gentle faded air. Buttermilk had been mixed into the paint to produce an age it had not earned. There were ancient trees of great size and greater cost that had outlived generations. The dog on the lawn was old and cranky, his coat in patches, his gaze milky, his tail bedraggled. Yes, indeed, Henry had made tradition where there was none. He had forced roots into sandy soil. Nothing belonging to him was transitory.

An ample Irish maid answered the door. Her apron was crisp, her expression matched.

"Yes?"

Stella indicated the cab waiting at the entrance to the drive. "Kindly pay him," she said. "Mr. Dillon is expecting me."

She swept past the woman into the hall, pausing for a moment to get her bearings. The furniture was old and gleaming with wax. A bouquet of roses, old-fashioned and pink, shed their petals in a fragile shower on the chest before her. There was a Pissarro on the wall, not one of the best but close to it, and a Renoir lady, plump and pearly, on the opposite side. Old Henry had made no mistakes.

Beyond were glass doors, brightly, brightly washed, leading into the garden and there, under the spread of an avocado tree, one plonking into the grass even as she approached, sat a family group. Henry Dillon, playwright extraordinaire. He might have been the paterfamilias of a New England primitive painting. An untutored artist would have delighted in the benign face with its plumped cheeks (did he conceal hazelnuts there?), his narrow nose, the foxy shrewdness of his eyes. And Alice? Artist, record Alice for posterity. Two round spots of color which nerves of delicate sensibility caused to blaze in her cheeks, dark brown eyes widened to assay the world around her, quick sparrow movements of the head bobbing away from imagined blows. Alice, taut and clever, whose mouth had pursed from years of blowing on Henry's flame. There was a quiet little boy, as well, spoon clutched in his fist, dreamily eating vanilla ice cream. There was birdsong. Dappled light. A tree house perched above their heads. Yes, paint them on a barn board in strong true colors. Immortalize them in all their probity and sweetness. They have posed for the portrait all their lives.

"My dear." Henry rose from his chair and came forward, arms outstretched. "My dear Stella." His kiss smelled of Sen-Sen and tobacco. "You look wonderful, wonderful."

Alice rose and kissed the air above her ear. "Stella, you haven't changed a bit."

The child was introduced. "Our grandson, Willie."

He put his sticky hand in hers and then hid behind his grandmother's knee.

"Sit down. We were just having tea."

Stella took her place in the arrangement, immediately disordering it. Her sprawl was ungainly, her dress food-spotted, her gaze harsh. Where did she fit in among the flowered teacups and the whisper of sprinklers sighing over the asters and begonias, the peonies and roses?

"It's nice of you to see me," she said.

Henry's reply was a soothing murmur. "My dear old friend," he said, "it's been far too long. You've stayed well?"

"I've stayed alive." She waved away the cup of tea Alice proffered. "I don't take tea."

Nothing else was offered. She might as well have something. "Well, a drop then." Her eyes swept around the garden, came to rest on the tree house beautifully balanced in the branches above them. "Is that yours?" she asked the little boy. He shook his head, dropped ice cream on his shirt front.

"It's mine," said Henry. "That's where all the work is done. A childhood dream fulfilled."

"In spades, considering the money you've made. Tons of it. My God, they must have backed up trucks, it must come in over the transom. You shimmy up a tree and the world's your oyster. Sixteen plays," she said, "and not a flop among them. Not a single stiff. English companies, French companies, Rumanian, Swahilian. It's awesome. Stupendous. Mind-boggling."

Alice sniffed criticism. Her voice rose. "Henry works harder than any man alive," she said.

"Alice," said Stella roughly, "I love Henry. I've known him since he was a humorless, good-natured, sturdy little boy. He lived

76

next door to me. We drank lemonade out of the same glass and showed each other our genitals in the garage. He took me to my first dance and left the print of his hand in sweat on my silk dress. I gave him German measles. I visited his rooms at Yale. I saw him off to war."

Alice drained her teacup as if it contained hemlock. "You've stayed away a long time for such an old friend," she said caustically. "We had one Christmas card, I believe, and a telegram from Mexico asking for funds. You can't blame me for feeling that perhaps the ties that bind aren't all that tight."

"Girls, girls." Henry was patient, avuncular. "Pax. Stella's a gypsy, a wild gypsy. She can't be expected to toe the mark. I wouldn't know her if she did."

Alice retreated, eyes blinking with the fervor of her defense. "It's just that I get sick of it," she said. "Henry's work has given pleasure to millions of people all over the world. They *lose* themselves in his plays. They laugh and cry. But there's always someone *carping*. They're not above taking from him. Oh my, yes. Just make a plea and out pops the checkbook. They don't carp about the writing when it's on a signed *check*. No, indeed. And there are plenty and plenty of those, I can tell you." Her cup chattered against the saucer. She set it down.

"Well, we're not here to talk about that." Henry hitched his chair closer to Stella. "You still write?"

"Yes."

"You've never sent me a copy, not a line. Shame on you."

"No."

"Why not? You know how proud I am of you." He patted her hand. "Really proud, Stella."

She regarded him for a long silent moment. Henry, standing on her doorstep with a gardenia in a cellophane box, Henry asking her in the dark, on the porch swing under a pale moon, what made a girl love a man and how to go about it. Henry, white as ashes, waving to her, gawky in a military cap too big for him, as his train took him away.

"You've always told me that you wanted to be an important

writer," she said. "Well, you've been very successful. The whole world knows your name. But I'm the writer, Henry. That's why you haven't seen my work. I spared you comparisons."

"I'm going in the house." Alice stood abruptly. "I have a headache." She turned to Stella. "You can let another ten years go by," she said, "or a lifetime. Come with Grandma, Willie."

They were alone. Henry stood up and jingled the change in his pockets. For a moment the set of his shoulders was stiff; then he turned back to her, shaking his head in wonderment.

"'My big brother is bigger than your big brother,'" he chanted. "'I'm a better writer than you are, Henry.' Still the same arrogant, blunt, rude, marvelous Stella you ever were." He took his chair again, carefully hitching his trousers against creases. "I can't afford to agree with you, Stella. You were right not to send your work. I don't want to see it."

She stood up, knocking over her chair. "I've made a mess of this," she said. "I'd better go home." She stopped in her tracks. "I *can't* go home till I get what I came for. Damn, shit, hell," she raged.

"Sit down, sit down. You're digging up my turf with all that clumping around. What do you want? Tell me."

"Money, money, money, money!" she yelled at him.

"Nothing simpler. How much?"

"You'd give it to me? After the way I've dumped on you?" She struck her forehead with the flat of her hand. "Now I could tear out my tongue."

"Baloney," he said. "You meant every word of it. You think I'm a hack and you're a genius."

"I could kiss your hand," she said gleefully.

"You'd kiss my hand or my ass or my anything else to get what you're after. You don't have to. I've always loved you, Stella. Not sexually. You're too raw for me that way. But it reassures me to know you're around somewhere, swilling and swindling. I won't give you much this time. You'll drink it up. But enough to get by for a while." He reached into his pocket, extracted a battered wallet, peeled out some bills.

two children in her mother's garden in Vienna, she with a crown of flowers in her hair. But Nell was not to think of her as a little angel made of spun sugar, oh, no, she was to disabuse herself of that notion. For during the very service itself she heard the organist make a mistake in the wedding march and she scolded him for it afterward. She had her standards, she was stern, with herself as well as with him. And now, he was a vine without support, a tree bent. He sat, his long, thin hands hanging between his knees. "I can't make myself a cup of coffee. I can't keep a checkbook. I don't know where my collar buttons are. She drove the car, she spoke to the maid, to the lawyer . . ."

Nell waited in vain to hear more, to hear praise for the woman's spirit, hosannas for her mercurial temperament, a cry for lost lasciviousness, an amen for wit and beauty. But there was only the melancholy catalogue of domestic inconvenience. Her own eyes filled with tears. Lovely Eda Lowenthal, whose vitality promised that age could be graceful and stylish. A lost friend, a lost light. Thieving Death.

"I'll drive you home," she said, "but let me have a word with Amos first. I'll meet you downstairs."

He blew his nose; he mopped his eyes. "Yes, that would be good. I came in a taxicab. A neighbor called it." He stopped in the doorway, stagnant in his grief. "Her things? Her wedding ring?"

"I'll bring them along."

"Bring the candy boxes also. I have a sweet tooth."

Amos hugged her to him in the hallway, glaring over her head at a student nurse who showed too much curiosity by turning to gawk at them. "I'm sorry as hell," he said. "She was a fine lady."

"I promised her she'd be all right. So much for promises."

He patted her. "Why don't you go home for the rest of the day? I'll mind the store."

"Would you? I feel I'd just like to sit down and think about her. George will cry a little and take a nap and watch some television, and by tomorrow be on the lookout for a plump widow who understands the care and feeding of diabetics and is willing to float her dentures in a water glass next to his." She turned her coat collar up, dug in her purse for her car keys. "If I lived a lifetime with a man I'd want to mean more to him than nursemaid and chambermaid. Yes, I'm going home."

She left George to the long-faced neighbors gathered on his front porch, carrying Pyrex dishes of macaroni and cheese and chocolate cakes and strudel.

A light rain began to spatter. The ocean turned gray.

At Marina One the sun umbrellas flapped damply in the breeze. A light aluminum chair toppled into the swimming pool and bobbed like a life raft with no survivors. Stella's cat curled itself under a balcony, nursing his ill will toward the world. Somewhere in the far reaches of the complex a daytime soap opera played out its dolor. The fire pits were smokeless. The sails on all the masts were furled. The ladies had been driven indoors. They were even now being comforted by the hairdryers in the beauty salon, warming their hands in sudsy manicure water, watching with too excessive an interest their own reflections in the long pink-tinted mirror.

Nell passed Jake Cooley's door. It stood open. He was sitting under the light of a Tensor lamp, an embroidery frame in his lap, sewing, his hand describing a graceful arc of needle and thread. He looked up at her. "You're home early."

"Yes."

"Anything wrong?"

"A friend died."

His cool blue eyes lingered on her. "Want to be alone?"

"Yes and no."

"Sit here for a while." He stood and beckoned her in. She walked into the neat apartment. He surrendered the best chair and she took it. The air was perfumed with vegetable soup, steaming in the kitchen beyond.

"I cook soup on rainy days." He put aside the flowered panel and stuck the needle like a careful housewife into a strawberry pincushion.

She sank back and closed her eyes. Some of the physical discomfort of wet and cold left her. As often as she had seen death she had never become reconciled to it. A close look bred fear. Fly blithely when you are not the pilot. Live boldly when you don't know the hundred different ways the body shuffles off its coil, hemorrhage and shock, blood clot and cardiomyopathy, kidney failure, pulmonary edema . . . The list stretched on — miles of tombstones. On bad days she saw her own. Here Lies Nell Willis . . . Beloved of Whom?

"You're a long way from it," Jake said suddenly.

She opened her eyes. "A long way from what?"

"Your own end. That's what you're looking at, isn't it?"

"You're reading my mind."

"Some of my friends have gone, which makes me thoughtful. A thirty-five-year-old forester, a fifty-year-old professor. The wind chill factor at those funerals was seeing myself in their overpriced coffins, seeing the worms at me. It turns your bowels to water to confront mortality at my age . . . at any age."

"It makes you examine your books," she said. "Debits, credits, miscalculations. You see all the mistakes, all the ink blots. You see the total."

He began to sew again. A spray of lilac began to bloom beneath his clever fingers. "Well, I guess it behooves us all to live with a flourish. The part I always like best in Will Shakespeare is 'Enter with Drums and Trumpets.' A man might well advance with trumpets clearing a path for him. Don't know anyone who blows one, but I hear 'em in my head . . . I've stepped off a lot of curbs to that sound. Want some soup?"

"Yes," she said, "I would. Let's have it for dinner. Bring it upstairs. I'll make a pie."

"Set out some bowls if you've got them and I'll be up with the kettle."

She hurried upstairs. She heard no threatening footsteps or chariot wheels at her back.

Nell sat with a cognac warming between her cupped hands while Jake cleaned her kitchen. He dug into the corners like a

Dutch hausfrau while she lay back, eyes closed, listening to the efficient swish-swish of his dishcloth. She was amused. She had half expected to be lying with her face crushed into his hairy chest by now. Her fingers were almost alive with the tactile possibilities, rough, smooth, warm, hard. Could it be that his erotic fantasies included an Ajaxed sink, a floor swept and scrubbed? My God, the man was even wiping down the stove. She leaned against the back of the couch and watched with delight. How far would he go? He ran a sponge against the windowsill, rinsed the dishcloth, snapped the towel and hung it with an accurate toss. For some unaccountable reason she saw herself naked in a bathtub while he stood over her with a soaped cloth. He'd find every crevice. She broke into uninhibited laughter at the thought. Not dildos, not whips, not chains, but a darkly handsome man subduing her with soap and water.

She was tempted to drag him into the bathroom and put it all to work, right now. She put aside the liquor. Strong drink always made her randy and reckless.

"Can I hire you to come every Saturday?" she asked. "You don't have to do windows or ironing."

He sprawled into a chair opposite her and lit a large cigar. "It's habit," he said. "I was on a P.T. boat in the navy. They're small — there's a slot for everything and everything in its slot."

"True," she said. "True of the entire natural world."

He studied the ash forming on his cigar. "Winston Churchill could get a two-inch ash on a stogy," he said.

"Well, great men are capable of anything." She sat upright, brushing back her hair impatiently.

"I'm waiting for greatness to be thrust upon me," he said. "It's a little slow in coming."

It was her habit to question bluntly, professionally — "Are your bowels regular, do you sleep through the night?" — and out of female curiosity. "What do you do with your life, besides sit in a chair and sew a fine seam?" she asked him.

He slumped comfortably on his spine. "Well, I started out working for my daddy, who was a marine colonel and a building contractor. He felt if a building he put up lasted ten years, it was a monument comparable to the Parthenon. In essence, he was a cheap son of a bitch, but he's dead now and he left me money, so I try to speak kindly of him. He bought me a bulldozer when I was eighteen — I rampaged around in that thing like a demented hot rodder, tearing out hundred-year-old trees, slicing off hilltops — there wasn't a rabbit or a bird or an earthworm left a hole or a nest within a fifty-mile radius. Between us, we just about wrecked the look of this country, all the way from Torrance to Torrey Pines, putting up dry-wall condominiums and no-frill tracts. My daddy's motto was build 'em with spit, shit and speed; he lived and died by it. I'm living off those ill-gotten gains with some sense of shame — but not much."

"Were you ever married?"

"Yes, before I came into my maturity I had a fling at it. Care to hear about it? I come off as a horse's ass — but you'll see that for yourself."

She did want to hear about it, kicked off her shoes, cupped her chin in her hand and gave him her uninterrupted attention.

She had been a high-tailed little Texas girl who wore white duck pants with nothing underneath. She spoke with a lisp which made him concentrate on her mouth and wonder, in the comparative innocence of his youth, what many, many things she might do with it. She had long curved nails which he felt like the lash of pure lust down his back and she fell open like a disintegrating flower whenever he put a hand on her. She grieved over John Garfield's death and voted for Dwight David Eisenhower because he looked like her daddy. She kept a cheerleader's pompon pinned over their bed with streamers that blew in the wind and reminded her of the one year she'd spent in high school in Waco. She loved the big Rexall drugstore with its racks of gothic romances and its pink douche bags. She would sometimes spend a whole afternoon there with one strawberry soda spilling over onto the counter in front of her. She read every religious tract left on her doorstep by Jehovah's Witnesses and other peripatetic evangelists. She felt her role in life was to make her bed with flowered sheets and striped pillowcases and lie on it, her pubic hair white with Cash-mere Bouquet bath power, her perky breasts pointing to the ceiling. His penis had gone limp, his mind dark. It lasted three weeks.

"Did it sour you?" she asked.

He chewed on the cigar stub, working it from one side of his mouth to the other, and reflected. He was judicious, not to be rushed into an answer.

"On balance, no," he said. "A good marriage has a lot to be said for it. I've seen a couple that have worked just fine — my brother Adam, my first cousin Jonas. A little forbearance, a healthy mutual passion, some money, a reasonable sense of humor — all glue to hold it together." He cocked his head at her. "You ever try it yourself?"

"No, I seem to stay with short-term arrangements. Going to bed isn't a very complicated business; marriage is. Besides, I'm a handful. I've been told that I'm cold, perfunctory, spoiled and willful."

"All by the same man?"

"Different men, same criticism. So it seems wiser to just come and go, before the charm wears off."

He dipped the chewed end of his cigar in the remains of her drink and tucked it back in his mouth. "It's a funny business," he said. "You pick your friends after you know something about them. What their golf handicap is, how they hold their booze, what they think of Karl Marx, what they'd do if the house caught fire. But we head into our love affairs catch as catch can, two bodies on a collision course. It's a shame. Tell you what," he said to her agreeably. "Let's start out friends and see where it gets us. Put the building up on a good foundation. Care to do that?"

It was a new tack. The unfamiliar had always appealed to her. Intimacy and coolness, they made for interestingly defined boundaries. Familiarity before fellatio — why not?

"You're on," she said. "I play poker, skeet shoot, understand football, trawl for bass. I can build a campfire, I can Indian wrestle."

"Oh, I'm sure there's more to you than that, and all of it of considerable interest. Spend a little time with me. We'll take a walk in the woods or read some Shakespeare or wash the dog — whatever. I'm a handy fellow to have around in case a light bulb burns out or your toilet doesn't flush. The passage of time, no display of ire, no rancor of any sort, no payment on demand might very well bring us to a pleasant conclusion."

"It's as good an offer as I've had all year." She held out a hand and he took it and raised it to his lips.

"To the buddy system," he said, and he grinned at her.

The phone rang insistently. He got up to go but she held up a detaining hand. He lingered at the door.

A Mrs. Scheinbaum was on the line. Her voice was loud and apologetic. She was sorry to disturb the doctor but she was becoming a little alarmed; her tenant, Mr. Solomon, was running a temperature, had been for most of the day. He had spurned her boiled chicken, he loved boiled chicken; it struck terror to her heart. Nell was soothing; she told the woman to keep him warm and covered, she would arrive within ten minutes.

She hung up. "I've got to go to Venice to see a patient."

"I'll drive you."

"I don't know what I'll find. I may be a while. It could be the whole night."

He shrugged. "I've got it." He held the door for her.

Venice, California, was no kin except in name to that other lovely, fabled city. The loop of lights stringing this shore glittered over taco stands and addict shelters, Chicken Delight stalls and men's and women's urinals standing like fetid little houses on the beach. There was a small amusement park, the steeds on its merry-go-round prancing to a scratchy amplified record. Girls with short flowered skirts and fine legs rode them like Valkyries, hair flying, minds stoned. There were photograph booths with strips of film on the outside showing pimply adolescent boys and winos wearing their battered hats at rakish angles. There was a fortuneteller, a gassy old man who cursed his hemorrhoids, his hard chair and his hard lot while he promised sailors and spinsters

love and marriage, fertility and futures for a buck-fifty a throw.
And all around was the sea rolling forward in foam-edged waves
which stank of oil and sewage.

Mr. Solomon lived above a family grocery store. Its stock was
sparse, its aisles dotted with rat droppings, unswept and unno-
ticed. His apartment at the front had two salt-crusted windows
overlooking the beach.

Mr. Solomon's zealous pursuit of life, God and Mammon were
to be seen in the prayer shawl draped like a sheik's tent, in the
Shabbat candles melting to greasy stubs in tarnished holders of
some beauty, in the racing forms strewn across the floor.

Mr. Solomon, sunbrowned and skeletal, sat in his bed, his thin
white hair bristling over a high domed pate. He held the bed-
clothes up under his chin and looked at Nell and Jake warily.

"A house call costs more than an office call. That nosy
landlady sticking a thermometer in my mouth — let *her* pay
the bill."

Nell sat on the edge of the bed and placed a stethoscope against
his chest, prying down his protesting fingers. She listened, she
probed, she palpated. He wiggled under her hands like a recalcitrant child. "Who's your gentleman friend?" he demanded.

"Just that. My gentleman friend."

"He's new."

She ignored him. "You have the flu, Sam. You're underweight.
You have high blood pressure. And you're no spring chicken. I
think I want you in the hospital and have a pretty nurse rub your
back."

"I'll die first. I'm staying here!"

"If you do you'll have to let Mrs. Scheinbaum go with you
when you go to the toilet. You understand that."

His old head waggled, his eyes went sly with pleasure. "She's
already seen my thing on other occasions."

"Do tell."

He looked at Jake. "If you don't use it, you can't use it," he
warned.

"That's right, friend." Jake was an instant ally.

Nell wrote a prescription, tore it off and put it by the bedside table.

"How old are you, Sam?"

"Seventy-five." He tapped his nose and winked at her. "You're asking yourself am I a liar about Mrs. Scheinbaum. The answer is no. I join the company of Picasso and Toscanini, Rubinstein, that Senator Thurmond with his babies and Bertie Russell — he had women till he was eighty and *he* was a philosopher!"

You and me, Sam, she thought, I know it's curative powers. Better than two Alka-Seltzer tablets, more soothing than wine.

"Stay in bed. Lots of fluid. Light diet. And keep your hands off your crotch and off Mrs. Scheinbaum until your temperature is back to normal." She tucked him in. She didn't wish him sweet dreams. If anyone had them he did.

They came out into the nearly deserted walk fronting the beach.

They were hit from behind. She saw Jake throw his hands up in the air and then twist into what seemed to be a slow endless collapse to the ground. Two arms clamped her, one around her waist, lifting her from the ground, the other around her neck. She felt the blood pulse behind her eyes as her wind was cut off. She felt the heavy, irregular thumping of a man's heart. Her hand still clutched her medical bag, which flapped against her legs as he whipped her one way and then another in a ferocious, punishing, jolting motion. Then she was being dragged away from the limp figure on the sidewalk. She felt a concrete wall scrape her knee. She tried to make herself go limp, to fight against the impulse to claw and scratch. She felt his slippery hands. A spray of his sweat hit her in the face.

His breath was wrenched from a heaving, overtaxed chest. He set her down, grabbed her hair and pulled her face back. She saw blank green eyes, a broken nose. There was a knife in his hand.

"I was afraid you'd be old," he said. "They're all old around here. Old Yids."

He held her out at arm's length. "Won't do no good to yell. They don't come out anyhow. Scared."

"I won't yell," she said, hardly able to talk, her mouth dry.

"What's in the bag?"

"Medicine."

"You carrying any money?"

"No."

"I'll get it off him. Later. You know what we're gonna do now?" He suddenly stuck a grimy finger into her mouth, forcing it open. "You're gonna suck me and then I'm gonna pee on you and then we're gonna make it right here in this alley with the garbage for a pillow."

She didn't let a fraction of a second go by. "All right," she said. "We'll do what you say. But I have to tell you. I have syphilis." She spoke very distinctly. "Syphilis. Advanced. Virulent. Contagious."

The green eyes blinked. "You're shitting me."

"It's true. I'm very sick. I'm running with pus." She didn't move a muscle, returning his hard look without blinking. "You're going to be sterile. You're going to have a fever and a rash. You're going to feel as if your balls are falling off every time you have to urinate."

"You dirty cunt," he said.

"Yes."

He hit her with the flat of his hand. She felt the bag wrenched from her and then heard him running, running down the alleyway as if pursued. It was then a terrible palsy overtook her. She let it rattle through her frame as she tried to keep from passing out. Head down. She directed herself as if she were apart from the scene, looking on. Head between the legs. Then she was on all fours, then on her feet. She had wet her pants. She stopped to pull them off, leaving them sodden on the street.

When she got to Jake he was doubled over, his head in his hands. She knelt beside him, ran her fingers through his hair. There was a fast-rising bump but not blood. She pried his eyelids wide and turned his head to the light, examining his eyes.

Recognition flooded into them. He put out a hand to her. "You? . . . What happened to you?"

She told him, letting him rest his head in her lap. He struggled to rise. "Which way? Where'd he go?"

"Never mind. He's gone."

They were arm in arm then, supporting each other as they staggered for the car. Once inside she turned to face him, her teeth chattering. "Well," she said, close to hysteria, "if we're not friends now, we never will be."

He pulled her close.

Impatience with fear, Nell decided, was a good remedy for it. She elected not to lock her car door on the way to the hospital in the morning, or to buy a gun or to go looking for an attack dog. There were other strengths to go to. After all, she told herself, she was a Willis. A stalwart bloodline, staunch and stubborn and combative. There had been a sod-buster from Montana and a labor organizer in the lettuce fields of Salinas. There had been a renegade priest, a hanging judge, a San Francisco madame rarely acknowledged in the family and a clever felon who had never seen the inside of a jail. Rapists, leary lovers, her own goblins — she could handle them all.

Her tire went flat. She burst into angry tears.

The boy at the station gave her a lift to the hospital. He was a Mexican youngster with a soft deferential air and when she told him she was a doctor he became even more ceremonious, delivering her to the door as if she were a nun returning to a convent. She pressed a tip on him, which he held in his hands as if it were a talisman, staring at her with dark, brimming eyes.

"I fix your car for you, doctor. Myself."

"Thank you, Carlos."

"My mother is a midwife."

She saw now that she was in celestial company. Women who nurtured and birthed and bossed.

"Sixty-five babies." He volunteered the number proudly.

She was out of the car. "Don't you add to it," she said. "Viva zero population growth."

"But I'm Catholic. An altar boy at Saint Joseph's by the Sea."

"Fudge a little," she advised him, and added another dollar to the one he held.

The young man who accosted her in the hallway was Protestant, vasectomized and frantic.

"Dr. Willis — you got a minute? —"

"One." She paused in her forward motion. The intern was pale, his collar wrenched open, flecks of blood on his white coat. "I'm in trouble," he said urgently. He trotted alongside her as she strode down the hallway.

"Where's your resident?"

"Off today."

"What's the problem?"

"I've got a sixty-year-old woman oozing white foamy stuff from her mouth. I'm not talking about a trickle either. She's gushing."

"Let's get there." They were almost at a run now. "Have you got a history?"

"I didn't have time. I shoved a suction tube into her."

"Did you get a stethoscope on her?"

"Lady, I tried. I'm not sure what I heard. She was pounding away like a jackhammer, I can tell you that."

She took hold of his arm. "You're Vincent, aren't you?"

"That's right."

"All right, Vincent, what orders did you give?"

He was sallow, young, with an unruly cowlick standing up like a coxcomb. He seemed close to tears. "Uh ... uh ... aminophylline, to be given I.V."

They were at the door of the room. She gripped him by the shoulders and shook him. "Pull yourself together. A woman in paroxysm is not likely to be cheered by that face. You're an airline steward, Vincent. When the plane is crashing, you smile. Smile, Vincent."

A grimace twisted his face. "I guess that'll have to do," she said, and went in ahead of him. The nurse stood aside for her as she approached the bed, moving quickly, snapping out orders.

"Adjust that oxygen mask. Turn it up. Get tourniquets on her legs. Get me some injectable digitalis and a sixth grain of morphine. Also get out of my way." This last was aimed at Vincent, who stood helplessly in her path. She grabbed the tube and jammed it deep into the woman's lungs. The flood of mucus and blood hit them both.

"Oh, *Christ.*" The young intern turned away and gagged.

The big black nurse grinned at her. "Looks like they sent a boy to do a man's work."

"You just sweep your own corner," Nell told her coldly. "I see where you tried to get that I.V. into six different places. This woman looks like Swiss cheese."

"They're hard to find on her," the nurse said sullenly.

The patient's color had returned, her breathing was easier. Nell beckoned the intern into the hall.

"Get an EKG later this morning. If you're not sure when you've read it, I'll take a look."

Vincent sagged against the wall. "I was scared shitless."

Her glance flicked off him. "If this scares you, sonny, you better get into dermatology."

"Can I buy you a cup of coffee?" he asked.

"You can buy me bacon and eggs and coffee."

The cafeteria smelled as damp and soggy as a Chinese laundry. Her food was expensive, cold and unappetizing. She ate heartily nonetheless while he watched like a seasick traveler.

"This is a lousy life," he said. "If I had it to do over I'd have gone into Beverly Hills real estate."

Nell sipped the bitter coffee. "You may yet," she said, looking at him over the cup.

"You love the life, huh?"

"Some days."

He tilted back in his chair. "I noticed it in med school. The women were hell-bent. I mean they didn't take time to change their Kotex pads."

"Listen," she said to him flatly, "you're not going to push me into delivering you a diatribe on women and how they won the West. I can only speak for myself. I wanted to be a doctor. I waited tables, tutored assholes, went sleepless, hungry and mostly unlaid for the better part of six years. I missed concerts, theaters, holidays and home life in the process. I'm unmarried, in debt, harassed and cynical, but I'm here. Like old Harry said, 'If you don't like the heat get out of the kitchen.' And thanks for breakfast." She got up.

"Want to see a movie Saturday night?" His grin was engaging.

"No, and neither do you. Stay home and read some medical journals. You're sloppy."

She left him slamming his napkin into her egg-stained plate.

"Oh, God, oh, God, Dr. Willis — ?" Ellen met her at the top of the stairs as she approached her office.

"What is it?"

The girl stood before her, wringing her hands, mouth opening and closing as if she were choking on a stone.

"For Christ's sake, girl, speak up. Is it my grandfather? Has there been an accident? What is it!"

"The office — somebody — the drug cabinet . . . it's a robbery — "

She pushed past the girl and into the waiting room where two patients looked up idly from their magazines. She smiled stiffly at them and muttered a good morning. Ellen followed hard on her heels, her hair damp with sweat.

"Where's Amos?"

"He hasn't come in yet."

She went into the lab on a run. The drug cabinet was wrenched open, one door hanging by a broken hinge. She could see at a glance that all the hard stuff was gone, the morphine and heroin, the Demerol, the amphetamines; bottles and capsules spilled out onto the floor, broken glass syringes crunched under her feet. She checked the shelves, sweeping the debris out of her way. The two lab technicians, Sally and Mavis, sat on a bench against the wall, their faces totally devoid of color.

"Who found it like this? Who was the first one in?"

"I was." It was Ellen. She was leaning against the wall with the glazed look of a soldier about to be shot. Suddenly she sighed and slipped to the floor in a dead faint. She fell like a rag doll, revealing bikini panties and an ugly purple bruise on her thigh — a love bite or the sharp edge of a kitchen table? One of the other girls gave a little squeak of dismay and started to rise. Nell motioned her back.

"Just stay put!" She crushed an ammonia capsule between her fingers and thrust it under Ellen's nose. The girl rolled her head from side to side to escape the fumes. When she opened her eyes, tears filled them.

She grabbed beseechingly for Nell's hand. "I had nothing to do with it, Dr. Willis. I swear on Saint Anne and the Mother of God!"

Nell pulled free and rose to her feet. She exploded at them.

"An enormous quantity of morphine and Carbrital has been taken from the drug cabinet in this office. Only the staff and Dr. Steinberg and myself have keys to the office." She began to pace back and forth in front of them. "The cold facts are that someone here is hooked, a thief, a liar, a junkie! Understand me," she went on harshly. "We're not talking about rifling a purse or stealing a credit card. We're talking about hard drugs. I'm giving you fifteen minutes to come in and tell me who is responsible. And whoever it is who walks through my office door had better know this. I'm not going to throw an understanding arm around you and ask you how come. I'm going to call the Santa Monica police and have you arrested. If the other two know who it is and don't speak up in the same time limit, they're out of this office and on the street by six o'clock tonight. No references, no paycheck. Just gone. That's fifteen minutes." She slammed the door furiously behind her.

Her office was stifling. She turned on the air conditioner and then sank into her chair, her head in her hands. Where the hell was Amos? She needed him to handle this. She went back over the past weeks, digging into her memory. Who had seemed jazzed, intense, hyped-up? Who had been careless at work? Who had stayed late or arrived early?

She saw Ellen's red-rimmed eyes wide with fear, swearing on her protecting saints. Ellen, who lived alone and went to night and morning Mass. Had she found that the pretty little wooden statue was just that? Had she prayed in vain?

The other two. Mavis, a Wisconsin dairymaid, plodding, efficient, humorless. Married. No children yet. Working so she could afford them. She suffered from migraines. Nell had treated her and finally suggested a psychiatrist. It had been her mother-in-law nagging her, she had told Nell. She lived in the same house, slept in the room next door, listened with her ear to the wall. She couldn't make love to her husband for weeks at a time knowing the old woman was there, sleepless, avid, listening.

And Sally. She was fairly new. She was clever, quick, crocheted bikini tops while she ate her diet lunch. She joked with the patients; she had a sure gentle touch with a needle. Had she used one on herself? Damn Amos for being late!

A sparrow lit on the windowsill. Another joined. They swirled around each other in a mating flight. A boy whistled off-key in the street below. The air conditioner hummed its one monotonous note. Nell snapped a pencil in two and waited.

She got to her feet, leaned out the window. A woman in a blue police uniform ticketed a car, her blond hair spilling from her crash helmet. An ice cream wagon cruised by, its bells jangling. She sat down again with her back to the door.

When she turned Amos stood before her. He had not shaved. He was coatless. Sweat ringed his armpits — she caught a whiff of him all the way across the room, a stench.

"Poor Nell," he said. "Poor Amos."

She stared at him.

"I was going to tell you, Nellchick. Some day."

He collapsed into a chair, his hands hanging limply over the arms, his legs spread wide in front of him. He tipped his head back, closed his eyes. She might have been looking at his corpse. She saw the dark rings under the eyes, the heavy pulse beating in the throat. When he spoke again she recognized the tone. She had heard it at the scene of an accident when someone was led, bleeding and dazed, away from the wreckage. She had heard it in hospital corridors when pronouncement of death was made to someone who had gone sleepless for days.

He spoke listlessly. It had started in medical school. All that white hot brilliance had come from a needle used in the back seat of his car, in a toilet cubicle, once even near a city dump with the garbage steaming and smoking like an inferno. It had begun with arrogance. Wanting his brain to race ahead of the others, wanting insights and perceptions and visionary truths ahead of the others. He had been a man enmeshed in the dark memories of his family, bound and held in the horrors of their past. His mother still wore short sleeves so that her concentration camp number could be visible to all. His father took scraps of bread and meat to conceal in his bed, until the putrescence revealed them to the disgusted maid. He had been afraid to be without food.

The melted bones of an incinerated family had been the ashes of his youth. To be a Phoenix, to rise through that powdery dust, took help. He had found help.

The raid on the office had been made to look like a robbery. Ordinarily he simply picked out a phony name, wrote out a prescription in triplicate, presented it at a neighborhood pharmacy. But in the early hours of the morning he was a man in despair, a man without alternatives. His face was waxy, his head sagged, his chin resting on his chest. A hanged man, a dead man. "What are you going to do with me?"

Her throat closed. There were no words. She bolted from the room.

His straw hat had been battered into a shape that pleased him by being left in the rain and the sun and to the ministrations of a teething puppy. It rode low on his brow, a white fringe boiling from beneath its brim, giving him the look of a beneficent impoverished monk. She noted also that he was sockless in his worn, English, handmade shoes. His thin anklebones were visible beneath the cuff of his pants. The hat, the shoes, the trousers he considered old and honorable extensions of himself. He never threw anything out.

She remained on the verandah watching for a moment. He was scattering bread crumbs for the birds, speaking aloud in the voice of a martinet.

"Territorial imperative, if I ever saw it. Get off her, you predator." This last was to a swooping blue jay. "There's enough for all. Don't crowd. Observe a pecking order. Be reasonable."

The birds fed voraciously, clustering, chattering, darting at each other. He was not pleased by the disorderly scene before him; he believed that both man and nature must come to terms. He flung the last of the crumbs and picked up the book that lay beside him in the grass.

Nell approached from behind and dropped a kiss on the bristly back of his neck. He turned. He saw in the look of her face and the weary way she sank into the grass at his feet, hugging her knees and staring away across the garden, that she suffered in some way.

"This is a nice surprise," he said, letting a hand rest on her shoulder.

"It's a crisis."

He knew her to be sensible. She was not given to hyperbole. A cloud passed over the sun. He saw a shadow fall on her from within and without.

"Well, what is it?"

She buried her face in the rough cloth covering his knees. It was an attitude she had taken as a child when a confidence had appeared to her to be too horrendous, too private, too chilling to be told face to face.

First she had been stunned, then angry. How dare Amos have betrayed his monkey-clever mind, his jocular spirit, his talent for medicine? How had he dared to turn his back on their old astringent, knowing, forgiving relationship and have hidden this dirty secret? She appealed to her grandfather. Didn't he remember how it had been with them? Amos lying on her bed, crumbs from chocolate cake scattered on the cover as they lay there, heads bent over the open texts, studying till morning? Hadn't he witnessed Amos in the library of this very house, striding back and forth, whacking his thighs with a folded newspaper, making her a learned Galatea as he chanted facts at her in a sonorous, professorial voice? Hadn't she listened to his siren song, calling her to attention from stuporous hours of study: "You can, you will, you must."

And all the other fragments in the mosaic of their friendship . . . the birthday flowers, hideous spiked gladioli in a hideous beribboned basket, the concert tickets given to applaud a pass mark in chemistry, the box of fudge which they consumed to the point of nausea in the hope of jogging their exhausted minds with sugar, the sweat of their hands intermingling as they peered anxiously at deans' lists and honor rolls. Who was this unknown man with the dark guilty face, with whom she had had impromptu pleasures and binding links?

Her grandfather heard her out silently and remained silent. She knew of old that he came slowly to judgment. He fished for a pocket handkerchief, snapped it open. The suggestion of lavender rose in the air. There were sachets almost as old as herself lying in the drawers of the house. Her grandmother had put them there and they remained undisturbed, with only a ghost of their scent remaining.

"I think," he said slowly, polishing his glasses, "that you are more dismayed for yourself than you are for him."

"Not true." She was on her feet, defensive.

"How is it that you didn't know till now? Could it be you weren't paying attention, Nell?"

A chipmunk ran along a bough above her head, flicked a tail and disappeared into the tree. Then its face reappeared, framed by a clump of leaves. He waited. Her grandfather waited.

"We're not children anymore. He had to know what he was doing. He's grown-up. I'm not his caretaker."

"Friend." The word hung on the air. It reminded and accused. She saw his standards raised before her like a bar high off the ground. She was expected to take its measure, to fly over it, to land unharmed on the other side.

"Stop trying to soften me up."

"Am I?"

"He's got track marks on his arm," she shouted. "Like any other hophead. He's practicing *medicine*, for Christ's sake. He has to rely on his judgment, make evaluations, use his goddamn head."

She marched back and forth in front of him, digging her heels into the grass, ruining it.

"I can't countenance it," she said flatly. "I won't."

"What will you do?"

"Throw him out."

"Then why did you come here?"

"To hear what you had to say, if you ever descend from that fucking Buddha calm and *speak.*"

"Please put that divot back in the grass. It's unsightly."

She dropped to her knees in front of him. "I hate him for being weak. He was always larger than life-size to me. Now he's Tom Thumb. What the hell do I do?"

She walked away from him to the end of the garden. "You're making me wild," she said across the intervening space.

He rose stiffly from his chair, the last crumbs in his lap spilling on the ground. "I went to Yale," he began, "with a fellow who killed his wife. She ran her car into his greenhouse and destroyed all his bedding plants. He came to me the night he did it and I called the police. Afterward I found an attorney, a sharp fellow who got very high fees, to represent him. He lost the case but they later judged the man insane. I went to see him twice a week at the asylum until he died. He said I reconciled him to life. I intend to use that statement to get myself into heaven."

He started for the house. She ran after him, caught him at the steps and followed him into the gloomy hall. "You want me to stand by him. Is that the point of your story? To help?"

"Have you any other good deed to your credit?" he asked, looking at her sharply.

"I'd have stood for anything but this."

"That's up to you. Are you staying for lunch?"

"Do you take lunch?" she said acidly. "You're so spiritual I'm surprised it isn't a communion wafer and wine."

"It's lamb cutlets," he said, "and I'd be glad of your company."

Amos was not in the office when she returned. Ellen fluttered in to tell her Dr. Steinberg had cleared everything up. He knew who the culprit was, a young patient of his, a badly disturbed young man. He had taken steps to have the boy sent to Synanon. The hen roost was soothed, the barnyard quieted to its customary clucking, the fox, with its bloodied muzzle, driven off.

"He said we could all go home early. Will that be all right?"

"He told all of you to go?"

"Yes."

"Who's left for me to see?"

Ellen was puzzled. Dr. Steinberg had said she was to cancel all of Dr. Willis' afternoon appointments.

The news made Nell uneasy. She felt all her muscles tightening, coiling, as though in defense against an attacker. "Well, run along then. Tell the other girls."

"I saw a darling two-piece knit in the mall. Blue with a kind of yellowish piping on the jacket. I told the girl to hold it for me." Ellen was like a child let out of school. "I never wear blue. What do you think, Dr. Willis?"

"Yes, by all means, buy it." She was abstracted. She saw the office empty, late afternoon sun streaming through dust motes. The girls would leave everything in order; there would be neat piles of paper on her desk, manila envelopes, all the histories for tomorrow's patients ready for her. There would be a hospital gown draped on its hanger in the examining room. The scale resting at zero. Blood shining like dark wine in specimen bottles. The calendar from the insurance agent heralding spring. There was nothing whatever to fear.

"Put the calls on the service," she told Ellen.

"Dr. Willis . . ."

"Yes?"

"I heard Dr. Steinberg crying in his office."

She sat behind her desk without replying for a moment, her hands in her lap. Then she stirred. She knew she could manipulate the girl with a word. "The toilet makes that noise. It's been driving me crazy for a week. We'll call a plumber in the morning."

"Oh — "

"Be on time tomorrow. Big day."

"Of course. And doctor?"

"Yes?"

"Am I too washed out for light blue?"

White's your color, my girl, she thought. Virginal white, sacrificial white, shroud white. "You'll look very nice in blue," she said.

Ellen was gone, clumping down the hall in her sensible shoes, calling to the others to turn out the lights and lock the back door.

Nell remained very still in her chair; she felt blank, oddly suspended. The phantoms of childhood seemed to be in the room with her. They had not been fear of the dark, or solitude or the faces of strangers. No. They had been formless, shapeless, the rushing of black water, the white flash of lightning, spaces that converged and crushed, noises that deafened. Her mother and father had died in a car, rolling over and over to rest in a deep river. They had tumbled together, pushed into a final, fearsome embrace. There had been the rending of steel, the last bright flash of sunlight, then death. She knew the shape of the stakes driven into her heart.

"Stop it," she said aloud to herself.

Footsteps sounded in the corridor outside her office. She swung her feet up on her desk, pushed up her glasses and presented a demeanor of complete composure to Amos as he opened the door.

He had shaved and changed his shirt and he didn't smell any longer but it only seemed to intensify his diminished look. She was reminded of the cadavers they had studied together, bodies on slabs with the gray hue that spoke of finality and terrible conclusions.

"Come in, Amos." Her voice was matter-of-fact and flat. He

advanced into the room, but he did not take a chair or look directly at her.

"This is the end, you know," she said. "I'm throwing you out."

She waited for protest, explanation, appeal. He rocked back and forth on the balls of his feet and stared over her head as if he were witnessing someone else's fate. Another man was confronting a sheer cliff, an impossible barrier.

Struggle, she demanded, thrash, answer for what you are.

"You're a cold bitch."

She sighed. He had no center to go to — the only weapons at hand were sticks and stones. Jack and Jill went up the hill. They had done that, she and Amos, and now it was Jack falling, sliding, flat on his ass.

"You're not the first to have noted it. You probably won't be the last."

"I've always been in love with you. That's what I tripped over."

It was a false turning, the wrong key. She was suddenly furious.

"Hell, don't lay this at my door. You're a spoiled brat. I'm not your German governess promising *Liebchen* a *Mandelbrod* if he eats his spinach like a good boy or goes potty like a big boy. If you came unglued you did it without any help from me!"

He dug into his pocket, came up with a handful of change which he jingled absently. It went back into the pocket. His hand followed, hangdog, caught.

"There's no appeal in this court, I see. Friends for fifteen years, partners, colleagues, but it's guilty as charged."

"You're right," she said. "I don't trust you anymore."

He gave a little laugh, a small, dry, mirthless attempt that died away into a nervous cough. Nell clasped her hands in front of her, rather ugly hands, she thought, ringless, scrubbed, freckled.

"It'll be best for both of us if we go our separate ways. You'll get your fair share of the money and the practice and the furniture." She made him meet her eyes by the unblinking directness of her own.

"Get some help, Amos. Get some good professional help. That's for old time's sake . . ."

He shuffled his feet but remained standing before her as if he'd grown into the carpet. An almost playful expression passed across his face, transforming him from culprit to gamin.

"What'll you do about the music of a German band?" he asked.

"What are you talking about?"

"We used to go folk dancing to the music of a German band. And you got flushed and thirsty and drank beer out of a stein and hung around my neck with both your hands. And what will you do for dirty limericks which make you laugh and for long talks on the telephone in the middle of the night? And where, Nellchick, will you get a dose of bitter truth when you need one?"

"There are lots of comics around," she said, "and fancy dancers. And as for the truth, bitter or otherwise, I don't think I would have gotten it from you in any event."

"Oompa-pa, oompa-pa, oompa-pa!" He waltzed in a circle, his arms flung wide till he bumped into the door. "I hope you're always right about everything," he said, and like a performer he bowed himself out. She heard his crazy singing in the hall for another moment and then it was quiet again.

She picked up her purse off the desk and dug for a mirror. She stared at the face reflected there; a severe woman with cold blue eyes stared back. Who had been sacrificed in this encounter? She allowed the question, put off the answer. Some day she would probe it, yes, some day she would have to know why it had been so easy.

6

THE BARMAN at the Glass Slipper was named Harold; he made lovely tongue sandwiches on thin buttered bread which he kept under the counter for Eunice. When time allowed, he clumsily carved a radish rose. There was always parsley.

He charged her fifty cents more than the same sandwich would have cost at the delicatessen down the street, but he steered her right nine times out of ten and the four bits covered the time away from other customers.

"Mustard?"

"If you've got that yellow kind. Like you get at the baseball games."

"Brown mustard. You want brown mustard on a sandwich like that."

Eunice twined her legs around the barstool, daintily lifted the bread and rearranged the meat. "So?" she said looking through her false eyelashes. "Who's who?"

Harold brought his face close to her. A dozen small veins had broken under his skin, making a bloody freeway across his nose.

"See that guy down the other end of the bar? The one with the Harris tweed jacket?" His breath, stale beer, wafted toward her. He kept a glass at the ready under the bar.

"Yes. I saw him when I came in. He's got hair growing out of his ears."

"What about it?" Harold was aggrieved. He had hair growing out of *his* ears.

"He doesn't look special."

"Beverly Hills lawyer. Tax lawyer. House in Newport Beach, house in Encino. Royal Oaks. Doesn't booze. One martini with a twist and he makes it last an hour. He's not in here for action. I figure what he wants is to meet a nice lady and buy her lobster tails and French fries. Okay?"

"What're you gonna do," asked Eunice resentfully. "Slide me down the bar into his lap?"

"You know better'n that. Don't I always introduce you? Don't I find a topic of interest to get you started? What's wrong with you tonight?"

Eunice chewed on a hangnail and wondered why she felt lighter than air. Alan had told her she was putting on weight so she had gone all day on black coffee and a cheese Danish. Or maybe it was a dismal sense of déjà vu. Here was Harold with his beer breath computerizing her life. That one's a dentist. This one's a cartoonist. Look over there. He's a pilot. He's a piano player. This one wants to talk. That one bites. The one in the corner is borderline psychotic — or maybe already there.

"A lawyer?" Lassitude made her slump on her elbows.

"Big lawyer."

She craned past a woman in a large hat to look again. "Is he tall or short? I can't tell when he's sitting down."

"What's the difference?" Harold became mildly threatening. "You wanna go home alone, go home alone. I'm being mister nice guy but if you don't want any, you don't get any."

She pushed the sandwich aside. If she went home she would straighten her drawers and wash her hair. There was a whole lemon pie in the refrigerator. She'd eat that. All of it — and the Oreo cookies and some graham crackers and dry corn flakes and soda crackers and butter. She'd eat until she sat with a mouth full of food and her gorge rising behind it. Hortense would be at Booker's, lying in bed with him, flowing over and under and around him like a spill of chocolate syrup. There were all those long empty hours to fill. Alan had been too busy to boff, as he so elegantly put it. Well, she knew the taste of lemon and defeat. What did the man at the end of the bar taste like?

"Bring him on," she said. "But not till I finish my sandwich."

His name was Harvey Medford. He spelled it for her, first name and last. He spoke slowly, as if he were controlling a stammer, but he had a nice smile and very white teeth. She told herself that must mean something. He took the time to get them cleaned or perhaps he rubbed peroxide on them before he went to bed. He was very pleased that she was free for the evening. And it was interesting that she was a Dodger fan. He had been a Dodger fan ever since the team had come out here from Brooklyn. Of course, he'd lost a little of his zest for the game after Sandy Koufax retired, but it was a great team and he had great hopes for it.

"Harold says you watch all the games. That's unusual for a woman."

"He just told you that to get us started. I don't know first base from second. He thinks you have to *launch* people, like satellites." She focused her attention on the white teeth. "Otherwise we might just float by each other."

Her retort gave him a desperate moment. Whatever they had in common was going. "Well, that's all right," he said. "I go to the games with my next-door neighbor."

She knew instantly that he was not a lawyer, he was a bookkeeper in Studio City. She knew his house was redwood with a birdhouse perched on the roof. She knew he opened a can of Campbell's Manhandler soup most nights for dinner and ate it lukewarm from the pan. She knew that he went to the laundromat on Saturday morning and measured out the soap in a cup, that he had just begun to let his hair grow when everyone in his office was now beginning to cut his. He would have his license in his hand before a cop got off his motorcycle. He would stay off the grass and observe the No Smoking signs in elevators.

Shame extorted a confession before she had turned a single screw.

"He told you I was a lawyer, didn't he? I'm not. I'm a store manager for Safeway. The one on Laurel Canyon and Riverside. Do you know it?"

Go home, she told herself, take a warm bath and put on some perfume and get into bed and make yourself come. Otherwise it was going to be a long night short on talk and a dry kiss just wide of her mouth and maybe dinner at the Tail of the Cock, soup and salad included.

"Well, that's a good job."

"What do you do?"

Tell him, she thought dully. Tell him you go down on a vain little peacock of a movie director who talks on the phone while you're doing it. Tell him how long it takes for you to climax because they've sucked so many fetuses out of you with that little vacuum cleaner they use now. Tell him about Yoga and Zen and *est* and needlepoint and exercise classes. Tell him about psychiatrists who fuck you and make you pay the bill and gynecologists who fuck you and won't take Blue Cross. Tell him about Harold who wants to hear all about it the next time you come into the bar with his big pouty mouth hanging open at every word. Tell him not to be afraid of performing for you. You'd welcome the missionary position as a change from all the variations that make your lower back ache.

"I'm a secretary. Just a secretary."

"Most of the guys who come in here say they're doing some kind of important work. I didn't mean to put you on or anything. I guess there's nothing wrong in managing a grocery store. I came up from box boy."

"I'll buy my milk from you from now on," she said restlessly. "You might as well have the business." He was going to sit on the barstool for the rest of the night, eking out his confidences, one at a time. She fought a yawn by patting it daintily to death with her hand.

"There's a nice little smorgasbord restaurant up the street," he said. "It's clean and not too crowded. Could you have dinner with me?"

"I'd love to."

The peroxided smile flashed brightly. "That's great. And you don't have to worry. I can talk about things besides baseball. It's getting over this first hump . . ." His voice trailed off. She saw him make a tentative move toward his left hand as if to twist a ring. A white line circled it where the gold had been.

"How long have you been divorced?"

"Oh. Well, it's a couple months now. Fifty-four days."

She picked up her bag and swung herself down from the barstool.

"I fuck like a rabbit," she said. "You'll feel better soon."

They made love three times during the night in a little bedroom with daisy-strewn wallpaper and two scratchy Hudson's Bay blankets on the bed. The third time Harvey's transport stained the sheet. He sat up, a flush dyeing his fair skin, and muttered something about how sorry he was and how happy he was and would she excuse him a minute — he'd get a wet washrag and clean it up. She watched him as he scrambled from bed. Something about his small tight buttocks, the thin line of blond hair downing his stomach made him seem like a boy.

His gulping eager response in bed was not dissimilar to that of a gawky young newsboy she had once had in Seattle when she had gone there to try to get an Avon line of cosmetics to sell. He had been standing in front of the Empire Hotel in the rain and she had bought all his papers and the rest of his afternoon for twenty dollars and for a cup of hot cocoa she had sent to the room; he had gobbled her up like a bag of popcorn.

Harvey, in his sad maturity, had gone a step further. In the dark middle of the night he had whispered his gratitude. He had begun to envision a monkish abstinence in his life. He was afraid no one would see anything in him. He had even thought of placing an ad in one of those newspapers or magazines that carried them, advertising the few virtues he could summon up. He ticked them off for her. He was, he thought, of good character, average height, unquarrelsome disposition. He hesitated to include a passionate nature, but he would mention intelligence and kindliness, and last but not least, solvency. He had kissed her nipples with pride at being the sole and only owner of the ranch house they slept in. Now she heard the sound of his electric toothbrush and a discreet hawking as he cleared his hay-fever-ridden sinuses.

She looked around the room and knew why there had been no vice in the night. The woman who had furnished it came clearly to mind. She was probably small. The slipper chair was undersized, the ornaments on the dresser itsy-bitsy Japanese shepherdesses and little dogs with gilt ruffs around their foolish faces. The curtains had had the life washed out of them. They hung at the window, stiff with starch and shrunken, two inches from the sills. Eunice sniffed. Doubtless the lady of the house had marched poor Harvey into the bathroom and washed and scrubbed him until he too had shrunk into the man who called out, "Oh, golly," as he spilled his seed onto the bed.

She scratched her thigh and blew a strand of hair away from her face. She thought idly about washing herself but she knew it wasn't necessary. She always woke in the morning with a sweet breath, as though the sex act scented her through and through. She ascribed it to nature. Your hair either curled or it didn't. You had clear, healthy skin or you didn't. You had head colds or you never had a sick day in your life. Eunice was all clover and rainwater and regular bowels.

The bedroom door opened cautiously. A small boy stood there regarding her with solemnity. She drew the rough blanket up to her chin and stared back.

"God Almighty, who the hell are you?" It was not said with irritation, but it was not friendly either.

"Archer."

"Archer *who!* It's seven-thirty in the morning."

"Archer Medford." He had the rabbity look of prepuberty, large green eyes, long legs, short torso.

"Is my father up yet?"

She nodded toward the bathroom and the noises coming from within.

"My grandmother sent me home to get some clean underwear before I go to school." He stood for a moment and then edged toward the bathroom door. He looked over his shoulder at her while he knocked politely.

"Yes?" The voice came from within. "I'll be out in a minute, honey."

"Daddy. It's me."

The door was flung wide. Harvey stood there, stark naked and dashed to bits. "Archie? What are you doing here?"

"Grandma says I have to have decent underwear to wear to school. Today's gym day and everybody will see it." He spoke with poise and clarity.

Harvey ducked back into the bathroom, groping for a towel to cover his loins and an explanation that would suffice.

"Didn't you have some shorts and stuff with you?"

"Yes, but they've got holes. She said they were disgraceful and I couldn't wear them. She said I should walk home and get some without holes or I couldn't go to school. I have a test today."

"This is Eunice, Archie. She missed a bus and stayed all night." He bobbed his head in her direction. "Eunice, this is my son, Archie."

"Archer." The boy amended it formally.

Eunice plumped the pillow behind her back. "Have you got a middle name?"

"Wayne."

"Like John Wayne?"

"For my Grandfather Wayne. He was a minister at the First Congregational Church."

She asked him then if he would kindly go out of the room for a minute so she could get up and get dressed and make everybody a nice breakfast.

"I can make the breakfast. I take cooking."

Harvey excused himself. He would just climb into his clothes and then they would sort everything out. He left the two behind him taking stock of each other.

"What can you cook?"

"French toast. Blueberry muffins. Jell-O chocolate pudding. Blueberry muffins."

"You said blueberry muffins already."

"We had to make them twice. They didn't come out right the first time."

"Make French toast," she said. "Not too brown."

"How many pieces do you eat?"

"Three."

He walked slowly toward the door. Eunice did not intend to lose an opportunity. "Archer — where's your mama?"

"In Glendale. Working things out."

She was not sure she had heard him correctly. Was he being sage beyond his years or smart-ass or parroting what he had heard?

"What's she doing there?"

"Working things out. She's doing it in Glendale and my daddy's doing it here. I'm staying with my grandmother till they're finished."

"Swell. Well, get cracking on the toast. I'll make the coffee."

It seemed perfectly equitable to him. He left her without a backward glance.

Harvey came to the table in a tie and jacket. Eunice and Archer sat across from one another nicely washed and combed. They might have been the family from a Cheerios commercial, so bright, polite and sunny were they to each other. Harvey made appreciative noises over the French toast and interrogated his son like a kindly but nagging schoolmaster. Was he all right at his grandmother's? Yes, he was. Did he have enough allowance to get by on during the week? Yes, he did. Was he cutting down on sweets, did he say prayers before bedtime, did he still wet his bed? This last was offered as a gentle admonition. The boy turned fiery red to the tips of his ears and looked imploringly at Eunice.

"I peed in bed till I was thirteen," she said promptly. "It's nerves and you outgrow it."

"Well, of course, it's not his fault," Harvey said. "Things have been pretty upsetting for him. It's just that his grandmother is quite old and . . ."

"*I* change the sheets," Archer said in a small voice.

"There's got to be something else to talk about at the breakfast table," Eunice told them firmly. "This French toast isn't bad."

"I did it better last time," Archer said. "It doesn't always come out the same."

He slid from his chair with an apologetic sideways glance at his father. "I've got to go to school now."

His picked up his jacket which was dark green and dusty looking and a brown paper bag containing respectable underwear.

"Well, so long," he said.

"Hey?" Eunice's voice stopped his progress toward the back door. "You like to go swimming?"

He thought it over. "I don't know how."

"You don't know how to *swim?*"

"No."

"What if you got swept down a storm drain? What if you fell in a river?"

"There's no water in the Los Angeles River," he said patiently. "And there's no storm drain anyplace around this neighborhood."

Eunice wouldn't have it. She wanted him imperiled and part of the drama. "I know a man," she began darkly, "who fell asleep in his bathtub, slipped under the water, and glub, glub, he was gone."

"My grandmother sits on the toilet seat in the bathroom with me when I take a bath." He had a lawyer's neat and methodical logic.

"You're too old for that. Lock her out." A thought dawned. "I'll tell you what. This Saturday you get on the Olympic Boulevard bus with forty-five cents exact change in your hand and ride it all the way out to the Marina. You get off and walk one block to the big apartment building that's staring you right in the face. At ten o'clock in the morning you'll find me by the swimming pool, ready to teach you to swim and save your life from any accidents that might befall you."

He looked to his father, who beamed. "Well, Archie, that seems like a generous offer. What do you say?"

"I'll try it."

Eunice was in high spirits. "We'll go off the deep end together," she said exuberantly.

Doubt and fear instantly shadowed Archer's face. She saw it and she grinned. "We'll start out in two feet of water. I'll hold you up by your bellybutton."

Sensing that something untoward, something bristling with

possibilities had overtaken him, his face cleared, his head bobbed, and he went out the screen door running, allowing it to slam behind him.

Harvey hardly knew how to let her see what was flowering in his heart. He had been loved all night, his son had been nurtured in the morning. She evoked sunlight and madonnas at his breakfast table. What could he say? She divined sentiment in the air and banked the fires before they could catch, let alone burn.

"I've got to toddle off myself. I'll be late to work." She sipped the last drop of her coffee and rose, stacking the dishes on her arm like a harassed waitress.

He protested that he would clean the kitchen. It was his daily and accustomed task. He rose to help her, paused to kiss the soft nape of her neck, causing her to spill syrup on her blouse.

She pushed him off and blotted the stain. "That's enough now, Harvey," she said as if she were fending off a nipping puppy.

"Eunice, Eunice, Eunice." He sang her name in concert with the birdsong outside, his chant the more piercing of the two. "I can't believe any of this."

She peered under the sink for soap and splashed it over the piled dishes. "You're almost out of Tide," she said.

He was not to be put off.

"I'll pick you up tonight. We'll ride out to the beach. I have a blanket in the car."

She envisioned sandy carnality under a pier and winced.

"I have a Spanish lesson tonight." She turned to face him and saw the hopeful light in his blue eyes. "Not true. I haven't got a Spanish lesson, Harvey. I just don't want to get all clogged up before I think this over."

Harvey martialed his forces right and left. But she had gone to bed with him, right off the bat. They had made love only one hour and fifty minutes after they had met. And the beauty of it. She must consider the beauty and the rightness of it. Hadn't it been as if they had always known each other? Hadn't they been in perfect harmony, perfect rhythm? Why, he had been married half a lifetime and never spent a night like the one he had just passed.

No, his wife had taken hot milk and aspirin tablets on those rare occasions when he sought her under her Sears Roebuck cotton pajamas. She had come out in bright red spots like giant hives, which made her look like a victim of measles and brutality at one and the same time. He had tugged, she had thrashed, and all the while she had grown blotched and bellicose. How often he had closed his eyes and conjured a milk white nymph, naked as a jaybird and pliant as silk. How often had he turned away from her nightclothes puddled on the floor like discarded Dr. Dentons and wished for her death and his. But now all that was at an end. He caught Eunice's hand, brought it to his lips. She was beneficence, she was balm in Gilead.

"Goddamn," said Eunice. "I'm in a hole *again.*" She pulled free and started for the bedroom. He followed, cracking his shin smartly on the table leg in his haste.

She was already making the bed as he entered, flinging the blankets about and plopping the pillows by crushing them against her bosom. She had been in many beds and never left one unmade. It was a matter of pride.

"Stand on the other side and grab hold," she said. Meekly, he complied. "Somebody hand-crocheted the lace on this sheet. My mother did that stitch."

"Eunice, please, I beg you. Don't just walk out of my life."

"Miter your corners," she directed. "Otherwise they pop out in the middle of the night and leave your feet cold."

"I won't get in your hair. I promise you that. But I can see that you need care, Eunice. I can *see* that."

She gave a final smoothing pat to her side and took her coat off the chair.

"I know how to balance a bank statement, Harvey, and change a sparkplug. I left home when I was sixteen with twelve dollars and a hatpin with a jet knob on top of it in my purse in case I was accosted in a bus station. I never spent the twelve dollars and I never used the hatpin. So it's as plain as the nose on your face that I can look out for myself."

He used his last weapon as she trotted toward the front door.

"What were you doing in that bar then?"

She took a deep breath. The question had been asked before. "I was saving somebody the waltz," she said flatly.

"I won't call till the weekend. If you just want to go to lunch that'll be fine . . ."

"You'll find lots of girls at scientology or folk dancing," she suggested. "You'd probably find just what you're looking for."

"I've found her, Eunice, I've found her."

She took out a lipstick and swept it across her mouth expertly. "You don't know how crazy I am," she said. He paid no heed. She gave in then. She always did.

"I'm at Burbank Studios. We can eat Chinese across the street."

By some kind of common unspoken consent the men stayed away from the damp, warm cauldron of the laundry room on Saturday mornings. They sat around the pool reading newspapers or worked out in the gym, grunting and puffing with the unaccustomed effort. They courted hernias and heart strain as they lifted weights, rowed machines on mechanical tracks and pumped stationary bicycles on long trips to nowhere.

The ladies of Marina One had the room to themselves, and the oversized glass-walled dryers tumbled with bras and panties and machine-washable knits. They came wearing their bunny-rabbit slippers and pink plastic curlers and terry-cloth robes, faces free of make-up, mouths without lipstick, giving some an air of innocence, others the denuded look of age. It was a gathering that reached back in time to riverbanks and rushing streams. Pursuing cleanliness, eschewing godliness, they let their hair down.

Stella was the earliest arrival. She sat on her bundle of disgracefully dirty sheets, a beer-stained sweater, an unraveling nightie, and, cigarette drooping, she bided her time. Someone would show up with two quarters for the machine and she would insinuate her laundry together with her victim's.

She was surprised and discomfited by the sound of sobbing. It was a scale of woe rising from a high note to a low one and then to a rush of shallow sobs much like a drunk in the throes of hiccups. Stella heaved herself upright and peered into the far reaches of the room. The weeping Niobe was an airline stewardess she remembered vaguely as a cream-slathered, inert figure browning in the sun, navel, loins and the faint hint of pubic hair for all the world to see.

"You sound like a cat with it's tail in the wringer. What is the matter with you anyhow?"

The girl's face dripped tears. She was a bloody leaking faucet.

"Oh," she sobbed, and, "oh," again and that was all that was to be had out of her.

"I don't want to know anyway," Stella said. "You're making a hell of a racket considering the state of my head this morning."

The girl inched back further into the corner and wept on.

Stella hunkered on her pile of clothes and smoked gloomily.

Hortense and Eunice came through the door carrying a plastic wash basket heaped high. They gave the snuffling figure a curious glance, and then began sorting their wash in neat piles on the floor. Stella gave them a decent amount of time to organize and then she descended upon them.

"As is usual with me," she began, "I'm out of money. I've gotten as dirty as I can without becoming disgusting to myself and I need a load of wash done. Perhaps you'd throw my things in with yours."

Hortense lifted her head. She knew Stella's cadging ways.

"It's sure all hand to mouth with you, isn't it?" She knew the answer but a mild irritation caused her to pose the question.

"I never think about it," Stella said. "The ravens have always fed me and I trust will continue to do so. Will you take my wash?"

"Throw it in." Hortense turned to Eunice. "Plenty of Clorox. She's been in those duds for a month."

Eunice made a shushing motion at her friend. She felt that Stella, despite her granite, had feelings which could be hurt and nothing could have dissuaded her from that view.

"It's all right," she said. "Just toss the stuff over and we'll get you nice and clean."

Stella had no further use for the steamy intimacies of the washroom. "You can bring them up to me when they've run through," she said.

Eunice was about to acquiesce when Hortense stopped her.

"Just whoa up," she said. "We don't mind doing you a little favor but neither one of us is your maid. You just wait and take up your own bundle."

"I've left important work," Stella said.

"It's not gonna run away while your undies wash. You're one funny lady, you know that? It's always, 'Get me this' or 'Give me that,' like you were born to it." She was not chiding so much as probing into the source of Stella's colossal nerve. She was never grateful, never suppliant, never apologetic. Hortense marveled at her.

"I must put first things first, it's as simple as that," Stella replied. "I've always known my order of priorities. I just follow it." She scratched her ear and looked complacent. "I don't know why it makes people bridle. Not you, Hortense. You've always been very helpful. Yes, I've got you marked down as a helpful one."

"I'll bet." Hortense was mild again.

The girl in tears blotted her damp cheeks and sidled past them to the door, hugging her pile of neatly folded towels. Something in her pale, woebegone face spoke across the room to Eunice. She had begun many a morning with wet eyes and a bitter mouth.

"Is something wrong?" she asked. "Are you late with the curse? What's the matter, honey?" She searched for other possible disasters. "Are you knocked up? Has someone died?"

The girl looked at the others. The lure for her was the sympathy in the voice, the eyes wise with understanding, the shoulder to lean on. There was the memory of pajama parties and sorority sisters and best friends and maids of honor. Wasn't there always a woman across the chicken salad sharing your agony and the check? Didn't the manicurist hold your hand and the secrets of your heart? Hadn't your mother brushed your hair and hushed your tears? It came out in a rush.

She had received her final divorce papers in the morning mail along with an advertisement for a sale at the May Company and an appeal from a day-care nursery. It had been a terrible marriage. Not sexually. It had been all right on its back but on its feet, God, on its feet. She had never gotten a single cent from him that wasn't meant for the grocery bill. She had had to ask her mother who was seventy years old to send her clothes and Kotex and even postage stamps. She had never been able to offer a gift or walk into a store or buy a flat of pansies to plant in her front yard. He made good money. He wore nice clothes and drove a BMW. But he cut the phone pad in half to make it last longer and bought chickens in the downtown Central Market that were old and blue and hairy and made her eat them for a whole week at a time.

"The first paycheck I made," she said, "I spent every single cent in one day. I bought ice cream and lipstick and a red setter puppy and sling pumps in three colors and . . ." She stopped abruptly. "I'm crying," she said, "because it took me ten years to get the piece of paper that came this morning. Ten years," she said dully. "They say everything that goes wrong in a marriage is sex. It isn't. It's money. It's fighting about money."

"It doesn't come as any surprise to me that men are worms," Stella said. "Of course they'll take advantage if you let 'em. Nothing new in that. I'd say blow your nose and forget him. Spilt milk." She rose. "I'll come back for my wash. It would be convenient if you folded it." She started to go and looked back at the girl. "You should have shoved his bankbook up his ass." And she loped out, banging the door behind her.

"Amen," Hortense said.

"That woman's always drunk," the girl said with lofty disdain.

"She's got craw."

"I think she's crude," said the girl.

Hortense bent a sour look on her. "I say she's right. I say if you eat shit there's no good wailin' 'cause it ain't caviar. I ain't ever gonna beg from any man 'cause his hangs out and mine's tucked in. Not this girl."

"Tote that barge, lift that bale," Eunice said. "Miss Independent."

"It beats sniffing around the garbage pails like you do."

"*What* garbage pails?"

"The *men,* honey. The men you dig up out of the banana peels and the tomato juice cans!"

The washroom conviviality was suddenly gone, a wrangle erupting, caused in Hortense by the tides of the moon, in Eunice by her needful alliance with losers.

The stewardess beat a retreat. Cat fights were her daily diet; she could do without the one shaping up before her.

"Some people can't be big, black, strong, make-it-on-your-own types. Some people don't want to end up with a teacher's pension and a dildo for company. Some people want to love and be loved. I'm prepared to take chances."

"Child," Hortense said, "you've taken more chances than a Chinese lottery, and so far zilch, zero. Don't forget I've stuffed cotton between your legs when you were bleeding and cleaned up puke after you were sick. I know where you're at and it's trash city. Now if I ain't earned the right to say that to you as a friend, I want my door key back and goodby, whitey."

"You're one mean nigger today," said Eunice.

"Go clean the bathroom," Hortense told her. "It's your turn."

Eunice pranced past her, spirits restored. Horty on the boil was as good as a dose of castor oil, nasty but cleansing.

She spotted the moldy green jacket clear across the pool area. He was standing stiffly, staring straight ahead as if his head had frozen to his neck.

"Yoo-hoo!" Her raucous call caused him to turn around. He raised a tentative hand and gave it a tentative waggle.

She beckoned him to her side. He came slowly, scuffing his sneakers along the coping. She saw that his jacket was zipped to his chin, a ratty quilted cocoon concealing the butterfly beneath.

"Hi, Archer."

"Hi."

"Aren't you too warm in that jacket?"

He shook his head.

"I see you got here okay."

"Yes."

"Well, where are your trunks? You can hop upstairs and climb in 'em and we'll dive right in."

"I didn't bring any."

"How come?"

"I don't have any."

She looked at his solemn face. "Well, if it was just you and me and God in his heaven we'd go in starkers, but since it isn't we'll go into Santa Monica and buy you something zingy at Henshey's."

"I haven't any money."

"Honey, till Master Charge catches up with me, you're with the last of the big-time spenders."

He sat silently beside her in the car, rivulets of sweat pouring down his back. His heart hammered in his chest and in his ears. Eunice whistled through her teeth while she drove. He wondered if a gap between those fine white teeth produced the sound. He was afraid to look directly at her.

"Take off that damn jacket," she said. "I'm roasting just looking at you in it."

He tugged manfully but the zipper stuck. She reached across and whoosh, the jacket fell apart, revealing his Mickey Mouse shirt.

"Whatcha been up to all week? Have you gone to the movies? Have you fallen in love with anybody? Have you grown a mustache? What's new?"

"I pasted Blue Chip stamps in for Grandma." It was the best he had to offer.

"Uh huh. Well, that didn't take you all week, did it?"

"I watched *Stella Dallas* on television."

"With Barbara Stanwyck?"

"I don't know."

"Did you cry?"

"No."

"How come?"

He wanted to tell her that all his tears had been used up with the departure of his mother. Emotion now produced only a stinging between his eyes and a dry heaving. Sometimes he curled his toes inside his sneakers until they ached. Sometimes he bit the inside of his lip.

"It wasn't too sad," he said.

"I'm a big crier myself. I believe in it. I boo-hoo-hoo at least once a day."

He wondered if he should commiserate.

"Most girls cry," he consoled her.

"They've got plenty to cry about, believe me, baby."

He nodded. He didn't know what he was agreeing to, but it seemed friendly.

They drove in companionable silence to the store.

The saleslady measured his waist while he stared at the ceiling in an agony of embarrassment. His stomach roiled with gas and excitement. What if he let wind and she smelled it. He tightened his buttocks and submitted to the will of God.

"You're a little fellow for your age, aren't you?" She was an old woman with glasses dangling from a black cord and a sprinkle of dandruff on her rusty black dress.

"He's twenty-one," said Eunice, winking at him. "Hey, I like that red satin number. How about you, Archer?"

"I guess so."

"Well, whip into the dressing room and let's see 'em on you."

He went off clutching the trunks. The curtains of the cubicle thrashed and billowed as he struggled into them, wondering desperately where he should put his wienie. Ah. There was a little knitted pouch. He stuffed it in with both hands and then peered into the glass to make sure there was no bulge. There was none, but there was goose flesh clearly visible on his skin from the air conditioning.

He rubbed at himself in the hope that that chicken look would leave him. He needed to blow his nose, but there was nothing at hand. He snuffled and then used the back of his arm. He'd been in here for at least five minutes. He was expected to come out.

He cleared his throat and emerged like a man on his way to the firing squad.

Eunice sat on a counter swinging one brown leg. She did not laugh or whistle or catcall. He swallowed the spit pooling in his mouth and advanced further. Her steady regard made him forget to suck in his stomach. He was sure that it swelled in front of him like a basketball with his bellybutton protruding and ugly for all to see.

"Archer," she said, "you've got a swell build."

He loved her from that moment on.

He was rocked in the cradle of the deep. He was rocked in an ammonic womb. He gulped water, he thrashed, he made it across the pool and turned, a drowned rat, wreathed in smiles.

She clutched him by gathering up a handful of his swimming trunks. He bumped into her breasts, grabbed at her neck.

"I opened my eyes," he said.

She hoisted him up on the coping, where he sprawled panting. She was beside him, shaking out her wet hair, the water spattering his heaving chest.

"Did you like it?"

"Yes."

"Next time we'll go in the deep end."

"Sure," he said. He was as bold as brass. Hadn't he seen her through the veil of water as a mermaid shape beckoning him on and on? Hadn't he felt her encircling arm? There was no depth he feared; no perilous height either. Could he have grown an inch or two this afternoon? He felt if he stood now he would tower over her.

The late afternoon sun fled away, cooling the pool area with shadows. There was the stinging slap of a breeze off the ocean. Eunice hugged her knees and felt a bud of melancholy open slowly inside her. This was an empty hour. Others stretched ahead.

"Hey," she said. "Do you have a date tonight?"

He thought of sitting over a plate of cooling creamed tuna with his grandmother sitting opposite, teeth clinking like a tiny metronome as she ate. He thought of early bedtime with the summer light still washing over his bedroom walls and the sound of a ball game being played in the lot next door.

"We go to bed early on Saturday so we can get up for church on Sunday." He watched her like a kitten about to pounce on a string.

"Let's eat hamburgers and go to the pier and get our pictures taken and see a double bill. Let's do that instead."

"I'd have to ask." His mind raced ahead to possible refusal. Nails whacked into a coffin. The earth split. The sky fell. His knees trembled visibly.

"I'll call." Eunice was on her feet. "I'll say I'm a distant relative of your daddy's. I'll say you might inherit a fortune if you play up to me. I'll say I'm blind and you have to lead me across the street. Leave it to me."

They went up to the apartment. Hortense had propped a note on the coffee table. She was out for the night with Booker. Eunice should not get into bed without bolting the door. She should throw out the crab meat in the refrigerator. It was doubtless toxic by now. She should sleep well and alone. There was a scrawl of x's across the bottom of the page and a round face drawn with a down-turned mouth as a signature.

Eunice dried Archer off with a beach towel, stripping him with one yank on the red trunks. He felt a shock of surprise and then pleasure. His skin tingled. He jumped as her hand approached his groin but the swipe she made at it was practical and purposeful. He was warm and dry in a jiffy and sitting on the bed in her bathrobe while she showered with the door open, yelling to him above the rushing water.

"Look in the *Times* for the Venice Theater and call for when the show comes on. One's mushy and one's roller skating. I want to see all of the mushy one."

He pawed through the paper and squinted at the print. He had only been allowed to see G-rated pictures. Now he saw the sprawled and licentious figure leaning out of the ad toward him.

His nose was pressed to a shelf of bosom. He made a quick and sidelong comparison with Eunice as she emerged from the shower. She kicked the door shut, but he had decided in her favor during that instant she had been in view

He thought of strawberries crushed sweetly against the roof of his mouth and the down of peaches furring his tongue. He thought of the warm underbelly of his cat when he put his face against it and the disturbing lurch of his heart when he lay, belly down, in his bed. Oh, he was happy.

"We are proud to present a double feature starring Raquel Welch and . . ." The tinny, recorded voice foretold the delights to come and the scheduled showings as well.

"It's eight o'clock for *Kansas City Bomber,*" he told her as she emerged tugging a sweater over her head.

"Do you like chili on your burger and onions and Russian dressing? Do you like French fries and a root beer float?"

His mouth watered. His grandmother served lumpy mashed potatoes and string beans floating in greenish water. His palate roared to life. Panic followed. He only had bus fare home. Did she mean for him to pay his share? He could say he wasn't hungry. He could have a stomachache.

"My treat," she said.

"Thank you very much."

She sat on the bed next to him. "Are you ever going to call me by my name?"

"Thank you very much . . . Eunice."

"You're welcome . . . Archer."

She tossed his clothes at him. "Hurry up. I want to be there at the beginning."

It was after midnight when they came out under the starry sky. Little belches arose in Archer, recalling onions and Hershey bars and cherry drink and bubble gum. His head ached dully and his bladder sloshed with liquid. He thought of the long jolting bus ride home and groaned inwardly. He'd have to sit with his legs crossed all the way and what of the walk to the house when he got off? He would go behind a billboard and pee a stream that would wash away the ground under his feet. He hardly heard what she was saying.

"Listen, it's too late for you to go on the bus now. You'll sleep at my place. I'll call your grandma again."

That was a bad plan. His grandmother awoke cranky, he told her. Her teeth floated in a water glass by her bed. Her glasses with their thick lenses glinted beside them. Her hearing aid rested on the bureau. She was helpless, lurching, groping, bound to be unfriendly.

"She's afraid to be alone in the house," he said. "We lock up right after supper. She's afraid she'll die in the night from her emphysema."

"Then I'll take you home."

A bad plan again. He saw his grandmother peering through a cautious slit in the door at Eunice in her tight blue sweater with a gold chain separating her high breasts. She would smell that scent of cloves and cinnamon and see the red-painted toenails poking through her sandals. She would drive her from the door, shrieking Jezebel in her wake. His grandmother spoke of Sodom and Gomorrah more often than San Francisco or San Diego.

"I'll just catch the bus."

"Aren't you scared?"

How did he know? He had never been on a bus at this hour of the night. And what were his defenses? He had a pocketknife with a snapped-off blade and a Christian prayer learned at Sunday school to fend off the devil. Neither seemed enough. He swallowed hard.

"It's okay," he said with a squeak of fear in his voice.

She saw that he had made a test, a crucible of it. He had laid his undersized balls on the line.

"Well, you're not a little kid, are you?"

"No." He was both grateful and appalled. She was going to let him go alone.

She gave him an approving whack across the shoulders. "I bet you would have hopped on that bus, but I'm not going to let you. I'm going to dump you right down on your doorstep. But you know what's plain to me, Archer?" she added. "What's plain to me is that you've got a steel rod right up your spine from your ass to your hairline, and I'm proud of you."

She hugged him to her and they walked to the car, bumping hips all the way.

Alan waited until she brought him his coffee, black, with two sesame wafers and some honey; waited until he ate them to the last seed; waited until he sucked his tooth clean. Then he looked up from *Variety* and fired her.

He moved around the room gesticulating like a Turkish rug merchant, bowed over by the weight of it all, alert with cunning. The thing was, he told her, rubbing his hands together, they had put the screws to him. Somebody upstairs had gotten righteous and closely questioned the charges he had put on his last picture. They built houses for executives and put in sprinkler systems and raised walls of old brick, but they were pissed off by a side trip he had taken to Mexico City. That and a bill for a new motor in the Jaguar and a little tailoring done by a rip-off limey on a couple of suits. They figured he could use a secretary from the pool until he checked off the lot. She should look at it this way; if his days were numbered, so were hers. Get off the *Titanic* before it sank, right?

Eunice stood in front of his oversized desk and felt her face stiffen into that cold wet mask it became before she fainted. Her mind raced wildly through dunning letters and lawyers' threats. It sorted stacks of bills — the antique dealer who let her pay off the amethyst beads because she pretended not to notice that he was rubbing his erection against her hip when she bought them, the Saks charge, the Standard Oil charge, the goddamn Spanish boots she had snapped up on impulse. Christ, she even had an unpaid tab at Art's Deli. She tried to slam the Pandora's box shut, but it was overflowing. The florist. Her masseuse at the gym. Horty. She owed Horty fifty dollars for something or other.

Alan was droning on about references. A dirty grin accompanied his promise to describe her various services in glowing terms.

"You little prick" — she cut him off short — "stuff your references. I've been with you for five years! I've taken your laundry and called your chicks and blown you under your goddamn desk! I'm going where you go, buster!"

He leaned back in the leather chair and stroked his stubbled chin judiciously. "Sweetheart," he said, placating her, "I'd say yes in a minute, but it isn't good for *you*. You're the best. You've been the crème de la crème, but what's happening here isn't good for you. It's not healthy." He was a physician, solemnly prescribing a necessary tonic. "You know how you are. An arranger walks through the door, you're going down on him the next night. I use a talented English writer, you ball him till he can't write his name. Even the mail kids aren't safe. Sweetheart, you need a quiet backwater. A nice insurance office, a nice real estate office. Out of trouble. Eunice" — he was paternal now — "you're getting older, baby. It's settling-down time."

She stared at him in disbelief. This little crumb with his sexual itches furtively scratched was telling her how to live?

"I want the rest of this week's salary. In cash. And I'm leaving as soon as I can clear out my desk." She moved stiff-legged with fury toward the door. "One other thing, Alan. Your picture stinks. They're saying it all over the lot. That house you just bought? It'll go. The new car? They'll pick it up for payments. That little cunt at the Château Marmont? Bye-bye. I'll see you at the unemployment window."

She slammed the door and leaned against it, shaking. Then, as if pursued, she ran to the phone. Scotty. Scotty knew thousands of people. She broke a nail dialing and shouted at the girl who told her he was out of town on location.

"Give me a number. I've *got* to reach him."

He didn't leave a number. He'd be gone for a month.

She sat tapping the desk with the pencil. Horty. She'd call Horty. No. Horty had laid down the law about being called at school. Only an accident would make it permissible. And that meant her head through the windshield, not rear-ending or anything minor.

Alan burst through the door, his face aggrieved.

"I am not able to pay you in cash. If you'll accept my check?"

"You're overdrawn, shit-heel!"

"Eunice," he said with a pained look, "I think we should try for a dignified parting. After all, we have been something to each other. I think I may have been instrumental in broadening your view of life, culturally, humanly. You've seen me at my best, and, yes, at my worst. You've been a confidant and a friend."

"Get the cash up," she said, emptying her drawer onto her desk.

"Listen, cooze, don't threaten me!" He edged toward her, an ugly flush suffusing his face.

"I take karate lessons three times a week," she said holding her ground. "If I kick you where I'm thinking of kicking you, you're a disabled veteran."

He winced. "Charming." He took out his wallet and threw some bills at her. "Don't keep in touch."

She went into the washroom to cry and changed her mind. She phoned Harvey at the store with just the hint of an ordeal in her voice. She hated to take him away from work, but after what had just happened she wasn't feeling very well or thinking straight. He would be there, he promised her fervently, in twenty minutes. They would go to his house. He would give her some sherry. She would tell him all about it. The comforting net he threw settled around her.

The house was stuffy and hot and smelled of the morning's fried bacon. She sat on the vinyl couch with the springs twanging under her and took tea and sympathy. The tea was too strong. The hand patting hers was too hairy and freckled. She tried to compose herself by closing her eyes and going limp. For a moment, boredom with him and her own plight almost tipped her into sleep. He waited patiently.

"Well, I'm broke," she said loudly. "Fired and broke."

"You know what I think?" he said. "I think it's all for the best. You've got shadows under your eyes and you're pretty nervous. You've been working too hard."

She thought of the long afternoons at the office while a picture was away on location when she yawned over a book and did her nails. She'd even brought an afghan from home and napped on the army cot in the ladies' room.

"He expected a helluva lot."

"Eunice," he said, "I don't know how to put this so it won't offend you. Look. I'm doing pretty well right now. Why don't you let me take care of you for a couple of months till you get settled? You know how I feel about you . . ."

She sat up and took life. She debated naming a figure and settled for a look of profound gratitude. "You're very sweet, Harvey."

"You could move in here."

Her eyes swept the twelve-by-eighteen-foot room. The abyss yawned wider. She saw herself tamed, penned, bundled into domesticity, condemned to one bathroom. "You have to think about how it would look, Harvey. Let's just leave things the way they are. The time will probably come when I'll have to call on you. That'll probably be tomorrow night at the latest." She put a gentle hand on his arm.

"I'll try not to be a burden, Harvey."

He was a conservative politically with a strong sense of fiscal responsibility. He nodded approval.

"I'll make you an allowance," he said. She wondered if it would be more than Archer got.

"Thank you." The next question followed without a beat. "How much?"

He cleared his throat. "What do you usually spend for pocket money?"

She hadn't heard that expression since she'd left home.

"I'll leave it to you, dear."

He named a sum. It would take her and Archer to the movies a couple of times and leave enough over to buy arsenic to poison him.

"That's a beginning," she told him sweetly. "I'll take in ironing to make up the rest."

Booker told her a story that made her laugh. It was an old joke and she'd heard it before, but she laughed anyway. It was either that or scream.

He sat on the kitchen table munching an apple, dressed in his tennis whites with a towel knotted ascot style in the deep opening of his shirt. Eunice noticed his dimples for the first time. She had a passion for dimples. She had once slept with a button pressed to her cheek for a month trying for those delicious little hollows.

"It's a bitch, your getting fired."

She was fascinated to see that he ate the core of the apple and all the seeds as well. She sat in front of the boiled egg she had fixed for her own lunch and looked at its runny interior with disgust.

"Fat troubles and lean pickings, that's the story of my life." She dabbed at the egg and then threw down her spoon. "I should have stayed in Kelso and gone to work in the salmon-canning factory. I'd have married a lumberjack by now and had a houseful of kids."

He turned a chair around, swung his long legs over it and rested his head on bent elbows. "You've got the glooms, baby," he told her.

Harvey came to mind, with his milky glance and his milky kindness. She saw herself being led into Chamber of Commerce dinners on his arm. She saw herself serving coffee and Ralph's coconut cake in his neat kitchen to his neat friends as they planned camping trips and compared sleeping bags. She saw him preparing for bed with an extra wash under his armpits and a careful gargling with Listerine. He would lay a towel under her hips to save the mattress and turn out the lights to save on the electric bill. He would take out the garbage and repair alarm clocks and recount the news she had already read in the daily paper. Harvey was the prize in the Cracker Jack box. Harvey was her fate. She sighed.

"You've got it made, Booker. You climb into those white shorts and that Izod shirt and zap around the courts and drink Gatorade and suck up to the ladies . . ."

The dimples disappeared. The friendly smile, white teeth and porcelain caps, was gone. "You been listening to Horty? That's the shit she lays on me all the time."

"I wish I was a man."

"You ain't, baby."

She ignored him and rambled on. "I'd be somebody's son-in-law living the *good* life. Yes, sir, I'd grow a *Viva Zapata* mustache and hunt for a bucktoothed dentist's daughter. I'm surprised you aren't in that slot right this minute, the way you look and all."

She cocked her head to one side and studied him. "I guess Horty keeps you in line."

He corrected her coldly. "Maybe Horty tells you what to do, girl, but *nobody* tells me!"

"Uh huh." Eunice twisted a lock of her hair and stared at him. He went to the refrigerator and rummaged through it noisily, looking for a beer. There was none. He drank a whole quart of milk from the carton, head thrown back, throat glistening with drops of sweat. She followed the course of one in her mind's eye. Down the throat, down the muscled chest, down the groin, down, down, down. She had spent an hour lying in a hot bath before he got there and now everything seemed warm and loose and open.

"Where the hell is Hortense, anyway? That woman's always keeping me hung up. She's fifty goddamn minutes late." He glanced at his very thin gold watch.

"Maybe she's at a PTA meeting."

"Pee Tee Asshole meeting!"

"You aren't bothering me."

He slung dark glasses across the bridge of his nose and became an expressionless stranger with no eyes to read.

"You're bothering *me,"* he said.

"Well," she drawled, "if I am . . . I am."

She got up and went into the living room. She had been home all day and the place was a litter of papers and magazines. Her bed, visible in the next room, was unmade next to Hortense's with the covers and pillows in order. She went to the record player, shuffled a stack of records, found one and dropped it into place.

"La la la la." She sang with the music as she closed her eyes and moved in languorous circles. She knew he was in the room with her now. She had seen a cat watching a sparrow, tense and hungry and dangerous. The bird had dared fate by swooping and fluttering until it was mirrored in those yellow eyes. She swooped and fluttered.

She threw her arms above her head and yawned, her skimpy sweater hitching up and revealing her skin. Still she kept her eyes closed. If she stumbled she would stumble blindly. If she fell she would fall far.

His arms encircled her from behind.

"Let's just do it, baby." His hands rose to her breasts. They moved on them slowly. "Let's just play fuck the fucker."

Bad dreams followed good times, she knew that, but she wanted to know what she didn't know and right now. Right this minute. She didn't turn around to face him. She merely stared out at the late afternoon sun shining through the windows Hortense had washed on Sunday morning.

"Don't talk to me about it afterward," was all she said.

They knew they had forgotten to close the bedroom door when they heard a resounding crash from the living room. Eunice, dazed and wet-mouthed, stared past Booker at Hortense. A package had fallen from her arms and she stood in the middle of the room looking right at them.

Booker rolled off Eunice and onto his feet in one swift motion. He stood like an antlered buck staring down the muzzle of a shotgun. Hortense raked him with a glance from head to toe.

"She's crazy," she said, "so that makes you an even bigger shit."

She took off her coat and threw it on a chair behind her.

"Put something over that damp dick and get in here." She swung her attention to Eunice, who sat bolt upright, shielding her nakedness with a copy of *Time* magazine.

"You'd better go take a douche and stay out of my way for a while."

She turned then and went into the kitchen and ran herself a glass of water. It was lukewarm and brackish. She sipped it slowly, as if she had nothing else on her mind. After a moment she sensed Booker's presence. He was behind her, fingering his warm-up jacket and staring at the tops of his Adidas sneakers. She let him dangle while she rinsed the glass and broke a dead leaf from a geranium plant.

"Say it and lemme outta here!" he yelled, goaded by her impassive calm.

She set the glass down carefully and walked by him into the living room. He had been mortified in the past by that unseeing, unnoticing passage. She had stepped over him drunk in the bushes. She had ambled around his inert bloody body when he had been beaten in a fight. She had sashayed past him as he lay caught in the sticky embrace of a prom queen in an empty gymnasium. Always with her nose in the air. Always with that delicate disdain stiffening her nostrils as if something were rotting directly beneath them. Now she was settling into a comfortable chair, plumping a pillow behind her back, lighting a cigarette and smoking reflectively. He charged after her and stood splay-legged in front of her.

"Yeah, yeah, yeah!" he shouted in mindless defiance. She merely glanced at him.

"It's your fault, goddamn it, you cold-assed righteous bitch." Shame made him sputter. "You've hauled me around by the ear ever since I was seven years old. I had to smoke behind the fuckin' barn. I had to drink behind the fuckin' barn. I had to jack off behind the fuckin' barn because I was afraid of you. That's right, Mama. Your fishy eye has been on me from the day I first saw you. You've been whacking at me with a big stick long enough."

"You finished?"

"No," he wailed. "This was no big deal, Hortense. I went for a dip, that's all. That's all it was."

"You're either a child," Hortense said, "messin' his pants whenever he feels like it or you knew what you were doing. It doesn't much matter which because you're out of my life either way. *Repeat.* Out of my life, Booker. That means don't call me when you're hangin' on the ropes. You can't lean on me, lay me, or love me from here on in. You'll notice I'm not screaming, I'm not crying, I'm not calling you names. I'm just shoveling the dirt in on you, Booker, because you're dead."

He was almost hopping now in his frenzy. "God, Horty, what're you doing to me?"

The other side of the coin came into view. Hortense teaching him to read, Hortense holding his hand at his mama's graveside in the rain, Hortense murmuring love and truth in the dark.

"Get your perfidious black ass out of here," she said quietly.

He had fallen from the tree. She had pelted him with apples and driven him from Eden.

Eunice showered for an hour before she crept into the living room to see how far she had fallen from grace. She had scrubbed herself so fiercely, washing her hair, her ears, her buttocks with such flagellant thoroughness that now she wore a drowned, mangled look.

Hortense was rigid in her chair, had not moved. She was sorting her emotions, balancing anger against reason, wrath against an inclination to yawn in the face of it all. Eunice made herself as small as possible, curling herself into a tight wary knot in the least comfortable chair in the room.

She knew instinctively that tears would not appeal and that contrition would get her nowhere. She relied instead on those ancient links between women who defy men even while they succumb. Hadn't they both raged against appetites which had led them to doubtful beds and dubious ends? Hadn't they both smiled mysterious smiles as lovers heaved and panted above them and their minds fled down cool corridors of thought as chaste and manless as a nunnery?

Just understand, her glance told Hortense, and I'll get off scot-free, because you see the absurd humor in it.

"I like you a lot better than Booker," she declared emphatically, "and it was just simple cunt itch that got me in this mess. You're my best friend, the best I ever had and worth three dozen of him." A tick began to pulse in her left eye, a nervous flutter which beat whenever her character was under scrutiny. "I always spoil things," she added wistfully.

"I'm not surprised by any of it." Hortense got up from her chair and walked the room, her hands clasped like a headmaster behind her back. "You stole my earrings when you first moved in with me and took money out of my purse. You're a liar. You cheat at backgammon. You're greedy. You always take the biggest lamb chop and the largest slice of cake. You weasel out of your fair share of the work and the only emotion you know is self-pity."

"It's all true. So true."

Hortense threw her hands up to silence her. "Just shush," she commanded and continued to prowl about the room. Eunice felt a rush of unease. If the jury was out too long she would be hanged. She knew that.

"Think of the good laughs we've had." She scuttled to bolster her case. "And you've said yourself a thousand times that I have a cheerful disposition." There was no response. She saw herself scattered to seed. She gnawed on her thumb and wondered if she had any real charm for anybody.

"Horty?"

"Girl, just let me be. I'm thinking this over."

"You're responsible for me," she insisted. "You are. Without you around you know that I get dippy and do crazy things." She muttered an inward prayer that she had hit pay dirt. Hortense was maternal in a cranky, unwilling sort of a way. It was her best chance. She got up and trotted after her, getting underfoot in the process. Hortense paused and putting her hands on her shoulders shoved her down on the couch.

"You're more trouble than you're worth."

"I know."

"I don't like slyness," she snapped. "I don't like sluts."

Eunice wiggled like a child grasped by an angry mother's hand. She chewed a strand of hair, sucking on it noisily; she shifted from one buttock to the other; she flounced, flopped and fluttered. Hortense stood over her with unwavering severity.

"I haven't heard one word of sorry out of you."

"Well, God," Eunice cried, "if that's what you want I can apologize till I'm blue in the face. I'll start right now." She drew a deep breath. "I'll put saltpeter in my food," she offered. "I'll be as sexless as grass. I'll take the padding out of my bras and be ugly. Anything you say, Horty. Anything at all."

"If you hadn't lost your job," Hortense told her, "you'd be out on your ass, bag and baggage."

Pardon was finally in view and yet Eunice found herself vexed. To be kept on as a charity case was merely to be tolerated. She wanted more than that. She wanted either mortification, punishment, Sturm und Drang — or reconciliation, preferably accompanied by a tearful hug. Hortense had no sense of drama. If she was going to be coldly practical there would be no heat in it at all. And no fun. She gave her an impudent look.

"I can always move into the Y.W.C.A.," she said. She meant to draw her out and see where it led, but it was a match tossed into dry grass. Hortense flared.

"I catch you lapping up and down my man with a tongue like an anteater and you have the brass to sit there and look put-upon! They wouldn't have you in the Y.W.C.A. They wouldn't have you at the city *dump.*"

Eunice made a hasty retreat.

"I just meant I wouldn't have anyplace else to go. I haven't got any money."

The plain truth, plainly spoken, put out the fire. Hortense sat down beside her, shaking her head. "Next you're gonna tell me you'll have to sell apples on the street corner. Shit." She pulled a cigarette out of her skirt pocket and let it hang, unlit, from her aggressive lower lip. "You're no damn good to me. You've lost me my childhood buddy and the best fuck I know."

"He'd come running back if you'd let him."

"I won't."

Eunice never dealt in absolutes. She was slightly in awe of people who drew lines and slammed doors. Possibly it was because she had no dignity to affront, no pride to humble.

"But you love him."

The word seemed weightless and trivial. It moved Hortense not one inch.

"I don't like him." She snapped a match on her thumbnail and puffed on her cigarette. "And when I don't like somebody, they ain't got a prayer."

Eunice shriveled under the cold blast like an oyster touched with lemon juice. "What about me?" she asked as meekly as she could manage.

"We'll see about you."

There wasn't much comfort in it, but Eunice drew hope and wrapped it around herself like a tattered blanket. Hortense would doubtless make life hell. She was not sentimental and she had ample experience with erring children. They got rapped on the head and cracked with a ruler. They were made to see the error of their ways. Well, there was nothing for it. She would have to clean Hortense's drawers and cook her those sandy grits she loved for breakfast. Penitence might be good for her once she got the hang of it.

7

STELLA KNEW the jig was up the moment she saw the nurse with red hair and a temper to match in close conference with the dog-faced doctor. She had marked them for the enemy ever since she'd been coming here. She was usually in and out without a word to anyone, collecting her fee and out onto the street before they noticed her. Let the others pause for the nasty lemonade served in paper cups with the seeds still floating on top. She would give herself something a great deal nicer than that. It was usually a whiskey toddy pleasantly warmed and drunk slowly, not to revive her but to make it last. She watched them with their heads together and heard the nasal whine of the girl accusing her.

"This is twice in two weeks, doctor. I don't know how she's gotten away with it."

She lay back and stared at the ceiling, making an airy pretense of whistling. Nothing much came out of her but breath hissing through her teeth. Never mind. She squeezed on the rubber grip and urged her blood through the tube into the glass jar attached to the bed beside her. Pity she couldn't turn a tap and have it rush out and be done with it.

She planned her day after the snippy girl stuck a piece of tape on her and let her go. She would have an idle stroll along the sea front and find a windless corner to write a line or two on the scrap of paper in her pocket. Then the promised toddy and then perhaps a bench provided by a considerate mortuary on a corner with the traffic hurrying past in a noxious-smelling but soothing stream. She liked the spectacle of people rushing to and fro on their frantic business while she sat like an island in their midst. The tapestry she wove in her head could be made anywhere, but it pleased her to let it form in the bickering noise of the street. Wordsworth could have his host of bloody daffodils. She was content with Mercury Monarchs and Impalas with their garish metallic paint.

"I am speaking to you."

She let her head loll to one side and took the least possible notice of the starched girl at her side.

"Yes," she said haughtily. "What is it?"

"The doctor wishes to speak to you as soon as you're finished. You must not leave without seeing him."

She disregarded her and watched her blood drip like falling red petals and marveled at its rich color. If that's what was coursing through her veins she would live to be a hundred and confound them all. She speculated on who might be lucky enough to be transfused with that lovely ruby elixir. Who knows? . . . she might be transmitting some of her gifts along with it and some pale aborted girl or a sad student with a failed kidney might begin to dream dreams and rampage out of their daily rounds.

She was fussed with and then freed. The hands which pulled her upright were unfriendly. She peered woozily about her and patted her tangled hair into further disorder.

"My hat," she demanded. "I came in a spectacular felt hat."

"It's where you left it." The girl pointed it out as if it had some kind of unpleasant life of its own. Stella plopped it on her head and bowed majestically.

"The doctor is waiting for you," the nurse said in a doomsday voice.

Stella lurched past her on unsteady feet. "They better pay me," she warned as she passed, "or I'll come back and drink the goddamn stuff down again."

The doctor sat tapping a pencil on the desk before him. The rapping warned of a short fuse and even shorter shrift. He beckoned her in but made no motion toward a chair. Tap, tap, tap, and then he was launched on a tirade.

"We've checked on you. I have the records right here before me. We know what you're up to."

She took the chair without an invitation. The smell of sanctity and self-righteousness was making her lightheaded.

"I never said I was a volunteer." Stella's glance pierced him through. "It says quite clearly you can volunteer or you can get paid. I'm one who gets paid. Under other circumstances I might be more generous and donate my blood, but in my position it's quite impossible. I might add that the blood you're getting is very, very blue. I am distantly related to the Cabots of Boston and there was a senator in the family somewhere."

The doctor thrust a muzzle toward her. Yes, it was a muzzle; with that wispy beard and those sharp little protruding teeth it could not be called anything else.

"You've been sneaking in here twice a month, lying about your name. It's quite clear that you are recklessly disregarding our rules about the number of times you may give blood — no oftener than once every eighty-four days. We have had experience with drunks before."

Why, the silly little cur was all but snapping at her. She buttoned up her sweater the wrong way and got to her feet.

"Don't be an ass," she told him. "Alcohol kills germs. I never intended my vital fluids to be passed on to prigs or Puritans. I only wish to save an interesting life, if any. Label me one hundred proof and pump me into somebody who knows a good thing." She made for the door. "And hereafter," she offered as a final threat, "I'll go where I'm appreciated."

She would really have liked to stop and use the ladies' room, but she felt it the better part of wisdom to take the money and run. The woman in charge handed her the bills with the tips of her fingers. Stella riffled through them and handed back a torn and taped dollar.

"They won't take them like that at my watering hole," she said in elegant measured tones. "Dig up another."

"Really!" The woman behind the desk flung another bill in her direction.

"Thanks very much." She examined the disapproving face before her. "You look a bit peaky. Why don't you help yourself to a corpuscle or two?" She was out the door on light feet before she could be answered.

Most of the afternoon went in an unimpressive bar on the boardwalk. It had a beery smell and was none too clean, but there was a booth and the barman was properly morose and silent. Stella established herself so she could see a blue slice of sea through the open door and composed herself to work. It was not precisely a meditative process. Harshly she rummaged through the baggage of her life, ferreting out the moments of fate and passion, terror and delight. What had been the look on her mother's face as she died? What curses had her grandfather flung at age as he walked, bent double in the little shuffling pilgrimages he took to buy the cigar that finally choked him? What was the knotted meaning in her sister's mutterings as she shattered in a midlife breakdown? Sighs and whispers. She had cocked an attentive ear to them all. Not for her the raunchy celebration of sex so fashionable with younger writers. No hysterical accusations flung at life enclosing one in glass jars. No, she addressed herself to bad smells and clenched fists. She sifted through ashes and smoking ruins. She braced herself against floods and cataclysms of all sorts, the more Biblical the better. Crossed wires, missed trains, false starts, broken promises, swindles, the grim reaper, the power and the glory. She had a word for all of them.

By the time the sky darkened and the six o'clock news mired the world in traffic accidents and shootings, suicides and revolutions, she had written four lines of a sonnet she totally approved of. She had also consumed a fifth of bourbon and one hard-boiled egg in case an ulcer lurked somewhere in her gut. She paid her blood money for the booze, told the barman to cheer up as life was indeed a bowl of cherries, and sauntered into the dusk.

Marina One was ablaze with lights. Gas torches flared as if illuminating some ancient Hellenic rites. She felt a pleasant kinship with the rest of the tenants as they tanked up to get through the night. It was always the same. The men emptied their pockets on their bureaus and tried to stuff the day's troubles into the hamper with their socks and shorts. The women cried tears induced by charcoal smoke and ennui. They would huddle in the recreation hall after dinner like refugees, dancing cheek to cheek or playing quarrelsome bridge for stakes they could ill afford. Some of the women who worked would have their hair done in the beauty salon, hoping the Clairol color and the careless curls would lead to good sex and sleep without Seconal. To this end hi-fi's blared throughout the complex, salads were tossed with and without garlic, assignations were arranged with a minimum of small talk and life went on and on.

There was a man in her apartment. She never locked her door, for there was nothing worth stealing. She saw him through the window as she approached. He was gigantically tall; he overflowed her stiff kitchen chair. He appeared to have a huge brindle beard and a great jutting nose, presented to her now in profile.

She stood speculating before her door. Bill collector? Not in that horse-blanket plaid jacket. Distant relative? Her line had pinched patrician faces and were generally undersized. Reformer, sent by an interested friend? She had none who gave a damn about her habits. Lover encountered in a run-down hotel, long since forgotten? She had kept to herself for some years now — at least that's the way she remembered it. A lawyer with a legacy? She thought not — he didn't look munificent. Rapist, robber, Hebrew scholar?

She barged in, swinging her handbag as if it contained a blackjack.

"Who are you and what do you want?" She felt it sensible to get right to the point.

"My name is Caleb Crown. You should know it."

"I don't."

Her ignorance of him did not go down at all well. He had been interviewed and photographed and widely quoted. He was used to being accosted in the street and supplicated on the telephone.

He was annoyed. "I am a publisher," he said, "of the best writers in this country. I am famous for discovering and nurturing talent. I pay poorly, promote brilliantly, and eight novels of note are dedicated to me in gratitude and affection. Where have you been that you don't know who I am?"

"Out of town," she said.

"Your friend Henry Dillon is in my stable. He must have mentioned my name to you."

"Stables are for horses. No, he hasn't."

"I've made him rich."

"I'm sure he's done the same for you." She dismissed discussion of Henry peremptorily. "Very well, you're a publisher. What of it?"

He pulled his beard and glowered. "Henry thinks you're gifted. He says you may be a genius."

She shrugged. "A tired word."

His look was that of a man whose nerves were being rubbed by sandpaper. "He asked me to look you up. I have done so, though I'm not sure to what end." He wheezed irritably. "Why do you live in this garish place like an eccentric crone with a kitchen table and one chair?"

Stella hitched out of her sweater and removed her hat. "It's furnished with words," she said in perfect possession of herself. "I am a poet. Poorly paid and advertised not at all."

"I know who you are," he huffed crankily, "or I wouldn't be here. And you're drunk," he added abruptly. "I can smell you clear across the room."

"You smell drink because I've been drinking. I am never drunk. People often ascribe capacity to the Irish. I am not Irish. I hold my liquor without any help from ancestry. What do you want with me?"

He stood up, groaning from his long sit. He had an almost Falstaffian girth, but it sat firmly on his frame.

"Turn some lights on," he commanded. "And some heat. I detest this California chill that comes with night."

She shrugged and flipped the light switch. He had fine ruddy skin and eyes of almost sinister intelligence. He advanced on her and inclined his head to get a better view of her.

"You're not much to look at," he said emphatically.

"When I'm at my best I'm better than average," she retorted without ill will. "I'm simply not vain. I have an excellent constitution and energy to burn. Staying power is all that counts in my line."

"Not for people who have to look at you."

"I didn't ask you here, did I?"

"But I am here. Well, never mind. Do you eat at all or do you just drink?"

"I eat lightly and drink heavily. Why? Are you going to invite me to dinner?"

"Well, I want to talk to you. It might as well be over dinner." He rubbed his arms and shuddered. She did not know whether to ascribe it to cold or distaste. From the way he was scrutinizing her, rumpled hair to scuffed shoes, she felt it was more likely distaste. As she meant to get a really good bottle of wine out of him she let him squint on as long as he liked.

"It's a mistake to judge a book by its cover," she remarked, leaning against the table. She left the chair for him in case he should want to sit again.

"I'm a very entertaining talker. Are you a good listener?"

"No. *I* like to talk."

"We'll take turns." She tried a smile on him. He did not return it. He kept looking about as if he had found himself in a puzzling maze. She felt obliged to see what he saw.

It was a perfectly good room. It had windows and doors. It had a lumpish bed in the corner and plenty of paper and pencils. She was fond of pencils and bought them in all colors by the dozen. They were quite pretty, really. The walls were blank, of course, but art quickly exhausted itself, in her view. Had she dusted lately? No. Well, dust swirls had a puffy grace, blowing here and there across the floor. Had she flushed the toilet? Certainly! She was a lady. What else did he expect from a woman with eternal verities on her mind?

"I can't take you to a decent restaurant looking like that, no matter how brilliant you are. Do you have another dress? A washrag? Some face powder? A comb?"

She folded her arms akimbo and glowered, annoyed finally. "You'd better tell me your business right here and now. I have no time to waste primping."

He hooted at that. "Primping! You look like you've been in a coal mine for a month. See here. I have not eaten since lunch and that was only a lettuce leaf and three small shrimp. I am a big man. I am a hollow man. I don't want to talk business until I've dined. Come along or not, but I have something to say to your advantage."

He smoothed the old-fashioned chain which lay across his belly, hauled out a weighty gold watch and scanned its face.

"I'll come back in an hour. I'm punctual to the minute. Don't keep me waiting."

He moved his bulk to the door. "You have remarkably limpid eyes," he said and lumbered away.

Stella marshaled her forces like a good general. It was as obvious as the nose on his face that Mr. Crown was devoted to the pleasures of the flesh. He had not garnered that girth by dainty picking, and his last remark to her about her eyes hinted at other appetites as well.

She determined that she would serve herself forth as appetizingly as a suckling pig with an apple in its mouth. One had to give to get.

She examined the contents of her closet with a critical eye. The old brown skirt with the safety pin holding the waist was in tatters. Two sweaters were clearly the victims of moths and time. She threw them aside and dug deeper. There was a gray dress with a sagging hem and the forlorn remains of peasant embroidery, but it too had seen better days. One pair of slacks with a gaping hole and a Japanese kimono completed her wardrobe. She considered the blouse she was wearing. It might do if she found a brooch to hold open the neckline, but the lace collar was torn and if truth be told it did smell a trifle high.

She rummaged in her drawers, flinging aside her washed-out underclothes. She found a silk rose as faded as the last one of summer and held it coquettishly to her bosom. Ghastly. She tried sticking it in her hair. Worse. The only jewelry yielded by further search was a paste pin with a stone missing, and a George McGovern button. She thought of going naked, with her pubic muff in proud curls and a Venus smile on her lips. She liked herself best stripped to the buff, with her hair hanging in a tangle, but it would hardly do to be as honest as all that.

She decided to bum off Nell. She had been vaguely aware of elegance in her clothes and they were both tall. She scurried off like a determined pack rat.

Nell opened the door to her insistent rap.

"Hello. Isn't it too chilly for you to be out without a coat?"

"I'm here to borrow one," Stella said. "And a dress and shoes and lipstick."

Nell grinned and stood aside. "Come in."

Stella loped past her and turned to make a comparison between them. She had bigger tits than Nell, that was immediately apparent, but she could leave buttons open wherever necessary.

"We hardly know each other," she began, "but this is an emergency. You can say no if you like but I'll regard it as very unfriendly if you do."

"Then I won't. What's the occasion?"

"A man is taking me to an expensive dinner. The poor dolt doesn't know how expensive, but that's beside the point. The point is I've got to look human. What do you own that would give me an air?"

"Anything would be an improvement." Nell was tart.

"You pick. I don't really give a damn."

Nell led her to the bedroom. Stella saw at a glance that she had come to the right place. This one had a sense of style. There were flowers on her night table and a silk robe thrown on the bed. The pillow slips had lace and the books were leather-bound. She forgave her the luxury because of the books. There were a lot of them. Nell paused at the closet door.

"I'm not prying," she said, "but just what effect are you after? Girlish, soignée, seductive, horsy? I must say I'm surprised that you're making any effort at all."

"He's rich," Stella confided. "And powerful. He can do me a world of good."

Nell studied her. "It seems out of character."

"Strategy," Stella said. "A glimpse of boobs goes down like candy with all of 'em."

Nell dragged out an armful of clothes and dumped them on the bed.

Stella wriggled out of her dreadful garb in a flash. She wore nothing underneath. Her body was beautiful, strong, as pure as Greek sculpture. Her neck was dirty.

Nell sighed and sank down on the bed. "You do yourself a great disservice," she said. "You're really a pretty woman."

"Balls." Stella snatched up a beige dress and held it under her chin. "Is this a good color for me?"

"No. It makes you sallow. Try the yellow."

Stella found it and pulled it over her head, ripping the seam in her haste.

"Damn, it's too small."

"Try the green, then."

Stella wriggled into a clinging green jersey and settled the folds around her hips. She minced to the mirror and pursed her mouth at the reflection. "I wouldn't burn the topless towers of Ilium, but it isn't bad, is it?" She turned awkwardly to see herself from all sides.

"You look very dishy." Nell leaned on an elbow, amused.

"This, then, and thank you very much. What over it?"

Nell tossed her a white coat. Stella flung it about her shoulders. There was just the suggestion of preening now as beauty triumphed over beast.

"My God," she said staring. "Maybe I'll just stay at home and make love to myself."

Nell took her firmly by the arm and marched her into the bathroom.

"This is soap," she said picking up a scented bar, "and this," as she turned on the tap, "is water."

"I intended to bathe all along," Stella said sulkily, "since it's an occasion."

"Do."

She thrust a jar into her hands. "Deodorant." She picked up a bottle. "Perfume."

"Sweat is sexual." Stella thrust them both away. "It arouses *me* every time."

"There's no accounting for taste," Nell said. "Sit down and let's see what can be done about your hair."

Fifteen minutes later she had just gotten the snarls out. She tried piling it on Stella's head, tucking it behind her ears and finally decided to draw it back severely to show her noble brow. Stella fidgeted throughout.

"Enough. Enough. I'm far too good for him right now."

The two women returned to the living room, Stella clutching her loot. "There's one other thing."

"Don't hesitate," Nell said dryly.

"A drink. To bring the roses to my cheeks."

Nell selected her second-best Scotch, took a water glass instead of crystal, poured sparingly and handed it to her. Stella flopped on the couch, threw her head back and closed her eyes.

"You're a good sort," she said.

"I want the clothes back," Nell countered, "after you've had them dry-cleaned."

"You shall have them." She opened her eyes again. "I saw the table set for one. Are you between men or off them?"

"Neither. I'm just enjoying an evening alone."

"It can't be easy for you with men. You're intelligent. Proud. Maybe even arrogant."

"How is it with you?"

"Me?" Stella thought it over. "I like a good time in bed. I don't want to be bothered out of it. Men don't like that."

She swallowed her drink in two gulps. "The better friendship is with women. I had a fine friend once in my youth.

She had a mind as sharp as an ax. And wit. And character."

"Are you friends still?"

"She died of cancer at twenty-nine. I have all her letters. They're as good as Swift's."

Stella held out her glass. "One more to see me into my bath."

Nell shook her head. "You'll drown in it if I do."

"Yes," said Stella getting to her feet. "I like you. I may take you up."

Nell laughed. "You'll wear out my clothes and drink my booze. I'm not sure I'll allow it."

Stella looked at her shrewdly. "You'll find we have things to say to each other. And in due time, you'll be able to boast of knowing me. I'll be famous. Get in on the ground floor."

"I'll consider it."

Stella started to go and then bethought herself. "Shoes," she cried. "I can't go in these brogues." She held a foot out in front of her.

"You're out of luck. You're at least a size nine. I have small, aristocratic feet."

"Who has boats to fit me, then?"

"Try Jake."

She put her arm through Stella's and urged her out. Stella held back one last time.

"Jesus," she cried, "what if we fall into bed tonight? I haven't a nightdress fit to be seen."

"Glory in thy nakedness," Nell told her and put her out on the doorstep like a reluctant cat.

When Caleb arrived and saw her done up in her borrowed finery he confined himself to an approving nod and muttered, "That's better."

She was a little put-out. She had been quite dazzled by the sight of herself in the sea green dress a dryad might have worn. She thought very well of the way her hair swirled, and her legs seemed to her to be extremely handsome. She had managed to get some shoes from Hortense, and they gave her a swaying walk that was quite Italian and sexy.

She made of their crossing through the gardens to his car a kind of regal progress, putting her nose in the air and holding his arm as if he were a consort. It gave her satisfaction to see Jake poke his head out of his door and take notice of her, and one or two other tenants around the barbecue seemed visibly impressed.

She was even more imperious in the restaurant, following the headwaiter to their table with condescension and hauteur. It had become a kind of amusing game, one she had never played before, and by the time he had ordered her a vermouth cassis (she had wanted Scotch but to no avail) she felt she might well be Queen of all the Russias.

"So money buys all this, does it?" She looked at the white linen and the perfect rose on the table. Then she hitched around in her chair and surveyed her fellow diners. They were a classy lot, no doubt of it.

"Come now," he said peering over the huge menu. "Don't play-act. There's nothing naive in you at all. If you had been diligent in your work all these years you might well have had all the high life you could handle."

She bristled at that. "I work slowly because what I produce is perfect of its kind." She snuffled and touched her nose with the damask napkin. She had forgotten a hankie. "There's no way I can be hurried. None."

He made no reply to that. He adjusted his glasses to peer at the hand-lettered bill of fare. A waiter had appeared on silent feet and stood by his side with an air of subservience.

Caleb asked his name.

"George, sir."

"Very well, George. Tell me when the sole was caught."

"Today, sir."

"What time?"

The waiter shrugged. "They get it every morning."

"Then we'll have it. And watercress salad dressed with walnut vinegar and oil, haricots verts done no more than three minutes, and I will see the wine list."

"I hate fish," said Stella.

"I am dieting. It would be self-centered of you to gorge in front of me." He tucked his napkin into his waistcoat and looked like a stern Victorian father. Stella downed her aperitif, swigging it like a sailor.

"That's to be sipped," he admonished her.

She sneered at him. "Ah, you're one of those who make a fuss about food and drink. Get it down, get the benefit, and get on to other things is the way I look at it."

"Primitive point of view." He nibbled at a piece of Melba toast, studying her all the while. "I have plans for you," he said, crunching toast. "Good sensible plans."

Stella lifted an eyebrow. "You understand, don't you, that while I look years younger, I'm forty. I have plans of my own."

He beckoned the wine steward. "Batard-Montrachet seventy-one and not too chilled, please." He turned back to her. "Very well, you're forty. You look it, by the way. You've published two slim volumes of verse by an obscure little West Coast company which also turns out party books and map folders. Harold Bloom doesn't know who you are nor does Stephen Spender or anyone else who should. It's my business and has been for thirty years to bring new people to light. That doesn't necessarily mean you will have a wide sale. It does mean critical attention for your work and care in bringing you along. It means notice of you in the *New York Times*. It means judicious advertising and dignified promotion. It means a discerning editor to watch over you and keep you from flagging. Are you listening?"

Stella pushed aside the rose so she could peer at him closely. She did so, leaning her elbows on the table.

"Go on."

"It's obvious that it's recognition you're after. You can have it. You should have it, it's your due. I'll see, to the best of my ability, that you get it."

"Who do I have to kill?" Stella was leery.

"You have to accept a modest advance and commit to a reasonable delivery date. I am fairly lenient about that. I understand you cannot whip your Muse, but I will expect you to drink less and write more. Our books are beautifully designed and printed. If you work hard and in good faith, in no time you will have a cult, your picture in a news magazine, looking untidy, and an inflated sense of your own importance." He patted his mouth with his napkin.

"How *much* money," demanded Stella.

"I'm a fair man. I have a reputation for it. You won't be swindled."

"I've been sucked up to before." She leaned back in her chair and looked at him combatively.

He maintained his calm. "You're not easy to deal with, are you?"

"Yes, I am," she said promptly. "Think of a sum of money to offer me and then double it." She took the dregs of his drink and sipped it with nice restraint.

Caleb folded his arms. "Now see here. I cannot put Midas' gold in your pocket. We do not enrich our Sapphos, our Emily Dickinsons, our Amy Lowells. I would be happier if we did but such is not the case. You must content yourself with a laurel wreath."

Stella flared. "I know your ilk," she trumpeted. "Try paying your plumber one cent less than twenty bucks an hour and see what happens. Try offering your *garage* mechanic a laurel wreath. You'll get a monkey wrench up your ass is what you'll get!"

"You'll get a small advance," he retorted. "Growing smaller by the minute."

"Perhaps I'll get a better offer from someone else." She took on the sharp look of a fishwife haggling over the price of haddock.

"You'll get the best you can command from me," he said shortly.

He watched the waiter with a critical eye as dinner was ceremoniously served. The fish was laid open, the bony skeleton whisked rapidly aside, steaming butter spooned with care. The waiter lingered as if he would like a taste of the dish himself, but a look from Caleb sent him backward to the kitchen.

They were alone again. Caleb looked at his plate a moment and then pushed it aside.

"You're damned difficult," he said, "and you've spoiled my appetite."

"You need to lose weight," she said. "There's too much of you."

The hint of a smile came into his eyes. "So. You've taken notice of me, have you?"

"You're not easy to miss."

"Stella," he said, "I find you quarrelsome and suspicious and churlish, but your work is splendid. You'd do well to put yourself in my hands."

She looked at the crisply curled fish on her plate. She looked out the window. She looked at the main chance.

"I'll sleep on it," she said.

A bottle of wine was brought in a frosted silver bucket; two glasses were put before them, glacially misted. She perked up considerably at the sight and decided to be charming.

"Are you married?" she asked.

"Widowed. I've been alone five years. I'm a man who likes to be fussed over. I haven't adjusted to solitude."

She conjured up a vision of his wife, a mothering, serving presence. She doubtless embroidered house slippers for him with his monogram emblazoned in red silk and read aloud to him in a high thin voice. She saw her placing a gout stool and offering milk white breasts to his weary head. It made her chuckle aloud.

"Something amuses you about my bereavement?"

"You're over it," she said. "You wouldn't have that great belly if you weren't."

"She was a sweet woman. Not bright, but very spiritual." His eyes met hers with a sardonic gleam. "And you? Are you involved with anyone?"

"Free as a bird." She rested her chin on her hand.

"I'm sixty years old," he said, frowning at her. "And you're a handful. That's plain to see."

"Well," she taunted, "if your fires are banked, they're banked. There's nothing I can do about that."

He grasped her wrist then, and not lightly either. "Don't prod, my dear," he warned. "This old turtle can still stick his head out of the shell and snap." He let her go and picked up his wineglass, tasted, chewed appreciatively, drank.

"I like a contest of wills. But I like other things more. I like tenderness and good will toward my bed partner. I'd rather dry tears than cause them. I would like someone to understand the autumnal melancholy I sometimes feel in the midst of happiness. I would like someone skillful enough to remind me of my youth. I would find all kinds of ways to show my gratitude."

"I turn on my side and go to sleep," said Stella.

"Perhaps you have — to date."

"Well," said Stella, "we're not going to decide anything here and now."

"That's to come," he said, calling for the check. She sat in nonplused silence all the way home.

Over her protest that she could perfectly well find her way to her own door (hadn't she done it blind drunk a hundred times?), he insisted on seeing her up. She paused halfway up the stairs to remove the shoes which by now pinched the life out of her. She listened, with a certain malicious interest as they climbed, for heavy breathing from him, but he went up like an antelope.

"I won't ask you for coffee," he said, "because you probably don't have an uncracked cup to serve it in."

She thought it over. "You're right. I haven't."

He took her hand and held it in his. "Now then, my dear, think over all I've said. I'm staying at Henry's for a week or so. I'll want your decision before I return east." He patted the hand he held and returned it to her. "Have you your key?"

"I don't lock the door. That's how you got in in the first place."

He clucked disapproval. "You live very recklessly."

She gave him a sly smile. "You don't."

"You're the worse for wine," he said, "and I'm a gentleman." He stroked his jaw and fixed her with a long look. "Give me every credit for restraint. I'm very unsettled, looking at your pretty mouth."

"Talk!" she sniffed.

"When I was a boy," he said soothing her, "I seduced the Irish maid in my father's house. I remember shucking off my clothes on the stairs, so great was my haste. My father found us on the landing, rolling about the floor in transports of youthful high spirits. I remember him coming out of his room with a pince-nez on the bridge of his nose. He had on a Sulka dressing gown. I don't know how long he stood there, but finally he spoke to me. 'Caleb,' he said, 'this is not appropriate.' " He patted her shoulder. "I think he might have said the same thing now."

He started away and then suddenly turned back. "It occurs to me that you haven't said thank you for the very expensive dinner I bought you."

She shrugged. "I don't bother with formalities."

"It's not your manners I deplore. I'm already aware that you haven't any. It's something else entirely." She did not encourage him to go on; he needed no encouragement. "You must come down from the heights, Stella, and move among us. Admit to a common humanity. It's sometimes humbling, but what of it? It's healthy to be able to say thank you. It's pleasant. It's openhearted. You've been surly too long, I think. *Try* saying it, whether you mean it or not."

"It wasn't even a very good dinner." She showed him the stubborn set of her jaw.

"Come, come." He urged her like a recalcitrant child. "You smiled during the meal. You may even have laughed. Yes, I think you definitely laughed. I remember admiring the whiteness and the evenness of your teeth. You enjoyed yourself, admit it."

"I don't deny it" — she flounced — "but I don't intend to make a fuss about it either."

"Stella, Stella," he said, "you mean to win the war, but you've lost the battle. You're almost smiling now."

"Oh, hell . . . if you're going to go on and on about it. Thank you for the dinner." It was begrudged all the way.

"A crack in the dike," he said, and he beamed at her. "I'm pleased."

She sulked. "What's Henry's number if I want to talk some more?"

"He's a modest man. You'll find him in the book."

The look in his eyes could not be read in the dark. He stood there as if he had all the time in the world and wanted it spent near her. A night bird sang. Someone in the apartment above slammed a door. Diana Ross, on a record, sang of disappointed love.

"I imagine," he said, "that you sleep on your back, with your arms flung above your head."

Stella pulled the pins that held her hair. It fell about her shoulders. She was tired of being done up.

"Either come in or go home," she told him.

He merely smiled and turned, moving away through the dark, his footsteps heavy and measured on the creaking wooden steps. She went to lean over the balcony to watch him.

"Look where you're going," she called, "or you'll end up head over ass in the swimming pool."

He looked up at her, a corpulent Romeo to her raddled Juliet. "I can see very well in the dark." He waved and was gone.

Stella woke before dawn to think him over. She got up, padded into the kitchen to fill a wineglass and brought it back to bed, hoping its fumes would open her eyes and clear her mind. The cat occupied the warm hollow she had left. She tossed it out and settled in with the blankets drawn to her chin. She didn't particularly like what she was feeling. Her encounter with Caleb was like a mote in her eye she was unable to blink away.

The cat came back and tried to make friends. It purred against her breast.

"Scat," she said. "I don't intend to settle for *you.*" She sipped the wine, but it tasted cheap and raw on her tongue. At her age she had to do better. She put it aside and watched the dawn lighten the wall opposite her. Somewhere in her mind was a hazy catalogue of men. They were shadow figures, one notable for his red suspenders and the bandana he wore to bed, another for the sea chanties he sang in her ear, a third who was blind and felt his way with wicked fingers. She realized now that she had never really spoken to any of them. Indeed, she had wanted it that way. She valued her mind over her body. She had never shared her thoughts.

She picked up the phone and aroused Henry's entire household.

"My God, Stella, it's five o'clock in the morning. Caleb is fast asleep and so was I." Henry was definitely cross.

"Then you're missing the best part of the day. Let me talk to him."

"This is outrageous."

"Put him on."

She heard cursing and stumbling away. Then Caleb was on the line.

"I don't see you as a madcap, Stella," he said coldly.

"What are you doing today?" she queried, thoroughly unchastened.

"I am going to visit my mother in San Diego." His tone was even shorter.

"I'll go along. I like the drive by the ocean."

"She is ninety years old. You're too much for her. You're too much for me. I'm standing here in my bare feet. I'm chilled to the bone. I'm annoyed, Stella."

It was a long drive, she thought, holding the phone away from her. At the end of it she would know more.

"Sleep is death," she said. "Pick me up at nine." She hung up before he could reply.

Her back ached. Bed became intolerable. She dragged on her old Japanese kimono and headed for the sauna. She used it more than any other tenant in the building, but then no other tenant had so much sauce to sweat out of his system.

Steam rose over the warm pools. The early morning light had a pearly sheen. Water stood in the cups of the hibiscus blossoms and rusted the frames of the deck-side chairs. The frond of a palm tree crackled dryly in a small lifting wind. She padded on, enjoying the damp concrete underfoot. She had obstinately waded in puddles as a child.

Jake was naked in the sauna, stretched out with his eyes closed. A towel had twisted off his body and lay on the floor. Stella stood in the doorway and looked. She envied him his taut flat belly and his handsome feet with their straight toes. Hers had bunions. Yes, everything about him was nicely made and placed. Very nicely.

"Jesus." He saw her and sat up. "This place belongs to the men from six to nine-thirty. What the hell are you doing up at this hour, anyway?"

"I've come to get rid of the poison." She sat on the bench next to him in a companionable, confiding way. He hitched over to make room.

"The way you keep staring at it," he said, "I'm afraid it'll fall off." Then he grinned, picked up the towel and knotted it around his waist. "Well," he said to her, "as long as you're here, stay."

"Ach, my mind's a thousand miles away." She sat back and listened to the hissing of the steam.

"Who was your fat friend last night?" He closed his eyes again. She told him only the facts, reserving the feelings for herself. He knew Stella of old. He let her hide them.

"If anything comes of it," he warned her lazily, "you have to start paying rent."

They were silent for a while, enjoying the opening of their pores and the lassitude the heat induced. She wondered if she should discuss Caleb with Jake. She knew he had had a long career of amorous adventure; what could he tell her about running before the wind without peril, what of crossing the finish line first, with pennants flying?

"Jake?"

"Hmmmm?"

She thought better of it and backed away.

"Nothing. Never mind."

In the long run she knew she would submit to no opinion but her own, anyway.

And what did she think of this other one, this great galumphing bear of a man with his Brahmin mind and his sonorous piss-elegant voice? There was sex in it somewhere. She had felt her hackles rise like a cat approached by a tom. She had felt an odd familiar tingle in the tip of her nose which always occurred when she was horny. And she had speculated boldly about him. Did the

159

gallantry drop away when he lowered his well-tailored English trousers? Did he know a string of obscenities of Elizabethan roundness and rarity? Did he, looking into the last quarter of his life, lash himself to perform mightily — or did he rest on garnered laurels?

Another thought nagged. Did he mean to pack her into a new and unfamiliar mold and turn her out, altered, for the worse?

She recalled disturbing words: discipline, sobriety, responsibility. She balked at each and every one. There was some kind of bargain he meant to drive with her, she knew it. Well, he'd have to get up early in the morning to best her. She hadn't made her way this far, penniless and just slipping past her prime, without knowing her way around.

"Open your eyes and look at me," she told Jake.

He opened one.

"Would you say, my age and condition taken into account, that I'm attractive? Think of me, mind, tarted up and reeking of perfume. Holding my blue-veined breasts in my hands and lifting them toward you." She turned her beet red face toward him as if he were Paris at his judgment of Beauty.

He was prompt in his reply and not very flattering. "I've seen better. I've seen worse."

"I agree. But tell me plainly. Would you throw me out of your bed? Would you invite me in in the first place?"

He scratched the furry patch on his chest and reflected.

"We'd never even come close. I don't know whether that's because I've known you for ten years without laying a hand on you or because you're a rummy."

He leaned over and patted her flank. "I'd have to proceed platonically with you, sweetheart. No hard feelings."

"I couldn't seduce you under any circumstances whatsoever?" She pressed him like a shyster lawyer cross-examining.

"Jesus, Stella, what's with you?"

"Yes or no?"

"No." He wiped his brow. "No," he said again.

"Fair enough."

He was cross. "You want to open a can of peas? . . . Okay, I'll open it. I'll tell you what isn't attractive, Stella. What isn't attractive is the way you corner a man. It wouldn't kill you if you came in at an angle once in a while. Everything with you is head on."

"Why are you uncomfortable?"

"Because I love you," he said grumpily, "and I don't like this conversation a helluva lot."

He was right, of course. It wasn't necessary to be graded like a prize heifer for the soundness of her carcass, the size of her udders, the tonality of her "moo." She knew who she was. She always had.

He tried to make amends.

"Come take a shower with me. I'll wash your back."

"No, the booze in me is only half boiled away."

He lingered. "Stella," he said.

"Yes."

He grinned. "If I was alone on a desert island. Okay?"

"Better than nothing," she retorted, and turned her back to him.

Caleb had borrowed Henry's beautifully kept Lincoln Continental and had transformed it into a Dutch still life with gifts for his mother. A garden rake stuck out the back window, a flat of yellow pansies bloomed like scraps of bright yellow velvet and a bag of potting mix evoked deep woods, moss and harvest.

Beside him on the front seat was a brown paper bag neatly rolled down to reveal a dozen green pippin apples still dewed with water, ready for crunching should his impatient appetite overtake him.

The attire of the bon vivant had been replaced as well. He wore an elegant but faded shirt open at the collar and a hat of ancient vintage, battered, stained and utterly rakish.

Stella, in her shabby gray sweater, looked like a tramp he had obliged with a ride. She too wore a hat, black, squashed and tugged over one eye, giving her a sinister look that, together with dark glasses and a drooping cigarette, might well have led to her arrest had she been standing on a street corner.

He handed her into the front seat and she caught a pleasant

whiff of soap and shaving lotion. He was obviously a man who tended himself with care. He had a morning freshness of manner as well, energetic and confident.

"Now, then," he began, snapping her seat belt for her, "I drive very fast but very skillfully. I would appreciate it if you did not squeal or call out warnings or jam your feet into the floorboard. I have been driving for forty years without a single unpleasant incident of any kind." He settled himself comfortably behind the wheel. "I will say further that I'm as nice as pie about stopping for calls of nature. No problem there. However I will not stop at souvenir stands or antique shops. My late wife was addicted to them and I vowed on her death never to indulge another woman in that way."

"You talk a lot in the morning, I see," Stella said, rolling down her window.

"My dear," he said, swinging the car into the traffic without looking, "at my age I feel the need to get it all said." He narrowly missed a boy on a motorbike and had a rude remark shouted at him for his trouble.

He tore onto the freeway and from that moment Stella began to review her life like a drowning woman coming to the end of it.

It was a ride of such surpassing recklessness that it became almost exhilarating. They sped along as if pursued by the hounds of Hell. Caleb loved the horn and used it with gusto. A matron, patting her bouffant hairdo and idling along, was raucously honked out of their path. A diesel truck was beep-beeped into the slow lane with an arrogant crescendo. He blasted out warnings to Greyhound buses and Winnebagos. Stella reasoned that since the landscape consisted mostly of mean little housing tracts and shopping centers it was just as well to have it all skim by in a blur. When she spotted a black and white highway patrol car she held her tongue. Since they were not dead amid strewn wreckage it was obvious that Caleb was the darling of the gods. They would certainly not be arrested for mere speeding. They were not.

Caleb further narrowed the odds by turning away and digging

into the bag beside him for an apple. He offered one to her. The wind rushed through the car and tore the hat from her head. It sailed away out the window and was lost.

"That's my best hat!" she protested wrathfully. She had often flung it over garden walls, but to lose it like this was another matter.

"Unbecoming," he replied, maneuvering the car into a space almost too narrow for it.

"I expect you to pay for it!" She was shrieking now over the din, the wind, the honking, the traffic.

"Certainly."

Stella began to feel cheerful. She had discovered nerves of steel on this harrowing journey, unaided by even one nip or tipple. The smell of oil and exhaust and hot pavement bothered her not at all. She loosened her collar and rolled up her sleeves, admiring the delicate tracery of her veins. She thought of flinging all her clothes out the window and riding Highway 5 like a soaring bird in the company of the eagle who was Caleb. Perhaps there was something aphrodisiac in jouncing along like this. The warm sun spilled in on her and confirmed it. Yes, she would like to pull off the road and take another kind of ride, astride the man next to her.

A boy and girl passed them in a car painted with a fiery streak along its side. The girl nuzzled into the boy's shoulder; his hand cupped her breast, proving with bravado that he could do two things at once. They were indifferent to the whole world. Stella turned around to stare and met the boy's sleepy look. He made a kissing motion into the air which she took to be directed at her. She waved back jauntily. Caleb accelerated and left them behind too. She regarded him with possessive eyes, but he looked straight ahead, munching one apple after another. She made a humble pleasure out of watching. Such gusto. Such concentration.

"Let's turn off and ride by the ocean." He snapped his directional signal too late and was grazed by an enormous van. They rocked down the off ramp and came into the quiet of the road by the sea.

She offered mild praise. "Well. We got off alive."

"Churlish drivers in this state. Shameful."

The sea was a spoiled blue, dulled by kelp and oil spill, but there were sailboats with immaculate sails and fields of tomatoes showing red and green on the palisades overlooking the water's edge.

The contest appeared to be over. Caleb slowed down and pronounced the landscape very pretty indeed.

"Stop," Stella commanded. "I have to go into the bushes."

He complied with alacrity, skidding fifty feet or so to the brink of a ditch. He came around and opened the door for her and promised to turn his back until she called out.

It was a ruse. Stella had the kidneys of a camel. She walked off into a grassy meadow, waited a suitable length of time and then sat down, searching warily for poison oak before she did so.

"Come out here. You can see a fisherman on the beach."

He walked briskly toward her, as if stubble and rock were his native habitat. She noted that big men often move with grace. He surveyed the scene like a Spanish explorer coveting the sweep of land before him.

"Splendid," he said. "Really splendid." He remained standing over her.

Stella showed herself to advantage. She lay back, clasping her arms behind her head, displaying aggressive breasts and availability with one and the same gesture. She knew her eyes darkened with desire. She opened them wide so that he might see. She was, she thought smugly, an odalisque — overlooking, of course, the soup stain on her skirt and the hole in her stocking.

"Ah," she murmured, looking up at him. The little sigh promised pliability and yielding. It got her exactly nowhere.

"Stella," he said with instant comprehension of her purpose, "copulation in the grass at our age is out of the question. In the first place, there are ants. They are crawling on your skirt this very moment. In the second place, I require bedsprings to assist my weight. In the third place, I am expected to breakfast at my mother's house and she mustn't be kept waiting. Lastly" — he held out a hand to pull her up — "there are two small boys standing on the ridge behind us, waiting to see a comic turn.

I can't speak for you, but as for me, I cannot make love to laughter."

She snapped her head around and saw the audience, sly-faced and watchful. She put her finger in her mouth, pulled and produced a horrendous grimace. The children fled. She scrambled up.

"I know a cheap motel near San Diego," she said.

"Why cheap? I'm rich."

"It's what I'm used to." She walked ahead and seated herself in the car again. He got in on his side but left the key unturned in the ignition.

When he spoke it was calmly. "It's childish to rub my nose into it," he said. "When we do have a night, and we will, I think we owe ourselves every comfort. The comfort of clean linen and tender beginnings. Whatever is used in your life you can keep to yourself. I'll do the same. I look forward to it," he added and started the car.

They drove for half an hour or more in total silence. When he spoke again it was to brief her on the coming visit.

"My mother is a socialist," he told her as they drove down a shabby side street, searching for her house. "She voted for Eugene Debs and insisted that my father do the same. She was arrested in Selma at the age of eighty, not only for marching for civil rights but also because she bit a piece out of a policeman's ear. My father adored her but died young from the strain of living with her. She had too many opinions for a harmonious married life. She is the reason I married a timid soul, as far a departure from her as possible, a mistake I will not make again."

He slammed on the brakes. They had stopped before a white frame house of no distinction, standing in a garden which redeemed it in a flurry of roses and blossoming lemon trees. A shutter had torn loose and sagged beside a window. A broken cane chair furnished the porch. A green and yellow parrot squawked invective in a cage: "Fuck you, fuck you." His mother made an appearance in the doorway, a tiny woman, old but unwasted, the size of a child but invincible.

His face lit up at the sight of her. "She has lost her glasses," he said, almost to himself. "She probably sat on them. Mother!" he called and rushed from the car to embrace her, leaving Stella to manage for herself.

She saw him swing the woman from the ground and waltz her down the path, causing her to cry out sharply and demand to be put down instantly. He gave her a final approving shake and a smacking kiss that appeared to rock her off her feet. She pushed him away and peered toward Stella. The car was too far distant to satisfy her curiosity. She tottered toward it with remarkable speed.

"Come out," she called, and Stella obeyed. The woman thrust out her hand and shook Stella's with enthusiasm.

"I'm glad you've come," she began. "I have much to say to you. Before anything else I wish to tell you I consider you an extraordinary writer. Radical. Militant. Angry. Everything any woman of sense would be. Come in and have coffee."

The inside of the cottage spoke of a persevering spirit. The oak kitchen table had been scrubbed to whiteness by an energetic hand and the worn pink and gray linoleum had been mopped and waxed diligently. The kitchen towels, hand-embroidered with cheerful maxims, were all folded the same way and hung neatly to boot.

The stove top was clean. One would look in vain for a spatter of grease lurking in the burners. The chipped kitchen tile had been tended by a battered toothbrush standing in a glass; the counter had been given the gleam of well-cared-for dentures.

Stella was blind to her own surroundings but eagle-eyed in her observation of others'. She took in the beauty of the lily blooming in a jelly jar. She saw the sweet potato sending forth its pretty shoot of green in a cracked majolica pitcher of swirling brown and yellow. She sensed, in the faint lingering smell of cinnamon and nutmeg and mace, that Christmas cakes had been baked here, wrapped in fine white linen napkins and offered as gifts. Tea had been brewed here as well, probably strong to bitterness and sipped in the deep silence of early morning. Smiles had been offered in these rooms, and courtesy, and certainly the grocery boy or the day maid had gone home feeling subtly cheered, though they may not have known why. She was pleased by the sight of a violin and a music rack with a score spread open upon it. She saw a deck of cards laid out in a game of solitaire, family pictures in silver frames, a dog dish on the floor, bottles of French wine and, astonishingly, a clay pipe packed and ready to smoke on a table. She saw, sitting opposite her, a kindred spirit.

"The scones are just out of the oven. There's real butter. I hate margarine, I don't give a damn what they say about it. There's jam — those berries are from my garden. I'm full of thorns from picking them. There are no eggs. I'm allergic to them."

Caleb took his place after holding the chairs for both of them. The old lady ate heartily, nodding her head as if she were in accord with her own light hand with pastry and the excellence of her coffee. She dispensed the food lavishly, and when they were served she treated them to a show of emotion which was equally ample.

"I'm glad you came," she said briskly. "I've been lonelier than usual lately. I've taken to talking to myself and the dog and I find that disturbing. I was going to call you long-distance to find me the services of a good young analyst at the college here. I don't want to drift into senility just because there's no one interesting to talk to."

"Bosh," said Caleb. "You don't want a companion, you only want ears. Ears to fill up with your political palaver and what-have-you." He buttered his scone heavily, defying his arteries.

His mother turned to Stella. "Men are dense," she said. "He doesn't understand that old age is exile. Exile from ferment and creativity and sex and anything else that counts for much. You agree?"

"I'm not old," said Stella, "but I'm willing to be warned."

"Sensible. I knew you were sensible. I said so."

Caleb beamed at his plate, letting them decide between them what life was all about. He took a kind of harem pleasure in the empathy he felt between them; it made for a pleasant meal and good digestion following. Mrs. Crown left him to himself while she talked on.

"I want to speak of your work," she said to Stella.

Stella took this as her due and leaned back in her chair, ready to be praised.

"There are black holes in space," said Mrs. Crown. "Your poems look into them. I won't read them at night because they disturb my sleep. But I enjoy being terrified by day. At my time of life nothing is worth reading that doesn't send a chill down your spine. He," she said, indicating her son, "is a romantic. He likes books with happy endings. Like his father. His father," she added with a dry smile, "was an indulgence of mine. I should have married a labor organizer."

Caleb rose and patted her white head. "I'm going outside to put up chicken wire around your vegetable garden. The rabbits eat better than you do. Perhaps you'll be kind enough" — this last to Stella — "to dry the dishes for her. She makes me do it as a rule and I don't enjoy it."

He turned sideways to squeeze through the narrow kitchen doorway and went off whistling.

"Where did you get my book?" Stella queried. "Were there a lot of them on sale? Was it marked down?"

Mrs. Crown took her measure. "I won't lie to you. I bought it for twenty-five cents. You went unsold, you see. You were on the remainder shelf. Booksellers are quite ruthless."

Stella shrugged.

"No," Mrs. Crown said emphatically, "you mustn't let it go. You have to demand. Demand of yourself. Demand of others. When you get where I am all you can do is assent."

She rose, gathering up the dishes with the careless ease of a carhop, and stacked them in the sink.

"You've just met Caleb?"

"This week."

"What do you make of him."

"Nothing yet. Well . . ." She hesitated.

"You'd like to sleep with him. Almost all women want to. It's odd . . . he's gotten quite pudgy in the last few years. Perhaps it's nostalgia. Women see him as a great kewpie doll. He isn't."

"I never played with dolls," said Stella. "Tell me, what can I expect from him?"

"Almost anything you want, providing you don't wheedle. He takes positions on principle. His own are very high. He was charming to his wife. He's not ashamed of sentiment. You mustn't hector him or cheat him or he'll toss you down the stairs on your bum. I'm pleased he's my son. What else can I tell you?"

"How can I get him in bed?" Stella said, licking the jam spoon.

"How should I know? We're not oedipal in this family."

She tossed Stella a towel. "Do dry these. I hate having dishes stand about in a rack."

Stella did as she was told, lazily dabbing at plates and cups as if she didn't know how. They worked side by side. Through the window Caleb could be seen bending and stooping at his work. The garden was laid out in neat rows of lettuce and beans and a flower thrust here and there for frivolity. He might have been a figure from an illustrated book of hours, a peaceful big-bellied peasant. He paused to wipe his forehead on a monogrammed Irish linen handkerchief. The peasant image vanished. He called to them. "Come sit outside. I'd like company."

The two women went out of the house and arranged themselves on the wooden back steps. Mrs. Crown steadied herself with a fine dry hand laid on Stella's shoulder. When they were seated Stella had a strange urge to lay her head in Mrs. Crown's blue cotton lap. It was a fleeting moment. She had not been a loving child, but somewhere there was a remembered caress she sought again.

She sat up straight instead and stared ahead of her. She refused to be lulled into bathos by the sight of an old lady taking the sun. Next it would be priests or shrinks.

"I'd like a glass of wine if you have such a thing," she said.

"Oh," said Mrs. Crown, "so that's the way it is."

Obligingly she scurried into the house after Stella's drink. She was out again in a moment, brandishing a handsome green bottle and a glass. Caleb's sensitive ears caught the pop of the cork. He paused, raised both a hoe and his voice.

"No, no, no, none of that!" he called. He lumbered to the porch, shaking his head. "The sun is out, things are growing, we are here to enjoy nature. If you wish to drink, bend over the garden hose. Meanwhile, come out into the patch and work up a sweat."

Stella's eyes fastened on the bottle as Mrs. Crown held it uncertainly, wavering between hospitality and doubt.

Finally she set it down. "I'll give it to you with lunch." She was conspiratorial in her tone.

Caleb leaned down to Stella and pulled her upright. "You have the pallor of prison." He grasped her face and turned it to the sun. "I like dark, gypsyish women. Let's turn you into one." She was trundled down the garden path and a rake was thrust into her hands. She dug her heels into the dirt like a mule and glowered at him.

"What kind of goddamn silliness is this?" she snapped.

"Sunshine and exercise are healthy for you. I am preserving you for posterity."

"You want a peon to clean up your mess. That's what you want."

He paid no attention and shoved her along the row of runner beans. "Look at you, woman," he said. "Here is a world of good smells and birdsong, tender buds and green shoots. Try to be in harmony with it. And rake thoroughly, there are snails."

"I thought you were a city man or I would never have come with you." Stella made wild swipes with the rake, destroying everything in her path.

He crouched ahead of her, weeding with quick sure hands.

"Submit nicely," he told her. "Give yourself to it, and I will take you wading in the ocean. I will make ham sandwiches with sharp mustard and we'll have pears and cookies and all the wine you can drink."

"I have to go to the bathroom." She was as stubborn as a child in her determination to outwit him.

"You don't. You went on the road."

"I feel faint."

"Flop backwards, then; the earth is nicely turned behind you."
She swung the rake around her like an armed samurai, decapitating a dahlia as she did so. He let her fulminate while he examined a ladybug in the palm of his hand.

"These are said to be lucky. Shall I give it to you?"

She turned an angry back to him. He came close, all gentleness. The little insect was carefully deposited on her shoulder. "Make a wish," he said.

She rounded on him. "Very well. I want a boilermaker. Right now. *That's* my wish."

He was despotic but kind. "Finish the row, Stella, and I'll let you off."

Something in his manner, a kind of paternal tolerance, deflated her. She felt foolish. She gathered together a little mound of snails. Then another. Not one escaped her. She began to enjoy it, to anticipate her reward. She even bent double to search under the leaves. Death to the intruders!

"I've got the little buggers," she called triumphantly. A bee stung her.

"Goddamn sonofabitch!" she howled, jumping on one foot, then on another. "Look what you've done now. I'm poisoned."

He pulled her hair up and examined the mark. Then he moistened his finger with saliva and applied it. "Stand still. You're not Cleopatra. It's not an asp. You'll live."

She wrenched free of him and marched toward Mrs. Crown, whose face was pursed with sympathy. The old woman put an arm around Stella and led her into the house, making motherly noises about men and what eternal fools they were.

Stella had two drinks for her trouble and was on her third when Caleb came in from the garden. His mother stood holding a bottle of Scotch, warding him off. "Don't say a word," she cautioned.

"I'd like some of that myself. In a glass. With ice." He went to the sink to wash the garden loam from his hands while Stella moaned behind him. "You're a big baby," he said.

"No, you are," his mother corrected him sharply. "This woman has heard the music of the spheres. And you have her pulling weeds. It's ridiculous."

"Listen to your mother," said Stella, feeling somewhat better for the drink. "Always listen to your mother."

He smiled on them both and laid out plans. They would all go to the beach. He would, if he could still fit into them, wear the bathing trunks of other years. His mother would take her umbrella and a blanket and he would make a splendid lunch. If they found a secluded spot Stella was to pin her skirts up and join him in the water. He would lave her neck with some. The salt would sooth the sting she suffered and cheerfulness would prevail. He was already rummaging in the refrigerator. They were swept into compliance.

Mrs. Crown's sun hat had been fashionable in nineteen twenty-six. It had been refurbished some years ago with a ten-cent store rose. Sitting upright, presenting her patrician profile to the sea, she recalled Renoir and summer days lost in time. Beside her a picnic basket made the air odorous with garlic and cheese and fresh-pulled scallions from the garden. A rain-stained volume of Eliot lay open in her lap. She was sleeping, overcome by the sounding sea and the finger of sun which had found her under the pink umbrella.

In the water Caleb breasted the waves, thrashing and ducking, rolling and snorting like a playful dolphin. His gray hair curled tightly against his head; the gray patch on his chest matted. He became a Triton roaring at the sea and sky in a delirium of pleasure.

"Good, good!" he shouted to Stella. She stood at the water's edge, her skirt clasped gingerly in her hands, suffering the waves to lap her toes.

"Ugh," she said.

A jellyfish tumbled through the shallows and lay at her feet, a translucent blob shifting this way and that, a pale relic of life. She discredited its simple beauty and that of the trees cresting the hills and even the shattered remains of the ivory-covered shells on which she stood. Either nature or the morning Scotch was giving her heartburn.

"Ho!" cried Caleb. Now he rode the foamy crest of a wave, tumbling through it like a sea beast, showing his teeth and flailing his arms, battling the rush of water.

Stella regarded the bluish chill of her flesh and said nothing. He thrashed toward her. In his vigor he seemed to loom over everything in sight. He exhaled power.

"Glorious, glorious," he cried. "Isn't it glorious, Stella!"

Stella lifted one foot like a wounded crane. "I'm turning to ice," she said coldly.

Suddenly, wordlessly, he snatched her up and bore her out to sea. She gasped as her clothes were drenched through and through and gasped again as they submerged into a roaring green world. It was a whirling vortex of light and dark, air and choked breath, struggle and surrender. Wind or song or blood beat in her ears. They rolled over and over, clasped together in a mating of contortions and outcries. Good Christ, he was out of his trunks and into her in one writhing motion as the sea tossed them up and down. Her legs straddled his waist, barely meeting behind his girth. Fluids of all sorts became her element. She was alive. She was dying. She was filled to the brim and emptied. She clung like a child, a woman, a whore. Finally, he cradled her in his arms, made feather light by the buoyancy surrounding them. They rocked in the deep like two survivors of a shipwreck delighted with life.

"I surprise myself," he said, and kissed her throat.

"God Almighty," she cried out. "I feel tuned like a fiddle."

They came softly to the side of Mrs. Crown, whose hat now dipped over her eyes. She slept on, oblivious of them as they lay side by side on the sand. They might have been medieval tomb figures, so still were they, so joined.

Stella stared up into the empty bowl of the sky and wondered at herself. Her mind slept, she was all feeling. Could the rotund man next to her have caused this strange unsettling afterglow that left her as limp as a stroked cat? Could he have imposed himself between her and her certainty in one damp encounter? If so, she did not know herself. And if that was true it needed looking into. It was permissible to lose her purse or her bus ticket but certainly not herself.

The afternoon passed. Daylight fought dusk with streaks of pink and orange and blue. A somber edge of gray lowered the temperature and chilled the sand. A man came onto the beach with a rod and a line to cast into the darkening sea. He set a folding chair down with care, then a galvanized bucket, and stood with his hands on his hips, staring at the ocean, as if he at last commanded something worth having.

Mrs. Crown stirred and awoke. Caleb opened his eyes. Salt had dried his skin. He looked as if he had been altered in the water into some encrusted creature of the deep. Civilization had not produced him. Tiny fish had flipped gossamer fins and slid past him, staring into his eyes. He had risen out of waving sea grass; he had surfaced through streaming bubbles, bearing a conch shell aloft.

"We'll all be stiff as boards in the morning," he said, coming with a groan to his feet. "Let us head for liniment and hot baths."

He gathered them up, blanket, basket, umbrella, and shooed them to the car. Stella trailed after him in silence. She felt herself in the presence of myths. Would she freeze into a Daphne Laureola and twist roots into the ground, while an amorous god snatched a last embrace? Would she be impaled on Neptune's fork and be waved as a trophy above his hoary head? She sneezed violently. She would catch cold! She hurried after him.

No one seemed hungry. Mrs. Crown turned on the kitchen light and heated canned tomato soup, which they sipped from mugs, sitting around the table. Stella's damp clothes had been hung on the wash line outside to dry. She wore an old dressing gown of Mrs. Crown's, a dainty Edwardian garment of ecru lace and faded silk. It gave her an unbuttoned, languorous air, as though she had just stumbled from bed and dreams of unbridled sensuality.

"I think I'll play the violin," said Mrs. Crown. No one disputed her. She went to the music stand and dragged it close, so she could see without searching for her glasses.

She played Mozart with labored sweetness, closing her eyes and trembling to the music like a reed in the wind. A moth flew in the window and beat around her head, as if her white hair were a flower it could not resist. In the middle, she stopped.

"I'm tired," she said.

Caleb scraped back his chair. "Into bed with you."

She dropped the bow. It had become too heavy to hold. "Leave the cups; I'll wash them tomorrow. Come back sometime." She threw the invitation at Stella. "I like you."

Her son came forward to embrace her. He wrapped her in his arms until she almost disappeared from view. Stella saw her white thin hand on his wide back, patting him as if he were an overgrown baby hanging over her shoulder.

"Send me books and candy," she ordered him. "Be happy."

He would not let her go. He showered warnings and admonitions on her. "Lock your door. Don't leave the iron plugged in. Put the rubber pad in your bathtub before you step in. Don't smoke your pipe in bed. I love you."

"Yes, yes, yes, yes," she said, and looked imploringly at Stella. "Take him away." She yawned widely, rudely.

"We're going." Caleb motioned to Stella.

"Your dressing gown." Stella began to peel out of it.

"Keep it. Put your sweater over it in case you're arrested for speeding. I'll iron your clothes and send them to you, although they really belong in the ash can."

Stella was reckless. "Throw them out." She wanted to say more. "You have style," she told the old woman, and that was as far as she went by way of thanks.

They walked slowly through the garden. Caleb seemed reluctant to go. He glanced over his shoulder, and when the light went out he sighed audibly. Night jasmine bloomed richly on the night air. He tore a leaf from a plant, crushed it, sniffed his fingers. He wished to take something tangible from the place. The life inside the house was painfully ephemeral. He sought Stella's hand.

"She's very old," he said.

Stella did not know how to comfort. "She'll outlast both of us."

"My resources come from her. I'm not ashamed to say it."

"I get along on my own," Stella said, stung with unworthy jealousy.

He put a heavy arm around her shoulders. "That is over," he said.

Stella huddled on her own side of the car, erecting a wall of silence behind which she examined the day. He drove at a terrible clip and now she wanted to call out and implore him not to cut her off in a tangle of blood and crumpled steel from the satisfaction she meant to have out of him. Or would it be better to be snuffed out and never have to weigh the price of surrender, because that was the pill to be swallowed. Nothing less would do. Surrender.

"Stop at the first motel," she said suddenly.

"Are you tired?"

"No," she said. "I want to see if it was a fluke."

8

NELL'S OWN PHYSICIAN was named Douglas Stuart Colin Mac-Farland, and each and every name appeared sprawled in a bold legible hand on his prescriptions. He was a friend of her grandfather's and had looked after her in his dour Scottish way from her twelfth birthday on. He had told her about menstruation and about sex with great clarity and no nonsense, sitting on the edge of her bed with his large hands clasped in his lap. She was not to be frightened, he told her, about blood or about men. Nature's plan included both and nature was sensible and often beautiful. When she was ill she quite looked forward to his coming, hanging out the second-story window, searching the street for his battered car. He would roll up, waving a greeting to her, while his radiator boiled over, leaving a dark stain on the drive. He timed his visits so he could have breakfast in the kitchen and quarrel vociferously with her grandfather about gardening and man's fate, manure and manners. Often, when she lay flushed with fever, she had been forced to wait till they settled a question between them, and if he lost a point he would storm into her room with a black face and lecture her on clear thinking while he thumped her chest and peered down her throat. On those occasions sticky bottles would emerge from his worn leather bag and malodorous doses would be poured into a monogrammed soup spoon and thrust into her gagging mouth.

There had been hot summer afternoons when he felt lazy.

Then he would draw up her dainty wicker chair and arrange himself in it and keep her wide-eyed and headachy as he told her that for a skinny stick of a girl, she had a good mind and should put it to use. He had no children of his own and so it was that he fastened himself on her. If she excelled she was in favor. If she failed he relegated her to an early marriage and drudgery and mediocrity.

When she was fifteen and told him she was going to be a doctor, he gave her a twenty-dollar gold piece, which he considered magnanimous and overly indulgent, but he was pleased and moved to be generous. Her grandfather shared her grudgingly with him only because he had seen her safely through diphtheria, measles and hives brought on by sexual frustration before she took her first lover.

Now he was approaching his seventy-fifth birthday like a rampaging bull, energetic, angry and not to be trifled with. He saw his practice in the front rooms of his home, a plain frame house in Santa Monica. The smell of oatmeal porridge hung over his consulting room like wet flannel. His bookshelves were jammed to overflowing with tattered volumes of Robert Burns and Milton and Victorian novels of obscure authorship. There were no medical texts. His memory was a matter of pride with him. All he needed to know about medicine was recorded in his head somewhere between lyric poems and Gothic romances. A rubber plant with engorged leaves grew to horrendous proportions in the corner of the room, dust settling over it in a ghostly gray film. The temperature was kept well below sixty degrees, causing patients to shiver with chill as well as fear at his pronouncements. He had been born to a cold climate and believed in its efficacy. Sunshine spoke of Paradise — in his view, there was no such thing. Hell, by all means.

Nell had come to him for her annual physical. She dressed in the large tiled bathroom, wondering what the doctor looked like afloat in the claw-footed tub, lying on his back. She noted a long-handled brush and a cake of yellow soap. There was no sybaritic lingering here. Doubtless he dug into his ears and scrubbed his toes, searching out lurking dirt like a zealot. Amused by her own curiosity she slid open a drawer. There was nothing in it but a comb and a jar of liniment.

"What are you doing in there?" His voice was impatient. "I wish to speak to you in here with your clothes on. You can primp later. Come out."

She hesitated, hearing a familiar note. It was the voice he had used in her girlhood to tell her she had an inflamed ovary, an abscessed tooth, a deep cut. It was the voice of anxiety.

She paused to use her lipstick, hating the feeling of it caked on her stiff mouth. She wiped it away and saw that her hand was shaking slightly.

"Well, woman?"

"Keep your shirt on. I have to use the toilet."

She stood in the middle of the bathroom, the white tile glaring all around her. She remembered now a strange scowl on his face, a frown which brought his heavy brows together and made him look like a prophet of doom. Where in the examination? Her mind raced back. She remembered how his hands passed over her, paused, moved again.

She opened the door.

"Take a chair." He waved her toward one and waited only long enough for her to settle into it.

"You've got a lump in your right breast," he said bluntly. "It has no business being there. How you missed it yourself I'll never know. Surely you caution your patients to examine themselves monthly. You're careless. Negligent. Stupid." He paused, agitated. "I want you in the hospital tonight. Saint Joseph's. I'm not a Catholic, but the nuns there are used to my ways and don't speak back to me. I'll do a biopsy first thing in the morning and if it's malignant I'll want to operate right then and there. You're a doctor. I needn't mince words." He pulled off his glasses and closed his eyes. "I don't suppose you go to church," he said.

"It appears to be too late now," she answered.

He rose to his feet and clumped back and forth across the room. His shoes were stout and worn, the shoes of a workingman. He bought them in the Army and Navy Store and wore them till they cracked.

"It surpasseth understanding," he said bitterly. There was lamentation in his voice. Divine goodness had been challenged.

She had seen the disease often enough, identified it, prescribed for it, treated it. She had saved some patients, snatched them away, found them reprieves and acquittals, and she had lost others — weary old women, no longer willing to struggle, disbelieving men in their middle years, wasted young boys, bewildered girls. And now it was her turn. Would she lose the breast, lose both? The lymph glands, the muscles of her chest? Would she burn under the radiation treatments, suffer nausea and dizziness, lose her hair? Would she live?

"I'm going to smoke," she said, rummaging in her bag. "I know you disapprove but I'm going to anyway."

He held a light for her. "You needn't hang onto yourself in front of me, you know."

She glanced up at him with mocking eyes. "When I'm apprehensive I wet my pants. I've done that already."

He let that go with a deprecating wave of his hand. "It's nothing to be ashamed of. I've wept. At a sad ending. Over a woman . . . I've tended you since you were a wee thing. You can howl if you like."

She heard his voice echo across the years. Spit. Cough. Open. Shut. Breathe in. Breathe out. Little did he know what would result if she did as she was told now. Howl? She would wail like a banshee. She would flood the room. Anger burned in her. The goddamned random idiocy of it happening to her. She had only begun to make choices in life. I'll have this. No, thank you, to that. How dare fate hurry her? She wanted age with its eccentricities. She wanted time to squander. She searched for invective, not tears; for sticks and stones to hurl. How could she ever have soothed those patients she had condemned, with their x-rays and cardiograms lying before her on her desk? How could she have offered rest and diet and pills and potions? Rage, *rage* at the dying of the light. Dylan had said it all with sublime boozy brilliance.

Dignity had no charm for her; patient submission even less. Oh, how she would exhort those poor souls in her care now. Drink, carouse, climb the mountain, ford the stream, take, flee; fate is gaining on you. Indeed, she wept, for the men she hadn't loved, for the places she hadn't seen, for articles left unbought, for municipal bonds falling due in midlife, for sunsets, for honors never to be bestowed for flights to distant stars never to be undertaken. She had meant to learn French. To go to Africa. To dye her hair red, to win a Nobel Prize. And what in lieu of all this? A harp, a narrow grave, a sudden ending. Damn, damn, damn.

"I'll give you a drink of Scotch. I was saving it for Christmas, but I'll spare you a glass. A small glass."

"Parsimonious as usual," she said. "No thanks. I'll take your dose the way you've always given it to me. Unpleasantly." She glared at him ferociously.

"You're not dead yet," he snapped.

"I'm scared. That's worse."

"I think you should try to be brave," he said sternly.

"Who's watching?"

"I am."

"I don't intend to bother, just for you."

He went to sit behind his battered desk. There was a jar of hard candy in front of him. His teeth were quite rotten, but he refused to give them up. He pawed through them, found a lemon drop, unwrapped it, sucked greedily. Then he recollected himself and held one out to her.

"Douglas," she said impatiently, "don't give me one of your damned lemon drops. Give me a fighting chance."

He crunched the sweet fiercely. "I am not God," he said, "but I am a believer. Better a man of faith holding the knife. Cling to that."

Nell was reminded of the steaming broth he had spooned into her during girlhood illness. Taste this. All will be well. She had doubted then. She doubted now.

The wall clock ticked heavily behind her. The newsboy thumped the paper on the front porch. She sat brooding, examining the possibilities with cold precision. She looked straight into the face of death sitting in his corner. I'm too choice a morsel for you, she thought. Had she not been tangled in a weedy creek and surfaced to life and sunlight? Had she not survived the exploding firecracker, the Asian flu, a burst appendix, a broken heart? She would be damned eternally if she would go with docility into those bony arms. Centered in her, somewhere in the recesses of her soul, was a rock, a weapon. She stretched to her utmost. She had it in hand.

"I'll tell you what pathologist I want. It's my hide. I don't want any mistakes."

He took her wariness with bad grace. "I don't make any. I've got plenty walking around to give testimony to my skills."

"I'd better be one of them."

A faint burr came into his speech when he was annoyed. "You can get another opinion. It's your right."

The sick have no rights, Nell thought sourly. No choice. No appeal. Numbly they submit.

"I want two days. Then you can have me."

He was outraged. "Out of the question. What for? Are you a gambler as well as an atheist?"

"I want to make love to a man while I've got two breasts to show him. I don't intend to make amends or make a will, just love. All day and all night, Douglas."

He shuffled the papers in front of him, swung around in the ugly oak chair he refused to throw out, rubbed the end of his nose. He was disapproving but curious.

"How will you keep your mind on it, girl? I wonder at that, with the sword of Damocles hanging over the bed. I should think there'd be more comfort on your knees."

"Why, I may be there, too," she said, "but not in prayer."

He was stern, but a faint smile washed across his face. "I understand you well enough. Don't think I don't. I've had some offer themselves to me, here, on my examining table. I swear on the Testament, should you doubt it."

"And?" She taunted him.

"What do you take me for? I understand the younger fellas take that kind of advantage these days. I prescribed a sedative and sent them on their way."

"Their loss."

"Hah." He was silent a moment, watching her moodily. "Another woman would ask a hundred questions of me. You know the answers, of course. Still . . . if there's anything I can say that will help . . ."

"Say it's all a mistake."

She saw his eyes fill up as she gathered her remaining strength to cross the door. She felt like a jointed doll moving clumsily at the pull of a string. She would suppress the tremors if it killed her on the spot. She very nearly heaved on his worn carpet with the effort. The door handle was at last within her grasp. When she spoke again her voice was sullen and aggrieved.

"Remember not to bill me," she warned him. "I'm a member of the club."

She fled to her grandfather's house; she would gather courage there, recover herself, be steadied. Among the things stored in the old man's heart would be a remedy for this day; what was dark would become bright and what was fearful would become acceptable.

She noted with surprise the beginnings of a Japanese rock garden near the fence. The rocks were arranged with some charm, but the whole thing had a tottery, insubstantial look, as if it were not intended to last the week. It drew her close with its strange, climbing shape, so at odds with the daisies and the snapdragons and the full-blown roses. It had a gay and careless air, as if someone in the house had been taken by a whim and rushed out to pile stone on stone. Above it all, tied to a green garden stake, was a paper kite, a gaudily colored fish with one large watchful black eye, roundly staring. It breasted the currents of air, bobbing, floating, puzzling the birds.

This could not be the work of Mrs. Keitel; the housekeeper kept her duties as narrowly defined as she dared. She hated and feared nature. Her nose reddened with allergy. Her sparse gray hair snaked into ugly disarray with the slightest breeze. She never set foot outside except to air the blankets or beat the rugs, and then she was darting and furtive, as if she were stark naked, whacking away at the carpets with a kind of fury. Most days she kept to the kitchen with the green blinds half pulled and a dishrag wrung out and hanging limply over the sink. There she made endless cups of watery junket or embroidered pillow cases with sprays of flowers in muddy colors.

It was too early for dinner, but Mrs. Keitel sat by a cold stove eating corn flakes out of a chipped blue dish. A glass of water and two soda crackers on a plate made a picture of Spartan self-denial. There was no book propped open before her, no newspaper, no distraction. Her mind was as dry as her dinner, her eyes fixed on the empty wall opposite.

Nell stood in the doorway observing her. Someone in Mrs. Keitel's past had made a point of proper mastication. A tyrannical aunt, perhaps, interrupting a silent meal to admonish her to eat without haste. Slowly, slowly, she munched the corn flakes, thirty little chews per bite, pause, thirty more. Her mouth was open and Nell could see the nasty pulp she was making of it, shifting it from side to side.

Mrs. Keitel sipped her water, patted her lips. She would rinse the two plates and the glass and walk up the backstairs and remove her clothes, and, in a faded nightgown, with her hair braided and all her prayers said, she would lie on her single bed, daylight still suffusing her room, waiting to sink into dreamless sleep. There need be no resurrection for her, Nell thought grimly; there had never been any life.

"Is he home?"

Mrs. Keitel put her spoon down and turned her head stiffly, startled. "Oh. It's you."

"There's no dinner cooking, I see."

"No." Mrs. Keitel was sparing of speech. Speech, like food, was not to be wasted.

Nell was used to the obstacles the woman strewed in her path. Where is the needle? Where it belongs. Where is my sweater?

Where you left it. Who ate the last slice of cake? You know as much as I do.

"I'm not feeling well," Nell told her. "In fact, I'm quite tired and cross, so please tell me where my grandfather is and why there's no dinner for him."

Mrs. Keitel was not to be budged. It would be her way or not at all. She remained stonily silent.

"If you muck around with me," Nell said, her temper rising, "I'll take that bowl in front of you and upend it on your gray head."

Mrs. Keitel was now pleased. The blood was up, the lines drawn. She had never liked Nell and she meant to show it at every opportunity.

"You'd better see to him, is all I can say," she remarked darkly.

Nell hurried from the kitchen toward the broad flight of stairs, a flutter of panic taking her breath away. The terror begun in the doctor's office widened. He was ill. She had let two weeks go by without calling and that meddlesome old woman had let him decline and fail. He had a cold. He had fever. He had worse. She nearly tripped in her haste to get to his room.

He was on the balcony, cutting the hairs out of his nose with a little curved scissors. On the bed lay a new gray suit, a striped shirt, a silk tie the color of a dove's wing. Beside them, ready to be taken up and clapped on his head, a fine new Panama hat. The air was rich with limewater. He turned this way and that, snipping, studying his reflection in a hand mirror, and then, thinking himself unobserved, he strutted a step or two.

He had taken her once as a child to see a parade. She remembered a white-haired old man, very tall, baton in hand, legs kicking, leading a band down the street. He was that very figure now, chest thrown out, legs straight, and God knows what his cock was doing. She saw instantly that the jaunty figure before her could not be involved in her fate; he had taken new life from some mysterious force and was no longer what he had been. He had turned off the path leading to his grave and was bounding through leafy woods with cloven hoof and the hairs of his nose nicely disposed of. He was a bright plant pushing upward. She was a weed. Her bones would bleach and burn. His would dance a jig.

"Look at you," she said with some resentment. "What in God's name is this?"

He favored her with a wide smile, a little bow from the waist. "My dear."

Her tone was faintly accusatory. "You've got a new suit. It looks expensive. It looks tailor-made." She rushed on, discomfited by his smug look of pleasure. Gray suits. Silk ties. He must be spending money madly. His business of course, but on whom? And why? She saw polish on his shoes. Wasn't that a flower on the bureau, waiting to become a boutonniere? He'd never worn a flower in his life. Where was his brown jacket with the hole in the lapel? Where were his scuffed bedroom slippers? Who had cut his beard to make him an Edwardian dandy?

He came into the room and patted her head on the way to his dressing table. He took up two ancient silver brushes and stroked his hair into a fine mane. A cowlick refused to lie down. It stood above his head like a small horn, confirming him as a satyr.

Nell sank onto the bed. Who was this man with his own buoyancy, his own happiness? She felt stiff, quenched, alone.

He picked up his trousers and hauled them over his skinny haunches, and then, with his accustomed delicacy, turned his back to zip them. The shirt followed and the tie, knotted with a flourish.

"I cut quite a figure, don't I?" He solicited her approval.

"And how."

But he saw that she was less than pleased. She had never liked surprises and he was not given to them himself, in fact. He sat beside her and took her hand.

He began an explanation, speaking to her in the low soothing voice which had once called her out of closets and lured her down from rooftops and the dangerous high branches of trees. It was the special voice, the sweet voice, that had imparted lore and fantasy, had told stories bringing her safely to the edge of sleep, had explained and reasoned and reassured.

them. To mark a gain against time. It rose and fell, rose and fell. She heard him stir behind her, jump to his feet, examine his watch.

"My goodness, I'll be late." He swept up his hat and strode toward the door. He turned then, to look at her across the room, outlined by the blue light against the window. Beyond her a tree bloomed white. She seemed very far away.

"Did you come for any special reason?" he asked.

"No."

"We'll visit next time, my darling."

"Yes."

He went out.

Nell bought a bottle of Scotch and headed for Stella. She knocked on her door and heard a bellicose voice shout out.

"I'm not at home!"

"Yes, you are. Let me in."

Stella peered out at her with the look of a bear prodded from its cave.

"It's you."

Nell held the bottle aloft. It made an immediate difference. Stella stood aside and waved her in. The room was a shambles, close, hot, dark. Stella wore men's pajamas. Her feet were bare, her glasses pushed up into her hair. Nell picked her way through the strewn books and papers, lifted the cat from the chair and sat in it. Stella remained standing; she offered no greeting.

"Call it forced entry. Call it whatever you like," Nell told her. "I felt like talking to you."

She set the bottle down on the floor. Stella swooped it up and read the label. "If this is meant for me you can talk all night long."

She padded into the kitchen for glasses. Drawers were pulled, cupboard doors slammed. There were mutterings, table silver was emptied with a clatter on the floor, there was an outcry as she stepped on a fork. "Shit!"

Nell saw two huge baskets of fruit rotting on a table. The banana skins had turned quite black, the apples were shriveled, one orange, half peeled, had fallen to the floor. Under its pink bows and yellow cellophane the fruit had turned to garbage.

Stella stood at the kitchen door, squinted at the label on the bottle, worked the cap free. She filled the two glasses she had found and was at hers before she came back into the room.

"This is lovely drink," she said, and handed the shorter measure to Nell.

"What's all that?" Nell indicated the baskets.

"Ah, that. A man sent it. I've got one hanging around, you know." She seemed to ponder the fact with some astonishment. "Are you surprised?"

Nell knew Stella would not be easily deceived. Stella would bite the coin to test its worth, would throw a lie in her teeth. Respect kept her honest. "Yes," she said.

"So'm I. I don't know what it will come to. He spends money on me. Calls, send presents. That fruit." She sniffed disdainfully. "I hate fruit. It's all core and peel and seeds. If it would ferment into something useful it would be worth having."

"Is *he* worth having?" It was good to wander away from herself into gossip.

Stella scratched her nose, grew wary. She hunched her shoulders, narrowed her eyes, fidgeted. "One day at a time for me," she said. "Then I'll see where I'm at."

"He might get away."

"Nobody wiggles off my line," Stella corrected. "If they're gone it's because I've tossed 'em back into the sea."

When the forces of women gathered, Nell thought, Stella should be at their head, mounted, armed, a powerful arm flung forward in defiance, promising victory. Her banner would be blood red, her mind white hot. Yes, she would draw them from their kitchens, snatch them from the bridge games, summon them from the tennis courts and the golf courses, from the psychiatrists and the beauty parlors, and the day would be hers. Nell very nearly cheered aloud.

The liquor coursed warmly down her throat. Stella threw herself into a chair, her feet planted, her face incurious, in no hurry to sound her out. In the shadows she seemed like a great stone totem, solid, ugly, impervious. Her prominent veins stood out on her forehead, her heavy gray hair hung loose around her wide and bony shoulders. She was a sight.

"There's a damn mosquito in here. I hear it buzzing." Stella sprang to her feet, grabbed a magazine and stalked the room, swatting at the walls. "There." A tiny spot of blood appeared among the other stains.

"Snuffed out," Nell said, swigging. "I hope we don't all go like that."

Stella's gaze bored through her like a drill. "That's a dark remark and you have a dark look about you. If you have something sticking in your craw, spit it out. You have a chance of being understood here."

"It won't go away by talking about it." Reticence was an old habit with Nell. Turn it this way. Turn it that. Work it out for yourself.

"That's a ninny's attitude," snapped Stella. "That's what's wrong with us in this country. A tight lip and a tight asshole. It's the purest shit. Look at nature, woman. Warts, scars, cracks, fissures, slime, green fungus, boiling gasses, poisoned wells, toads and warthogs, the lame, the halt, the blind. It all hangs out to be seen. Nothing hidden. Out in the open where you can deal with it. Tell me or don't tell me — but set it out in the landscape. It won't be bigger than any other mess you see before you. And that's all I have to say."

"I doubt it," Nell said, but the knot inside unraveled by at least one thread, perhaps two. Canonize Stella, she thought, the fiery prophet of the possible.

"Well." Stella hefted the bottle. "Let's get on with it. You've interrupted my work as is."

"I brought the bottle, don't forget."

"It doesn't entitle you to all that much."

They drank on, both silent, each with her own thoughts. A pleasant flush began to go through Nell . . . and more. It erected a barrier around her that nothing could penetrate. Nothing at all.

Down demons. Away threats. She poured another for herself.

"Here, now, don't get ahead of me." Stella held out her glass and guided Nell's hand until she got it filled to the brim. She's piggish, thought Nell. She could see her shoving her way to the head of a line, grabbing the only vacant seat on a bus under the nose of a crippled old woman, taking the first piece of candy out of the box. Oh, yes, that great lout of a woman was doubtless a bully in school, jumping for the volleyball, shouting to be heard above all others. It was remarkable how precisely personality came into focus with a tot or two or three.

"We should eat something," Nell said.

"I don't see why."

"Neither do I." They bumped heads as they both made a lunge at the bottle.

"Manners," Nell admonished.

"Go ahead then, if you're going to swill."

"Hoity-toity," said Nell, and helped herself first, leaving only a drop or two for her hostess. Stella stared sourly at the dregs, heaved to her feet, disappeared into the bathroom and emerged with another bottle. She plunked it down between them. "That is not tap water, for your information. Keep it in mind."

They made hefty inroads with the first pouring. Nell felt a cheerful buzzing in her blood. When had she been drunk last? At her high school prom. Yes, that was it. The quarterback on the football team had tried to get into her pants under the stairs and she had hit him with a copy of Milton. Give me back the hour, she thought dreamily, and you would have your due, you great, hulking, pimply boy. And when else? By herself when she was thirteen. Solemnly. Experimenting. She had ended up naked in the backyard, running through the sprinklers while the gardener called on the saints and debated raping her.

"I'll have a bit more," she said.

Stella poured grudgingly. "I'll freshen mine too." The bottle wavered now over the glasses. Nell reached out and steadied her hand.

"You're spilling."

"You moved the glass."

They drank on. Now the warm dark was as soothing as an embrace, the smell of rotting fruit strange and wonderful. A street in Rome had smelled like that. Had there been a man in the doorway? Had she said yes to him or no? Had she ever been to Rome at all?

"Have you ever been to Rome?" By now she had slid to the floor. Her head rested on the seat very near to Stella's lap.

"Do you think I'm made of money? How would I get there? Why would I go? I get pinched on the behind here. In the Safeway market."

"It's not the same, you dolt." She has no soul, Nell thought. She's a tunnel closed at both ends. No, that was not fair. Looking at her, upside-down to be sure, but still, studying her, she had a sad maternal air. Weren't they the best of friends, drinking the night away? I like her, she thought, and she must like me as well. We're both clever. We achieve. Achieve greatly. Hurrah for the two of us. The great achievers.

"Why are you lying on the floor?" Stella asked.

"Is that where I am?"

"You're a sloppy drunk. You give way." Stella was very superior. "You'll notice that I am bolt upright in this chair."

"You're listing," Nell told her, "way over to the left. If you don't know that, you're drunker than I am."

Stella straightened. "If I go to the bathroom will you swear on your honor not to take another drop till I come out?"

"Certainly."

"I'm going to leave the door open all the same," she threatened, and made for the bathroom. Nell rolled over on her stomach and saw her majestically enthroned on the toilet seat.

"Kings often received their courts while sitting on the pot. Did you know that?"

Stella's voice was haughty and seemed far away. "Information of that sort is of no use to me." She rose, flushed and walked carefully back into the room.

"You didn't wash your hands. You could spread hepatitis."

"Mind your own business." Stella seated herself again and took up her drink.

Nell drained hers. How safe, how cradled she was. How big and brave. She was full of wonder at it. While she mused Stella had slipped yet another good slug into her glass.

"Your health," she said.

"Ah," Nell replied, reminded. "That's what I came about."

Stella leaned down to peer at her. "You look all right to me — and if you aren't, put it out of your mind."

"Of course. Nothing simpler."

"Yes." Stella was firm, brooking no disagreement. "I intend to live to be a hundred and beyond. That's my intention and let no man meddle with it." She burped loudly.

"How are you going to manage that?"

Stella rose to her feet and declaimed, as though facing a huge, unseen audience. "Once, when I was a girl, and God knows that's a way back, I rode on a roller coaster."

"You were speaking of living to be a hundred . . ."

Stella roared on. "A roller coaster, lifting up into the sky like a big colored snake. I didn't have the price of the ticket but I meant to ride. There was a small boy standing there with a fistful of tickets. His father had bought them. I think the man hoped the boy would be thrown off and dashed to pieces. He was a nasty boy with a nose running snot and mean little eyes. I said, 'Give me one of those tickets, sonny. If you use them all yourself the fun will go out of it.' He said something rude but I grabbed one out of his hand and before he could do anything away I went." She raised her glass above her head.

"Sweet Jesus, what a ride. The women screamed. The hairpins flew out of my hair. My heart popped out of my mouth. Everybody clutched the bars in front of them or clutched each other or simply clutched. One girl got hold of the hair on her man's chest and you could hear him yell for a mile. We were jolted and thrown and thrown and jolted and up and up and then we were at the very top. The people below were little pepper specks, sprinkled about, that's all they were. Then came the second before the last plunge. You know how a hawk rides the air, hovering? That's what we did. And then we hurtled down, the wind singing and screeching, the breath torn out of us, we plummeted like a rock. Then's when I made up my mind. I said, remember this, Stella, my girl, because this is the way you're going to live your life from this day forward, up and down and banged around and thrills all the way."

"You could have fallen off," Nell said, now flat on her belly, her head resting on her arm.

"I didn't," said Stella, "as you can see, if you're still able to see at all."

Nell didn't answer. She had passed out, quite peacefully, where she lay.

Just before dawn she awoke, every muscle crying in outrage. Stella, her head thrown back, her mouth wide open, snored loudly. The cat made its morning toilet, licked its paws with a darting pink tongue; then, tail held aloft, approached her, sniffed, backed away, offended. She yawned, groaned, dragged herself to her feet. She went to the window, raised it and stuck her head out into the first light. A hummingbird trembled above the Copa D'Oro, beating its wings in nervous flight. A small scruffy dog lifted his leg and destroyed the grass, then scrabbled with his forepaws to make amends. Birds began a busy chattering; a truck rumbled heavily in the street. The yellow eye of a flashing signal paled before the rising sun.

Nell knelt by the sill and let herself be washed by the air. She meant to accept this day with calm, but a nagging thought discomfited her. Patients frequently died in the early hours of the morning. She had been at their bedsides, sleepy, awed, helpless. She had lowered eyelids over sightless eyes with her own hand and wondered: Had they resolved to keep the sight of an unblemished sky? Had they come to some final truth that needed no confirming by the passing of another day? Had they cried out as they went: test me no longer?

Stella stirred, hawked, coughed. Stella, comrade beside the fires as they burned low, stalwart, breasting the wave at her side as it engulfed her. Bleary, blowsy sister, wake and brace the troops. But she merely shifted and slept on. Nell left her to it, closing the door quietly behind her.

Jake collided with her as she passed his door. He had come thrusting through it, loaded with fishing gear, swaddled in oilskins, clumsy in heavy boots.

"Oof," she said as she slammed into his chest. She knew by his rude robust air that he had been up for an hour. He had showered. He had shaved. He had eaten a huge breakfast, moved his bowels, made his bed. He had doubtless sat under his desk lamp sorting through the bright flies that now adorned his hat and jacket, giving him a raggedy peddler's look. He would skim the sea, plunder its depths, listen to the clamor of the gulls and be very pleased with himself. Let others go their lunatic rounds, he would have this day, rare and fine and exactly to his taste.

A lure grazed her cheek and something, she couldn't tell what, entangled itself in her hair. "Turn me loose," she cried.

"Don't wiggle, you'll only make it worse." She felt his deft fingers in her hair. "Damn, stand still." She heard his rod clatter to the floor. He swore. "This'll teach you to come lurching home, swacked, at the crack of dawn."

He freed her and held her away to look at her.

"I was drunk," she said. "Awfully drunk."

"Do you any good?"

"A world of good."

"You look like hell," he observed pleasantly.

"I do, don't I." She patted her crushed dress ineffectually. His gray eyes questioned how she passed the night. She let him speculate for a moment and then put him straight. "Stella and I tied one on. If it had gone on much longer I suppose we might have gone off and enlisted in the navy together."

He gathered up his gear. "Something must have got your wind up. I have time to listen."

She sagged against the wall then. Her head hurt, her stomach was sour and unkind to her. Dutch courage, she saw, was short-lived. I have time to listen. So say the faceless priests in the dark of the confessional. But a line forms behind you and the stories are old and often heard and nobody stays with you to the end.

"I'm a good sailor," she said. "Take me with you."

"I'd like nothing better."

She hurried for a jacket, made a call to her exchange, pleaded illness, arranged for the young Korean doctor on the floor above to cover her and put out of her mind the awful speed of time.

They bought enough groceries for a trip to China. Nell thought of cold bird and wine picnics out of fitted wicker baskets from Abercrombie & Fitch while he grabbed peanut butter and Heinz sweet pickles and potato chips and chili peppers. As he moved up and down the aisles, dumping doughnuts and strawberry soda into his cart, she saw him as a boy, in brown cords and torn sneakers, stoking up for a summer day by a pond or a stream or in a cave dangerously hollowed out of a hillside. It would seem the coarse appetite of youth had never left him. Ice cream sandwiches, that awful icy vanilla mush tucked between spongy chocolate layers, followed to complete the repast. She suggested apples and cheese. He threw in a dozen apples and a wheel of cheese with the lordly gesture of a gourmand.

Still, he was in touch with something, with this lunatic shopping, because she began to have the stir of excitement from her own childhood, when she had stuffed herself with Mallomars and maple nut fudge, washed down with a drink of warm water from the garden hose. All that sugar burning in her blood had sent her under the house with a neighbor boy and their kisses had been peppermint and carmel and astonishingly carnal for their age.

She was curious to know if they solved the same mysteries at the same moment in life. Had he wandered into a garage and found, in the depths of the galvanized tin ash can, one of those soft paper books, bound with string, with smudged, inky, erotic couplings flowering on every page? Had he sat in the garage, knees to chest, with the smell of leaking gas from an old Packard choking him, and turned those pages with their entwined figures, every orifice gapingly revealed, and marveled at the astounding agility? Had his heart pounded as he sat, flushed and unhungry at the dinner table, deaf to conversation, wondering how they did those things and what the sensations were that accompanied them? What was the child like before the man and why did she care?

"Do you like baked beans?"

"Love 'em."

"Will you eat them cold out of a can with a spoon?"

"Of course."

What if she had met him then, at twelve or thirteen, when she was thin as a slat and rude and forthright? He would have appeared in her life, suspicious and unsmiling, to watch her at a distance. He would have moseyed closer as he heard her fiery debates in the school auditorium, defending the Scottsboro boys and Sacco and Vanzetti, or seen her drive her first car recklessly into the school parking lot. He would have vied with her in classes and slouched by her silently in the halls. He would have appeared on her doorstep without invitation and argued hotly with her for weeks about euthanasia and Hemingway, before he grabbed her and kissed her without permission, jamming his tongue into her mouth, both their chins wet with spit, ignoring a cold sore in his passion. They would have been scrappy and abrasive; he would have wandered off after a softer girl. He would have wandered back.

"You're quiet." They were riding toward the boat slip.

"I'm speculating about you," she said. Her head lay against the back of the seat. She felt peaceful and lazy.

"Go ahead."

"What kind of a boy were you?"

He thought it over. "I guess I was a handful. Big for my age. Short fuse. Mistrustful — worried that someone would sneak up behind me or try to sneak one by me. Hungry for girls. Nothing special."

"Were you smart?"

"No, dumb. Illiterate. I'm a late bloomer. Never read a book till I was twenty-one. As it is, I'm only down to T for Tolstoy."

He turned around and groped for a poplin windbreaker on the

back seat. He tossed it to her. "You'll need it on the boat."

She took off her jacket and pulled it on. It smelled of stale smoke and baby powder. Is that what he used, baby powder? She told him she fancied herself in men's clothes. She had worn her grandfather's yellow slicker to school, slinking along in its ample folds, feeling slim and supple and sinuous. She had looked grotesque, there was a snapshot bearing witness, but she had been happily unaware of it.

He told her that if his windbreaker made her feel slim and supple and sinuous, she had better keep it. What were her other peculiar crotchets?

She would tell him later. They had arrived.

His boat had no name. It was anchored among the *Deirdres* and *Annabellas* and *Spindrifts* in austere anonymity. He expected her to lug her fair share and she did so, trotting back and forth from car to boat, storing the bundles neatly as he directed. A girl, belly exposed in a pink bikini, watched her from the deck of a nearby sailboat. Nell went back and forth. The bikini-clad girl turned to toast on the other side.

Finally, sweat trickling down her back and all stowed to Jake's satisfaction, he pointed out a seat.

"There's some chop out there today. How good's your gut?"

"Cast iron."

"All right. But if it doesn't hold up, puke downwind. I keep a clean ship."

The motor thundered to life and they were off, bucking the waves, a bronco ride on the back of a skittish horse. Nell turned her face into the spray, posing like a figurehead, but only until the curl left her hair and her mascara streaked darkly under her eyes. Then she grasped the railing and wondered about the sagacity of this entire venture. He pointed to a gull overhead that raced with them out to sea. Lovely, she mouthed, not meaning it. She stared down at the water. The waves were Botticelli scallops, white lines curling in folds of foaming green. The wind cried around her. Jake spun the wheel and stared ahead. Land receded. She speculated on shipwreck. Life on an island. Life in company with him.

Would there be conversation enough for eternity? He cut the motor.

They drifted alone at the far edge of the world.

She soon saw that Jake intended to go about the business that had brought him here. He had pulled on a gray woolen cap fuzzy with loose threads and was now deeply engrossed in baiting his line. He had come to fish and she was expected to fend for herself. She was like that, too; when she sat over a book or wrestled with the writing of a paper, she barely tolerated the presence of anyone else in the room, would offer the merest grunt by way of acknowledgment.

"My Uncle Tyler Cooley expressly left me this rod in his will," he said to her suddenly. "He left half a million dollars to a Mexican lady he was fond of, but he left me this rod."

He seemed disposed to reminisce. Nell encouraged him.

"A favorite uncle?"

"Never would have gotten to my manhood without him."

He told her then of the man who had given him his first taste of whiskey, his first Havana cigar, his first conviction that life was worth living. He had made a fortune in auto parts before he was thirty-five and had devoted the rest of his short and colorful life to having a good time. He liked Jake because of all his nephews, and he had seven, Jake kept his counsel and did not pick his nose in public. He would send an airplane ticket for him, first-class, and Jake would fly to Montana every summer, getting off the plane more than half drunk, having had two cocktails and a bottle of wine with his lunch. His Uncle Tyler would meet him in an old yellow Stutz Bearcat and they would go up to his lodge, where there was nothing but thick steaks and cold beer and time. His uncle would wake him at four in the morning and give him coffee laced with Old Grand-Dad bourbon and they would get in the car and bump down empty country roads till they came to a stream. They would put on old rubber boots that smelled as if someone had died in them and stand in the icy water and talk and fish.

There was usually more talk than fish but that was all right with Jake. Uncle Tyler was a great talker. His view of life, which he expounded in a whiskey-raw voice, was that it was meant to be a pleasing business. That meant the company of decent men and bad women. It meant saying what you meant to anybody, high or low, and never, on any account, selling yourself in return for a dirty buck. There were things he approved of and things he didn't. He didn't see why you shouldn't kiss a man if you had reason to love him. He often kissed Jake, a great wet smacking buss on the cheek, and Jake never wiped it dry in his presence either. He believed in giving to the poor but if they said thank you he screeched to a halt and never did it again. He didn't think any man should be beholden to any other. He hated Republicans and said so at a lot of dinner parties. He loved his old mother to distraction and sent her all kinds of beaded dresses and high-heeled shoes from Helena, which she was unable to wear, but she was buried in one of the dresses because he insisted on it. He bought Jake his first woman, a nice girl who waited table in a café, and he waited outside to see if it came out all right. He wrote him a letter every week of his life and enclosed a twenty-dollar bill, with directions to squander it any which way he wanted. He died of a ruptured spleen two days before his forty-eighth birthday and Jake had wept so inconsolably that they had sent for the family doctor. He felt his Uncle Tyler would have been glad of the tears. He loved a show of genuine emotion.

"I think you take after him," Nell said.

"I do, I do," he said and went back to his rod.

She left him alone. She found a spot free of gear, and wadding his coat under her head she stretched out at full length. The wide empty sky, the wide empty sea, they suited her. The very vastness rebuked fear. If death meant a restoration to this kind of harmonious infinitude it could be faced. The thought no sooner came than she was instantly annoyed with herself. She had not come here to test life against mortality. She was here with an attractive man. She was in her prime. She was aware of desire and curiosity. She would most certainly see how it all came out in the end.

She shucked her shoes and stockings, rolled up her shirt sleeves, gave herself to the sun. Jake hoisted himself onto a stool. She noted a tear on the seat of his pants. He had applied a neat patch, but it was just wide of the mark. He wears blue shorts, she observed, the color of this very blue sky. How well he matches. The boat rocked. Small waves tapped like gentle fingers against the sides. Everything became beautifully simple. What is beyond human power is beyond it. White clouds rolled overhead. She slept.

When she awoke she was alone. She sat up, frowning, her skin prickling with sudden fear. He was not in the bow. She scrabbled for her shoes, unable to see clearly with the light stabbing off the water. She peered down the hatch, but it was black below. A curious red haze seemed to hang before her. She blinked.

"Jake? Cooley? Where are you?"

Silence.

"Where the hell are you?" She cracked her shin against a metal box. It was some kind of joke. She was annoyed.

"Jake!"

He emerged from the hatch. "Yo."

"Where were you?"

"In the head."

"Ah. I just woke up. I saw myself abandoned out here . . . drinking seawater . . . going mad." She saw the sun was much lower on the horizon. She must have slept for hours. She felt dazed, dry, out of sorts. He showed her two black bass, mouths agape, lying rigidly on a bed of ice. "Dinner."

"Not if I have to cook them."

"You don't. I will." He studied her flushed face. "You've had too much sun. Let's go below and get a salt tablet into you." He herded her down the steps into the narrow space below. There were two bunk beds, stacks of old magazines, a picture of Fujiyama in cold solitary beauty taped to the wall. There was a littered table, the smell of brine. She sat down and rubbed her eyes with her fists. He handed her a large tablet and a glass of water. Dust motes floated in it. He sat opposite, watchful. The tablet stuck in her throat. She choked, coughed, beat the air with her hands. He leaned across and gave her a solid whack. Eyes swimming, she nodded thanks. He resumed his place. Why the sharp blow between her shoulder blades should have done it she couldn't imagine, but quite suddenly a vivid explicit sexual image crossed her mind. She was, in a moment, sensitive in every part of her body. In heat, she thought, give it its name, in heat, spongy, willing, persuadable, in a hurry. In another moment, she speculated, I will be peeling him out of his shirt and pants. Image followed image. There was biting, scratching, licking, a whole marvelous and expert tangling, slick acrobatics, anointment with oils, the shape of his mouth here and there and bloody well everywhere. It had to be sunstroke.

"Wash your face and come topside." He started up the stairs. "I'll fix you a peanut butter and jelly sandwich."

Hah, she thought, comfort me with apples — and with sandwiches and candy bars filled with stale nougat and rancid nuts. Well enough, for now. She combed her hair a different way that pleased her. She sprayed scent behind her ears and then, somewhat absently, between her breasts. If he should find his way there, surprise, it would smell of lilac.

They had a silent and altogether greedy meal. She found she was starved and made way with the better part of what was in the basket. He lit his customary cigar and filled the air with smoke as he puffed tranquilly.

"You're an interesting woman," he began. It was a statement, not flattery. "No commitments. No marriage. How come?"

What could she tell him that might be edifying? That she was an only child of long-dead parents, that she had been petted and cosseted by a doting old man? That she was impatient and self-sufficient and judgmental, even arrogant? That she was often pleased in bed and rarely out of it? Dared she insult him by telling him that most men were irrelevant, guilty, frightened, foolish? Dared she let him see the scope of her demands where men were concerned: wit, good sense, good sensibilities, firmness, fairness? And how could she, at the same time, let him know the delight she took, how very much she liked his sex? How pleasingly sentimental they could be, how fond, how faithful. How unpetty and unpatronizing.

"I've been badly spoiled," she said. "I'm not proud of it but

I'm afraid it's the truth. I took prizes in school. The best home-raised rabbit. The best drawing of a cow. The best chocolate fudge cake made from scratch. Moreover, my teeth came in straight while others wore braces. The boys with the bluest eyes always asked me out and presented me with gardenias which cost them half their allowance. I could ride a horse bareback and jump a high hurdle at close to six feet. I was proposed to twice before I was eighteen; one of them went on to be a Superior Court judge, the other buys guns in West Germany and sells them in Brazil. I made Phi Beta Kappa, even though it was a matter of pride with me never to crack a book till finals, and my chemistry professor fell wildly in love with me and was prepared to desert a wife, three children and a mistress." She paused, ruminated. "I think it must have all gone to my head. Too clever by far, too fond of myself to live. What can I tell you? Narcissus loved himself."

"Never met your match?"

"I probably did. Too smug to know it."

He tore the top off a soft drink can with his teeth and drank deeply. "What's your body count to date?"

She made an impatient movement. "Are you asking me about my love affairs?"

"Change the names. Protect the innocent."

"You won't learn anything. God knows I didn't."

"It's not important," he said. "I'd handle you differently, anyway."

He gathered up the sandwich wrappings, the bottles, the paper napkins, and stowed them neatly in the basket.

"Well, we've dawdled along for some weeks now," he said. "Don't you think it's time we moved this relationship along one square? Isn't it time we got into bed and grappled with each other? And it doesn't have to be a bed, Nell — I'd willingly lie down with you on a cornhusk mattress or in the tall grass. The bulge in my trousers would do credit to an adolescent boy at a burlesque show. You're thorny, bright and troublesome, but I consider that the final riddle of you lies between your legs, and I'd like to solve it."

Why hold back, she thought? Have me today, have me tomorrow, the day after is up for grabs.

She offered a warning. "You realize, don't you, that there'll be two of us in that bed. I wake early and I study my partner."

"I'm at my best asleep," he said.

She liked the prospects. Couple and grapple. No holds barred. Each in his corner, sweating, primed. Sound the bell. Shake hands. Mix it up and carry off the trophy to prop open the door. And if he won on points? Why, he most likely would put a large, bare, emphatic foot square on her stomach and proclaim victory to all the world. It was a narrow bed that waited below and it was a narrow beginning, but why not?

Then she hesitated, remembering what she knew and he did not. Very well. She would see how tough he was.

"Sit down," she said, patting the place next to her. "I have something to tell you."

The anesthesiologist was a bustling little man with hands so cold they gave her goose bumps. He called her "Doctor" respectfully and stared disapprovingly at her pretty lavender nightgown, as if he considered it inappropriate for the occasion. He gave her a shot to make her sleep easily through the night and then shifted from one foot to the other as he searched for a pleasantry to offer her. He came up with a weather report. It was going to be hot the following day. He'd heard it on the radio. And smoggy. He was allergic to smog.

She told him that as she was going to be asleep for most of it, it didn't really matter, did it?

No, he told her, it really didn't. He hesitated before leaving. He was going to play golf the next day; he would hold good thoughts for her.

"I trust it won't throw your game off," she said.

"No, it won't," he said. He left her.

A little black nurse with a high saucy behind and huge tilted eyes came in to write up her chart. She lingered to offer solace and confidences while Nell's eyes grew heavier. Her mama had

had this surgery a year ago and she was off in Texas with a new husband and feeling just fine. Of course, the Texas fellow knew her mother had savings bonds but she didn't really think that's why he had proposed. He had a three-legged dog, he said, and he was used to there being some parts missing.

Nell observed that she might have to find a fellow like that for herself, if her luck didn't hold.

The little nurse said that any man who was worth shit wouldn't be the least put off.

"What's your name?" Nell asked her drowsily.

"Serena Alice."

"I'm glad you're on duty on this floor, Serena."

Serena concurred. Nell could have gotten one of the big nurses who were bulldykes. There were two around here and they were mean, mean. Their back rubs were more like beatings, and they plopped the old ladies on cold bedpans.

She plumped Nell's pillow and Nell caught a whiff of potent perfume and something else.

"Serena," she said, "you've been smoking a joint in the ladies' room."

"You can't do this job on your own legs. You need a little extra boost."

Serena whisked up a glass and gave the bed a crank or two. "I'm down the hall if you want me. Just ring and I'll come." And Serena floated away, a stoned Florence Nightingale.

Nell burrowed under the blankets and thought about Jake and what a rare old time they'd had. It had been like love in the middle of an old and comfortable marriage. There had been lots of talk, easy, unhurried, good-natured talk. He would like to see her happy. She had only to tell him what it took and he would find the means to provide it. If she liked a garden, he would plant it. Rings for her fingers? He would adorn her. Let there be no sadness kept to herself, no fear of growing old. He wanted to take a hand in all her troubles. In return she had only to learn to play bridge and allow him to smoke his cigars in bed. If she agreed he would proceed to put her picture in his wallet.

And he, she had inquired, what would he like?

He would like to have her on a bed of fallen maple leaves, red and gold ones piled deep. When his Uncle Tyler had gone off to make love to his Mexican housekeeper in the upstairs bedroom on a resplendent brass bed crested with angels, Jake had wandered up in the hills. He had lain under a maple tree, looking down at the darkened windows, and had vowed that when he had a woman of his own he would make love on those prickly leaves, and if the ticks got him it would still be worth it. To date he hadn't found a lady willing; they preferred hotel suites at the Hilton.

In that case they were made for each other, she responded. She had crawled under the dark green shelter of a mulberry tree and clasped the boy who delivered for the cleaners ardently in her arms, trying to get him to touch her nipples, but he was a Seventh-Day Adventist and scared to death to do anything but take the barrette out of her hair. It seemed plain that they would have to find a forest and roll from tree to tree in remembrance of things past.

Oh, Jake, cheerful lover, who had scratched his belly afterward and floored her with his avowal that, one tit or two, she suited him better than any woman he'd ever come across.

Only mean it, she thought, and they can cut off my head.

She was deep in a turbulent dream in which she was hurtling toward an unyielding wall, certain to be shattered on impact, and she struggled to free herself, thrashed and fought and strained to surface again, dimly felt clouds dispelling, swam up out of darkness to find Douglas leaning over her bed and whispering, "Benign: I threatened to leave the church if it weren't. Apparently He heard me — He could ill afford to lose me."

Her voice was thick, her mouth parched, the ordeal still reverberated along her nerve ends. "I'll always be optimistic, from this day forward," she said. She was too exhausted to say more, but she reached for his hand. He grasped it and held it.

"Go to sleep," he told her. "I have five other patients to see."

"Stay a while," she said groggily. "Stay . . ."

"What a lot of trouble you are to me," he told her as he settled back to watch over her. She closed her eyes. There was no pain any longer; the vista was wide and green and consoling. She was shepherded by Douglas, holding her fast in his large, calloused hand. She slept.

It was rather like an unseasonal Christmas. Jake had contributed a lively myna bird that called "Good morning" and "Do you like San Francisco?" over and over again. Hortense and Eunice had wandered in bearing an old Sinatra recording of "My Funny Valentine." Stella came lugging a jug of California burgundy, having already opened it for sampling. It was she who made the toast, lifting her glass to Nell, who again sat tucked up in her own bed in her own apartment, with its sliver of the Pacific Ocean visible from the window.

"To narrow squeaks," Stella said, "and I'm glad it wasn't me."

The ladies lounged around her bedside, sipping the wine, sharing Nell's reprieve, each silently thanking her own guardian angel that the ordeal had not been hers. Still, it had brought them closer and they were keyed up and noisy, getting drunk, getting sentimental.

"God," Eunice said, gulping her drink. "It makes you stop and think."

"Women get all the shit," Hortense announced loudly. "Menstruation, menopause, mastectomy, melancholy. God's a man. There's no damn question about it."

"Don't be a complaining fool," Stella said. "We outlive them, we outfox them, we outclass them. We have to suckle them at the start and lay them out at the end. Fathers, uncles, nephews, lovers, they've had their heads in our laps from the Madonna to Marilyn Monroe. I pity the poor buggers. I salute us." She swirled the wine in her glass and splashed it down the front of her dress.

"You'll never get that stain out," Eunice said in a slurred voice, sitting on her spine, hugging her knees, pondering her fate. What if it had been she?

She would never have survived it like Nell, all steel nerves and cool self-control. Sleeping pills for me, she thought, handfuls, washed down with diet Cola, thinking of her figure to the last; and then blankets of striped carnations and a handsome young preacher hastily summoned and a eulogy selected at random for those who die early. She very nearly wept for herself then and there. As soon as she left she would call Harvey. She would be very, very nice to Harvey, so that when fate stalked her he would be there to ward it off with his strong freckled hands.

Stella passed among them refilling the glasses. Hortense put her palm over hers. "No more for me. I'm getting bluer by the minute." She tossed off what remained of her drink.

"You ought to call Booker," Eunice said sharply. "That's what's bothering you."

"You ought to button your big mouth," Hortense flared.

"Can't we get drunk like ladies!" Stella bellowed. The other two subsided. Stella glared at them and continued, "Our friend here went to the edge of the precipice. She has been hauled back. I rejoice for her. Now either *rejoice* or get the hell out of here!"

Eunice held out her glass. "The trouble is," she said, "this thing has got us all thinking. My mama's dead and so is Hortense's. Yours, too," she said, pointing at Nell, "and I don't know if Stella ever even had one. We're all thinking who'd come running if we needed them and how long would they stay? We're just neighbors in the apartment house."

"More than that," Nell said.

"Just neighbors in an apartment house," Eunice repeated dolefully. She wandered off into the kitchen looking for ice. The wine was warm, probably because Stella kept the jug between her knees. In any case, she hated warm wine.

She cracked ice cubes out of their tray and found she was feeling terribly sorry for herself. Nell's close call had triggered long-buried memories and emotions; that period when she had first come to town, lugging her favorite picture, "The Dream of Saint Ursula," under her arm, looking for work, making endless applications, standing in long lines at the unemployment office.

She was in the little apartment by the steam room then, and

one night she had come home from her latest fruitless foray, turned on the gas oven, put her head in it and waited for Saint Ursula's jazzy little angel to show up. She remembered the shock of the explosion, lumber and light fixtures and plaster raining down on her head, and the big black girl from across the way grabbing her by her underwear and hauling her out, all the while yelling, "What the fuck have you done, what the fuck is this!" She had taken her to her own place and chewed her out for the rest of the night and kept her on. She'd been there ever since. With Horty. Of course, she paid half the rent now, she wasn't a charity case. But she was some kind of a case; that much she admitted to herself.

She returned to the others as Nell shifted wearily in her bed and said, "I'm going to throw you all out now. I'm drunk and tired. Thanks for rallying around . . ."

"Don't leave your dirty glass," Hortense directed Eunice. "Put it in the dishwasher. And take mine."

She came to Nell's side. "We're all glad you got off."

"I know you are."

"God," Stella cried impatiently, "next thing you know we'll be bawling and kissing each other and forming a goddamn sorority. I'm taking the rest of this wine with me. I've got a long night to get through."

She lurched toward the door with her finger hooked through the handle of the bottle, bearing it over her shoulder like a lumberjack on a spree, off to her lair.

Eunice emerged from the kitchen and followed her. She paused in the doorway and informed them that from now on she was going to burn the candle at both ends, seeing how easily it could be snuffed out.

Hortense offered her a parting shot. "You've used that candle for everything else, honey. You might as well start burning it."

Eunice thumbed her nose at Hortense, blew Nell a kiss and departed.

Hortense lingered. "You want the light out?"

"Yes, please."

She snapped it off. The two women were silent in the dark for a moment.

"Tonight I miss my mama," Hortense finally said. "Tonight I'd like to sink down by her chair and feel her hand on my head and hear her say 'Child' to me. I could always feel the callus on her hand she got from chopping wood and hoeing."

She continued then in a low murmurous voice and Nell saw, as she spoke, the muscular, tough little woman Hortense longed for. She had kept a lump of sugar lodged in her cheek for as long as Hortense could remember. She popped it in with her morning coffee and kept reserve lumps in her apron pocket. Hortense thought as a child that the reason they went into her cheek all day long was to sweeten her words as they passed through her mouth. She had written her daughter every week, half a page only, but words that were pithy and comforting. There was often a lace doily slipped into the envelope, or a pot holder or dried herbs or a river agate.

Once she had called long-distance from Texas, bringing a mayonnaise jar full of nickels and dimes and quarters into the phone booth so she could talk to her heart's content. It had been her one and only long-distance phone call, and she hadn't said much except that the garden was full of slugs, that she had planted a mess of sweet peas, that the tree frogs kept her awake at night. Only after the operator had warned her that her time was up had Hortense heard her call out over the hundreds of dusty miles that separated them, "I love you, Horty."

She had died two weeks later.

"The trouble is," Hortense said, "I've grown up but I don't believe it."

Nell heard her close the door quietly behind her. She drew the blankets up to her chin and stared through the dark.

She thought of them all, the departed ladies, and of herself. She thought of them borne along on a surging stream, moving swiftly, clinging to a frail raft; here one slipped, there one flailed; catch me, hold me, bear me up; a hand stretched out, a hand clasped.

Would the waters close over their heads? Was the shore too distant?

The myna bird asked if she liked San Francisco, and when there was no reply, asked again.

9

HENRY DILLON stood at his study window and looked down on the top of Alice Dillon's head as she scurried about the garden below, exhorting the men stringing lights into the trees to be careful not to break the branches. A dove cooed, balancing her shrillness with its soft reiterated cry. She scurried here and there, tugging the pastel cloths into place over the many little tables set out on the lawn, dropping a nervous hand on the flower arrangements, shifting them just out of line so they no longer had the perfect air the florist had sought. Henry saw with some dismay that the predominant color of the decorations was pink. Alice ran to candy colors. He never knew whether it was an attempt at gaiety or if she were colorblind. It was most likely the latter. She was not good at festivities of any kind, and although there were any number of services for her to command she insisted on tending to every detail herself.

Grimly she awoke that morning to have a cross meeting with cook and the gardeners. Her brow furrowed with headache as she ate her abstemious breakfast of dry toast and a half a cup of tepid coffee. Then off into the garden to stare around her, blinking at the showy flower beds. She would not allow them to be cut, so the table arrangements were the stiff little knots of flowers she ordered for every occasion, jammed into their baskets with wires and decorated with satin bows more appropriate to funeral designs than a dinner party under the stars. Moreover, she would not use the good china, a pattern of surpassing ugliness she had ordered when they were young and poor, buying one piece at a time like a miser accumulating a horde. It was white Lenox with a heavy gold band and there were crystal goblets to match. Henry, who loved Italian pottery and wine drunk from thick green glasses, had shuddered at her choice even then, but he was gentle with Alice's delicate sensibilities and for years had pushed the pale and creamy food she favored around on the plates he abhorred. The caterer had supplied the tableware for the party.

Below, she fluttered. She had a peculiar paleness in the morning, as though the night had drained her. She never resorted to cosmetics, so that in the bright, sharp sunlight she had a ghostly look. Dear Alice, poor Alice, the two designations had juggled in his mind from the day they had married.

Her little dog bounded out of the house and followed at her heels. Henry had given it to her as a birthday gift, thinking, as he matched the small yapping animal to his small anxious wife, how often dogs resembled their masters. Ashamed of the thought, he had tucked a diamond bracelet in its collar. Alice never wore it, but the dog had been a huge success. She had a tiny sleigh bed made and it was kept in their bedroom. The dog's snuffling often kept Henry awake. It would not eat unless Alice put the food in its dish and when they traveled she carried it with her in a ventilated box, warning stewards and pursers that if anything happened to it they would answer to her.

He had told her he wanted a fete by Watteau in honor of his friends Caleb and Stella. He had envisioned a beribboned and dainty picnic, perfect grapes and pears heaped on the tables, Mozart softly played under the trees and the other middle-aged and corpulent guests moved by the joy and lightness of it all, wandering along the mossy paths hand in hand. His plays often incorporated such a scene to the delight of the ladies who packed the matinees year after year. If he had not feared undoing Alice altogether it would have been something more Bacchic, with wine fountains and folk singers and silk pillows strewn on the grass. But Alice was not up to that. She had even been dubious about the fairy lights in the trees. They drew gnats and mosquitoes. She would, he knew, come down to the party smelling faintly of citronella. Mosquitoes attacked her fiercely and raised great red welts on her transparent skin.

"It looks quite nice, darling," he called down to her. She squinted up at him, shading her eyes, frowning.

"I don't know." She looked about her, as if she were, somehow, at the wrong address. "What if it rains?"

"It won't."

"If you want to talk," she said, "please come down. I have a sore throat. I can't shout."

The sore throat he had anticipated. Sometimes it was a slight fever, a pain in the lower back, a sense of giddiness, but something always overtook Alice when a party was planned. Her little dog yapped. It hated Henry. Alice scooped it up in her arms, kissed its wet nose, whispered into its silky ears. Henry, watching from above, thought ruefully that he had never had such treatment at her hands. How dry her kisses were.

"We've ordered far too much food," she announced.

"We can afford it," he said with mild humor.

She did not respond. She took everything he said quite literally.

"Please come down, Henry. I want to go over the guest list again."

"We've done that several times, my dear."

There were only three people of their acquaintance she felt comfortable with, a slightly deaf and rather eccentric old aunt of hers, an elderly and effeminate lawyer who lived alone and grew orchids, and a young, angry and very ambitious Hollywood writer who sat at her feet and told her she was the only lady in a world of cunts. She permitted the word because in her heart of hearts she believed he was absolutely right.

The rest of their wide circle she viewed with disdain, keeping an exact count of the number of times she and Henry were invited to dinner each year in return for her own hospitality, as well as of Christmas cards, birth announcements, congratulatory wires and gifts. She knew precisely who had given the silver bonbon dish she had seen on sale in Beverly Hills, stacked by the dozens in a window. She knew if the candies sent from New York were stale and reposed in someone's drawer, to be dragged out and presented to her as a hostess gift. She knew when the needlepoint pillows went to others and she received a machine-made monstrosity hastily purchased in Spain. Her chilly thank-you notes went out on heavily embossed stationery from Cartier's written in a large, hysterical hand: Henry and she had been pleased to receive the donors' gift. Since they had not seen them in six months, a year, for quite some time, she had not been able to express her appreciation in person. She hoped their families were quite well. Had their son recovered from his divorce? Was their daughter finding herself at last or was she still unheard from in Saudi Arabia?

Woe to the senders of these tokens and mementos. Alice, sitting stiffly in their drawing rooms, heard every nuance, registered every hastily concealed pain. She saw the sleepy eyes of the gangly son of the house nodding from the poppy. She heard the high-pitched quarrel carried on in far reaches of the upper floors. She saw the tears, just dried, in the wife's eye; she counted the host's drinks. Had Henry been privy to all she knew his plays would have come far closer to life.

Henry met her in the garden, draped an arm around her.

"Don't overtire yourself," he said. "I want you to enjoy yourself tonight."

She shrugged off the remotest possibility of it. "I don't really see why we're doing this. The most Caleb has managed for us in New York is dinner in a restaurant. This all seems very extravagant to me. And what we'll do with Stella I'll never know. She'll probably come in a thrift-shop dress with liquor on her breath. I cannot believe for one moment that Caleb has any interest in her at all."

Henry led her to a garden bench too recently painted to sit on with comfort. He tested its sticky surface, sighed, sat down, pulling her down alongside him.

"I don't know why I should tell you this now, my darling, but it's so long ago. I was never really attracted to Stella, but when I was a boy I thought of asking her to marry me."

A large butterfly danced by. Alice followed its flight. She did not wish to hear what he was saying.

"It's not her beauty, if she has any at all. It's the wonderful working of her mind. Stella at her best is like some glorious fun house, full of mazes, bright with mirrors and distortions, frightening, amusing. Don't you see that?"

"I haven't thought about it," said Alice. "And why tell me all this now?"

He patted her hand. "Only to explain why Caleb is tempted."

She turned to him and he was struck with the sharp and pointed planes of her face. "If you were a true friend," she said, "you'd dissuade him before it goes any further."

Not I, my good and faithful Alice, thought Henry. In his mind's eye he had followed the course of the affair from moment to moment, like a putto in an Italian painting, peering down from the green foliage of the trees at Mars, sprawled on his back, while naked Venus, barebosomed and self-satisfied, watched him in his surfeited sleep. Oh, the beauty of it, autumnal love in the rich golden light of late afternoon. Impede it? Thwart it? Never!

The party was almost over. The remains of small cold Cornish game hens were left on the plates. Wine stained the tablecloths. The musicians, tired and chilled, played what they hoped was the last waltz of the evening. Two waiters moved wearily, speaking softly to each other in Spanish. A young actress fretted in the driveway over the loss of an earring. She went down on all fours pawing in the leaves, cursing, accusing. A film producer waited for her with the motor of his car running, striking himself in the chest where a strange pain had persisted all evening and muttering, "Don't quit on me now, you sonafabitch" to his rebellious heart. In the kitchen the catering crew packed away the petits fours and the pastry shells and imported chocolates to feed to their children. The cook quarreled loudly with a waitress, who burst into tears. Crab shells and lobsters left off ice made an odious smell. The drawing room was already darkened except for two young men who made promises to each other in the shadows; they were overheard by the houseboy who sniggered, causing their hasty exit.

In the garden Stella nursed a drink and brooded. The evening had been long and dull. Sometime, hours back, the wife of a director, a woman with a sad and ravaged face, had placed a hand on her knee, and then on her thigh. She had silenced the conversation with her loud announcement that she was not Sapphic — but could steer the lady to those who were. The table was made skittish; the talk after that veered nervously into tennis matches and recent operations. Pride of place went to two open-heart surgeries. They had the gruesome accounts through dessert and into coffee and brandy. Now they were all departed, the felonious businessman, the actress with the pronounced tremor, the musicia with a disfiguring birthmark on his cheek, all gone to Valium and prayers or to tense all-night wakefulness.

Stella glared across the lawn at Caleb, collared by a film director who clutched his arm and proposed a ruinous arrangement with one of his writers. He droned on and on, his manner hectic, his accent Hungarian. Caleb's head, she could see, bobbed like a mechanical doll's. Kick him in the shin and come and get me, thought Stella, I've been too long at the goddamn fair.

She hadn't wanted to come in the first place. She had sulked and balked, but Caleb had been implacable. Henry had wished to bestow some kind of bounty on them and he was an old and valued friend. Poor Henry had few occasions for ceremony in his life. He had been passed over by the Pulitzer committee. He had never stood before the King of Sweden to be lauded for his contributions to literature. He had graduated from a correspondence college in his youth so there had been no cap and gown, no sonorous baccalaureate address. His opening nights were spent sitting beside Alice in hotel rooms while she vomited and begged him to let her buy a farm in Oregon where she could live in peace. He had seen Caleb's passion for Stella. He wished to scatter flowers before them, to have music played sweetly in their hearing, to give them his catered food and his best wishes. They had arrived early and stayed late.

Stella sipped her wine. It had tasted tannic and unpleasant at the first of the evening; now it seemed mellow. Perhaps they'd gotten to the good stuff at last. She slipped out of one shoe, scratched where a belt buckle bit into her flesh, slid down in her chair until she looked as limp as a rag. A cloud covered the moon. The night had a threatening empty blackness. Gone the reckless laughter. Gone the silken dresses and the flash of jewels. The rich cigar smoke hung stalely in the air. The pianist lifted his hands from the keyboard in a violent fit of coughing. The last horn wailed away into silence. Stella's head felt heavy on her neck, her lids heavy on her eyes. She had not said a dozen words all evening beyond "Yes, more" to the doe-eyed young Mexican waiter with the crucifix peering from under his shirt and "I haven't been to a movie since *Rin Tin Tin*" to the insistent and pimpled film critic who had sat at her right. She felt rust in her throat and gloom in her soul. She was certain she would have a head cold by morning. A moth plummeted into a dish of puddled ice cream. She lifted it out on the end of a matchstick; she peered closely to study it; she burped aloud. She drank on.

Alice emerged from the house and looked this way and that. She raised a nervous hand to her hair. The strings of lights began to be extinguished; pop went the green, pop went the pink. The musicians looked like figures cut from black cloth. Now she spotted Stella and wandered toward her, trailing a scarf behind her, a wavering flutter of blue chiffon.

"Stella?" She peered through the dark, leaning forward a bit, uncertain, hesitating.

Stella grunted.

"Ah, you're all alone." She sank heavily into a chair at her side. Across the garden Henry stood seeing the last of the guests out, bidding them good night in a jovial tone that was neither weary or diminished by the lateness of the hour.

"They've trampled my lawn," Alice said dispiritedly, "and nobody liked the food."

Stella tipped her head back and stared into the star-studded sky.

"The tower of Babel," she said reflectively. "Much said, nothing meant. Why do you do it?"

She heard Alice's shallow breathing. One day she would have sarcoidosis or a dark patch on her lungs. She was, Stella thought, fated to come to a miserable end.

"Why?" Alice pondered the question. "Henry loves people. They love him."

"Vultures." Stella was impatient. "Fools. There was a man at this table wearing a diamond pinkie ring and a gold bracelet. I wouldn't piss on him if he were on fire. Perfect idiot."

"Yes," said Alice, "I know the one."

"Erect a barricade," said Stella. "Dig a moat."

Alice didn't seem to hear her. "Once," she mused, "we had a party here for two hundred. I remember I had a swan carved out of ice. And nothing but white flowers. White begonias, white carnations, white lilies. There was a senator here and a Russian dancer and a blind duchess whose male secretary cracked walnuts and popped the meat into her mouth for her. He said his fingers were often bitten but he was well paid. They were all here, that night. Right in the middle of it I went upstairs, put on my nightgown, braided my hair and got into bed. The windows were wide open. I could hear the laughter and the chatter and someone singing lieder. They never knew I was gone." She brushed the crumbs from the table into her hand and folded a soiled napkin with care. "It's strange," she said. "As if I didn't exist."

She looked away. Caleb and Henry now walked arm in arm near a flowering hedge. Water splashed musically into a pool. Stella pushed a wine bottle toward Alice.

"Have a drink," she said. "Drink gives you presence when nothing else does. You'll come into being fast enough after you've belted a few."

"I'm not allowed wine. I have an ulcer." She gave Stella a pale smile. "I'm sure you guessed that."

"I could see there was something gnawing," said Stella. She felt misgivings as soon as the words were out of her mouth. She felt there would be a rush of confidences, confessions, complaints — and the hour was late.

Alice selected a chocolate from a silver dish at hand and nibbled at the sweet with little rabbit bites.

"If I were you," she remarked thoughtfully, "I would run away from Caleb before it's too late."

Stella sipped wine and look impassive.

"Yes," Alice went on, "I would run away. You ought to listen to me, Stella. I've been an appendage to a man for thirty years. I've heard people say of me, 'That dark little woman is the wife.' The 'wife!'"

She clasped her hands, put them in her lap, then on the table, then against her flushed cheeks. "When I was eighteen I studied art in Paris. I went there quite by myself with a portfolio and presented myself to a great teacher in his studio. He had a fearsome reputation for savaging people, but he looked at my drawings and said get warm underwear and come here and study with me. I had the most wonderful winter of my life, all chilblains and timidity, but I worked . . . oh, how I worked and at the end the teacher bought one of my canvases for his own collection." She ate another candy, gulping it down fiercely, as if, like her life, it must perforce be swallowed. "It all ended when I married Henry. There was so much to do about Henry. I had to find him tax exemptions and a barber who could cut his hair the way he liked it. I had to put up lugs of strawberries to make jam because his mother did that and he liked homemade jam on his toast. I designed his study, the furniture and the curtains and even the pictures on the wall. I had his suits made and got pregnant the moment he said he wanted a child." A night wind ruffled her hair, revealing her broad brow, the furrows etched there.

"I joined the causes he believed in. I had my face lifted before I was forty-five because he had a young secretary with no lines at all. I sat beside him during interviews wearing proper little suits and heard them ask him about his work. They asked me what my favorite color was. There was a profile of us done once in a national magazine. They quoted Henry as saying that life was an art he was trying to master. They quoted me as being fond of children and English tea."

"Well," Stella said gruffly, "I'm sorry for you. It's not right. It's not just."

"I've always thought I disliked you." Alice touched her pearls with delicate nervous fingers. "But just tonight, when I saw you sitting out here so stubborn and dauntless, I realized it was envy. My goodness, Stella, we might have been friends all these years and I could have learned how you do it."

"I'll tell you now," said Stella. "Give no quarter. You can't cleave a rock unless you're God and even He hasn't tried it with me yet. No quarter, Alice. Write it on a piece of paper and stick it between your boobs, and when you falter, haul it out and read it aloud. Defend what you are. Live for it. Die for it." She flung out a hand for her glass. "Now. Is the wine all gone or could I have a sip for the road?"

"The wine is finished," Alice said. She looked around the disordered garden. An umbrella sagged and flapped, flowers wilted, fine ashes blew through the air.

"It will take me all day tomorrow to put things right," she said. "Do go home now. Henry is cross if he doesn't get enough sleep."

"Henry again. Always Henry."

"Yes," she murmured, "and you'd best be careful about Caleb. His last wife embroidered house slippers for him. Just think, Stella — petit point house slippers."

Before Stella could reply Alice called across to the men, her voice high and thin on the night air.

"The party's over," she cried. "All over."

Caleb flatly refused to bed down in Stella's apartment. He was, he said, mortally offended by her lumpy bed, which he insisted would serve only for the mortification of a nun in penance. He demanded his comfort. Moreover, though he did not wish to insult her, he had to point out that her place was none too clean. He took her instead to a seaside hotel. She had sat silently by his side on the way from the party, her chin sunk on her chest, saying little.

She had, in fact, confined herself to two questions. What had he been talking about with Henry? And how many days had he left before his departure?

He was more than willing to tell her about his conversation with Henry. It had, of course, been about her. Henry had made solicitious inquiries as to his emotional state; he had responded enthusiastically with his new-found sense of well-being. He had told Henry that they, he and Stella, would turn out wonderfully. He expected, he told Stella, that she would do her part.

Stella did not smile. She felt, in the sullen early-morning hours, that he was swaggering. Inordinately proud of himself. Smug. She wanted nothing to do with happiness. She had another purpose.

"When are you leaving?"

"Far too soon. In three days." He drove recklessly, one hand on the wheel, the other stroking her hair.

The hotel loomed before them, a big pseudo-Spanish pile, looking as if it had been built yesterday and would not last till tomorrow. Stella hated the sleepy attendant with his Ruritanian uniform of red and gold. She hated the dapper elevator attendant, who had big horse teeth and a sallow yellowish complexion. Everything seemed false and fabricated. She slouched after Caleb to their room like a captive concubine, shuffling her shoes, her eyes downcast. She felt an inch from death. It was too much wine, but nobody could have told her that. She knew death when she felt it.

There were flowers in the room and a basket of oranges and a pile of sandwiches, cut thin.

Caleb moved about swiftly, leaving her standing by the door, still in her coat, still drooping and unwilling. He opened a window, patted the bed, lit the lamps, every gesture claiming the room for his own. He even paused to pull a daisy from the floral arrangement and tuck it into his buttonhole. Stella watched in wonder. He was turning the place into a goddamn love nest.

At last he came toward her, grasped her hand and drew her into

223

the center of the room, where the huge chandelier rained a hard light down upon her. He pulled her free of her coat and tossed it on the bed. He took her face between his hands and studied her.

"Worse for drink but very lovely."

"I'm not going to look like a houri at this hour in the morning." She spoke fretfully. "Which bed do you want? I'm going to fall in mine right now."

He would see about that later. He left her standing and went into the bathroom. She heard water being drawn into the tub. She remained rooted where she was, too tired to move, feeling captive, hostile.

"Stella," he called, "come in here."

God, she thought, if he has any water frolic in mind I'll kill him. She appeared in the doorway, her face looking sharp and impatient. The tub steamed with hot water, frothed with bubbles. He had his sleeves rolled up. His cheeks had turned a beautiful cherubic shade of pink.

"Off with your clothes," he ordered cheerfully.

"I'm in no mood for water sports," said Stella. "I'm awash with wine and dead tired, so whatever you have in mind you can just forget."

He shook his head, took hold of her and unbuttoned her blouse.

"Do what I tell you," he said pleasantly, "and be quick about it. The temperature's just right."

He'll have me wallowing like a porpoise in there, and then Christ knows what next. She shucked her clothes, leaving them pooled at her feet, and stared at him with cold eyes.

Without a word he scooped her up and deposited her in the depths of the tub. Then he lifted up her mane of hair and piled it atop her head. He bent toward her and she felt his sucking, biting kisses raining on her, and just as she shuddered at the sweetness of it, he was at her suddenly with a soapy face cloth, scrubbing ferociously where his mouth had just been. Be damned if he wasn't cleaning her ears, peering into them to see that the job was well done. Next his hands cupped a breast, lifted, caressed. He murmured something about great ripe apples and took a nibble to see if it was truly so. He fancied apples. The other breast felt his tongue as well. He lathered her bush, twisted its tendrils into peaks and curls and then stood back to admire the sculpture he had made with suds. He lifted a foot hidden in the green depths, held it aloft and nuzzled the instep against his cheek. And then to work again until she was as clean as a hound's tooth. Stella bobbed and turned in his hands like a rubber doll, astonished. Then out she came and was enveloped in a huge towel and dried from head to foot. Caleb groaned a little with the exertion of it all but went at it with the dispatch of an English nanny. Then off they marched to the other room, the cool air washing Stella's body, and the bed was turned down and she was slid under the sheets and warmly blanketed.

Then he undressed himself, depositing each article of clothing with particular neatness on the chair by the bed. A second later he disappeared and there were gargling sounds and snortings and snufflings and he was back, turning off the lights, raising a second window to the breeze, which ruffled his hair into white foam. Big and sturdy, he loomed at the window, making some sort of quiet communion with the night. Stella felt very still and suspended as she watched him. She felt foolish and wise at the same time, and for once, quite speechless. He came to her side, nudged her to make room for him, and then he was stretched out next to her, his girth making the bed sag and creak.

"Ah," he said.

Excitement rose in Stella. She put her hand between his legs, stroking, encouraging; the soft bud became a stalk.

"So you've come to life, have you?" His voice was loud and amused.

"All that warm water," she muttered. "What do you expect?"

"Well, my dear, tonight I have other needs."

Stella's ears pricked up. If it was to be anything athletic she would have none of it. At his age he needn't be too imaginative.

His encircling arm pulled her close to him, her head bumped against his broad shoulder.

"All safe . . . all serene. Dear Stella." She felt his chest rise and fall with quiet contented breathing. "Now I think we should find each other out. Tell me about your childhood and if I'm not fast asleep by the end of it, I'll tell you mine."

Stella struggled upright. "You want to *talk?*"

"You are too detached, my dear," he said. "Exchange of confidences binds. Connect me with your twelve-year-old self, and you shall have me as the roguish boy I was. Backwards from middle age we go. Begin."

Stella rolled away on her side and pounded her pillow. He could have her from the front or from the back or standing on her head, but she was outraged at this other surrender.

"I'm a private person," she remarked huffily, "and we'll get along better if you remember it."

"Tosh," he said. "You're a stingy person, parceling out your favors with a little leg here, a little backside there. I want more than that. I mean to have more." He settled himself, pulling most of the covers off her to envelop him.

She was suspicious. "Why should I tell you things you can use against me?"

"In the first place, I won't use anything you tell me to hurt you. In the second, people who are intimate must be vulnerable to each other. It's an act of trust."

In the dark Stella smiled a fierce and ominous smile. "I slept with the parish priest when I was thirteen," she trumpeted. "And very good he was, too."

"Unlikely if not untrue," said Caleb firmly.

"I stole money. From my father's pockets. From my mother's purse."

"Of little interest." Caleb was not appeased.

"What then? What?" Stella was becoming flustered, hot, uneasy. He probed like her dentist.

"The first poem," he said.

Stella thrashed, flung out an arm, gave him a glancing blow.

"On toilet paper." She laughed suddenly. "The whole bloody family was in the house on a Sunday morning. Bikes were piled up on our front porch. My aunts were sitting on their fat bottoms, shelling peas for dinner, the men swilling beer and talking shop, and I went to the bathroom and locked the door and sat there writing in blue ink that came through the other side of the paper. God, masturbating was nothing to what I felt then. Nothing. I came out all red and splotchy, with tears in my eyes. I think one of the aunts thought I'd been diddled by a cousin and had gone in there to wash it away. The next day I read it and it was the worst drivel you ever saw. I tore it to bits and stuffed it down the drain. Then I reasoned that inspiration in a smelly bathroom had been the cause of its being so terrible. So I waited till the feeling came on me again and I hiked off into the woods in search of beauty. A farmer, out hunting woodchucks, nearly blasted my head off with his shotgun, and I ran home, wetting my pants with the close call I'd had. No poem from that, I can tell you. Then I decided that the whole thing was a mystical experience and I went to church after the last Mass was said, and it was dark and cold and I knelt down and put my scrap of paper on the floor, and by the light of the guttering candles I scratched out something. Then I waltzed into the confessional, lit a match, and just as I was being transported by my own genius the priest popped in the other half and asked me what I was up to. Poetry, I told him, and full of pride I shoved it across for him to read.

"He said it was sheer doggerel and as he was young and a Jesuit my heart turned to stone. Later, I decided he was just jealous. Not much poetry in what he had to do day after day. I never stopped trying after that. Before I was deflowered. After. When my mother died. When I was put in jail for lifting a bottle of bourbon from the grocery store. And other occasions which are none of your business."

He was silent.

"Caleb?"

By Christ, he was asleep, the damned inquisitive bastard was sound asleep. Stella thrust herself against his bulk, left a kiss in the hairy tangle of his chest and closed her eyes.

Stella sat in a chair, swinging her leg up and down in a fretful motion. A run laddered her stocking from her ankle to her knee, she noticed. She bent over, moistened her forefinger with spit, and stopped the unraveling threads. When she looked up again she saw the secretary behind the desk watching her curiously, trying to place her in the hierarchy of the clientele: was she a stripper in trouble, an abandoned wife, a litigious hooker? Caleb, seated next to her, cleared his throat.

"Let it be," he said. "I'll buy you a new pair as soon as we're finished here."

Stella slumped in her chair. The secretary answered the phone, chanting the firm's name in a bright, lilting voice: "Keller, Keller, Keller and Wainwright — good afternoon."

Caleb lit a cigar. When the girl was free again he questioned her pleasantly: "He knows we're here?"

"He'll just be a moment. He's finishing a long-distance call."

Caleb nodded and folded his arms.

The door opened then and a small man rushed out to them, energetic, precise, pleated folds under his eyes, a pince-nez bobbing on a ribbon against his chest, extending his hands in greeting.

"Forgive me, forgive me." He clasped Caleb in a warm embrace and beamed at Stella. "Do come in, come right in." He ushered them into the room behind him, standing aside with a little half bow to Stella.

His office was huge, and though sumptuous it contained small, homey touches: an old-fashioned muffler hung behind the door even though it was nearly summer, a striped one, yellow and white wool, surely uncomfortable, sure to scratch. The remains of lunch were on a table, a spiral curl of apple peel, shiny black seeds, a little pearl-handled fruit knife; and a glass of mineral water respirated, tiny bubbles breaking, a ring of lemon floating on its surface. A frugal lunch, the lunch of a man with a monkish view of life, moderate, close.

Stella clumped inside deliberately and dropped into the first chair at hand without waiting to be asked. She stared boldly around her. She avoided offices at all costs. No good, in her opinion, was to be got out of them. If you did find yourself in one there was always a dentist with a drill lurking there, or a doctor with dire warnings. Lawyers, with their ponderous legal tomes and their welter of closely written documents, were the worst of a bad lot.

She hiked herself up in the huge leather chair, revealing a badly soiled slip and three inches of thigh, and she glared first at Caleb and then at the tidy and compact little man behind the desk, who offered a tidy and compact little smile to match his appearance.

"Stella, my dear, this is Moses Keller, my close friend of forty years. He flourishes as the green bay tree. He is the father of six sons, and his second wife is often mistaken for his daughter, a thing that makes him proud as punch."

Mr. Keller rose and bobbed at her. "A pleasure, a genuine pleasure." He beamed. "So gifted, so talented, such an accurate ear, such soaring, confident flights. 'Ode to Hymen,' 'Cantos for a Long War in Southeast Asia,' 'The New Lysistrata.' I know the product, you see."

He sat down again, shuffling a few papers with small, rapid fingers, his smile slowly disappearing, as if it might somehow interfere with the serious business at hand.

Stella was not encouraging. She made a sniffling sound that might or might not have acknowledged him. Mr. Keller began to have an anxious look. He washed his hands dryly, rubbing one over the other. Caleb had extolled a glorious woman to him. This one looked as though she carried a concealed weapon. Perhaps not concealed. Her eyes, flashing at him, were dangerous and quite out in the open. He lined up paper clips on the neat surface of his desk and waited. Caleb went on.

"He's drawn you an excellent book contract at my request. I've looked at and found it to be in order. Moses loves the written word."

"I aspire dimly myself." He permitted himself a small chuckle.

"Confess, Moses. There was a bad novel in your twenties."

"Well, fortunately for all, the law is my first mistress."

Stella thought blackly of liens and foreclosures, of suits and countersuits, of quitclaims and summonses.

"He works for you," she said flatly.

"He does indeed." Caleb smiled.

"Well," she said harshly, "that's where the shit hits the fan."

Mr. Keller unbuttoned his jacket, revealing a damp shirt and a heavy gold watch chain. He felt as if he were baring his bosom to an asp. He should, he reflected, have left this one to his son, Anthony. Anthony defended radicals and lettuce growers, murderers and child molesters. He longed for Anthony. Anthony, alas, was cruising the West Indies to quiet his ulcer and deepen his tan.

Stella lapsed into a stony silence. She took in the Georgian desk with cold and calculating eyes, the silver inkpot, the French paperweight. She carefully noted the Morocco bindings and the fine view from the lofty window. She saw the framed photograph of the stiffly coifed woman, whose neck was encircled with perfectly matched pearls and whose look of satisfaction bespoke, at the very least, well-trained attack dogs, steam-heated greenhouses, efficient housemaids, obliging young lovers.

And beside her sat Caleb, puffing on his cigar, admiring the ash that grew at its end; shrewd and merry Caleb. An image rose in her mind. The two of them, Moses Whatsisname and Caleb, frockcoated, sly, laying out walnut shells before her and urging her, as they manipulated them cunningly, to tell them where the little pea lay. Is it here? No? Then here? No? We seem to have fooled you.

She peered at them from under her heavy brows. Not so fast. They'd have to rise early in the morning to swindle her. Fleecing? She knew all about fleecing. Hadn't her daddy, resplendent in his straw hat and his flowered bow tie, sold off Florida real estate sodden with seawater to unsuspecting widows in the twenties? Hadn't he seated himself on their front-porch gliders with colored folders in his hands, extolling beautiful sunsets and inimitable views? The sky is light till ten o'clock and the sea stretches to infinity, somewhere or other, dear ladies. Yes, he had drunk their lemonade, squeezed just for him, and palmed the seeds with ever so much finesse, blowing them with such a refined little phut into his curled palm, and he had patted their hands, he intended to buy himself, right next door, perhaps; he would grow petunias and fish from the pier as the sun sank in the West, verily burned itself out as it sank in the West.

Hadn't her Uncle Ed, with the cowlick and the bulbous nose, run for the state senate on money which came to his house in thick white envelopes bearing no return address? She had seen him many a summer morning with his beefy arm draped around an innocent in the barber shop, murmuring promises into an ear sharply outlined by a fresh haircut. And her cousins. Christ's bleeding wounds, her cousins. George Harris and William Benjamin, sandy-haired and blue-eyed, nails short and clean, deodorant under their armpits, their private parts talcumed, alike as two peas in a pod. Why, they had gone through agricultural college on the friendly poker games they got up in the neighborhood, one dealing with a flourish while the other signaled by a little obbligato of coughs behind his hand. Not to mention her brother Valentine, who leaned on his butcher's scale with a scabby elbow while he smiled at his customers and inquired after their health with a gold-toothed grin; charging for bone and gristle he'd gotten rich. And the lesser felons, second cousin Harris, who signed his father-in-law's name to checks, and David Allen, who stole his mother's tea service the night before he went off to the navy. What a family of thieves. But they had made her wise to the game.

Try me, lawyer, she thought wickedly, just try me.

"This is a standard contract," Mr. Keller told her soothingly. "Nothing very complicated. It includes, of course, the terms of the advance as well as the entire royalty structure. The territory of publication, both hard-cover and soft-cover, U.S. rights, English-speaking rights, foreign rights, the usual indemnity respecting privacy and defamation, stipulations covering accounting procedures and an agreement to negotiate in good faith, which really amounts to no more than a first look, on your next book." He ventured a smile at her. "Everything is clearly stated in plain English. We try not to obfuscate in this office. Still, if anything puzzles you, just draw it to my attention. I'm here to help in any way I can."

Stella thrust out her jaw. "The lawyer who gets my business," she said, leaning forward in her chair pugnaciously, "has an office over a drugstore. You have to walk up three flights of stairs to get to it and when you arrive it's about as big as a rabbit hutch. It has a battered wooden desk which he bought secondhand thirty years ago from a junk shop. It has a chair. Just one. Anyone else in the room aside from him has to stand. He answers the telephone himself, if he feels like it. If not, not. He's worn the same suit as long as I've known him and that's an age and a half. It's dark green. That may or may not be the color — I personally think it's mold. He doesn't own a car; it's shanks' mare for him, rain or shine. He brings his lunch in a brown paper bag and it's usually a peanut butter sandwich and a brown-spotted banana. That's *my* lawyer."

She leaned back and folded her arms across her chest. Caleb was watching her, his mouth pursed thoughtfully.

"Is there some particular point you're making, Stella?"

Stella waved an arm about, encompassing the paintings, the conference table, the gleaming walnut bar, the walls of books.

"Somebody," she said, feeling snippy as hell, "paid through the nose for all this."

Mr. Keller looked to Caleb in alarm. "I don't understand," he said weakly.

Caleb puffed, puffed again. "I believe Stella is questioning your probity, Moses," he said. He turned a chiding gaze on her. "I'm sure you appreciate that it would be insulting for me to vouch for Mr. Keller any further than I have. I'm sure you see that, Stella."

Stella laid on the scourge, flailing right and left. "You speak for him. He speaks for you. Humpty and Dumpty. It looks like I'm the only disinterested person in sight." She rummaged in her bag, found a handkerchief, blew her nose triumphantly.

Mr. Keller rose on his short legs, his face scarlet. He reached for a glass of water, which he swallowed in long, nervous gulps.

"This is extraordinary," he said aloud to no one in particular.

Stella leaped to her feet and stomped back and forth across the room. "It takes me years to make my poems," she said vehemently, "years of tyrannical work. I'm not giving them up, not a line, not a word, not a strophe, till I strike a bargain that suits me right down to the ground. I'm not one of those idiots who'll sell their souls for a fig." She shook her head to emphasize the point. Hairpins rained down.

". . . My dear Miss . . ." Mr. Keller struggled to interrupt her, but she charged on, plunging, rearing, neighing.

"I'm not finished with what I have to say." She rounded on Caleb, included him. "It'll take more than a romp in the hay or my pants hurled off the Palisades or peaches out of season or lobster cocktails or suites of rooms in hotels with twenty-four-inch television sets; it'll take bundles and stacks more than that to get me into camp, don't think it won't."

Mr. Keller needed to go to the bathroom. Mr. Keller wanted to go to the bathroom. "Would you excuse me just a moment," he said to Caleb. "I won't be a moment."

He scurried out. The door closed with a little click on his agitated back. Stella stood fuming in the middle of the room while Caleb tapped his ash calmly into the tray before him.

"Well, well," he said. "Apart from your customary paranoia, your profoundly held conviction that the entire world wants to cheat and abuse and hoodwink you, could you explain what you're up to? I'm at a loss myself."

Stella flounced one way and then another. "I'm not delivering myself up to the unknown put together by the unscrupulous. There's nothing hard to understand about that!"

"No," Caleb said mildly, "not if you're dealing with charlatans. As it stands, however, you are dealing with me, your devoted admirer, your intimate friend, as well as with an honorable and upright attorney at law. Or perhaps not." His voice grew steely. "I'm not patient with your shenanigans, Stella; with tantrums of any sort. You will either sign this contract with me or you will not. That's up to you. But what is not up to you is the apology you will offer my friend. That I insist on. Moses and I go back a long way, as far back as Harvard College. He was best man at my wedding, his eldest son is named after me. His name is stainless, his reputation unsullied." Caleb paused for a moment. "Now. Whatever offense I may have taken at this unseemly display I will overlook. You need not say you are sorry to me, though it would be graceful of you if you did." Again he paused, but Stella remained mute. "I believe," he continued, "that there is a fountain pen on the desk. Your signature is required on all three copies. In ink, my dear Stella, not in blood."

"Not so fast, not so fast!" Stella cried, snatching the contract from the desk. "I'm going to crawl over this line by line, with my own legal counsel looking over my shoulder. The one I told you about, the *honest* one above the store. If we're satisfied, we'll be in touch with you."

Caleb reached into an inner pocket, withdrew his wallet and extracted some bills from it. He held them out to her.

"Take a taxi home. I will speak to Mr. Keller on your behalf. It's clear to me that you don't know how to say you're sorry. Good afternoon, Stella."

Stella grabbed the papers and stormed out, crying that a retreat was not a rout, not by a long shot. She marched toward the elevator, her face flushed, nostrils flared with anger. She had never been bested in a horse trade yet. She wouldn't be now.

Stella lay in her bed, her arms behind her head, a glass of whiskey balanced on her belly. Papers were scattered on the counterpane, an ashtray overflowed and spilled onto the sheets. She had not bothered to turn on the lights; her thoughts were better suited to glum darkness. Not that she was given to introspection. She had little or no patience with self-analysis, self-evaluation; deeds done needed no excuses, those undone even less review. When she was off balance for one reason or another, and those times of doubt and misgivings were rare, she treated herself to a good bottle, drunk slowly. On occasion she ground her teeth violently, she cracked her knuckles — a sure sign of unease with her. Do it or don't do it, get over it, get done with it — this was her litany, recited in a voice thick with liquor, taken in solitude. Remorse was a soppy, ashen angel, weeping crystal tears from empty eyes. Fuck it. If she set her foot on the wrong path she would climb it to the end, briars, nettles, stinging weeds notwithstanding.

She reared up, swung her feet to the floor, grasped the bottle and lurched to the mirror. She scanned her reflection. Why, only look, it was a face to turn heads still, it had character, it was a rare old face. She lifted the bottle in a toast. Some number of cells died suddenly in her brain at that moment; the earth sloped, dizziness made her unsteady on her feet. A breath from an open grave rose damply in her nostrils. She dismissed it; it was merely hunger, she hadn't eaten. Phantoms and beasts came out of the forest when five or six meals were forgotten. Had she breakfasted? That was millenniums ago. No, she had not. She had been in Caleb's bed, legs splayed out, empty-headed, replete, like any other prisoner of love awakening to the toastmaster, to the laundry, to the morning soap opera. Caleb?

The very name became a target. She stormed through the room, sweeping up the papers from the floor, bringing them up before her shortsighted eyes, yelping aloud in rage. A contract? It wasn't rich enough for her gifts, the conniving bastard. What did he think she was, a fire sale, a rummage sale, a bloody flea market? She peered at the papers, muttered, dropped them underfoot and ground them under her heel. Back to the bed she went, sloshing the blankets with the open bottle. She knotted a pillow under her head, made ugly faces at the ceiling. Caleb. Caleb. He was a plug in the spout, that's what he was. A cork, shutting off that whirling, swirling outpouring of the unconscious that was her real self. What had she to do with languishing and soul kissing and soft stroking and secrets? Christ, what had she been up to? She wanted her old hard self back again. Make way, clear the streets, curb your dogs, Stella is abroad in the land. Yes, she wanted to walk the beach and be deaf to the enormous roar of the waves, be blind to the sun. She wanted her own landscape, the rocky, boiling, stormy country where she alone ruled. Caleb, the shepherd. Caleb, the spoiler. He had cut her down with a scythe: she was no longer grass springing greenly from the ground, she was hay, dry, baled, bound, fodder for cows.

A heavy tread sounded outside her door. There was a muffled

pounding — muffled because her head had ducked under a pillow.

"There's a plague in here," she called out in a booming voice. "Move on!"

The knocking became insistent. Outside, Caleb's voice was raised in command. "Don't keep me standing here, Stella."

"Who is it?" she inquired in a la-de-da voice.

"Stella, be quick!"

She gathered her sweater around her with a majestic gesture and crossed the room with mincing steps, bare feet slapping on the floor, ending with her ear against the door. "Yes?" she said. "You wish to see someone?"

She heard his impatient grunt. "I'm too old for this."

Her combative face appeared in a narrow crack. Her eyes, narrow and mean, swept over him. "You've got on an Alpine hat," she accused, "with a red feather in the band. Disgusting." She flung the door wide, staggering backward.

He removed the offending hat and came inside, striding past her to toss it on the couch. She pursued him aggressively, put her face up to his.

"Slave trader!" She spat the word at him and then grinned, pleased with herself.

He grasped her by the arm with a rough hand, dragged her across the room and threw her down on the bed so hard that she felt something jar in her spine.

"You are drunk and foolish," he said with utter coldness.

Stella was very grand, gathering herself up with what she considered immense self-control. "If you are going to take that tone with me," she announced, "I will have to show you the door."

He loomed over her. "Any other man," he said, "would slap you silly."

"You dare!"

"Don't tempt me."

She sniffed.

Then she reached up and waggled a finger under his nose. "You'll never get me up on the block. Never." She pulled her lip up, showing her teeth. "Sound teeth." She thumped her chest. "Sound of wind." She tapped her forehead. "Sound, sound, sound of mind." She rose, ducked under his restraining arm and made for the kitchen, stumbling in the dark. The light from the refrigerator lit her face as she peered into its depths. "Rat cheese," she said petulantly. "There's nothing but rat cheese."

Caleb was beside her in two strides, taking her by the shoulders and shaking her. "I won't have this," he said emphatically. "I will not have this!"

She flounced free of him and then, crouched and ferocious, she fought back. "Damn you. I'm finished with you. Heaving your great carcass on top of me, shoving and pushing and humping. And there I am like an idiot squashed beneath you, and yelling for you to do it some more. And all the while my mind is blank. *Blank.* You great prick, you've shrunk me. You've diminished me. There's nothing in my head but burst grape skins, fish scales, skeletons. A night with you and I'm nothing. An inane smile, soft eyes, puddles. Where's the thunder? Where's the lightning? What am I doing whispering in the dark into your cauliflowered ear? You're just a man. I've had 'em by the dozens, had 'em and gone on my way with a hay and a ho, and thank God I don't have to see your hairy backside again. You want me to be a soft gray mouse in your pocket. You want me to be a sweet child and sit on your lap with your hands cupping my dumpling buttocks. You want to stroke my hair and twine it around your fingers. Tame Stella, Stella on her back, Stella in love. Not for me!"

Caleb's roar shook the windows. "Silence!" Anger ripped over him in waves. He was a mountain of hot ash and lava, thrusting up out of an earthquake. He stomped toward her, all his great bulk aquiver with rage. Stella inched back a step or two. Caleb advanced, a clenched fist raised before him.

"You are a greedy, willful, destructive, monomaniacal and totally intolerable woman! I can only ascribe my having anything whatever to do with you to the onset of senility! Any twenty-dollar whore in any flophouse is your superior in every way. You say I've stolen your divine fire by making love to you — as insane a display of ego as I've ever encountered. What smarts here, my girl, is not your banked fires but the price I put on them." He took hold of her and shoved her angrily before the mirror. "Look at yourself — drunken, lazy, self-indulgent, the hide of a water buffalo. The Muse has gone elsewhere, has she? I don't blame her. Who would want to live in your company? The laurel crown on your unwashed hair? I don't think so."

He picked up his hat, put it on again, snapped the brim. Stella watched him, her mouth slack in astonishment. The eagle had swooped and pecked out her eyes.

"You're going?"

He almost smiled at that. "Indeed I am. Before we get to sticks and stones."

"Go on, then," she cried hotly. "I don't care."

"You will," he told her sternly. "But it will be far too late."

She hung out the window, watching his retreating figure. Far too good for him; she was far too good for him. But *wait!* . . . He was out of sight.

10

HORTENSE THOUGHT with longing of the little buggers from John Muir Junior High School. She had transferred away from there to Leland Stanford High after principal Harry Saul had cornered her in the cloakroom late one rainy afternoon, the other teachers gone, all the children gone, custodians gone, and had kissed her wetly, crying that his life was a ruin, that he was growing older and less and less sure of himself with every passing moment, that only she of all the people he knew could lead him in his progress from morbidity to bliss, starting right there and then on the dusty floor scored with the heel marks of ten thousand kids. She had retrieved the glasses that fell from his high-bridged nose and were nearly crushed underfoot in his amorous frenzy, had observed the shiny and scaling bald spot on his remorsefully hung head, and told him to piss off. He saw that he had misjudged her, saw the possibilities of disaster if she talked, clasped his hands in a fervent and doleful appeal for her silence and wrote her a glowing letter to take with her.

And so she had been six weeks at the high school. It took sheer brute strength of will to get from the first class to the last. She acquired it, but only at the cost of the first strands of gray in her hair and a coarse and hoarsened voice. She carried a can of hair spray in her pocket to ward off attack and learned to leave her jewelry at home. Someone, with the light, quick touch of an accomplished cutpurse, had snatched a gold chain off her neck as she bent over a drinking fountain. She had been goosed at the same time. She had admired the dexterity but deplored the loss. She had also had pornographic notes of almost dazzling lewdness left in her box. She had been, in her passage through the halls, tweaked, fondled, massaged, and tripped. Summer had not come a moment too soon.

Now it was bust-out day. The kids packed the halls, butting into each other, jiving, lounging against the walls, the boys with the sassy looks of little bulls, in their bright blue and yellow and poison green satin shirts, the girls with apple-hard buttocks straining their jeans. The Hondas and the Pintos with rust-raked fenders waited outside, stacked with surfboards and cases of illegally purchased beer. There was grass artfully concealed under hub caps and blankets and sun cream and AM-FM radios. There were knives, short-bladed and wicked, and a bone-handled razor or two. There was Vaseline and K-Y jelly and Trojans and a few sexual oddities made in Mexico and purchased by the boldest for use on the most innocent. It was summer, sand up the crotch, lust in the heart, larcenous. Long, hot summer.

Hortense swung down the hall to a chorus of whistles and rhythmic poundings. Every undulation of her hips was greeted with appreciative cries, yelps, wolf calls, yips. Some of the girls, those who subsisted on Fudgsicles and Coca-Cola and ran to fat around the middle, watched her sullenly: surely, on her sleek black skin there had to be a blemish like those that spotted their faces. One of the more reckless youths, who felt the brush of her hand as she cleared a path for herself, was transported into a fantasy so carnal it made his ears ring, his eyes water.

"Yeah, okay, fine, swell." Hortense plunged through them. "Just take it easy." She made the door of her classroom, only to be stopped by a muscular brown arm thrust in front of her, barring her way. He was a big galoot with pretty blue eyes, bad teeth and nerve.

"Baby, baby," he crooned. "I don't eat nuthin' but chocolate."

She slapped him away, riffled a pack of report cards she carried under his nose.

"These'll take the hubba-hubba out of you, hot stuff," she said. "You are F for failed, baby." She unlocked the door and was propelled into the room by the bucking mass behind her.

Someone had written "Summer Sucks" large upon the blackboard. She left it unerased and took her seat, pounding on the desk with a book until the babble subsided. In the back of the room a guitar twanged. Hortense wiped the offender out with a single dark glance.

"Okay," she said. "Before everybody rushes off to get V.D., parking tickets and polluted, I have something to say. I've had you in this class for six weeks and this is what I've concluded: there's no hope for you kids. Let me repeat: no hope, none."

There was a growl and a catcall. Hortense banged the book again. "Shut up. You need to hear this and you're going to hear this. This school was vandalized three times this semester. Three. Once with fire. Once with water. Once with an *ax!* Six merchants in the neighborhood were ripped off to the tune of two thousand dollars in shoplifted goods. Only two people in this class can fill out a job application in halfway literate or even legible English. There are enough crabs among you to start a cannery. Three of you are pregnant and nine of you have been aborted more than once. One of you slashed the tires on my car. Three of you have been arrested for drunk driving. One of you jumped your mama and damn near killed her. Four of you have helped yourselves out of my purse every Friday afternoon like clockwork. What I'm trying to say is — get out of my sight — and if you're not in the slammer, I'll see you next fall."

A cheer rose. A willowy, silky-haired girl in elaborately embroidered denims came forward, holding a bouquet of wilted daisies in front of her. She tendered them to Hortense with a melting smile.

"These are for you, Miss Washington, from the class. We all got up the money for it. Maybe some of it was stolen, like you said, but everybody contributed. It was like, man, we just love Miss Washington. I mean, we all got it on with you, even if you do chew our asses out more than any other teacher in the school.

241

And we all feel we learned a lot from you. You ask any kid and he goes, 'Yeah, she's got it together, she's in the right space,' so what we want to say is have a real cool summer, and keep the faith." She thrust the rank flowers into Hortense's hands, jiggled so the boys in the front row would know she was not wearing a bra and took her seat.

Hortense held the flowers under her nose; then, with a weary sigh, she chucked them on her desk, first leaning forward to retrieve the condom tucked neatly among them. She held it aloft for all to see.

"You kids have real class," she said.

"We was just funnin', teach."

"Yeah, it's a joke, unless you got somebody you wanna fit it on."

Foot stamping and cheers greeted the last sally.

Hortense held up her hand, raised her voice. "If more of you used these things the world would be a healthier, happier, cleaner place." She flung it away disdainfully. It was neatly fielded in midair and pocketed.

She held up the report cards. "All right. Line up for the bad news. C's, D's and F's are as far as we go in the alphabet."

Moments later they were gone, filling the air with whoops, spilling out of the yard and into the streets, wild, free.

Hortense waited until the din receded. She meant to empty her desk drawers, return the textbooks to the library. Instead she sat, resting her chin on her hand, staring through the dusty windows at the cars stenciled with swastikas and other obscenities. Summer.

Summer was Texas, lying in a torn hammock with a water-stained copy of *Pride and Prejudice* bleeding blue onto her cotton dress, slapping at mosquitoes, digging out chiggers, struggling to keep the cool and witty presence of the nineteenth century in a backyard littered with dog turds and chicken feed.

It was climbing past the No Trespass sign, up a swaying iron ladder, to drop into the reservoir tank with the name of the town in white paint on its side, wearing her pink bra and rayon panties, to slide into the dusty water and float on her back and stare up into a sky the color of dirty linen.

It was squeezing jelly bags tied to the loop of pipe under the kitchen sink, while the gnats hummed in the air and the juice and sugar boiled to thickness with soft plopping sounds on the stove. It was peach ice cream with slivers of the fruit crushed in it, eaten on the back porch with a sticky-handled spoon, the night sullen with lightning, heavy with humidity. It was going into town where the drugstore signs flashed with every other bulb burned out and cowboys lounged against the buildings, shifting tobacco wads, waiting for the Western movie to come on. It was standing in the bus depot, where an old man blew his nose between his fingers and stared at her as she read the names of other places and composed farewell notes in her head. "Mama, I'll send for you. If I end up where it's cold you'd better think twice about coming, but I'll never do real good unless you're someplace close."

Summer was Booker. Booker, rattling over the backcountry roads in his old Chevy, held together with baling wire, boasting his head off about how he could take Tony Trabert or Ken Rosewall or Dennis Ralston if he could ever get out of this shit-ass town and do something besides deliver milk for the Alco Dairy. Booker, putting his cheek against hers and asking guilelessly how much she had saved; sister, he had said, I need dollars; he had to get away, away from the two cracked cement courts in Ida Hays Memorial Park on which grass and weeds sprouted; he needed coaching, pros to play against, proper courts with night lights so he could practice around the clock. Lend me your dollars, he had begged, so I can ankle on out of here.

"We're going together." She had been flinty. "And you're getting up your share. If you start living off me now, you'll live off me from now *on.*"

Booker. Suddenly she wanted Booker. Ted Todson waited for her instead.

Hortense was used to dealing with men. She was harsh and dismissive with sexual advances unless she was really interested, canny and sharp-tongued if business was involved, and impatient and unyielding on almost every other level. The belly-pinching years had made her jealous of her time; it was not to be wasted.

Her life with Booker had suited her. It was she who had begun it when they were children, winnowing him out from the sea of eager adolescent boys who had longed for her, hauling him into maturity after her like a dawdling puppy pulled on a leash. She had hatched him. She had shaped him. She had made him her own. She was bored by the probings necessary in other relationships with men, the slow, sensuous evaluations, the fencing, the parrying. Bored! She scorned the humiliation of being appraised, being judged. Banter wearied her. Flattery embarrassed her. She got her bearings by direct confrontation. It did no good to nibble her ear. Those who had succeeded with her, and there had been a few aside from Booker, had laid it on the line; they were rewarded with laughter and consent.

Ted Todson got off on the right foot.

"I wanted to see you again. That's why I'm here. I wasn't just passing by. I tracked you down."

He was waiting for her in the yard as she came down the steps of the auditorium. The school was deserted, one lone, gangly boy stuffing baskets on the court in the distance, the hoop loose and chattering faintly with every shot.

She noted that Todson had not bothered to shave, that he wore unbecoming pants with a pleated waist and a shabby jacket. He motioned to his car parked by the school fence. It was old and unwashed.

"Come take a ride with me," he said.

Hortense thought of Booker. He was out of her life and had been for weeks. He knew of old that she was not easily appeased. He knew her wrath. There had been no sign of him. Coldly, she had dismissed him from her mind, replacing him with work and halfhearted domesticity. She had painted the kitchen, relined the drawers, oiled the sewing machine. She had read a history of England, *The Decameron*, a cookbook. She had lain awake until morning, watching television, nursing anger. Eunice had made herself scarce, staying out most nights. Jake had shared his dinner on one or two occasions. She had gotten drunk once with Stella. She had gone shopping with Nell. For the rest, she had seen some bad movies, made herself a skirt, polished furniture, repaired an alarm clock. She had taken cold showers, clamped down on her sexual fantasies to the point of obliterating them, except in her dreams, felt resentment. She had stopped just short of self-pity, distracting herself with new records, an expensive house plant, a chocolate cake consumed to the last morsel in solitary gluttony.

The sudden appearance of Todson made her wary. When vulnerable she was more cautious than ever.

"Let's just hold our horses a minute," she said, coming to a halt in the middle of the yard. It was hot. Her dress stuck to her back. The kids had tired her. She was cross.

"Just what do you want with me exactly?" She hitched up her school satchel under her arm and regarded him steadily. That level gaze had caused passion to die in a score of men.

"Can we talk in the shade?" His hand cupped her elbow. She found herself walking beside him, glancing at him sidelong. A dusty red-pepper tree cast shadows on the ground. He leaned against it, watching her. She stood with a hip thrust out. The book satchel smelled rankly of old leather.

He seemed to be in no hurry to explain, stooping to pluck a blade of grass which he chewed on for a moment or two while she grew uneasy.

"Well?" she demanded.

His reply came smoothly. "I got a helluva kick out of watching you handle Booker that day at my house. Looking down your nose at the house, the tennis court, the whole layout. Climbing up that hill, your back like a ramrod . . . I half expected you to turn around at the top and give us all the finger."

"If you're looking for a put-down," Hortense told him, "you've already had it from me." She fished a cigarette from her pocket, snapped a match on her fingernail before he could get his lighter out.

"I run a big ad agency," he said. "Lots of clients. Lots of accounts. You've been bad for my business."

"I've got nothing to do with your business. I got nothing to do with you."

"Wrong." His smile was wide. "You've taken my mind off it. I sit in conferences and I wonder about you. I'm supposed to be thinking about dog food and cold cream. I've been thinking about you. So here I am."

"So here you are," Hortense said. She was not encouraging. He hunkered down under the tree. It was the move of a man totally at his ease. Hortense felt too tall and awkward looking over him. He squinted up at her.

"Your nose is shiny," he said.

"That's 'cause I'm sweating." She was huffy. "You're making me sweat with all this sucking around. Listen, mister," she went on impatiently, "this is my vacation. My vacation started today. I'm going home and put my feet in a bucket of cold water and I'm going to turn on my electric fan and eat ice cream. I'm gonna do the *New York Times* crossword puzzle. From what I can tell, you don't fit in *no*where."

He was not rebuffed. "Come have a cup of coffee. I'll tell you the story of my life."

"Let me tell you," she said. "You're white. You're married."

She did not wait for his reply or for anything else. She turned and walked away from him. It was a long way back across the school yard and she traversed it without looking around. It wasn't necessary to look around. She knew he was still there.

The apartment was stifling and musty. She opened the windows and rummaged in her closet for an old and voluminous housecoat. She took off her clothes and walked naked into the kitchen to take some meat from the freezer, returning to pull the robe over her head, leaving the top buttons open to expose her skin. She padded around the house, watering plants, thinking. She was not beguiled by Todson's account of his attraction. His pursuit of her had a kind of annoying arrogance. Still, there was a disturbing tug and pull in her. It came, she thought crankily, from not having had any lately, from the hot, still day, from walking barefoot and undressed through the silent apartment. She was suffering a self-imposed chastity. Booker's been in bed twenty times since we broke up, she thought darkly, thrusting, reaming, getting his dick wet, restoring his self-esteem. She knew Booker He would never let his fires die into ashes. Son of a bitch, he would haul 'em. Damn Booker. Damn men.

Her front doorbell rang. She moved heavy-footed to the door and shouted through it.

"Who is it!"

There was no answer. Suddenly, she swung the door open. She glowered.

It was Todson, almost obscured by a bouquet of flowers.

"I used to sell books from door to door," he said. "It conditioned me never to take no for an answer." He moved past her into the room, into the kitchen beyond, flowers in one hand, searching for a vase with the other.

"These need deep water. Have you got a big vase? A bucket?"

She flounced after him, pausing in the doorway to watch him in disbelief. "Hey!" she cried. "Hey, what is this?"

"Persistence." He put the flowers in the sink, pushed the stopper in, ran some water. Then he turned to her and grinned. "Come on, let's be friends." He brushed past her into the living room, took a chair and crossed his legs indolently. There was a hole in the bottom of his shoe.

"Hortense," he said, "I like you. I like you, Hortense. I haven't said that to a woman in years."

She edged back into the room, sighed, sat down. "So?"

"I think at this moment I'd rather get into your mind than into your bed."

"You're not going to get into either."

"You know, I was brought up by a woman like you," he said lazily. "My father died when I was a kid. He had a Mobil gas station in Portland, Oregon. My mother took it over. I can see her now, in some kind of a printed cotton dress with gloves on to protect her hands from grease, standing in that station, pumping gas, wiping windshields, selling tires. She had a high, fluty voice, a society voice they used to call it, and she'd stand there asking truck drivers if they needed their batteries checked as if she were inviting them to a ritzy tea party. She never gave a nickel's worth of credit to anybody, not even the local minister. She had me print up a sign saying 'Cash Only, No Exceptions.' One night a punk kid drove in and tried to hold her up. I was in the back, scared shitless. I saw her pick up a tire wrench and brain him with it. He dropped like a poleaxed steer. He was still out cold when the police came." He paused and thought about the past a moment. "When it rained she wore an old flowered garden hat. Christ, she was a sight. She put me through Oregon State College, and if I ever fell below an A average she cut off my allowance. Once I went three weeks on Wonder bread and Hershey bars. I couldn't drink, smoke, spit, fuck or swear till I left home, and the day I did I cried like a baby."

Hortense drawled in reply. "I'm sure she was something else, honey, but if you're looking for your mama, pass by me." Her voice got flat. "I think you'd better do that anyway. I'm black clear through. Black skin, black soul, black disposition. And where men are concerned, black's my favorite color."

He looked at her for a moment, sitting across the room, pugnacious and implacable. "Booker wants a job from me," he said without inflection.

"Is that right?" She smiled, but it was a smile that did not reach her eyes. "Well, if Booker wants a job with you, let *him* kiss your ass for it. He's on his own these days. Dumb move," she added tartly. "You almost had me going, what with your mama and all."

"You're right," he said. "It was dumb. Dumb, because it didn't work."

Foxy, Hortense thought. Admit your errors. Take defeat gracefully. But keep the eye contact. Don't press. She grinned at the expertise, finally amused.

"All right," she said, "you've got your foot in the door. Just one of 'em."

He sat back, satisfied. "One's all I need."

Todson's offices took up the top floor of a high-rise building on the edge of Beverly Hills. He looked down upon Spanish villas and lavish ranch houses, a Rolls-Royce agency, an expensive sea food restaurant. Lights spread below like tilled fields, here dark, there bright. Potted trees and flowering plants banked his terrace. A small stone cherub spat water. French park chairs evoked Paris.

He walked her through the premises, stopping at the refrigerator in the middle of a well-stocked bar. "Have some fruit juice, carrot juice, celery juice, spinach juice. I keep all the tonics. I take all the pills. Faulkner said there was a pill for every ill except the last . . ."

She shook her head, no, thanks; he remained standing for a moment, his head cocked to the side, absently jiggling some change in a pocket. "I find that friends of mine are beginning to keel over; men just fifty, or a couple years older, are dying like flies all around me. Where are the three score and ten we were promised?" He shook his head, bemused. "I've walloped the world — now I'd better live in it a little."

He led her on, throwing doors wide so that she might see how he provided for his staff. There was a series of rooms, all well appointed, containing hand-rubbed walnut desks. Jars of sharpened pencils were placed neatly beside sleekly designed Italian typewriters. Wastebaskets were conspicuous and copious — apparently he allowed for mistakes. There were water carafes and good pictures, piped music, footstools, humidors, silent wall clocks. Nine to five had been made as painless as possible, ulcers were mollified by decor.

His own office abruptly reversed the concept. The desk was ugly varnished wood, scarred by burning cigarettes, stained, littered. There was a badly reproduced print of Michelangelo's *Creation*, God's outthrust hand instilling life into Adam. What inspiration he drew from that she could only surmise. The Supersalesman charging the supersalesman? There was an old mohair couch, a battered coffeepot, an ancient Underwood typewriter. There were no family pictures anywhere. The light source was fluorescent tubing, a hard hot light that suggested interrogation.

He saw by her sour look that she was not taken in. "I'm the

Clarence Darrow of the advertising world — sloppy but shrewd."

She shrugged.

"You're right, it's all deliberate. Brings me in on people's blind side. It hasn't hurt business." He paused a moment.

"You're a smart girl, Hortense. It fools a lot of people. Last spring *Playboy* had a profile on me: Todson, a man in touch with his roots, Todson, manipulating the public in a frayed shirt. Hell, there are a dozen handmade English shirts hanging in that closet over there, three dozen more at home. I have my shoes made by a cobbler who takes a year to deliver a pair. I've got a Porsche motor under the hood of my Dodge. I own a block of real estate on this strip. And so on and so on."

"Uh huh," Hortense said. She shifted to get comfortable in the cracked leather chair. He sat across from her, enjoying his revelations, a magician pulling cards from his sleeve.

"It's all a sell — a hard sell or a soft sell." His tone mocked his own duplicity. "I got to this town in forty-nine. I had twenty bucks in my wallet, a duffel bag with some clean shorts, a nickel pack of gum in my pocket and larceny in my soul. I got off the Greyhound bus at eight o'clock in the morning, headed for the Beverly Hills Hotel, checked into a suite with a patio, went to the barber shop, charged the haircut, went to the pool and looked around for a lady who could foot the bills. And there she was, a hundred and twenty pounds, just over thirty, divorced, chain-smoking, drinking vodka for breakfast, as easy to knock off as a sitting duck. She's the present Mrs. Todson. She's a nice lady with loose screws, cold feet, big heart, and she's learned, after all these years with me, to take a somewhere ironic view. I've been reasonably faithful, I've doubled her money, I've left her alone, except for one weekend in Acapulco which produced my daughter and separate bedrooms thereafter for us. The business works, the marriage works. I'm bored." His grin was mirthless.

Hortense yawned visibly. She didn't bother to pat it. "You call that a hard-luck story? You had twenty bucks? I had a dollar. One green folded-up dollar stuck in the waistband of my panties. I had the clothes on my back and they'd already been there two years.

No nickel gum, no nickel anything. I checked into the Y.W.C.A., in a room with an alcoholic getting over a six-month binge, a religious nut and a girl with the worst acne I ever saw. I walked thirty blocks to the employment office with my teacher's credentials in a manila envelope and got put to work at McDonald's frying hamburgers. You know that sign they've got up? — eighteen billion hamburgers sold? Well, I fried seventeen billion of 'em. It took me three years to get a teaching job. You want to know what's under the hood of my Ford car? A Ford motor, with a burned-out transmission and a leaking fuel pump. You know what I've got in my closet at home? Moths. My shoes cost six ninety-eight and I got 'em at Sears." She rose to her feet abruptly. "What am I doing here trading true confessions with you, anyhow?"

"We're getting to know each other," he said.

"You're bad news," she answered irritably. "I know it in my bones. You come at me one way, then you come at me another. When I was ten years old I got hold of a string of firecrackers. There was a nice little old man lived next door to us. He said, 'Child, don't mess with those crackers,' but I went right on and put a match to them. They went up in blue fire and I got good and burned." She shoved up a sleeve and rubbed the old, puckered scar. "Well, I ain't ten anymore and I don't play with fire anymore. So you can ride me home or put me in a cab — but I'm going."

He groaned and shook his head. "Hortense," he said, "you're a pain in the ass. Grow up. There's some kind of attraction between us. Maybe it's because we're a couple of carpetbaggers, but whatever it is, it's there. We'll probably both get over it. If not, we'll do something about it. Now if you want to go home, I'll take you."

Hortense snorted. She was piqued that he discerned willingness, however faint. "Mister," she said, "I run a little fever now and again when a pretty man passes by, but it don't mean nuthin'. You're just a little fever, about ninety-eight point nine. I'll take two aspirin and you'll be gone."

"Maybe."

They left it at that.

The restaurant was dimly lit, party to obscure the bad food and the small portions and party because the management was convinced that low wattage encouraged an atmosphere appropriate to clandestine meetings. The fact that women met there more often than men was stubbornly overlooked. So it was that the ladies fumbled through plates of creamed something or other and drained their pitifully meager daiquiris. There were added insults. The bread was always slightly stale, the tab inordinately large. The waiters were rude to single women and unspeakable to those in pairs, going on the assumption that only men could be sufficiently bellicose to demand attention, malignant enough to make life trying for them.

They did not mess with Mrs. Todson, however. She snapped her fingers under the nose of a majestic maître d' and made her wants known in her harsh and aggressive voice. She waved a ten-dollar bill in the air, rather like a trainer creating an obedience situation with a small dog. It was not discreetly palmed or surreptitiously handed over; it was brandished.

"If you expect to get this," she announced, "I want a good table by a window, a waiter with clean fingernails and the speed of a whippet. I don't want anybody to hover or ask me how I'm enjoying my meal. There's no possibility of that in a place like this anyway. I'm expecting a young woman to join me. Don't keep her hanging around when she arrives. She's black and impressive, so you can't miss her. I want a cup of coffee as soon as I'm seated."

The bill was held slightly out of reach, but with a small lunge the man had it in hand.

"Leave it to me, madame," he said. "You'll be well looked after."

"I am," she answered. "That's why I can be as rude as I am."

She took her seat at the table and stared out at the waves lapping the pier. She did not like water; it was not her element, unless it was to be found heated in a Jacuzzi.

Hortense spotted her across the room, her elbows on the table, her nose sunk into a steaming cup of coffee. She threaded her way through the tables with her long determined stride and stood over Mrs. Todson until she looked up, blinking with her wide gray eyes like an awakened cat. The ashtray smoldered with half-dead butts. Hortense was late. She had agreed to come when Mrs. Todson had phoned much too early in the morning, with the burr of sleep or whiskey still in her voice.

"Let's have lunch, Miss Washington. A real old-fashioned ladies' lunch. I've got a lot to talk over with you. It's about you and Ted. Now listen, before you get rattled. I liked you when I met you. I still do. I just think we'd better put our heads together. Could you come to that crummy Tiger's Lair at the beach? The food's lousy, but it's dark and my neighbors aren't likely to show up there."

Hortense had done little but acquiesce to the place and the hour. She had wrestled with herself on the question of dress and then thought to hell with it. A black sweater and pants would do for what was bound to be a hair-pulling number. A touch of vanity made her add a silver chain. She did not wear lipstick. The perfume was for herself. She never went without it.

She slid into the chair opposite Mrs. Todson and pushed the cutlery out of her way.

"Okay," she said, "I'm here."

Mrs. Todson thrust a strong dry hand across the table. "My front name's Gail. Can I call you Hortense?"

Hortense returned a firm grip. "Nobody's stopping you."

"Do you want a drink?"

"No."

"I've had two already. Then let's order." She pulled a pair of heavy-rimmed glasses from her bag, stuck them on and peered at the menu. Hortense set hers aside unread.

The waiter appeared with marvelous alacrity and stood, pencil in hand, ear inclined.

"Yes, girls, what'll it be?"

Mrs. Todson bestowed a long, insolent stare upon him. "We're not girls," she drawled. "We were once but not anymore, alas. The fact is, I would have considered you overly familiar at sixteen."

The man nodded silently, a little shaken, and she became brisk again. "I want a patty of chopped meat, rare to the point of cannibalism. I want one sliced tomato. Sugarless tea. Forgive me" — she turned to Hortense — "but what I eat is so nasty I want to get it out of the way as quickly as possible."

Hortense gave her order. The waiter sped away.

The two women took each other's measure, Hortense over the rim of her water glass, Gail as she struck a match to her cigarette. It was a hasty, furtive and totally accurate appraisal, each of the other.

She's tough but not bitchy, probably easygoing until riled. She's stood up well against time. She won't take any shit. She's probably dished plenty in her time. She smokes too much. Some part of her defenses don't hold up. I bet she's never cried. That ring she's wearing is my salary for a year. She's had her nose fixed. So mused Hortense.

She's nobody to mess with. She's smart but skeptical. She'd probably blister you if you crossed her. She's had to fight for every inch of her life. She has beautiful eyes. She's never retreated from a situation. She doesn't suffer fools gladly. Her figure is good but she could lose a few pounds. Thus Gail.

Hortense plunged first.

"He has the hots for me," she said bluntly. "I've seen him twice. We haven't gotten near a bed. I don't know if I'm to blame for any of it or not. He didn't get any invitation — but maybe I give off a smell or something. I don't like him much. Sometimes you don't have to like them much. I don't want to mess with your life; I don't want to mess up mine. I'm not going to tell you I'm ashamed or anything like that. When I'm ashamed it's over a big issue. That's all. That's all I've got to say." She leaned back in her chair, one arm draped over the back of it.

"Very nicely put," Gail said. The waiter set their plates before them; blood was pooled around the meat patty.

"Lovely," she said. "Raw meat is my dish today." She tucked into it with gusto. When she spoke her mouth was full; her manners were not elegant but they were individual.

"The trouble is not with us, as I see it. It's with men. Maybe they're pricks because they've got pricks. I don't know. You're younger than I am, with more energy and more stamina. I don't want to get into a fight with you over Ted. I do want to hang on to him because I've got most of the kinks worked out of my marriage — believe me, there were a lot of them. You stay around for all those years and you raise up quite an edifice. There's a daughter, two houses, cars, boats, a terribly complicated tax structure and a cold-eyed view of what you both are. In our case, not much.

"He's probably told you we don't live together. A woman would have kept that to herself. But that's neither here nor there. Ted's after you. And lady, look out when Ted's after you. If you were my best friend, and he's knocked off a couple of those, too, I'd warn you about good old Ted. You're not, so you're more or less on your own. What I will tell you is that he's given Booker a job. He's going to want to be thanked for that." Her gray eyes were the color of stone. "He takes a lot of gratifying," she said.

The waiter sidled up, bearing coffee. The women were silent as the cups were filled.

"Dessert? We have German chocolate cake, a lovely lemon mousse, ice cream."

Gail waved him away. "Just go get the bill and add it twice before you give it to me." She held out her cigarette case to Hortense. Hortense shook her head.

"I'll leave him be," she said slowly. "The only thing is Booker. I'm finished with Booker but I don't want him hung out for bait. He's as weak as boiled spaghetti, the fool. He thinks because he's got all those pectoral muscles and big white shiny teeth and curly hair that everybody loves him."

"You love him," Gail said.

"No, ma'am. I'm used to him."

Ice clinked in the water glasses around them. The ladies surrounding them at the other tables murmured to each other across the slowly fading rosebuds in the plated vases; they delayed the grocery store, the laundry, the car wash. They stole an hour.

Hortense stared into her cup and found herself far away. Booker stood against the barn wall, a chalk stripe marked above his head.

"Am I tall now? Have I grown now? Horty, look at the mark. Where's it at?"

"Five foot, dumbbell. You're a shrimp. A little shriveled shrimp. You ain't never gonna do nuthin' but bump your head on my chin."

"I'm gettin' bigger!"

"No, you ain't."

"Then measure my pecker. Why don't you measure my pecker?"

Gleeful laughter. And she had. And it was a limp little worm. How crestfallen, his face, how dimished his dream of manhood.

"Listen, Booker, that's gonna get bigger. You don't have to worry none about that."

He had tucked it back in his pants, solemnly, silently. He had wandered off without speaking to her. She had stayed behind to erase the smudge on the barn wall. To put it higher, higher. They had never measured again. Sadly, she knew that he had never reached the mark.

"Hortense?"

She was recalled by Gail Todson, who had risen to her feet.

"I've got to run. I've taken care of the bill. Oh, hell," she added abruptly. "Why do I hang on? I used to be kind of a dignified lady. Let's hope I haven't made a complete ass of myself today."

Hortense gave a little. "Two cats in a closet aren't all that much fun — but you were all right."

The other woman nodded. Then she turned and walked away. Hortense noted with a smile that the tip she left was miserly, half of it in pennies.

The calls began shortly thereafter. Hortense would be roused from sleep by the phone ringing. It was often two or three in the morning when everything seemed at low ebb. Her heartbeat felt slow and heavy, her mind numb. Eunice, in the bed next to hers, groaned at the sounds, woke, swore vilely, slept again, so that Hortense was left alone in the sooty dark, listening to him. She hated being caught this way, sluggish, fatigued. She began to have the feeling that he never slept, that he was there somewhere in the city, in a room blazing with lights, staring out into the empty corridors, talking, talking, talking. She saw the outlines of his hard face tight with determination. That his energy never wavered was as disturbing as the calls. He seemed to be telling her that he could pursue her endlessly, that he could pervade her life, night or day, night *and* day. At first she was mildly annoyed, then belligerent, then brusque. Finally, profane and furious.

Eunice, her eyes gummy and sunken, sat upright in bed and urged her on. Who the hell did this bastard think he was? What the hell was he up to? Where did the fucker get off, hassling her like this? Her high, nervous voice joined Hortense's in outrage. She began to see it as malevolent.

"Horty, he's crazy. Those big guys get like that. Let's disconnect the phone. I'm getting afraid of him."

Hortense dismissed her fears. Men like Todson saw themselves as a blind force of nature. Opposition was to be blown away, bowled over, bent or broken. It *was* a kind of insanity, come to think of it.

She told him so on the tenth call in the flat, harsh voice she used with unruly kids. There had been a curious silence on the line when she finished.

"Look," she said, "I don't know how all this got started but I'm stopping it. Cold."

"Are you?" His voice was low. She had to strain to hear. "Are you stopping it?"

She hung up on him, slamming the phone into its cradle. Eunice shivered, clutching the blankets.

"Maybe he's on something?"

"He is. It's called an ego trip. Go to sleep, Eunice. Forget it. It's handled."

In the following nights she found herself waking suddenly,

listening. But the phone was silent. He had tired of bullying her. The thought of him brooding over the rejection was almost as unpleasant as the calls had been. Then she became impatient with herself. She was making melodrama out of a man's ugly conceit. Another woman might have been flattered. Still, his total silence weighed on her.

She took to rising early in the morning, pulling on a light sweater and making for the beach. Once there she ran, streaking across the sand with the wind at her back, hearing Todson's heavy, insistent voice suggesting, insinuating. She brought herself up short. It had to be put into perspective. He was merely a sulky, thwarted man, neither sinister nor mad. A schmuck. That was all. But she fled the house anyway, passing most of the day out on the beach.

It was there she came across Stella quite early one morning. She saw her, at some distance, in her shapeless cardigan and battered felt hat. She saw further, as she approached, that Stella was engaged in some kind of strange ritual. There she sat, on the damp sand, surrounded by a ring of stones, each weighting a fluttering piece of white paper. The whole world, Hortense decided, had gone crackers.

There was something huddled and limp about Stella that made Hortense suspect she had been there all night. "Hey, Stella," she called as she came up to her. "You up early or out late?"

Stella peered up at her. "How long have I been here? I have no idea."

Hortense hugged herself. "It's pretty cold. June, and it's freezing. What's all this?" She indicated the strange druidic circle.

"Those are blank pieces of paper," Stella growled, "weighted with rocks. They are symbolic of my present state of mind. Emptiness pressed down with stone. I'm blocked. Silenced. Constipated."

Hortense hunkered beside her. She saw, at close quarters, a pinched grayness in Stella's face. She recalled then seeing the blinds drawn over the windows of Stella's apartment for some days now. She had not seen her making her customary sallies to the corner bar.

"Are you all right?"

"Of course I'm not all right. I haven't written a word in weeks. Nothing'll come. I'm on a rack. I'm roasting over hellfire. Also, my slacks are wet from sitting on this goddamn sea-drenched strand."

"Then get up," Hortense said with admirable good sense. "Go home."

"Verse is my home," Stella said grandiloquently.

"You're a little sozzled, aren't you?"

"Comment on the obvious is boring."

Hortense sat beside her, pulling up her knees and hugging them with wrapped arms. The sea hissed at their feet. A sandpiper minced in front of them, leaving tiny perfect tracks in the sand.

Stella showed signs of age. Circles ringed her eyes like kohl, there was a sad droop to her mouth, the locks of hair blowing untidily about her face were as gray as her skin. The nails on her hands were jagged and broken. Her stomach growled loudly. Hortense thought of a stray dog, skittish, abandoned. She felt a wave of pity which she knew Stella would despise.

"Are you going to sit here all day?"

"Yes." The reply was obstinate. "All this day. All the next."

"There's got to be another way to turn on," Hortense said. "You've got sand all over you. You look like a barnacle."

"I don't give a hoot about my appearance. That should be plain. A battle is taking place here. Here I stay till it's won."

She rooted around in her capacious pocket and came up with a quart of bourbon with only a drop remaining. She tippled daintily, closing one eye and crooking a finger as if it were a teacup.

Hortense watched her. She saw clearly that Stella could not be cajoled or comforted.

"Wanting is a bad thing," she said half to herself.

"Nonsense." Stella's voice rang out strongly. "When my desires go, the worms can have me and welcome. What doesn't work is *two* desires at once. That's what I'm plagued with. That's what I won't have."

She flung the bottle into the water. She had surprising strength; it sailed high and far before it splashed.

"What happened to the fat man?"

"Ah. Him. Sent packing."

"And you miss him."

"I don't waste time on thoughts of the absent." Stella's voice finally lacked conviction.

They sat side by side, like two harpies, Hortense thought, and the waves broke and receded in front of them. There seemed nothing else to say.

It was Saturday afternoon. The poolside was crowded; on every deck chair a body browned in the sun. Ice melted in Scotch, in orange juice, in diet soda. One young woman had abandoned the top of her bathing suit. The diving board cracked and resonated, a diver shouted as he hit the water, belly first. Laughter was loud, conversation continuous.

Booker took the stairs to Hortense's apartment three at a time, and when he came through the door he wrenched off his tie and squirmed out of his plaid jacket, flinging it away. Sweat had marked large circles under his arms and stood out in drops on his forehead.

She was at the sewing machine, wearing an old pair of slacks, a man's shirt, her hair a tight screw on top of her head. There were pins in her mouth which prevented a greeting, even if she had deigned to offer one. She didn't. She merely looked up at him for a while.

She saw the change in him. He stood before her hesitant and subdued, like a man rising out of bed after a long illness. The muscles in his back, in his neck, were bunched and tense, and he had a curious new gesture, his hand wandering to his mouth as if he wanted to stifle what he was about to say.

She knew Booker of old. When dismissed or chastised he had always visibly declined, sleeping badly, eating badly, peanut butter slathered on crackers, beer, ice cream bars, food snatched at random. It was as if he were saying: "See what's become of me, out of your care." She was familiar with that hangdog dejection.

Once she had caught him stealing money from the poor box in church. He had nearly fainted at the flaying he got. He had cringed under her castigation. She had warned him darkly that he needn't fear God's eye — but hers. *She* was watching him. He had to deal with *her*.

He had that same look now, as if he still heard her thundered "Thou shalt not!"

"Well," she finally said, her voice cold, "look what the cat dragged in."

She saw his eyes shift nervously around the room. "She here? You alone?"

She continued to feed the cloth under the needle, paying him not the slightest attention until she was finished. Then she bit off a piece of thread, folded the blouse and set it aside.

"Yes, I'm alone. Didn't you have a dime on you to call, before you come bustin' in here?"

She took a sharp tone with him. In the past he had found that bracing, even comforting. It put him at the center of her attention, where, in his childish vanity, he insisted on being. He had often goaded her into severity. He liked her best in this role, chiding, warning, scolding. To come from that to her acceptance had always delighted him. Her scorching judgment was more pleasing than another woman's caress. He was proud of her inflexibility; it was as inseparable a part of her as her harsh laughter, her mocking gaze. All his life he had submitted to it with glee. You can't get around Hortense, no sir, no way. The fun was in the trying. She had her little susceptibilities and finding them out was sweet. Her cry of "Get off, Booker!" or "You quit that right this minute, Booker!" were the triumphs of his boyhood.

"I didn't have no dime." When he was uneasy he lapsed into the careless speech of long ago.

He sat down in the nearest chair, his hands capping his knees. The humble posture evoked other times. Hortense saw him sitting in just that way on the porch of his house, while the minister intoned prayers over his mother's casket. She had come outside, sick from the thick air clouded with the scent of lilies, sobered by

261

the sight of the cheap pine coffin balanced on the kitchen table, pressed by the packed bodies, and had sat beside him, both of them swinging their bruised and scabbed legs over the side of the porch.

He had slept in her bed that night, clinging to her all through the humid hours till daybreak, the two of them plastered together, sticking together with sweat and the fear of death.

She tapped a cigarette out of a pack, popped it in her mouth, tossed one across at him. He didn't attempt to catch it, and it fell on the carpet at his feet.

"Well, smoke it or pick it up, one or the other," she called sharply to him.

"I'm not smokin' anymore. I quit."

"You enjoying life so much you want to live a long one?" She chuckled briefly at her own joke and slammed the cover on the sewing machine.

Booker sighed deeply. She was impervious to his sighs.

"You're lookin' fine," he said. "Real fine."

She was impervious to his compliments as well. She threw him a glance over her shoulder as she went to the kitchen. "It's lunchtime. You want something to eat or not?" It was an offer but coldly proffered.

"I'm not hungry."

"Well, I am." She hummed a little tune as she went. Let him see that both her appetite and her appearance were unimpaired by his long absence. "You want to talk to me, come in here."

She had her head in the refrigerator, dragging out bread, tomatoes, lettuce, milk, hugging it all to her bosom. He hovered in the doorway.

"Sit down on that stool. You're making me crazy, standing in the door like that."

She found herself thinking what a clutter some men made by just standing around, hands hanging, waiting to be pushed or pulled. He had annoyed her before when they made a bed together, often after sleeping in it, holding his section of the sheet limply in his hand until she directed him irritably, "Tuck it in, fold it over, miter the corner." He had always made a botch of tasks, cutting himself on tin cans, banging his thumb with hammers. He had stood over stuffed drains, unflushed toilets, burst pipes, with the same helpless air, until she had shoved him aside and done the work herself. Only in bed had he been the great athlete that he was.

She pulled out the breadboard and set about making the sandwiches, cutting the tomatoes in thick slices, spreading mayonnaise in swirls.

"You've got a lot of nerve showing up here. I said I was through with you. You must be hard of hearing or something."

"I heard you." Again the sigh.

She felt a stab of impatience. "Make yourself useful. Put out the mats and the napkins. Pour the milk." She ordered him about in a loud voice. Meekly he opened drawers and cupboards.

"Those are the wrong glasses. The big ones are for milk."

Awkwardly, he arranged the table. She watched him.

"You look like you've been eating standing up for a month. You're scrawny. Peaked. You still in your old place?" She managed to keep her tone disinterested.

"Yeah."

"Anybody ever clean it — or are you living up to your neck in dirty socks?"

"I clean it. Sometimes."

She slid the sandwiches onto plates, then shoved him out of her path as she put the food on the table. "Don't get under my feet."

She leaned against the sink and folded her arms. "Yes," she said, "you're real brave coming back here." Her nostrils flared with the possibility of a fray. "I thought I put you in your place once and for all. I don't remember telling you I'd changed my mind. I don't remember asking you to come over here. I guess you're just here on straight nerve."

He grabbed her then, held her emphatically. "Don't be so goddamned rough on me!"

She disengaged herself, as if she were brushing off a housefly. "Keep your hands to yourself."

Then she drew out a chair and seated herself at the table, looking up at him sourly. "I didn't make that sandwich to throw it out. Sit down and eat. God!" This last was a snort as he tucked his napkin in his shirt front.

"I would've thought by now you would've learned to put it in your lap. You're traveling with the high and mighty these days. You don't see them sticking their napkins under their chins like no baby's bib."

He snatched it away, crumpled it into a ball and threw it. Then he pushed his plate aside, his face heavy with misery. Shrieks rose from the swimmers outside. A voice wah-hooed, there was the sound of splashing.

"Why do you live in this goddamn place anyhow? A bunch of honkies lapping up booze and pinching fannies, potbellied old farts wearing their rugs into the swimming pool. Shit. They all make me sick."

He grabbed up his glass of milk and gulped it, leaving his mouth rimmed with white.

"Wipe your mouth," she said. "You've got a milk mustache."

He used the back of his hand. "A bunch of honkies," he said again.

"You're working for one, from what I hear." Hortense stared at him coldly.

He got up from the table and slammed the window shut, muffling the noise. He stood leaning against the pane, as if to cool his skin at the touch of the glass.

"Yeah," he said. "I'm working for Todson." He let a moment pass. "I've got my car outside. Let's go for a ride. I can't breathe in this goddamned apartment."

"Nope," she said. "I'm going to finish sewing my blouse, bake a pineapple upside-down cake, wax the kitchen floor, and then I'm going to lie down and take me a nice nap with the radio playing at my ear. After that I'm going out to dinner and a picture show. Can't go for no ride with you because my day's all taken up."

A strand of hair made a pretty curl at the back of her neck. She pinned it severely in place. He watched her closely. Her brows met in a frown, forbidding desire. She saw on his face that he wanted her and felt anger that he should. The spoiled little brat. Marching in here with his melancholy look. It gave her satisfaction that he was afraid of her. Oh, he had reason to be. She half wished that he had appeared in his old guise, with his wheedling charm, his certainty, his laughter. He might have brazened it out, won her around. Might have? He *would* have. Often he had persisted through her anger, placing a kiss lightly on her forearm, blowing his warm breath against her ear. She had a taste for his wiles but not for this damp supplicating air.

"I see you got yourself a new thin watch," she said contemptuously.

He mumbled an answer. "It was on sale."

"Uh huh. I see you got a new ring, too. Some other kind of sale, I guess."

"All right," he said harshly, "so I got a couple of nice things. At least I don't look like somebody's washlady."

She hooted at that. "You've rolled around plenty with this old washlady, boy. Not for some time, of course. And why would I care what you think of my looks? What you think of anything?"

He made a despairing gesture. "I didn't come here to fight with you. You just won't have it any other way."

He seemed so deflated she became less pugnacious. "If you're here to put the bite on me, I won't lend you money."

"I didn't come for money either."

She felt a pang of anxiety. "You sick?"

"No, I ain't sick." His voice was dull.

Her good will was gone as quickly as it had come. Booker was up to tricks. He had plagued her with them endlessly, a frog in her lunch basket, a mousetrap in her bed, lies, he knew all sorts of sly antics. He was concealing something now.

"You're up to something," she said sternly. "What is it? You'd better tell me right quick."

Booker swallowed with effort. "Todson wants you," he said. "I'm supposed to fix it up."

There was a moment's silence. Then Hortense shook her head as if she had not heard.

"Say that again."

"This is all coming from him. I'm just saying what he said." He fell still again.

"You mean you're just a dummy, sitting in his lap. Charlie Dumb McCarthy."

He struggled on. "I know he comes on strong, but that's the only way he knows. He's really crazy about you. He talks about you all the time. Wants to put you in a big apartment, a big car. Wants to fix you up with credit cards. Said to tell you whatever you want is yours. Said to tell you 'good times and hard dollars.' And if any of that made you mad, to say, 'Don't get mad, Horty, he's really sold on you, all the way.'"

He was finished. He stopped and gulped air. He did not look at her, but he felt the burn of her look on him.

"So," she said, "part of your job is pimping, huh? Well, well. Isn't that cute? If I'd known that's where you were heading I wouldn't have wasted my time teaching you to read and write and long divide. I could have just bought you a white fedora and some tight shiny pants and turned you loose on any street corner." She lit a cigarette, blew the smoke into the air, watched it curl away. "I wonder why he picked you out. Must be he saw what kind of work you would do best. Yes, sir, you're a nice-looking boy with a little bit of swagger and a little bit of style. Not too smart but that's all right. Smart would just get in the way. I expect he watched you sucking around him, kissing ass, tugging on your cap, and he said to himself, 'Why, this cream wants to rise to the top in the worst possible way. That makes him my boy. I'll just give this boy an office and a telephone with punch buttons and some papers to shuffle around, and when I've got him good and housebroken I'll send the little pup sniffing to fetch her.' And damned if you aren't here. Dropping turds at my feet." She made a clicking sound with her tongue. "Tsk, tsk. You've made a mess, all right. A nasty, smelly mess. I should rub your nose in it. But I won't. I think I'll just pick you up by the scruff of your neck and set you outside the door and close it and lock it."

He started to speak. "Horty —"

She held up a hand instantly. "I'll be doing all the talking right up till you leave. There isn't much more to say, actually. Except that this finishes it. It's in a box, the hole is dug, it's buried."

The finality in her voice made him frantic. "Horty, don't kill me. Don't. Gimme another chance. I'll quit the job. I'll shove his face in."

"I don't give a shit what you do. You can believe that, Booker, if you never believe another thing the rest of your life."

He burst into tears then, a child's snuffling and bawling. She watched him as he leaned against the wall, his head buried in his arms.

"Stop that," she said. "Booker, stop that right now. It won't do you any good, you know that. Now go in the bathroom and wash your face with cold water before you leave."

"Horty," he cried, "I'm nuthin' without you."

"Nuthin' with and nuthin' without, baby."

He stumbled away from her then into the bathroom. She heard his tears for some time after.

Eunice knew Hortense of old. It would not do to offer her the slightest sign of sympathy; she would immediately infer from any gesture that she was to be pitied. She had a way of squaring her shoulders and setting her mouth which said all too eloquently that she was scornful of interference in her affairs. Plainly, her stance declared, I'll handle things myself.

The small African violet, damp in its pot, thrust into her hands, was as far as Eunice dared go. She would have liked something more dramatic, some little tableau, her arms around Hortense, Hortense's head inclined to her shoulder. She had always longed for an older sister, seeing her as someone perpetually lovely, combing and brushing her hair, presenting an image like her own in the glass, the same eyes, the same mouth. She dreamed of them sharing dresses, confidences, boyfriends, heartache. She had often composed letters in her head which were dispatched to imaginary farms, villages, distant cities.

"Dear Sister: I've enclosed a snapshot of me. You can see I've lost weight. The pin I'm wearing is the one you sent; I'm never without it. Do you like my blond hair? Oh, I wish we were together so we could have a good talk. If you were here, I know I would sit by your side and tell you all my troubles. Don't worry about me, though; I am well and will visit you at the first opportunity." And so on and on.

"What's all this in honor of?" Hortense bent over the rich purple bloom.

"A man was selling them on the corner. He had a terrible birthmark on his cheek and I felt sorry for him. Then he short-changed me. It just goes to show you."

Hortense laid aside the book which had gone unread in her lap for the last hour. She took off her glasses. Her shrewd glance came to rest on Eunice, who looked away furtively.

"I think I'll get ready for bed," Eunice said, rising and darting into the bathroom, leaving the door open as she wiggled out of her clothes. Where they fell, they lay, to be kicked out of her path as she came and went, to be stumbled over by anyone less agile.

The subject of Booker lay heavily on the air. She had awakened the night before to find Hortense sitting up in the dark, smoking, staring into space, her face deeply thoughtful. She had wanted to say something then, but at night, in the dark, Hortense appeared even more formidable and unapproachable than usual. She hated not knowing where matters stood. Curiosity and fear of Hortense's wrath warred.

She returned to the living room and made herself like a little girl at Hortense's feet.

"Would you brush my hair for me? I have a migraine headache. I'm so tired."

Hortense took the brush from her and began the long, even, sweeping strokes.

"That's lovely." Eunice closed her eyes and rested her head on Hortense's knee.

"Horty?"

"Hmm?"

The restful stroking continued.

"Have you sent Booker away for good?"

"Yes. Away for good."

"I know you hate me to ask . . ."

"But you will anyway."

"Horty, you're my best friend. My very best. You've been so sad these last couple of days."

"I have the curse," Hortense said crossly.

Eunice twisted around so they faced each other. She saw with some shock that Hortense looked old, ground down, weary. She always suffered from lassitude herself, but to see Hortense like that was unfamiliar. It was frightening. Hortense, who always had such a current of energy flowing through her.

"Can't we talk?" Eunice implored. "Can't we?"

"We never stop." Hortense laid aside the brush, rose and walked to the window. She ran her finger along the sill. It was just as she thought. Eunice had not dusted all week and it was her turn. She smoothed her hair away from her face. She knew Eunice would persist until all was laid bare, every twist and turn of event, every pang, every remorse. She was like a child, tugging at her skirts.

"Okay," she said. "There's not much to it. Things between Booker and me were just getting old, I guess. He came back and tried to make it up. I'd had enough." Instinctively and from long habit, she continued to protect him.

Eunice listened intently to every word. It was important to understand about survival; you never knew when your own endurance would be tested.

"But you've known him all your life."

Hortense sat down heavily on a chair. "I guess you could say it took me all my life to know him." Her voice was dry. "I do now."

She sat with her legs apart, her skirt straining over them, her hands resting limply in her lap. Eunice had seen women in that posture waiting at bus stops, a day's hard work bowing their shoulders. Where was the other Hortense, the one who could sweep her up, make her see all kinds of possibilities? Oh, where was she?

"Maybe," she said tentatively, "maybe you were too hard on him. You know you can be hard, Horty."

Hortense scowled. "Watch out I don't turn it on you."

Eunice rushed on recklessly. "Maybe your expectations were too high. I don't see how you can turn your back on all those years. Look at all you invested. Look at all that happened between you. Why, I can remember as plain as plain your telling me how you went into J C Penney and got Booker some new clothes, so when he came up north he wouldn't be ashamed of himself. How you took him into a restaurant and ordered a meal for him and just a cup of coffee for yourself; telling him to cut his meat in bites before he stuffed it in his mouth, not to butter the whole piece of bread at once, to leave a dime for the waiter. You told me all that, Horty. You taught him his manners."

"Did I? That boy still picks up a steak bone in his fist."

"How can he do without you? How can you do without him?" she asked unhappily. Hortense and Booker had been a certainty in an uncertain world, a fixed star to be guided by. Eunice floundered. Nothing remained from her own past. Her emotional history had ended in two weed-covered graves: Here lies George Wilson, at Peace with Jesus. Here lies Helen Wilson, Heaven is her Home.

"How will we do?" Hortense echoed her question. "I don't know."

"You love him."

"Liking him cuts more ice with me — and I didn't." Hortense clasped her hands behind her head and suddenly laughed raucously. "I guess if I'd kept after him the way I was going, he wouldn't have liked me very much either. No, sir. We were gonna buck heads anyway."

Eunice was appalled. She saw that Hortense was beginning to regain her ground, beginning to recover. It offended her sense of the romantic. She allowed her tone to become aggrieved. "I don't understand you."

Hortense snapped back. "You don't have to, baby. I understand myself and that's enough for me."

"What if you end up alone?" It was the fear that threatened her and haunted her.

"Well, what if?"

"I'm afraid to be by myself. Why isn't it all right to settle for a little less than what you want? Everybody does. Everybody in the whole world."

"Don't talk everybody to me," Hortense growled. "I'll tell you about settling. Dust settles. Ashes settle. What's underneath is buried. You go settling, honey, you're gonna be in big trouble."

"Where are you?" Eunice couldn't resist the barb. "Just tell me that."

"Me? I'm young, I'm healthy, I got my own teeth. I'll manage. Now go to sleep — I don't want to hear your voice another minute."

Eunice got to her feet. She needed yet another reassurance. Now that things were finished between Hortense and Booker, might Hortense not pack up and go, might she not shake the dust of this place and take off?

"Will you be going away, Horty?"

Hortense shrugged. "I ain't settled on anything just yet. Why? You want my green coat? You've been after it ever since you moved in here."

"I don't want the coat."

She wanted Hortense. Hortense made her feel safe and protected.

"Are you going to stay up late?" She lingered in the doorway.

"I'll be along pretty soon. Turn the lights out. You left 'em on in the bathroom all night. You're running up our bills."

Hortense picked up her book, slid her glasses back on. "Go on, don't stand there staring at me. You aren't going to see anything happen by staring at me. I ain't gonna come out in spots."

"Please come soon. I hate to go to sleep by myself."

"Stop being such a baby, Eunice. Good night. And thanks for the violet. It gives me hay fever but thanks anyway."

Eunice blew her a kiss and disappeared into the bedroom. She sank down on her bed, hugged herself, feeling disconsolate, feeling tears in the offing. Suddenly she snatched up the phone and dialed rapidly. It rang two, then three, then four times.

"Hello?"

"Hello, Archer, this is Eunice."

She heard his dazed, sleepy voice respond. "Hello, Eunice."

"I know it's late. It's after eleven, isn't it?"

"It's twelve thirty-five."

"Is everybody asleep?"

"Yes."

"Listen, Archer, tomorrow's Sunday. Let's go to the zoo. We'll eat lunch with the monkeys. That would be fun, wouldn't it? Would you like to do that?"

"We go to church on Sunday."

"After church. Get the taste of it out of your mouth."

She heard a faint chuckle from him.

"I heard you laugh, Archer." She suddenly felt merry, elated, seeing already the jig and jog of tomorrow. "Don't tell me I didn't because I did. I'll bring lunch and meet you on the corner."

"Is my dad coming?"

"No. Just you and me, Archer. Just you and me against the world."

She could almost see the shape of his smile, curved, shy, pleased.

"Okay," he said. "I'll see you then."

Somewhere he had found a pair of dark glasses which all but engulfed his face. They were the ninety-eight-cent variety to be found on dusty racks in the back of drugstores. He had, in fact, bought them that very morning, with some vague idea that they would make him look older and like an airline pilot. He had tried on several kinds, but most were too large, sliding down on his nose, and those that did fit made him feel giddy, the bright green and blue and purple lenses making everything waver before him.

His final choice had been these, with pink glass, and now the world was the color of strawberry sherbet. He had kept them in his pocket, hidden from his grandmother, until he was well away from the house, and then popped them on as he approached his rendezvous.

Water from his hair dripped onto his collar. He had paused, cutting across the neighbor's yard, to wet his celluloid comb under the garden tap. He made a part down the center, felt with his fingers to be sure it was straight, slicked it down on both sides. His grandmother always combed it back from his forehead, giving him a peeled and naked look. He felt his way enhanced him greatly.

All else was in order, with the possible exception of his tennis shoes. They smelled. He knew that because he had sniffed them critically before donning them and there was definitely a rubbery odor emanating from them. He had scrubbed them hard with a bar of Lifebuoy soap, with the result that his feet now felt damp and cold.

When he saw Eunice coming toward him with her pretty, swaying walk his heartbeat accelerated and he felt a nervous desire to sneeze. He wished desperately that he had gone to the bathroom before leaving the house. He wished he had grown taller since he saw her last. He wished the awful pinkness before him would go away, the pink dog crossing the pink street to lift a leg under a pink tree; it was making him sick to his stomach.

She was by his side now. She wore a ruffled skirt and a large straw hat that swooped fetchingly low over her eyes. There were flowers scattered over her blouse, which was unbuttoned to show the cleft between her breasts. Little silver birds rose and fell there on a chain. She had added false eyelashes and he was dazzled by the feathery shadow they cast on her cheek. He wondered how they had come about — her lashes had been blond and stubby last time.

He shifted back and forth in his squishy shoes and waited for her to speak first.

"Hi, Archer," she said. "I love your shades."

"Hello, Eunice."

He felt her arm drop fraternally around his shoulder. "I'm parked around the corner."

He was hugged up against her hip as they walked toward the car. It made his shirt ride up and bunch under his shoulder blades but he didn't dare disengage himself to pull it down; it would, he thought, seem unfriendly, as if he were trying to pull free. He worried frantically lest his damp hair leave a blot on her blouse. It seemed to take forever before they arrived at the car. Dimly he knew it was lovely to be crushed up against her, to smell her talcum powder and feel her warm skin, but anxiety spoiled it: his hair, his shoes, the pinkness of it all.

"Hop in." He was turned loose and clambered in. The hot air in the car almost overcame him. His glasses slid slickly down his nose. He shoved them back.

Eunice rolled down the windows, flipped on the radio, tooled the car expertly through the traffic. He found himself speechless, numb, searching for something to say. He sorted through possible topics, the weather, her appearance, wondering all the while why he couldn't just say he was glad to see her: that's what he wanted to say.

"Are you glad to see me?"

He jumped visibly. "Yes," he said, and then wanting to adorn it, to enrich it, he repeated: "Yes, it's nice to see you."

She took off the hat and flung it on the seat behind them. Now he remembered how wonderful her hair was, full of red glints and curled tendrils.

"I was beginning to think that it was out of sight, out of mind with you, Archer."

He was almost offended by that. How many nights had he gone sleepless while her face rose before him, obscuring the figure of Jesus in the print on the wall, obscuring the geometric pattern of the wallpaper, obscuring everything.

"I guess you've been pretty busy," he said, making an accusation of his own.

"I don't know where the time flies to, but it goes, goes, goes."

She took a sidelong glance at him. "I lost your phone number, Archer. That's why you haven't heard from me. Yes, I lost your phone number and my car keys and an opal ring, all in one month."

He knew it was a lie, not even a very convincing one. "That's okay," he said.

"No, it isn't, baby. Listen, I've been going out with your father a lot. That's what it is. I'm out late. I sleep late in the morning. Then I get up and drink coffee to get started and go get my hair done and come back and watch the afternoon television shows . . . do you ever see 'As The World Turns'? You get hooked on that damn show, believe me; it's like eating peanuts."

"Well," he said defiantly, "I've done a lot of stuff, too. I made a vegetable garden in our backyard. Peas and tomatoes and beans. I made a model airplane from a kit. And a lot of other stuff."

He thought heavily about all the long afternoons sitting on the porch while his grandmother slept upright in a wicker chair, her mouth hanging open, little puffs of breath bubbling out of her. Once his father made his daily call to see how he was, there was nobody else to talk to, nobody to play with. He hadn't made a model plane at all. Or a garden either. You couldn't call one row of puny radishes that the snails got to and spoiled a garden.

"I got invited to a birthday party next door," he said, inventing it on the spot, "and I learned to dance. A girl taught me. There were more girls than boys there." He would have willingly gone on but he could not possibly imagine what might have happened next. "There was ice cream, too — Neapolitan — and two kinds of cookies." No doubt about that being lame but it was the best he could do.

"Sounds like you had a ball."

"Yes."

They had arrived at the zoo. Eunice took a huge lunch basket from the trunk and he pulled himself free of the sticky vinyl seat and followed her up a winding path bordered with trees. There was the smell of cut grass in the air and people had spread picnics out on all sides of them. Here a red-checkered cloth was flung, there a blue and orange beach towel. He saw quartered watermelons and big kitchen bowls of potato salad. He saw the shells of hard-boiled eggs and smelled milk just beginning to sour in the sun. Somebody blew on a silver whistle. A baby, plump and diaperless, toddled down the slope, chasing a pigeon which waddled complacently in front of him. A boy tipped oil in his hand and stroked and stroked it over the bare back of a pretty girl.

He was eager to know what they had for lunch, and apprehensive as well. He had only been to one other picnic in his life and that had been in the church basement on a rainy day. He could only recall the skin of a boiled chicken lying on the paper plate before him, with little hairs still springing from it, and rice pudding so slithery he could not swallow it for the life of him.

"We'll see the animals and then we'll find a shady tree and have lunch. There's turkey and meat loaf and celery and fudge brownies and oranges — and mint Life Savers so we can digest it all." She pointed ahead of her. "That's a good spot right there. Let's put the basket down so nobody else'll grab it."

She handed it to him and he scurried ahead, planting it under the tree as if he were claiming the ground for them and no other. He saw that there were ants swarming about, but he would have died rather than say anything. She had designated the place. Here it would be.

The aviary resounded to the staccato chatter of birds, lapwings and speckled pigeons, red-eyed doves, mousebirds; there were tiny hummingbirds in whimsical flight, spoonbills standing and sleeping, bearded vultures with black bristle beards, storks and saddlebills, African ducks, showing their rigid tails to females while pumping their necks full of air. Lost on Archer, behind his pink curtain, were the colors, the flamboyance of it all, the bitter greens, the sharp yellows, the dawn grays, until Eunice suddenly snatched the glasses from his nose. He almost breathed his satisfaction aloud. The world was normal again.

"Oh," he said as the rainbow flashed and glowed before him, "they're pretty."

He was familiar with one particularly loud and aggressive blue jay which lorded it over the sparrows in his garden, a noisy quarrelsome bird staring at him in disdain as he pulled weeds without hope from among his radishes. But never had he seen anything like these jewels hurtling through the air before him.

Eunice pursed her mouth and strange chirping noises issued forth. Archer saw, in wonder, a parakeet inching toward them on a bar, tipping an inquiring head, responding. A chill ran through him. It only confirmed what he already knew. She had special powers to charm. He looked around proudly to see if anyone had taken note of her feat. A small boy standing next to them lapped a dripping ice cream cone, and then blew a loud raspberry at the flock of birds nearby, scattering them. His stony glance at Archer said, don't worship false idols; I have powers of my own.

Archer hated the mockery. At that moment, tongued too far, the ball of ice cream toppled into the dust. Archer smiled, a little flush of pleasure staining his cheeks. So much for the heretic.

Eunice led him on, taking his sticky hand in her own. He marveled at the warm dryness of her touch. Didn't she perspire, ever?

The baboons hunkered on cement blocks and displayed their mimicry of humankind. They smiled mirthless smiles. They scratched endlessly. They showed their red bottoms, looking over their shoulders with round, insolent eyes. They picked their noses, cradled their young and, in plain view, they mated.

Terror and fascination struggled in Archer. He found a spot on the ground and riveted his attention there, certain that the thudding beat of his heart was clearly audible. What shocked him was the openness of it all. He thought of how he undressed in the bathroom with the pale yellow light of the bulb overhead barely lighting his mirror. Nakedness was a forbidden and surreptitious thing in his grandmother's house. She was never seen in a dressing gown, never glimpsed in the slightest disarray. He was expected to hurry through his bath, wash down there and be done with it. What would her displeasure have been had she known how he gazed and gazed at himself in the soapy water? He often felt his throat tighten with something close to tears that no one else saw him like this, that no other hand but his own caressed or stroked. The cat licked her kitten, he had seen it. There was other mothering in evidence everywhere. So, he reasoned, there's that love and then there's another kind. He knew very little of either.

"Do you know about love, Archer?"

There, she'd done it again, dipped into his mind.

"We have Health at school," he said cautiously. "Mrs. McKinley teaches it."

She led him to a bench and settled on it with a sigh. She rummaged in her straw bag, took out a compact, a soiled powder puff, dusted her nose.

"What did they tell you?" she asked casually.

"About our organs. About babies."

"That's all?"

Her arm had crept along the back of the bench. Now it touched him ever so slightly.

He felt this conversation could only result in failure. What could he wring out of Mrs. McKinley's lesson? He saw her standing in front of the class, sternly dealing with their wretched curiosity, her pale, slightly bulging eyes seeing straight into the very depth of their depravity.

Yes, her look had said, you're a bunch of dirty little boys and girls, but I'll set you right. It hurts to have babies. They arrive by means of gross appetite and the subjugation of females. This goes here. That goes in there. It's an utterly ridiculous plan. I had nothing to do with it. Ever.

Surely his father had kissed his mother. Dimly he remembered embraces cut short at his appearance. It wasn't much to go on. Had there been anything else to refute Mrs. McKinley's account? Nothing he could recall.

He saw again the charts snapping down as the teacher unfurled them. There was a drawing of a baby in a womb. He had stared at it, thinking of himself attached to his mother in that way. Always with her, always inside her, carried wherever she went, night and day. Yes, he had been pleased by that part of it.

"There isn't very much to it," he confessed to Eunice. "You can hear it all in one period."

"Oh, yeah?"

He nodded. He hoped he sounded poised and sure of himself. Would she laugh at him if she knew how baffled he was?

"Did you go to Health, too?" He made it a club in which they might have mutual membership.

"No, I never did," she said, "and I wish you hadn't either."

At once he had a presentiment that he would hear more, much more than Mrs. McKinley ever dreamed of.

She got up then and tucked his arm into hers. They strolled past the spider monkeys, the lion-tailed monkeys, the dusty leaf monkeys with their climbing games, their wrestling matches and their roughhouse play, the babies taking long, long leaps to cling securely to their mother's fur; past the purple-faced langurs, with the hair on their heads shaped into caps, hoods, bowls, fringes and other hairstyles. And all the while she talked about that mysterious business.

Away, caution. Away with Mrs. McKinley's charts. Now he followed Eunice through forests and glades where flowers sprang up in their footprints. He heard the thin, piping sound of Pan of Arcadia playing on a reed. He heard the hoofs of horses, bulls and goats, saw bronze masks brandished on poles, listened to the splash of water poured in libations, made out the faint rustle of the first sprig of corn. There were the sounds of a festival, lyre and lute, a glimpse of sacred prostitutes, and nymphs in a mossy clearing, punishing unresponsive lovers and stealing away young men for themselves. His own head rested on flesh that was smooth and milky and entwined in garlands. He felt like laughing at the clarity of it. It was so simple. So deep.

Generously, he forgave Mrs. McKinley her ignorance. No one had ever trusted her enough to impart these secrets to her. He wondered if he should write it all down anonymously and leave it on her desk.

The murmur of Eunice's voice died away.

"Well, thank you very much for telling me," Archer said. "It was interesting."

"It should wait a while," Eunice concluded. "Just open a drawer in your mind and drop it in. Then when you're ready, you'll be ready."

Oh, soon, he thought. But then he saw that his head barely touched her shoulder.

He ate the picnic lunch with enormous appetite.

Harvey left early in the morning, tiptoeing from the room so as not to awaken her. He made a little ritual of arranging the breakfast table for her, orange juice, sugared breakfast cereal, the newspaper carefully folded and propped up at the entertainment page, for Eunice was not political, had no interest in sports, did not care whether it rained or shone. Sometimes he added a blighted rose, sometimes a geranium leaf. On occasion there was a note. "Would you like to eat out tonight? — I think it's too hot for you to cook." "Don't bother to defrost the refrigerator — I've already done it." "You looked so pretty last night — I couldn't stop looking at you." There were always two or three twenty-dollar bills discreetly tucked into the paper napkin, demonstrating his tact. The business of keeping a woman worried Harvey. He would have felt better about expressing his feelings in some other, more tender way, but he sensed that Eunice preferred the money. He waited in vain to be thanked.

He often stopped to lean over her in the bed before leaving the house, breathing cautiously, marveling. She was so flowerlike, so perfectly pale, so delicately wrought. The very air about her held a dying and delicious memory of perfume and bath soap. He resolved to quarter her in castles, to feed her caramels, to rub her back and plait her hair. He would command song for her. He would halt traffic so she might pass. He would deck her in broaches and speak to her in verse. The mere sight of her made him feel blessedly singled out and favored. He put it to himself that he was the luckiest man on earth.

And what of the sleeper? Beneath her shadowed lids, feigning sleep, Eunice could barely wait to have him gone. Barely awake, her mind was stuffed with grievances. She would chide where he would love. Must the shower go on precisely as the clock struck seven, to hiss and steam like a nest of disturbed snakes? Must he lather and shave and hum, all at the same time, with spirits so hearty her very toes curled under the blankets? What narrowness drove him to the same habits morning after morning? Why make the coffee first every time? Why not throw caution to the winds and squeeze the orange juice first? Might not some glorious experience result from such a reversal? . . . Orange juice and *then* coffee? Think with glee of a bran muffin for a change, instead of a slice of toast, medium brown. Change your chair. Sit with your back to the wall clock so that time's tyranny relented. Watch the sparrows bicker instead of reading the stock market report. Even wander in the garden, cup in hand, letting the dew fall lightly upon you as it does on bush and bramble. Run naked, for God's sake, to snatch up the morning paper and thrill and astound the neighborhood. Any or all of these, but go forward, I pray you, with a difference.

Fat chance. He made love in the same ordered way. First the apologetic crawl that brought him under the blankets with her. Had he hit her with his knee? She must excuse his clumsiness. Was his elbow in her eye? He was chagrined if indeed it were. His cold feet he could do nothing about. Then came the kiss on the neck, the kiss on the lips, the kiss on the breast, the kiss between the legs, all in the same careful manner, as if he were afraid of disturbing or awakening her. He hadn't yet.

At last the front door closed behind him. Quietly. A malaise fell upon Eunice. A mood of little pouts and sulky glances. She sat up, throwing back the sheets, naked, flank and thigh, and she confronted the day. Should she buy a large picture hat of Milanese straw adorned with a rose of palest cream? Should she seek a yellow scarf and bind it around her head to make of herself a harem lady? Should she paint her nails green and her mouth burgundy and astonish the lads in the park? Should she go without panties and try on shoes and see the face of the salesman color with confusion and lust as she hiked up her skirt and waggled her foot this way and that?

What was she doing here anyway? She belonged back at the Marina with Hortense, with terrible Stella, with cool Nell. Yes, it would be nice there, all of them sitting under the shade of the Italian umbrella, spooning Italian ices, pulling their thin dresses away from their moist skin, and talking in low, skeptical voices about all manner of things.

She wandered instead around the house, dust rag trailing from her hand like a limp ribbon, flicking idly at the furniture as she passed. What sense did it make to polish furniture of such hideousness, so dark and cumbersome, all yellow varnish and thick legs? Better to burn it in a consuming fire, replace it with a sand-colored Japanese mat and one fragile tulip in a glass vial. Flick, flick, and so much for that.

Well, then, nature. And so into the garden, to move peckishly among the few gaudy nasturtiums and the bowed hibiscus. Near the fence, knees cracking to bend and pick a tiny pansy of perfect blue, she heard a sigh. She stood tiptoe to peer over the garden fence, and there on the other side stood the young widow who lived in the house next door, wan and lonely. She was hanging the wash — a white nightgown, a white slip, a single white towel. She spent half an hour in desultory conversation with her and heard a lament that clearly echoed her own. The days were so long, so long. As she leaned against the fence and talked to the other woman, as the breeze carried their mournful conversation, they became sisters in ennui, kindred spirits.

"I'm going to paint the fence this afternoon. I hope the smell won't bother you."

Paint the fence, paint the Sistine Chapel, it's all the same to me, Eunice thought. "No," she said, "I'll be indoors. I think I'll bake a cake, a lemon surprise cake. The surprise will be if it turns out."

"Do you use a mix?"

"Betty Crocker."

"Save me a piece. I never bake for just myself."

"I will," she said tenderly, for now she felt sad and sorry for the widow who must eat cupcakes because she was alone.

"Goodby then," she called on her way back to the house, and "Goodby" she heard in return as she closed the door.

She had meant to stay only a week or so — Hortense was cranky, had told her to get out of her hair for a few days. Archer was to have come over for company, but his grandmother fell and broke her wrist, so he was captive in another house just as she was captive in this one. Sometimes they talked on the phone, comparing television shows, telling jokes. Sometimes she was met with an awkward silence at the other end of the line; then she knew he was not alone and did not want to explain her call.

Finally it drove her to serious housework. She found silver in a china cabinet, a Victorian teapot, an ornate platter, a candy dish with a fretted rim, and she piled them on a table. She imagined them coming as wedding gifts, the pot from Uncle George, who expected to be invited to Sunday dinner, the platter from distant cousins, who hoped to be asked to a leg of lamb, the dish because someone in the family had two of them. They were all tarnished now and set aside, along with the family ties that no longer bound.

She thought about polishing them. She changed her mind. They would only darken again. Why bother? She found a bucket and liquid wax and waltzed across the kitchen floor, whistling "Night and Day" through her teeth, swirling a mop over the dirt she had not swept up. She arranged the tin cans in the cupboard so that all the labels presented themselves in orderly rows, cat food, string beans, pineapple and peaches. She bathed the cat, who retaliated by scratching her. She turned the hose on the windows and swabbed them down with wadded paper towels, but it made her back ache so she left the inside for another time.

The closets intrigued her. She rummaged through the one in the spare bedroom, shoving aside old raincoats and abandoned jackets and umbrellas with broken handles and torn webbing. It was then she found the cardboard carton.

She lifted it down and sat on the floor, looking intently at pictures of people she did not know. There were pictures of Harvey as well, young and homely, staring stolidly at the camera, teddy bear, bat and ball, bicycle handles, pony's reins held stiffly in his hands; Harvey, older and sadder in an army uniform; sadder still in a blue serge suit with a white carnation, standing with his vivacious bride behind a mountainous wedding cake.

She even read his letters. They had been kept without much sentiment, bundled together carelessly and held by a thick rubber band.

Dear Helen,

We got to Paris yesterday but I didn't get to see much as I had a bad cold. I sent you a bottle of French perfume, which I can get at the PX at quite a good saving. Put some behind your ears and think of me. This sure is a beautiful city from what I've seen of it. I'm going to try to get to Notre Dame tomorrow and will send you a post card from there.

Best love,
Harvey

Dear Dad,

I guess I don't have to tell you about this place as you were here in the last war, but I thought you might like a view of Napoleon's Tomb. Thanks for sending me the baseball standings. I don't think the Giants have much of a chance this year. I've thought about what you said about my GI loan and I guess I will buy a house if we can find something Helen likes. I hope your shoulder isn't giving you too much trouble. Take care of it so we can get us some mountain trout fishing in when I get back.

Lots of love,
Harvey

Dear Mom,

I'm sorry my letter to you got lost, but the mail gets loused up all the time. I guess it's because it has to come from such a long way. I guess I did forget your birthday. I sure didn't mean to hurt your feelings and I'm sorry I have. I know you have a lot of worry about me being over here. I asked Dad to get you a new purse from me. He said you needed one. Maybe Helen can help you pick it out. Anyhow, many happy returns, even though late.

Love,
Harvey

Dear Helen,

It's a beautiful fall night here. The trees are just starting to lose their leaves. I took a walk along the Seine and you could see the moon in the water. It was beautiful. I thought about you and wished you were here with me to enjoy it all. Maybe if things go right we could come back here after we are married.

All my love,
Harvey

And then there was a journal, a cheap nickel notebook, the writing precise and minuscule:

"Sometimes I think about killing myself. I walked around in the rain all yesterday afternoon thinking about it. I don't know what there is to go back to there. I don't know what I'll be or what will happen to me. Not much, that's for sure. It's funny, I'm young, but I don't feel young. I feel a thousand years old, as if I know everything I'll ever know. The only surprise would be if I shot myself. I'm going to bring home a gun and put it away."

And the gun was there, in his bottom drawer, among the neatly folded T-shirts and boxer shorts. Eunice stared at it for some time, afraid to touch it.

This was Eunice's view of life: If you can still be surprised by events large or small you are all right. If something troubles you, hide it with two sweeps under the nearest rug and think determinedly of other things.

If the morning sun kisses your face it will be a good day, and an even better one if you find a safety pin and pick it up. Don't ever make decisions on Tuesday. Four-leaf clovers don't mean a thing, so it's folly to pick them and preserve them in lockets of gold. Far better if you pluck a hair from the head of someone you love for luck. Don't step on cracks in the sidewalk. Do make love in the moonlight whenever possible, with your pillow at the foot of the bed, even if it occasions some comment from your partner.

Always eat food from the sea in preference to food grown on land. The number three is very desirable. The number ten is to be avoided at all costs. You can see the outlines of your life in a teacup, but you are foolish if you accept it as gospel. Wash your hair out of doors; there are gamma rays that penetrate the brain and make you smart.

That was what she was doing when Harvey drove up in the new car. He hallooed to her from the rolled-down window and she lifted her dripping head, getting soap in her eyes which stung and burned.

"What?" she responded crossly. "What? . . . I can't see a damn thing!"

His voice was full of cheer and high spirits. "Come see what I bought for you."

She bound her dripping hair in a huge towel and swayed down the front path and there, spanking in the bright sunlight, was a white Buick with a shiny black top. He turned off the motor and dangled the keys in his hand, smiling widely.

"My God," she said.

"Power steering and power brakes," he chanted. "Factory air conditioning, AM-FM radio, white side walls, heater, and it's all yours, bought and paid for."

"My God," she said again. Now the soap ran down her back and a little chill followed in its wake. He leaped from the car and ran to grab her hand, pulling her into the street. Frantically she clutched at the towel. It fell away and her hair spilled around her shoulders in soapy, snaky ropes.

"Wait," she cried.

"No," he urged and pulled her along. Up went the hood so she could peer stupidly at the huge exposed motor. Up went the trunk so she could gawk into it. The doors swung back to reveal red leather upholstery which gave the whole interior a hellish gleam. Moreover, the key ring was a huge silver "E" and from it the keys dangled smartly.

He snapped the lights off and on. He pushed the radio buttons.

He showed her how smoothly the front seat slid back and forth and how, if one wished to ruminate under some lovely spreading tree, one could tilt the passenger seat back, making it a kind of cushioned bed. And then there was the smell. That ineffable, unreproduceable smell of animal hides and lamb's wool, of motor oil and something else she couldn't define. Together they cocked an ear at the good stiff creak of the doors and the solid satisfying thunk as they shut them.

"It's gorgeous," she said, "absolutely gorgeous. Oh, let's go get Archer and drive down Wilshire Boulevard and blow the horn and get the jump on everybody at the stoplights. Let's do *that!*"

"Well," he said, "I don't know. I took off work."

"Call in and say you're sick. Say your daddy died. One day won't matter. It's the first brand-new car I've ever had in my entire life."

"I would have bought a Rolls," he said expansively, "but they didn't have any in white."

She hugged him in a crushing, exuberant embrace. "I'm going to learn to change tires and sparkplugs and everything. I'm going to wash it every day with baby shampoo. Oh, please, clean out the garage. It *has* to be parked in the garage."

He murmured assurances that he would, on Sunday, right after breakfast; he would throw out all the old newspapers and the baby crib; he would hose it down. She made plans rapidly. She would bind her hair in a scarf and alert Archer that they were coming. They would spend the whole day, even till dark, riding around the city. She would drive past the Marina so everyone could see her. Hurry, hurry, she admonished him, so this most wonderful, most unexpected of days could begin.

She got Archer on the line and spoke so rapidly that for fully three minutes he thought he was talking to a madwoman.

"Who is this?" he kept inquiring plaintively as she babbled at him.

"Me, me, Eunice. It's white, Archer, it's pure white, like the driven snow. We're going all over town. Put on a nice shirt and comb your hair. I'll come by and beep for you."

"When are you coming," he asked slowly, "so I can be ready?"

"Listen for the horn, honey. I've got to jump into my clothes."

In fact, she took off her clothes and stood naked before Harvey, her pink nipples pointing at him.

"You gave me a present," she said, "and I'm going to give you one. Stay right there."

She dashed away from him into the kitchen, flung open the cupboard doors, scrabbling until she found what she was looking for. Back she raced, clutching in her hand a large jar of strawberry jam. Harvey stood rooted to the spot, a little alarmed.

"Take off your clothes," she commanded. "Take off everything."

Mesmerized by her sure and authoritative manner, he did as he was told.

"I'm going to put jam on your cock," she said happily. "I'm going to spread this delicious goop all over you and lick it off again. Have you ever done that?"

He had not. Such a thought had never occurred to him.

"It's lovely," she promised him. "Lovely for you and lovely for me."

She removed the bedspread. No point in having to wash it afterward.

"Now," she said, "lie on your back. Don't be nervous, Harvey. You're going to be thrilled out of your socks."

He lay like a blind man, his eyes closed, experiencing her by her touch and by her breathy, excited voice.

"Isn't it nice?" she called to him brightly. "Isn't it nice, Harvey?"

He felt himself lathered, felt cool and sticky. The scent of strawberries recalled the peanut butter and jelly sandwiches of his youth. They had been made by his mother. He went limp with shock at what he was doing, at what was being done to him.

"Never mind, you'll be up again in a second," she said, enclosing him with her open mouth, and then, "Oh, I don't know which tastes better, you or the jam."

Her little cries of pleasure made him feel as if he were an item ordered from a menu. Then his whole being exploded.

"Oh, Christ!" he shouted at the top of his voice.

He saw her red, smeared mouth; he felt her busy tongue. His hands pulled at her hair, clamped on her ears.

"I can't stand it," he said. "Eunice, I can't, I can't!"

Nor was she through with him then, although he lay winded and spent on the bed, wondering idly if the seeds had caught in her teeth. He almost laughed aloud at that. There were two kinds, those of the berries and those he had spilled into her mouth.

"Wait," she whispered. "I'll show you some other things." She danced around the bedroom. "I saw this trick once in a carnival," she told him. "You had to pay a dollar to get in. A boy I knew said he'd pay my way if I would do what she did afterwards. Look." He saw with amazement a disappearing act. A tube of cold cream slid between her legs and was seen no more.

"Go after it," she whispered, and when he did she bit him on the neck and called him names that he hadn't heard since the army.

"The boys in high school nicknamed me the vacuum cleaner," she said solemnly, "which wasn't nice, but I guess not many girls have muscles down there like me."

He agreed. Fervently he agreed.

"Well," she said, "the rest will have to wait."

He burrowed his face against her belly. "Oh, Eunice," he said at length, "I want to give you the world."

"Okay," she said, "but let's go for a ride now."

They roared down the street toward Archer's house with Eunice at the wheel. She drove at full tilt, narrowly missing a mangy brown dog and a fire hydrant as she slued around the corner. Harvey, belted in and nervous, kept a weak smile on his face. He was already burdened by the lie he had told, calling into the store to say in an apologetic voice that there was illness in his family. He had coughed a series of little nervous coughs. He had spoken in a low tone. The clerk, upon hanging up, had winked at another clerk, and then had hurried off to make a report to someone higher up.

But the knot of guilt was gone as he careened along by her side.

They were lovers riding the back of a white swan through the glassy waters of a looping stream. He heard the call of the meadowlark where there was none. He was a man bewitched.

"Hey," she shouted jubilantly as they approached Archer's house. "Hey, everybody, we're here!"

She saw the lace curtains part, making a little crack. She saw an old and sour face peer out at her. She stuck out her tongue. The curtains closed abruptly. Then Archer came down the steps, holding his hand aloft in a tentative wave.

"Jump in," she cried, "and away we go."

"Hello, Daddy."

"Hello, son."

"This is a nice car."

He clambered into the back seat, struggled with belts, secured himself, all the while staring around him.

"A nice car, a nice car," Eunice mocked feverishly, "is that all you can say?"

"It's a Buick," he added hurriedly, "with two hundred and five horsepower and a four-hundred-and-fifty-five-cubic-inch displacement. It gets twelve miles in city driving and sixteen to eighteen on the road, depending on your personal driving habits." He sat back nervously.

"Just watch my smoke" was her only reply as they burned rubber and tore off down the road.

It was a daylong odyssey, broken by lunch in a drive-in because Eunice could not be persuaded to dismount her steed and eat at a counter. She confided to the carhop that the car was hers and just acquired.

"He gave it to me," she said, jerking a finger at Harvey, who immediately turned brick red.

"That's neat," said the little girl with the tight rump and a freckled, saucy face. "I love white cars. That's three hamburgers, no dressing, three Cokes, three fries, right?"

"What kind of a car do you have?" Eunice was not ready to leave the subject.

"I ride on the back of my boyfriend's Honda. It's making me bowlegged, too."

Harvey looked to confirm it. Archer scrunched down in the seat and looked uncomfortable.

She made dire threats to them if they spilled anything on the leather. She made them tuck napkins under their chins and eat their entire lunch bent over their plates. But she was mellow and magnanimous as the sun turned red in the late afternoon, bounteous and generous, for she let Archer drive.

They were out in the deep valley on a quiet street when the great moment came.

"Climb over here and try it out," she said, turning to look at him in the back seat.

Harvey protested. "Eunice, I don't think . . . he's too small to see over the wheel . . ."

She was adamant. "He's going to drive this car," she said firmly. "Are your hands clean, Archer? I don't want to get the wheel sticky."

He wiped them on his cords. "Yes," he said.

She hauled him over then, grasping his shirt in one hand and his crotch in the other. Then he was positioned in that hot and embarrassing place between her thighs, crushed into her soft bosom, and with his eyes starting and his breath coming rapidly he took the wheel between his hands. Stretching to the utmost, his foot found the gas pedal; the car moved.

"Stay on your own side," she whispered into his ear. "That's right. Turn a little to the right, a little, not too much, and press the pedal. Uh huh, you've got it. This kid," she said, turning to Harvey, "is a natural-born driver. Don't run into the curb, Archer. There's plenty of road in the middle."

They went around the block three times before the cop spotted them and waved them to the curb. Harvey groaned. Archer foresaw years in prison and tears filled his eyes.

"I'll do the talking," Eunice said. "You guys just button up and let me handle it."

The officer took a long time coming around the car, drawing out a huge pad of citations as he approached.

"Good afternoon," he said. He had bright yellow hair and a virile and energetic air. "Out for a little ride?"

Eunice took a moment to set Archer aside. Then she smiled.

"He's underage," she said, "and it's against the law, I know that as well as the next person, but we just got this car this morning and I thought it would be something he'd remember all his life if he was the first to drive it. I think memories are important — and he'll never forget this one."

The officer smiled at Archer, who had been wondering if he could hold his breath until he died on the spot.

"How's it handle?" he asked.

Archer choked something in reply which sounded like "Fine."

"May I see your license?" This was directed at Eunice, who promptly emptied her purse in her lap. Among the hairpins and the cigarettes, the Tampons and two or three peanuts in their shells, she produced what he wanted and handed it over.

"And may I see the registration?"

Harvey hurriedly retrieved the slip from the glove compartment, cutting a finger on the hinge in the process.

"I'm sorry, officer. About the boy . . . it was just a block or two."

The policeman leaned on the car window. He looked at Archer. Archer looked away and blinked rapidly.

"How old are you, son?"

"Nine. I'm nine." Was it a crime? He was sure it was.

"I've got a boy just about your age."

Archer tried to nod, but his head was immovable on his neck, frozen there.

"He rides a bike."

"I usually walk where I'm going," Archer said numbly.

"Yes," the officer said. "Old shanks' mare isn't a bad way to get around. All right, folks," he continued, "enjoy the rest of the day. Here's your ticket. You can handle it through the Automobile Club or if you want to contest it you can appear in Municipal Court."

Eunice flared. "You have a heart of stone," she said coldly.

"Yes, ma'am." He touched his cap and walked away.

"I've been arrested," Archer said in a stunned voice.

"No," Eunice said, "I have. But never mind. Put it out of your head. Nothing's going to spoil our day if I have anything to say about it. Ready?" She looked at the two of them. "Okay. We're off again." And they roared away, scattering a flock of sparrows into wild flight.

Sunset found them on the beach beside a smoking fire, eating hot dogs that were charred on the outside and cold and raw within. A fat man ran down the beach grunting, his belly heaving over tight blue shorts. A blond, bronzed boy emerged from the sea in a rubber wet suit and swaggered by them, carrying a surfboard high over his head. Newspapers and sandwich wrappings blew over the sand.

They were left to themselves, weary now, sand fleas swirling around them, conversation contracted to small remarks. Each of them felt the melancholy of approaching dusk. A woman came to the edge of the embankment above and called out crossly to the jogging man:

"Fred. It's time to go. Fred?"

The man ran on, as if in flight from the sound of her nagging voice.

Eunice made a mess of the meal, dropping the food into the fire, pulling it out again with cries of pain as she scorched her fingers. Sand gritted in their teeth, a cool wind blew away what warmth remained, the day wound down.

Eunice poked the fire with a stick. Embers shattered and fell into fragments. She waited for the moon to show, hoping that under its clear white eye some of the earlier intoxication would return.

"Let's go wading," she proposed.

Harvey hauled out his pipe and said he would just smoke if she didn't mind; perhaps Archer would accompany her.

Archer had been tunneling in the sand, but now the fragile bridge broke and the holes filled swiftly with fine white drifts. He was getting bored, he was getting tired.

He followed her to the water's edge, saw the white flash of her skin as she peeled out of her stockings and hung them around her neck. He did not care to remove his own shoes and socks; he had a crooked big toe and she would see it.

"Come on," she said impatiently. "What are you waiting for?"

The water was dark, inhospitable; what might lurk in it? "I'll watch," he said.

"Do what you want. I don't care."

But as she moved into the waves he followed, first tucking his socks carefully into his shoes, leaving them lined up neatly on the sand.

He hated the icy sting of the water. He wished she would hold his hand. Instead she stood transfixed, staring at the horizon.

"China's out there," she said.

His calf muscles knotted, his foot cramped. He did not care about China. A lone bird winged out to sea. He wondered if it would finally sleep on the water, wings folded, tranquil until dawn.

"I knew a girl who drowned once," Eunice said. "Her name was Nancy Ellis Quinn. She sang soprano in the glee club."

"That's too bad." He didn't particularly want to hear stories of death and disaster just then. But it was strange and startling.

"She got pregnant in the back seat of a car. Her family was furious, so she went to the beauty parlor and got her hair done, and then she went to the river and jumped in. They asked me to give the speech at her funeral, because I was her best friend."

"What did you say?"

"I said she was a lovely person with a lovely voice, and I said if they didn't want things like this happening every day of the year they'd better get hold of Marvin Bicker and scare the shit out of him, since he was always trying to get girls in the back seat of his car. The next day his father drove him to the post office where they had a marine recruiting office and made him join. He wrote me a nasty post card from Guam." She smiled brightly at Archer. "I fixed him," she said.

Archer looked up at her thoughtfully. Eunice as avenger was a stranger to him. "I have a pain in my foot," he said, backing away. "I think I'll go up on the dry sand and stamp on it."

She followed him and watched as he hopped up and down, trying to ease the cramp, arms windmilling to maintain his balance.

"Oh, sit down. I'll fix it." She grabbed his foot in her hand, spilling him backward onto the ground, and before he could protest she was leaning over him, loose breasts under the blouse swinging, alternately blowing her warm breath on his chilled foot and massaging the taut smooth skin over his thin calf.

"I'm fine," he said, red with embarrassment. "It's fine now, it's okay."

She hung on. "You've got awfully big feet for your age."

He tried to draw away, offended. He could say something about those great mounds hanging from her chest; he was simply too polite to do so.

"It embarrasses you to be touched, doesn't it?"

Now she was more outrageous than ever.

"No," he said. He wished a huge wave would come and carry her out to sea, that she would drown like Nancy Ellis Quinn before his eyes..

"Yes, it does, and the sooner you get over it the better. If you crawl in your shell like a snail how is anyone ever going to know that you have tender feelings? How, unless you stretch out your hand and say, 'I'm Archer'? Do you want to be left at the post, while everyone else in the world goes prancing around, hugging and kissing each other? How will you ever get a wife so full of you that she lets the pot roast burn and the book fall out of her lap unread, just for the thinking about you? Throw out your arms, Archer, and the more who fall into them, the better. If you close them, you just hug yourself."

"I don't care," he said defiantly.

"But I do. Now give me a kiss. Here on the cheek — and I'll tell you if you'll pass muster or not."

She offered him her face. She smelled of brine and sweat and hot dogs. He pecked.

"Thrilling," she said. "Now let's go home."

He maintained a moody silence in the back seat until they drew up in front of his grandmother's house. He had things to think about and was prepared to leave them without a word, but his father gave him a look which clearly warned him that he was neglecting his manners.

"Did you have a good time, son?"

His mouth still burned from the kiss. How could that be called a good time?

"Yes," he said.

Eunice turned and grinned at him. "Want to give us another kiss?"

"I have to go now; I have to go to the bathroom."

"All right," Harvey said, opening the door for him. "Off with you."

He ran up the path, as if hurling himself into the house.

That night Harvey lay stiffly on his side, listening to the rumble of the pipes which followed each flushing of the toilet. Eunice returned to bed and lay beside him in silence. She heaved herself over on her stomach, twisted on her back again. The sheets rustled as she tossed and turned and flailed. At last she sat up abruptly and cried out accusingly at him: "Why did you want to kill yourself, Harvey? Why?"

He did not ask her how she knew. It didn't seem important. Perhaps that desire was always on his face for all to read.

"I've forgotten now," he said. "Since you came."

"I tried once," she told him. He took her hand and held it. She sank back on her pillow and they lay in the dark together.

During the course of the next few weeks Harvey presented Eunice with a red fox jacket lined in white satin, three thin gold bracelets, a ruby ring. She found herself in a state of constant excitement, running from the closet to her jewelry case half a dozen times a morning, draping herself in the coat before a mirror, adoring the fuzzy, tartish look it gave her. The clink of the bracelets sliding up and down her arm became her favorite sound; more than once she roused herself from sleep at night to hold the ring under the lamp and study it, like a drop of blood pricked from a finger.

She went to any length to please him. She chopped onions for fried liver, though she detested it, sewed buttons on his shirt sleeves, washed his back in the tub, made popovers. They wandered through the department stores at night, hand in hand, and picked out a new lamp with a pleated paper shade and a hunting scene encircling the base. They bought a reclining chair in leather, testing it first, she on his lap, giggling as they tipped this way and then that. They cleaned leaves from the rain spout, he on a ladder, she with her arms around his legs, propping him up to keep him safe.

She thought she felt the first stirrings of love. Not love, really, but pleasure at the sight of him, reading, smoking, balancing his checkbook with his tongue lodged in his cheek. She wanted it to be love, she willed it to be. It was reassuring to turn down the bed at night, to darken the house, to lie close, back to front. Breakfast at eight, dinner at six, bed at ten seemed like little barricades erected to keep her from wandering off. She'd been a vagabond long enough. Stay a while, she told herself. It's not the most exciting time in the world, but you've been off the wall too long.

So they played Monopoly under the lamp light and walked arm in arm in the rain. She cut his toenails and trimmed his hair where it grew ragged around his collar. They installed squares of kitchen linoleum on their knees. They canned a lug of peaches, Harvey fishing the bottles out of the scalding water, she peeling and stoning the fruit. They painted a bureau and stenciled it with field flowers. They pasted stamps in an album he had kept since boyhood and she marveled at stamps from Mozambique and Morocco and New Zealand. They had grown parsley in a window box. They invented names for each other which embarrassed him and made her laugh. He removed a sliver from her wrist. He fixed her watch. She bought him a terry-cloth bathrobe and pipe cleaners.

The visitor arrived just before ten in the morning. She always peered through the curtains when the doorbell rang. The papers were full of horror stories, housewives raped and murdered; only this morning, sucking in her breath and shaking her head in disbelief, she had read of a woman who had opened her door to an innocent blond child of fifteen with long ironed hair down her back who had proceeded to cut her and stab her in the very doorway of her home with a thin carving knife. She kept an ice pick handy on the drain board — though she knew very well she would have been unable to use it on anything but an ice cube.

But her curiosity overcame her and she opened the door to him. His hair was thin and lay in wide, parted strands, as if the comb he used had broken teeth. There was a light rain of dandruff spotting his lapels and a piece of white tape holding the earpiece of his glasses. A careless man, in a hurry.

"My name is Galloway," he said to her. "Charles Galloway. My credentials."

And he pulled a slick black wallet from his pocket and flipped it open.

Which transgression was this? She thought of parking tickets torn into bits and scattered into the wind, library books unreturned, cherries sampled from fruit stands, and then panic overtook her.

Many months before she had been in a department store, killing time. She had seen a red and white scarf, striped like a barber's pole, and had carried it out into the street to see if she liked it in the sunlight. At that moment Hortense had come by, blowing the horn at her, startling her, hurrying her. She had climbed into the car still clutching it. My God, it was just a dollar scarf; she wasn't a kleptomaniac, it was merely her inertia, her damnable vague, lazy way that made her drift off with it instead of returning it. She had never worn it, not once.

She paused long enough to concentrate on what Mr. Galloway was saying. He had removed his hat, was patting his forehead with a large and rather dirty handkerchief, was saying something about making an example of Mr. Medford in order to deter others, and suddenly she saw the shape of it all.

She grabbed for the doorjamb then and heard her own voice,

high and babbling, one word tripping over another. They were just foxtails, she told him, not even good skins; the ring was just a tiny little stone, just a chip, hardly visible; the bracelets turned her arm green. He could have them back this very moment, oh, please, take them back.

Fate had found her, had dogged her, come around corners, tracking her, searched her out even in this miserable little cul-de-sac with its yellow sign which plainly read "Dead End." And Harvey, poor wheyfaced Harvey, who only meant to be kind. Well, she wasn't surprised. Everything in her life turned out this way. Dresses bought on sale unraveled at the seams, prizes in a Cracker Jack box were always tacky and made in Hong Kong, her snapshots faded, her hopes died. Harvey would go to jail and sit in the prison library and think despairingly of his lost life. She would write him post cards and come on visiting days with apples and they would touch fingers and cry.

Why, she thought desperately, hadn't she told him she would be content with a cuticle scissors, a hair ribbon, a shower cap! Spring would come with dandelions, summer with dry grass, fall with burning leaves, and she would be alone.

It's a test of character, she thought, to see what I'm made of. She resolved to be steadfast. She would not recriminate or scold, and if she wept it would be in the clothes closet with her face buried in his coat, unheard.

In the kitchen, with a lamp chop cold and greasy on the plate before him, he said only this: "Never mind, Eunice, it was worth it."

11

"IF YOU THINK it's outrageous, kindly do not say so."

Her grandfather stood before the full-length cheval glass in his
bedroom, looking every inch the Edwardian dandy. Nell came to
stand behind him, thinking that she looked rather handsome
herself in her unaccustomed finery, flowered French silk dress,
large picture hat, good pearls. She thought they might be taken
for a pair out of a Henry James novel, living in some elegant
watering spot, Bad Godesberg, perhaps, mistaken for royalty by
Europeans and whispered about over teacups. Who is that distin-
guished-looking gentleman and that ravishing creature with him?
Is it a liaison of disparate years? Is it sinister? Is it sanctioned?

"I think," Nell said, "that it's remarkable you're up to it."

She came around in front of him and gave his tie a firm tug.
He batted her away impatiently.

"Don't fuss with me. I'm not the center of attention. It doesn't
matter how I look."

"As I'm your only relative present," she remarked, "I would
like to have a sense of family pride. Therefore, pull up your socks;
they're slumping over your shoes."

She seated herself on the edge of his large, lumpy, dark bed.
She had spent so many hours in this room, in tears and laughter,
pique and rage. She felt it ought to be sealed off like a tomb,
housing all the emotions of her childhood. But the old intimacy
was slipping away. Today would end it. Well, her behavior would

be exemplary. She was no longer of an age when she could thrust out her lower lip, allow her eyes to brim with tears, demand that she come first in all things. She rather wished that were not so. In the old days she would have stared at him defiantly, announcing in sulky tones: "I don't want you to." And moreover she might very well have had her way. Well, hey and ho for those days — they were no more.

She told him what a dashing figure he cut and wasn't it lucky that everything in the garden had come out in a rash of bloom. She wandered to the window to confirm it. The summer roses had a velvety look, and one or two bushes, unwilling to be merely pretty, were fiery red. The lilies were tubes of ivory, folded over themselves like fine, ancient parchment, the hedge a silver gray. She saw with a pang that he had left a book under a tree, its pages ruffling in the breeze. It might have slipped from his lap as he dozed there, aging and disorderly and familiar to her. She saw that he had removed the old split cane chair. Had he thought it shoddy or did it recall his more sedentary days, when he sat in the shade and peeled figs and sought no company but his own? Now three gentlemen tuned their violins under the tree looped with ribbons, and there was a punch bowl centered on a white cloth, bobbing with summer fruit. There were a dozen gilt chairs standing on the lawn and a maid in a white apron and a cap and nurse's shoes to spare her feet.

Matters were slow and stately below. Two waiters, one young with a scampery walk, one old and shuffling, brought out silver trays laden with sandwiches, cucumbers cold and green on rounds of bread, shrimp curled pinkly, watercress and cream cheese. She saw the boy take a shrimp and cover his theft with parsley. She saw the wine bottles frosting in the huge tubs of ice and the cake, a virginal white and doubtless poisonous if it stood much longer in the sun. She scanned the sky and frowned at the ashen look of some clouds beginning to build up over the trees, but all in all it was festive, gleaming, a credit to everyone.

"What kind of present did you get me?" her grandfather demanded. He was finished with his dressing now and sat in a straight chair, as if he feared disarranging his finery. He smoked his pipe, puffs coming out as if his lungs were bellows.

"Something very expensive. Something you'll love."

"What? So far it's been cut glass ashtrays and salad tossers."

"Balzac. *La Comédie humaine* in blue leather, gorgeously tooled. I can hardly bear to give it up. I intend to borrow it back."

"Very nice. Can you afford it?"

"Not really. Still, you don't get married every day."

He held his pipe in his hand and looked at her in some wonder. "In a way, this vindicates my whole life ... mind and body still good for something."

"Yes," she said, "you're a ripe old cheese, there's no mistake about that."

"What time is it? Do we have time to talk before they all get here?"

"Yes, plenty of time."

He beckoned her. "Draw a chair up close. Sit beside me."

She complied. He brushed ash carefully from his coat. It fell on his trousers and stayed there.

"I'm giving you this house," he said. "And it's furnishings and the services of Mrs. Keitel — if you can stand her."

Nell pulled off her hat. She did not know whether she felt burdened or grateful, consoled or abandoned.

"Aren't you going to live here?" The house without him was inconceivable.

"We've decided on Frances' house — there are no stairs to make me wheeze. There's also her place in Provence — I may just get a beret and settle down there." The very thought seemed to infuse him with energy. "And drink wine and bathe in the blue Mediterranean. Is that goatish enough for you?"

"Yes, indeed. Randy as hell." She felt as if he had raced past her, hurtled a garden wall and disappeared.

"Hmm." He peered at her. "I know that look of yours. You're not pleased."

"Don't be silly."

"No, I see something's not right with you."

"Well," she said wryly, "it's just that I begin to see myself as a kind of Mrs. Havisham, shut up in a great house with cobwebs hanging from the furniture. Hanging on me as well."

She remembered the time when he had gone east to bury his brother. He had not wanted to take her on such an occasion, and she had stood in the depot watching the train pull away, lighted window after lighted window, gathering speed and rushing by her until she was alone in the dark.

His face grew stern. He wagged a long finger. "Nell, I won't have it."

"What won't you have?"

"You musn't cling to me. You may *not* cling to me."

"You're right, you're right, you're right," she said.

He went on, scolding her. "I don't believe in self-sacrifice. It's unhealthy, it's morbid. Now, look here. You'll have this house. You'll have some money from me if I don't spend it all, which, incidentally, I very well may. You're young and when you're not sullen, you're beautiful. You may wish to marry or you may not, but in either event, I want to see you behave with style."

"Go get married, why don't you, and leave me in peace."

"That's exactly the way I wish to leave you, my darling. In peace."

A murmur of voices rose from below. Nell craned out the window, glad of the interruption. "They're here," she said, "and some lady's slip is showing."

The violins swept into a waltz. The birds sang in response. She rested her head on her chin and gazed down. "Dr. MacFarland's all spiffed up in a green suit," she said, and she thought: Why has everybody gotten so old? So old.

He came and stood beside her and he spoke in a softened tone. "There's Frances."

A gray-haired woman in floating blue lace waved and called. "Hello, you two. It's time to come down. It's time, William."

They moved away from the window together. He did nothing ceremonious, he gave her no special embrace. He did not even touch her. But he did look at her under his heavy, winged eyebrows, directly, humorously.

"Well, granddaughter, will you give me away?"

"Yes," she said, and added to herself, if I must.

The ladies sat under the ilex tree, their heels digging into the grass. The afternoon sun was high and merciless, the cake had been too rich, but still it was a party and in their diminishing ranks there were so few occasions for celebration. So they drank the wine and looked across the garden at their husbands, those whose husbands were still alive, and wished the music would go on until dark. The bride's bouquet had been handed with a flourish to the oldest among them and she sat holding it carefully, while the white petals trembled and fell in her lap.

In the drawing room a few brave souls moved cautiously, heads inclined to catch the beat of the music, holding each other fearfully.

Dr. MacFarland was a dreadful dancer, but he loved to dance and would not turn Nell loose. He said the marriage of his old friend had so shaken him that he must without delay take his mind off it; he didn't know if he was embarrassed by this late-in-life mating, or jealous or abashed. Unnerved he was.

And so he grasped Nell by the waist and refused to let her go, pulling her tight against his tweed suit, swooping, darting and stomping with her in a lumpy, stiff-gaited waltz.

"Loosen up," he told her. "Give yourself to the music. *One*, two, three — *one*, two, three . . .

"Well," he said, "so he's off to a new life. It makes me wonder about mine. There's not much to it these days. My patients, of course, some of whom I've been treating for fifty years; that hasn't changed. And a few friends, those who have managed to survive; not many, one or two. We play bridge, quarrel over the cards, and afterward it's stale pound cake, weak tea and bed. If it weren't for Horace Walpole and Sir Walter Scott I'd be in serious trouble. I'm seeing a psychiatrist, you know," he said abruptly.

"I didn't. Whatever for?"

"Depression. Sleeplessness. Loneliness. I've come to a time in life where I'm left by myself, and I'm bad company for myself. It's costing me a fortune to be told in addition that I'm no good at relating to people, that I'm arrogant and judgmental. I knew all that before I went. Now I'm going to dip you back, so hang on."

Nell did, afraid that they would collide with the furniture. He was being rash the way he was tossing her about.

"Yes, it's quite terrifying to find yourself old and alone, and discover you have a bad character to boot. We have terrible arguments, that mind man and me. I say it's because my wife up and died on me and he says, 'No, it's because you're rigid and repressed and narrowminded' . . . Am I?"

"Yes."

"Your grandfather and I have been friends for half a century. How do you explain that if I have no charm?"

"He has."

"So do you and it hasn't gotten you anywhere."

"Thank you very much. And look out — you're headed into that table."

He jarred her backbone as he swerved clumsily to avoid it.

"Look here," he said, "a while back you came to me in trouble. You were given a reprieve. What are you going to do with the life you got back?"

"Live it."

"How? I'm willing to listen, it's not too late to learn. You see, I have an open mind after all. I can take a new tack. Melancholy is a nasty business. Almost all my friends are dead — or have I said that already?"

"Not me. I'm alive and devoted to you."

"I'm too truculent for you. And you're too giddy for me."

"Giddy? I'm a serious young woman."

"Not so young. You're in your thirties. I know *where* in your thirties, too."

They revolved in the center of the room, spinning like a top, out of step with the music. People retreated to give them more room. He clutched her even closer and she pushed at his chest.

"Don't hold me so tight. Your jacket's prickly."

"Sorry." He moved back a bit. They danced on.

"I had an affair once," he announced with a slightly braggadocio air. "With my music teacher. It went badly."

"Really? Why?"

"I was young and fractious. She didn't entirely please me so I set about molding her. She didn't want to be molded."

"I should think not."

"How do you conduct those matters these days?"

"Hit or miss, the same as you did."

He was sweating alarmingly.

"Douglas," she said, "sit down and loosen your collar. You've overdone. I'll get you a glass of champagne."

She steered him to a chair, saw him settled into it, helped him with his knotted tie and then threaded her way through the guests, pausing to smile, to speak, to acknowledge good wishes. A woman in a violet dress with violets pinned to her shoulder in a damp clump seized her hand.

"William is remarkable. I think he's so brave to marry at his age."

"You're next, Mrs. Starling."

The woman flushed with pleasure and laughed nervously. "I don't know. Oh, I don't think so. Oh, I think not."

She saw her grandfather in the next room, sipping a drink, smiling, speaking to his friends; he caught her eye and waved to her over their heads.

She stopped a waitress and took two glasses from the tray. When she returned to him, Douglas was slumped in the chair, mopping his brow.

"That's warm work," he said, and he patted the seat beside him. She sat there, handing him the brimming glass.

"Have I depressed you with my problems? I think I depress everyone these days, except my cleaning woman, and she's deaf as a bone. Perhaps that's why she's exempted."

"I'm worried about you," she told him, casually placing her fingers on his wrist to feel his pulse.

"Getting old is very nasty. I tell you that so you'll make the best of being young. Are you making the best of it?"

"Well, I'm having a very nice time currently with a very nice man. We sleep together, which keeps me from being tense and unruly, and for the most part we don't get on each other's nerves. I don't know him very well. I'm not sure I need to or even want to. I'm a stubborn woman. I like having my own way. I don't want to be compelled to justify or explain anything I do. Most men won't put up with that. They needn't. I won't put up with anything less than that. So there we are."

"Women are fierce creatures," he said. "Far stronger than my own poor sex. I go to the old peoples' home, you know, to look after them. There are the ladies, bright as dollars, finger painting and making pots, eating with good appetite, and there are the men, staring into the air and plucking at the bed sheets." He drained his glass, gulping steadily.

"Whoa," she cautioned. "That's vintage. What's your hurry?"

"It goes down like water. No bite to it at all." He sighed deeply. "Piety," he said. "I'm left to my piety and constipation."

"They may be one and the same thing," she told him with a smile.

He ignored her. "I wish your old cock of a grandfather had stayed behind with me, that's what I wish. He'll never hold up, having to shine every minute, the way you must with a woman. You have to keep up to the mark with them, perform, they judge you very stringently. He'd have done better to stick with me. We were going to build a dovecote this summer; I've already bought the lumber and the wire. We were reading *Martin Chuzzlewit* aloud — I read aloud very well. It was my habit to come by here after the clinic and have a glass of something with him and sit out in that garden and read the better part of a chapter a day. And what of the fishing? Every Sunday, off the pier, with bait in the bucket and a bottle. I doubt if that woman will be able to put up with his chess game. I couldn't. But he was a good talker, your grandfather. He knew everything about Voltaire and quite a lot about that fellow Proust. Too effete for me. Still, you don't find a well-read man under every rock."

"Why do you use the past tense?" Nell asked. "He's still alive."

"Not to me." The old doctor scowled and then held out his glass to her. "Pour a bit of yours in there. I've got a terrible thirst from the dancing."

She obliged him.

"I'm weary of it all," he said tonelessly. "I don't notice things anymore. I have aches and pains. I have bad breath. I give people black looks. I sleep with the light on all night."

"So do I," she told him.

"But you're sure of the morning. I'm not." He closed his eyes momentarily. "You'll have to drive me home. This drink has befuddled me."

She shook him lightly. "Douglas?"

"Yes, yes . . . what is it?" He made an effort to sit upright.

"I forbid you to be like this." Her voice was angry.

His huge head fell back against the cushion. "Do you indeed? Then I'll stay with that Viennese head meddler and struggle on." He seemed too weary to pursue it further. "They're playing a nice waltz. But I won't dance anymore."

Lucidity, she decided, comes afterward; after things are over and done with and one's time is spent asking how and why things happened in just that particular way. In the same way, she concluded that "lovers" was a foolish and inadequate designation for two people sharing bed, board and one bathroom. One is not wildly in love at seven in the morning when a man grunts and wakes beside you, smelling brackish and musty, and shows you his furred buttocks as he takes over the bathroom at the very moment you wish to use it yourself. One is not passion's slave at the breakfast table when conversation is monosyllabic and mundane, having to do with bacon and eggs and the stuffed-up garbage disposal. Nor is one blind to the whole world as small quarrels erupt about money or laundry or one's taste in friends.

It was true, Nell conceded, that she had lived cheerfully enough with Jake. Cheer easily maintained, she added, because little or no pressure had been put upon him. She yielded in small things.

His cooking was better than hers. She admitted it and ate his Irish stew with as much gusto as he did. He *was* neater, although she came to detest the way he folded a damp bath towel in exactly three quarters and let it hang sodden on the towel bar. He took his own sweet time at everything, love, talk, meals. She sometimes had the urge to prod him to the end of a sentence or the end of foreplay or the end of a crust of bread, but he was not to be moved from his deliberate pace.

He was not a rancorous man. He *was* a lazy one. She thought him prodigal with his time. An hour with the morning paper seemed excessive to her. A hour in the shower maddening. His day could begin at one o'clock as well as at eight in the morning. Hers began at six, confronted by a dozen decisions, a dozen appointments, a dozen put off to be met at the very first free moment. His sense of laissez-faire insulted her view that things must not be left alone just to happen, but she prudently kept impatience to herself. It seemed to her imbecilic to try to alter a grown man; futile as well.

She was kept from smugness by his view of her, which he expounded on with candor. He found her too tart, verging dangerously on the sour. Except in bed, where she was erotically complicated, her head ruled her heart. He found her authoritative about altogether too many things. He could damn well work the *New York Times* crossword puzzle as well as she. She often commanded where a request would have done the job. He would have preferred her to be moody instead of icy when displeased. All irritating but tolerable because he also found her witty and bawdy, generous and dashing, rarely, if ever, a bore.

They were rather like a couple driving down a country road, in a pastoral setting, with a cow or two, a barn, a stream, nothing to impede or halt or endanger them. A pleasant, drowsy journey, with the possibility that one or the other might nod off.

And yet he surprised her. It came in the area of surprises — they were in bed. He sat up, stuffed a large, black cigar in his mouth, the first of the day, removed it to bite off the end, patted her flank and made a pronouncement.

"I had to get up to pee in the night three times last week," he said, "and that tells me something. What does it tell you?"

"You have prostate trouble," she told him.

"It tells me," he went on, "that I'm getting older. You remember my story about my Uncle Tyler?"

"A remarkable man," she muttered into her pillow. "What about him?"

"He died at forty-eight. Tomorrow is my forty-eighth birthday." He struck a match and puffed the foul smoke into the room.

"We'll have a cake," she said. "I'll buy you a handsome tie."

He waved her into silence. "I've come to a conclusion, and since it affects you I'm going to tell you what it is. I expect, at the outset, to come up against your tight-ass view of things, but I'll ask you for once to hold off and listen carefully to what I have to say."

"I only wish to remind you that it's Monday morning and I can't lie around in bed. But I'm listening."

"What's life about?" he asked her, shifting his bulk. "Don't answer, I'm going to tell you." He puffed again. The air was filthy now.

"It's about getting and spending and laying waste our powers. It's about heart attacks and breakdowns and larceny of every description. It's about sharp practice, political villainy, sexual dysfunction. In the main it's shit, right?"

"Not in my view," she said, "but go on."

"I would say the major color is gloom. I would say we're walking a tightrope over a sea of excrescence. I would say if chicanery doesn't get us, the mortician will. The young are bootless, the old imperiled, the poor ever with us. The streets stink, the air reeks and I have a bad morning cough. Therefore," he said, "I have taken steps which my Uncle Tyler took before me, but far too late to save his hide. I am about to chuck it — and I invite you to come along."

She glanced at her watch and threw back the covers. "Keep talking while I brush my teeth. I'll leave the door open."

He sat on the edge of the bed, raising his voice over the running water.

"I've bought an island in Juan De Fuca Strait. It's got a house, a chicken run, a dock, an Airedale pup, four apricot trees and sanity. There's one other family living there. They're of Portuguese descent, Catholic, and have five lively kids. The mail boat comes over from Seattle twice a month. The captain is a pretty good storyteller and a fine drinker. There are any number of things to do on that island. You can watch the birds, grow herbs, whittle a soft stick and turn your mind over while sitting on a rock in the ocean. The fog is bad, the fishing is good. There's enough room so that if one of us gets a little ornery he can hike a mile down the beach and be out of the other's way. There's nothing to lose, everything to gain, and I'm putting this place up for sale tomorrow. In the main I love you, Nell, but with or without you I'm going to Juan De Fuca Strait."

She finished brushing and rinsed her mouth, carefully placing the glass on the sink. Then she came out and leaned in the doorway, looking at him.

"Well," she said, "in the main I love you, too, Jake, and I'm going to let you go."

He ground out his cigar and pulled at the end of his nose. "I mean it," he said. "I'm not fooling around here."

She came into the room and gathered up her clothes. He leaned back against the headboard and looked across the room at her with a lopsided grin.

"Just so long, Jake?" he asked her. "Just like that? You won't even think about it?"

"Afraid not."

"You think it'd wear out?"

"No. We'd probably get on very well indeed, flopping on the beach, sleeping in the sun, making mud pies." She smiled at him.

"Well, why the hell not? My Uncle Tyler was a happy man. And he never saw a soul except his Mexican lady, me, and the veterinarian. That man knew about living, I'm telling you. He had those misty blue hills in sight night and day. He took his bath in a river where he could watch the fish between his toes. He picked daisies in the meadow and put 'em on his dining room table in a soup can. He was an elegant man. A remote man. A smart man.

And he would have been an old man if he'd started sooner." He paused. "Nelly, hang up your shingle and let's go dig earthworms. Come with me."

"Mmm," she said, brushing her hair and pulling it severely into place.

"What'll happen to you," he said shortly, "is you'll stay on here and keep on handing out pills. You'll get older and that sharp edge you've got now will get honed like a razor blade. A lot of men will come and go and you won't give a damn either way. Be my girl. Let me get two tickets."

She was dressed now. She put her keys and cigarettes and note pad into her purse. "What you say may all be true," she told him, "but who's going to take out the garbage?"

She went into the kitchen. He climbed out of bed and loped after her in his bare feet, stood in the doorway watching her as she poured her coffee.

"What does that mean?"

"Just that. Who's going to take out the garbage if we all head for the nearest island? Who's going to change the bedpans and the light bulbs? Who's going to sell potatoes? Aspirin? Diaphragms? Who'll drive the bus? Who'll mop the floor? Who'll teach the multiplication table? Who'll dance Giselle? Who'll make jelly and penicillin?"

She sat down and cupped her hands around her coffee mug. He stood disheveled and disgruntled.

"Somebody elected you, did they?" He glowered.

"Have some coffee, Jake. You sound cranky."

"You think if you turn off the stove the whole goddamn world stops cooking? Christ, lady, you've got a real ego going there."

"We can make it a fight," she said quietly. "I'd rather not."

"No. I'm not looking for a fight either. I guess you are what you do — and there's no way I'm going to get around that." He stood a while regarding her, shaking his head and scratching his belly.

"Are you gonna miss me?" he asked.

"Oh, yes. Are you really going?"

"You'd better believe it."

"Principles are fine," she said ruefully, "but you can't fuck them on a rainy night, can you?"

"But you'll stand on 'em?"

"I guess so."

"Well," he said.

"Well," she echoed.

They were already cut adrift, already embarked on separate journeys.

"If it thins out," he told her, "I can always be reached. I'll have to take a boat and take a walk and take a ferry, but I can always be reached."

"Providing the tide is right." She smiled at him. "Goodby, Jake."

"Nelly."

He moved forward to kiss her, to persuade her, to beguile her, but she was out the back door before he could get across the room, and he had only one leg in his trousers when he heard the short, sharp coughs and then the roar of her souped-up Triumph as she pulled out of the carport, late for her rounds and already speeding though she was still backing up, tires squealing as she turned and negotiated the narrow alley and then raced for the highway and was gone. He stopped, then, all thought of chasing after her leaving him, and he got all tangled up in his feet, hopping about like a crazy person until he fell back on the bed again, one leg still in his pants, one out.

12

STELLA STUDIED the photograph in the newspaper and concluded that Pritchard's features resembled her own except for his eyes, round eyes like bits of chocolate, dark and sweet.

She was faintly elated to discover that he was still alive. He was her brother, after all, and while she hadn't seen him since 1951, she was pleased to note that his hair was not white, that the passing of time had left him looking still boyish and full-cheeked.

His recent notoriety, if one could call it that, had to do with his raising the largest pumpkin in California. He was pictured with his arms straining around the huge orb, a proud smile on his face, as if he had unlocked some mysterious secret of nature.

Stella reasoned that if he had time to spend in his garden, his tiny, tense, religious wife must be dead. No loss. Stella remembered her scattering mothballs in every corner of the house and praying at the dinner table until the meal was cold muck in front of them. She had been a deaconess in her church and a wet blanket at home. Further, his son, who was a canny corporation lawyer in San Francisco, with a house near the Presidio and a French cook in his kitchen, regarded his father as a rube and had cut off all communication with him except for sending a loudly checked jacket, too large and unsuitable, as a Christmas present and his discarded English overcoats from Burberrys on Father's Day.

Vaguely she wondered why she hadn't stayed in touch with

him herself. Of all her family she had always been fondest of Pritchard.

He had ridden her to school on the back of his bicycle with his strong legs pumping and the wind fresh and cool in their faces. He had saved the tinfoil in cigarette packages and had given her a large, heavy ball of it to weight papers on her desk. He had made her a swing from a piece of orange crate and a strong rope.

And so he had grown to mild young manhood, spending most of it tending the odorous mulch pile he cherished the way other boys of his acquaintance were beginning to cherish girls, feeding choice morsels of garbage, lettuce leaves and carrot tops into it until it was a dark, rotting syrup. He had a gulping, hearty laugh which rose above all other laughter when a joke was told. He carried old ladies' packages for them and refused the dime they pressed into his palm. He believed in a just and merciful God. He watered his neighbors' lawns should they be out of town. He rubbed his mother's back and shoulders should she complain of headache. He never quarreled.

Stella hoped he had money. She knew he was industrious. He had worked at the same neighborhood hardware store for years, sweeping the street in front of it, waiting on trade, arranging rakes and hoes, trowels and garden hoses into beautiful patterns on the walls. He had bought the business when the owner died, crying inconsolably at the man's funeral, catching everyone there by the lapels to tell them that his boss was a dear, dear fellow and the world would not soon see his like again.

He was not a man to indulge himself except for Burpee seed catalogues and flats of bedding plants. He treated himself to a cigar only twice a year, once on his birthday, again on Thomas Jefferson's birthday. He admired Jefferson greatly.

He had always been tentative with Stella. Stella as a young girl, locked away in her room, lying flat on her belly, her hair uncombed, her gaze fiery and intent on a book, caused him to tiptoe carefully past her door, unless she required him to fix a light cord or repair her headboard so it would not wobble.

Bright women blinded him with their brilliance. In consequence he had married a dim woman, dim in color, dimmer yet in perception. He had never had a happy day with her.

Over the years he had sent post cards with cryptic messages so that his sister might not feel alone in the world.

"Cabbages as big as melons this year." "I'm wearing dental plates now." "You wouldn't recognize me anymore, I'm afraid." "My roses are the talk of the street."

Only once had she answered. "I'm working my head off. If anyone dies, my number is OLdfield 10404."

Once, when the gas company had shut off the utilities, she had thought of calling on him for help; but something had intervened, she couldn't remember what, and they had lost touch.

Now she had something in mind that needed cold hard cash, and there was no blinking the fact that she had worn out every source on this side of town.

So it was that she thumbed the pages of the telephone book and found him, Pritchard Carver, on Broadway, in Glendale, California.

To show Pritchard she respected his hard-won position in life she washed her hair and took a bath. She borrowed carfare from Jake, and taking a cheese sandwich to eat on the bus and a pencil and a piece of paper, she crossed the city to what remained of the bosom of her family.

She had to walk two or three blocks from the bus stop and her brassiere strap broke on the way, forcing her to duck behind a hedge and tie a knot in it. She didn't intend to appear in front of her older brother jiggling like a tart.

A little girl stood on the front porch of the house and inquired nasally what she was doing.

"Get off," Stella said.

The little girl stared.

"Get off, I say."

The little girl thrust one finger up her nose. "This is my lawn. You get off."

Stella bared her teeth and the child fled.

Stella finished adjusting her underclothes and marched on,

staring at the house numbers with a nearsighted squint. She suddenly recognized an old dark green wicker chair of her mother's on the porch. Her mother had rocked in it every night, staring into the starry sky, thinking her own thoughts. They all left her alone, accommodating that darkness which overcame her from time to time. Stella decided she recouped something of her life, gazing into the heavens on those solitary evenings. Sitting in this green wicker chair, which now had a hole in it.

She approached the house, smelling the turned earth. The gate was blistered and in need of paint, but beyond every care had been expended. The garden ran amuck with peas and tomatoes, stalky corn, squash in yellow curves, huge phallic cucumbers of a pale green. There were two figures in among the orderly rows of growing things, a scarecrow and a man, hoeing. They resembled one another. The man had a red bandanna handkerchief knotted around his neck and suspenders holding up his earth-stained trousers.

"Pritchard," she said, "is that you?"

He turned, and shading his eyes he stared into the street. "Yes," he said. "Who is it?"

She passed through onto the garden path laid out in stepping stones.

"It's your sister Stella."

The hoe dropped from his hands.

"Stella?"

"Don't gawk. I'm remarkably unchanged from my youth, so there's no need to gawk."

"Oh, my," he said, wiping the dirt from his hands onto his pants. "Oh, my goodness."

She slouched toward him, thrusting out her hand.

"Well," she said, "I'm tired and I'd like to sit down."

He winced at the sight of her, the shapeless dress, the odd necklace of seeds and beads, the cracked leather purse. The gray of her hair was too painful to look at. He blinked shyly and took her hand.

"Well, what do you know," he said. "Little Stella."

"Big Stella. Thirsty Stella. Hot Stella. Do we have to stand here? Your neighbor's peering at us from under her window shade."

He ushered her into his front room, hand under her arm. It was close and hot and dark. There was a three-piece suite of golden oak furniture, a stiff little oval picture of her father and mother on the fireplace mantel and the famous pumpkin resting on the hearth. There were no books. There was no air. She sat down and waved him into the chair across from her.

"This is remarkable," he said slowly. "You won't believe this, but I had a dream about you last night. Yes, you came to me in a dream, wearing a beautiful hat and carrying some peonies in your hand. I never have much luck with peonies. Not enough shade. You came into the backyard and said, 'Pritchard, it's ending. Hurry up and do something with your life.'" He paused a moment, and he shook his head. "I had beans for supper. They don't agree with me so that might account for it. Stella, my goodness."

"It's not the second coming of Christ, Pritchard. It's just me."

He drank her in. "You still have dark good looks, Stella. You always had those dark good looks."

"I saw your picture in the paper, holding that thing you grew."

"The biggest in the county. The biggest in the state."

"Is that what you've been doing all these years? Growing big things?"

"It's my hobby. You could say it's my hobby."

"Jean's dead, I take it?"

"Yes. I have her planted next to Mother and Dad."

"Planted?"

He nodded.

"Well. So you're alone?"

Her brother had a look of utter content. "I'm out in the yard from dawn till dark," he said brightly.

"You haven't got any money buried out there, have you? I need some money." She wasted no time. "I'm glad to see you, of course, but I wouldn't have turned up here like a bad penny unless I had something in mind, would I?"

As always he expected nothing; he was entirely forgiving. "You always did go your own way."

"Well, I can't *pay* my own way, that's the problem, Pritchard. That's the problem with sister Stella. I've come to put the bite on you."

His face saddened. He pulled a burr from his shirt and shook his head. "I've got my social security, and I get twenty-five dollars a month from my son's wife, who's a very decent girl. There's nothing else." He was embarrassed by his impoverishment.

"You owned the hardware business," Stella insisted.

"The bookkeeper stole it from me, bit by bit. Mrs. Adams. Of course you never knew her. Embezzled it all away. Never suspected her. Kept a lovely coleus on her desk. Grew ivy in the ladies' room in a water glass. I was very surprised at her, I must say."

She leaned back and groaned. "Damn," she said. "I was two hours getting here." Then she had a thought. "Papa's watch, his gold watch. You have that, don't you?"

"Why, no, John got that when he graduated from law school."

Her frenzied gaze rolled around the room. "You must have something somewhere!"

He was crestfallen. "There's only the greenhouse. I bought it after Jean died. To make up for everything," he said defensively. "It's out in back. Would you like to see it?"

"All right," she said irritably. "Show me the goddamn thing."

The gentle hiss of steam filled the greenhouse, taking the curl and the starch out of her. He led her along the rows of miniature plants, curled, green, tender to the touch. His voice, when he spoke, seemed prayerfully lowered, as if they had come into a sacred grove.

"Everything does well in here. Isn't it fine? No wind disturbs them. No insects. They can't be bruised or harmed. I call it 'The Peaceable Kingdom.'"

"It's hot as hell in here," she replied. "My armpits are running."

She stalked up and down the rows and then out the door,

leaving it ajar. He followed her, running to catch up with her rapid stride.

"Are you in trouble, Stella?" he asked anxiously.

"Never out of it," she said, walking on.

"I'll make you some lemonade." Now that she had come he wanted to keep her, he was unwilling for her to go again.

"With gin?"

"I don't keep spirits."

"I have to catch the bus," she said shortly.

"We've hardly had a talk. Father and Mother, Selma and Orville, Mattie and Tom, the twins, Alice and Eugene, John and his wife and their three children . . . there's so much to catch up on."

Yes, she thought, we could sit knee to knee, but my history would shrivel your skin and yours would bore me to death.

She paused to give him a kiss on the cheek. He smelled of fertilizer.

"Keep America green, Pritchard," she said, submitted to his bony hug and then pulled free.

"Come again," he said. "I'm always home. I'll pick you some peas next time."

Stella thwarted was Stella rampant. She tried, on three different occasions, to reach Caleb by phone and was told at his office, his club and his home that he was not available to speak to her. She had engaged in a heated conversation with his houseboy, beginning with extravagant claims of extreme need: she was starving, she was being evicted, she was ill. The houseboy remained unmoved, and was then treated to a string of profanity so Irish and archaic he thought her mad. The lackey had hung up on her.

She had then composed a letter on her twenty-nine-cent pad in a bold scrawl, but she was dissatisfied with its tone, unable to strike just the right balance between imperiousness and reconciliation. In addition, she was certain it would go unread.

Thus it was that she sold the stove and the refrigerator out of the apartment, neither of which belonged to her, to a man she met in a bar, warning him that he must come late at night to take them away, no questions asked. The man was larcenous, mounted the backstairs after midnight with a seedy-looking companion, disconnected the appliances, paid her a measly forty dollars and went off into the dark, telling her that they were always in the market for transactions such as these.

Without further ado she gathered up her nightie, her toothbrush, her toothpaste, a fistful of pencils and a moldy rain slicker and stashed them in a large brown paper bag. She left a note for Jake propped on the kitchen table, saying she expected to return in style and that she would reimburse him handsomely for having made off with his property. She then stationed herself at the entrance to the Santa Monica Freeway, heading east, holding up a large cardboard sign which read: I AM ENTIRELY HARMLESS. KINDLY GIVE ME A RIDE TO YOUR FURTHEST DESTINATION.

She got no takers for the better part of two hours, sweltering and scowling as cars whizzed by her.

At last a diesel truck slowed, the driver squinted to read the sign and then stopped, throwing open the door to the cab.

"Okay," he said. "Hop in."

She clambered up with agility, deposited her greasy bag, the toothpaste having already squirted inside, and settled back with a sigh.

"Man is a wary beast," she said. "I've been standing on this on-ramp all morning. I'm Stella Carver."

"Joe Polanski. That's some sign you got there."

"The truth is not convincing or I would have been to Denver by now. How far are you going?"

"Salt Lake City."

"I'm agreeable to Salt Lake City. How far is it?"

"Seven hundred and forty miles. We ought to get to know each other pretty good."

She studied him. He was close to fifty, with a square, stubborn face, dark, bushy brows, intelligence in his eyes and the faintly pugnacious air of a man fending off the troubles of his life with brute strength.

"I'm going to tell you something at the outset so we won't have to deal with it later. I do sleep with men but not at random. I have a long, arduous journey in front of me and I'm going to need all my energies at the end of it. You may or may not have had that in mind, but I'd rather be clear at the beginning than have to tussle and pummel and knee you in the crotch at some rest area along the way. If that doesn't suit you, let me out at the next exit."

He gave her a sour look. "I've got all the women I can handle," he said. "One in L.A., one in Yonkers. Enough."

"You're not married?"

"Married in L.A., not married in Yonkers. Understand?"

"Certainly. Is it okay with you if I roll down the window? I'm boiling."

"Sure."

She did so and turned her face to the breeze.

Mr. Polanski was a man of discretion and rectitude. They rode in silence for almost an hour before he asked a question. "How come you didn't take a bus where you're going? Only the kids bum."

"I'm set on my course and I have no money. When I'm washed and combed I'm quite presentable. I have an engaging smile. I have a thumb. And, as you see, I'm riding down the road at this very moment." She was pleased with herself and smiled at him. "Determination's the thing, my friend, in every endeavor."

He was in accord with her. He liked women of substance, formidable women. He took a pack of cigarettes from his pocket, shook one into his mouth. "You tied up with somebody?"

"I'm involved. Neither tied up or down."

He struck a match under his nail and bent over the flame, keeping one eye on the rushing traffic. "How come he lets you tramp across the country? There're a lot of wild people roaming around, you know."

"He's not my custodian."

"Think you can handle yourself, huh?"

"Who but a fool would rely on anyone else?"

"You want to hear something?" he asked, turning in the seat and giving her a solemn look. "I told you I got two ladies I do business with? Each of those ladies has seen me blubbering in her lap and I ain't ashamed to say it. Last year I lost my job. I'm new with this outfit. A whole year I was out of work. First I thought, hell, I been working all my life, I got a workshop fixed up in my garage, I'll make a dog kennel or something like that. Two weeks later I was going crazy. Every day down to unemployment to see if they got anything. Every day reading the classified ads in the newspaper. Looking everywhere. Trying everything. Finally I took a mop and a pail and some of my wife's cleaning stuff and I went around knocking on doors, asking could I wash windows. I made eight dollars doing that. That night I was bawling in my wife's lap. The same back east with the other one. She was going to leave me and marry some car salesman. Same thing, cried like a baby. Don't tell me you don't need somebody. I need somebody."

"Two somebodies, it would appear," Stella said.

"Okay. I got a lot of emotion. It's the way I am. You want a cup of coffee?"

"I'd rather have a beer."

"At ten o'clock in the morning?"

"I never take anything stronger until lunch," she said primly.

"Ah-hah, I think I know about you, lady. I think I know about you." He wagged a finger at her. "I got drinkers in my family," he said.

"Splendid," Stella said. "Then you know how they hate to be meddled with."

"You want to get juiced, get juiced. Only I don't pay."

"I'll accept coffee. Coffee and toast. Perhaps an egg."

"Okay, I see how you operate. Breakfast on me."

The heat during the afternoon was intolerable. Mr. Polanski removed his shirt. Stella unbuttoned her blouse and took off her shoes. The landscape was oppressive; tire factories, bottling plants, anonymous stucco suburbs elbowed each other for miles. She dozed for a long time, her head back, heard herself snoring when they hit a bump and struggled awake. The hot interior stank

323

of sweat and motor oil. The road seemed to wind before them endlessly, now cutting through brown hills stubbled with brush and pocked with outcroppings of stone. The truck was so large, the cab so high, that she had the impression she was flying over the highway rather than riding on it.

She knotted a handkerchief around her brow. It gave her a raffish and slightly drunken air. She found herself swaying with the movement of the truck. The heat had sapped her.

"I got some salt tablets in the dash. Swallow a couple — here's the thermos . . ."

She was limp. "I like dark, cool places," she said. They had slowed to go through the hamlet of Littlefield. She looked longingly out the window at the signs of various bars: Pete's, The Kick-Off, The Tap Room. The truck rumbled by and she stared out the window, imagining the cavelike interiors, seeing only blue neon scroll reading "Coors Beer."

She straightened again. She saw a brush fire in the hollow of a far-off hill smudging the blue sky with a sullen cloud.

"Look," she said. "The burning bush. God's voice next, no doubt."

She reached into her bag, withdrew her paper pad and fanned the still air against her fiery face. "I think," she said, "that I am going to faint."

Mr. Polanski took her at her word and thrusting out one arm he pushed her head between her gaping knees. Her face was within an inch of the rubber mat, fumes assailed her, her ears rang.

"I'm getting off the road. Sit tight."

The next she knew she was lying in a field with Mr. Polanski's jacket wadded under her head. A jack rabbit peered alertly at her through the gorse; the sky was bright white and cruel overhead.

"That's all right, that's all right," Mr. Polanski murmured, patting her hand. "You're okay now."

She came up woozily on an elbow, dismissing his ministrations. "Don't fuss, don't fuss."

She struggled to sit up, pushed her heavy hair back from her face, slapped sand from her blouse and her skirt. She felt the taste of bile in her mouth, grit in her teeth — she spat. Then she pushed his assisting hand aside and hauled herself up on unsteady feet.

"Let's move on. I've got this whole bloody country to get across."

"Wait a minute," he said to her. "We've got to work something else out. You passed out on me, I've lost a lot of time. Look, I'm not in the transportation-of-ladies business; I'm not even supposed to pick up riders, my insurance doesn't cover it. I haul freight for a mean sonofabitch who'll have my ass if this load comes in late. So what do you say? — we call it quits and no hard feelings."

She looked around her in disgust. "Well, if you're only going to think of yourself — "

He exploded. "Who the hell am I supposed to be thinking about, lady? I pick you up. I schlep you. I spend my own dough feeding you. You've cost me time. And now I'm supposed to apologize for trying to shake you off and get my fucking job done. You're a pain in the ass, you know that?"

"You have a point. I'm just trying to get where I'm going, but I see the justice in what you say."

"I'll drop you in Cedar City."

"Very well. Cedar City. Whatever that may be."

But he stopped to give her one last meal in Cedar City, a tough steak curled in grease and a cheap bottle of wine. She left the meat untasted, put the bottle in her purse, grunted meager thanks and took up her place under a traffic light with her thumb stuck out. He waved as he drove by. She did not return the gesture. Hail and farewell, Mr. Polanski.

The car that stopped for her was a white Cadillac with gold hub caps and wheel spokes; the statue of a Remington cowboy welded to the radiator cap saluted the breeze with a Stetson held aloft. A sequined band down the side proclaimed it to be the property of Don Burden, The Texas Moonstar. The driver aimed the car so close to her she was forced to jump up on the curb, cursing him soundly in the bargain.

"Hayou," he cried in a merry voice. "Hayou?"

It took her a full moment to realize he was not hailing her but inquiring after her well-being. "How *are* you?" How was she indeed! Pissed off at being nearly run down. He flung open the door and beckoned her in, his hands fiery with gemstones. She saw another figure in the back seat, slumped under a huge, creased cowboy hat, a pair of elaborately tooled boots propped up on the seat in front of him. She noted, in passing, that the man's fly was open, but as he was fast asleep she was not concerned.

"Give you a lift, little lady?"

"Where are you heading?" she asked.

"Kearney. I got me a spread in Kearney. You riding or standing there?"

"I'm riding, thank you," she said, and positioned herself in the front seat, her disreputable bag in hand.

He looked like a fat child grown thin, not quite handsome but close enough to it, with a cocky air of self-satisfaction, as if applause resounded in the air about him, cries and whistles and little girls' shrieks.

He was instantly voluble. She ought to know him, he made that plain at the outset, because, hell, his records were on every juke in the country; they were played in France, in Australia, and the Irish Free State, too. That fellow behind there, sleeping on his tail bone, was Cal Everly, his lifelong friend, business manager and asshole buddy. They were good old Texas boys with two and a half million green American dollars stashed away in a Swiss bank. That brought them just about all the fucking and drinking and good times they could handle. He put a hand on her knee to punctuate his pleasure in living.

"Off with the hand," Stella said. "Pronto." She looked at him pleasantly.

The man whooped. "We got us a buckin' bronco here. Hey!" He swiveled his curly head around to the back seat. "Hey, Cal, wake up, we got us a smokin' pistol in here."

"I heard. I hate a big mouth on a woman." The voice from the back was gravelly with drink.

"What's your name, little girl?"

Stella turned to bend her coolest, blackest gaze on him. "My name," she said, "is Marie de Rabutin Chantal, marquise de Sévigné, more commonly known as Madame de Sévigné. That would be an accent acute on both e's."

"That's more handle than I got on my pump," he said.

"Also," she went on, "tell your friend in the back seat that I find him offensive; and, if you will, that his pecker is out for the world to see. Considering its diminutive size, its pallid color and general lack of tone, he would be well advised to put it back in his pants, as he only lays himself open to ridicule by displaying it."

She reached into her bag, took out the wine bottle and had a satisfying swig.

With a roar the man in the back sat up, stuffed himself back into his pants, yanked up his zipper and vented his spleen.

"What are you dragging that along for? Fucking old bitch with a bottle! Pick up something nice and round if you're gonna pick up. Shit, my dog wouldn't get up on her from behind!"

"Hell, Cal, she's salty, and I like salt on my meat. She's a whole shakerful."

"Well, I don't know about you, but I'm gonna gag her before I eat her. Take me to some quiet place and I'll show you."

Stella corked her bottle with an emphatic splat and turned to look at them both with an unblinking stare of profound and intense purpose. It was a moment before she spoke.

"If you touch me," she said, "I'll ruin you. I'll hound you and reduce you to cinders. I've never made an idle threat in my life. I'd do it if it took me thirty years. I have reservoirs of force, of vigor, of competence and potency that I haven't even begun to tap yet, and it would be focused on you two. That's the validity it would have. I'd come to the door of your house in Kearney with police and attack dogs. I'd find you through your secretary, your agent, your PR man, your music publisher, your booker. I'd come at you with lawyers, FBI men, security guards, Pinkertons, and a kitchen knife in my hand. If either one of you so much as touch me."

The one in the back seat shrieked, "Get rid of her!" and the driver replied, "Cowboy, she's gone!"

The car squealed and skidded to a halt, pulverized rock spraying over the hood and the windshield. A high, wide plateau broiled all around them. The air was still, the road ran off to nowhere. She got out stiffly, slamming the door behind her.

The driver leaned over, speaking through the open window. "It's miles from anyplace, but you brought it on yourself. You could've rode all the way with us, with just one little stop on the prairie for fun, but have it your way."

"So long, amigos," she said.

They roared off, clouds of dust and stinging sand billowing back in her face.

She was alone. She knew there was life all around her, snakes, lizards, birds, beetles, kangaroo rats, coyotes; knowledge and intuition told her there was a plethora of life sharing this uniform and monolithic place with her. But she felt alone, she disliked the immensity of the desert under its clear, fading sky and the heat was making her ill again.

"This is a dangerous journey," she said to herself, aloud but undaunted. "And why not? All life is."

She sat down on a rock to wait. It was getting dark. She drank the rest of the wine just to pass the time.

The farmer who picked her up during the cold night hours was a brittle old man, frayed and taciturn, a man who would chop wood slowly, would bend painfully to retrieve a bucket, a dogged, unflagging man. The car was an ancient Pontiac, shock absorbers long since gone, front seat sprung, but he made no apology for it.

"You're between towns. It's pretty late to be out on this road."

She looked him over carefully. He waited out the scrutiny and then said, "You'll be all right with me. I ain't nothing more than I look — a dirt farmer."

He drove slowly, both hands on the wheel at all times, gripping it as if he held the reins of a skittish horse. He spoke only twice more. Once to tell her his destination, Rock Springs, and once to offer her a peach from an open bag on the seat between them.

He had a faint asthmatic wheeze which bubbled through the quiet night like a kettle on the boil. Stella found the sound comforting. She slept.

It was dawn when they approached the town. The old man shook her awake and took his hand away swiftly as soon as her eyes opened.

"Lady," he said, "I live down this road. I'd invite you to the house for a cup of coffee, but my missus is bedridden and don't like company. You can take the rest of them peaches if you want."

She got out and paused a moment to lean in the window. "What's your name?" she asked.

"P. J. Walker."

"Well, Mr. Walker, you're a decent man to spend a night with. I can't say that occurs often in my experience. I'll take the peaches."

A young sailor on leave from a nuclear submarine took her from Rock Springs to Point of Rocks, and two little old ladies, one of whom crocheted in the back seat while the other chattered endlessly of her sister-in-law's bad cooking and her poor brother's destroyed stomach, gave her a lift from Point of Rocks to Rawlins.

An Indian laborer stopped outside of Rawlins to wave her into the back of his truck, where she rode wedged between a lashed-down cultivator and a panting, salivating, tail-thumping red setter, who sniffed her crotch and licked her face.

He took her to Sinclair, where she flagged down a young girl in pink plastic curlers, whose crying baby squalled and wet her lap all the long, tedious afternoon, while her hair grew wet at her nape and sweat trickled continuously between her breasts.

At Laramie a minister offered her a ride and half of his sardine sandwich. She gagged after one bite and hid it in her pocket, where it smelled rankly all the way to Pine Bluffs.

There she was picked up by a woman close to her own age, with a soft, cloudy beauty, good clothes, good scent. The car was black, air-conditioned, quiet. The woman's hands on the wheel were narrow, ringless, with short, unpolished nails. She could take her to North Platte, she told her, in a dry, inflectionless voice. Stella peeled off her stockings, jammed her slicker behind her head, made a disorderly nest for herself. She edged toward sleep but was roused by the feeling that she was being watched in some disturbing, ambiguous way.

"Why are you staring at me?" she asked crossly.

"I'm sorry," the lady said.

Stella had no appreciation of prudence. "What's there to stare at?"

"You're a handsome woman."

"Handsome." Stella echoed the word flatly. "Ah. I think I see what I'm into here. My dear," she said, "I've lived a reckless, some even say a rash life. I understand appetite. I approve of it. I don't think, however, that mine is the same as yours."

The woman's grin was wide and engaging. "How quick you are," she said.

"Yes, yes," Stella replied, "there's no question that *I'm* quick. The thing is, how quick are you?"

"Very."

"Then you'll understand quickly when I tell you I don't go to bed with women. Some charming ladies have invited me to get over my obstinacy from time to time, but it's an experiment I've never made."

"There's a lovely inn in the country not far from here," the woman said. "Very cool, with beautiful rooms overlooking a garden. We could bathe and rest."

"It's bad manners to persist," Stella told her.

The woman put a gentle hand on Stella. "I would do nothing to embarrass you, nothing to startle you. You would hardly know you were seduced until you were."

"It's all right for school girls, I guess, to get up to something with their gym instructors. But after fifteen it's narcissism. You might just as well look into a pool of water."

"Come look," the woman said, her touch moving lightly up Stella's arm. "Let's lean over the edge and look together."

Stella did not debate it. When they stopped to get gas on the outskirts of North Platte and the woman went into the washroom, Stella left the car and walked around the block out of sight, raising her thumb again. She did not wish to reproach or be reproached, judge or be judged. Nor did she care to romp with sloe-eyed ladies in flowered bed sheets. She just wanted to move on. She had a place to go.

A fairground operator took her to Kearney, complaining of business; folks didn't want to see cootch shows anymore; they were nothing compared to what they could watch in their downtown picture shows. There was a sudden wind and a drenching rain outside the city, thunderheads standing out sharply in the sky. She was driven to shelter under a tree, where a car packed full of amiable college fraternity boys found her and took her to Grand Island, shifting her boisterously from lap to lap all the way. A drunk endangered her life from there to Council Bluffs, hurling beer cans at fence posts the entire distance. She got lucky with a long ride to Iowa City in the company of a beekeeper who rented honeybee colonies to farmers who needed pollination for their crops, went on to Elkhart with a Boy Scout leader in short pants and knee socks, got lucky again with a sheet and pillowcase salesman for Wamsutta, horny and downhearted, who traveled six days a week, nine months a year, and was afraid he would die all alone in a hotel room somewhere. He took her into downtown Scranton.

She spent part of the forty dollars for a cheap motel room, the rest on a good bottle of Scotch and two tacos. She filled a bathroom water glass, propped it on the tub, bathed, drank and schemed. She slept in a bed for the first time in three nights, restless and fitful, and was out on the highway again before dawn.

A stock clerk at Macy's took her the rest of the way, warning her darkly to put whatever money she had in her shoe, to buy a hammer and carry it at all times, not to ride in the subway, not to walk in the park, never, ever to get into an elevator alone: everyone was the enemy. He took her across the rest of Pennsylvania, across New Jersey, past the swampy, steaming junk yard of

Jersey City, through the Holland Tunnel, and let her off near Times Square, calling a final warning that it was full of hookers and pimps and addicts: take care!

It was hot, the temperature at a hundred, the humidity near a hundred, the tar in the streets had begun to run, sticking to the soles of her shoes. Garbage cooked in green cellophane bags; the people looked pale and wet and cross.

She asked for directions, was ignored, refused to be ignored, accosted and collared five different passers-by before she was told which way to go. She walked forty blocks, scanning the city to see if it suited her. It did not. The buildings made the people Lilliputian, the traffic was an abomination, the Guggenheim was pompous, lacking wit, the Metropolitan might be possible, she would decide after she had been to see it. Windows were grimy, pigeon shit ate the façades of buildings, motes blew into her eyes.

The side streets were better. Window boxes bloomed, the houses had panache, there were signs saying "Curb Your Dog." She approved of that.

Caleb did well for himself. His was the biggest house on the street, brass doorknobs polished, tubbed trees perky, front steps swept, garbage cans lidded and labeled — Caleb's own general tone prevailed.

The houseboy was unaccustomed to the likes of Stella. She stood in the doorway like flotsam cast up by a turbulent sea and with hauteur undiminished said: "Tell him it's Stella and that I will not leave until I see him."

She pushed past the astonished young man and sat down in a gilt and red plush chair, legs out, arms dangling, looking about her. How immensely rich Caleb must be, how darkly opulent were the polished Jacobean chests and the bronzes in massive groups upon them. How acquisitive he was. She counted the Hellenic torsos — there were five, spotlighted. The floor had been laid for a Renaissance prince in Carrara marble, the stairway for ducal entrances and exits. She thought what the silver urns would bring in a pawnshop and pursed her mouth in a silent whistle.

Then she heard his heavy tread, and her gaze rose to the top of the stairs. And there he was. Her heart kicked in her chest, she heard a cry that must have been her own, and with the blood surging through her veins she ran up, taking the steps two and three at a time, and she flung herself on him. She slammed into his chest, very nearly toppling him backward, and she held him in a hectic, viselike embrace until his arms finally rose and encircled her.

"Well," he murmured into her tangled hair. "Well. And well again. What have we here?"

Smothered against him, the words spilled out of her. "I crossed the whole goddamn country. I want my book contract. I want my advance. I want my publication date. I want you," she cried.

He held her out at arm's length and shook his head. "The order of priorities is typical of you, my dear. But welcome." And he kissed her brow.

She clung to him like a barnacle. "Don't be a fool," she said with savage intensity. "I've been out of my head without you. No good to myself, no good to my work, mad with longing. All links broken. Punished. Stagnant. Sniveling. You have only to look at me to see the state I'm in. My God, man, I'm in love, and it's gall and wormwood and pain in every bone of my body. I can't work, I can't sleep, even drink's not what it was. You've ruined drink for me! It's grotesque, I tell you, what's befallen me. Words shamble through my head. What's a poet without words, you unfeeling prick! Am I nothing to you that you chop me down? Heal me, I tell you. Restore me! — Or roast in hell forever!"

"How daintily you woo me," Caleb said, letting go of her.

"I believe in plain speaking," Stella said. "I don't give a fig for pride or dignity either. I have to get back on my feet, that's all I know. I begrudge the time I spend mooning over you. I want you where I can get my hands on you. I want to be appeased and purged, sated, freed! I have to have you back."

"You figure very largely in that speech," Caleb told her dryly. "I appear in the role of a prescription, to be taken to lower the temperature, to restore the brain to clarity. A pill, in fact — a term of mild contempt used by my children to designate a fool."

"Must we stand here discussing it? I want to sit in a chair. I'm exhausted. Do you know what I've been through?"

He was immediately his old solicitous and courtly self, helping her into a room filled on all four walls with books, and where there were no books there were heroic portraits, battle scenes, Venus reclining, Venus and Eros. He rang for tea. He poured a good measure of Scotch into a glass and handed it to her.

"I've been completely miserable without you," he said quietly. He sat down behind a huge desk halfway across the room from her. "My heart has been quite broken. Don't accept it smugly as your due, Stella. You haven't earned my feelings. By right, you shouldn't have them. The truth is I can't withhold them from you."

"But you have," she cried hotly. "I abased myself. I humbled myself. I called endlessly. And paid for the calls, too. And where were you? Out to lunch. Out to bloody lunch!" She was fierce in her outcry. "*I* came to *you*. Further abasement. I've made a hegira to you, across this entire, benighted, franchised country. And damn — we're quarreling already. There's some best in me somewhere, Caleb; for God's sake bring it out."

"Come to my arms," he said softly. "Come to me, my wicked, my devious, my ungrateful Stella."

All that afternoon, while the light washed the walls with gold, she lay across his lap, looking up into his wise and weary face. She felt torpid, as though she lay on a riverbed with waters moving gently over her head, fracturing sunlight and sky, dulling sound. She studied him idly, the stroke of his eyebrows, the long curve of his mouth, the lines that creased his forehead, his imperial Roman nose. But he seemed detached from her somehow, apart from her, a mythical figure, wine-clad, besotted, ravished with love and wine, a Bacchus, withered cherries hanging from his ears, trailing away from her through a green and darkened wood, retreating, vanishing, leaves closing after him. She called him back.

"Take me to bed," she commanded.

It was, she thought, waking some hours later, pure delight, like a pure ideal, to put aside her superior self and to melt into this great old man. He had awesome gifts as a lover, but beyond that she could sit in his shade a while, rest and renew herself. She prodded him awake.

"Don't sleep."

"You've tired me out."

"I've watched you sleep for an hour, you great whale. You're almost beautiful when you sleep. Though you bulge here and there. Put your arms around me and tell me something delectable."

"Well," he said, heaving himself up on the pillows, "we must decide what to do with you."

"Palaver? More talk? Let's just be, for Christ's sweet sake." She put her face against his huge belly. "How your guts rumble."

"Disquietude," he said, "as I see our future together."

"Why get your wind up? It's a piece of cake." Stella was emphatic. "I'll function as I always have. You'll be the rock. All else will be hot flesh and straddling until you are too old for it. Then I'll spoon-feed you and rub whiskey on your gums and cosset you in every possible way."

"I shan't ask for that."

"What, then?"

"Time." He stroked her hair.

"Eons," she said. "We have eons. Put your hand on the small of my back. Just there. Your hand was made to fit where my spine sags."

"I am older than you, very much older."

She grew impatient. Matters were growing morbid. A small terror plucked at her and she staunched it with abuse.

"Don't try to weasel out of marrying me. Yes, I want marriage. The ring, the words, a settlement, everything. I didn't make this wretched pilgrimage for nothing."

"I have some say in it, I trust?" He looked at her with his dark, heavy-lidded eyes, his all-seeing gaze.

"You don't. You must have me. For better or worse." She flailed at him, pounding on his massive chest, hurting him. He caught her hands.

"Then I will. If I must, I will. Peace, Stella. I will have you."

She rolled on top of him, locked her legs around his, ground her hips on him, clutched, sniffed, bit, licked, tongued, kissed.

"Speedily," she said.

"Yes," he answered, looking over her head at something far away and unnamed. "Speedily."

They flew through the night back to California. Stella lay curled up against Caleb all the way, lapping champagne in the first-class compartment, first from a chilled glass held aloft in a series of extravagant toasts, then sloshed jovially into her water tumbler, then slopped into her coffee cup, and for the last thousand miles or so drunk manfully from the bottle. She had to be assisted upon arrival.

It was too late to go to a hotel, so over Caleb's mild protest they went back to her apartment. It stank dreadfully of cat and mold. Stella had left food uncovered on the drainboard before her hasty departure and the result, after eight days, pits and cores, stems and peelings, was a pyramidical fantasy of rot.

"Never mind," she said, flinging open all the windows to try and stir the hot, motionless air. "It's just for one night. I'll put clean sheets on the bed."

She went to the linen closet. "One clean sheet, as I don't seem to have two."

"You have an incomparable flair for disorder. I thank God I'm a rich man and you need never do anything for the rest of your life but sit on a silk cushion and soil it. Is your bathroom fit to use?"

"The water runs. There's soap."

"If this were our first consummation," Caleb told her, "it wouldn't take place, that I can assure you. There, there," he added, "I love you, sloven though you are. Come kiss me."

She did so fiercely. "We'll darken the room. You won't see anything. There'll just be you and me, naked and amorous. Hurry up."

"I was hoping," he said dryly, "that you were thinking of bathing, too."

"Yes, yes," she said impatiently. "Tomorrow. I'll wash my feet."

"That's reassuring."

He took his bag and went into the bathroom. She heard him singing as the water ran into the tub. Hastily, she swept the clothes and the papers and the books under the bed, righted a lamp shade tilted at a crazy angle, killed a fly with her shoe and rummaged frantically for a decent nightgown. She found one that was stretched and faded and slipped it over her head. She lit a candle and stuck it into a saucer, so that the room had a pleasant, shadowed light. She tied up her hair with an old belt and arranged herself in bed with the air of an odalisque, or as near to that attitude as she could manage, with her gown sliding off her shoulders and the pillows lumped and knotted behind her, down escaping to float in the air each time she punched one.

He came into the room smelling baby-sweet, his hair neatly brushed and still damp.

"The candle's a charming touch," he said, and climbed in beside her. "May I blow it out? The danger of fire."

"Let there be darkness," she said.

They lay side by side, his hands composed and folded on the counterpane, on the clean sheet she had promised. Their voices were murmurous.

"You are my beloved," he told her. "I see what an excellent woman you are and I'm touched that you want to be by my side."

"You've unsettled me," she said, "but I don't care. I love you. Move your leg, please, I'm getting numb down one side."

"My love, my sweet," he said. "Ah, Stella, what a maze you are to wander through, thorny, green, puzzling. What a delight. To be happy and amused, both at once, what man can say the same? You'll never want for loving, my dear, as long as I live. You may take that as a promise."

"I'll hold you to it," she said passionately. "To the very letter of it. Never another. Not a hand on a buttock. Not a stray thought. Only Stella. Ever Stella."

"Ever Stella," he agreed. "Now turn over and fit yourself against me."

"You're so fat," she said. "A mountain range."

"God bless you."

"He must," she said, and grasping him around his pillowy middle she fell asleep.

Caleb died in the night.

In the last moment he dreamed he was young again, with birds wheeling around his head and a sounding sea at his back. He seemed in touch with a special slant of wisdom that cast a mild and warming light over his entire life. He felt himself gathered in and made eternally cheerful. All that he had ever known or thought or read or championed or cared for was distilled like stones shining and clearly seen in water, and he regretted nothing.

Stella awoke, her eyes still gummy from sleep, to find him marble cold beside her, leaned over him, saw cessation in his face, saw that he was already on another journey.

Time passed as if she were apart from it, smothered in webs and in veils; it was figmental, preposterous. She was aware of the sound of her own voice, howling, of people in the room, crowds of people; Jake was there, Hortense, others, packing in, stampeding, surging. A siren shrieked, there were two attendants in white. For a moment she thought them murderous, storming at the body on the bed; one leaped up on him, mounted him, struck him with his fist on the chest, hammering him repeatedly. The action seemed manic, insane. She thought she saw a kiss bestowed; it was the other, kneeling at Caleb's head, mouth on his mouth, bellowing air.

She saw a narrow white cot trundled past her on squeaking wheels, saw the heavy body transferred to it, strapped into place; she moaned as it wheeled past her and stood to follow, savage, raging. Jake held her back; she struck him.

She felt the prick of a needle in her arm. Nell was there, leading her to the couch, settling her, covering her. It was unbelievable. She had been so smug with the certainty of life. Of health. Of continuance. Hers. His. Theirs. The knife stroke of it. So sudden and final. No recourse, no redress. They were going to grow old, be quarrelsome, accustomed, bound. She battled despotic sleep. She drifted.

So he had died on her. Without farewell, without ceremony, with no by your leave at all, he had gone out of the game.

I must make something of this, she thought to herself, because if I cannot, if I do not . . . For a moment she lost her train of thought.

Caleb, how you suited me. Suited me. How clever you were. How insinuating and rowdy, such a juicy plum. I never expected the likes of you, rolling into view like a great wallowing ship. You were a summer evening, soft air, zephyrs. And tart as rind. Flavorsome. Erect and lascivious. Strong and stubborn and full of dignity as a parson. Chiding and corrective, willing me to be what I was not. Oh, friend. With your probity and slyness, your steely mind and courtly airs, your sumptuous tastes, your unabashed greed. What a fanciful man; how you nourished me, maddened me, made me laugh. How sweetly you forbore. Nothing base in you. All honor. God knows I never had one like you before. And God knows I never will again. Ah, Caleb. Fat prince.

At that, she cried aloud in pain, and Nell, dozing in a chair in the corner, came to her side.

13

THEY WOULD ALL remember the day in differing ways, but each with the realization that the road had diverged and that their lives would now take other turnings. They wished to embrace each other, to reinforce each other, to affirm they found much to admire, each in the other. During this hour they would smoke too many cigarettes, drink too much coffee, cry, blow their noses and say "What the hell" to fate. In concert and in sisterhood it all seemed so much less threatening.

Stella had a new place at the top of the apartment and Jake had made her a condition of the sale of the building. She was to stay there as long as she liked, and the rooms already suffered the battering of her presence, with the familiar litter rising on the floor and her gray cat spitting nervously in the corner. She would not now, would not ever, care where she was. She went about her old business in her old way with one alteration only: she had given up drink for food and was already growing portly, short-winded and odorous from the peanuts and the chocolates and the crackers she carried in her pockets.

The ladies had gathered for breakfast, yielding the place of honor to Eunice. She had bought a new straw hat and smart red luggage which waited packed at the door. Smoke spiraled in the air, cups chattered against saucers, their talk rose and fell: what had been, what would be, arrivals and departures.

Hortense was acerbic and bracing.

"Just remember," she told Eunice, "no is a word, too. Use it once in a while. No, I won't sleep with you just because you bought me a chicken dinner. No, I can't give you any of my money. No, I don't mess with married men. No, honey, you're too young. No, mister, you're too old. No, you can't have my house key. No — no way. Think you can remember any of that?"

"No," Eunice said, grinning at her.

"I got to be crazy, letting you go off to Alaska."

"Let her go," Nell said. "She's a big girl now, Hortense."

"We're big girls — she's still a runt . . . Tell me again, Eunice. You got yourself a job *where?*"

"In a camp at the pipeline, outside of Fairbanks. You get a lot of money and big tips and opportunities. You *do*, Hortense, don't look at me like that."

"Uh huh. Opportunities."

"They have long nights," Stella said. "Can you get through a long night, child?"

"I have so far."

"Zonked on Seconal."

"I feel strong," Eunice said. "I honestly do. It's going to be a new life."

"It's the old life in a new place, you mean." Hortense was cranky.

"It'll be different," Eunice said with confidence. "I *know* it's going to be different."

"That's right," Nell told her. "Go around the next corner."

"Is that what you've got in mind for yourself?" Hortense looked at Nell with lifted eyebrows.

"For myself." Nell pondered the question. "Well," she said, "I don't think I care to live entirely on remembered bliss. I think as time passes I may very well come to admire a little compromise as a sensible and rational way to live. So . . . I think I'll take a teaching appointment at S.C. and write a paper on kidney disease — and seasonally, when the geese honk overhead and the leaves fall, I'll put in a long-distance phone call to Jake and we'll meet halfway, say in Sacramento, in a Ramada Inn in a room overlooking the parking lot. He'll bring me a quart of Washington blueberries, leaking through the wrapping paper. I'll bring him a box of cigars. He'll say I've gained weight. It won't be true. We'll take off our clothes and brush our teeth and crawl into a bed that vibrates if you drop in a quarter. We'll make love and talk and be full of good will. On Sunday morning, when it's time to go, we'll be irresolute. I'll leave a bedroom slipper behind. He'll forget his razor. We'll stand looking at each other. He'll say, 'See you on May Day; I'll bring fudge.' I'll reply, 'The kind with walnuts in it.' He'll call from a pay phone in Tacoma that night to say that the sun is going down and the sky is gorgeous; he just wanted me to know. I'll write him the next day to say miraculously my sinus condition has cleared; bless him."

She looked around at the women who were watching her, willing her to a conclusion. Eunice gnawed her lower lip fretfully.

"I hate to be left dangling. How will it end?"

"Not badly, I trust. Not at all badly." She turned to Hortense then. "And you?"

"Pay my money, take my chances."

They looked to Stella, seated in a rocking chair. They all thought of Caleb, that force, that presence, making grass on a plot green now with his bones and his marrow.

"Work," Stella said bluntly in the silence that fell. "Work, work, work and again work."

"I suppose you're through with men," Eunice inquired fearfully of Hortense.

"I haven't locked the door, but it sure as hell ain't going to be easy to get in."

Stella stared out into the bright blue day. "Speaking for myself, I am not bent on death and destruction. I say yes to life when asked."

They thought of what she said and were pleased by it. Each knew the excellence of it, fine spring rain, books, jokes, orgasms, poetry, hot baths, linked arms, tulips, children, the whole fine flourishing shape of it.

"I'll write to you all," Eunice said brightly.

"No, you won't," Hortense told her. "You'll forget to buy stamps. You won't be able to find the mailbox. You'll be in love."

"God, I sure hope so! Well," she said, looking at her watch, "I've got to toddle."

She stood up and looked around with a tremulous smile. "Oh, shit," she said, "I'm going to miss you all."

"You're gonna miss your bus is what you're gonna miss." Hortense set her mouth. "Get someplace on time for once."

Eunice looked at them, Hortense, Stella, Nell, in the bright sunlight and her heart went out to each in turn.

"Will you be all right?" she cried.

Stella answered for them all. "The direction is forward," she said.

The bus depot seized Archer's imagination and turned it over and over again, like the time he had been caught in a wave at the beach, hurtled upside-down, seeing sky, sandy bottom, green rushing water. People were milling around, dragging suitcases in all states of repair, one with brown tape crisscrossing it, and some of the people sat on the hard benches and stared as if they were leaving life itself. He saw one old man drinking something from a bottle in a brown paper bag and another crying in the corner, his thin shoulders heaving — a moment of separation had undone him altogether.

The place was dirty, too. The very seat he sat on was littered and sticky and popcorn had been spilled and crunched under his new shoes. Every other moment a voice blared a destination or a departure in tones so harsh he could not make out a single word, and he watched Eunice anxiously, hoping her ears were sharper than his.

He excused himself and walked to the water fountain, his mouth feeling like old socks from the excitement of it all, but the water tasted of rust and he saw what looked like a blob of mucus and was quite sure somebody had spat in the basin.

When he sat down again Eunice asked him about his clothes,

inquiring if he really wanted to wear that celluloid clip bow tie and that green wool jacket all the way to Alaska. Wouldn't he like a nice, roomy T-shirt, which she could purchase at the news stall? They were going to an unbuttoned life, to the end of the U.S. Highway system, to the end of the road. No reason not to get off on the right foot.

He explained carefully that the outfit he was wearing had been his grandmother's choice, reserved in the back of his closet for funerals and visits to third or fourth cousins. The tie was, in fact, biting into his chin with its sharp edges, reminding him of his grandmother's last embrace and fiery caution: "I'm going to die soon, Archer, but I'll know what you're up to from the grave and beyond." This was followed by a kiss smelling of paregoric — and thus he had been relinquished and released from her care.

Eunice was already on her feet; a moment later she was back, unfurling a shirt that said "Win With The Dodgers" and a large pin reading "Digging For Gold Beats Gold Digging." She said she thought it was singularly appropriate, considering where they were going, and right then and there she whisked off the tie, the jacket, unbuttoned the shirt and stripped it from him, told him to hold his arms straight above his head — and the new shirt slid over him, ending somewhere near his crotch. The air blew on his body; there was room to wiggle.

"Thank you," he said.

Eunice flung an arm around his shoulders. "Isn't it goofy, Archer, the way things turn out?"

He acquiesced tentatively.

"We know your daddy has to be away for four or five years, and there's your grandmother getting her place in the old peoples' home, which she's had her eye on forever, and your mother moving to Tuscaloosa, in a house too small for any number over two. So guess who was left to take care of you? Me. After all the discussion and the long-distance phone calls your daddy said, 'Listen, Eunice, you and Archer get along swell and Alaska's part of the United States of America, the last frontier, and a boy ought to see that, so why don't you take him up there with you and put him in school and teach him to play poker, so when I get back he'll know a thing or two?' "

"Yes," Archer said, "it was a surprise."

"Yeah, in a way, but to tell you the truth, Archer, I had my eye on you from the beginning. I mean it could have come to kidnapping if all this other stuff hadn't fallen into line. I'm pretty determined when I want something, you know."

"Uh huh," Archer said. He looked at his shoes and wished they were two-tone brown and white instead of all brown.

"I for one," Eunice said, "think we'll have a ball. We'll go to a lot of movies and get a bowl of goldfish and learn to ski and look for whales in the ocean off of Captain Cook's Outlet. I'm good company, you know. I know fourteen different Polish jokes."

"I know some, too."

"That's what I mean. We both know a lot of jokes."

"Yes," Archer said.

"Okay, then."

They both fell silent while a woman's nasal voice urged everyone headed for San Diego to get a move on.

"Listen," Eunice said, "there's something else I want to tell you. When you're sunk, sad about anything, I'll know it. I mean, you don't have to put a smile on your face every minute of the day. I can tell when things aren't copacetic. You can even cry if you feel like it."

"No, I won't have to cry."

"No?"

"I enjoy your company," Archer said.

Eunice nodded. "Most men do," she said.

Their bus pulled in and it was announced. Archer carried both their bags and Eunice let him. He selected their seats and was willing to give her the one closest to the window. She let him have it. He asked her where the toilet was in case he needed to use it and she pointed it out and also showed him how the lights over their heads could be brightened or dimmed.

They put their lunch, cream cheese and pimento sandwiches, in the overhead rack and they put their heads against the little white doilies pinned to their seats. The air conditioning went on as soon as the bus rolled away and its hum made Eunice sleepy.

"When we get out in the country, look for the Burma Shave signs," she told him. "They're a gas." She closed her eyes.

Archer pressed his face against the glass to watch out for them. He looked northward and far, far beyond.

37

shouted "Sit dow", cross your legs", I didn't unde-
stand the last part but they anyway crossed
my legs. "Head down!" pushing my head
against the b rear end of another detainee.
like a chicken. A female voice was shouting
all the way to the Camp, No Talking", and
a male voice, "Do not talk", and an
Arabic translator ▮▮▮▮▮▮▮▮ [1,3]
▮▮▮▮ [1,3] "Keep your head down",
I was completely annoyed by the American
way of talking I hoped I had the option
not to listen to those guards, and stayed
that way for **GUANTÁNAMO** I got cured
by meeting **DIARY** erican people.
Although I " giving orders
with two different way "DO NOT TAK" or
"No talking". It was interesting. Now, the
chains in my ankles cut the blood off to my
feet. My feet became numb. I heard only
moaning and crying of other detainees.
Beating was the order of the trip. I was
not spared, the guard kept hitting me
on my head, and squeeze my neck against
the rear end of the other detainee. But
I don't blame him as much as I do the
poor, and painful detainee, who was crying, and
kept moving, and so nose raised my head.
Detainees told me so that we took a fairy
during the trip, but I didn't notice.

ALSO BY LARRY SIEMS

The Torture Report: What the Documents Say
about America's Post-9/11 Torture Program

Between the Lines: Letters between Undocumented Mexican
and Central American Immigrants and Their Families and
Friends

'This Guantánamo detainee's harrowing memoir is a tremendous achievement – and a grave warning against ignoring the rule of law'
Observer

'A sobering, often chilling, read. Slahi's story deserves to be widely read'
Independent on Sunday

'Slahi's ordeal is at the heart of *Guantánamo Diary*, but the book is about much more. It is a chilling story of the United States' worst abuses in the post-9/11 era. It is an account of other countries' complicity in these abuses. It is a terrible example of what happens to innocent people when the rule of law is suspended. In the words of Larry Siems, the book's editor, it is "an epic for our times"'
Huffington Post

'Compelling'
The Economist

'The fact that you are able to read his account of his time in America's most notorious prison is a testimony to his intelligence, his entrepreneurial spirit and determination'
Independent

'Slahi's book offers a reminder that the struggles we face in these difficult times involve real individuals, not faceless creatures who are to be characterised as members of one or other hated group. That he has resorted to words, the mightiest of weapons, even as his incarceration continues, makes his experience all the more relevant today'
Financial Times

'*Guantánamo Diary* . . . will leave you shell-shocked'
Vanity Fair

'Necessary reading for those seeking to understand the dangers that Guantánamo's continued existence poses to Americans in the world . . . a fluent, engaging and at times eloquent writer even in his fourth language of English'
Washington Post

GUANTÁNAMO DIARY

MOHAMEDOU OULD SLAHI

Edited by **LARRY SIEMS**

CANONGATE
Edinburgh · London

This edition published by Canongate Books in 2015

First published in hardback in Great Britain in 2015 by Canongate Books Ltd,
14 High Street, Edinburgh EH1 1TE

www.canongate.tv

1

First published in the United States by Little, Brown and Company, Hachette
Book Group, Inc, 1290 Avenue of the Americas, New York, NY 10104

British Library Cataloguing-in-Publication Data
A catalogue record for this book is available on
request from the British Library

ISBN 978 1 78211 285 3

Printed and bound in Great Britain by Clays Ltd, St Ives plc

Mohamedou would like to dedicate his writing to the memory of his late mother, Maryem Mint El Wadia, and he would also like to express that if it weren't for Nancy Hollander and her colleagues Theresa Duncan and Linda Moreno, he couldn't be making that dedication.

you keep me in jail so why should I cooperate?
I said so not knowing that Americans use torture
to facilitate interrogation. Of course, I was very
tired from being taken to interrogation
every day. My back was just conspiring against
me. I sought Medical Help, "you're not
allowed to sit for so long time" said the ▮▮▮
▮▮▮ physiotherapist, "Pls, tell my interrogators
so they make sit for long hours almost every
day", "I will write a note but I can not
sure whether it will have effect" she replied.
Feb 03 ▮▮▮ washed his hands off me, "I am
going to leave but if you're ready to talk
about ~~my~~ your telephone conversations request
me. I'll come back" he said, "~~Be sure~~ I
assure you that I am not going to talk ~~about~~
anything unless you answer my question - why I
am here?", ▮▮▮ asked me to dedicate an
English copy of Koran to him, which I
happily did, and off he went. I never heard
about ▮▮▮ after that, ▮▮▮ and I
to "not" working together but he was an over-
baring person. I don't think in a negative way.
▮▮▮ just had tons of reports with all kind
of evil theories. The ~~a~~ mis-mash of what-ifs
was mainly fueled with prejudices, ~~and~~
hatred, and ignorance toward the Islamic
Religion. "I am working on showing you
~~UNCLASSIFIED~~

Contents

80

I hungrily started to read the letter but soon I
got chocked. The letter was a cheap forgery, it
was not from my family. It was the production of
the Intel community. "Dear brothers, what I
received no letter, I am sorry!", " Bastards,
they have done so with other detainees" said a
detainee. But the forgery was so clumzy and
un professional that no fool would fall for it.
First, I have no brother of mine with that name,
second, my name was misspelled, third my family
doesn't live where the correspondent mention but
close enough, forth I know not only the handwriting of every single member of my family,
I also know every phrases his ideas. The letter
was kind of a sermon, "Be patient like
your ancestors, and have faith that Allah
is going to reward you". I was so mad at
this attempt to fraud me, and play with my
emotions. Next day, ▪ pulled me for
interrogation. "How is your family doing?", "I hope
they're doing well", "I've been working to get
you the letter!", "Thank you very much,
good effort, but if you guys want to forge
a mail let me give some advices", "What are you
talking about?", I smiled "I don't really
know is okay, but it was cheap to forge a
message and make me believe I have contact
with my dear family!" I said handing him

A Timeline of Detention

January 2000	After spending twelve years studying, living, and working overseas, primarily in Germany and briefly in Canada, Mohamedou Ould Slahi decides to return to his home country of Mauritania. En route, he is detained twice at the behest of the United States—first by Senegalese police and then by Mauritanian authorities—and questioned by American FBI agents in connection with the so-called Millennium Plot to bomb LAX. Concluding that there is no basis to believe he was involved in the plot, authorities release him on February 19, 2000.
2000–fall 2001	Mohamedou lives with his family and works as an electrical engineer in Nouakchott, Mauritania.
September 29, 2001	Mohamedou is detained and held for two weeks by Mauritanian authorities and again questioned by FBI agents about the Millennium Plot. He is again released, with Mauritanian authorities publicly affirming his innocence.
November 20, 2001	Mauritanian police come to Mohamedou's home and ask him to accompany them for further questioning. He voluntarily complies, driving his own car to the police station.
November 28, 2001	A CIA rendition plane transports Mohamedou from Mauritania to a prison in Amman, Jordan, where he is interrogated for seven and a half months by Jordanian intelligence services.

July 19, 2002	Another CIA rendition plane retrieves Mohamedou from Amman; he is stripped, blindfolded, diapered, shackled, and flown to the U.S. military's Bagram Air Base in Afghanistan. The events recounted in *Guantánamo Diary* begin with this scene.
August 4, 2002	After two weeks of interrogation in Bagram, Mohamedou is bundled onto a military transport with thirty-four other prisoners and flown to Guantánamo. The group arrives and is processed into the facility on August 5, 2002.
2003–2004	U.S. military interrogators subject Mohamedou to a "special interrogation plan" that is personally approved by Defense Secretary Donald Rumsfeld. Mohamedou's torture includes months of extreme isolation; a litany of physical, psychological, and sexual humiliations; death threats; threats to his family; and a mock kidnapping and rendition.
March 3, 2005	Mohamedou handwrites his petition for a writ of habeas corpus.
Summer 2005	Mohamedou handwrites the 466 pages that would become this book in his segregation cell in Guantánamo.
June 12, 2008	The U.S. Supreme Court rules 5–4 in *Boumediene v. Bush* that Guantánamo detainees have a right to challenge their detention through habeas corpus.
August–December 2009	U.S. District Court Judge James Robertson hears Mohamedou's habeas corpus petition.
March 22, 2010	Judge Robertson grants Mohamedou's habeas corpus petition and orders his release.
March 26, 2010	The Obama administration files a notice of appeal.
November 5, 2010	The DC Circuit Court of Appeals sends Mohamedou's habeas corpus case back to U.S. district court for rehearing. That case is still pending.
Present	Mohamedou remains in Guantánamo, in the same cell where many of the events recounted in this book took place.

Notes on the Text, Redactions, and Annotations

This book is an edited version of the 466-page manuscript Mohamedou Ould Slahi wrote by hand in his Guantánamo prison cell in the summer and fall of 2005. It has been edited twice: first by the United States government, which added more than 2,500 black-bar redactions censoring Mohamedou's text, and then by me. Mohamedou was not able to participate in, or respond to, either one of these edits.

He has, however, always hoped that his manuscript would reach the reading public—it is addressed directly to us, and to American readers in particular—and he has explicitly authorized this publication in its edited form, with the understanding and expressed wish that the editorial process be carried out in a way that faithfully conveys the content and fulfills the promise of the original. He entrusted me to do this work, and that is what I have tried to do in preparing this manuscript for print.

Mohamedou Ould Slahi wrote his memoir in English, his fourth language and a language he acquired largely in U.S. custody, as he describes, often amusingly, throughout the book. This is both a significant act and a remarkable achievement in itself. It is also a choice that creates or contributes to some of the work's most important literary effects. By my count, he deploys a vocabulary of under seven thousand words—a lexicon about the size of the one that powers the Homeric epics. He does so in ways that sometimes echo those epics, as when he repeats formulaic phrases for recurrent phenomena and events. And he does so, like the creators of the epics, in ways that manage to deliver an enormous range of action and emotion. In the editing process, I have tried above all to preserve this feel and honor this accomplishment.

At the same time, the manuscript that Mohamedou managed to compose in his cell in 2005 is an incomplete and at times fragmentary draft. In some sections the prose feels more polished, and in some the handwriting looks smaller and more precise, both suggesting possible previous drafts; elsewhere the writing has more of a first-draft sprawl and urgency. There are significant variations in narrative approach, with less linear storytelling in the sections recounting the most recent events—as one would expect, given the intensity of the events and proximity of the characters he is describing. Even the overall shape of the work is unresolved, with a series of flashbacks to events that precede the central narrative appended at the end.

In approaching these challenges, like every editor seeking to satisfy every author's expectation that mistakes and distractions will be minimized and voice and vision sharpened, I have edited the manuscript on two levels. Line by line, this has mostly meant regularizing verb tenses, word order, and a few awkward locutions, and occasionally, for clarity's sake, consolidating or reordering text. I have also incorporated the appended flashbacks within the main narrative and streamlined the manuscript as a whole, a process that brought a work that was in the neighborhood of 122,000 words to just under 100,000 in this version. These editorial decisions were mine, and I can only hope they would meet with Mohamedou's approval.

Throughout this process, I was confronted with a set of challenges specifically connected with the manuscript's previous editing process: the government's redactions. These redactions are changes that have been imposed on the text by the same government that continues to control the author's fate and has used secrecy as an essential tool of that control for more than thirteen years. As such, the black bars on the page serve as vivid visual reminders of the author's ongoing situation. At the same time, deliberately or not, the redactions often serve to impede the sense of narrative, blur the contours of characters, and obscure the open, approachable tone of the author's voice.

Because it depends on close reading, any process of editing a censored text will involve some effort to see past the black bars and erasures. The annotations that appear at the bottom of the page throughout the text are a kind of record of that effort.

These notes represent speculations that arose in connection with the redactions, based on the context in which the redactions appear, information that appears elsewhere in the manuscript, and what is now a wealth of publicly available sources about Mohamedou Ould Slahi's ordeal and about the incidents and events he chronicles here. Those sources include declassified government documents obtained through Freedom of Information Act requests and litigation, news reports and the published work of a number of writers and investigative journalists, and extensive Justice Department and U.S. Senate investigations.

I have not attempted in these annotations to reconstruct the original redacted text or to uncover classified material. Rather, I have tried my best to present information that most plausibly corresponds to the redactions when that information is a matter of public record or evident from a careful reading of the manuscript, and when I believe it is important for the overall readability and impact of the text. If there are any errors in these speculations, the fault is entirely mine. None of Mohamedou Ould Slahi's attorneys holding security clearances has reviewed these introductory materials or the footnotes, contributed to them in any way, or confirmed or denied my speculations contained in them. Nor has anyone else with access to the unredacted manuscript reviewed these introductory materials or the footnotes, contributed to them in any way, or confirmed or denied my speculations contained in them.

So many of the editing challenges associated with bringing this remarkable work to print result directly from the fact that the U.S. government continues to hold the work's author, with no satisfactory explanation to date, under a censorship regime that prevents him from participating in the editorial process. I look forward to the day when Mohamedou Ould Slahi is free and we can read this work in its entirety, as he would have it published. Meanwhile I hope this version has managed to capture the accomplishment of the original, even as it reminds us, on almost every page, of how much we have yet to see.

Introduction

by Larry Siems

In the summer and early fall of 2005, Mohamedou Ould Slahi handwrote a 466-page, 122,000-word draft of this book in his single-cell segregation hut in Camp Echo, Guantánamo.

He wrote it in installments, starting not long after he was finally allowed to meet with Nancy Hollander and Sylvia Royce, two attorneys from his pro bono legal team. Under the strict protocols of Guantánamo's sweeping censorship regime, every page he wrote was considered classified from the moment of its creation, and each new section was surrendered to the United States government for review.

On December 15, 2005, three months after he signed and dated the manuscript's last page, Mohamedou interrupted his testimony during an Administrative Review Board hearing in Guantánamo to tell the presiding officers:

> *I just want to mention here that I wrote a book recently while in jail here recently about my whole story, okay? I sent it for release to the District [of] Columbia, and when it is released I advise you guys to read it. A little advertisement. It is a very interesting book, I think.*[1]

But Mohamedou's manuscript was not released. It was stamped "SECRET," a classification level for information that could cause serious damage to national security if it becomes public, and "NOFORN," meaning it can't be shared with any foreign nationals or intelligence services. It was deposited in a secure facility near Washington, DC, accessible only to those with a full security clearance and an official "need to know." For more than six years, Mohamedou's attorneys carried out litigation and negotiations to have the manuscript cleared for public release.

During those years, compelled largely by Freedom of Information Act litigation spearheaded by the American Civil Liberties Union, the U.S. government released thousands of secret documents that described the treatment of prisoners in U.S. custody since the September 11, 2001, terrorist attacks. Many of those documents hinted at Mohamedou's ordeal, first in the hands of the CIA, and then in the hands of the U.S. military in Guantánamo, where a "Special Projects Team" subjected him to one of the most stubborn, deliberate, and cruel interrogations in the record. A few of those documents contained something else as well: tantalizing samples of Mohamedou's voice.

One of these was in his own handwriting, in English. In a short note dated March 3, 2005, he wrote, "Hello. I, Mohamedou Ould Slahi, detained in GTMO under ISN #760, herewith apply for a writ of habeas corpus." The note concluded simply, "I have done no crimes against the U.S., nor did the U.S. charge me with crimes, thus I am filing for my immediate release. For further details about my case, I'll be happy for any future hearings."

Another handwritten document, also in English, was a letter to his attorney Sylvia Royce dated November 9, 2006, in which he joked, "You asked me to write you everything I told my interrogators. Are you out of your mind? How can I render uninterrupted interrogation that has been lasting the last 7 years? That's like asking Charlie Sheen how many women he dated." He went on:

Yet I provided you everything (almost) in my book, which the government denies you the access to. I was going to go deeper in details, but I figured it was futile.

To make a long story short, you may divide my time in two big steps.

(1) Pre-torture (I mean that I couldn't resist): I told them the truth about me having done nothing against your country. It lasted until May 22, 2003.

(2) Post-torture era: where my brake broke loose. I yessed every accusation my interrogators made. I even wrote the infamous confession about me planning to hit the CN Tower in Toronto, based on SSG ▓▓▓▓▓▓▓ advice. I just wanted to get the monkeys off my back. I don't care how long I stay in jail. My belief comforts me.[2]

The documents also included a pair of transcripts of Mohamedou's sworn testimony before detainee review boards in Guantánamo. The first—and the first sample of his voice anywhere in the documents—is from his Combatant Status Review Tribunal (CSRT) hearing; the date is December 8, 2004, just months after his so-called "special interrogation" ended. It includes this exchange:

Q: *Can I get your response to the very first allegation that you are a member of the Taliban or al Qaida?*

A: *The Taliban, I have nothing to do with them whatsoever. Al Qaida, I was a member in Afghanistan in 91 and 92. After I left Afghanistan, I broke all my relations with al Qaida.*

Q: *And you've never provided them money, or any type of support since then?*

A: *Nothing whatsoever.*

Q: *Ever recruited for them?*

A: *No, not at all; no trying to recruit for them.*

Q: *You said that you were pressured to admit you were involved in the Millennium plot, right?*

A: *Yes.*

Q: *To whom did you make that confession?*

A: *To the Americans.*

Q: *And what do you mean by pressure?*

A: *Your honor, I don't wish to talk about this nature of the pressure if I don't have to.*

Q: *Tribunal President: You don't have to; we just want to make sure that you were not tortured or coerced into saying something that wasn't true. That is the reason he is asking the question.*

A: *You just take from me I am not involved in such a horrible attack; yes I admit to being a member of al Qaida, but I am not willing to talk about this. The smart people came to me and analyzed this, and got the truth. It's good for me to tell the truth, and the information was verified. I said I didn't have anything to do with this. I took and passed the polygraph, and they said I didn't have to speak of this anymore. They said please don't speak of this topic anymore, and they haven't opened it up to this topic for a year now.*

Q: *So no U.S. authorities abused you in any way?*

A: *I'm not willing to answer this question; I don't have to, if you don't force me to.*[3]

The other transcript comes from the 2005 Administrative Review Board hearing where he announced he had written this book. A year had passed since the CSRT hearing, a year when he was finally allowed to meet with attorneys, and when he somehow found the distance and the stamina to write down his experience. This time he speaks freely of his odyssey, not in fear or in anger, but in a voice inflected with irony and wit. "He was very silly," Mohamedou says of one of his interrogator's threats, "because he said he was going to bring in black people. I don't have any problem with black people, half of my country is black people!" Another interrogator in Guantánamo known as Mr. X was covered head to toe "like in Saudi Arabia, how the women are covered," and wearing "gloves, O.J. Simpson gloves on his hands." Mohamedou's answers are richly detailed, for deliberate effect and for an earnest purpose. "Please," he tells the board, "I want you guys to understand my story okay, because it really doesn't matter if they release me or not, I just want my story understood."[4]

We do not have a complete record of Mohamedou's effort to tell his story to the review board at that hearing. Just as he begins to describe what he experienced in Guantánamo during the summer of 2003, "the recording equipment began to malfunction," notes a boldface interruption in the transcript. For the lost section, in which "the detainee discussed how he was tortured while here at GTMO by several individuals," the document offers instead "the board's recollection of that 1000 click malfunction":

> The Detainee began by discussing the alleged abuse he received from a female interrogator known to him as ▋▋▋▋▋▋▋. The Detainee attempted to explain to the Board ▋▋▋▋▋▋ actions but he became distraught and visibly upset. He explained that he was sexually harassed and although he does like women he did not like what ▋▋▋▋▋▋ had done to him. The Presiding Officer noticed the Detainee was upset and told him he was not required to tell the story. The Detainee was very appreciative and elected not to elaborate on the alleged abuse from ▋▋▋▋▋▋.
>   The Detainee gave detailed information regarding the alleged abuse from ▋▋▋▋▋▋ and ▋▋▋▋▋▋. The Detainee

xxi

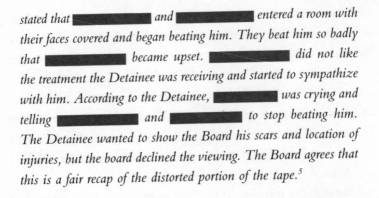

stated that ▮▮▮▮▮ *and* ▮▮▮▮▮ *entered a room with their faces covered and began beating him. They beat him so badly that* ▮▮▮▮▮ *became upset.* ▮▮▮▮▮ *did not like the treatment the Detainee was receiving and started to sympathize with him. According to the Detainee,* ▮▮▮▮▮ *was crying and telling* ▮▮▮▮▮ *and* ▮▮▮▮▮ *to stop beating him. The Detainee wanted to show the Board his scars and location of injuries, but the board declined the viewing. The Board agrees that this is a fair recap of the distorted portion of the tape.[5]*

We only have these transcripts because in the spring of 2006, a federal judge presiding over a FOIA lawsuit filed by the Associated Press ordered them released. That lawsuit also finally compelled the Pentagon, four years after Guantánamo opened, to publish an official list of the men it was holding in the facility. For the first time, the prisoners had names, and the names had voices. In the transcripts of their secret hearings, many of the prisoners told stories that undercut claims that the Cuban detention camp housed "the worst of the worst," men so dangerous, as the military's presiding general famously declared as the first prisoners were landing at the camp in 2002, they would "gnaw hydraulic lines in the back of a C-17 to bring it down."[6] Several, like Mohamedou, broached the subject of their treatment in U.S. custody.

The Pentagon doubled down. "Detainees held at Guantánamo are terrorist trainers, bomb-makers, would-be suicide bombers, and other dangerous people," a military spokesman again asserted when the transcripts became public. "And we know that they're trained to lie to try to gain sympathy for their condition and to bring pressure against the U.S. government."[7] A year later, when the military released the records of Guantánamo's 2006 Administrative Review Board hearings, Mohamedou's transcript was missing completely. That transcript is still classified.

Mohamedou's manuscript was finally cleared for public release, and a member of his legal team was able to hand it to me on a disk labeled "Slahi Manuscript—Unclassified Version," in the summer of 2012. By then, Mohamedou had been in Guantá-namo for a decade. A federal judge had granted his habeas corpus petition two years before and ordered him released, but the U.S government had appealed, and the appeals court sent his petition back down to the federal district court for rehear-ing. That case is still pending.

Mohamedou remains to this day in the same segregation cell where he wrote his Guantánamo diary. I have, I believe, read everything that has been made public about his case, and I do not understand why he was ever in Guantánamo in the first place.

Mohamedou Ould Slahi was born on December 31, 1970, in Rosso, then a small town, now a small city, on the Senegal River on Mauritania's southern border. He had eight older sib-lings; three more would follow. The family moved to the capi-tal, Nouakchott, as Mohamedou was finishing primary school, and his father, a nomadic camel trader, died not long after. The timing, and Mohamedou's obvious talents, must have shaped his sense of his role in the family. His father had taught him to read the Koran, which he had memorized by the time he was a teenager, and he did well in high school, with a particular aptitude for math. A 2008 feature in *Der Spiegel* describes a popular kid with a passion for soccer, and especially for the German national team—a passion that led him to apply for, and win, a scholarship from the Carl Duisberg Society to study in Germany. It was an enormous leap for the entire family, as the magazine reported:

Slahi boarded a plane for Germany on a Friday in the late sum-mer of 1988. He was the first family member to attend a university—abroad, no less—and the first to travel on an air-plane. Distraught by the departure of her favorite son, his mother's goodbye was so tearful that Mohamedou briefly hesitated before getting on his flight. In the end, the others convinced him to go. "He was supposed to save us financially," his brother [Y]ahdih says today.[8]

In Germany, Mohamedou pursued a degree in electrical engineering, with an eye toward a career in telecom and com-puters, but he interrupted his studies to participate in a cause that was drawing young men from around the world: the insur-gency against the communist-led government in Afghanistan. There were no restrictions or prohibitions on such activities in those days, and young men like Mohamedou made the trip openly; it was a cause that the West, and the United States in particular, actively supported. To join the fight required train-ing, so in early 1991 Mohamedou attended the al-Farouq train-ing camp near Khost for seven weeks and swore a loyalty oath to al-Qaeda, the camp's operators. He received light arms and mortar training, the guns mostly Soviet made, the mortar shells, he recalled in his 2004 Combatant Status Review hearing, made in the U.S.A.

Mohamedou returned to his studies after the training, but in early 1992, with the communist government on the verge of collapsing, he went back to Afghanistan. He joined a unit com-manded by Jalaluddin Haqqani that was laying siege to the city of Gardez, which fell with little resistance three weeks after Mohamedou arrived. Kabul fell soon thereafter, and as Moham-edou explained at the CSRT hearing, the cause quickly turned murky:

Right after the break down of [the] Communists, the Mujahiden themselves started to wage Jihad against themselves, to see who would be in power; the different factions began to fight against each other. I decided to go back because I didn't want to fight against other Muslims, and found no reason why; nor today did I see a reason to fight to see who could be president or vice-president. My goal was solely to fight against the aggressors, mainly the Communists, who forbid my brethren to practice their religion.

That, Mohamedou has always insisted, marked the end of his commitment to al-Qaeda. As he told the presiding officer at his CSRT:

Ma'am, I was knowledgeable I was fighting with al Qaida, but then al Qaida didn't wage Jihad against America. They told us to fight with our brothers against the Communists. In the mid-90's they wanted to wage Jihad against America, but I personally had nothing to do with that. I didn't join them in this idea; that's their problem. I am completely out of the line between al Qaida and the U.S. They have to solve this problem themselves; I am completely independent of this problem.[9]

Back in Germany, Mohamedou settled into the life he and his family in Nouakchott had planned. He completed his degree in electrical engineering at the University of Duisburg, his young Mauritanian wife joined him, and the couple lived and worked in Duisburg for most of the 1990s. During that time, though, he remained friends or kept in touch with companions from the Afghanistan adventure, some of whom maintained al-Qaeda ties. He also had his own direct association with a prominent al-Qaeda member, Mahfouz Ould al-Walid, also known as Abu Hafs al-Mauritani, who was a member of al-Qaeda's Shura Council and one of Osama bin Laden's senior theological advisers. Abu Hafs is a distant cousin of Mohamedou, and also a brother-in-law through his marriage to Mohamedou's wife's sister. The two were in occasional phone contact while Mohamedou was in Germany—a call from Abu Hafs, using bin Laden's satellite phone, caught the ears of German intelligence in 1999—and twice Mohamedou helped Abu Hafs transfer $4,000 to his family in Mauritania around the Ramadan holidays.

In 1998, Mohamedou and his wife traveled to Saudi Arabia to perform the hajj. That same year, unable to secure permanent residency in Germany, Mohamedou followed a college friend's recommendation and applied for landed immigrant status in Canada, and in November 1999 he moved to Montreal. He lived for a time with his former classmate and then at Montreal's large al Sunnah mosque, where, as a *hafiz*, or someone who has memorized the Koran, he was invited to lead Ramadan prayers when the imam was traveling. Less than a month after he arrived in Montreal, an Algerian immigrant and al-Qaeda member named Ahmed Ressam was arrested entering the United States with a car laden with explosives and a plan to bomb Los Angeles International Airport on New Year's Day, as part of what became known as the Millennium Plot. Ressam had been based in Montreal. He left the city before Mohamedou arrived, but he had attended the al Sunnah mosque and had connections with several of what Mohamedou, at his CSRT hearing, called his classmate's "bad friends."

Ressam's arrest sparked a major investigation of the Muslim immigrant community in Montreal, and the al Sunnah mosque community in particular, and for the first time in his life, Mohamedou was questioned about possible terrorist connections. The

Royal Canadian Mounted Police "came and interrogated me," he testified at his 2005 Administrative Review Board hearing.

> *I was scared to hell. They asked me do I know Ahmed Ressam, I said, "No," and then they asked do you know this guy and I said, "No, No." I was so scared I was shaking. . . . I was not used to this, it was the first time I had been interrogated and I just wanted to stay out of trouble and make sure I told the truth. But they were watching me in a very ugly way. It is okay to be watched, but it is not okay to see the people who are watching you. It was very clumsy, but they wanted to give the message that we are watching you.*

Back in Mauritania, Mohamedou's family was alarmed. " 'What are you doing in Canada?' " he recalled them asking. "I said nothing but look[ing] for a job. And my family decided I needed to get back to Mauritania because this guy must be in a very bad environment and we want to save him." His now ex-wife telephoned on behalf of the family to report that his mother was sick. As he described to the Review Board:

> *[She] called me and she was crying and she said, "Either you get me to Canada or you come to Mauritania." I said, "Hey, take it easy." I didn't like this life in Canada, I couldn't enjoy my free-dom and being watched is not very good. I hated Canada and I said the work is very hard here. I took off on Friday, 21 January 2000; I took a flight from Montreal to Brussels, then to Dakar.[10]*

With that flight, the odyssey that will become Mohamedou's *Guantánamo Diary* begins.

It begins here because from this moment forward, a single

force determines Mohamedou's fate: the United States. Geographically, what he calls his "endless world tour" of detention and interrogation will cover twenty thousand miles over the next eighteen months, starting with what is supposed to be a homecoming and ending with him marooned four thousand miles from home on a Caribbean island. He will be held and interrogated in four countries along the way, often with the participation of Americans, and always at the behest of the United States.

Here is how the first of these detentions is described in a timeline that U.S. District Judge James Robertson included in his declassified 2010 order granting Mohamedou's habeas corpus petition:

Jan 2000	*Flew from Canada to Senegal, where brothers met him to take him to Mauritania; he and brothers were seized by ▬▬▬▬ authorities, and were questioned about the Millennium plot. An American came and took pictures; then, someone he presumed was American flew him to Mauritania, where he was questioned further by Mauritanian authorities about the Millennium plot.*
Feb 2000	*Interrogated by ▬▬ re Millennium plot*
2/14/2000	▬▬▬▬▬ *released him, concluding there was no basis to believe he was involved in the Millennium plot.*

"The Mauritanians said, 'We don't need you, go away. We have no interest in you,'" Mohamedou recalled, describing that release at his ARB hearing. "I asked them what about the Americans? They said, 'The Americans keep saying you are a link but they don't give us any proof so what should we do?'"

But as Judge Robertson chronicled in his timeline, the Mauritanian government summoned Mohamedou again at the United States' request shortly after the 9/11 terrorist attacks:

9/29/2001	*Arrested in Mauritania; authorities told him* ███████ ███████ *arrest because Salahi was allegedly involved in Millennium plot.*
10/12/2001	*While he was detained, agents performed a search at his house, seizing tapes and documents.*
10/15/2001	*Released by* ███████████ *authorities.*[11]

Between those two Mauritanian arrests, both of which included interrogations by FBI agents, Mohamedou was living a remarkably ordinary and, by his country's standards, successful life, doing computer and electronics work, first for a medical supply company that also provided Internet services, and then for a similarly diversified family-owned import business. But now he was nervous. Although he was free and "went back to his life," as he explained to the ARB:

> I thought now I will have a problem with my employer because my employer would not take me back because I am suspected of terrorism, and they said they would take care of this. In front of me while I was sitting [there] the highest intelligence guy in Mauritania called my employer and said that I was a good person, we have no problem with [him] and we arrested him for a reason. We had to question him and we have questioned him and he is good to go, so you can take him back.[12]

His boss did take him back, and just over a month later, Mohamedou's work would take him to the Mauritanian Presidential Palace, where he spent a day preparing a bid to upgrade President Maaouya Ould Sid'Ahmed Taya's telephone and computer systems. When he got home, the national police appeared again, telling him he was needed once more for questioning. He asked them to wait while he showered. He dressed, grabbed his keys—he went voluntarily, driving his own car to police headquarters—and told his mother not to worry, he would be home soon. This time, though, he disappeared.

For almost a year, his family was led to believe he was in Mauritanian custody. His oldest brother, Hamoud, regularly visited the security prison to deliver clean clothes and money for Mohamedou's meals. A week after Mohamedou turned himself in, however, a CIA rendition flight had spirited him to Jordan; months later, the United States had retrieved him from Amman and delivered him to Bagram Air Base in Afghanistan and, a few weeks after that, to Guantánamo. All this time, his family was paying for his upkeep in the Nouakchott prison; all this time, the prison officials pocketed the money, saying nothing. Finally, on October 28, 2002, Mohamedou's youngest brother, Yahdih, who had assumed Mohamedou's position as the family's European breadwinner, picked up that week's edition of *Der Spiegel* and read that his brother had by then "been sitting for months in a wire cage in the U.S. prison camp in Guantánamo."

Yahdih was furious—not, he remembers, at the United States but at the local authorities who had been assuring the family they had Mohamedou and he was safe. "Those police are bad people, they're thieves!" he kept yelling when he called his family with the news. "Don't say that!" they panicked, hanging up. He called them back and started in again. They hung up again.

Yahdih still lives in Düsseldorf. He and I met last year over a series of meals in a Moroccan restaurant on Ellerstraße, a center for the city's North African community. Yahdih introduced me to several of his friends, mainly young Moroccans, many of them, like Yahdih, now German citizens. Among themselves they spoke Arabic, French, and German; with me, like Yahdih, they gamely tried English, laughing at one another's mistakes. Yahdih told a classic immigrant's joke, in Arabic for his friends and then translating for me, about an aspiring hotel worker's English test. "What do you say if you want to call someone over to you?" the applicant is quizzed. "Please come here," he answers. "What if you want him to leave?" The applicant pauses, then brightens. "I go outside and tell him, 'Please come here!'"

In Düsseldorf, Yahdih and I spent an entire meal sorting and labeling photographs of siblings, sisters- and brothers-in-law, nieces and nephews, many living in the family's multigenerational household in Nouakchott. During his 2004 CSRT hearing, Mohamedou explained his disinterest in al-Qaeda after he returned to Germany by saying, "I had a big family to feed, I had 100 mouths to feed." It was an exaggeration, but only by half, maybe. Now Yahdih bears a large share of that responsibility. Because activism can be a risky business in Mauritania, he has also assumed the family lead in advocating for Mohamedou's release. During our last meal together, we watched YouTube videos of a demonstration he helped organize in Nouakchott last year outside the Presidential Palace. The featured speaker, he pointed out, was a parliament minister.

A few days before I visited Yahdih, Mohamedou had been allowed one of his twice-yearly calls with his family. The calls are arranged under the auspices of the International Committee of the Red Cross and connect Mohamedou with the family household in Nouakchott and with Yahdih in Germany. Yahdih told me he had recently written to the Red Cross to ask if the number of calls could be increased to three a year.

The first of these calls took place in 2008, six and a half years after Mohamedou disappeared. A reporter for *Der Spiegel* witnessed the scene:

At noon on a Friday in June 2008, the Slahi family convenes at the offices of the International Red Cross (IRC) in the Mauritanian capital Nouakchott. His mother, brothers, sisters, nephews, nieces and aunts are all dressed in the flowing robes they would normally wear to a family party. They have come here to talk to Mohamedou, their lost son, by telephone. The Joint Task Force in Guantanamo has granted its approval, with the IRC acting as go-between. Thick carpets cover the stone floor and light-colored curtains billow at the windows of the IRC office.

"My son, my son, how are you feeling?" his mother asks. "I am so happy to hear you." She breaks into tears, as she hears his voice for the first time in more than six years. Mohamedou's older brother speaks with him for 40 minutes. Slahi tells his brother that he is doing well. He wants to know who has married whom, how his siblings are doing and who has had children. "That was my brother, the brother I know. He has not changed," Hamoud Ould Slahi says after the conversation.[13]

From what Yahdih tells me, the conversations remain more or less the same five years later, though two things have changed. The calls are now Skype calls, so they can see one another. And they are now missing Mohamedou's and Yahdih's mother. She died on March 27, 2013.

The lead editorial in the *New York Daily News* on March 23, 2010, was titled "Keep the Cell Door Shut: Appeal a Judge's Outrageous Ruling to Free 9/11 Thug." The editorial began:

It is shocking and true: a federal judge has ordered the release of Mohamedou Ould Slahi, one of the top recruiters for the 9/11 attacks — a man once deemed the highest-value detainee in Guantanamo.

That ruling was Judge James Robertson's then still-classified memorandum order granting Mohamedou's habeas corpus petition—the petition Mohamedou handwrote in his Camp Echo cell five years before. Without access to that order or to the legal filings or court hearing that resulted in the order, the newspaper's editorial board nevertheless conjectured that a judge was letting "a terrorist with the blood of 3,000 on his hands" go free, adding contortedly, "he possibly being a man whose guilt was certain but unprovable beyond a reasonable doubt thanks to squeamishness over evidence acquired under rough treatment." Expressing confidence that Mohamedou was "squeezed appropriately hard after 9/11" and that his treatment made the country safer, the editors urged the Obama administration to appeal the order, adding, "What was the rush to release? The judge could have waited, should have waited, for the country to understand why this had to happen before exercising his legal authority."[14]

Two weeks later, the court released a declassified, redacted version of Judge Robertson's order. A section of the opinion summarizing the government's arguments for why Mohamedou must remain in Guantánamo included a footnote that might have surprised the newspaper's readers:

> *The government also argued at first that Salahi was also detainable under the "aided in 9/11" prong of the AUMF, but it has now abandoned that theory, acknowledging that Salahi probably did not even know about the 9/11 attacks.*[15]

That certainly would make it a stretch to call Mohamedou a "9/11 thug." It is also a stretch, by any measure, to call a

---

* The AUMF, or Authorization for Use of Military Force, is the September 14, 2001, law under which Guantánamo operates. It authorizes the judgment ordering a man freed nine years after he was taken into custody a "rush to release." But there is a truth at the heart of that *Daily News* editorial—and much of the press coverage about Mohamedou's case—and that truth is confusion. Nine years is now thirteen, and the country seems to be no closer to understanding the U.S. government's case for holding Mohamedou than when Judge Robertson, the one judge who has thoroughly reviewed his case, ordered him released.

This much seems clear from the available record: Mohamedou's time in U.S. custody did not begin with allegations that he was a top 9/11 recruiter. When he was questioned by FBI agents on his return to Mauritania in February 2000, and again a few weeks after the 9/11 attacks, the focus was on the Millennium Plot. This appears to have been the case for his rendition to Jordan as well: "The Jordanians were investigating my part in the Millennium plot," Mohamedou told the Administrative Review Board in 2005. "They told me they are especially concerned about the Millennium plot."

By the time the CIA delivered Mohamedou to Jordan, though, Ahmed Ressam had been cooperating for months with the Justice Department in the United States, and by the time the CIA retrieved Mohamedou eight months later, Ressam had testified in two terrorism trials and provided the names of more than 150 people involved in terrorism to the U.S. government and the governments of six other countries. Some of those people were Guantánamo detainees, and the U.S. government has used Ressam's statements as evidence against them in their habeas cases.

---

president "to use all necessary and appropriate force against those nations, organizations, or persons he determines planned, authorized, committed, or aided the terrorist attacks that occurred on September 11, 2001, or harbored such organizations or persons, in order to prevent any future acts of international terrorism against the United States by such nations, organizations or persons."

Not so with Mohamedou. Ressam "conspicuously fails to implicate Salahi," Robertson noted in his habeas opinion.

The CIA would have known this. The agency would also have known if the Jordanians had uncovered anything linking Mohamedou to the Millennium Plot, the September 11 attacks, or any other terrorist plots. But the CIA apparently never provided any information from his interrogation in Amman to Guantánamo prosecutors. In a 2012 interview with the Rule of Law Oral History Project at Columbia University, Lt. Col. Stuart Couch, the Marine prosecutor assigned to build a case against Mohamedou in Guantánamo, said that the CIA showed him no intelligence reports of its own, and most of the reports the agency did share with him came from Mohamedou's Guantánamo interrogation. "He had been in their custody for six months. They knew I was the lead prosecutor. They knew we were contemplating a capital case. If we could have found his connection to 9/11, we were going to go for the death penalty."

"So something must have gone on," Stuart Couch surmised in that interview. "Slahi was in the custody of the CIA, and they must have felt like they got as much information out of him as they could, or the information they had didn't pan out to his significance, and they just kind of threw him over to U.S. military control at Bagram, Afghanistan."[16]

There is a chilling passage in the 2004 CIA inspector general's investigation report *Counterterrorism and Detention Interrogation Activities, September 2001–October 2003*, one of only two unredacted passages in a four-page blacked-out section of the report headed "Endgame." It says:

> *The number of detainees in CIA custody is relatively small by comparison with those in military custody. Nevertheless, the Agency, like the military, has an interest in the disposition of*

detainees and a particular interest in those who, if not kept in isolation, would likely have divulged information about the circumstances of their detention.[17]

In early 2002, not even Mohamedou's family knew he was in Jordan. Few people anywhere knew that the United States was operating a rendition, detention, and interrogation program, and that it was doing so not just with the assistance of long-standing allies like the Jordanian intelligence service but also with the cooperation of other, shakier friends. Mauritania was such a friend. In 2002, Mauritania's president and multi-decade ruler Ould Taya was under fire internationally for his country's human rights record, and at home for his close cooperation with the United States' antiterrorism policies. That Mohamedou had been questioned by FBI agents in his own country in 2000 had been controversial enough to attract the press. What if he had returned to the country in mid-2002 with stories that he had been turned over to the Americans without extradition proceedings, in violation of an explicit Mauritanian constitutional protection; that the CIA had delivered him in secret to Jordan; and that he had been interrogated for months in a Jordanian prison?

In any case, there is no indication that when a U.S. military C-17 carrying Mohamedou and thirty-four other prisoners landed in Guantánamo on August 5, 2002, the thirty-one-year-old Mauritanian was an especially high-value detainee. He would have stood out if so: an article published two weeks later in the *Los Angeles Times* titled "No Leaders of al Qaeda Found at Guantánamo Bay, Cuba" quoted government sources who said that there were "no big fish" in custody there, and the island's nearly six hundred detainees were not "high enough in the command and control structure to help counter-terrorism

experts unravel al Qaeda's tightknit cell and security system."[18]
A top secret CIA audit of the facility around the same time
reportedly echoed those conclusions. When journalists visited the camp that August, the commander of Guantánamo's
detention operations told them his own uniformed officers
were questioning the continuing designation of detainees as
"enemy combatants" as opposed to prisoners of war entitled to
Geneva convention protections. The Pentagon's solution was to
replace that commander and ratchet up the camp's intelligence
operations.

Almost immediately a schism opened between military interrogators and the FBI and Criminal Investigation Task Force
agents who had generally been leading prisoner interviews in
Guantánamo. In September and October, over the fierce objec-
tions of the FBI and CITF agents, the military set up its first
"Special Projects Team" and developed a written plan for the
interrogation of the Saudi prisoner Mohammed al-Qahtani. That
plan incorporated some of the "enhanced interrogation techniques" the CIA had been employing for several months in its
own secret prison. Under the plan, which was implemented in
fits and starts through the fall and finally, with the signed authorization of Defense Secretary Rumsfeld, in a harrowing fifty-day
barrage starting in November, military interrogators subjected
Qahtani to a round-the-clock regime of extreme sleep deprivation, loud music and white noise, frigid temperatures, stress positions, threats, and a variety of physical and sexual humiliations.

It was during this time, as the struggle over interrogation
methods was playing out in the camp, that a link surfaced
between Mohamedou Ould Slahi and the 9/11 hijackers. "September 11, 2002, America arrested a man by the name of Ramzi
bin al-Shibh, who is said to be the key guy in the September
11th attacks," Mohamedou recounted at his 2005 ARB hearing.

It is exactly one year after September 11, and since his capture my life has changed drastically. The guy identified me as the guy that he saw in October 1999, which is correct, he was in my house. He said that I advised him to go to Afghanistan to train. Okay, then his interrogator ▮▮▮▮▮▮▮▮▮ *from the FBI asked him to speculate who I was as a person. He said I think he is an operative of Usama Bin Laden and without him I would never have been involved in September 11th.*[19]

Bin al-Shibh had been the target of an international manhunt since 9/11 for his alleged role in coordinating the "Hamburg cell" of hijackers. He was transferred to CIA custody immediately after his capture in a shoot-out in a suburb of Karachi and was held first in the CIA's "Dark Prison" in Afghanistan and then, through the fall, in a prison near Rabat, Morocco. During interrogations in one of those facilities, bin al-Shibh told of a chance meeting with a stranger on a train in Germany, where he and two friends talked of jihad and their desire to travel to Chechnya to join the fight against the Russians. The stranger suggested they contact Mohamedou in Duisburg, and when they did, Mohamedou put them up for a night. "When they arrived," the 9/11 Commission recorded in a description drawn from intelligence reports from those interrogations, "Slahi explained that it was difficult to get to Chechnya at the time because many travelers were being detained in Georgia. He recommended they go through Afghanistan instead, where they could train for jihad before traveling to Chechnya."[20]

Bin al-Shibh did not assert that Mohamedou sent him to Afghanistan to join a plot against the United States. Lt. Col. Couch, who saw the bin al-Shibh intelligence report, recalled in the 2012 interview, "I never saw any mention that it was to attack America. I never saw the fact that Ramzi Bin al-Shibh had said, 'We told him what we wanted to do, and he said, "This is where you need to go train." ' It was sort of, 'This is where you can get training.' "[21] During Mohamedou's habeas proceedings, the U.S. government did not argue that he had persuaded the men to join bin Laden's plot; rather, the government alleged that in suggesting that the men seek training in Afghanistan — something Mohamedou had learned was necessary to join an earlier fight involving Russians — he was serving in general as an al-Qaeda recruiter. Judge Robertson disagreed, finding that the record showed only that "Salahi provided lodging for three men for one night in Germany, that one of these was Ramzi bin al-Shibh, and that there was discussion of jihad and Afghanistan."[22]

Stuart Couch received bin al-Shibh's intelligence reports when he was assigned Mohamedou's case in the fall of 2003. The reports, and the assignment itself, had particular significance for the former Marine pilot: his close friend Michael Horrocks, a fellow refueling tanker pilot in the Marines, was the copilot on the United Airlines flight that the 9/11 hijackers used to bring down the World Trade Center's South Tower. That event had drawn Stuart Couch back to active service. He joined the Guantánamo military commission's team of prosecutors with a purpose, hoping, as he explained in a 2007 *Wall Street Journal* profile, "to get a crack at the guys who attacked the United States."[23]

Soon he was looking at batches of intelligence reports from another source, Mohamedou himself, the fruit of what military interrogators were already touting as their most successful Guantánamo interrogation. Those reports contained no information about the circumstances of that interrogation, but Lt. Col. Couch had his suspicions. He had been told that Mohamedou was on "Special Projects." He had caught a glimpse, on his first visit to the base, of another prisoner shackled to the floor in an empty interrogation booth, rocking back and forth as a strobe light flashed and heavy metal blared. He had seen this kind of thing before: as a Marine pilot, he had endured a week of such techniques in a program that prepares U.S. airmen for the experience of capture and torture.

Those suspicions were confirmed when the lieutenant colonel's investigator, a Naval Criminal Investigative Service (NCIS) agent, gained access to military interrogators' files. Those files included the Special Projects Team's daily memoranda for the record, the interrogators' detailed accounts not only of what was said in each session but also of how the information was extracted.

Those records remain classified, but they are summarized in the U.S. Senate Armed Services Committee's 2008 *Inquiry into the Treatment of Detainees in U.S. Custody* and the Justice Department's own 2008 review of interrogations in Guantánamo, Afghanistan, and Iraq. Those reports document a "special interrogation" that followed a second painstaking, Rumsfeld-approved plan and unfolded almost exactly as Mohamedou describes it in his *Guantánamo Diary*. Among the specific documents described in those reports are two that, when Stuart Couch uncovered them in early 2004, convinced him that Mohamedou had been tortured.

The first was a fake State Department letter Mohamedou had been presented in August 2003, which was clearly meant to exploit his close relationship with his mother. In its report, the Senate Armed Services Committee describes "a fictitious letter that had been drafted by the Interrogation Team Chief stating that his mother had been detained, would be interrogated, and if she were uncooperative she might be transferred to GTMO. The letter pointed out that she would be the only female detained at 'this previously all-male prison environment.'"

The second was an October 17, 2003, e-mail exchange between

one of Mohamedou's interrogators and a U.S. military psychiatrist. In it, the committee found, the interrogator "stated that 'Slahi told me he is "hearing voices" now.... He is worried as he knows this is not normal.... By the way ... is this something that happens to people who have little external stimulus such as daylight, human interaction etc???? Seems a little creepy.'" The psychologist responded, "Sensory deprivation can cause hallucinations, usually visual rather than auditory, but you never know.... In the dark you create things out of what little you have."[24]

In a 2009 interview, Lt. Col. Couch described the impact of these discoveries:

> *Right in the middle of this time, when I had received this information from the NCIS agent — the documents, the State Department letterhead — and it was at the end of this, hearing all of this information, reading all this information, months and months and months of wrangling with the issue, that I was in church this Sunday, and we had a baptism. We got to the part of the liturgy where the congregation repeats — I'm paraphrasing here, but the essence is that we respect the dignity of every human being and seek peace and justice on earth. And when we spoke those words that morning, there were a lot of people in that church, but I could have been the only one there. I just felt this incredible, alright, there it is. You can't come in here on Sunday, and as a Christian, subscribe to this belief of dignity of every human being and say I will seek justice and peace on the earth, and continue to go with the prosecution using that kind of evidence. And at that point I knew what I had to do. I had to get off the fence.[25]*

Stuart Couch withdrew from Mohamedou's case, refusing to proceed with any effort to try him before a military commission.

No charge sheet has ever been drawn up against Mohamedou

Ould Slahi in Guantánamo, no military commission defense attorney was ever appointed to his case, and it appears there have been no further attempts to prepare a case for prosecution. The *Daily News* editorial decrying Judge Robertson's habeas decision attributes this to "squeamishness" over using "evidence acquired under rough treatment," but it is not at all clear that Mohamedou's brutal Guantánamo interrogation yielded any evidence that he had a hand in any criminal or terrorist activities. At his 2005 ARB hearing, he told of manufacturing confessions under torture, but the interrogators themselves must have discounted what they knew to be induced confessions; what they passed along in their scrubbed intelligence reports consisted instead, Stuart Couch has said, of a kind of "Who's Who of al Qaeda in Germany and all of Europe."[26]

Just as his extreme treatment is often cited as an indicator of his guilt, so those intelligence reports have come to serve as a kind of after-the-fact proof that Mohamedou himself must be among the Who's Who. And yet, Stuart Couch has suggested, Mohamedou's knowledge seems to have been little better than his interrogators'. "I think, if my recollection is right, that most of them had already been known to the intelligence services when he was being questioned," Couch noted in the 2012 interview, adding:

I've got to be clear on something. When you read the intelligence reports given up by Slahi, he doesn't implicate himself in anything. The only way he implicates himself is by his knowledge of these people. He never implicates himself in any of what I would consider to be an overt act that was part of the al-Qaeda conspiracy to attack the United States on 9/11.[27]

Nor, it seems, have U.S. intelligence services unearthed anything else implicating Mohamedou in other terrorist plots or attacks. In a 2013 interview, Colonel Morris Davis, who became chief prosecutor for the Guantánamo military commissions in 2005, described a last-ditch effort, almost two years after Stuart Couch withdrew from Mohamedou's case, to develop some kind of charge against Mohamedou. Colonel Davis's real target at the time was not Mohamedou, who by then hardly even registered on the prosecutorial radar, but rather the prisoner the military had moved into the hut next door to Mohamedou's to mitigate the effects of his torture and almost two years of solitary confinement. That prisoner would not accept a plea bargain, however, unless Mohamedou received a similar offer. "We had to figure some kind of similar deal for Slahi," Colonel Davis said in that interview, "which meant we had to find *something* we could charge him with, and that was where we were having real trouble."

> When Slahi came in, I think the suspicion was that they'd caught a big fish. He reminded me of Forrest Gump, in the sense that there were a lot of noteworthy events in the history of al-Qaida and terrorism, and there was Slahi, lurking somewhere in the background. He was in Germany, Canada, different places that look suspicious, and that caused them to believe that he was a big fish, but then when they really invested the effort to look into it, that's not where they came out. I remember a while after I got there, in early 2007, we had a big meeting with the CIA, the FBI, the Department of Defense, and the Department of Justice, and we got a briefing from the investigators who worked on the Slahi case, and their conclusion was there's a lot of smoke and no fire.[28]

When Mohamedou's habeas corpus petition finally came before the federal court in 2009, the U.S. government did not try to argue that he was a major al-Qaeda figure or that he had a hand in any al-Qaeda plans or attacks. As the DC Circuit Court of Appeals wrote in its subsequent review of the case:

> *The United States seeks to detain Mohammedou Ould Salahi on the grounds that he was "part of" al-Qaida not because he fought with al-Qaida or its allies against the United States, but rather because he swore an oath of allegiance to the organization, associated with its members, and helped it in various ways, including hosting its leaders and referring aspiring jihadists to a known al-Qaida operative.[29]*

When Judge Robertson heard Mohamedou's petition in 2009, the DC district courts presiding over Guantánamo habeas cases were judging the question of whether a petitioner was part of al-Qaeda based on whether the government could show that the petitioner was an active member of the organization at the time he was detained. Mohamedou had joined al-Qaeda in 1991 and sworn a loyalty oath to the organization at that time, but that was a very different al-Qaeda, practically an ally of the United States; Mohamedou has always maintained that the fall of the communist government in Afghanistan marked the end of his participation in the organization. In his habeas proceedings, the government insisted that his occasional contacts and interactions with his brother-in-law and cousin Abu Hafs and a handful of other friends and acquaintances who had remained active in al-Qaeda proved that Mohamedou was still a part of the organization. While a few of those interactions involved possible gestures of support, none, Robertson suggested, rose to the level of criminal material support for terrorism, and overall, Mohamedou's contacts with these people were so sporadic that "they tend to support Salahi's submission that he was attempting to find the appropriate balance—avoiding close relationships with al Qaida members, but also trying to avoid making himself an enemy."

Judge Robertson's decision granting Mohamedou's habeas corpus petition and ordering his release came at a critical moment: as of April 1, 2010, the U.S. government had lost thirty-four out of forty-six habeas cases. In appeals of several of those cases, the government persuaded the DC Circuit Court of Appeals to accept a looser standard for judging whether a petitioner was "part of" al-Qaeda; now, as the appellate court explained in reversing Judge Robertson's order and remanding the case to district court for rehearing, the government no longer needed to show that a Guantánamo prisoner was carrying out al-Qaeda orders or directions at the time he was taken into custody.

In its opinion, the appeals court was careful to delineate "the precise nature of the government's case against Salahi." "The government has not criminally indicted Salahi for providing material support to terrorists or the 'foreign terrorist organization' al-Qaida," the court emphasized. "Nor," it added, "does the government seek to detain Salahi under the AUMF on the grounds that he aided the September 11 attacks or 'purposefully and materially support[ed]' forces associated with al-Qaeda 'in hostilities against U.S. Coalition partners.'" Rather, when Mohamedou's habeas corpus case is reheard in federal court, the government will likely again be arguing that his sporadic interactions with active al-Qaeda members in the 1990s mean that he too remained a member. Under the new standard, the court wrote, "Even if Salahi's connections to these individuals fail independently to prove that he was 'part of' al-Qaida, those connections make it more likely that Salahi was a member of the organization when captured and thus remain relevant to the question of whether he is detainable."[30]

Ironically, when a district court rehears the case, the government will likely face questions about what it has always contended is the most damaging of those connections, Mohamedou's relationship with his cousin and brother-in-law Abu Hafs. As a member of bin Laden's Shura Council, Abu Hafs had a $5 million bounty on his head from the United States in the late 1990s, a figure that increased to $25 million after the September 11, 2001, terrorist attacks. For years, though, the United States has known that Abu Hafs opposed those attacks; the 9/11 Commission reported that he "even wrote Bin Laden a message basing opposition to those attacks on the Qur'an." After the attacks, Abu Hafs left Afghanistan for Iran, where Iranian authorities placed him under a soft form of house arrest for more than a decade. In April 2012, Iran repatriated Abu Hafs to Mauritania. He was held for two months in a Mauritanian prison, during which he reportedly met with an international delegation that included Americans, condemned the 9/11 attacks, and renounced his ties to al-Qaeda. He was released in July 2012 and has been living since then as a free man.

I have not met Mohamedou Ould Slahi. Other than sending him a letter introducing myself when I was asked if I would help to bring his manuscript to print—a letter I do not know if he received—I have not communicated with him in any way.

I did request to meet with him at least once before submitting the completed work to make sure my edits met with his approval. The answer from the Pentagon was brief and absolute. "Visiting or otherwise communicating with any detainee in the detention facility in Guantanamo, unless you are legal counsel representing the detainee, is not possible," a public affairs officer wrote.

"As you are aware, the detainees are held under the Law of War. Additionally, we do not subject detainees to public curiosity."

The phrase "public curiosity" comes from one of the pillars of the Law of War, the 1949 Geneva Convention Relative to the Treatment of Prisoners of War. Article 13 of the convention, "Humane Treatment of Prisoners," says:

> *Prisoners must at all times be humanely treated. Any unlawful act or omission by the Detaining Power causing death or seriously endangering the health of a prisoner of war in its custody will be prohibited, and will be regarded as a serious breach of the present Convention. . . .*
>
> *Prisoners must at all times be protected, particularly from acts of violence or intimidation and against insults and public curiosity.*
>
> *Measures of reprisal against prisoners of war are prohibited.*

I had proposed a confidential meeting, under strict security protocols, to make sure the edited version of Mohamedou's work—a work he specifically wrote for a public readership—accurately represents the original content and intent. For years that work itself was withheld, under a censorship regime that has not always served Geneva's purposes.

Censorship has been integral to the United States' post-9/11 detention operations from the start. It has been purposeful, not once but twice: first, to open a space for the abuse of prisoners, and then to conceal that those abuses happened. In Mohamedou's case, those abuses include enforced disappearance; arbitrary and incommunicado detention; cruel, inhuman, and degrading treatment; and torture. We know this thanks to a documentary record that was also, for years, rigorously suppressed.

I do not know to what extent personal and institutional

interests in covering up those abuses have contributed to Mohamedou's continuing imprisonment. I do know that in the five years I have spent reading the record about his case, I have not been persuaded by my government's vague and shifting explanations for why he is in Guantánamo, or by the assertions of those who defend his now-thirteen-year detention by saying he is almost certainly, or possibly, a this or a that. My own sense of fairness tells me the question of what this or that may be, and of why he must remain in U.S. custody, should long ago have been answered. It would have been, I believe, if his *Guantánamo Diary* had not been kept secret for so long.

When Mohamedou wrote the manuscript for this book nine years ago, in the same isolated hut where some of the book's most nightmarish scenes had very recently happened, he set himself a task. "I have only written what I experienced, what I saw, and what I learned first-hand," he explains near the end. "I have tried not to exaggerate, nor to understate. I have tried to be as fair as possible, to the U.S. government, to my brothers, and to myself."

He has, from everything I have seen, done just that. The story he tells is well corroborated by the declassified record; he proves again and again to be a reliable narrator. He certainly does not exaggerate: the record contains torments and humiliations not included in the book, and he renders several of those he does include with considerable discretion. Even when the events he recounts are at their most extreme, his narration is tempered and direct. The horrors of those events speak for themselves.

That is because his real interest is always in the human dramas of these scenes. "The law of war is harsh," Mohamedou writes early on.

If there's anything good at all in a war, it's that it brings the best and the worst out of people: some people try to use the lawlessness to hurt others, and some try to reduce the suffering to the minimum.

In chronicling his journey through the darkest regions of the United States' post-9/11 detention and interrogation program, his attention remains on his interrogators and guards, on his fellow detainees, and on himself. In his desire "to be fair," as he puts it, he recognizes the larger context of fear and confusion in which all these characters interact, and the much more local institutional and social forces that shape those interactions. But he also sees the capacity of every character to shape or mitigate the action, and he tries to understand people, regardless of stations or uniforms or conditions, as protagonists in their own right. In doing so, he transforms even the most dehumanizing situations into a series of individual, and at times harrowingly intimate, human exchanges.

This is the secret world of Guantánamo—a world of startlingly premeditated brutalities and of incidental degradations, but also a world of ameliorating gestures and kindnesses, of acknowledgments and recognitions, of mutual curiosities and risky forays across deep divides. That Mohamedou managed to experience all of this despite four years of the most arbitrary treatment imaginable and in the midst of one of Guantánamo's most horrendous interrogations says a great deal about his own character and his humanity. It says even more about his skills as a writer that he was able, so soon after the most traumatic of those experiences, to create from them a narrative that manages to be both damning and redeeming.

And yet this is not what impressed me most, as a reader and as a writer, when I first opened the file with Mohamedou's handwritten manuscript of *Guantánamo Diary*. What arrested me were characters and scenes far removed from Guantánamo: The hard-luck stowaway in a Senegalese prison. A sunset in Nouakchott after a Saharan dust storm. A heartbreaking moment of homesickness during a Ramadan call to prayer. The airport approach over Nouakchott's shantytowns. A rain-glazed runway in Cyprus. A drowsy predawn lull on a CIA rendition flight. Here is where I first recognized Mohamedou the writer, his sharp eye for character, his remarkable ear for voices, the way his recollections are infused with information recorded by all five senses, the way he accesses the full emotional register, in himself and others. He has the qualities I value most in a writer: a moving sense of beauty and a sharp sense of irony. He has a fantastic sense of humor.

He manages all of this in English, his fourth language, a language he was in the process of mastering even as he wrote the manuscript. This accomplishment testifies to a lifelong facility and fascination with words. But it also stems, it is clear, from a determination to engage, and to meet his environment on its own terms. On one level, mastering English in Guantánamo meant moving beyond translation and interpretation, beyond the necessity of a third person in the room, and opening the possibility that every contact with every one of his captors could be a personal exchange. On another, it meant decoding and understanding the language of the power that controls his fate—a power, as his twenty-thousand-mile odyssey of detention and interrogation vividly illustrates, of staggering influence and reach. Out of this engagement comes a truly remarkable work. On the one hand, it is a mirror in which, for the first time in anything I have read from Guantánamo, I have recognized aspects of myself, in both the characters of my compatriots and of those my country is holding captive. On another, it is a lens on an empire with a scope and impact few of us who live inside it fully understand.

For now, that power still controls Mohamedou's story. It is present in these pages in the form of more than 2,600 black-box redactions. These redactions do not just hide important elements of the action. They also blur Mohamedou's guiding principles and his basic purpose, undercutting the candor with which he addresses his own case, and obscuring his efforts to distinguish his characters as individuals, some culpable, some admirable, most a complex and shifting combination of both.

And it is present above all in his continuing, poorly explained imprisonment. Thirteen years ago, Mohamedou left his home in Nouakchott, Mauritania, and drove to the headquarters of his national police for questioning. He has not returned. For our collective sense of story and of justice, we must have a clearer understanding of why this has not happened yet, and what will happen next.

Guantánamo lives on unanswered questions. But now that we have *Guantánamo Diary*, how can we not at least resolve the questions in Mohamedou's case?

When we do, I believe there will be a homecoming. When that happens, the redactions will be filled in, the text will be reedited and amended and updated as Mohamedou himself would have it, and we will all be free to see *Guantánamo Diary* for what it ultimately is: an account of one man's odyssey through an increasingly borderless and anxious world, a world where the forces shaping lives are ever more distant and clandestine, where destinies are determined by powers with seemingly infinite reach, a world that threatens to dehumanize but fails to dehumanize — in short, an epic for our times.

103

comfort items, except for a thin iso-mat and
a very thin, small, and worn-out blanket. I was
deprived from my books, which I owned. I was
deprived from my Koran. I was deprived
from my soap. I was deprived from my
toothpaste — maybe —, I was deprived from
the roll of toilet paper I had. The cell —
better the box — was cooled down that I was
shaking most of the time. I was forbidden
from seeing the light of the day. Every
once in a while they gave me a rec-time in
the night to keep me from seeing or interacting
with any detainees. I was living litterally in
tenor, I don't remember having slept one
night quietly, and that if they gave me a break,
which was rarely. For the next seventy days
to come I hadn't known the sweetness of
sleeping. Interrogation for 24-hours, three,
and sometimes four shifts a day. I rarely
got a day-off, "If you start to cooperate you will have some sleep, and hot
meals" ▓▓▓ used to tell me repeatedly.
The last visit of ICRC: After a couple days of
my transfer ▓▓▓ from ICRC showed up at
my cell and asked me whether I wanted to write
a teller, "yes!" I said, ▓▓▓ handed a
paper and I wrote, "Mama I love you, I
just wanted to tell you that I love you!"

104

After that visits I never saw the ICRC for more
than a year. They tried to see me but in vain.
"You started to torture me, but you don't know
how much I can take. You might end up killing me
I said when ███████ and ███████ pulled me for
interrogation, "We do recommand things, but we
don't have 'the final decision" ███████ said, "I just
want to warn you, I am suffering b/c of the
harsh conditions you expose me to. I already
have sciatic nerve crisis attack. And torture
will not make me more cooperative", "According
to my experience you will cooperate, We are stronger
than you, a **GUANTÁNAMO** ces" ███████ said.
███████ never w **DIARY**   name, but he got
busted, when mistakenly one of un colleague called
him with his name. He doesn't know that I know
his name, but well I do. ███████ grew worse with
every day passing by. He started to lay me out my case—
He started with the story of ███████, and me having
recruit him for sep11 attack, "why should he lie
to us ███████ said, "I don't know". "All you have
to say is, I don't remember, I don't know, I have
done nothing. You think you are going to impress an
American jury with these word. If In the eyes of
Americans you are doomed. Just looking at you in
orange suits, chains, being muslim, and Arabic
is enough to convict you" ███████ said "That is
injust", "We know that you are criminal"

111

.I have a great body." Every once in a while ███ offered me to other side of the coin," If you start to cooperate, I am gonna stop harassing you? otherwise I will be doing the same with you and worse every day. I am ███████ and that why my gov't designated me to this job. I've been always successful. Having sex with somebody is not a considered as torture" ███ was leading the monolog ███████. Every now and then the ███████ entered the room, and try to make me speak, "You cannot defeat us, we have so many people, and we keep humilate you with American ███████ ", "I have a ███████ friend, I'm gonna bring tomorrow to help me" ███ said, "At least cooperate" said ███ wryly. ███ didn't undress me but ███ was touching my private parts with ███ body. In the late afternoon, an other torture squad started with other poor detainee. I could hear loud music playing. "Do you want me to send you to that team or are you gonna cooperate" said ███, but I didn't answer. The guards wryly used to call ███████ b/c the most of the torture took place in those buildings, and in the nights. When the darkness started to cover the sorry camp, ███ sent me back to my cell. "Today is just the begin, what's coming is worse and that is every day" ███████ Doctor Routine check: In order ██ to see how much torture a detainee

ONE

Jordan–Afghanistan–GTMO

July 2002–February 2003

The American Team Takes Over...Arrival at Bagram...
Bagram to GTMO...GTMO, the New Home...One
Day in Paradise, the Next in Hell

███████████, July ██, 2002, 10 p.m.*

The music was off. The conversations of the guards faded
away. The truck emptied.

I felt alone in the hearse truck.

The waiting didn't last: I felt the presence of new people, a
silent team. I don't remember a single word during the whole
rendition to follow.

---

* It becomes clear, from an unredacted date a few pages into the manuscript, that the action begins late in the evening on July 19, 2002. MOS
manuscript, 10. A Council of Europe investigation has confirmed that a
CIA-leased Gulfstream jet with the tail number N379P departed Amman,
Jordan, at 11:15 p.m. that night for Kabul, Afghanistan. An addendum to
that 2006 report listing the flight records is available at http://assembly.coe.
int/CommitteeDocs/2006/20060614_Ejdoc162006PartII-Appendix.pdf.
    EDITOR'S NOTE ON THE FOOTNOTES: None of Mohamedou
Ould Slahi's attorneys holding security clearances has reviewed the
footnotes in this book, contributed to them in any way, or confirmed or
denied my speculations contained in them. Nor has anyone else with access

A person was undoing the chains on my wrists. He undid the first hand, and another guy grabbed that hand and bent it while a third person was putting on the new, firmer and heavier shackles. Now my hands were shackled in front of me.

Somebody started to rip my clothes with something like a scissors. I was like, What the heck is going on? I started to worry about the trip I neither wanted nor initiated. Somebody else was deciding everything for me; I had all the worries in the world but making a decision. Many thoughts went quickly through my head. The optimistic thoughts suggested, Maybe you're in the hands of Americans, but don't worry, they just want to take you home, and to make sure that everything goes in secrecy. The pessimistic ones went, You screwed up! The Americans managed to pin some shit on you, and they're taking you to U.S. prisons for the rest of your life.

I was stripped naked. It was humiliating, but the blindfold helped me miss the nasty look of my naked body. During the whole procedure, the only prayer I could remember was the crisis prayer, Ya hayyu! Ya kayyum! and I was mumbling it all the time. Whenever I came to be in a similar situation, I would forget all my prayers except the crisis prayer, which I learned from life of our Prophet, Peace be upon him.

One of the team wrapped a diaper around my private parts. Only then was I dead sure that the plane was heading to the U.S. Now I started to convince myself that "every thing's gonna be alright." My only worry was about my family seeing me on TV in such a degrading situation. I was so skinny. I've been always, but never *that* skinny: my street clothes had become so loose that I looked like a small cat in a big bag.

---

to the unredacted manuscript reviewed the footnotes, contributed to them in any way, or confirmed or denied my speculations contained in them.

When the U.S. team finished putting me in the clothes they tailored for me, a guy removed my blindfold for a moment. I couldn't see much because he directed the flashlight into my eyes. He was wrapped from hair to toe in a black uniform. He opened his mouth and stuck his tongue out, gesturing for me to do the same, a kind of AHH test which I took without resistance. I saw part of his very pale, blond-haired arm, which cemented my theory of being in Uncle Sam's hands.

The blindfold was pushed down. The whole time I was listening to loud plane engines; I very much believe that some planes were landing and others taking off. I felt my "special" plane approaching, or the truck approaching the plane, I don't recall anymore. But I do recall that when the escort grabbed me from the truck, there was no space between the truck and the airplane stairs. I was so exhausted, sick, and tired that I couldn't walk, which compelled the escort to pull me up the steps like a dead body.

Inside the plane it was very cold. I was laid on a sofa and the guards shackled me, mostly likely to the floor. I felt a blanket put over me; though very thin, it comforted me.

I relaxed and gave myself to my dreams. I was thinking about different members of my family I would never see again. How sad would they be! I was crying silently and without tears; for some reason, I gave all my tears at the beginning of the expedition, which was like the boundary between death and life. I wished I were better to people. I wished I were better to my family. I regretted every mistake I made in my life, toward God, toward my family, toward anybody!

I was thinking about life in an American prison. I was thinking about documentaries I had seen about their prisons, and the harshness with which they treat their prisoners. I wished I were blind or had some kind of handicap, so they would put me in isolation and give me some kind of humane treatment and protection. I was thinking, What will the first hearing with the judge be like? Do I have a chance to get due process in a country so full of hatred against Muslims? Am I really already convicted, even before I get the chance to defend myself?

I drowned in these painful dreams in the warmth of the blanket. Every once in a while the pain of the urine urge pinched me. The diaper didn't work with me: I could not convince my brain to give the signal to my bladder. The harder I tried, the firmer my brain became. The guard beside me kept pouring water bottle caps in my mouth, which worsened my situation. There was no refusing it, either you swallow or you choke. Lying on one side was killing me beyond belief, but every attempt to change my position ended in failure, for a strong hand pushed me back to the same position.

I could tell that the plane was a big jet, which led me to believe that flight was direct to the U.S. But after about five hours, the plane started to lose altitude and smoothly hit the runway. I realized the U.S. is a little bit farther than that. Where are we? In Ramstein, Germany? Yes! Ramstein it is: in Ramstein there's a U.S. military airport for transiting planes from the middle east; we're going to stop here for fuel. But as soon as the plane landed, the guards started to change my metal chains for plastic ones that cut my ankles painfully on the short walk to a helicopter. One of the guards, while pulling me out of the plane, tapped me on the shoulder as if to say, "you're gonna be alright." As in agony as I was, that gesture gave me hope that there were still some human beings among the people who were dealing with me.

When the sun hit me, the question popped up again: Where am I? Yes, Germany it is: it was July and the sun rises early. But why Germany? I had done no crimes in Germany! What shit did they pull on me? And yet the German legal system was by far a better choice for me; I know the procedures and speak the language. Moreover, the German system is somewhat transparent, and there are no two and three hundred years sentences. I had little to worry about: a German judge will face me and show me whatever the government has brought against me, and then I'm going to be sent to a temporary jail until my case is decided. I won't be subject to torture, and I won't have to see the evil faces of interrogators.

After about ten minutes the helicopter landed and I was taken into a truck, with a guard on either side. The chauffeur and his neighbor were talking in a language I had never heard before. I thought, What the heck are they speaking, maybe Filipino? I thought of the Philippines because I'm aware of the huge U.S. Military presence there. Oh, yes, Philippines it is: *they* conspired with the U.S. and pulled some shit on me. What would the questions of *their* judge be? By now, though, I just wanted to arrive and take a pee, and after that they can do whatever they please. Please let me arrive! I thought; After that you may kill me!

The guards pulled me out of the truck after a five-minute drive, and it felt as if they put me in a hall. They forced me to kneel and bend my head down: I should remain in that position until they grabbed me. They yelled, "Do not move." Before worrying about anything else, I took my most remarkable urine since I was born. It was such a relief; I felt I was released and sent back home. All of a sudden my worries faded away, and I smiled inside. Nobody noticed what I did.

About a quarter of an hour later, some guards pulled me and towed me to a room where they obviously had "processed" many detainees. Once I entered the room, the guards took the gear off my head. Oh, my ears ached so badly, and so did my head; actually my whole body was conspiring against me. I could barely stand. The guards started to deprive me of my clothes, and soon I stood there as naked as my mother bore me. I stood there for the first time in front of U.S. soldiers, not on TV, this was for real. I had the most common reaction, covering my private parts with my hands. I also quietly started to recite the crisis prayer, *Ya hayyu! Ya kayyum!* Nobody stopped me from praying; however, one of the MPs was staring at me with his eyes full of hatred. Later on he would order me to stop looking around in the room.

A ▮▮▮▮▮▮▮▮▮▮▮▮▮▮▮▮▮▮▮▮▮▮ medic gave me a quick medical check, after which I was wrapped in Afghani cloths. Yes, Afghani clothes in the Philippines! Of course I was chained, hands and feet tied to my waist. My hands, moreover, were put in mittens. Now I'm ready for action! What action? No clue!

The escort team pulled me blindfolded to a neighboring interrogation room. As soon as I entered the room, several people started to shout and throw heavy things against the wall. In the melee, I could distinguish the following questions:

"Where is Mullah Omar?"

"Where is Usama Bin Laden?"

"Where is Jalaluddin Haqqani?"

A very quick analysis went through my brain: the individuals in those questions were leading a country, and now they're a bunch of fugitives! The interrogators missed a couple of things. First, they had just briefed me about the latest news: Afghanistan is taken over, but the high level people have not been captured. Second, I turned myself in about the time when the war against terrorism started, and since then I have been in a Jordanian prison, literally cut off from the rest of the world. So how am I supposed to know about the U.S. taking over Afghanistan, let alone about its leaders having fled? Not to mention where they are now.

I humbly replied, "I don't know!"

"You're a liar!" shouted one of them in broken Arabic.

"No, I'm not lying, I was captured so and so, and I only know Abu Hafs..." I said, in a quick summary of my whole story.*

"We should interrogate these motherfuckers like the Israelis do."

"What do they do?" asked another.

"They strip them naked and interrogate them!"

"Maybe we should!" suggested another. Chairs were still flying around and hitting the walls and the floor. I knew it was only a show of force, and the establishment of fear and anxiety. I went with the flow and even shook myself more than necessary. I didn't believe that Americans torture, even though I had always considered it a remote possibility.

"I am gonna interrogate you later on," said one, and the U.S. interpreter repeated the same in Arabic.

"Take him to the Hotel," suggested the interrogator. This time the interpreter didn't translate.

---

* Abu Hafs, whose name appears here and elsewhere in the manuscript unredacted, is MOS's cousin and former brother-in-law. His full name is Mahfouz Ould al-Walid, and he is also known as Abu Hafs al-Mauritani. Abu Hafs married the sister of MOS's former wife. He was a prominent member of al-Qaeda's Shura Council, the group's main advisory body, in the 1990s and up until the September 11, 2001, terrorist attacks in the United States. It has been widely reported that Abu Hafs opposed those attacks; the 9/11 Commission recorded that "Abu Hafs the Mauritanian reportedly even wrote Bin Ladin a message basing opposition to the attacks on the Qur'an." Abu Hafs left Afghanistan after the 9/11 attacks and spent the next decade under house arrest in Iran. In April 2012 he was extradited to Mauritania, where he was held briefly and then released. He is now a free man. The relevant section of the 9/11 Commission report is available at http://govinfo.library.unt.edu/911/report/911Report_Ch7.pdf.

And so was the first interrogation done. Before the escort grabbed me, in my terrorizing fear, I tried to connect with the interpreter.

"Where did you learn such good Arabic?" I asked.

"In the U.S.!" he replied, sounding flattered. In fact, he didn't speak good Arabic; I just was trying to make some friends.

The escort team led me away. "You speak English," one of them said in a thick Asian accent.

"A little bit," I replied. He laughed, and so did his colleague. I felt like a human being leading a casual conversation. I said to myself, Look how friendly the Americans are: they're gonna put you in a Hotel, interrogate you for a couple of days, and then fly you home safely. There's no place for worry. The U.S. just wants to check everything, and since you're innocent, they're gonna find that out. For Pete's sake, you're on a base in Philippines; even though it's a place at the edge of legality, it's just temporary. The fact that one of the guards sounded Asian strengthened my wrong theory of being in the Philippines.

I soon arrived, not at a Hotel but at a wooden cell with neither a bathroom nor a sink. From the modest furniture—a weathered, thin mattress and an old blanket—you could tell there had been somebody here. I was kind of happy for having left Jordan, the place of randomness, but I was worried about the prayers I could not perform, and I wanted to know how many prayers I missed on the trip. The guard of the cell was a small, skinny white ▇▇▇▇▇▇, a fact which gave me more comfort: for the last eight months I had been dealt with solely by big, muscular males.*

---

* Context suggests the guard may be female. Throughout the manuscript, it appears that the pronouns *she* and *her* are consistently redacted, and *he* and *his* appear unredacted.

10

I asked ▮▮ about the time, and ▮▮ told me it was about eleven, if I remember correctly. I had one more question.

"What day is it?"

"I don't know, every day here is the same," ▮▮ replied. I realized I had asked too much; ▮▮ wasn't even supposed to tell me the time, as I would learn later.

I found a Koran gently placed on some water bottles. I realized I was not alone in the jail, which was surely not a Hotel.

As it turned out, I was delivered to the wrong cell. Suddenly, I saw the weathered feet of a detainee whose face I couldn't see because it was covered with a black bag. Black bags, I soon would learn, were put on everybody's heads to blindfold them and make them unrecognizable, including the writer. Honestly, I didn't want to see the face of the detainee, just in case he was in pain or suffering, because I hate to see people suffering; it drives me crazy. I'll never forget the moans and cries of the poor detainees in Jordan when they were suffering torture. I remember putting my hands over my ears to stop myself from hearing the cries, but no matter how hard I tried, I was still able to hear the suffering. It was awful, even worse than torture.

The ▮▮ guard at my door stopped the escort team and organized my transfer to another cell. It was the same as the one I was just in, but in the facing wall. In the room there was a half-full water bottle, the label of which was written in Russian; I wished I had learned Russian. I said to myself, a U.S. base in the Philippines, with water bottles from Russia? The U.S. doesn't need supplies from Russia, and besides, geographically it makes no sense. Where *am* I? Maybe in a former Russian Republic, like Tajikstan? All I know is that I don't know!

The cell had no facility to take care of the natural business. Washing for prayer was impossible and forbidden. There was no clue as to the *Kibla*, the direction of Mecca. I did what I could. My next door neighbor was mentally sick; he was shouting in a language with which I was not familiar. I later learned that he was a Taliban leader.

Later on that day, July 20, 2002, the guards pulled me for routine police work, fingerprints, height, weight, etcetera. I was offered ▮▮▮▮▮▮▮▮ as interpreter. It was obvious that Arabic was not ▮▮▮ first language. ▮▮▮▮ taught me the rules: no speaking, no praying loudly, no washing for prayer, and a bunch of other nos in that direction.* The guard asked me whether I wanted to use the bathroom. I thought he meant a place where you can shower; "Yes," I said. The bathroom was a barrel filled with human waste. It was the most disgusting bathroom I ever saw. The guards had to watch you while you were taking care of business. I couldn't eat the food—the food in Jordan was, by far, better than the cold MREs I got in Bagram—so I didn't really have to use the bathroom. To pee, I would use the empty water bottles I had in my room. The hygienic situation was not exactly perfect; sometimes when the bottle got filled, I continued on the floor, making sure that it didn't go all the way to the door.

For the next several nights in isolation, I got a funny guard who was trying to convert me to Christianity. I enjoyed the conversations, though my English was very basic. My dialogue partner was young, religious, and energetic. He liked Bush ("the true religious leader," according to him); he hated Bill Clinton ("the Infidel"). He loved the dollar and hated the Euro. He had his copy of the bible on him all the time, and whenever the opportunity arose he read me stories, most of which were from the Old Testament. I wouldn't have been able to understand them if I hadn't read the bible in Arabic several times—not to mention that the versions of the stories are not that far from the

---

* Again, redacted pronouns suggest the interpreter is female.

ones in the Koran. I had studied the Bible in the Jordanian prison; I asked for a copy, and they offered me one. It was very helpful in understanding Western societies, even though many of them deny being influenced by religious scriptures.

I didn't try to argue with him: I was happy to have somebody to talk to. He and I were unanimous that the religious scriptures, including the Koran, must have come from the same source. As it turned out, the hot-tempered soldier's knowledge about his religion was very shallow. Nonetheless I enjoyed him being my guard. He gave me more time on the bathroom, and he even looked away when I used the barrel.

I asked him about my situation. "You're not a criminal, because they put the criminals in the other side," he told me, gesturing with his hand. I thought about those "criminals" and pictured a bunch of young Muslims, and how hard their situation could be. I felt bad. As it turned out, later on I was transferred to these "criminals," and became a "high priority criminal." I was kind of ashamed when the same guard saw me later with the "criminals," after he had told me that I was going to be released at most after three days. He acted normally, but he didn't have that much freedom to talk to me about religion there because of his numerous colleagues. Other detainees told me that he was not bad toward them, either.

The second or the third night ▇▇▇▇▇▇▇ pulled me out of my cell himself and led me to an interrogation, where the same ▇▇▇▇▇▇▇▇▇▇▇▇ Arabic already had taken a seat. ▇▇▇▇▇▇ ▇▇▇▇▇▇▇▇▇▇▇▇▇▇▇▇▇▇▇▇▇▇▇▇▇▇▇▇▇▇▇▇▇▇ ▇▇▇▇▇▇▇▇▇▇▇▇▇▇▇▇▇▇▇▇▇▇▇▇▇▇. You could tell he was the right man for the job: he was the kind of man who wouldn't mind doing the dirty work. The detainees back in Bagram used to call him ▮▮▮▮▮▮▮▮▮▮▮▮▮; he reportedly was responsible for torturing even innocent individuals the government released.*

▮▮▮▮▮▮▮▮ didn't need to shackle me because I was in shackles 24 hours a day. I slept, ate, used the bathroom while completely shackled, hand to feet. ▮▮▮▮▮▮▮▮ opened a file in his hand ▮▮▮▮▮▮▮▮▮▮▮▮▮▮▮▮▮▮ and started by means of the interpreter. ▮▮▮▮▮▮▮▮ was asking me general questions about my life and my background. When he asked me, "What languages do you speak?" he didn't believe me; he laughed along with the interpreter, saying, "Haha, you speak German? Wait, we're gonna check."

Suddenly ▮▮▮▮▮▮▮▮▮▮▮▮▮▮▮▮▮▮ ▮▮▮▮▮▮▮▮▮▮▮▮ the room ▮▮▮▮▮▮▮▮▮▮▮▮ ▮▮▮▮▮▮▮. There was no mistaking it, he was ▮▮▮▮▮▮▮ ▮▮▮▮▮▮▮▮▮▮▮▮▮▮▮▮▮▮▮▮▮▮▮▮▮▮▮▮▮ ▮▮▮▮▮▮†

"Ja Wohl," I replied. ▮▮▮▮▮▮▮▮ was not ▮▮▮▮▮▮▮ but his German was fairly acceptable, given that he spent ▮▮ ▮▮▮▮▮▮▮▮▮▮▮▮▮▮▮▮▮▮▮▮▮▮▮▮▮▮▮▮▮▮ ▮▮▮▮▮▮▮▮▮▮▮▮. He confirmed to his colleague that my German was "▮▮▮▮▮▮▮.

---

* At his December 15, 2005, Administrative Review Board (ARB) hearing, MOS described a U.S. interrogator in Bagram who was Japanese American and whom Bagram prisoners referred to as "William the Torturer." ARB transcript, 23. The lead interrogator here could be that interrogator. MOS's 2005 ARB hearing transcript is available at http://www.dod.mil/pubs/foi/operation_and_plans/Detainee/csrt_arb/ARB_Tran script_Set_8_20751-21016.pdf, p. 23 transcript, p. 206 in link.

† Context suggests the second interrogator addressed MOS in German.

Both looked at me with some respect after that, though the respect was not enough to save me from ▮▮▮▮▮▮ wrath. ▮▮▮▮▮ asked me where I learned to speak German, and said that he was going to interrogate me again later.

▮▮▮▮▮▮▮▮▮▮▮▮▮, "Wahrheit macht frei, the truth sets you free."

When I heard him say that, I knew the truth wouldn't set me free, because "Arbeit" didn't set the Jews free. Hitler's propaganda machinery used to lure Jewish detainees with the slogan, "Arbeit macht frei," Work sets you free. But work set nobody free.

▮▮▮▮▮▮ took a note in his small notebook and left the room. ▮▮▮▮▮ sent me back to my room and apologized ▮▮▮▮▮▮▮.*

"I am sorry for keeping you awake for so long,"

"No problem!" ▮▮ replied.

After several days in isolation I was transferred to the general population, but I could only look at them because I was put in the narrow barbed-wire corridor between the cells. I felt like I was out of jail, though, and I cried and thanked God. After eight months of total isolation, I saw fellow detainees more or less in my situation. "Bad" detainees like me were shackled 24 hours a day and put in the corridor, where every passing guard or detainee stepped on them. The place was so narrow that the barbed wire kept pinching me for the next ten days. I saw ▮▮▮▮▮▮▮▮▮▮▮ being force-fed; he was on a forty-five day hunger strike. The guards were yelling at him, and he was bouncing a dry piece of bread between his hands. All the detainees looked so worn out, as if they had been buried and after several days resurrected, but ▮▮▮▮▮▮▮▮ was a completely different story: he was bones without meat. It

---

* Context suggests the apology is directed to the interpreter.

15

reminded me of the pictures you see in documentaries about WWII prisoners.

Detainees were not allowed to talk to each other, but we enjoyed looking at each other. The punishment for talking was hanging the detainee by the hands with his feet barely touching the ground. I saw an Afghani detainee who passed out a couple of times while hanging from his hands. The medics "fixed" him and hung him back up. Other detainees were luckier: they were hung for a certain time and then released. Most of the detainees tried to talk while they were hanging, which made the guards double their punishment. There was a very old Afghani fellow who reportedly was arrested to turn over his son. The guy was mentally sick; he couldn't stop talking because he didn't know where he was, nor why. I don't think he understood his environment, but the guards kept dutifully hanging him. It was so pitiful. One day one of the guards threw him on his face, and he was crying like a baby.

We were put in about six or seven big barbed-wire cells named after operations performed against the U.S: Nairobi, U.S.S. Cole, Dar-Es-Salaam, and so on. In each cell there was a detainee called English, who benevolently served as an interpreter to translate the orders to his co-detainees. Our English was a gentleman from Sudan named ████████████████████. His English was very basic, and so he asked me secretly whether I spoke English. "No," I replied—but as it turned out I was a Shakespeare compared to him. My brethren thought that I was denying them my services, but I just didn't know how bad the situation was.

Now I was sitting in front of bunch of dead regular U.S. citizens. My first impression, when I saw them chewing without a break, was, What's wrong with these guys, do they have to eat so much? Most of the guards were tall, and overweight. Some of them were friendly and some very hostile. Whenever I realized that a guard was mean I pretended that I understood no English. I remember one cowboy coming to me with an ugly frown on his face:

"You speak English?" he asked.

"No English," I replied.

"We don't like you to speak English. We want you to die slowly," he said.

"No English," I kept replying. I didn't want to give him the satisfaction that his message arrived. People with hatred always have something to get off their chests, but I wasn't ready to be that drain.

Prayer in groups wasn't allowed. Everybody prayed on his own, and so did I. Detainees had no clues about prayer time. We would just imitate: when a detainee started to pray, we assumed it was time and followed. The Koran was available to detainees who asked for one. I don't remember asking myself, because the handling by the guards was just disrespectful; they threw it to each other like a water bottle when they passed the holy book through. I didn't want to be a reason for humiliating God's word. Moreover, thank God, I know the Koran by heart. As far as I recall, one of the detainees secretly passed me a copy that nobody was using in the cell.

After a couple of days, ███████████████ pulled me to interrogate me. ███████████ acted as an interpreter.

"Tell me your story," ███████████ asked.

"My name is, I graduated in 1988, I got a scholarship to Germany...." I replied in very boring detail, none of which seemed to interest or impress ███████████. He grew tired and started to yawn. I knew exactly what he wanted to hear, but I couldn't help him.

He interrupted me. "My country highly values the truth.

Now I'm gonna ask you some questions, and if you answer truthfully, you're gonna be released and sent safely to your family. But if you fail, you're gonna be imprisoned indefinitely. A small note in my agenda book is enough to destroy your life. What terrorist organizations are you part of?"

"None," I replied.

"You're not a man, and you don't deserve respect. Kneel, cross your hands, and put them behind your neck."

I obeyed the rules and he put a bag over my head. My back was hurting bad lately and that position was so painful; ▄▄▄▄▄▄▄▄▄ was working on my sciatic problem.* ▄▄▄▄▄▄▄▄ brought two projectors and adjusted them on my face. I couldn't see, but the heat overwhelmed me and I started to sweat.

"You're gonna be sent to a U.S. facility, where you'll spend the rest of your life," he threatened. "You'll never see your family again. Your family will be f**cked by another man. In American jails, terrorists like you get raped by multiple men at the same time. The guards in my country do their job very well, but being raped is inevitable. But if you tell me the truth, you're gonna be released immediately."

I was old enough to know that he was a rotten liar and a man with no honor, but he was in charge, so I had to listen to his bullshit again and again. I just wished that the agencies would start to hire smart people. Did he really think that anybody would believe his nonsense? Somebody would have to be stupid: was he stupid, or did he think I was stupid? I would have respected him more had he told me, "Look, if you don't tell me what I want to hear, I'm gonna torture you."

---

* At his 2005 ARB hearing, MOS indicated that an interrogator nicknamed "William the Torturer" made him kneel for "very long hours" to aggravate his sciatic nerve pain and later threatened him. ARB transcript, 23.

Anyway, I said, "Of course I will be truthful!"

"What terrorist organizations are you part of?"

"None!" I replied. He put back the bag on my head and started a long discourse of humiliation, cursing, lies, and threats. I don't really remember it all, nor am I ready to sift in my memory for such bullshit. I was so tired and hurt, and tried to sit but he forced me back. I cried from the pain. Yes, a man my age cried silently. I just couldn't bear the agony.

███████████ after a couple of hours sent me back to my cell, promising me more torture. "This was only the start," as he put it. I was returned to my cell, terrorized and worn out. I prayed to Allah to save me from him. I lived the days to follow in horror: whenever ███████████ went past our cell I looked away, avoiding seeing him so he wouldn't "see" me, exactly like an ostrich. ███████████ was checking on everybody, day and night, and giving the guards the recipe for every detainee. I saw him torturing this other detainee. I don't want to recount what I heard about him; I just want to tell what I saw with my eyes. It was an Afghani teenager, I would say 16 or 17. ███████████ made him stand for about three days, sleepless. I felt so bad for him. Whenever he fell down the guards came to him, shouting "no sleep for terrorists," and made him stand again. I remember sleeping and waking up, and he stood there like a tree.

Whenever I saw ███████████ around, my heart started to pound, and he was often around. One day he sent a ███████████ interpreter to me to pass me a message.

"███████████ is gonna kick your ass."

I didn't respond, but inside me I said, May Allah stop you! But in fact ███████████ didn't kick my rear end; instead ███████████ pulled me for interrogation.* He was a nice

---

* This appears to be the German-speaking interrogator who assisted in the earlier interrogation.

guy; maybe he felt he could relate to me because of the language. And why not? Even some of the guards used to come to me and practice their German when they learned that I spoke it.

Anyway, he recounted a long story to me. "I'm not like ██████████. He's young and hot-tempered. I don't use inhumane methods; I have my own methods. I want to tell something about American history, and the whole war against terrorism."

██████████ was straightforward and enlightening. He started with American history and the Puritans, who punished even the innocents by drowning them, and ended with the war against terrorism. "There is no innocent detainee in this campaign: either you cooperate with us and I am going to get you the best deal, or we are going to send you to Cuba."

"What? *Cuba?*" I exclaimed. "I don't even speak Spanish, and you guys *hate* Cuba."

"Yes, but we have an American territory in Guantánamo," he said, and told me about Teddy Roosevelt and things like that. I knew that I was going to be sent further from home, which I hated.

"Why would you send me to Cuba?"

"We have other options, like Egypt and Algeria, but we only send them the very bad people. I hate sending people over there, because they'll experience painful torture."

"Just send me to Egypt."

"You sure do not want that. In Cuba they treat detainees humanely, and they have two Imams. The camp is run by the DOJ, not the military."*

---

* Department of Justice. This is not true, of course. The Guantánamo Bay detention camp is located on the Guantánamo Bay Naval Base and is run by a U.S. military joint task force under the command of the U.S. Southern Command.

"But I've done no crimes against your country."

"I'm sorry if you haven't. Just think of it as if you had cancer!"

"Am I going to be sent to court?"

"Not in the near future. Maybe in three years or so, when my people forget about September 11." ▇▇▇▇▇▇▇▇ went on to tell me about his private life, but I don't want to put it down here.

I had a couple more sessions with ▇▇▇▇▇▇▇ after that. He asked me some questions and tried to trick me, saying things like, "He said he knows you!" for people I had never heard of. He took my email addresses and passwords. He also asked the ▇▇▇▇▇▇▇▇▇▇▇▇▇▇▇▇▇▇▇▇ who were present in Bagram to interrogate me, but they refused, saying the ▇▇▇▇▇▇ law forbids them from interrogating aliens outside the country.* He was trying the whole time to convince me to cooperate so he could save me from the trip to Cuba. To be honest, I preferred to go to Cuba than to stay in Bagram.

"Let it be," I told him. "I don't think I can change anything."

Somehow I liked ▇▇▇▇▇▇▇. Don't get me wrong, he was a sneaky interrogator, but at least he spoke to me according to the level of my intellect. I asked ▇▇▇▇▇▇▇ to put me inside the cell with the rest of the population, and showed him the injuries I had suffered from the barbed wire. ▇▇▇▇▇▇▇

---

* This could refer to agents of the German foreign intelligence service, the Bundesnachrichtendienst (BND). Press accounts indicate that MOS was interrogated by both German and Canadian intelligence agents in Guantánamo; later in the manuscript, in the scene where he meets with what appear to be BND interrogators in GTMO, MOS specifically references such a prohibition on external interrogations. See footnote on page 51; see also http://www.spiegel.de/international/world/from-germany-to -guantanamo-the-career-of-prisoner-no-760-a-583193-3.html; and http:// www.thestar.com/news/canada/2008/07/27/csis_grilled_trio_in_cuba.html.

approved: in Bagram, interrogators could do anything with you; they had overall control, and the MPs were at their service. Sometimes ▋▋▋▋▋▋▋▋ gave me a drink, which I appreciated, especially with the kind of diet I received, cold MREs and dry bread in every meal. I secretly passed my meals to other detainees.

One night ▋▋▋▋▋▋▋▋ introduced two military interrogators who asked me about the Millennium plot. They spoke broken Arabic and were very hostile to me; they didn't allow me to sit and threatened me with all kind of things. But ▋▋▋▋▋▋▋▋ hated them, and told me in ▋▋▋▋▋▋, "If you want to cooperate, do so with me. These MI guys are nothing." I felt myself under auction to whichever agency bids more!*

In the population we always broke the rules and spoke to our neighbors. I had three direct neighbors. One was an Afghani teenager who was kidnapped on his way to Emirates; he used to work there, which was why he spoke Arabic with a Gulf accent. He was very funny, and he made me laugh; over the past nine months I had almost forgotten how. He was spending holidays with his family in Afghanistan and went to Iran; from there he headed to the Emirates in a boat, but the boat was hijacked by the U.S. and the passengers were arrested.

---

* The interrogator's remark about military interrogators and MOS's reference to an interagency competition for control of his interrogation suggest that the interrogator may be from one of the civilian agencies, likely the FBI. The protracted interagency conflict between the FBI and the Pentagon's Defense Intelligence Agency over the military's interrogation methods has been widely documented and reported, most notably in a May 2008 report by the U.S. Department of Justice's Inspector General titled *A Review of the FBI's Involvement in and Observations of Detainee Interrogations in Guantanamo Bay, Afghanistan, and Iraq* (hereafter cited as DOJ IG). The report, which is available at http://www.justice.gov/oig/special/s0805 /final.pdf, includes substantial sections devoted specifically to MOS's interrogation.

My second neighbor was twenty-year-old Mauritanian guy who was born in Nigeria and moved to Saudi Arabia. He'd never been in Mauritania, nor did he speak the Mauritanian dialect; if he didn't introduce himself, you would say he was a Saudi.

My third neighbor was a Palestinian from Jordan named ████████████. He was captured and tortured by an Afghani tribal leader for about seven months. His kidnapper wanted money from ████████████ family or else he would turn him over to the Americans, though the latter option was the least promising because the U.S. was only paying $5,000 per head, unless it was a big head. The bandit arranged everything with ████████████ family regarding the ransom, but ████████████ managed to flee from captivity in Kabul. He made it to Jalalabad, where he easily stuck out as an Arab mujahid and was captured and sold to the Americans. I told ████████████ that I'd been in Jordan, and he seemed to be knowledgeable about their intelligence services. He knew all the interrogators who dealt with me, as ████████████ himself spent 50 days in the same prison where I had been.

When we spoke, we covered our heads so guards thought we were asleep, and talked until we got tired. My neighbors told me that we were in Bagram, in Afghanistan, and I informed them that we were going to be transferred to Cuba. But they didn't believe me.

Around 10 a.m. on August ██, 2002 a Military unit, some armed with guns, appeared from nowhere.* The armed MPs

---

* It is clear from an unredacted date later in this chapter, as well as from official in-processing records, that MOS arrived in Guantánamo on August 5, 2002, which would make this scene the morning of August 4, 2002.

were pointing their guns at us from upstairs, and the others were shouting at the same time, "Stan' up, Stan' up..." I was so scared. Even though I expected to be transferred to Cuba some time that day, I had never seen this kind of show.

We stood up. The guards kept giving other orders. "No talking...Do not move...Ima fucking kill yo'...I'm serious!" I hated it when ████████████ from Palestine asked to use the bathroom and the guards refused. "Don't move." I was like, Can't you just keep it till the situation is over? But the problem with ████████████ was that he had dysentery, and he couldn't hold it; ████████████ had been subjected to torture and malnutrition in Kabul during his detention by the Northern Alliance tribal leader. ████████████ told me that he was going to use the bathroom anyway, which he did, ignoring the shouting guards. I expected every second a bullet to be released toward him, but that didn't happen. The bathroom inside our shared cells was also an open barrel, which detainees in punishment cleaned every day for every cell. It was very disgusting and smelled so bad. Being from a third world country, I have seen many unclean bathrooms, but none of them could hold a candle to Bagram's.

I started to shake from fear. One MP approached the gate of our cell and started to call the names, or rather the numbers, of those who were going to be transferred. All the numbers called in my cell were Arabs, which was a bad sign. The brothers didn't believe me when I told them we were going to be transferred to Cuba. But now I felt myself confirmed, and we looked at each other and smiled. Several guards came to the gate with a bunch of chains, bags, and other materials. They started to call us one by one, asking each detainee to approach the gate, where he got chained.

"████████," one of the guards shouted. I proceeded to the gate like a sheep being led to her butcher. At the gate, a guard yelled, "Turn around!" which I did, and "Both hands behind!"

When I slid my hands through the bin hole behind my back, one of the guards grabbed my thumb and bent my wrist. "When you fuckin' move, I'm gonna break your hand." Another guard chained my hands and my feet with two separate chains. Then a bag was put over my head to blindfold me. The gate was opened, and I was roughly pushed and thrown over the back of another detainee in a row. Although I was physically hurt, I was solaced when I felt the warmth of another human being in front of me suffering the same. The solace increased when ████████████ was thrown over my back. Many detainees didn't exactly understand what the guards wanted from them, and so got hurt worse. I felt lucky to have been blindfolded, for one, because I missed a lot bad things that were happening around me, and for two, because the blindfold helped me in my daydreaming about better circumstances. Thank ALLAH, I have the ability to ignore my surroundings and daydream about anything I want.

We were supposed to be very close to each other. Breathing was very hard. We were 34 detainees, all of whom were Arab except for one Afghani and one from the Maldives.* When we were put in a row, we were tied together with a rope around our upper arms. The rope was so tight that the circulation stopped, numbing my whole arm.

---

* In-processing height and weight records indicate that thirty-five detainees arrived in Guantánamo on August 5, 2002. The records of that group are available at http://www.dod.mil/pubs/foi/operation_and_plans /Detainee/measurements/ISN_680-ISN_838.pdf. An official list of all Guantánamo detainees is available at http://www.defense.gov/news /may2006/d20060515%20list.pdf.

We were ordered to stand up, and were pulled to a place where the "processing" continued. I hated it because ▮▮▮ ▮▮▮▮▮▮▮▮▮ kept stepping on my chain, which hurt badly. I tried my best not to step on the chain of the man in front of me. Thank God the trip was short: somewhere in the same building we were set down next to each other on long benches. I had the feeling that the benches made a circle.

The party started with dressing the passengers. I got a headset that prevented me from hearing. It gave me such a painful headache; the set was so tight that I had the top of my ears bleeding for a couple of days. My hands were now tied to my waist in the front, and connected with a chain all the way to my feet. They connected my wrists with a six-inch hard plastic piece, and made me wear thick mittens. It was funny, I tried to find a way to free my fingers, but the guards hit my hands to stop moving them. We grew tired; people started to moan. Every once in a while one of the guards took off one of my ear plugs and whispered a discouraging phrase:

"You know, you didn't make any mistake: your mom and dad made the mistake when they produced you."

"You gonna enjoy the ride to the Caribbean paradise...." I didn't answer any provocation, pretending not to understand what he said. Other detainees told me about having been subject to such humiliation, too, but they were luckier; they understood no English.

My flipflops were taken away, and I got some made-in-China tennis shoes. Over my eyes they put really ugly, thick, blind-folding glasses, which were tied around my head and over my ears. They were similar to swimming goggles. To get an idea about the pain, put some old goggles around your hand and tie them tight, and stay that way for a couple of hours; I am sure you will remove them. Now imagine that you have those same goggles tied around your head for more than forty hours. To seal the dressing, a sticky pad was placed behind my ear.

Sometime during the processing we got a cavity search, to the laughter and comments of the guards. I hated that day when I started to learn my miserable English vocabulary. In such situations you're just better off if you don't understand English. The majority of the detainees wouldn't speak about the cavity searches we were subject to, and they would get angry when you started to talk about them. I personally wasn't ashamed; I think the people who did these searches without good reason should be ashamed of themselves.

I grew sick, tired, frustrated, hungry, nauseous, and all the other bad adjectives in the dictionary. I am sure I wasn't the only one. We got new plastic bracelets carrying a number. My number turned out to be 760, and my next ██████████████████. You could say my group was the 700 series.

████████████ used the bathroom a couple of times, but I tried not to use it. I finally went in the afternoon, maybe around 2 p.m.

"Do you like music?" the guard who was escorting me there asked when we were alone.

"Yes, I do!"

"What kind?"

"Good music!"

"Rock and Roll? Country?" I wasn't really familiar with these types he mentioned. Every once in a while I used to listen to German radio with different kinds of Western music, but I couldn't tell which one was which.

"Any good music," I replied. The good conversation paid off in the form that he took my blindfold off so that I could take care of my business. It was very tricky, since I had chains all around my body. The guard placed me gently back on the bench, and for the next couple of hours waiting was the order. We were deprived from the right of performing our daily prayers for the next forty-eight hours.

Around four p.m., the transport to the airport started. By then, I was a "living dead." My legs weren't able to carry me anymore; for the time to come, the guards had to drag me all the way from Bagram to GTMO.

We were loaded in a truck that brought us to the airport. It took five to ten minutes to get there. I was happy for every move, just to have the opportunity to alter my body, for my back was killing me. We were crowded in the truck shoulder-to-shoulder and thigh-to-thigh. Unluckily I was placed facing the back of the vehicle, which I really hate because it gives me nausea. The vehicle was equipped with hard benches so that the detainees sat back to back and the guards sat at the very end shouting, "No talking!" I have no idea how many people were in the truck; all I know is that one detainee sat on my right, and one on my left, and another against my back. It is always good to feel the warmth of your co-detainees, somehow it's solacing.

The arrival at the airport was obvious because of the whining of the engines, which easily went through the earplugs. The truck backed up until it touched the plane. The guards started to shout loudly in a language I could not differentiate. I started to hear human bodies hitting the floor. Two guards grabbed a detainee and threw him toward two other guards on the plane, shouting "Code"; the receiving guards shouted back confirming receipt of the package. When my turn came, two guards grabbed me by the hands and feet and threw me toward the reception team. I don't remember whether I hit the floor or was caught by the other guards. I had started to lose feeling and it would have made no difference anyway.

Another team inside the plane dragged me and fastened me on a small and straight seat. The belt was so tight I could not breathe. The air conditioning hit me, and one of the MPs was shouting, "Do not move, Do not talk," while locking my feet to the floor. I didn't know how to say "tight" in English. I was calling, "MP, MP, belt..." Nobody came to help me. I almost got smothered. I had a mask over my mouth and my nose, plus the bag covering my head and my face, not to mention the tight belt around my stomach: breathing was impossible. I kept saying, "MP, Sir, I cannot breathe!...MP, SIR, please." But it seemed like my pleas for help got lost in a vast desert.

After a couple minutes, ██████████████ was dropped beside me on my right. I wasn't sure it was him, but he told me later he felt my presence beside him. Every once in a while, if one of the guards adjusted my goggles, I saw a little. I saw the cockpit, which was in front of me. I saw the green camo-uniforms of the escorting guards. I saw the ghosts of my fellow detainees on my left and my right. "Mister, please, my belt...hurt...," I called. When the shoutings of the guards faded away, I knew that the detainees were all on board. "Mister, please...belt...." A guard responded, but he not only didn't help me, he tightened the belt even more around my abdomen.

Now I couldn't endure the pain; I felt I was going to die. I couldn't help asking for help louder. "Mister, I cannot breathe..." One of the soldiers came and untightened the belt, not very comfortably but better than nothing.

"It's still tight..." I had learned the word when he asked me, "Is it tight?"

"That's all you get." I gave up asking for relief from the belt.

"I cannot breathe!" I said, gesturing to my nose. A guard appeared and took the mask off my nose. I took a deep breath and felt really relieved. But to my dismay, the guard put the mask back on my nose and my mouth. "Sir, I cannot breathe . . . MP . . . MP." The same guy showed up once more, but instead of taking the mask off my nose, he took the plug out of my ear and said, "Forget about it!" and immediately put the ear plug back. It was harsh, but it was the only way not to smother. I was panicking, I had just enough air, but the only way to survive was to convince the brain to be satisfied with the tiny bit of air it got.

The plane was in the air. A guard shouted in my ear, "Ima gonna give you some medication, you get sick." He made me take a bunch of tablets and gave me an apple and a peanut butter sandwich, our only meal since the transfer procedure began. I've hated peanut butter since then. I had no appetite for anything, but I pretended I was eating the sandwich so the guards don't hurt me. I always tried to avoid contact with those violent guards unless it was extremely necessary. I took a bite off the sandwich and kept the rest in my hand till the guards collected the trash. As to the apple, the eating was tricky, since my hands were tied to my waist and I wore mittens. I squeezed the apple between my hands and bent my head to my waist like an acrobat to bite at it. One slip and the apple is gone. I tried to sleep, but as tired as I was, every attempt to take a nap ended in failure. The seat was as straight as an arrow, and as hard as a stone.

After about five hours, the plane landed and our ghosts were transferred to another, maybe bigger plane. It was stable in the air. I was happy with every change, any change, hoping for the betterment of my situation. But I was wrong, the new plane wasn't better. I knew that Cuba was quite far, but I never thought it to be that far, given the U.S.'s high speed airplanes. At some point, I thought that the government wanted to blow up the plane over the Atlantic and declare it an accident, since all the detainees had been interrogated over and over and over.

But this crazy plan was the least of my worries; was I really worried about a little death pain, after which I would hopefully enter paradise with God's mercy? Living under God's mercy would be better than living under the U.S.'s mercy.

The plane seemed to be heading to the kingdom of far, far away. Feeling lessened with every minute going by; my body numbed. I remember asking for the bathroom once. The guards dragged me to the place, pushed inside a small room, and pulled down my pants. I couldn't take care of my business because of the presence of others. But I think I managed with a lot of effort to squeeze some water. I just wanted to arrive, no matter where! Any place would be better than this plane.

After I don't know how many hours, the plane landed in Cuba. The guards started to pull us out of the plane. "Walk!... Stop!" I couldn't walk, for my feet were unable to carry me. And now I noticed that at some point I had lost one of my shoes. After a thorough search outside the plane, the guards shouted, "Walk! Do not talk! Head down! Step!" I only understood "Do not talk," but the guards were dragging me anyway. Inside the truck, the guards shouted "Sit down! Cross your legs!" I didn't understand the last part but they crossed my legs anyway. "Head down!" one shouted, pushing my head against the rear end of another detainee like a chicken. A female voice was shouting all the way to the camp, "No Talking," and a male voice, "Do Not Talk," and an Arabic translator, ████████████ ████████████████████████████, "Keep your head down." I was completely annoyed by the American way of talking; I stayed that way for a long time, until I got cured by meeting other good Americans. At the same time, I was thinking about how they gave the same order two different ways: "Do not talk" and "No talking." That was interesting.

By now the chains on my ankles were cutting off the blood

to my feet. My feet became numb. I heard only the moaning and crying of other detainees. Beating was the order of the trip. I was not spared: the guard kept hitting me on my head and squeezing my neck against the rear end of the other detainee. But I don't blame him as much as I do that poor and painful detainee, who was crying and kept moving, and so kept raising my head. Other detainees told me that we took a ferry ride during the trip, but I didn't notice.

After about an hour we were finally at the promised land. As much pain as I suffered, I was very happy to have the trip behind me. A Prophet's saying states, "Travel is a piece of torture." This trip was certainly a piece of torture. Now I was only worried about how I was going to stand up if they asked me to. I was just paralyzed. Two guards grabbed me and shouted "Stan' up." I tried to jump but nothing happened; instead they dragged me and threw me outside the truck.

The warm Cuban sun hit me gracefully. It was such a good feeling. The trip started ████████████████████ 10 a.m., and we arrived in Cuba around 12:00 or 1:00 a.m. ████████████████████, which meant we spent more than thirty hours in an ice-cold airplane.* I was luckier than a ████████████████ brother who froze totally. He happened to ask the guard to turn down the A/C on the plane. The guard not

---

* In this passage, MOS describes a five-hour flight, a change of airplanes, and then a much longer flight. A 2008 investigation by the British human rights organization Reprieve found that transfers of prisoners from Bagram to Guantánamo typically involved a stop at the U.S. air base in Incirlik, Turkey, and the Rendition Project has found that a C-17 military transport plane, flight number RCH233Y, flew from Incirlik to Guantánamo on August 5, 2002, carrying thirty-five prisoners. See http://www.libertyse curity.org/IMG/pdf_08.01.28FINALPrisonersIllegallyRenderedtoGuanta namoBay.pdf; and http://www.therenditionproject.org.uk/pdf/PDF%20 154%20[Flight%20data.%20Portuguese%20flight%20logs%20to%20 GTMO,%20collected%20by%20Ana%20Gomes].pdf.

only refused to meet his wish, but he kept soaking him with water drops all the way to Cuba. The medics had to put him in a room and treat him with a blazing fire.

"When they started the fire, I said to myself, here you go, now they start the torture!" he told us. I laughed when he recounted his story in the ████████████████ the next morning.

I could tell they had changed the guard team for a better one. The old team used to say "Wader"; the new team says "Water." The old team used to say, "Stan' up," the new team, "Stand up." The old team was simply too loud.

I could also tell the detainees had reached their pain limit. All I heard was moaning. Next to me was an Afghani who was crying very loudly and pleading for help ████████████ ████████████████████████████████. He was speaking in Arabic, "Sir, how could you do this to me? Please, relieve my pain, Gentlemen!" But nobody even bothered to check on him. The fellow was sick back in Bagram. I saw him in the cell next to ours; he was vomiting all the time. I felt so bad for him. At the same time, I laughed. Can you believe it, I stupidly laughed! Not at him; I laughed at the situation. First, he addressed them in Arabic, which no guards understood. Second, he called them Gentlemen, which they were most certainly not.

In the beginning I enjoyed the sunbath, but the sun grew hotter with every minute that went by. I started to sweat, and grew very tired of the kneeling position I had to remain in for about six hours. Every once in a while a guard shouted, "Need water!" I don't remember asking for water, but it's likely that I did. I was still stuck with the blindfold, but my excitement about being in a new correctional facility with other human beings I could socialize with, in a place where there would be no torture or even interrogation, overwhelmed my pain; that and the fact that I didn't know how long the detention was going to last. And so I didn't open my mouth with any complaints or moans, while many brothers around me where moaning and even crying. I think that my pain limit had been reached a long time before.

I was dead last to be "processed"; people who got hurt on the plane probably had priority, such as ███████████████ ████████. Finally two escorting guards dragged me into the clinic. They stripped me naked and pushed me into an open shower. I took a shower in my chains under the eyes of everybody, my brethren, the medics, and the Army. The other brothers who proceeded me were still stark naked. It was ugly, and although the shower was soothing, I couldn't enjoy it. I was ashamed and I did the old ostrich trick: I looked down to my feet. The guards dried me and took me to the next step. Basically the detainees went through a medical check, where they took note of everybody's biological description, height, weight, scars, and experienced the first interrogation inside the clinic. It was like a car production line. I followed the steps of the detainee who preceded me, and he followed somebody else's steps, and so on and so forth.

"Do you have any known diseases?" asked the young nurse.

"Yes, sciatic nerve and hypotension."

"Anything else?"

"No."

"Where did they capture you?"

"I don't understand," I replied. The doctor repeated the

nurse's question, but I still didn't understand. He spoke too quickly.

"Never mind!" the doctor said. One of my guards gestured to me, putting one of his hands over the other. Only then did I understand the doctor's question.

"In my country!"

"Where are you from?"

"Mauritania," I replied as the guards were dragging me to the next step. Medics are not supposed to interrogate detainees, but they do anyway. Personally I enjoy conversations with everybody and I couldn't care less about them breaking the rules.

It was cool and crowded inside the hospital. I was solaced by the fact that I saw detainees who were in the same situation as me, especially after they wrapped us in the orange uniform. Interrogators were disguised among the Medics to gather information.

"Do you speak Russian?" an old civilian, an Intel wreck of the cold war, asked me. He interrogated me a couple of times later on, and told me that he once worked with ██████████████, a Mujahideen leader in Afghanistan during the war with the Soviets who supposedly used to turn over Russian detainees to the U.S. "I interrogated them. They're now U.S. citizens, and among my best friends," he told me. He claimed to be responsible for a section of the GTMO Task Force. Interrogators like him were sneaking around, trying to converse "innocently" with the detainees. However, interrogators have a hard time mixing in with other people. They're simply very clumsy.

The escort led me to a room with many detainees and interrogators at work. "What's your name? Where are you from? Are you married?"

"Yes!"

"What's the name of your wife?" I forgot the name of my wife and several members of my family as well because of the persistent state of depression I had been in now for the last nine months. Since I knew that nobody was going to buy such a thing, I went, "Zeinebou," just a name that came to my mind.

"What languages do you speak?"

"Arabic, French, German."

"Sprechen Sie Deutsch?" asked the male interrogator in uniform who was helping ███████████████████████ typing in laptop.

"Bist du ███████████?" I asked him. ██████████████ was shocked when I mentioned his name.

"Who told you about me?"

"████████████, from Bagram!" I said, explaining that in Bagram ████████████ told me about ████████████ in case I needed a German translator in GTMO.*

"We'll keep the conversation in English, but very simple," he said. ████████████ avoided me for the rest of his time in GTMO.

I was listening to the interrogation of a Tunisian fellow detainee.

"Did you train in Afghanistan?"

"No."

"You know if you lie, we're gonna get the information from Tunisia!"

"I am not lying!"

The medical check resumed. A ████████████████████████ corpsman took a thousand and one tubes of blood off me. I thought I was going to pass out or even die. A blood pressure check showed 110 over 50, which is very low. The doctor

---

* MOS may be referring here to his German-speaking interrogator in Afghanistan.

immediately put me on small red tablets to increase my blood pressure. Pictures were taken. I hated the fact that my privacy was being disrespected in every way. I was totally under the mercy of somebody I didn't trust and who might be ruthless. Many detainees would smile for the camera. I personally never smiled, and I don't think that on that day, August 5th, 2002, any detainee did.

After the endless processing, the escort team took me out of the clinic. "Keep your head down!" It was already dark outside but I couldn't tell what time it was. The weather was nice. "Sit down." I sat outside for about thirty minutes before the escort team picked me up and put me in a room and locked me to the floor. I didn't notice the lock, nor had I ever been subject to it before. I thought the room was to be my future home.

The room was bare but for a couple of chairs and a desk. There was no sign of life. "Where are the other detainees?" I said to myself. I grew impatient and decided to go outside the room and try to find other fellow detainees, but as soon as I tried to stand up the chains pulled me down hard. Only then did I know that something was wrong with my assumptions. As it turned out, I was in the interrogation booth in ███████ ███████, a building with history.

All of a sudden three men entered the room: the older guy who spoke to me earlier in the clinic, an ███████████ ████████████████████████████, and a ██████████████ ████████████ who served as an interpreter.*

---

* The FBI led MOS's interrogations for his first several months in Guantánamo, waging a well-documented struggle to keep him out of the hands of military interrogators. "The FBI sought to interview Slahi immediately after he arrived at GTMO," the DOJ Inspector General reported. "FBI and task force agents interviewed Slahi over the next few months, utilizing rapport building techniques." At his 2005 ARB hearing, MOS described an "FBI guy" who interrogated him shortly after his arrival and told him,

"Comment vous vous appelez?" asked ████████ in a thick accent.

"Je m'appelle......" I answered, and that was the end of ████████████████████. Interrogators always tend to bring the factor of surprise as a technique.

I glimpsed one of the guy's watches. It was nearly 1 a.m. I was in a state where my system had gotten messed up; I was wide awake in spite of more than forty-eight hours of sleeplessness. The interrogators wanted to use that weakness to facilitate the interrogation. I was offered nothing such as water or food.

████████████ led the interrogation, and ████████████████ was a good translator. The other guy didn't get the chance to ask questions, he just took notes. ████████████ didn't really come up with a miracle: all he did was ask me some questions I had been asked uninterruptedly for the past three years. ████████████ spoke a very clear English, and I almost didn't need the translator. He seemed to be smart and experienced. When the night grew late, ████████████ thanked me for my cooperation.

"I believe that you are very open," he said. "The next time we'll untie your hands and bring you something to eat. We will not torture you, nor will we extradite you to another country." I was happy with ████████████ assurances, and encouraged in my cooperation. As it turned out, ████████████ was either misleading me or he was unknowledgeable about the plans of his government.

The three men left the room and sent the escort team to me,

"We don't beat people, we don't torture, it's not allowed." That would appear to be the lead interrogator in this scene—and perhaps also the "older gentleman" who appears in a subsequent session. DOJ IG, 122; ARB transcript, 23.

which led me to my cell. It was in ▮▮▮▮▮▮ Block, a block designed for isolation.* I was the only detainee who had been picked for interrogation from our entire group of thirty-four detainees. There was no sign of life inside the block, which made me think that I was the only one around. When the guard dropped me in the frozen-cold box I almost panicked behind the heavy metal door. I tried to convince myself, It's only a temporary place, in the morning they're going to transfer me to the community. This place cannot be for more than the rest of the night! In fact, I spent one whole month in ▮▮▮▮▮▮ ▮▮▮▮▮▮.

It was around 2 a.m. when the guard handed me an MRE. I tried to eat what I could, but I had no appetite. When I checked my stuff I saw a brand new Koran, which made me happy. I kissed the Koran and soon fell asleep. I slept deeper than I ever had.

The shoutings of my fellow detainees woke me up in the early morning. Life was suddenly blown into ▮▮▮▮▮▮▮▮▮▮▮ ▮▮▮▮▮▮▮▮▮. When I arrived earlier that morning, I never thought that human beings could be possibly stored in a bunch of cold boxes; I thought I was the only one, but I was wrong, my fellow detainees were only knocked out due to the harsh punishment trip they had behind them. While the guards were

---

* The March 3, 2003, Camp Delta Standard Operating Procedures instructed that arriving prisoners be processed and held for four weeks in a maximum security isolation block "to enhance and exploit the disorientation and disorganization felt by a newly arrived detainee in the interrogation process" and "to [foster] dependence of the detainee on his interrogator." The document is available at http://www.comw.org/warreport/fulltext/gitmo-sop.pdf (hereafter cited as SOP).

serving the food, we were introducing us to ourselves. We couldn't see each other due to the design of the block but we could hear each other.

"Salam Alaikum!"

"Waalaikum Salam."

"Who are you?

"I am from Mauritania...Palestine...Syria...Saudi Arabia...!"

"How was the trip?"

"I almost froze to death," shouted one guy.

"I slept the whole trip," replied ███████████████████.

"Why did they put the patch beneath my ear?" said a third.

"Who was in front of me in the truck?" I asked. "He kept moving, which made the guards beat me all the way from the airport to the camp."

"Me, too," another detainee answered.

We called each other with the ISN numbers we were assigned in Bagram. My number was ██████.* In the cell on my left was ████████████ from ████████████. He is about ████████ ████████████████████████████████. Though Mauritanian, he had never really been in the country; I could tell because of his ████████ accent. On my right was the guy from the ████████████. He spoke poor Arabic, and claimed to have been captured in Karachi, where he attends the University. In front of my cell they put the Sudanese, next to each other.†

---

* The number has already appeared unredacted, and the Department of Defense has officially acknowledged that MOS's ISN is 760. See, e.g., the publicly released DOD detainees list available at http://www.defense .gov/news/may2006/d20060515%20list.pdf.

† MOS may be referring here to Mohammed al-Amin (ISN 706), who was born in Mauritania but moved to Saudi Arabia for religious studies, and Ibrahim Fauzee (ISN 730), who is from the Maldives. Both arrived in

Breakfast was modest: one boiled egg, a hard piece of bread, and something else I don't know the name of. It was my first hot meal since I left Jordan. Oh, the tea was soothing! I like tea better than any food, and for as long as I can remember I've been drinking it. Tea is a crucial part of the diet of people from warmer regions; it sounds contradictory but it is true.

People were shouting all over the place in indistinct conversations. It was just a good feeling when everybody started to recount his story. Many detainees suffered, some more and some less. I didn't consider myself the worst, nor the luckiest. Some people were captured with their friends and their friends disappeared from the face of the earth; they most likely were sent to other allied countries to facilitate their interrogation by torture, such as the ███████████████████████████ ███████. I considered the arrival to Cuba a blessing, and so I told the brothers, "Since you guys are not involved in crimes, you need to fear nothing. I personally am going to cooperate, since nobody is going to torture me. I don't want any of you to suffer what I suffered in Jordan. In Jordan, they hardly appreciate your cooperation."

I wrongly believed that the worst was over, and so I cared less about the time it would take the Americans to figure out that I was not the guy they are looking for. I trusted the American justice system too much, and shared that trust with the detainees from European countries. We all had an idea about how the democratic system works. Other detainees, for instance those from the Middle East, didn't believe it for a second and trust the American system. Their argument lay on the growing

GTMO with MOS on August 5, 2002; both have since been released. See http://projects.nytimes.com/guantanamo/detainees/706-mohammad -lameen-sidi-mohammad; and http://projects.nytimes.com/guantanamo /detainees/730-ibrahim-fauzee.

hostility of extremist Americans against Muslims and the Arabs. With every day going by, the optimists lost ground. The interrogation methods worsened considerably as time went by, and as you shall see, those responsible for GTMO broke all the principles upon which the U.S. was built and compromised every great principle such as Ben Franklin's "They that give up essential liberty to obtain a little temporary safety deserve neither liberty nor safety."

All of us wanted to make up for months of forced silence, we wanted to get every anger and agony off our chests, and we listened to each other's amazing stories for the next thirty days to come, which was our time in ███████ Block. When we later got transferred to a different block, many fellow detainees cried for being separated from their new friends. I cried, too.

██████████████████ escort team showed up at my cell.

"█████████!" said one of the MPs, holding the long chains in his hands. ████████████ is the code word for being taken to interrogation.* Although I didn't understand where I was going, I prudently followed their orders until they delivered me to the interrogator. His name was ███████████ ████████████████████████████ wearing a U.S. Army uniform. He is an ████████████████████████████ ██████████, a man with all the paradoxes you may imagine. He spoke Arabic decently, with a ██████████ accent; you could tell he grew up among ██████████ friends.†

---

* The word is likely "Reservation." It appears unredacted elsewhere throughout the manuscript. See, e.g., MOS manuscript, 69, 112, 122.

† Around this time, FBI-led interrogation teams often included members of the military's Criminal Investigation Task Force (CITF) and military

I was terrified when I stepped into the room in ███████████ building because of the CamelBak on ███████████ back, from which he was sipping. I never saw a thing like that before. I thought it was a kind of tool to hook on me as a part of my interrogation. I really don't know why I was scared, but the fact that I never saw ███████████ nor his CamelBak, nor did I expect an Army guy, all these factors contributed to my fear.

The older gentleman who interrogated me the night before entered the room with some candies and introduced ███████ ███████████ to me, "I chose ███████████ because he speaks your language. We're going to ask you detailed questions about you ███████████████████. As to me, I am going to leave soon, but my replacement will take care of you. See you later." He stepped out of the room leaving me and ███████████ to work.

███████████████ was a friendly guy. He was ███████████ in the U.S. Army who believed himself to be lucky in life. ███████████ wanted me to repeat to him my whole story, which I've been repeating for the last three years over and over. I got used to interrogators asking me the same things. Before the interrogator even moved his lips I knew his questions, and as soon as he or she started to talk, I turned my "tape" on. But

---

intelligence agents. The DOJ Inspector General's report records that "in May 2002, the military and the FBI adopted the 'Tiger Team' concept for interrogating detainees. According to the first GTMO case agent, these teams consisted of an FBI agent, an analyst, a contract linguist, two CITF investigators, and a military intelligence interrogator." The IG found that "the FBI withdrew from participation in the Tiger Teams in the fall of 2002 after disagreements arose between the FBI and military intelligence over interrogation tactics. Several FBI agents told the OIG that while they continued to have a good relationship with CITF, their relationship with the military intelligence entities greatly deteriorated over the course of time, primarily due to the FBI's opposition to the military intelligence approach to interrogating detainees." DOJ IG, 34.

when I came to the part about Jordan, ▮▮▮▮▮▮▮ felt very sorry!

"Those countries don't respect human rights. They even torture people," he said. I was comforted: if ▮▮▮▮▮▮▮ criticized cruel interrogation methods, it meant that the Americans wouldn't do something like that. Yes, they were not exactly following the law in Bagram, but that was in Afghanistan, and now we are in a U.S. controlled territory.

After ▮▮▮▮▮▮▮ finished his interrogation, he sent me back and promised to come back should new questions arise. During the session with ▮▮▮▮▮▮▮, I asked him to use the bathroom. "No. 1 or No. 2?" he asked. It was the first time I heard the human private business coded in numbers. In the countries I've been in, it isn't customary to ask people about their intention in the bathroom, nor do they have a code.

I never saw ▮▮▮▮▮▮▮ in an interrogation again. The ▮▮▮▮▮▮▮ resumed his work a couple of days later, only the ▮▮▮▮▮▮▮ was now reinforced with ▮▮▮▮▮, ▮▮▮▮▮▮▮▮▮▮▮. ▮▮▮▮▮▮▮ was another friendly guy. He and ▮▮▮▮▮▮▮ worked very well together. For some reason, ▮▮▮▮▮▮▮ was interested in taking my case in hand. Although a military interrogator came with the team a couple of times and asked some questions, you could tell that ▮▮▮▮▮▮▮ had the upper hand.*

The team worked on my case for over a month, on almost a daily basis. They asked me all kind of questions, and we spoke about other political topics beside the interrogation. Nobody ever threatened me or tried to torture me, and from my side I

---

* As the DOJ IG report makes clear, the FBI maintained overall control of the interrogation of MOS throughout 2002 and early 2003. DOJ IG, 122.

was cooperating with the team very well. "Our job is to take your statements and send them to the analysts in D.C. Even if you lie to us, we can't really tell right away until more information comes in," said ▮▮▮▮▮▮▮▮.

The team could see very clearly how sick I was; the prints of Jordan and Bagram were more than obvious. I looked like a ghost.

"You're getting better," said the Army guy when he saw me three weeks after my arrival in GTMO. On my second or third day in GTMO I had collapsed in my cell. I was just driven to my extremes; the MREs didn't appeal to me. The Medics took me out of my cell and I tried to walk the way to the hospital, but as soon as I left ▮▮▮▮▮▮▮▮▮▮▮▮ I collapsed once more, which made the Medics carry me to the clinic. I threw up so much that I was completely dehydrated. I received first aid and got an IV. The IV was terrible; they must have put some medication in it that I have an allergy to. My mouth dried up completely and my tongue became so heavy that I couldn't ask for help. I gestured with my hands to the corpsmen to stop dripping the fluid into my body, which they did.

Later that night the guards brought me back to my cell. I was so sick I couldn't climb on my bed; I slept on the floor for the rest of the month. The doctor prescribed Ensure and some hypertension medicine, and every time I got my sciatic nerve crisis the corpsmen gave me Motrin.

Although I was physically very weak, the interrogation didn't stop. But I was nonetheless in good spirits. In the Block we were singing, joking, and recounting stories to each other. I also got the opportunity to learn about the star detainees, such as his excellence ▮▮▮ fed us with the latest news and rumors from camp. ▮▮▮▮▮▮▮▮▮

████████████ had been transferred to our Block due to his "behavior."*

████████████ told us how he was tortured in Kandahar with other detainees. "They put us under the sun for a long time, we got beaten, but brothers don't worry, here in Cuba there is no torture. The rooms are air-conditioned, and some brothers even refuse to talk unless offered food," he said. "I cried when I saw detainees blindfolded and taken to Cuba on TV. The American Defense Secretary spoke on TV and claimed these detainees are the most evil people on the face of the earth. I never thought that I would be one of these 'evil people,'" said

████████████████████████████

████████████ had been working as an ████████████

██.

He was captured with four other colleagues of his in his domicile in ████████████ after midnight under the cries of his children; he was pried off his kids and his wife. The same thing exactly happened to his friends, who confirmed his story. I heard tons of such stories and every story made me forget the last one. I couldn't tell whose story was more saddening. It even started to undermine my story, but the detainees were unanimous that my story was the saddest. I personally don't know. The German proverb says: "Wenn das Militar sich bewegt, bleibt die Wahrheit auf der Strecke." When the Military sets itself in motion, the truth is too slow to keep up, so it stays behind.

The law of war is harsh. If there's anything good at all in a war, it's that it brings the best and the worst out of people: some

---

* Context here suggests that the same Camp Delta block where arriving detainees were held for the first month also served as a punishment block for detainees from the general population.

people try to use the lawlessness to hurt others, and some try to reduce the suffering to the minimum.

On September 4, 2002, I was transferred to ███████████, and so the interrogators ended the isolation and put me in with general population. On the one hand, it was hard for me to leave the friends I'd just made, and on the other hand I was excited about going to a dead normal Block, and being a dead average detainee. I was tired of being a "special" detainee, riding all over the world against my will.

I arrived in ████████████ before sunset. For the first time in more than nine months, I was put in a cell where I could see the plain.* And for the first time I was able to talk to my fellow detainees while seeing them. I was put in ████████████ between two Saudis from the South. Both were very friendly and entertaining. They had both been captured ████████ ████████████████████. When the prisoners tried to free themselves from the Pakistani Army, which was working on behalf of the U.S., one of them, an Algerian, grabbed the AK47 of a ████████████ guard and shot him. In the melee, the ████████████ detainees asserted control ████ ████████████; the guards fled, and the detainees fled too—just as far as where another ████████████ U.S. division was awaiting them, and they were captured again. The

───────────

* By "plain," I think MOS may mean the Cuban landscape surrounding the camp. It appears from the manuscript that MOS was held in two or three different blocks in Camp Delta over the next several months, including one block that housed detainees from European and North African countries. MOS manuscript, 62. MOS indicated at his ARB hearing that he was being held in Camp Two's Mike Block as of June 2003. ARB transcript, 26.

▨▨▨▨▨▨▨ event caused many casualties and injuries. I saw an Algerian detainee who was completely disabled due to the amount of bullets he had taken.

I had a good time in ▨▨▨▨▨▨▨▨▨ at the beginning, but things started to get ugly when some interrogators started to practice torture methods on some detainees, though shyly. As far as I heard and saw, the only method practiced at first was the cold room, all night. I know a young Saudi man who was taken to interrogation every night and put back in his cell in the morning. I don't know the details of what exactly happened to him because he was very quiet, but my neighbors told me that he refused to talk to his interrogators ▨▨▨▨▨▨▨▨ ▨▨▨▨▨▨▨▨▨▨▨▨▨▨▨▨▨▨▨▨▨▨▨▨ also told me that he was also put in the cold room two nights in a row because he refused to cooperate.

Most of the detainees by then were refusing to cooperate after they felt they had provided everything relevant to their cases. People were desperate and growing tired of being interrogated all the time, without hope of an end. I personally was relatively new and wanted to take my chances: maybe my fellow detainees were wrong! But I ended up bumping into the same brick wall as anybody else. Detainees grew worried about their situation and the absence of a due process of law, and things started to get worse with the use of painful methods to extract information from detainees.

Around mid-September, 2002, an ▨▨▨▨▨▨▨▨▨▨▨ ▨▨▨▨▨▨▨▨▨▨▨▨▨▨▨▨▨▨▨▨▨▨▨ pulled me to interrogation and introduced themselves as the team that was going to assess me for the next two months.*

---

* Because this occurred within the period during which the FBI had overall control of MOS's interrogation, this would likely be another FBI-led interrogation team; see footnote on p. 44.

"How long am I going to be interrogated?"

"As long as the government has questions for you!"

"How long is that?"

"I can only tell you that you will not spend more than five years here," said ████████. The team was communicating with me through an Arabic interpreter who looked ██████ ████████.

"I'm not ready to be asked the same questions again and again!"

"No, we have some new questions." But as it turned out they were asking me the very same questions I had been asked for the last three years. Even so, I was reluctantly cooperating. I honestly didn't see any advantages in cooperating, I just wanted to see how far things were going to go.

Around the same time another interrogator ████████ ████████ pulled me to interrogation. He was ████████ ████████████████████, an organized goatee, and spoke ████████████████ accent. ████ ████████████████████████████████ He was straightforward with me, and even shared with me what ████████████████████████████████ about me. ████████████ was talking, and talking, and talking some more: he was interested in getting me to work for him, as he had tried with other North African Arabs.*

---

* This interrogator might be from the CIA. In 2013, the Associated Press reported that between 2002 and 2005, CIA agents in GTMO sought to recruit detainees to serve as informants and double agents for the United States. The CIA also helped facilitate interrogations by foreign intelligence agents in Guantánamo. Adam Goldman and Matt Apuzzo, "Penny Lane, GITMO's Other Secret CIA Facility," Associated Press, November 26, 2013, http://bigstory.ap.org/article/penny-lane-gitmos-other-secret-cia-facility.

"Next Thursday, I've arranged a meeting with the ████
██████████. Are you going to talk to them?"

"Yes, I am." That was the first lie I detected, because ████
██████████████████ had told me, "No foreign government is
going to talk to you here, only us Americans!"* In fact, I heard
about many detainees meeting with non-American interrogators, such as ████████████████████████████████████

██

█████████████████████████████ were helping the U.S.
to extract information from the ██████████ detainees. The
████████████████████ interrogators and the ████████████
██████ threatened some of their interviewees with torture
when they got back home.

"I hope I see you in another place," said the ██████████ interrogator to ████████████████████████.

"If we see each other in Turkistan, you're gonna talk a lot!"
the ██████████ interrogator told ████████████████████
████.†

But I was not afraid of talking to anyone. I had done no
crimes against anybody. I even wanted to talk to prove my
innocence, since the American motto was "GTMO detainees
are guilty until proven innocent." I knew what was awaiting

---

* Likely the "older gentleman" or one of his other FBI interrogators.

† The quotations appear to be directed to two different detainees. The
unredacted "Turkistan" in this passage suggests that MOS may be referring
to the interrogations of ethnic Uighur detainees by Chinese intelligence
agents in GTMO. These interrogations, which were reportedly preceded
by periods of sleep deprivation and temperature manipulation, were first
revealed in the May 2008 DOJ Inspector General's report, *A Review of the
FBI's Involvement in and Observations of Detainee Interrogations in Guantanamo
Bay, Afghanistan, and Iraq*. McClatchy Newspapers reported that the interrogations took place over a day and a half in September 2002. See http://www
.mcclatchydc.com/2009/07/16/72000/uighur-detainees-us-helped
-chinese.html.

me when it came to ███████ interrogators, and I wanted to get things out off my chest.

The day came and the guards pulled me and took me ████████████████, where detainees usually met ███ ████████████████████████. Two ██████ ██ gentlemen were sitting on the other side of the table, and I was looking at them, locked on the floor. ████████████ ██ ███████, who played the bad guy role during the interrogation. Neither introduced himself, which was completely against the ██████████████████; they just stood in front of me like ghosts, the same as the rest of the secret interrogators.*

"Do you speak German, or do we need an interpreter?" asked the ████████████.

"I am afraid we don't," I replied.

"Well, you understand the seriousness of the matter. We've come from ██████████ to talk to you.

"People have been killed," continued the older man.

I smiled. "Since when are you allowed to interrogate people outside ███████?"

"We are not here to discuss the judicial grounds of our questioning!"

"I might, sometime in the future, be able to talk to the press

---

* The visitors are likely German. In 2008, *Der Spiegel* reported that in September 2002, two members of the Bundesnachrichtendienst (BND) and one member of the Office for the Protection of the Constitution, Germany's foreign and domestic intelligence agencies, interviewed MOS for ninety minutes in Guantánamo. MOS appears to refer to two of those visitors, one older and one younger. John Goetz, Marcel Rosenbach, Britta Sandberg, and Holger Stark, "From Germany to Guantanamo: The Career of Prisoner No. 760," *Der Spiegel,* October 9, 2008, http://www.spiegel.de /international/world/from-germany-to-guantanamo-the-career-of -prisoner-no-760-a-583193.html.

and give you away," I said. "Though I don't know your names, I'll recognize your pictures, no matter how long it takes!"

"You can say whatever you want, you're not gonna hurt us! We know what we're doing," he said.

"So clearly you guys are using the lawlessness of this place to extract information out of me?"

██████ Salahi, if we wanted to, we could ask the guards to hang you on the wall and kick your ass!"* When he mentioned the crooked way he was thinking, my heart started to pound, because I was trying to express myself carefully and at the same avoid torture.

"You can't scare me, you're not talking to a child. If you continue speaking to me with this tone, you can pack your luggage and go back to ████████."

"We are not here to prosecute you or scare you, we would just be grateful if you would answer a couple of questions we have," said ████████████.

"Look, I've been in your country, and you know that I was never involved in any kind of crimes. Plus, what are you worried about? Your country isn't even threatened. I've been living peacefully in your country and never abused your hospitality. I am very grateful for all that your country helped me with; I don't stab in the back. So what theater are you trying to play on me?"

██████ Salahi, we know that you are innocent, but we did not capture you, the Americans did. We are not here on behalf of the U.S. We work for ████████████████████████, and lately we stopped some bad plots. We know you cannot possibly know about these things. However, we only want to ask you about two individuals, ████████████████████

---

* Probably "Herr Salahi." "Salahi" is a variant spelling of MOS's last name that is generally used in court documents in the United States.

████, and we would be grateful if you would answer our questions about them."

"It's just funny that you've come all the way from ████████ to ask about your own people! Those two individuals are good friends of mine. We attended the same mosques, but I don't know them to be involved in any terrorist operations."

The session didn't last much longer than that. They asked me how I was doing and about the life in the camp and bid me farewell. I never saw the ██████████ after that.

Meanwhile, the ██████████████████████████████ kept questioning me.

"Do you know this guy, ██████████████████?" asked ██████████.

"No, I don't," I honestly answered.

"But he knows you!"

"I am afraid you have another file than mine!"

"No, I read your file very thoroughly."

"Can you show me his picture?"

"Yes. I'm going to show it to you tomorrow."

"Good. I might know him by another name!"

"Do you know about the American bases in Germany?"

"Why do you ask me about that? I didn't go to Germany to study the American bases, nor am I interested in them in any way!" I angrily replied.

"My people respect detainees who tell the truth!" ██████████ said, while ██████████ took notes. I took the hint that he was calling me a liar in a stupid way. The session was terminated.

The next day ██████████ reserved me in the ████ ██████████████ and showed me two pictures. The first one turned out to be that of ██████████████████████, who was suspected of having participated in the September 11 attack and who was captured ██████████████████████████.

The second picture was of ▮▮▮▮▮▮▮▮▮▮▮▮▮▮▮▮▮ one of the September 11 hijackers. As to ▮▮▮▮▮▮▮▮▮▮▮▮▮, I had never heard of him or saw him, and as to ▮▮▮▮▮ ▮▮▮▮▮▮▮▮▮▮▮▮▮, I figured I've seen the guy, but where and when? I had no clue! But I also figured that the guy must be very important because ▮▮▮▮▮▮▮▮ were running fast together to find my link with him.* Under the circumstances, I denied having seen the guy. Look at it, how would it have looked had I said I'd seen this guy, but I don't know when and where? What interrogator would buy something like that? Not one! And to be honest with you, I was as scared as hell.

The ▮▮▮▮ team reserved me again the next day and showed me the picture of ▮▮▮▮▮▮▮▮, and I denied that I knew him, the same way I had the day before. My denial that I knew a man that I don't really know, I just saw him for a very short time once or twice and had no association whatsoever with him, gave fuel to all kind of wild theories linking me to the September 11 attack. The investigators were just drowning and were looking for any straw to grab, and I personally didn't exactly want to be that straw.

▮▮▮▮▮▮▮▮▮▮▮▮▮▮▮▮▮▮▮▮▮▮▮▮▮▮▮ said ▮▮▮▮▮. "▮▮▮▮▮▮▮▮▮▮▮▮▮▮▮▮▮▮▮▮▮▮▮▮ ▮▮▮▮▮▮▮▮▮▮▮▮▮▮▮▮▮▮▮▮▮▮▮▮▮▮ ▮▮▮▮▮▮▮▮▮▮▮▮▮▮▮▮▮▮▮▮▮▮▮▮▮

---

* The first picture is likely of Ramzi bin al-Shibh, who was captured in a shoot-out in a suburb of Karachi, Pakistan, right around this time, on September 11, 2002. At his 2005 ARB hearing, MOS told the panel, "September 11th, 2002, America arrested a man by the name of Ramzi Bin al Shibh, who is said to be the key guy in the September 11th attacks. It was exactly one year after 9/11, and since his capture my life has changed drastically." ARB transcript, 23.

███

███

████████████

"In the next few days!"

In the meantime I was transferred to ███████████████
where I met the ██████████████████████████████████
████████████████████████ for the first time. He was another one
of the star detainees. ████████████████ heard about my story, and
like any ██████████████████, he wanted to have more information. On my side, I also wanted to converse with cultured people. As far as I could tell, ████████████████ was a decent guy; I have
a hard time picturing him as a criminal.

I stayed in ███████████████████████ less than two weeks before
I was transferred to ████████████████████████████████ was filled
with European and North African detainees. For the first time
I got to know the ██████████████████████████████ and the ███
███.
███
███
███
███
███
███
███
███ in ███████
██████████████████████ before. I always wanted to know where
I was going and why. I remember one time when the escorting
team refused to tell me where I was going: I thought they
were taking me to my execution.* When I entered ███████████

---

* The extended redaction that follows is one of two multipage redactions
in the manuscript. The second one, which occurs at the end of chapter 6,

seems to correspond to a polygraph examination that MOS took in the late fall of 2003 (see footnotes on pp. 297 and 299). It is possible that this first extended redaction concerns a polygraph examination as well. At his 2005 ARB hearing, as he is describing his FBI interrogations through the winter of 2002, MOS said, "Then I took a polygraph and [Ramzi bin al-Shibh] refused to take a polygraph for many reasons. It turns out he is very contradictory and he lies. They said that to me themselves. They said my credibility is high because I took the polygraph." After his capture on September 11, 2002, Ramzi bin al-Shibh was held and interrogated at several CIA black sites. News reports suggest that bin al-Shibh was interrogated in a CIA-run facility near Rabat, Morocco, in late September and through the fall of 2002, and in 2010 the U.S. government acknowledged it possessed videotapes of bin al-Shibh's 2002 interrogation in Morocco. See, e.g., http://www.nytimes.com/2010/08/18/world/18tapes.html; and http://hosted.ap.org/specials/interactives/wdc/binalshibh/content.swf.

▓▓▓

was accompanied by an Arabic Interpreter ▓▓▓▓▓▓▓▓▓▓▓▓▓▓▓▓▓▓▓. He was very weak in the language. ▓▓▓▓▓▓▓▓▓▓▓▓▓▓▓

███████████████████████████████
███████████████████████████████
███████████████████████████████
███████████████████████████████

███████████████████████████

After a couple of days, I was taken to interrogation.

"How are you?" said ███████████. It had been a long time since I'd seen him.

"Good!"

███████████████ were in ███████████████, when you agreed ███████████████████████

███████████████████████████████
███████████████████████████████
███████████████████████████████
███████████████████████████████
███████████████████████████████
███████████████████████████████
███████████████████████████████
███████████████████████████████
███████████████████████████████
███████████████████████████████
███████████████████████████████
███████████████████████████████
███████████████████████████████
███████████████████████████████
███████████████████████████████
███████████████████████████████
███████████████████████████████
███████████████████████████████
███████████████████████████████
███████████████████████████████
███████████████████████████████
███████████████████████████████
███████████████████████████████

██████████████████████████████████

██████████████████████████████████

██████████████████████████████████

██████████████████████████████████

█████████████████████████████ latter's era, there were many issues, most of which were initiated by the desperation of the detainees. Endless interrogation. Disrespect of the Holy Koran by some of the guards. Torturing detainees by making them spend the night in a cold room (though this method was not practiced nearly as much as it would be in ████████████ time). So we decided to go on a hunger strike; many detainees took part, including me. But I could only strike for four days, after which I was a ghost.*

---

* Later in the manuscript, MOS writes that he participated in a hunger strike in September 2002, and news reports document a hunger strike in late September and October of that year (see, e.g., http://america.aljazeera. com/articles/multimedia/guantanamo-hungerstriketimeline.html, quoting an FBI document attributing that protest to anger over treatment by guards and the ongoing detention without trial or legal process). That hunger strike occurred toward the end of the tenure of Major General Michael E. Dunlavey, who was the commander of JTF-170, the intelligence operations in Guantánamo, from February through October 2002. He was succeeded by Major General Geoffrey D. Miller, who became commander of JTF-GTMO, which encompassed all Guantánamo operations, in November 2002. The Senate Armed Services Committee has documented at length the trend toward more abusive interrogations in October and November 2002, which included the development of the military's first "Special Interrogation Plan" for Mohammed al-Qahtani. On December 2, 2002, Secretary of Defense Donald Rumsfeld signed a memo authorizing interrogation methods including nudity, forced standing and stress positions, and twenty-hour interrogations. U.S. Senate Armed Services Committee, "Inquiry in the Treatment of Detainees in U.S. Custody," November 20, 2008, http:// www.armed-services.senate.gov/imo/media/doc/Detainee-Report-Final _April-22-2009.pdf (hereafter cited as SASC).

"Don't break, you're gonna weaken the group," said my Saudi neighbor.

"I told you guys I'm gonna hunger strike, not that I'm gonna commit suicide. I'm gonna break," I replied.

██. He was the kind of man to be picked for the dirtiest job, when many others had failed. ███████████ was a very radical hater. He completely changed the detention policies in GTMO in all aspects.

██
██
██
██
██
██
██
██
██
██ One day in paradise, and the next in hell. Detainees of this level are completely under the mercy of their interrogators, which was very convenient for the interrogators. ███████████████████

██
██
██
██
██
██
██████████████████████████████

I was like, what the heck is going on, I've never been in trouble with the guards, and I am answering my interrogators and cooperating with them. But I missed that cooperation meant telling your interrogators whatever they want to hear.

*   *   *

I was put once more in ███████████████ end ███████████.*

An escort team appeared in ███████████████ in front of my cell.

"760 reservation!" they said.

"OK, just give me a second!" I put my clothes on and washed my face. My heart started to pound. I hated interrogation; I had gotten tired of being terrified all the time, living in constant fear day-in and day-out for the last thirteen months.

"Allah be with you! Keep your head on! They work for Satan!" yelled my fellow detainees to keep me together, as we always did when somebody got pulled for interrogation. I hated the sounds of the heavy metal chains; I can hardly carry them when they're given to me. People were always getting taken from the block, and every time I heard the chains I thought it would be me. You never know what's going to happen in the interrogation; people sometimes never came back to the block, they just disappeared. It happened to a Moroccan fellow detainee, and it would happen to me, as you're going to learn, God willing.

When I entered the room in ███████████████, it was crowded with ███████████████ ████████████████████████████ ███████████████████████████.†

"Hi!"

---

* It is now around the end of 2002.

† The 2008 DOJ Inspector General's report identifies the two FBI agents who interview MOS from this point until he is turned over to the JTF-GTMO task force in May 2003 by the pseudonyms "Poulson" and "Santiago." Context suggests that the group in the room also includes a military interrogator and a French-speaking translator. According to the DOJ IG report, the team at this time also included a detective from the New York

"Hi!"

"I've chosen ██████████████████ based on their experience and maturity. They'll be assessing your case from now on. There are a couple of things that need to be completed in your case. For instance, you didn't tell us everything about ███████████████████████████████. He's a very important guy ████████████████."

"First, I told you what I know about ███████████████████, even though I don't need to be providing you information about anybody. We're talking here about me. Second, in order to continue my cooperation with you, I need you to answer me one question: WHY AM I HERE? If you don't give me the answer, you can consider me a non-existent detainee." Later on I learned from my great lawyers ████████████████████ ████████████████ that the magic formulation of my request is a Petition for a Writ of Habeas Corpus. Obviously that phrase makes no sense to the average, mortal man like me. The average person would just say, "Why the hell are you locking me up?" I'm not a lawyer, but common sense dictates that after three years of interrogating me and depriving me of my liberty, the government at least owes me an explanation why it's doing so. What exactly is my crime?

"It makes no sense: It's like somebody who quits a 10-mile trip after traveling nine miles," said ██████████████. It would have been more accurate had he said "a million mile trip after traveling one mile."

"Look, it's as simple as ABC: answer me the question and I'll cooperate with you fully!"

"I have no answer!" ██████████████ said.

"Neither do I!" I replied.

Police Department's Joint Terrorism Task Force, who interrogated Slahi with "Poulson" in January 2003. DOJ IG, 295–99.

"It says in the Koran somebody who kills one soul is considered to have killed all of humanity," said the French translator, trying to reach a breakthrough. I looked at him disrespectfully with the side of my face.

"I am not the guy you're looking for!" I said in French, and I repeated it in plain English.

██████████ started. "I am sure you're against killing people. We're not looking for you. We're looking for those guys who are out there trying to hurt innocents." He said this while showing me a bunch of ghostly pictures. I refused to look at them, and whenever he tried to put them under my sight I looked somewhere else. I didn't even want to give him the satisfaction of having taken a look at them. "Look, ████████ ██████████████ is cooperating, and he has a good chance of getting his sentence reduced to twenty-seven years—and ████████████████████ is really a bad person. Somebody like you needs only to talk for five minutes, and you're a free man," said ████████████. He was everything but reasonable. When I contemplated his statement, I was like, God, a guy who is cooperating is gonna be locked up for 27 more years, after which he won't be able to enjoy any kind of life. What kind of harsh country is that? I am sorry to say that ████████████ statement wasn't worth an answer. He and ████████████████ tried to reason with the help of the MI guy, but there was no convincing me to talk.

You could tell that the interrogators were getting used to detainees who refused to cooperate after having cooperated for a while. Just as I was learning from other detainees how not to cooperate, the interrogators were learning from each other how to deal with non-cooperating detainees. The session was closed and I was sent back to my cell. I was satisfied with myself, since I now officially belonged to the majority, the non-cooperating detainees. I minded less being locked up unjustly for the rest of my life; what drove me crazy was to be expected to cooperate, too. You lock me up, I give you no information. And we both are cool.

██████████████ the sessions continued with the new team. ██████████ rarely attended the sessions; "I won't come as long as you don't give us every piece of information you have," he once said. "Still, because we're Americans we treat you guys according to our high standards. Look at ████████████████, we're offering him the latest medical technology."

"You want just to keep him alive because he might have some Intels, and if he dies, they're gonna die with him!" I responded. U.S. interrogators always tended to mention free food and free medical treatment for detainees. I don't really understand what other alternatives they have! I personally have been detained in non-Democratic countries, and the medical treatment was the highest priority. Common sense dictates that if a detainee goes badly ill there will be no Intels, and he'll probably die.

We spent almost two months of argumentation. "Bring me to the court, and I'll answer all your questions," I would tell the team.

"There will be no court!" they would answer.

"Are you a Mafia? You kidnap people, lock them up, and blackmail them," I said.

"You guys are a law enforcement problem," said ██████████. "We cannot apply the conventional law to you. We need only circumstantial evidence to fry you."

"I've done nothing against your country, have I?"

"You're a part of the big conspiracy against the U.S.!" said ██████████.

"You can pull this charge on anybody! What have I done?"

"I don't know, you tell me!"

"Look, you kidnap me from my home in Mauritania, not from a battlefield in Afghanistan, because you suspected me of having been part of the Millennium Plot—which I am not, as you know by now. So what's the next charge? It looks to me as if you want to pull any shit on me."

"I don't want to pull any shit on you. I just wish you had access to the same reports as I do!" said ███████████.

"I don't care what the reports say. I'd just like you to take a look at the reports from January 2000 linking me to the Millennium Plot. And you now know that I'm not a part of it, after the cooperation of ██████████████████*

"I don't think that you are a part of it, nor do I believe that

---

* In this and the next paragraph, the subject could be Ahmed Ressam. Ressam was arrested as he tried to enter the United States from Canada in a car laden with explosives on December 14, 2000; he was convicted the following year of planning to bomb Los Angeles International Airport on New Year's Day 2001 as part of what became known as the Millennium Plot. In May 2001, after entering a guilty plea and before sentencing, Ressam began cooperating with U.S. authorities in exchange for assurances of a reduced sentence. A U.S. Court of Appeals later wrote that "Ressam continued cooperating until early 2003. Over the course of his two-year cooperation, he provided 65 hours of trial and deposition testimony, and 205 hours of proffers and debriefings. Ressam provided information to the governments of seven different countries and testified in two trials, both of which ended in convictions of the defendants. He provided names of at least 150 people involved in terrorism and described many others. He also provided information about explosives that potentially saved the lives of law enforcement agents, and extensive information about the mechanics of global terrorism operations." As MOS indicates here, Ressam never named or implicated him in any way in all those sessions. Ressam later recanted some of his testimony implicating others in the Millennium Plot. He originally received a twenty-two-year sentence with five years' supervision after his release. In 2010 the Ninth Circuit Court of Appeals ruled that sentence was too lenient and violated mandatory sentencing guidelines, and remanded the case to a federal judge for resentencing. The court's opinion is available at http://cdn.ca9.uscourts.gov/datastore/opinions/2010/02/02/09-30000.pdf.

you know ██████████████████" But I do know that you know people who know ████████████████" said ██████████████.

"I don't know, but I don't see the problem if it is the case," I replied, "Knowing somebody is not a crime, no matter who he is."

A young Egyptian who was serving as interpreter that day tried to convince me to cooperate. "Look, I have come here sacrificing my time to help you guys, and the only way to help yourself is to talk," he said.

"Aren't you ashamed to work for these evil people, who arrest your brothers in faith for no reason than being Muslim?" I asked him. "████████████, I am older than you are, speak more languages, I have a higher college grade, and I've been in many more countries than you have. I understand you're here to help yourself and make money. If you're trying to fool anybody, it's only yourself!" I was just so mad because he talked to me as if I were a child. ███████████████████████████ were just staring.

These conversation took place again and again in different sessions. I kept saying, "You tell why I am here, I'll cooperate; you don't tell me, I'm not gonna cooperate. But we can talk about anything else beside interrogation."

███████████████ welcomed that idea. He assured me that he was going to ask his boss to provide him the cause of my arrest, because he didn't know it himself. In the meantime he taught me a lot about American culture and history, the U.S. and Islam, and the U.S. and the Arab world. The team started to bring movies in; I saw *The Civil War*, Muslims in the U.S., and several other *Frontline* broadcasts regarding terrorism. "All of this shit happens because of hatred," he would say. "Hatred is the reason for all disasters."

███████████████████, he was interested in getting information as quickly as possible using classic police methods. He offered me McDonald's one day, but I refused because I didn't want to owe him anything. "The Army are fighting to take you to a very bad place, and we don't want that to happen!" he warned me.

"Just let them take me there; I'll get used to it. You keep me in jail whether or not I cooperate, so why should I cooperate?" I said this still not knowing that Americans use torture to facilitate interrogations. I was very tired from being taken to interrogation every day. My back was just conspiring against me. I even sought Medical help.

"You're not allowed to sit for such a long time," said the ▇▇▇▇▇▇▇▇▇▇▇▇▇▇▇▇ physiotherapist.

"Please tell my interrogators that, because they make me sit for long hours almost every day."

"I'll write a note, but I'm not sure whether it will have an effect," she replied.

It didn't. Instead, in February 2003, ▇▇▇▇▇▇▇▇ washed his hands of me.*

"I am going to leave, but if you're ready to talk about your telephone conversations, request me, I'll come back," he said.

"I assure you, I am not going to talk about anything unless you answer my question: Why am I here?"

---

* This may be the NYPD interrogator who the DOJ IG report indicates was part of the interrogation team in January 2003. The report describes an NYPD detective MOS identified as "Tom," who "told Slahi that if he did not explain certain phone calls he would be sent to a 'very bad place.'" DOJ IG, 299.

BEFORE

285

or crying. ~~thht~~ Ultimately I ended up doing both. I kept
reading the short message over and over. I knew it was for
real ~~from~~ my mom not like the fake one I got one year
ago. The only problem I couldn't respond the letter b/c
I was still then not allowed to see the ICRC.
was the one who handed me that historical piece of paper.
~~The First~~ Unofficial Laughter in the ocean of Tears.

████ kept getting me English
~~litterature~~ books I enjoyed reading, most of them
were Western. But I ~~remember~~ still remember one
book called The Catcher in The Rye that made me laugh
until my stomach hurt. I was a funny book. I ~~keep~~
tried to keep my laughter as low as possible and
pushing it down, but the guards felt something _ "Are
you crying?" asked me one of them _ "No, I am alright!"
I responded. And since interrogators are not professional
~~come~~ chains, most of the humour they, some ~~tug~~, came up
with ~~with~~ a bunch of lame jokes that really didn't
make me laugh, but I forced myself to always to an
official smile. ████

████ came on Sunday morning
and waited outside the building. ████ appeared
before my cell ████. I didn't recognize
him. I thought he was a new interrogator. But
he spoke I knew it was him. "Are ████" -
"Don't worry. Your interrogator is waiting outside
on you" - I was overwhelmed and terrified at
the same time. It was too much for ~~me~~. ~~Look~~
████ led me outside the building where

TWO

Senegal-Mauritania

January 21, 2000–February 19, 2000

The First Arrest in Senegal...An Escorted Homecoming...The First Interrogation in Mauritania...Getting Stuck in a Cul-de-Sac...The U.S. Dramatizes the Matter

A Mauritanian folktale tells us about a rooster-phobe who would almost lose his mind whenever he encountered a rooster.

"Why are you so afraid of the rooster?" the psychiatrist asks him.

"The rooster thinks I'm corn."

"You're not corn. You are a very big man. Nobody can mistake you for a tiny ear of corn," the psychiatrist said.

"I know that, Doctor. But the rooster doesn't. Your job is to go to him and convince him that I am not corn."

The man was never healed, since talking with a rooster is impossible. End of story.

For years I've been trying to convince the U.S. government that I am not corn.

It started in January 2000, when I was returning to Mauritania after living twelve years overseas. At 8 p.m. on ███████ ██████, my friends ████████████████████████████

dropped me off at Dorval Airport in Montreal. I took the night Sabena flight to Brussels and was continuing to Dakar the next afternoon.* I arrived in Brussels in the morning, sleepy and worn out. After collecting my luggage, I collapsed on one of the benches in the International area, using my bag as a pillow. One thing was sure: anybody could have stolen my bag, I was so tired. I slept for one or two hours, and when I woke up, I looked for a toilet where I could wash and a place to pray.

The airport was small, neat, and clean, with restaurants, duty-free shops, phone booths, Internet PCs, a mosque, a church, a synagogue, and a psych consulting bureau for atheists. I checked out all the God's houses, and was impressed. I thought, This country could be a place I'd want to live. Why don't I just go and ask for asylum? I'd have no problem; I speak the language and have adequate qualifications to get a job in the heart of Europe. I had actually been in Brussels, and I liked the multicultural life and the multiple faces of the city.

I left Canada mainly because the U.S. had pitted their security services on me, but they didn't arrest me, they just started to watch me. Being watched is better than being put in jail, I realize now; ultimately, they would have figured out that I am not a criminal. "I never learn," as my mom always put it. I never believed that the U.S. was evilly trying to get me in a place where the law has nothing to say.

The border was inches away. Had I crossed that border, I would never have written this book.

Instead, in the small mosque, I performed the ritual wash and

---

* MOS's 2004 Combatant Status Review Tribunal (CSRT) and 2005 Administrative Review Board hearing transcripts make clear the date is January 21, 2000. The CSRT transcript is available at http://online.wsj .com/public/resources/documents/couch-slahihearing-03312007.pdf. CSRT transcript, 6; ARB transcript, 16.

prayed. It was very quiet; the peacefulness was dominating. I felt so tired that I lay down in the mosque and read the Koran for some time and fell asleep.

I woke up to the movements of another guy who came to pray. He seemed to know the place and to have transited through this airport many times. ████████████████████████████ ████████████████. We greeted each other after he finished his prayer.

"What are you doing here?" he asked me.

"I'm transiting. I came from Canada, and am heading for Dakar."

"Where are you from?"

"Mauritania. What about you?'

"I'm from Senegal. I'm a merchant between my country and the Emirates. I'm waiting on the same flight as you."

"Good!" I said.

"Let's go rest. I'm a member of Club Such-and-Such," he suggested, I don't recall the name. We went to the club, and it was just amazing: TV, coffee, tea, cookies, a comfortable couch, newspapers. I was overwhelmed, and I spent most of the time sleeping on a couch. At some point, my new ███████████ friend wanted to have lunch, and woke me up to do the same. I was concerned I wouldn't be able to come back because I had no club card and they had just let me in because my ███████████ ████ friend flashed his membership card. However, my stomach's call was louder, and I decided to go outside and have some food. I went to the Sabena Airlines counter and asked for a free meal card, and found a restaurant. Most of the food was mixed with pork, so I decided on a vegetarian meal.

I went back to the club and waited until my friend and I were called to our flight, Sabena #502 to Dakar. I had chosen Dakar because it was by far cheaper than flying directly to

Nouakchott, Mauritania. Dakar is only about 300 miles from Nouakchott, and I arranged with my family to pick me up there. So far so good; people do it all the time.

During the flight, I was full of energy because I had had some quality sleep in Brussels airport. Next to me was a young French girl who lived in Dakar but was studying medicine in Brussels. I was thinking that my brothers might not make it to the airport on time, so I would have to spend some time in a hotel. The French girl benevolently enlightened me about the prices in Dakar, and how the Senegalese people try to overcharge strangers, especially the taxi drivers.

The flight took about five hours. We arrived around 11 p.m., and the whole formalities thing took about thirty minutes. When I took my bag from the baggage claim, I bumped into my ▮▮▮▮▮▮▮▮ friend, and we bid each other farewell.* As soon as I turned away carrying my bag, I saw my brother ▮▮▮▮▮▮▮▮ smiling; he obviously had seen me before I saw him. ▮▮▮▮▮▮▮▮ was accompanied by my other brother ▮▮▮▮▮▮▮▮ and two friends of theirs I didn't know.

▮▮▮▮▮▮▮▮ grabbed my bag and we headed toward the parking lot. I liked the warm night weather that embraced me as soon as I left the gate. We were talking, asking each other excitedly how things were going. As we crossed the road, I honestly cannot describe what happened to me. All I know is that in less than a second my hands were shackled behind my back and I was encircled by a bunch of ghosts who cut me off from the rest of my company. At first I thought it was an armed robbery, but as it turned out it was a robbery of another kind.

---

* Context and the events that follow make clear that this is the Senegalese businessman he spent time with in the Brussels airport.

"We arrest you in the Name of the Law," said the special agent while locking the chains around my hands.

"I'm arrested!" I called to the brothers I couldn't see any-more. I figured if they missed me all of a sudden it would be painful for them. I didn't know whether they heard me or not, but as it turned out, they had heard me indeed because my brother ███████████████ kept mocking me later and claim-ing that I am not courageous since I called for help. Maybe I'm not, but that's what happened. What I didn't know was that my two brothers and their two friends were arrested at the same time. Yes, their two friends, one who came with my brothers all the way from Nouakchott, and the other, his brother who lives in Dakar and just happened to ride with them to the air-port, just in time to be arrested as a part of a "gang": What luck!

I honestly was not prepared for this injustice. Had I known the U.S. investigators were really so full of it, I wouldn't have left Canada, or even Belgium when I was transiting through. Why didn't the U.S. have me arrested in Germany? Germany is one of the closest allies of the U.S. Why didn't the U.S. have me arrested in Canada? Canada and the U.S. are almost the same country. The U.S. interrogators and investigators claimed that I fled Canada out of fear that I was going to be arrested, but that doesn't really make any sense. First of all, I left using my passport with my real name, after going through all formali-ties including all kinds of registrations. Secondly, is it better to be arrested in Canada or Mauritania? Of course in Canada! Or why didn't the U.S. have me arrested in Belgium, where I spent almost twelve hours?

I understand the anger and frustration of the U.S. about ter-rorist attacks. But jumping on innocent individuals and making them suffer, looking for fake confessions, doesn't help anybody. It rather complicates the problem. I would always tell the U.S.

agents, "Guys! Cool down! Think before you act! Just put a small percentage on the possibility that you might be wrong before you irreparably injure somebody!" But when something bad happens, people start to freak out and lose their composure. I've been interrogated throughout the last six years by over a hundred interrogators from different countries, and they have one thing in common: confusion. Maybe the government wants them to be that way, who knows?

Anyhow, the local police at the airport intervened when they saw the mêlée—the Special Forces were dressed in civilian suits, so there really was no differentiating them from a bunch of bandits trying to rob somebody—but the guy behind me flashed a magic badge, which immediately made the policemen retreat. All five of us were thrown in a cattle truck, and soon we got another friend, the guy I had met in Brussels, just because we bid each other farewell at the luggage carousel.

The guards got in with us. The leader of the group sat up front in the passenger seat, but he could see and hear us because the glass that usually separates the driver from the cattle wasn't there anymore. The truck took off like in a Hollywood chase scene. "You're killing us," one of the guards must have said, because the driver slowed down a little bit. The local guy who came to the airport with my brothers was losing his mind; every once in a while he spat some indistinct words conveying his worries and unhappiness. As it turned out the guy thought that I was a drug dealer and he was relieved when the suspicion turned out to be terrorism! Since I was the starring actor, I felt bad for causing so much trouble for so many people. My only solace was that I didn't mean to—and also, at that moment, the fear in my heart overwhelmed the rest of my emotions.

When I sat down on the rough floor, I felt better surrounded by the warmth of the company, including the Special Forces agents. I started to recite the Koran.

"Shut up!" said the boss in the front. I didn't shut up; I lowered my voice, but not enough for the boss. "Shut up!" he said, this time raising his baton to hit me. "You're trying to bewitch us out!" I knew he was serious, and so I prayed in my heart. I hadn't tried to bewitch anybody out, nor do I know how to do it, but Africans are some of the most gullible folks I ever knew.

The trip took between fifteen and twenty minutes, so it was shortly after midnight when we arrived at the Commissariat de Police. The masterminds of the operation stood behind the truck and got involved in a discussion with my Brussels friend. I didn't understand anything; they were speaking in the local language ██████.* After a short discussion, the guy took his heavy bags, and off he went. When I later asked my brothers what he told the police, they told me that he said he had seen me in Brussels and never before, and that he didn't know that I was a terrorist.

Now we were five persons jailed in the truck. It was very dark outside, but I could tell that people were coming and going. We waited between forty minutes and an hour in the truck. I grew more nervous and afraid, especially when the guy in the passenger seat said, "I hate working with the Whites," or rather he used the word 'Moors,' which made me believe that they were waiting on a Mauritanian team. I started to have nausea, my heart was a feather, and I shrank so small to hold myself together. I thought about all the kinds of torture I had heard of, and how much I could take tonight. I grew blind, a thick cloud built in front of my eyes, I couldn't see anything. I

---

* The language is likely Wolof; it is named again without redaction a few pages later. MOS manuscript, 436.

grew deaf; after that statement all I could hear was indistinct whispers. I lost the feeling of my brothers being with me in the same truck. I figured only God can help my situation. God never fails.

"Get out," shouted the guy impatiently. I fought my way through and one of the guards helped me jump down the step. We were led into a small room that was already occupied by mosquitoes, just in time for them to start their feast. They didn't even wait until we slept; they went right away about their business, tearing us apart. The funny thing about mosquitoes is that they're shy in small groups and rude in big ones. In small groups, they wait until you fall asleep, unlike in big groups, where they start to tease you right away, as if to say: "What can you do about it?" And in fact, nothing. The toilet was filthy as it could be, which made it an ideal environment for breeding mosquitoes.

I was the only chained person. "Did I beat you?" asked the guy while taking off the handcuffs.

"No, you didn't." When I looked I noticed I already had scars around my wrists. The interrogators started to pull us one by one for interrogation, starting with the strangers. It was a very long, scary, dark and bleak night.

My turn came shortly before the first daylight.

In the interrogation room there were two men ████████████ ██, a male interrogator and his recorder.* The ███████████ Police Chief was in charge of the police station, but

---

* The cast seems to consist of two men and two women: the Senegalese interrogator and his recorder, both male; and the Senegalese police chief and an American, who the redacted pronouns suggest are both female.

██████ was not part of the interrogation; ██████ looked so tired that ████ fell asleep several times out of boredom. The American ████████ was taking notes, and sometimes ████ passed notes to the interrogator. The interrogator was a quiet, skinny, smart, rather religious and deep thinking ██████████.

"We have very heavy allegations against you," he said, pulling a thick stack of papers out of a bright yellow envelope. Before he had them halfway out, you could tell he had been reading the stuff many times. And I already knew what he was talking about, because the Canadians had already interviewed me.

"I have done nothing. The U.S. wants to dirty Islam by pinning such horrible things on Muslims."

"Do you know ██████████████████?"*

"No, I don't. I even think his whole story was a fake, to unlock the terrorism budget and hurt the Muslims." I was really honest about what I said. Back then I didn't know a whole lot of things that I do now. I believed excessively in Conspiracy Theories—though maybe not as much as the U.S. government does.

The interrogator also asked me about a bunch of other people, most of whom I didn't know. The people I did know were not involved in any crimes whatsoever, as far as I knew. Lastly, the Senegalese asked me about my position toward the U.S., and why I had transited through his country. I really didn't understand why my position toward the U.S. government should matter to anybody. I am not a U.S. citizen, nor did I ever apply to enter the U.S., nor am I working with the U.N. Besides, I could always lie. Or let's say I love the U.S., or I hate it, it doesn't really matter as long as I haven't done any crimes

---

* The question, given the pre-9/11 date of this interview and the reference to the Canadians, might refer to Ahmed Ressam. See footnote on p. 66.

against the U.S. I explained all this to the Senegalese interrogator with a clarity that left no doubt at all about my circumstances.

"You seem very tired! I suggest you go and have some sleep. I know it's hard," he said. Of course I was dead tired, and hungry and thirsty. The guards led me back to the small room where my brothers and the other two guys were lying on the floor, fighting against the most efficient Senegalese Air Force Mosquitoes ████████. I was no luckier than the rest. Did we sleep? Not really.

The interrogator and his assistant showed up early in the morning. They released the two guys, and took me and my brothers to the headquarters of the Ministère de L'Intérieur. The interrogator, who turned out to be a very high-level person in the Senegalese government, took me to his office and made a call to the Minister of Internal Affairs.

"The guy in front of me is not the head of a terrorist organization," he said. I couldn't hear what the minister said. "When it comes to me, I have no interest in keeping this guy in jail— nor do I have a reason," the interrogator continued. The telephone call was short and straightforward. In the meantime, my brothers made themselves comfortable, bought some stuff, and started to make tea. Tea is the only thing that keeps the Mauritanian person alive, with God's help. It had been a long time since any of us had eaten or drunk anything, but the first thing that came to mind was tea.

I was happy because the one-ton stack of paper the U.S. government had provided the Senegalese about me didn't seem to impress them; it didn't take my interrogator a whole lot of time to understand the situation. My two brothers started a conversation with him in Wolof. I asked my brothers what the conversation was about, and they said that the Senegalese government was not interested in holding me, but the U.S. was the one that was going to call the shots. Nobody was happy with that, because we had an idea of what the U.S. call would be like.

"We're waiting on some people from the U.S. embassy to show up," said the interrogator. Around eleven o'clock a black American ▬▬▬▬ showed up.* ▬▬▬ took pictures, fingerprints, and the report the recorder had typed earlier that morning. My brothers felt more comfortable around the black ▬▬▬▬▬ than the white ▬▬▬▬▬ from last night. People feel comfortable with the looks they are used to, and since about 50 percent of Mauritanians are black, my brothers could relate to them more. But that was a very naïve approach: in either case, black or white, ▬▬▬▬▬▬▬ would just be a messenger.

After finishing ▬▬▬ work, ▬▬▬▬▬▬▬▬ made a couple of calls, pulled the interrogator aside and spoke to him briefly, and then ▬▬▬▬ was gone. The inspector informed us that my brothers were free to go and that I was going to be held in contempt for some time.

"Do you think we can wait on him until he gets released?" my brother asked.

"I would suggest you guys go home. If he gets released, he will find his way." My brothers left and I felt abandoned and lonely, though I believe my brothers did the right thing.

For the next couple of days, the Senegalese kept interrogating me about the same things; the U.S. investigators sent them the questions. That was all. The Senegalese didn't hurt me in any way, nor did they threaten me. Since the food in jail was horrible, my brothers arranged with a family they knew in Dakar to bring me one meal a day, which they consistently did.

---

* Redacted pronouns suggest this, too, may be a woman.

My concern, as I say, was and still is to convince the U.S. government that I am not a corn. My only fellow detainee in the Senegalese jail had a different concern: to smuggle himself to Europe or America. We definitely had different Juliets. The young man from Ivory Coast was determined to leave Africa.

"I don't like Africa," he told me. "Many friends of mine have died. Everybody is very poor. I want to go to Europe or America. I tried twice. The first time I managed to sneak into Brazil when I outsmarted the port officials, but one African guy betrayed us to the Brazilian authorities, who put us in jail until they deported us back to Africa. Brazil is a very beautiful country, with very beautiful women," he added.

"How can you say so? You were in jail the whole time!" I interrupted him.

"Yes, but every once in a while the guards escorted us to look around, then took us back to jail," he smiled.

"You know, brother, the second time I almost made it to Ireland," he went on. "But the ruthless ██████████ kept me in the ship and made customs take me."

Sounds Columbus-y, I thought. "How did you get on board in the first place?" I wondered.

"It's very easy, brother. I bribed some of the workers at the port. Those people smuggled me onto a ship heading to Europe or America. It didn't really matter. I hid in the containers section for about a week until my provisions were gone. At that point, I came up and mingled with the crew. At first, they got very mad. The Captain of the ship headed to Ireland was so mad that he wanted to drown me."

"What an animal!" I interrupted, but my friend kept going.

"But after some time the crew accepted me, gave me food, and made me work."

"How did they catch you this time?"

"My smugglers betrayed me. They said the ship was heading nonstop to Europe. But we made a stop in Dakar and customs took me off of the ship, and here I am!"

"What's your next plan?"

"I'm gonna work, save some money, and try again." My fellow detainee was determined to leave Africa at any cost. Moreover, he was confident that one day he was going to put his feet in the promised land.

"Man, what you see on TV is not how real life looks like in Europe," I said.

"No!" he answered. "My friends have been successfully smuggled into Europe, and they have good lives. Good looking women and a lot of money. Africa is bad."

"You might as easily end up in jail in Europe."

"I don't care. Jail in Europe is good. Africa is bad."

I figured the guy was completely blinded by the rich world that deliberately shows us poor Africans a "paradise" we cannot enter, though he had a point. In Mauritania, the majority of the young people want to emigrate to Europe or the U.S. If the politics in African countries don't change radically for the better, we are going to experience a catastrophe that will affect the whole world.

His cell was catastrophic. Mine was a little better. I had a very thin worn-out mattress, but he had nothing but a piece of carton he slept on. I used to give him my food because when I get anxious I can't eat. Besides, I got good food from outside, and he got the bad food of the jail. The guards let us be together during the day and locked him up nights. My cell was always open. The day before I was extradited to Mauritania, the ambassador of Ivory Coast came to confirm the identity of my fellow detainee. Of course he had no papers whatsoever.

*   *   *

"We are releasing you!" the recorder who had been interrogating me for the last several days said happily.

"Thank you!" I interrupted him, looking in the direction of Mecca, and prostrating myself to thank God for being free.

"However, we have to turn you over to your country."

"No, I know the way, I'll do it on my own," I said innocently, thinking I didn't really want to go back to Mauritania, but maybe to Canada or somewhere else. My heart had been teased enough.

"I am sorry, we have to turn you over ourselves!" My whole happiness turned into agony, fear, nervousness, helplessness, confusion and other things I cannot describe. "Gather your stuff!" the guy said. "We're leaving."

I started to gather my few belongings, heartbroken. The inspector grabbed my bigger bag and I carried my small briefcase. During my arrest, the Americans had copied every single piece of paper I had and sent it all to Washington for analysis.

It was around 5 p.m. when we left the gate of the Commissariat de Police. Out front stood a Mitsubishi SUV. The inspector put my bags in the trunk, and we got into the back seat. On my left sat a guard I had never seen before, older and big boned. He was quiet and rather laid back; he looked straight ahead most of the time, only rarely scanning me quickly with the side of his eye. I hated it when guards would keep staring at me as if they had never seen a mammal before. On my right was the inspector who had been the recorder. In the passenger's seat sat the lead interrogator. The driver was a ████████████████████████████████ ██.[*]

---

[*] This character is described in the subsequent paragraphs, without redactions, as "the white driver," "the white guy," and "the American man."

From his tan you could tell he had spent some time in a warm place, but not in Senegal because the interrogator kept guiding him to the airport. Or maybe he was looking for best way, I couldn't tell. He spoke French with a heavy accent, though he was stingy in his conversation; he limited himself exactly within the necessary. He never looked at or addressed me. The other two interrogators tried to talk to me, but I didn't answer, I kept reading my Koran silently. Out of respect, the Senegalese didn't confiscate my Koran, unlike the Mauritanians, Jordanians, and Americans.

It took about 25 minutes to the airport. The traffic was quiet around and inside the terminal. The white driver quickly found a parking place. We got out of the truck, the guards carrying my luggage, and we all passed through the diplomatic way to the waiting room. It was the first time that I shortcut the civilian formalities while leaving one country to another. It was a treat, but I didn't enjoy it. Everybody seemed to be prepared in the airport. In front of the group the interrogator and the white guy kept flashing their magic badges, taking everybody with them. You could clearly tell that the country had no sovereignty: this was still colonization in its ugliest face. In the so-called free world, the politicians preach things such as sponsoring democracy, freedom, peace, and human rights: What hypocrisy! Still, many people believe this propaganda garbage.

The waiting room was empty. Everybody took a seat, and one of the Senegalese took my passport and went back and stamped it. I thought I was going to take the regular Air Afrique flight that was scheduled to Nouakchott that afternoon. But it didn't take very long to realize I had my own plane to myself. As soon as the guy returned with my stamped passport, all five of us stepped toward the runway, where a very small white plane was already running its engines. The American man gestured for us to stay behind and he had a quick talk with the pilot. Maybe the interrogator was with him, too, I can't remember. I was too scared to memorize everything.

Soon enough we were told to get in. The plane was as small as it could be. We were four, and barely managed to squeeze ourselves inside the butterfly with heads down and backs bent. The pilot had the most comfortable place. She was a French lady, you could tell from her accent. She was very talkative, and rather on the older side, skinny and blond. She didn't talk to me, but she exchanged some words with the inspector during the trip. As it turned out, I later learned she told her friends in Nouakchott about the secret package she delivered from Dakar. The bigger guard and I squeezed ourselves, knees-on-faces, in the back seat, facing the inspector, who had a little better seat in front of us. The plane was obviously overloaded.

The Interrogator and the American man waited until they made sure that the plane took off. I wasn't paying attention to the conversations between the pilot and the inspector, but I heard her at one point telling him that the trip was only 300 miles, and would take between 45 minutes and an hour, depending on the wind direction. That sounded so medieval. The inspector tried to talk to me, but there was nothing to talk about; to me everything was already said and done. I figured he had nothing to say to help me, so why should I talk to him?

I hate traveling in small planes because they're shaky and I always think the wind is going to blow the plane away. But this time was different, I was not afraid. In fact I wanted the plane to crash, and only me to survive. I would know my way: it was my country, I was born here, and anybody would give me food and shelter. I was drowned in my dreams, but the plane didn't crash; instead it was getting closer and closer to its destination. The wind was in its favor. I was thinking about all my innocent brothers who were and still are being rendered to strange places and countries, and I felt solaced and not alone anymore. I felt the spirits of unjustly mistreated people with me. I had heard so many stories about brothers being passed back and forth like a soccer ball just because they have been once in Afghanistan, or Bosnia, or Chechnya. That's screwed up! Thousands of miles away, I felt the warm breath of these other unjustly treated individuals comforting me. I stuck all the time to my Koran, ignoring my environment.

My company seemed to have a good time checking the weather and enjoying the beach we had been flying along the whole time. I don't think that the plane had any type of navigation technologies because the pilot kept a ridiculously low altitude and oriented us with the beach. Through the window I started to see the sand-covered small villages around Nouakchott, as bleak as their prospects. There definitely had been a sandstorm earlier that day; People were just gradually daring to go outside. The suburbs of Nouakchott appeared more miserable than ever, crowded, poor, dirty, and free of any of life's crucial infrastructures. It was the Kebba ghetto I knew, only worse. The plane flew so low I could tell who was who among the people who were moving, seemingly disoriented, everywhere.

It had been long time since I had seen my country last—since August 1993, in fact. I was coming back, but this time as a terrorism suspect who was going to be hidden in some secret hole. I wanted to cry out loud to my people, "Here I am! I am not a criminal! I'm innocent! I am just the guy you knew, I'm no different!" But my voice was oppressed, just like in a nightmare.

I couldn't really recognize anything, the city plan had changed so radically.

I finally realized the plane was not going to crash, and I was not going to have the chance to talk to my people. It's amazing how hard it can be for someone to accept his miserable situation. The key to surviving any given situation is to realize that you are in it. Whether I wanted it or not, I was going to be delivered to the very people I didn't want to see.

"Can you do me a favor?" I asked the Inspector.

"Sure!"

"I'd like you to inform my family that I'm in the country."

"OK. Do you have the phone number?"

"Yes, I do." The inspector, against my expectation, indeed called my family and told them about my reality. Moreover, the Senegalese made an official press declaration stating that they turned me over to my country. Both the Mauritanians and Americans were pissed off about that.

"What did you tell the Inspector?" the Mauritanian DSE, the Directeur de la Sûrete de l'État, asked me later.*

"Nothing."

"You're lying. You told him to call your family." It didn't really take David Copperfield to figure out that the telephone call was intercepted.

The handover was quick. We landed near the back door of the airport, where two men were waiting, the Mauritanian Inspector and another freakin' big black guy, most likely brought to take care of business—just in case!

"Where is the Airport Police Chief?" the Inspector wondered, looking at his black colleague. I knew the Airport Police

---

* The Directeur de la Sûrete de l'État, which MOS abbreviates as DSE throughout the manuscript, is the director of the Mauritanian intelligence service.

Chief: he had once been in Germany, and I gave him shelter and helped him buy a Mercedes-Benz. I hoped he would show up, so he could see me and put in a good word for me. But he never showed. Nor would he have put in a good word for me: Mauritanian Intelligence is by far the highest law enforcement authority. But I felt like I was drowning, and I would have grabbed any straw I encountered.

"You will be escorted to the hotel to spend the rest of the night," said the Inspector to his guests.

"How are you?" he said ungenuinely, looking at me.

"I'm fine."

"Is that all he has?" he asked.

"Yes that's it." I was watching all my belongings on earth being passed around as if I'd already died.

"Let's go!" the inspector said to me. The black guy, who never took his eyes off me, carried the luggage and pushed me before him toward a dirty small room at the secret gate of the airport. In the room, the black dude unfolded his dirty black 100 year-old turban.

"Mask your face thoroughly with this turban," said the Inspector. Typically Mauritanian: the Bedouin spirit still dominates. The inspector should have foreseen that he would need a Turban to wrap my head, but in Mauritania organization is almost non-existent; everything is left to whim and chance. It was tricky, but I hadn't forgotten yet how to fold a turban around my head. It is something people from the desert must learn. The turban smelled of piled-up sweat. It was just disgusting to have it around your mouth and nose. But I obediently complied with the orders and held my breath.

"Don't look around," the inspector said when the three of us stepped out of the room toward the parked Secret Police car, a ██████████████████. I sat in the passenger's seat, the inspector drove, and the black guy sat in the back seat, without saying a word. It was about sunset, but you couldn't tell exactly because the cloud of sand was covering the horizon. The streets were empty. I illegally looked around whenever the chance arose, but I could hardly recognize anything.

The trip was short, about ten minutes to the Security Police building. We stepped out of the car and entered the building, where another guard was waiting on us, ███████████████. The environment was an ideal place for mosquitoes, human beings are the strangers in that place: filthy toilet, dirty floor and walls, holes connecting all the rooms, ants, spiders, flies.

"Search him thoroughly," the inspector told ███████████.

"Give me everything you have," ███████████ respectfully asked me, wanting to avoid searching me. I gave ███████████ everything I had except for my pocket Koran. The inspector must have realized I would have one, for ███████████ came back and said, "Do you have a Koran?"

"Yes, I do."

"Give it to me! I told you to give me everything." By now the guard was growing afraid of being sent back again, so he searched me gently, but he didn't find anything but my pocket Koran. I was so sad, tired, and terrorized that I couldn't sit up straight. Instead I put my jacket on my face and fell on the inch-thick, worn-out 100-year-old mattress, the only object that existed in that room. I wanted to sleep, lose my mind, and not wake up until every bad thing was over. How much pain can I take? I asked myself. Can my family intervene and save me? Do they use electricity? I had read stories about people who were tortured to death. How could they bear it? I'd read about Muslim heroes who faced the death penalty, head up. How did they do it? I didn't know. All I knew was that I felt so small before all the big names I knew, and that I was scared to death.

Although the mosquitoes were tearing me apart, I fell asleep. Every once in a while I woke up and asked myself, Why don't they interrogate me right now, and do with me whatever they want, and everything will be over? I hate waiting on torture; an Arabic proverb says, "Waiting on torture is worse than torture." I can only confirm this proverb. I managed to perform my prayers, how I don't know.

Sometime around midnight I woke up to people moving around, opening and closing doors in an extraordinary manner. When the guard opened the door to my room, I glimpsed the face of a Mauritanian friend who happened to be with me a long time ago when I visited Afghanistan in 1992 during the struggle against communism. He looked sad and weathered, and must have gone through painful torture, I thought. I almost lost my mind, knowing for sure I was going to suffer at least as much as he had, given his close relationship with the Mauritanian president and the power of his family—qualities I don't have. I thought, The guy surely must have spoken about me, and that is the reason why they brought him here.

"Get up!" said the guards. "Put on your turban." I put on the dirty turban, gathered my last strength, and followed the guards to the interrogation room like a sheep being driven to its last destination, the slaughterhouse.

When I was driven past the guy I had seen earlier, I realized he was just a screwed-up guard who failed to keep his uniform the way it should be. He was sleepy and drowsy: they must have called him in the midst of his sleep, and he hadn't yet washed his face. It was not the friend I thought it was; anxiety, terror, and fear were dominating my mind. Lord have mercy! I was somewhat relieved. Did I commit a crime? No. Did my friend commit a crime? No. Did we conspire to committing a crime? No. The only thing we had done together was make a trip to Afghanistan in February 1992 to help the people fighting against communism. And as far as I was concerned that was not a crime, at least in Mauritania.

So why was I so scared? Because crime is something relative; it's something the government defines and re-defines whenever it pleases. The majority of people don't know, really, where the line is that separates breaking the law from not breaking it. If you get arrested, the situation worsens, because most people trust the government to have a good reason for the arrest. On top of that, if I personally had to suffer, I didn't want anybody to suffer with me. I thought they arrested my friend in connection with the Millennium Plot, if only because he had been in Afghanistan once.

I entered the interrogation room, which was the office of the DSE. The room was large and well-furnished: leather couch, two love-seats, coffee table, closet, one big desk, one leather chair, a couple of other chairs for unimportant guests, and, as always, the picture of the president conveying the weakness of the law and the strength of the government. I wished they had turned me over to the U.S.: at least there are things I could refer to there, such as the law. Of course, in the U.S. the government and politics are gaining more and more ground lately at the cost of the law. The government is very smart; it evokes terror in the hearts of people to convince them to give up their freedom and privacy. Still, it might take some time until the U.S. government overthrows the law completely, like in the third world and the communist regimes. But really that is none of my concern, and thank God my government doesn't possess the technology to track Bedouins in the vast desert.

There were three guys in the interrogation room: the DSE, his assistant, and his recorder. The DSE asked them to bring my stuff in. They thoroughly searched everything I had; no stone remained unturned. They didn't speak to me, they only spoke with each other, mostly in whispers, just to annoy the hell out of me. At the end of the search, they sorted out my papers and put aside the ones they thought interesting. Later on, they asked me about every single word in those papers.

"I am going to interrogate you. I just want to tell you as a forewarning that you better tell me the whole truth," the DSE said firmly, making a big effort to take a break from smoking his pipe, which he never took off his lips.

"I sure will," I answered.

"Take him back," the DSE dryly ordered the guards.

"Listen, I want you to tell me about your whole life, and how you joined the Islamic movement," said the DSE when the guards dragged my skeleton away from the mosquitoes and back into the interrogation room.

If you get arrested for the first time, chances are that you're not going to be forthcoming, and that's OK; even though you know you haven't done any crimes, it seems sensible. You're very confused, and you'd like to make yourself appear as innocent as possible. You assume you are arrested more or less on a reasonable suspicion, and you don't want to cement that suspicion. Moreover, questioning involves a lot of stuff nobody wants to talk about, like your friends and your private life. Especially when the suspicions are about things like terrorism, the government is very rude. In the interrogation you always avoid talking about your friends and your private, intimate life. And finally, you are so frustrated because of your arrest, and you really don't owe your interrogators anything. On the contrary, they owe you to show you the true cause of your detention, and it should be entirely up to you to comment then or to leave them be. If this cause is enough to hold you, you can seek professional representation; if not, well you shouldn't be arrested in the first place. That's how the civilized world works, and everything else is dictatorship. Dictatorship is governed by chaos.

To be honest with you, I acted like any average person: I tried to make myself look as innocent as a baby. I tried to protect the identities of every single person I knew, unless he or she was too well-known to the Police. The interrogations continued in this manner, but when they opened the Canadian file, things soured decidedly.

The U.S. government saw in my arrest and my rendition to Mauritania a once-in-a-blue-moon opportunity to unveil the plan of Ahmed Ressam, who back then was refusing to cooperate with the U.S. authorities. Furthermore, the U.S. wanted to learn in detail about my friends in both Canada and Germany, and even outside those countries. After all my cousin and brother ▬▬▬▬▬▬▬▬ was already wanted with a reward of U.S. $5,000,000.* The U.S. also wanted to learn more about the whole Jihadi issue in Afghanistan, Bosnia, and Chechnya.

---

* Ressam appears here unredacted. The wanted man, it is clear from context here and unredacted references elsewhere in the manuscript, is MOS's cousin and former brother-in-law Abu Hafs. Abu Hafs was wanted in connection with al-Qaeda attacks in the 1990s, with a $5 million reward under the FBI's Rewards for Justice Program. The reward for senior al-Qaeda figures increased to $25 million after the September 11, 2001, terrorist attacks. See, e.g., U.S. State Department, "Patterns of Global Terrorism," appendix D, May 21, 2002, http://www.state.gov/documents/organization/20121.pdf.

Expertise for free. For the aforementioned, and for other reasons I don't know, the U.S. drove my case as far as it could be driven. They labeled me "Mastermind of the Millennium Plot." They asked all countries to provide any tiny bit of information they possessed about me, especially Canada and Germany. And since I am already a "bad" guy, force must be applied to roast me.

To the dismay of the U.S. government, things were not really as they seemed, nor did the government achieve what it wanted. No matter how smart somebody plans, God's plan always works. I felt like 2Pac's "Me Against the World." And here's why.

All the Canadians could come up with was, "We have seen him with x and y, and they're bad people." "We've seen him in this and that mosque." "We have intercepted his telephone conversations, but there's nothing really!" The Americans asked the Canadians to provide them the transcripts of my conversations, but after they edited them. Of course it doesn't make sense to selectively take different passages from a whole conversation and try to make sense of them. I think the Canadians should have done one of two things: either refused to provide the Americans any private conversation that took place in their country, or provided them the whole conversation in its original form, not even translated.

Instead, out of the words the Canadians chose to share with their U.S. colleagues, U.S. interrogators magically stuck with two words for more than four years: Tea and Sugar.

"What do you mean by tea and sugar?"

"I mean tea and sugar." I cannot tell you how many times the U.S. asked me, and made other people ask me, this question. Another Mauritanian folktale recounts about a man who was born blind and who had one chance to get a glimpse of the world. All he saw was a rat. After that, whenever anybody tried to explain anything to the guy, he always asked, "Compare it with the rat: Is it bigger? smaller?"

Canadian intelligence wished I were a criminal, so they could make up for their failure when ▓▓▓▓▓▓▓▓ slipped from their country to the U.S. carrying explosives.* The U.S. blamed Canada for being a preparation ground for terrorist attacks against the U.S., and that's why Canadians Intel freaked out. They really completely lost their composure, trying everything to calm the rage of their big brother, the U.S. They began watching the people they believed to be bad, including me. I remember after ▓▓▓▓▓▓▓▓ plot, the Canadians tried to implant two cameras, one in my room, one in my roommate's. I used to be a very heavy sleeper. I heard voices but I couldn't tell what it was—or let's say I was too lazy to wake up and check on them. My roommate ▓▓▓▓▓▓ was different; he woke up and followed the noise. He laid low and watched until the tiny hole was through. The guy in the other room blew through the hole, and when he checked with his eye, he made eye contact with ▓▓▓▓▓▓▓.

▓▓▓▓▓▓▓ woke me up and told me the story.

"▓▓▓▓▓▓, I heard the same voices in my room." I said to him. "Let's check!" Our short investigation was successful: we found a tiny twin hole in my room.

"What should we do?" ▓▓▓▓▓▓▓ asked.

"We call the police," I said.

"Well, call them!" ▓▓▓▓▓▓▓ said. I purposely didn't use our telephone; instead, I went out and used a public phone, dialing 911. Two cops showed up, and I explained to them that our neighbor, without our consent, drilled two holes in our

---

* Again, the reference appears to be to Ahmed Ressam.

house, and we wanted him to be held for his illegal action toward us. Basically, we asked for a fair relief.

"Put some caulk inside the holes and the problem is solved," said one of the cops.

"Really? I didn't know that. Are you a carpenter?" I said. "Look! I didn't call you to give me advice on how to fix my house. There's an obvious crime behind this, trespassing and violation of our privacy. If you don't take care of us, we'll take care of ourselves. And by the way: I need you guys' business cards," I said. Each one silently produced a business card with the other cop's name and contact on the back of it. Obviously, those cops were following some idiot directions in order to deceive us, but for the Canadian Intel it was too late. For days to come we were just sitting and making fun of the plan.

The irony was that I lived in Germany for twelve years and they never provided any incriminating information about me, which was accurate. I stayed less than two months in Canada, and yet the Americans claimed that the Canadians provided tons of information about me. The Canadians don't even know me! But since all Intel work is based on what ifs, Mauritania and the U.S. started to interpret the information as they pleased, in order to confirm the theory that I was the mastermind of the Millennium Plot.

The interrogation didn't seem to develop in my favor. I kept repeating my Afghanistan Jihad story of 1991 and early 1992, which didn't seem to impress the Mauritanian interrogator. Mauritania doesn't give a damn about a trip to Afghanistan; they understand it very well. If you try to make trouble inside the country, however, you're going to be arrested, regardless of whether or not you've been in Afghanistan. On the other hand, to the American government a bare visit to Afghanistan, Bosnia, or Chechnya is worth watching you for the rest of your life and trying to lock you up. All the Arabic countries have the same approach as Mauritania, except the communist ones. I even think the communist Arab countries are at least fairer than the U.S. government in this regard, because they forbid their citizens to go to Jihad in the first place. Meanwhile, the U.S. government prosecutes people based on an unwritten law.

My Mauritanian interrogator was interested in my activities in Canada, which are non-existent in the criminal sense, but nobody was willing to believe me. All my answers to the question, "Have you done this or that while in Canada?" were, "No, No, No, No." And there we got completely stuck. I think I looked guilty because I didn't tell my whole story about Afghanistan, and I figured I had to fill that gap in order to make my case stronger. The interrogator had brought film equipment with him that day. As soon as I saw it, I started to shake: I knew that I would be made to confess and that they were going to broadcast me on the National TV, just like in October 1994, when the Mauritanian government arrested Islamists, made them confess, and broadcast their confessions.* I was so scared

---

* Throughout the manuscript, MOS refers several times to the political climate and events in Mauritania—in particular, to the close cooperation of President Maaouya Ould Sid'Ahmed Taya with the United States in the so-called War on Terror. Ould Taya came to power in a military coup in 1984 and became president in 1992. During his long tenure as head of state, Ould Taya carried out several waves of arrests of political opponents and Islamists like the one described here, in which more than ninety people, including a former government minister and ten religious leaders, were arrested and then amnestied after publicly confessing to membership in illegal organizations. A crackdown on Islamists in the army and education system led to a failed coup attempt in 2003, and Ould Taya was ultimately deposed in a successful coup in 2005. By that time, in part because of his support for U.S. antiterrorism polices, which included allowing the rendition of MOS, and his aggressive campaign against Islamists in Mauritania, Ould Taya had lost much of his public support. See http://www.nytimes.com/2005/08/08/international/africa/08mauritania.html?fta=y&_r=0; http://www.csmonitor.com/2005/0809/p07s02-woaf.html; and http://

my feet couldn't carry my body. You could tell there was a lot of pressure on my government.

"I've been very patient with you, boy," the interrogator said. "You got to admit, or I am going to pass you the special team." I knew he meant the torture team. "Reports keep coming every day from everywhere," he said. In the days before this talk I couldn't sleep. Doors kept getting opened and closed. Every move around me hit my heart so bad. My room was next to the archive, and through a small hole I could see some of the files and their labels; I started to hallucinate and read papers about me that didn't exist. I couldn't take anything anymore. And torture? No way.

"Look, Director! I have not been completely truthful with you, and I would like to share my whole story." I told him. "However, I don't want you to share the Afghanistan story with the U.S. government, because they don't understand this whole Jihad recipe, and I am not willing to put gas on the fire."

"Of course I won't," the DSE said. Interrogators are used to lying to people; the interrogator's whole job is about lying, outsmarting, and deception. "I can even send my recorder and my assistant away, if you'd like," he continued.

"No, I don't mind them around." The DSE called his driver and sent him to buy some food. He brought chicken salad, which I liked. It was my first meal since I left Senegal; it was now February 12, 2000.

"Is that all you're gonna eat?" wondered the DSE.

"Yes, I'm full."

"You don't really eat."

"That's the way I am." I started to recount my whole Jihad story in the most boring detail. "And as to Canada or an attack against the U.S., I have nothing to do with it," I finished. In the

www.ft.com/cms/s/0/23ab7cfc-0e0f-11da-aa67-00000e2511c8.html #axzz2vwtOwdNb.

days that followed I got, by far, better treatment and better food, and all the questions he asked me and all my answers were consistent in themselves and with the information he already knew from other sources. When the DSE knew that I was telling him the truth, he quit believing the U.S. reports to be the Gospel truth, and very much put them aside, if not in the garbage.

▮▮▮▮▮▮▮▮▮▮▮▮▮▮▮▮▮▮▮▮▮ showed up to interrogate me. There were three of them, ▮▮▮▮▮▮▮▮▮▮▮▮▮▮▮▮▮▮▮ ▮▮▮▮▮▮▮▮▮▮▮▮▮▮▮▮▮▮▮. Evidently the Mauritanian authorities had shared all of my interviews with ▮▮▮ ▮▮▮▮▮▮▮▮▮, so that ▮▮▮▮▮▮ and the Mauritanians were at the same level of information.*

When the team arrived they were hosted at ▮▮▮▮▮▮▮▮▮ ▮▮▮▮▮▮▮▮▮▮▮▮▮▮▮▮▮▮▮ gave me a forewarning the day they came to interrogate me.†

---

* Judging from MOS's 2005 ARB testimony, the date is around February 15, 2000, and these interrogators are likely Americans. MOS told the Administrative Review Board panel in 2005 that an American team consisting of two FBI agents and a third man from the Justice Department interrogated him over a two-day period near the end of his detention in Mauritania. His detention for questioning at the behest of the United States was widely reported in the local and international press; in a BBC report, Mauritanian officials confirmed that he was questioned by the FBI. ARB transcript, 17; http://news.google.com/newspapers?nid=1876&dat=20000 129&id=gzofAAAAIBAJ&sjid=5s8EAAAAIBAJ&pg=6848,4968256; http://news.bbc.co.uk/2/hi/africa/649672.stm.

† This might be the Presidential Palace. Elsewhere in the manuscript, MOS's American interrogators tout the United States' close relations with then-president Maaouya Ould Sid'Ahmed Taya, implying that they were hosted by the president and stayed at the Presidential Palace when they were carrying out investigations in the country. MOS manuscript, 130.

"Mohamedou, we have nothing on you. When it comes to us, you are a free man," he told me. "However, those people want to interrogate you. I'd like you to be strong, and to be honest with them."

"How can you allow foreigners to interrogate me?"

"It's not my decision, but it's just a formality," he said. I was very afraid, because I had never met American interrogators, though I anticipated that they would not use torture to coerce information. But the whole environmental setup made me very skeptical toward the honesty and humanity of the U.S. inter-rogators. It was kind of like, "We ain't gonna beat you our-selves, but you know where you are!" So I knew ▬▬▬▬ wanted to interrogate me under the pressure and threat of a non-democratic country.

The atmosphere was prepared. I was told what to wear and what to say. I never had the chance to take a shower or to wash my clothes, so I wore my some of my dirty clothes. I must have smelled terribly. I was so skinny from my confinement that my clothes didn't fit; I looked like a teenager in baggy pants. But as much as I was pissed, I tried to look as comfortable, friendly, and normal as I could.

▬▬▬▬▬▬▬▬▬▬ arrived around 8 p.m., and the interrogation room was cleaned for them. I entered the room smiling. After diplomatic greetings and introductions I sat down on a hard chair, trying to discover my new world.

The ▬▬▬▬▬▬ started to talk. "We have come from the States to ask you some questions. You have the right to remain calm. You may also answer some questions and leave others. Were we in the U.S., we would have provided you with a lawyer free of charge."

I almost interrupted his nonsense and said, 'Cut the crap, and ask me the questions!' I was like, 'What a civilized world!' In the room, there were only the ▇▇▇▇ interrogators with an Arabic interpreter. The Mauritanian interrogators stepped outside.

"Oh, thank you very much. I don't need any lawyer," I said.

"However, we would like you to answer our questions."

"Of course I will," I said. They started to ask me about my trip to Afghanistan during the war against communism, showed me a bunch of pictures, asked me questions about Canada, and hardly any questions about Germany. As to the pictures and Canada, I was completely truthful, but I deliberately withheld some parts of my two Afghanistan trips in January 1991 and February 1992. You know why? Because it is none of the U.S government's business what I had done to help my Afghani brothers against the communists. For Pete's sake, the U.S. was supposedly on our side! When that war was done I resumed my regular life; I hadn't broken any Mauritanian or German laws. I legally went to Afghanistan and came back. As for the U.S., I am not a U.S. citizen, nor have I been in the U.S. — so what law have I possibly broken? I understand that if I enter the U.S. and they arrest me for a reasonable suspicion, then I completely have to explain to them my position. And Canada? Well, they made a big deal out of me being in Canada, because some Arab guy had tried to attack them from Canada. I explained with definite evidence that I was not a part of it. Now F*ck off and leave me alone.

The ▇▇▇▇ interrogators told me that I wasn't truthful.

"No, I was," I lied. The good thing was that I didn't give a damn about what they thought. ▇▇▇▇▇▇▇▇▇ kept writing my answers and looking at me at the same time. I wondered, how could he do both? But later I learned that ▇▇▇ interrogators study your body language while you're speaking, which is nothing but bullshit.* There are many factors involved in an interrogation, and they differ from one culture to another. Since ▬▬▬▬▬▬▬ knows my entire case now, I suggest that ▬▬▬▬▬▬▬ should go back and check where he marked me as lying, just to check his competence. The U.S. interrogators also went outside their assignment and did what any interrogator would have done: they fished, asking me about Sudan, Nairobi, and Dar Es Salaam. How am I supposed to know about those countries, unless I have multiple doppelgängers?

▬▬▬▬▬▬▬▬▬ offered to have me work with them. I think the offer was futile unless they were dead sure that I was a criminal. I'm not a cop, but I understand how criminals can repent—but I personally had done nothing to repent for. The next day, about the same time, ▬▬▬▬▬▬▬ showed up once more, trying to get at least the same amount of information I had shared with the Mauritanians, but there was no persuading me. After all the Mauritanian authorities duly shared everything with them. The ▬▬▬▬▬▬▬ didn't push me in any uncivilized way; they acted rather friendly. The chief of the team said, "We're done. We're going back home," exactly like Umm 'Amr and her donkey.† ▬▬▬▬

---

* Because MOS's ARB testimony suggests this interrogation was led by the FBI, he may be referring here to the FBI in general and to one agent in particular. ARB transcript, 17. The FBI does list body language among possible deception clues in material posted on its website, and former FBI agents have written and spoken publicly on the subject. See, e.g., http://www.fbi.gov/stats-services/publications/law-enforcement-bulletin/june_2011/school_violence; and http://cjonline.com/news/local/2010-11-26/no_lie_ex_fbi_agent_spots_fibbers.

† The reference is to a pre-Islamic proverb about a cursed woman who is expelled from her tribe; the sense is of an unwanted person who goes away and is not seen again.

████████████ left Nouakchott, and I was released ████████
████████.*

"Those guys have no evidence whatsoever," the DSE said
sadly. He felt completely misused. The Mauritanians didn't
want me delivered to them in the first place, because it was a
no-win situation: if they found me guilty and they delivered
me to the U.S., they were going to feel the wrath of the public;
if not, they would feel the wrath of the U.S. government. In
either case, the President was going to lose his office.

So in the end, something like this must of happened under
the table:

"We found nothing on him, and you guys didn't provide us
any evidence," the Senegalese must have said. "Under these
circumstances, we can't hold him. But if you want him, take him."

"No, we can't take him, because we've got to get evidence
on him first," answered the U.S. government.

"Well, we don't want to have anything to do with him," said
the Senegalese.

"Turn him over the Mauritanians," the U.S. government
suggested.

"No, we don't want him, just take him!" cried the Mauritanian government.

"You got to," said the U.S. government, giving the Mauritanians no choice. But the Mauritanian government always
prefers keeping peace between the people and the government.
They don't want any trouble.

"You are free to go," said the DSE.

"Should I give him everything?"

"Yes, everything," the DSE answered. He even asked me to

---

* The *New York Times* reported that MOS was released from Mauritanian
custody on February 19, 2000. http://www.nytimes.com/2000/02/21
/world/terrorist-suspect-is-released-by-mauritania.html.

double-check on my belongings, but I was so excited I didn't check on anything. I felt as if the ghoul of fear had flown from my chest.

"Thank you very much," I said. The DSE ordered his assistant and recorder to drive me home. It was about 2 p.m. when we took off toward my home.

"You'd better not talk with journalists," said the inspector.

"No, I won't." And indeed, I never disclosed the scandal of foreign interrogators violating the sovereignty of my country to journalists. I felt so bad about lying to them.

"Come on, we have seen the ███████████████████ ████████████*God, those journalists are wizards.

"Maybe they were listening to my interrogation," I said unconvincingly.

I tried to recognize the way to my home, but believe me, I didn't recognize anything until the police car parked in front of our house and dropped me there. It had been almost seven years since I saw my family last.† Everything had changed. Children had become men and women, young people had become older. My strong mom had become weak. Nonetheless everybody was happy. My sister ████████████ and my former wife had hardly slept nights, praying to God to relieve my pains and sufferings. May God reward everybody who stood on my side.

Everybody was around, my aunt, the in-laws, friends. My family kept generously feeding the visitors, some of whom came just to congratulate me, some to interview me, some just to get

---

* MOS appears to be quoting a conversation with a particular journalist after his release.

† MOS left Mauritania in 1988 to study in Germany. He testified at his 2004 CSRT hearing that he visited his family in Mauritania for two or three weeks in 1993. CSRT transcript, 5.

to know the man who had made news for the last month. After the first few days, my family and I were making plans for my future. To make a long story short, my family wanted me to stay in the country, if only to see me every day and enjoy my company. I said to myself, Screw it, went out, found a job, and was enjoying looking into the pretty face of my mom every morning. But no joy is forever.

THREE

Mauritania

September 29, 2001–November 28, 2001

A Wedding and a Party...I Turn Myself In...Release
from Custody...The Camel Rests in Two Steps...The
Secret Police Show Up at My House... "Independence
Day"...A Flight to Jordan

I t was a very busy day:* for one, I was involved in organizing the wedding of my lovely niece ███████████████,
and for two, I was invited to attend a big dinner organized
by a very important man in my tribe named ██████████
████████████. This man had unluckily been involved in a
terrible car accident, and had recently come back after spending some time in the U.S. for medical treatment. ████████
████████████████████ enjoys a high respect among the people
from the South, and the dinner was to aid what we call The
Cadres of Trarza.†

In the morning I asked my boss to give me some money to

---

* The date, according to MOS's 2005 ARB testimony, is Saturday,
September 29, 2001. ARB transcript, 18.

† Trarza is the region of southern Mauritania that extends from the
Senegalese border north to the capital. It was also the name of a precolonial
emirate in the same region. The Cadres of Trarza appears to be a community organization.

help my sister with the wedding.* In Mauritania we have the bad habit of organizing everything on the whim, a heritage of rural life that all Mauritanians still deal with today. My job was to help transport the invited guests to the site where the wedding was taking place.

Weddings in the Islamic, Arabic World are not only different from one country to another, but within the same country there are all kinds of different customs. My niece's wedding followed the customs that are practiced by average prestigious families in southern Mauritania.

Most of the work is usually done by the guy. He investigates the would-be wife's background by unleashing the female relatives he trusts the most. The report of this "committee" will produce an assessment of the technical data of the girl, her attitude, her intellect, and the like; sometimes this investigation step can be skipped when the girl already has a good reputation.

The next step is dating, though that is different than the American model. The interested guy dates his would-be wife in her family's house, usually in the presence of other family

---

* MOS testified at his 2004 CSRT and 2005 ARB hearings that when he returned to Mauritania in 2000 he worked as an electronics and computer specialist, first for a medical equipment supply company and then, starting in July 2001, for a company named Aman Pêche in Nouakchott. "This is a French word for fish," he explained at his CSRT hearing. "This company was a company of people from my tribe, and they gave me more money to join them. They wanted to develop the business and to use me; I was just setting up at my office, because they didn't know what to do with me at first. They had many electronic devices they wanted me to take care of. I had just set up my office and installed the AC, and September 11th happened. Then America went crazy looking for leads; and I was the cousin of the right hand of Osama bin Laden, and oh, get him." CSRT transcript, 8; ARB transcript, 18.

members. The goal of these dates is for both to get to know each other. The dating can take between a couple of months and a couple of years, depending on the man and the girl. Some girls don't want to start a family before graduating from school, and some do — or let's say family pressure and the man compel her to start the family right away. On the other hand, most guys aren't ready for marriage; they just want to "reserve" the girl and go about their business until they are financially ready. The groom is usually older than the bride, sometimes even much older, but in a few cases the bride happens to be older, and sometimes much older. Mauritanians are relatively tolerant when it comes to age differences.

Before the guy officially asks for the hand of the girl, he secretly sends a good friend to the girl to ask her whether she might consider him. When that is established, the decisive step comes next: the guy asks the girl's mom whether she would accept him as the husband of her daughter. Guys only ask for the hand of a girl if they know they will more than likely be accepted, so sometimes the guy sends a trusted third person in order to avoid the embarrassment of being turned down. Only the mother of the girl can decide; most fathers have little say.

This step, though not official, is binding for both. Everybody now knows that ███████ is engaged to ███████. Premarital sex is not tolerated in Mauritania, and not only for religious reasons: many guys mistrust any girl who accepts having sex with them. They assume, If she accepts having sex with me, she would accept another man, and another man, in an endless sexual adventure. Although the Islamic religion treats males and females the same way in this regard, the society tends to accept premarital sex from men much more than women. You can compare it with cheating in the U.S.: the society tolerates it more if a man cheats than if a women does. I never met an American man who would forgive cheating, but I did meet many American women who would.

There is no party or engagement ring, but the fiancé is now entitled to give his wife-to-be presents. Before the engagement, a lady would not accept presents from a stranger.

The last step is the actual wedding, the date of which is set by agreement of both; each party can take as much as time as he or she needs, as long as it is reasonable. The man is expected to produce a dowry as a necessary formality, but it is not appropriate for the girl's family to ask for any sum; the whole thing must be left to the man and his financial possibilities. So dowries vary from a very modest to a relatively sinfully high amount. Once the man produces whatever his possibilities and judgment allow, many families will only take a small, symbolic amount and send the rest to the man's family, at least half of the dowry.

The wedding party traditionally takes place in the girl's family house, but lately some people have found a lucrative business in professionally organizing weddings in club-like houses. The Party begins with the *Akd*, the marriage agreement, which can be performed by any Imam or respected Sheikh. Mauritanians don't believe in governmental formalities, and so hardly anybody declares his marriage at a government institution unless it is for financial advantages, which rarely exist.

The wedding party equally drains both the groom's and bride's family. Traditionally, Mauritanians would party for seven full days, but the punishments of modern life cut those seven days back to one single night. Only the friends of the groom from his generation are allowed to attend the wedding, unlike women, who can be all different ages. At the party women don't mingle directly with men, though they can be in the same hall; each sex respects the spot of the other. However, all the attendants talk to each other and enjoy the same entertainment that takes place in the middle of the hall, such as sketches, music, and poetry. When I was a child, women and men used to pass coded messages back and forth targeting a particular individual who certainly understood the message; the messages usually unfolded a funny situation that could happen to anybody and that is somewhat embarrassing. The person's friends would laugh at him or her, and he or she would have to fight back targeting the anonymous person who sent the message. People don't do this teasing entertainment anymore.

During the wedding food and drinks are generously served. The party traditionally closes with what they call the *Taweez-Pillage*, which doesn't have anything with the literal meaning of the words. It just describes the plot by the women to kidnap the bride, and the brothers' efforts to prevent the act. The bride's female friends are allowed to conspire and kidnap the bride and hide her; it is the job of the groom and his friends to prevent this event, and should the men fail in preventing the abduction, it is their duty to find the bride and deliver her to her husband. The bride must cooperate with her female friends, and she usually does, otherwise she'll be branded with all kinds of bad adjectives. It sometimes takes many days for the males to find the bride.

When the man succeeds in getting the bride the party is over, and the bride is given to the groom. Both get escorted by their closest friends in a long rally leading to the house of the new family, while the rest of the attendants retreat to their own homes.

The wedding of my beloved niece ▮▮▮▮▮▮▮▮▮▮ would have gone more or less like this. I wasn't supposed to attend the party because I was way older than the groom, and in any case I didn't have time. I had another interesting party waiting on me. When I finished delivering the guests I checked with my mom on the situation. Everything seemed to be alright; my services no longer were required as far as I could see. The atmosphere of wedding was clearly going to take over.

When I got to the party, which was in the beautiful villa of ███████████████ in Tevrlegh Zeina, the warmth of companionship hit me gracefully. I didn't know the majority of the guests, but I spotted my beloved ████████████████████ ████████████ drowned in the middle of the crowd. I right away fought through the crowd and sat beside ███████████.

He was happy to see me, and introduced me to the most remarkable guest. We retreated to the margin of the party with a few of his friends, and ████████████████ introduced me to a friend of his, a young ████████████. The ████████████ asked ████████████ and me whether he could defend ███████████, who now was wanted by the U.S. authorities with a $25,000,000 reward.*

"What are you going to do for him? Reduce his sentence from 500 to 400 years?" I asked wryly. People in the other parts of the free world like Europe have problems understanding the draconian punishments in the U.S. Mauritania is not a country of law, so we don't have a problem understanding whatever the government does; even so, the Mauritanian legal code, when it is followed, is much more humane than the American. Why sentence somebody to 300 years when he is not going to live that long?

We were just talking like that, and enjoying the food that was generously served, when my cell phone rang. I pulled it out

---

* The conversation appears to center on Abu Hafs, who in the wake of the 9/11 attacks was now the subject of a $25 million bounty (see footnote on p. 94).

of my pocket and stepped aside. The display read the phone
number of the DSE, the Directeur de la Sûreté de l'État.

"Hi," I answered.

"Mohamedou, where are you?" he said.

"Don't worry! Where are you?"

"I'm outside of my front door! I'd like to see you."

"Fine. Just hold on, I'm on my way!" I said. I took ████
██████████████████ aside.

"Look, ████████████ called me, and I'm going to see him."

"As soon as he releases you, give me a buzz."

"Alright," I said.

The DSE was waiting in front of his house, but he was not
alone: his assistant stood beside him, which was not a good sign.

"Salam Alaikum," I said, stepping outside my car.

"Waalaikum Assalam. You're gonna ride with me, and somebody else is going to drive your car."

"Fine." The Inspector and I rode with the DSE and headed
toward the secret, well-known jail.

"Look, those people told us to arrest you."

"Why?"

"I don't know, but I hope you'll be free soon. This whole
9/11 attack thing is screwing up everybody." I didn't say a thing.
I just let him and his assistant make small talk, to which I paid
no attention. The DSE had already called and interrogated me
twice in the two and a half weeks since the 9/11 attack, but
obviously the American government was not satisfied with a
yard; they wanted a mile at first, and then the whole Autobahn,
as it turned out in the end.

They put me in the same room I had been in one and half
years ago. The Inspector went out to brief the guards, which
gave me the opportunity to give a quick call to ████████████
██████████████.

"I'm arrested," I whispered, and hung up without even waiting on his answer. Then I erased my whole phone book. Not that I had any hot numbers—all I had were some numbers of business partners in Mauritania and Germany—but I didn't want the U.S. government harassing those peaceful people just because I had their numbers in my phone. The funniest record I deleted read "PC Laden," which means computer store; the word for "store" in German just happens to be "Laden." I knew no matter how hard I would have tried to explain that, the U.S. interrogators would not have believed me. For Pete's sake, they always tried to pin things on me that I had nothing to do with!

"Give me your cell phone," the Inspector said when he returned. Among the belongings the Americans took back home with them later was that old, funny looking cell phone, but there were no numbers to check. As to my arrest, it was sort of like political drug-dealing: the FBI asked the U.S. President to intervene and have me arrested; in turn George W. Bush asked the vanishing Mauritanian President for a favor; on receiving the U.S. president's request, his Mauritanian colleague moved his police forces to arrest me.

"I really have no questions for you, because I know your case," the DSE said. Both the DSE and his assistant left, leaving me with the guards and oodles of mosquitoes.

After several days in the prison, the DSE came to my cell.

"Look! Those people want to know about ████████████ ████████████, and they said you were a part of the Millennium Plot."

"Well, ████████████████████████ are my friends in Germany, and as to the Millennium Plot, I had nothing to do with it."

"I'll give you a pen and paper, and you write whatever you know."

*   *   *

After two weeks of incarceration in the Mauritanian prison, two white U.S. interrogators ██████████████████████████ ███████████ came to the jail late one afternoon to interrogate me.*

Before ██████████████████████████████████ met me, they asked the police to storm my house and office and confiscate anything that could give leads to my "criminal" activities. A special security team took me home, searched my house, and seized everything they thought might be relevant for the Americans. When the team arrived my wife was asleep, and they scared the hell out of her: she had never seen police searching somebody's house. Neither had I, for that matter, but I had no problem with the search except that it bothered my family. My neighbors didn't care much, first because they know me, and second because they know that the Mauritanian police are unjust. In a separate operation, another team searched the company where I worked. As it turned out, the Americans were not interested in any of the garbage except my work computer and the cellphone.

When I entered the interrogation room, the two Americans were sitting on the leather sofa, looking extremely angry. They must have been FBI, because the stuff they confiscated ended up on FBI's hands back in the States.

"Hi," I said, reaching out my hand. But both my hand and my "Hi" remained hanging in the air. ████████ seemed to be the leader. He pushed an old metal chair toward me.

"Do you see the picture on the wall?" ████████ said, pointing

---

* In his 2005 ARB testimony, MOS dates this interrogation as October 13, 2001, and speculates that these two interrogators are FBI, though "they are American, they may be anything." Accompanying the lead interrogator is an interrogator who "spoke German adequately but not very good," and "with a bad accent," who interprets during the interview. ARB transcript, 18.

at the President's picture, with ▇▇▇▇▇▇ translating into German.

"Yes," I answered.

"Your president promised our president that you are going to cooperate with us," ▇▇▇▇ said. I thought, How cheap! I personally don't give a damn about either president; to me both are unjust and evil.

"Oh, yes! I surely will," I said, reaching for a drink on a table filled with all kinds of drinks and sweets. ▇▇▇▇▇ jerked the drink out of my hand.

"We are not here for a party," he said. "Look, I am here to find the truth about you. I'm not here to detain you."

"OK! You ask and I'll answer."

In the midst of this discourse, the tea guy surged into the room, trying to accommodate his angry guests. "Fuck off!" said ▇▇▇▇▇. ▇▇▇▇▇▇▇▇ very disrespectful toward poor people, an idiot, and a racist who had one of the lowest self-esteems in the world. For my part, I ignored all the curses he addressed me with and just stayed cool, though very thirsty, because the session lasted the whole night.

"Before 9/11 you called your younger brother in Germany and told him, 'Concentrate on your school.' What did you mean with this code?"

"I didn't use any code. I always advise my brother to concentrate on his school."

"Why did you call a satellite company in the U.S.?"

"Because we have our Internet connection from the U.S., and I needed support."

"Why did you call this hotel in Germany?"

"My boss asked me to make a reservation for one of his cousins."

"How many computers do you have?"

"Only my work computer."

"You're lying! You have a laptop."

"That's my ex-wife's."

"Where is your ex-wife living?"

"The DSE knows."

"OK, let's check this lie out." ▇▇▇▇▇ disappeared for several minutes, asking the DSE to search my ex-wife's house and seize the laptop.

"What if you're lying?"

"I am not."

"But what if?"

"I'm not."

Of course he threatened me with all kinds of painful torture should it turn out I was lying. "You know we have some black motherfuckers who have no mercy on terrorists like you," he said, and as he proceeded, racial references kept flying out of his mouth. "I myself hate the Jews..."—I didn't comment—"...But you guys come and hit our building with planes," he continued.

"That's between you and the people who did it. You must resolve your problem with them; I have nothing to do with it."

Every once in a while ▇▇▇▇▇ received a call, obviously from a lady. During that time the other German-speaking idiot came up with the most stupid questions.

"Check this out. This is a German newspaper writing about you guys," he said. I scanned a newspaper article about the extremist presence in Germany.

"Well, ▇▇▇▇▇▇▇▇ that's none of my problem. As you can see, I'm in Mauritania."

"Where is ▮▮▮▮▮▮▮▮▮▮? Where is Noumane?" ▮▮▮▮▮▮
asked angrily.*

"I am not in Afghanistan, I'm in Mauritania — in prison.
How can I possible know their whereabouts?"

"You're hiding him," he said. I was going to say, "Check up
my sleeves," but I realized my situation didn't allow it.

"▮▮▮▮▮▮▮▮▮▮▮▮▮▮▮▮ said that he knew you!"

"I don't know ▮▮▮▮▮▮▮▮▮▮▮▮▮▮▮▮▮. There is nothing
to change about that fact." In the meantime, the DSE and his
assistant came back with my ex-wife's laptop. They weren't
allowed into the interrogation room; they knocked at the door
and ▮▮▮▮▮▮▮▮ stepped outside. I looked with the side of my
eyes and recognized the laptop bag. I was happy that they found
the "big secret."

▮▮▮▮▮▮ returned. "What if I told you that they didn't find
the laptop," he said, trying to be smarter than he is.

"All I can tell you is that I have no laptop," I said, letting him
believe that I hadn't seen the case. He didn't ask anymore
about the laptop after that. They mirrored all the hard disks and
took them home, just to waste four years popping their eyes out
of their heads looking for non-existent treasure. Tough luck!

"We have invaded Afghanistan and are killing everybody.
Do you think that's OK?" ▮▮▮▮▮▮ asked.

"You know best what you're doing," I said.

---

* The "Noumane" in the interrogator's question may refer to Noumane
Ould Ahmed Ould Boullahy, whose name appears in a footnote to Judge
James Robertson's opinion granting MOS's habeas corpus petition. The
footnote reads, "The government asserts that Salahi swore the oath to
Osama bin Laden, and did so at the same time as Noumane Ould Ahmed
Ould Boullahy, who went on to become one of bin Laden's bodyguards.
There is no evidence that Salahi maintained, or that he ever had, any rela-
tionship with Boullahy." The opinion is available at https://www.aclu.org
/files/assets/2010-4-9-Slahi-Order.pdf.

"Do you know Houari?"*

"No!"

"The Canadians said that they saw him with you. Either I am lying to you or they lied to me — or you're lying."

"I don't know him, but in the mosque, and in the café beneath it, I was always around many people I don't know."

"Why do you think we picked you up out of more than two million Mauritanians?"

"I don't know why. All I know is I haven't done anything against you."

"Write your name in Arabic." I wrote my name. For some reason, he kept taking pictures during the session. He really confused the hell out of me.

"Why did you call the UAE?"

"I didn't."

"So you think I am lying to you?"

"No, but I don't remember calling the UAE." As it turned out he did lie, but maybe unintentionally. I didn't call the UAE, but I did receive a call from a female friend of mine, ████████ ████████████████, who tried desperately to bring me and my ex-wife back together. I couldn't remember this during the session, I was so nervous. But when I was released, my family helped me remember, so I went to the police on my own and explained the call to them, and another call my ████████ ████████████████████████ made to France to contact his medicine supplier in Paris. In real life, if I give my phone to somebody I trust, I don't ask him about the details of his call. But if you get arrested, you have to lay out your whole life, and something like "I don't remember" doesn't work.

During the session, ████████████ called my family and me

---

* This name is written "Houari" in the manuscript. The interrogator may be referring to convicted Millennium Plot co-conspirator Mokhtar Hauoari.

all kind of names, and forbade me to drink from the goods that my people paid for—it was, after all, our taxes that made the U.S. guests comfortable. At the end of the session, when I was about to dehydrate, ███████████ hit me in the face with 1.5-liter water bottle and left the room. I didn't even feel the pain from a blow that almost broke my nose because of the relief of ███████████████ leaving. ███████████
███████████ didn't write anything, which struck me as strange because interrogators always want to write, but I believe that they recorded the session. ███████████ tried his best to repeat the curses that ███████████ was generously producing. I think that ███████████ was worthless to Mr. ███████; he just brought him along as a translator.

The Americans left ███████████, and the next day, the Mauritanian government released me without any charges. Furthermore, the DSE went to the Media Center and informed them that I was innocent and acquitted of every charge. The DSE's boss, the Directeur Général de la Sûreté Nationale,* offered me a loan in case I had any problems getting back to my job, and at the same time, the DSE called the President and Director General of my company and assured him that I am innocent and must resume my work.†

"We never doubted him for a second. He is welcome any time," my former boss answered. Still, the government was ordered by the U.S. to keep me under house arrest with no reason besides injustice and the misuse of power. I wasn't wor-

---

* Directeur Général de la Direction Générale de la Sûreté Nationale is abbreviated here and a few pages later in the manuscript as DG and spelled out in a footnote the second time. The Sûreté Nationale is the Mauritanian national police force; its director general is the country's top law enforcement official.

† In the manuscript, this is abbreviated PDG, short for the French title *président-directeur général*, the equivalent of president and CEO.

ried about getting a job after jail because I knew that Mauritanians were growing tired of Americans jumping on innocent people all around the world and trying to incriminate them. In fact, I got more job opportunities than I ever had in my life. My only worry was for my sister ███████████, who was suffering from depression and anxiety. My family of course was very happy to have me back, and so were my friends and relatives who kept coming to greet me and wish me good luck.

But the camel, as they say, rests in two steps.

Legend has it that an urban dweller rode a camel with a Bedouin. The Bedouin sat in front of the hump, and the urban dweller behind it so he could steady himself by grabbing the Bedouin. When they arrived home, the camel bent his front legs to come to rest, and the Bedouin, caught off guard, lost his equilibrium and fell to the ground. The urban dweller couldn't help laughing at the Bedouin.

The Bedouin looked at his friend and said, "Too soon to be happy: the camel rests in two steps." And indeed, as soon as the camel bent his rear legs to come to his final rest, the urban dweller fell on his face.

As far as I can remember, I never fell off a camel; however, as soon as I resumed my life, the U.S. government started conspiring with the Mauritanian government to kidnap me.

It was around 4 p.m. when I got back from work about a month later. It had been a long day, hot, and humid: one of those days. The Islamic calendar read Ramadan 4th, and so far everybody in the family was fasting except for the kids.*

---

* Ramadan 4th was Tuesday, November 20, in 2001.

It had been a remarkable workday. My company sent me to assess a relatively big project for our small company: we had been asked to give an estimate to network the Presidential Palace for both computers and telephones. I had made an appointment with the project coordinator for early that morning, and waiting outside his office was the order of the first half of the day. There are two things all government officials have in common: they don't respect appointments, and they never start work on time.

During Ramadan, most people party nights and sleep days. I hadn't partied last night, but I had stayed up late for another reason: namely I had a little familial fight with my beloved wife. I hate fights, and so I was depressed and couldn't sleep the whole night. As drowsy and sleepy I was, I still managed to be on the site of my rendezvous, though not punctually, with time enough to beat the coordinator by hours. His office was closed, and there was no free chair in the corridor, and so I had to put up with squatting on the floor with my back to the wall. I fell asleep many times.

Around noon ██████████████████████ showed up and took me to the Presidential Palace. I thought there would be a lot of formalities, especially for a "terrorist suspect" such as myself, but nothing like that happened. You had to give your name the day before, and when I showed the guards my ID they verified the visitors' list, where my name appeared with the appropriate clearance. I was shocked. But after all, only the Americans suspect me of terrorism, no other country. The irony is that I have never been in the States, and all the other countries I have been in kept saying, "The guy is alright."

As soon as I entered the sanctuary of the palace, I felt as if I were in another country. There was a garden inside with all kinds of flowers. Water fountains created a light drizzle. The weather was just cool and fine.

We went right to business. I went through many rooms on different floors and took some measurements, but we were stopped and advised to leave the actual palace because there was an official visit. We could stay inside the compound, and so I used that time and went to the palace's central telephone exchange to check on the infrastructure. The ████████████ ████████████████████████ and as friendly as most people from Atar. He was more of a security choice; the president trusts his own people most, which makes perfect sense. I felt depressed because the whole project needed much more work than what it said in the papers, and I needed help, professional help. I didn't want to mess around with the Presidential Palace. I would rather retreat completely than start selling them made-in-Timbuktu hi-tech equipment.

The ████████████████ showed us the things we needed to see and disappeared to his guests. It was late, and the project coordinator asked for another appointment to finish the measurement work and the assessment of the needed infrastructure. ████████████████████ and I left with the intention of coming back tomorrow and finishing the work. By the time we left the gate, I was already tired, and like, Get me the hell outta here. I made a call to my boss and briefed him, and I even went to the office after that and told my colleagues what happened.

On the way home, ██████████████████████████ called me to make sure that I would be at dinner in his house. ██████ ██████████████ is a ████████████████████████████ ██ ██████████. Besides, ██████████████████ is an old friend of the family; I knew him and played cards with him when I was a child. Today ████████████████ was organizing a big dinner for his friends, including my brother, who was on vacation with us from Germany, and me. Right when ██████████████ called, my car had a breakdown. I hated it when my As-Old-As-My-Grandpa car did that.

"Do you need me to come to you?" ████████████████ asked.

"No, I can see a garage not far from me. I'm sure they'll help me."

"Don't forget our Dinner Party, and remind ██████████ ██████████████!" he said.

A mechanic from the garage found that the benzene pipe to the carburetor was broken, and fixed it. In Mauritania people fix everything; in Germany, people replace everything. The mechanic wanted me to pay him more than I thought he ought to be paid, and so I did the thing I hate the most, negotiation, and paid him the amount we agreed on. One thing I like about Germany is that you don't need to negotiate; everything is labeled with a price. You could be mute and nonetheless be treated justly. The thing about negotiation is that most of the time somebody is going to be disadvantaged. Personally, I just want a fair price for both parties that makes each party happy.

When I arrived at my mom's home around 4 p.m., only my ██████████████ and my sister ████████████ were there, and both were asleep.* My mom had gone outside to gather her scattered sheep; it was feeding time. I went inside the house and put on my bathrobe. On my way to the shower, my mom and two secret police guys surged almost simultaneously into the house.

"Salahi, the Director General wants to see you!"

"Why?"

---

* It becomes clear in a few paragraphs that the first family member mentioned here is an aunt.

"We don't know," said one of the guys.

"OK. I'm going to take a shower and change my clothes."

"OK!" said the guy, stepping out. "We're gonna wait on you outside." The secret police respected me highly since I turned myself in a couple of weeks ago; they knew I am not a person who flees. I had basically been under house arrest since 2000 but I could have fled the country anytime; I didn't, and didn't have any reason to. I took my shower and changed. In the meantime my aunt woke up because of the noise. My sister didn't wake up, as far as I remember, and that was good, because I was only worried about her and the extreme depression she had been suffering.

"I think the police called you because you bought a new TV, and they don't want you to watch TV. Don't you think?" said my mom innocently.

I smiled and said, "I don't think so, but everything is going to be alright." My mom was referring to the new satellite antenna I installed the night before to have better TV reception. The irony is that the ▮▮▮▮▮▮▮▮▮▮▮▮▮▮▮▮▮ was the one who helped me install the antenna.* When I was in prison the month before, he had asked me to find a job for him because the police paid him miserably. I promised him I would, and in the meantime, I wanted to offer him an opportunity to do some work for me, so I called him to help fix my antenna, and paid him adequately. That was the only way for a man like him to survive. I helped him get some work, and we were sipping tea and joking in my house.

"I didn't bring you to my house to arrest me," I said jokingly.

★ That is, it appears that one of the officers who has been dispatched to bring MOS in for questioning was in MOS's home to help him install the satellite antenna the previous evening.

"I hope you will never be arrested," ████████████████████
said.

My mom's house is next to my brother's, with a short wall
that separates them. I could simply have jumped to my brother's
house, and escaped through his door that opens to a completely
other street, and guess what? There would be no finding me,
not only because so many people would shelter me, but also
because the police agents would not have been interested in
finding me. I even believe that the government would have
been much happier saying to the U.S., "He fled, we couldn't
find him."

You should know, Dear Reader, that a country turning over
its own citizens is not an easy deal. The President wished he
hadn't had to turn me over. I wonder why? After all it cost him
his office afterward. I understand that if the U.S. captures me
in Afghanistan and takes me to GTMO for whatever reason,
my government cannot be blamed because I chose to go to
Afghanistan. But kidnapping me from my house in my country
and giving me to the U.S., breaking the constitution of Mauritania and the customary International Laws and treaties, that
is not OK. Mauritania should have asked the U.S. to provide
evidence that incriminates me, which they couldn't, because
they had none. But even if the U.S. did so, Mauritania should
try me according to the criminal code in Mauritania, exactly
as Germany does with its citizens who are suspected of being
involved in 9/11. On the other hand, if the U.S. says "We have
no evidence," then the Mauritanian response should be something like, "Fu*k you!" But no, things don't work this way.
Don't get me wrong, though: I don't blame the U.S. as much
as I do my own government.

The secret police agents obviously wanted me to flee, especially ████████████████. But I wanted to keep it real—not to

mention that the government itself assured my family that I had done nothing, and so my family always wanted me to go to the police whenever they asked to see me. The funny thing about "Secret Police" in Arab countries is that they are more known to the commoners than the regular police forces. I think the authorities in Arabic countries should think about a new nomenclature, something like "The Most Obvious Police."

There were four of them when I stepped outside the door with my mom and my aunt. My mom kept her composure, and started to pray using her fingers. As to my aunt, that was her first time seeing somebody taken by the police, and so she got crippled and couldn't say a word. She started to sweat heavily and mumbled some prayers. Both kept their eyes staring at me. It is the taste of helplessness, when you see your beloved fading away like a dream and you cannot help him. And same for me: I would watch both my mom and my aunt praying in my rearview mirror until we took the first turn and I saw my beloved ones disappear.

"Take your car, we hope you can come back home today," one of the guys had instructed me. "The DG might just ask you some questions." ████████████ occupied my passenger seat, as sad as he could be.

"Salahi, I wish I were not part of this shit," he said. I didn't respond. I kept following the police car that was heading toward the secret, well-known jail. I had been incarcerated a couple times in the same illegal prison, and knowing it didn't make me like it. I hated the compound, I hated the dark, dirty room, I hated the filthy bathroom, and I hated everything about it, especially the constant state of terror and fear.

"Earlier today the Inspector was looking for you. You know the DSE is on a trip in Spain. The Inspector asked us who has your phone number. But I didn't say anything, even though I have it," ████████████, trying to make himself feel better. The only other guy who had my phone number was the DSE, and obviously he didn't give it to anybody.

So here we are, at the gate of the resented prison. The ████████████ was in his office, looking at me with his dishonest smile, which he quickly changed into a frown.*

"We didn't have your phone number. The director is on a trip. He's coming in three days, and meanwhile we are going to hold you in contempt."

"Why? I'm really growing tired of being arrested for no reason. What do you want from me now? You've just released me," I said, frustrated and angry, especially since the guy who knows my case was not in the country.

"Why are you so scared? I never knew you like that," the ████████████ said.

"Look, you arrested me after 9/11, and the U.S. interrogators came here and interrogated me. After that you, when you realized that I'm innocent, you released me. I sort of understand the mass arrest after 9/11, but this arrest right now is not OK."

"Everything is gonna be alright. Give me your cell phone," the Inspector lied, smiling his usual forced smile. ████████████ had about as much clue as I did about the goal of my arrest because the government wouldn't have shared anything with him. I don't think that the Mauritanian government had reached a resolution on my case; the main guy ████████████ ████████████ was on a trip, and without him a decision could hardly be made. What the ████████████ and I both knew back then was that the U.S. asked Mauritania's then–president

---

* This person could be the "Inspector" referred to several times elsewhere in this scene.

to hold me; the Mauritanian president asked his Directeur Général de la Sûreté Nationale—who is now the president—to arrest me; and he in his turn ordered his people, led by the Inspector, to hold me in contempt.*

However, I think that the U.S. wasn't making a secret of its wish, namely to have me in Jordan, and so at the point of my arrest ▮▮▮▮▮▮▮▮▮▮▮▮▮▮▮▮ two people knew the plan: the Mauritanian president and his DG. But since the U.S. was asking so much from its ally, the Mauritanian government needed some time to digest and confer. Turning me over to Jordan involved some serious things. The Mauritanian constitution would have to be broken. The Mauritanian President was hanging onto his office by a spider's thread, and any trouble would shake him heavily. The U.S. hadn't asked the Mauritanians to turn me over to them, which would make more sense; no, they wanted me in Jordan, and that was a big disrespect to the sovereignty of Mauritania. The Mauritanian government had been asking for evidence, any evidence, and the U.S. has failed to provide anything, and so arresting me in itself was burdensome for the government, let alone sending me to Jordan. The Mauritanian government sought incriminating evidences from the countries I had been in, Germany and Canada, and both countries provided only good conduct reports. For these and other reasons, the Mauritanian President needed his trusted guy, the DSE, before he took such a dangerous step.

I handed my cell phone to the Inspector, and he ordered the

---

* Mauritania's Directeur Général de la Sûreté Nationale in 2001 was Ely Ould Mohamed Vall. Vall, who served as director of the national police under President Maaouya Sid'Ahmed Ould Taya, seized power himself in a bloodless coup when Ould Taya was out of the country on August 3, 2005.

guards to take care of me and left. So I had to party with the guards instead of ███████████████ and the rest of my cousins.

In Mauritania, the guards of secret detainees are part of the Secret Police, and as much as they might sympathize with you, they would do anything they were ordered to, even if it involved taking your life. Such people are resented in the society because they are the arms of the dictatorship; without them the dictator is crippled. They must not be trusted. And yet I didn't feel any hatred toward them, just bad for them; they had the right to be as miserable as the majority of Mauritanians. Most of them knew me from previous arrests.

"I divorced my wife!" a young guard told me.

"Why, man? You have a daughter."

"I know but I don't have enough money to rent a place for my wife and me, and my wife got fed up with living in my mom's house. They just couldn't get along."

"But divorce? Come on!"

"What would you have done in my shoes?" I couldn't find any answer, because the simple Math was against me. They guy's salary was about 40 or 50 dollars a month, and in order to have a somewhat decent life he needed at least $1,000. All my guards had something in common: they all lived way below the poverty line, and without a supplementary job none of them could make it to the end of the month. In Mauritania, the gap between leading officers and enlisted agents is just too big.

"We have seen many people who have been here and ended up occupying very high level jobs in the government. We're sure you will, too," they always teased me. I'm sure they aspired to better jobs in the government, but I personally don't believe in working with a government that's not righteous; to me, the need for the miserable wages is not an excuse for the mischief they were doing under the color and authority of an unjust regime. In my eyes, they were as guilty as anybody else, no matter what excuses they may come up with.

Nonetheless, the Mauritanian guards, without exception, all expressed their solidarity with me and wished they didn't have to be the ones who had to do the job. They showed me all kinds of sympathy and respect, and they always tried to calm me down because I was worried about being turned over to the States and sent to a Military Tribunal. By then, the U.S. President was barking about putting terrorist suspects before military tribunals, and all kinds of other threats. I knew I would have no chance to be tried justly in a foreign military tribunal. We ate, prayed, and socialized together. We shared everything, food, tea, and we had a radio receiver to hear the news. We all slept in a big room with no furniture and an oodle of mosquitoes. Since it was Ramadan, we ate nights and stayed awake for the most part, and slept during the day. They were obviously directed to treat me that way; the ▮▮▮▮▮▮▮▮ sometimes joined us to check on things.

As scheduled, the DSE came back from his trip. "Hi," he greeted me.

"Hi."

"How are you doing?"

"Fine! Why are you arresting me?"

"Be patient! It's not a fire!" he said. Why did he speak about fire? I wondered. He didn't look happy at all, and I knew it wasn't me who was causing his unhappiness. I was completely depressed and terrorized, and so I fell sick. I lost my appetite and couldn't eat anything, and my blood pressure dropped gravely. The DSE called a doctor to check on me.

"You cannot fast. You have to eat," he said, prescribing some medicine. Since I couldn't stand up I had to urinate in a water bottle, and as to anything else, I didn't need to because I hadn't eaten anything. I really got very sick, and the Mauritanian government was completely worried that the Merchandise was going to vanish before the U.S. client took it. Sometimes I tried to sit up in order to eat a little bit, but as soon as I sat straight, I started to get dizzy and fell down. All that time I drank and ate what I could while lying on a thin mattress.

I spent seven days in Mauritanian custody. I didn't get any visits from my family; as I later learned, my family was not allowed to see me, and they were denied the knowledge of my whereabouts. On the eighth day, November 28, 2001, I was informed that I was going to be shipped to Jordan.

November 28th is Mauritanian Independence Day; it marks the event when the Islamic Republic of Mauritania supposedly received its independence from the French colonists in 1960. The irony is that on this very same day in 2001, the independent and sovereign Republic of Mauritania turned over one of its own citizens on a premise. To its everlasting shame, the Mauritanian government not only broke the constitution, which forbids the extradition of Mauritanian criminals to other countries, but also extradited an innocent citizen and exposed him to the random American Justice.

The night before the multilateral deal was closed between Mauritania, the U.S., and Jordan, the prison guards allowed me to watch the parade that was coming from downtown toward the Presidential Palace, the bands escorted by schoolboys carrying lighted candles. The sight awoke childhood memories of when I took part in the same parade myself, as a schoolboy, nineteen years before. Back then I looked with innocence at the event that marked the birth of the nation I happened to be part of; I didn't know that a country is not considered sovereign if it cannot handle its issues on its own.

* * *

The Secret Service is the most important government corps in the third world, and in some countries in the so-called free world as well, and so the DSE was invited to the ceremonial colors at the Presidential Palace in the morning. It was between 10 and 11 o'clock when he finally came in, accompanied by his assistant and his recorder. He invited me to his office, where he usually interrogates people. I was surprised to see him at all because it was a holiday. Although I was sick, my blood pressure rose so much from the unexpected visit that I was able to stand and go with them to the interrogation room. But as soon as I entered the office I collapsed on the big leather black sofa. It was obvious that my hyperactivity was fake.

The DSE sent all the guards home, and so I was left with him, his recorder, and his assistant. The guards gestured to me happily as they left the building, as if to say, "Congratulations!" They and I both thought that I was going to be released, though I was skeptical: I didn't like all the movements and telephone conversations that were going on around me.

The DSE sent his assistant away, and he came back with a couple of cheap things, clothes and a bag. Meanwhile the Recorder collapsed asleep in front of the door. The DSE pulled me into a room with nobody but us.

"We're going to send you to Jordan," he announced.

"Jordan! What are you talking about?"

"Their King was subject to a failed assassination attempt."

"So what? I have nothing to do with Jordan; my problem is with Americans. If you want to send me to any country, send me to the U.S."

"No, they want you to be sent to Jordan. They say you are the accomplice of ███████████████████████, though I know you have nothing to do with ████████████ or with September 11."

"So why don't you protect me from this injustice as a Mauritanian citizen?" I asked.

"America is a country that is based on and living with injustice," was his answer.

"OK, I would like to see the President!" I said.

"No, you can't. Everything is already irreversibly decided."

"Well, I want to say good-bye to my mom," I said.

"You can't. This operation is secret."

"For how long?"

"Two days, or maximum three. And if you choose, you don't need to talk to them," he added. "I really have no problem with that." I knew that he was speaking out of his rear end, because I was destined to Jordan for a reason.

"Can you assure me of when I'll be coming back?"

"I'll try. But I hope this trip to Jordan will add another positive testimony in your favor. The Senegalese, the Canadians, the Germans, and I myself believe that you're innocent. I don't know how many witnesses the Americans need to acquit you."

The DSE took me back to his office and tried several times to call his boss, the DG. When he finally reached him, the DG could not give a precise date for my return but assured him that it would be a couple of days. I don't know for sure, but I believe that the Americans outsmarted everybody. They just asked to get me to Jordan, and then there would be another negotiation.

"I don't know exactly," the DSE told me honestly when he got off the phone. "But look: today is Wednesday. Two days for interrogation, and one day for the trip. So you will be back here Saturday or Sunday."

He opened the bag that his assistant brought and asked me to try on the new cheap clothes. I put on the complete suit: a t-shirt, a pair of pants, jacket and plastic shoes. What a sight! Nothing fit; I looked like a skeleton dressed in a new suit. But who cared? At least I didn't.

Between the time when I got the decision and the time the U.S. turned me over to the Jordanian Special Forces, I was treated like a UPS package. I cannot describe my feelings: anger, fear, powerlessness, humiliation, injustice, betrayal.... I had never really contemplated escaping from jail, although I had been jailed unjustly four times already. But today I was thinking about it because I never, even in my dreams, considered I would be sent to a third country that is known throughout the world as a torture-practicing regime. But that was my only bullet, and if I used it and missed I would look very bad in the eyes of my government. Not that that mattered; they obviously would still comply with the U.S. even if I was an angel in their eyes. After all, I had turned myself in.

I looked around for ways to escape. Let's say I managed to get out of the building: I would need a taxicab as soon as I reached the main road. But I had no money on me to pay a cab, and I couldn't take one to a place where somebody knew me because those are the first places they're going to look. When I checked the doors, there was only one door that I would not have any reason to approach, so I asked to use the bathroom. In the bathroom I trimmed my beard and meditated about the other door. It was glass, so I could break it, but I knew the plan of the building; that door would lead to an armed guard who might shoot me dead right away. And even if I managed to sneak past the guard, I had to go around the Ministry for Internal Affairs that neighbors the main street, where there are always guards watching people coming and going. It would be impossible to go through the gate. Maybe, just maybe there's a possibility of jumping the wall, but was I strong enough to do that? No, I wasn't. But I was ready to pull all my strength together and make the impossible possible.

All these plans and thoughts were going through my head when I was using the bathroom. I looked at the roof, but there was no way to escape there; the roof was concrete. I finished cleaning and shaving and left. Outside of the bathroom there was a hall without roof; I thought I could maybe climb the wall and leave the compound by going from one roof to another. But there were two constraints: one, the wall was about 20 feet tall and there was nothing to grab onto in order to climb; and two, the whole compound could be encircled in a matter of minutes by the police, so that no matter where I landed I would be secure in police hands. I realized escape would remain an unrealized dream for somebody who suddenly found all doors before him closed except the door to heaven.

The DSE kept making calls to the incoming flight that carried the special mission team. "They should be here in about three hours. They're in Cyprus now!" he said. Normally he was not supposed to tell me where the plane was, or who was on the plane, or where I was going to be taken; the Americans wanted to maintain the terrorizing factors as harshly as possible. I should know nothing about what was happening to me. Being taken to an airport blindfolded, put in a plane, and taken to country that is an eleven hour flight away together make enough horrible factors that only people with nerves of steel would survive. But the DSE didn't care about telling me everything he knew. Not because he was worried about me, but because he knew for a fact that agreeing to such a horrible operation was at the same time agreeing to give up power. The turmoil against the Mauritanian President was already there, but the DSE knew this would certainly break the camel's back. I knew the same, and so I kept praying, "Oh, Lord please don't let people spill blood in my name!"

The DSE learned from the tower that the plane was expected around 7:00 or 7:30 p.m. The Recorder had been sleeping the whole time, so the DSE sent him home. It was around 6:00 p.m. when the DSE, his assistant, and I took off in the Director's luxurious Mercedes. He called the airport watch one more time to make the necessary arrangements to smuggle me securely without anybody noticing. I hoped his plan would fail and somebody would rat the government out.

The DSE headed in the opposite direction of the airport: he wanted to waste time and arrive at the airport about the same time as the Jordanian delegation. I was hoping that their plane would crash. Even though I knew it was replaceable, I wanted the plan to be postponed, like if you got news of your death and you wanted to postpone it. The DSE stopped at a grocery store and went in to buy some snacks for us to break the fast; sunset was going to catch us at the airport about the time of the unwelcome arrival. In front of the store stood a white U.N. truck. The driver had entered the store and left the engine running. I thought, with some luck I could possibly hijack it, and with some more luck I could get away, because the Benz would have little chance against the stronger body of the Toyota 4-wheel drive truck.

But I saw some drawbacks that discouraged me from the attempt. The hijacking would involve innocent parties: in the cab sat the family of the truck driver, and I was not ready to hurt innocent people. A hijacking would also involve neutralizing the Benz, which could cost the lives of two police officers. Although I wouldn't feel guilty about them getting themselves killed while trying to unjustly and illegally arrest me, I didn't want to kill anybody. And was I really physically able to execute the operation? I wasn't sure. Thinking of the operation was sort of daydreaming to distract myself from the horrible unknown that was awaiting me.

I should mention that in Mauritania the police don't have the Americans' extremely paranoid and vigilant technique of blind-folding, ear-muffing, and shackling people from head to toe; in that regard Mauritanians are very laid back. As a matter of fact, I don't think anybody is as vigilant as the Americans. I was even walking free when we arrived at the Airport, and I could have easily have run away and reached the public terminal before anybody could catch me. I could at least have forcibly passed the message to the public, and hence to my family, that I was kidnapped. But I didn't do it, and I have no explanation for why not. Maybe, had I known what I know today, I would have attempted anything that would have defeated the injustice. I would not even have turned myself in to begin with.

After the grocery stop, we took off straight to the airport. There was hardly any traffic due to the holiday; people had retreated peacefully, as usual on this day, to their homes. It had been eight days since I last saw the outside world. It looked bleak: there must have been a dust storm during the day that was just starting to give way in favor of the ocean breeze. It was a situation I had seen a thousand and one times, and I still liked it. It's like whenever the dust storm kills the city, the ocean breeze comes at the end of the day and blows the life back into it, and slowly but surely people start to come out.

The twilight was as amazing and beautiful as it had always been. I pictured my family already having prepared the Iftar fast-breaking food, my mom mumbling her prayers while duly working the modest delicacies, everybody looking for the sun to take its last steps and hide beneath the horizon. As soon as the Muezzin declares, "God is Great" everyone would hungrily grab something to drink. My brothers prefer a quick smoke and a cup of tea before anything; my sisters would drink first. None of my sisters smoke, smoking for a lady in my culture is not appropriate. The only absent person is me, but everybody's heart is with me, everybody's prayers are for me. My family thought it would be only a matter of several days before the government released me; after all, the Mauritanian authorities told my family that I have done nothing, they were just waiting until the Americans would see the truth and let me be. How wrong was my family! How wrong was I to put my faith in a bunch of criminals and put my fate in their country! I didn't seem to have learned anything. But regret didn't seem to help either: the ship had sailed.

The Mercedes was heading soundlessly to the airport, and I was drowned in my daydreams. At the secret gate, the Airport police chief was waiting on us as planned. I hated that dark gate! How many innocent souls have been led through that secret gate? I had been through it once, when the U.S. government brought me from Dakar and delivered me to my government twenty months earlier. Arriving at the gate put an end to my dreams about a savior or a miraculous sort of a superman who would stop the car, neutralize the police officers, and carry me home on his wings so I could catch my Iftar in the warmth of my mom's hut. There was no stopping God's plan, and I was complying and subduing completely to his will.

The Airport Police Chief looked rather like a camel herder. He was wearing a worn-out Boubou, the national dress, and an unbuttoned T-shirt.

"I told you I didn't want anybody to be around," said the DSE.

"Everything's alright," the chief said reluctantly. He was lazy, careless, naïve, and too traditional. I don't even think he had a clue about what was going on. He seemed to be a religious, traditional guy, but religion didn't seem to have any influence of his life, considering the wrong conspiracy he was carrying out with the government.

The Muezzin started to sing the amazing Azan declaring the end of the day, and hence the fast. "ALLAH is Great, Allah is great." "I testify there is no God but God," once, twice, and then twice, "I testify Mohamed is the messenger of God." "Come to pray, Come to pray, Come to flourish, Come to flourish," and then, twice, "God is Great" and "There is no God but God." What an amazing message! But guess what, dear Muezzin, I cannot comply with your call, nor can I break my fast. I wondered, Does this Muezzin know what injustice is taking place in this country?

There was no clean place around. All the miserable budget the government had approved for the restoration of the airport had literally been devoured by the agents the government put its trust in. Without saying anything, I went to the least dirty spot and started to perform my prayer. The DSE, his assistant, and the chief joined in. After I was done praying, the DSE offered me water and some sweet buns to break my fast; at that same moment the small business jet hit the runway. I had no appetite anyway, but the arriving plane sealed any need to eat. I knew I was not going to survive without eating, though, so I reached for the water and drank a little bit. I took a piece of the sweet bread and forced it inside my mouth, but the piece apparently landed in a cul-de-sac; my throat conspired against me and closed. I was losing my mind from terror, though I tried to act normally and regain my composure. I was shaking, and kept mumbling my prayers.

*   *   *

The ground crew directed the small airplane toward the Benz. It came to a stop inches away, the door opened, and a man ██ ██ ████ stepped down the accommodation ladder with steady steps. He was rather ████████████████████████████████ ███████████. He had one of those ████████████████████████ that keeps drowning in anything they drink. Oh Lord, I wouldn't share a drink with one of those people, not even for a million dollars. As soon as I saw the guy, I gave him the name ████████.*

When he hit the ground he scanned us standing before him with his fox's eyes. He had a ████████████████████████, and the habit of tweaking his ████████████████, and he kept moving his eyes, one wide-opened and the other squinted. I could easily see the shock on his face because he didn't seem to find the person he was looking for, namely me. But you could tell it was not the first time he led an abduction operation: he completely maintained his composure, as if nothing big was happening.

"We've brought people here in bags," his associate ████████ ████████████ told me later in Jordan.

"But how did they survive the trip without suffocating?"

"We make an opening for the nose to facilitate a continuous oxygen supply," ████████████████ said. I don't know about the bags story, but I do know cases of kidnapping terrorist suspects to Jordan.

████████████ was expecting his prey to be shackled, blindfolded,

---

* MOS's nickname for the leader of the Jordanian rendition team, who greets him here, seems to be "Satan," which appears unredacted twice later in the scene. Context suggests the thing "that keeps drowning" might be a mustache.

earmuffed. But me, standing before him in civilian clothes with eyes wide open like any human being, that struck him. No, that is not the way a terrorist looks — especially a high-level terrorist who was supposedly the brain behind the Millennium plot.

"Hi," he said; he obviously wasn't used to the beautiful Muslim greeting, "Peace be with you!" He quickly exchanged words with the DSE, though they didn't understand each other very well. The DSE wasn't used to the Jordanian dialect, nor was the Jordanian guest used to the Mauritanian way of speaking. I had an advantage over both of them: there is hardly any Arabic dialect I don't understand because I used to have many friends from different cultural backgrounds.

"He said he needs fuel," I explained to the DSE. I was eager to let my predator know *I am, I am.* I took my bag and showed my readiness to board, and that's when ████████ realized that I was the meager "terrorist" he was sent to pick up.

The DSE handed him my passport and a thin folder. At the top of the accommodation ladder there were two young men dressed in Ninja-like black suits who turned out to be the guards who were going to watch me during the longest eleven-hour trip of my life. I quickly spoke to the DSE in a manner I knew the ████████ wouldn't understand.

"Tell him not to torture me."

"This is a good guy; I would like you to treat him appropriately!" the DSE said vaguely.

"We're going to take good care of him," answered the ████████ in an ambiguous statement.

The DSE gave me some food to eat during the flight. "No need, we have enough food with us," the ████████ said. I was happy, because I liked the Middle Eastern cuisine.

I took the seat that was reserved for me, and the leader of the operation ordered a thorough search while the plane was rolling on the runway. All they found was my pocket Koran, which they gave back to me. I was blindfolded and earmuffed, but the blindfold was taken away to allow me to eat when the plane reached its regular altitude. As much as I knew about the basics of telecommunication tools, I was terrorized when they put on the earphone-like earmuffs: I thought it was a new U.S. method to suck intels out of your brain and send them directly to a main computer which analyzes the information. I wasn't worried about what they would suck out of my brain, but I was worried about the pain I may suffer due to electrical shocks. It was silly, but if you get scared you are not you anymore. You very much become a child again.

The plane was very small, and very noisy. It could only fly for three to three-and-a-half hours, and then it had to take fuel. "They are in Cyprus," the DSE told me several hours before their arrival in Nouakchott; I figured the return would be by the same route, because such crimes have to be perfectly coordinated with the conspiring parties.

███████████ offered me a meal. It looked good, but my throat was stiff and I felt like I was trying to swallow rough stones. "Is that all?" ████████ wondered.

"I am alright, ████████," I said. ████████ literally means somebody who has performed the pilgrimage to Mecca, but in the Middle East you respectfully refer to anybody you don't know as ████████.* In Jordan they call every detainee ████████ in order to keep the names secret.

"Eat, eat, enjoy your food!" ████████ said, trying to give me some comfort to eat and stay alive.

"Thanks, ████████, I've eaten enough."

---

* It appears from the context that MOS is referring to the honorific "Hajji."

"Are you sure?"

"Yes, ▬▬▬," I replied. ▬▬▬ looked at me, forcing the most dishonest, sardonic smile I ever saw, exactly like he did when he stepped down out of the plane back in Nouakchott airport.

The guards collected the garbage and placed the tray table in the upright position. I had two of them watching me, one right behind my neck, and the second sitting next to me. The guy behind me was staring at me the whole time; I doubt he ever blinked his eyes. He must have been through some rough training.

"In my training, I almost lost my composure," one young recruit later told me in the Jordanian prison. "During the training, we took a terrorist and slew him in front of all the students. Some couldn't take it and burst out crying," he continued.

"Where did you guys train?" I asked him.

"An Arabic country, I cannot tell you which one." I felt nauseous, but tried my best to act in front of the guy as if everything were normal and he were a hero. "They want us to have no mercy with terrorists. I can kill a terrorist who is running away without wasting more than one bullet," he demonstratively claimed.

"Oh, that's great! But how do you know he is a terrorist? He might be innocent," I gauged.

"I don't care: if my boss said he is a terrorist, he is. I am not allowed to follow my personal judgment. My job is to execute." I felt so bad for my people and the level of cruelty and gruesomeness they have fallen into. Now I was standing for real before somebody who is trained to kill blindly whomever he is ordered to. I knew he wasn't lying, because I met a former Algerian soldier once who was seeking asylum in Germany, and he told me how gruesomely they dealt with the Islamists, too.

"During an ambush, we captured a sixteen-year-old teenager, and on the way to the jail our boss stopped, took him off the truck, and shot him dead. He didn't want him in jail, he wanted revenge," he told me.

I wondered why there was so much vigilance, given that I was shackled and there were two guards, two interrogators, and two pilots. Satan asked the guard who was sitting beside me to empty his seat, and ███████ sat beside me and started to interrogate me.*

"What's your name?"

"Mohamedou Ould Salahi."

"What's your nickname?"

"Abu Musab."

"What other nicknames do you have?"

"None!"

"Are you sure?"

"Yes, ███████!" I wasn't used to an interrogator from the Sham region, and I had never heard that accent in such a scary way. I find the Sham accent one of the sweetest in the Arabic language, but ███████ accent was not sweet. He was just evil: the way he moved, spoke, looked, ate, everything. During our short conversation we were almost shouting, but we could hardly hear one another because of the extremely loud whining of the engines. I hate small planes. I always feel as if I'm on the wing of a demon when I travel in them.

"We should stop the interrogation and resume it later on," he said. Thank you, old engines! I just wanted him out of my face. I knew there was no way around him, but just for the time being.

███████████████ around midnight GMT we landed in

---

* "Satan" appears here unredacted in the manuscript.

Cyprus. Was it a commercial airport or the military airport? I don't know. But Cyprus is one of the Mediterranean paradises on Earth.

The interrogators and the two pilots put their jackets on and left the plane, most likely for a break. It looked like it had been raining; the ground looked wet, and a light drizzle was caressing the ground. Every once in a while I stole a quick glimpse through the small, blurry window. The breeze outside gave away the presence of a cold winter on the island. I felt some noises that shook the small plane; it must have been the fuel cistern moving. I drowned in my daydreams.

I was thinking, Now the local police will suspect the plane, and hopefully search it. I am lucky because I'm breaking the law by transiting through a country without a transit visa, and I'll be arrested and put in jail. In the prison, I'll apply for asylum and stay in this paradise. The Jordanians can't say anything because they are guilty of trying to smuggle me. The longer the plane waits, the better my chances are to be arrested.

How wrong I was! How comforting a daydream can be! It was my only solace to help me ignore and forget the evilness that surrounded me. The plane indeed waited long enough, about an hour, but there was no searching the plane. I was non-existent in the passengers' list that the Jordanians gave to the local authorities. I even thought I saw police in thick black uniforms coming near the plane, but I was not to be spotted because I was sandwiched between two seats and had to keep my head down, so I looked like a small bag. I might be wrong though, and just saw them because I wanted the police to come and arrest me.

███████, his associate, and the two pilots came back and we took off. The pilots switched places. I saw the fat pilot sitting in front of ██████████; he was almost as broad as he was tall. ██████████ started a conversation with him. Although I couldn't hear the talk, I assumed it to be a friendly discussion between two mature men, which was good. ██████████ grew tired like everybody else, except for the young guard who kept his never-blinking eyes pointed on me. Every once in a while he made a comment like, "Keep your head down!" and "Look down," but I kept forgetting the rules. I had the feeling that this would be my last flight, because I was certain I wouldn't make it through the torture. I thought about every member of my family, even my far nephews and nieces and my in-laws. How short is this life! In a blink of an eye, everything is gone.

I kept reading my Koran in the dim light. My heart was pounding as if it wanted to jump out of my mouth. I barely understood anything of what I was reading; I read at least 200 or 300 pages unconsciously. I was prepared to die, but I never imagined it would be this way. Lord have mercy on me! I think hardly anybody will meet death the way he or she imagined. We human beings take everything into consideration except for death; hardly anybody has death on his calendar. Did God really predestinate for me to die in Jordan at the hands of some of the most evil people in the world? But I didn't really mind being killed by bad people; before God they will have no case, I was thinking.

██████████████████████ around 4 a.m. GMT. A fake peace dominated the trip between Cyprus and my unknown present destination. The bandits seemed to be exhausted from the previous day trip from Amman to Nouakchott, and that was a blessing for me. The plane started to lose altitude again, and finally landed in a place I didn't know. I think it was an Arabic country somewhere in the Middle East, because I think I spotted signs in Arabic through the small windows when I stole a quick glimpse off my guarding demon. It was still nighttime, and the weather seemed to be clear and dry; I didn't see any signs of winter.*

This time I did not hope for the police to search the airplane, because Arabic countries are always conspiring with each other against their own citizens. What treason! Nonetheless, any leak of information wouldn't hurt. But I didn't give that daydream a second thought. We didn't stay long, though we went through the same procedure, ███████ and his two pilots going for a short break, and the same noises of taking on fuel that I heard in Cyprus. The plane took off to its final destination, Amman, Jordan. I don't think that we made any more stops, though I kept passing out and coming to until we arrived in Jordan.

Over ninety percent of Jordanians are Muslim. For them, as for all Muslims from the Middle East, fasting during Ramadan is the most important religious service. People who don't fast are resented in the society, and so many people fast due to social pressure even though they don't believe in religion. In Mauritania, people are much more relaxed about fasting, and less relaxed about prayer.

"Take your breakfast," said the guard. I think I had fallen asleep for a moment.

"No, thanks."

"It's your last chance to eat before the fast begins."

"No, I'm OK."

"Are you sure?"

"Yes, ████." They started to eat their breakfast, chewing like cows; I could even hear them through my earmuffs. I kept

---

* MOS indicated that the flight left Amman on the evening of November 28, so it would now be early in the morning of November 29, 2001.

stealing glimpses toward the small windows until I saw the first daylight prying the darkness open.

"████, I'd like to perform my prayer," I said to the guard. The guard had a little conversation with ██████████, who ordered him to take off one of my earmuffs.

"There is no opportunity to pray here. When we arrive, you and I are going to pray together," said ██████████. I was sort of comforted, because if he prays that was a sign that he was a believer, and so he wouldn't possibly hurt his "brother" in belief. And yet he didn't seem to have knowledge about his religion. Prayer must be performed on time in the best manner you can, at least in your heart. You cannot postpone it except for the reasons explained in the Islamic scriptures. In any case, the promised prayer with Satan never took place.*

---

* Again, "Satan" appears here in the manuscript unredacted.

FOUR

Jordan

November 29, 2001–July 19, 2002

The Hospitality of My Arab Brothers... Cat and Mouse: ICRC vs. Jordanian Intel... The Good News: I Supposedly Attempted to Kill the Mauritanian President... Bodybuilding Center: What I Know Kills Me... Unjust Justice

▬▬▬▬▬▬▬▬▬▬▬, around 7:00 a.m. local time.*

The small plane clumsily started to fight its way through the cloudy and cold sky of Amman. We finally hit the ground and came to a standstill. Everybody was eager to get the hell out of the plane, including me.

"Stand up," said one the guards, taking off the metal handcuffs that had already built a ring around my wrists. I was relieved, and sat silently talking to myself. "Look, they're friendly. They just wanted to make sure that you didn't do anything stupid in the plane; now that we arrived, there is no need for cuffs or earmuffs." How wrong I was! They just took the handcuffs off in order to handcuff me again behind my back and put on bigger earmuffs and a bag over my head, covering my neck. My

---

* It is still the morning of November 29, 2001 (see footnote on p. 148).

heart started to pound heavily, which raised my blood pressure and helped me to stand steadier on my feet. I started to mumble my prayers. This was the first time that I got treated this way. My pants started to slip down my legs because I was so skinny and had been virtually without food for at least a week.

Two new, energetic guards dragged me out of the plane. I twisted my feet when I reached the ladder; I couldn't see anything, nor did the stupid guards tell me anything. I fell face down, but the guards caught me before I hit the ladder.

"Watch out!" said ███████████████████, my future interrogator, to the guards. I memorized his voice, and when he later started to interrogate me, I recognized it from that day. I now knew that I had to step down the ladder until my feet hit the ground, and an ice-cold winter breeze hit my whole body. My clothes were not designed for this weather. I was wearing the worthless, made-in-a-cheap-country clothes I got from the Mauritanian authorities.

One of the guards silently helped my feet get into the truck that was parked inches away from the last step of the ladder. The guards squeezed me between them in the back seat, and off took the truck. I felt comforted; it was warm inside the truck, and the motor was quiet. The chauffeur mistakenly turned the radio on. The female DJ voice struck me with her Sham accent and her sleepy voice. The city was awakening from a long, cold night, slowly but surely. The driver kept accelerating and hitting the brakes suddenly. What a bad driver! They must have hired him just because he was stupid. I was moving back and forth like a car crash dummy.

I heard a lot of horns. It was the peak time for people who were going to work. I pictured myself at this very same time back home, getting ready for work, enjoying the new day, the morning ocean breeze through my open window, dropping my nephews off at their respective schools. Whenever you think life is going in your favor, it betrays you.

After about 40 or 45 minutes of painful driving, we took a turn, entered a gate, and stopped. The guards dragged me out of the truck. The cold breeze shook my whole body, though only for a very short time before we entered the building and I was left near a heater. I knew how the heater looked even with my eyes closed; I just sensed it was like the ones I had in Germany. Later on, I learned from the guards that the prison facility was built by a Swedish company.

"Do not move," said one of the guards before they both emptied out of the place. I stood still, though my feet could hardly carry me and my back hurt so bad. I was left there for about 15 or 20 minutes before ████████████████ grabbed me by the back of my collar, almost choking me to death. ██████████████████ pushed me roughly up the stairs. I must have been on the ground floor, and he pushed me to the first.

Legend has it that Arabs are among the most hospitable folks on the face of the earth; both friends and enemies are unanimous about that. But what I would be experiencing here was another kind of hospitality. ██████████████████ pushed me inside a relatively small room with a desk, a couple of chairs, and another guy sitting behind the desk and facing me. I baptized ████████████████ as soon as I saw him. He was a ████ ██████████████████████████████████████. Like the rest of the guards, he was dressed in ████████████ ██████████ had a high-and-tight haircut.* You could see that he had been doing this work for some time: there were no

---

* At his 2005 ARB hearing, MOS indicated that throughout his time in the Jordanian prison, everyone on the prison staff wore military uniforms. ARB transcript, 22.

signs of humanity in his face. He hated himself more than anybody could hate him.

The first thing I saw were two pictures on the wall, the present King Abdullah and his extinguished father Hussein. Such pictures are the proof of dictatorship in the uncivilized world. In Germany I never saw anybody hang the picture of the president; the only time I saw his picture was when I was watching news, or driving around during elections, when they hang a bunch of candidates' pictures. Maybe I'm wrong, but I mistrust anybody who hangs the picture of his president, or any president who wins any elections with more than 80%. It's just ridiculous. On the other wall I read the time on a big hanging clock. It was around 7:30 a.m.

"Take your clothes off!" said ███████████████████. I complied with his order except for my underwear. I was not going to take them off without a fight, no matter how weak it would be. But ████████████████ just handed me a clean, light blue uniform. Jordanians are materially much more advanced and organized than Mauritanians; everything in the prison was modest, but clean and neat. It was the first time I put on a prison uniform in my life. In Mauritania there is no specific uniform, not because Mauritania is a democratic country, but maybe because the authorities are too lazy and corrupt. A uniform is a sign of backwards and communist countries. The only so-called "democratic" country that has this technique of wrapping up detainees in uniforms is the U.S.; the Jordanians have adopted a 100% American system in organizing their prisons.

The young guy behind the table was rather fat. He was acting as a clerk, but he was a horrible one.

"What's your name? What's your address in Amman?"

"I am not from Amman."

"Where the hell are you from?"

"I am from Mauritania," I answered.

"No, I mean where do you live here in Jordan?"

"Nowhere!"

"Did they capture you while transiting through the airport?"

"No, Hajji took me from my country to question me for two days and bring me back."* I wanted to make it sound as harmless as possible. Besides, that's what I was told, even though I had the feeling now that I was being lied to and betrayed.

"How do you spell your name?" I spelled out my complete name, but the guy didn't seem to have gone to primary school. He wrote as if with Chinese chopsticks. He kept filling out one form after another and throwing the old ones in the garbage can.

"What have you done?"

"I've done nothing!"

Both burst out in laughter. "Oh, very convenient! You have done nothing but you are here!" I thought, What crime should I say in order to satisfy them?

I presented myself as a person who came all the way from Mauritania to provide intels about my friends. "▬▬▬▬▬ told me he needed my help," I said. But then I thought, What a silly answer. If I were going to provide information freely, I could do so in Mauritania. The guards didn't believe me anyway; what criminal benevolently admits to his crime? I felt humiliated because my story sounded weird and untruthful.

In the bureaucratic chaos, the prison's commanding officer took the process in hand. He took my wallet and copied my personal data from my ID. He was a serious looking officer in his late thirties, light blond, Caucasian looking, with a dry face. It was obvious he was married to the cause. During my sojourn in the Dar Al Tawqif wa Tahqiq House† for Arrest and

---

* "Hajji" appears here unredacted.

† The Arabic phrase itself appears to be a transliteration of the phrase "house of arrest and detention." In its 2008 report "Double Jeopardy: CIA

Interrogation, I kept seeing him working day and night and sleeping in the prison. Most of the guards do. They work ▇▇

▇▇▇▇▇▇▇▇▇▇▇▇▇▇▇▇▇▇▇▇▇▇▇▇▇▇▇▇▇▇▇▇▇▇▇▇▇▇

▇▇ rarely left the facility. I would catch him sneakily trying to look through the bin hole without me noticing him.*
▇▇▇▇▇▇▇▇▇▇▇▇▇▇▇▇▇▇▇▇▇▇▇ was an ▇▇▇▇▇▇ in what they call the al Jaish Al Arabi, the Arab Legion. I was thinking, What a masquerade! If this is the protector of us Arabs, we screwed up! As an Arabic saying has it, "Her protector is her assailant."

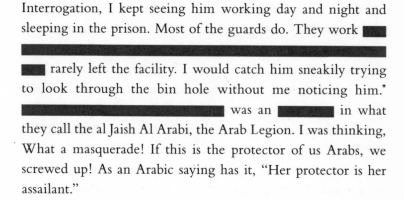

Renditions to Jordan," Human Rights Watch recorded that "from 2001 until at least 2004, Jordan's General Intelligence Department (GID) served as a proxy jailer for the U.S. Central Intelligence Agency (CIA), holding prisoners that the CIA apparently wanted kept out of circulation, and later handing some of them back to the CIA." Human Rights Watch reported that MOS and at least thirteen others were sent to Jordan during this period, where they were "held at the GID's main headquarters in Amman, located in the Jandawil district in Wadi Sir. The headquarters, which appear to cover nearly an acre of land, contain a large four-story detention facility that Human Rights Watch visited in August 2007."

Researchers who carried out that visit recorded that "the administrative offices and interrogation rooms are on the second floor of the building, while visiting rooms are on the ground floor. During the period that Human Rights Watch inspected the facility, all of the detainees in custody were held on the second floor. There are also many cells on the ground floor and third floor, however, as well as a small number of cells on the fourth floor, which includes a few collective cells and what the director called the "women's section" of the facility. In addition, the facility has a basement where many prisoners have claimed that they were brought for the most violent treatment. Prisoners in GID detention at Wadi Sir are kept in single-person cells and are prohibited from speaking with one another, but some have managed to communicate via the back window of their cells. (Each cell faces onto the central courtyard, and has a window looking out on the yard.)." Double Jeopardy, 1, 10–11. The Human Rights Watch report is available at http://www.hrw.org/sites/default/files/reports /jordan0408webwcover.pdf.

* This behavior may be the basis for the nickname "I'm-Watching-You," which appears unredacted later in this chapter.

"Why do they call you guys the Arab Legion?" I asked one of the guards later.

"Because we are supposed to protect the entire Arab world," he responded.

"Oh, that's really great," I said, thinking that we'd be just fine if they protected us from themselves.

After they had finished processing me, ███████████ ███████ handcuffed me behind my back, blindfolded me, and grabbed me as usual by the back of my collar. We got in the lift and I felt it going up. We must have landed on the third floor. ████████████████████████ led me through a corridor and took a couple turns before a heavy metal door opened. ████████████████████████ uncuffed me and took off the blindfold.

I looked as far as my eyes could reach. It was not far: about 8 or 9 feet to a window that was small and high so detainees could not look outside. I climbed up once, but I saw nothing but the round wall of the prison. The prison was in the shape of a circle. The idea was smart, because if you succeeded in jumping out of the window, you would land in a big arena with a 30 or 40 foot concrete wall. The room looked bleak and stark, though clean. There was a wooden bed and an old blanket, a small sheet, and that was about it. The door closed loudly behind ████████████████████████ and I was left on my own, tired and scared. What an amazing world! I enjoyed visiting other countries, but not this way.

I performed my ritual wash and tried to pray standing, but there was no way so I opted to pray sitting down. I crawled over to the bed and soon trailed off. Sleep was a torture: as soon as I closed my eyes, the friends I was potentially going to be asked about kept coming to me and talking to me. They scared the hell out of me; I woke up numerous times mumbling their names. I was in a no-win situation: if I stayed awake, I was so dead tired, and if slept I got terrorized by nightmares to the point that I screamed out loud.

Around 4:30 p.m., the guard on watch woke me up for food. Meals were served from a chariot that goes through the corridor from cell to cell, with the cook passing by again later to collect the empty plates. Detainees were allowed to keep one cup for tea and juice. When the cook showed up for my plate, he saw that I hardly ate anything.

"Is that all?" As much as I liked the food, my throat conspired against me. The depression and fear were just too much.

"Yes, thanks."

"Well, if you say so!" The cook quickly collected my plate and off he rolled. In jail it's not like at home; in jail if you don't eat, it's OK. But at home your parents and your wife do their best to persuade you. "Honey, just eat a little bit more. Or should I prepare you something else? Please, just do it for my sake. Why don't you tell me what you'd like to eat?" In both cases, though, you more than likely won't eat more—in jail because they scare the hell out of you, and at home because you're spoiled. It's the same way when you feel sick. I remember a very funny case when I was really hurting; it was either a headache or stomach ache.

"I'm in so much pain! Can you please give me some medication?"

"Fuck you, crybaby," the guard said. I burst into laughter because I remembered how my family would be overreacting if they knew I was sick.

After giving my trash back I went back to sleep. As soon as I closed my eyes I saw my family in a dream, rescuing me from the Jordanians. In the dream I kept telling my family that it was just a dream, but they would tell me, "No, it's for real, you're home." How devastating, when I woke up and found myself in the dimly lit cell! This dream terrorized me for days. "I told you it's a dream, please hold me and don't let me go," I would say. But there was no holding me. My reality was that I was secretly detained in a Jordanian jail and my family could not even possibly know where I was. Thank God after a while that dream disappeared, though every once in a while I would still wake up crying intensely after hugging my beloved youngest sister.

The first night is the worst; if you make it through that you're more than likely going to make it through the rest. It was Ramadan, and so we got two meals served, one at sunset and the second before the first light. The cook woke me up and served me my early meal. Suhoor is what we call this meal; it marks the beginning of our fasting, which lasts until sunset. At home, it's more than just a meal. The atmosphere matters. My older sister wakes everybody and we sit together eating and sipping the warm tea and enjoying each other's company. "I promise I will never complain about your food, Mom," I was thinking to myself.

I still hadn't adjusted to Jordanian time. I wasn't allowed to know the time or date, but later when I made friends among the guards they used to tell me what time it was. This morning I had to guess. It was around 4:30 a.m., which meant around 1:30 a.m. back home. I wondered what my family was doing. Do they know where I am?* Will God show them my place? Will I ever see them again? Only Allah knows! The chances looked very low. I didn't eat a lot, and in fact the meal was not

---

* In fact, it would be almost a year before MOS's family learned where he was—and only because a brother in Germany saw an article in *Der Spiegel* in October 2002 that reported that MOS was in Guantánamo. See "From Germany to Guantanamo: The Career of Prisoner No. 760," *Der Spiegel*, October 29, 2008.

that big; a pita bread, buttermilk, and small pieces of cucumber. But I ate more than I did the night before. I kept reading the Koran in the dim light; I wasn't able to recite because my brain was not working properly. When I thought it must be dawn I prayed, and as soon as I finished the Muezzin started to sing the Azan, his heavenly, fainting, sleepy, hoarse voice awakening in me all kind of emotions. How could all those praying believers possibly accept that one of their own is buried in the Darkness of the ███████████████████████████ House of Arrest and Interrogation?*

There are actually two Azans, one to wake people to eat the last meal, and the other to stop eating and go to pray. It sounds the same; the only difference is that in the last one the Muezzin says, "Prayer is better than sleeping." I redid my prayers once more and went to bed to choose between being terrorized while awake or asleep. I kept switching between both, as if I were drunk.

That second day passed without big events. My appetite didn't change. One of the guards gave me a book to read. I didn't like it because it was about philosophical differences between all kinds of religions. I really needed a book that would give me comfort. I wished we had a little more peace in the world. I was between sleeping and waking at around 11 p.m. that evening when the guards shouted ████████████ and opened the door of my cell.

"Hurry up!" I froze and my feet numbed, but my heart pumped so hard that I jumped off my bed and complied with the order of the guard. The escort guards handcuffed me behind my back and pushed me toward the unknown. Since I was blindfolded I could think about my destination undisturbed, though the pace of the escorting guard was faster than my

---

* See footnote on p. 154.

anticipation. I felt the warmth of the room I entered. When you're afraid you need warmth.

The guard took off both the handcuffs and the blindfold. I saw a big blue machine like the ones in airports for scanning luggage, and some other object to measure height and weight. How relieved I was! They were just going about taking the traditional prisoner data like fingerprints, height, and weight. Although I knew there was no getting around the interrogation session, I both wanted to get through it as soon as possible and was so afraid of that session. I don't know how to explain it, it might not make sense, I'm just trying to explain my feelings then the best way I can.

Another day passed. The routine was no different than the days before, though I gathered one vital piece of information: the number of my cell was ████████████████████████. After the Iftar fast-breaking meal, the guards would start calling a number, a door would open loudly, and you could hear the footsteps of the taken-away detainees. I figured they were being taken away for interrogation. I imagined I heard the guards shouting my cell number about a hundred times, and after each I went to the toilet and performed a ritual wash. I was just so paranoid. Finally, around 10 p.m. on Saturday, a guard shouted ███████████████████ for real.* I quickly went to the bathroom. Not that I needed to, I really hadn't drunk anything and I had already urinated about half a gallon, but the urge was there. What was I going to urinate, blood?

"Hurry up, we don't have time," said the guard who stood at the opened heavy metal door. Later on, I learned ████████ ██ ██

---

* MOS arrived in Jordan on Thursday, November 29, so it would now be the evening of Saturday, December 1, 2001.

████████████ The sergeant handcuffed and blindfolded me, and pushed me off. We took the lift and went one floor down, took a couple of turns, and entered a new area; a door opened and I went down a step. The odor of cigarette smoke hit me. It was the interrogation area, where they smoke relentlessly, like an old train. It's disgusting when the smoke keeps adding up and dominates the odor of a house.

The area was remarkably quiet. The escorting guard dropped me against a wall and retreated.

"What people did you send to Chechnya?" ████████████ ████████████ shouted at a detainee in English.

"I ain't sent nobody," responded the detainee in broken Arabic, with an obvious Turkish accent. I right away knew the setup: This interrogation was meant for me.

"Liar," shouted ████████████.

"I ain't lying," the guy responded in Arabic, although ████████████ kept speaking his loose English.

"I don't care if you have a German or American passport, you're going to tell me the truth," said ████████████ ████. The setup fit perfectly, and was meant to terrorize me even more. And even though I knew right away it was a setup, it worked.

"Hi, ████████████," said ████████████.

"Hi," I responded, feeling his breath right in front of my face. I was so terrorized that I hadn't realized what he was saying.

"So your name *is* ████████████," he concluded.

"No!"

"But you responded when I called you ████████████," he argued. I found it idiotic to tell him that I was so terrorized that I didn't realize what name he called me.

"If you look at it, we all are ████████████," I correctly

answered. ███████████ means "God's servant" in Arabic.* But I actually knew how ████████████████ came up with that name. When I arrived in Montreal, Canada on November 26, 1999, my friend ██████████ introduced me to his room-mate ████████████ by my given name. Later on I met another ████████████████████ who I'd happened to see when I visited the year before. He called me ██████████ and I responded because I found it impolite to correct him. Since then ████████████████ called me ██████████, and I found it cool. I wasn't trying to deceive ████████████; after all, ████████████ had keys to our common mailbox and always collected my official mail, which obviously bore my given name.

That was the story of the name. Obviously the Americans tasked the Jordanians with investigating why I took the name ██████████ in Canada, but the Jordanians understand the recipe far more than Americans, and so they completely ignored this part of the interrogation.

"Do you know where you are?" asked ████████████████.

"In Jordan," I responded. He was obviously shocked. I shouldn't have been informed about my destination, but the Mauritanian interrogator must have been so angry that he didn't exactly follow the orders of the Americans. The initial plan was to send me from Mauritania to Jordan blindfolded and not inform me about my destination, in order to plant as much fear and terror in my heart as possible to break me. But as soon as I answered the question, ██████████████████ knew that this part of the plan was broken, and so he took off my blindfold right away and led me inside the interrogation room.

It was a small room, about 10 x 8 feet, with an old table and

---

* It appears that the interrogator addressed MOS as "Abdullah," which means "servant of God."

three weathered chairs. ████████████████████ was in his
██
████. His assistant ██████████████████████ was a ██████████
██. He was obviously
the type who is ready to do the dirty side of any job. He also
looked ████████████████████. I scanned both back and forth and
wondered about these guys.* The whole problem of terrorism
was caused by the aggression of Israel against Palestinian civilians, and the fact that the U.S. is backing the Israeli government
in its mischiefs. When the Israelis took over Palestine under the
fire of the British Artillery, the invasion resulted in a mass migra-
tion of the locals. Many of them ended up in neighboring countries, and Jordan received the lion's share; more than fifty percent
of Jordanians are of Palestinian origin. To me, these interrogators just didn't fit in the vests they were wearing: it didn't make
sense that Palestinians would work for Americans to defeat the
people who are supposedly helping them. I knew that these two
interrogators standing before me didn't represent any moral values, and didn't care about human being's lives. I found myself
between two supposedly fighting parties, both of which considered me an enemy; the historical enemies were allied to roast
me. It was really absurd and funny at the same time.

████████████████████████ played a vital role in the Americans' War against Terrorism. He was charged with interrogating
the kidnapped individuals the U.S. delivered to Jordan and
assigning them to the different members of his team. He also
personally came to GTMO to interrogate individuals on behalf
of the U.S.†

---

* Context suggests that both the interrogator and his assistant appear to
have Palestinian backgrounds.

† MOS's 2005 ARB testimony indicates that he had three interrogators
during his secret detention in Amman; he profiles the three interrogators

██████████████████████ opened a medium-sized binder; it turned out to be a file on me that the U.S. had turned over to the Jordanians. He started to ask me questions that were not related to each other. It was the first time I ever experienced this technique, the goal of which is to quickly bring the liar into contradiction. But ████████████████████████ obviously was not briefed enough about my case and the history of my interrogation: it wouldn't have mattered whether I was lying or telling the truth, because I had been questioned so many times about the exact same things by different agencies from different countries. Should I have lied, I would have been able to lie again and again and again, because I had had enough time to straighten my lies. But I hadn't lied to him—nor did he doubt my truthfulness.

First he showed me the picture of ████████████████ ████████████ he had been interrogating earlier, and said "If you tell me about this guy, I am going to close your case and send you home." Of course he was lying.

I looked at the photo and honestly answered, "No, I don't know him." I am sure the guy was asked the same question about me, and he must have answered the same because there was no way that he knew me.

████████████████ was sitting on ████████████████ left and recording my answers. "Do you drink tea?" ████████ ████████████████ asked me.

"Yes, I like tea." ████████████████████ ordered the tea guy to bring me a cup, and I got a big, hot cup of tea. When the caffeine started to mix with my blood I got hyper and felt so comforted. Those interrogators know what they are doing.

"Do you know ████████████████ asked ████████ ████████████. I had been asked about ████████████████ a

---

in more depth later in this chapter. This one appears to be the senior interrogator who only interrogates him once. ARB transcript, 21.

thousand and one times, and I tried everything I could to convince interrogators that I don't know that guy: if you don't know somebody, you just don't know him, and there is no changing it.* Even if they torture you, they will not get any usable information. But for some reason the Americans didn't believe that I didn't know him, and they wanted the Jordanians to make me admit it.

"No, I don't know him," I answered.

"I swear to Allah you know him," he shouted.

"Don't swear," I said, although I knew that taking the Lord's name in vain is like sipping coffee for him. ▇▇▇▇▇▇▇▇▇▇ ▇▇▇▇▇▇▇▇▇▇ kept swearing. "Do you think I am lying to you?"

"No, I think you forgot." That was too nicely put, but the fact that the Americans didn't provide the Jordanians with any substantial evidence tied the hands of the Jordanians mightily. Yes, Jordanians practice torture on a daily basis, but they need a reasonable suspicion to do so. They don't just jump on anybody and start to torture him. "I am going to give you pen and paper, and I want you to write me your resumé and the names of all of your friends," he said, closing the session and asking the guard to take me back to my cell.

The worst was over; at least I thought so. The escorting guards were almost friendly when they handcuffed and blindfolded me. There is one common thing among prison guards, whether they are American, Mauritanian, or Jordanian: they all reflect the attitude of the interrogators. If the interrogators are happy the guards are happy, and if not, then not.

---

* This again could be Ahmed Ressam, about whom MOS has by this time been repeatedly questioned. At his 2005 ARB hearing, MOS testified, "Then they sent me to Jordan.... The Jordanians were investigating my part in the Millennium plot. They told me, they are especially concerned about the Millennium plot." ARB transcript, 20.

The escorting guards felt some freedom to talk to me. "Where are you from?"

"Mauritania."

"What are you doing in Jordan?"

"My country turned me over."

"Are you kidding me?"

"No, I'm serious."

"Your country is fucked up." In the Jordanian Prison, as in Mauritania and GTMO, it was extremely forbidden for the guards to interact with detainees. But hardly anybody followed the rules.

"You are starving, man, why don't you eat?" one of the escorting guards asked me. He was right. The shape of my bones was clear, and anybody could tell how serious my situation was.

"I am only going to eat if I get back home. I'm not interested in prison food. I'm interested in my mom's food," I answered.

"God willing, you're going to get out, but for the time being you got to eat." I don't want to make him look good, his type of job already defines his personality, but he felt that his country was not just. I needed any comforting word, and so far he had done a good job with me. Other guards joined us in the corridor and asked him where I'm from.

They opened the door to ████████████. I felt as though a big burden was taken off my back. "It's only a matter of days, and then they'll send me back home. The DSE was right," I thought. The Jordanians were as confused about the case the U.S. had given them as I was. The U.S. government obviously hadn't given any substantial material to help the Jordanians to do their dirty job. The painful fear started to diminish, and I started to feel like eating.

Sneaky I'm-Watching-You appeared at the bin hole of my cell and gave me thirty numbered pieces of paper. The coordination between the interrogators and guards was perfect. I immediately wrote both assignments. I was tasked by ███████ ████████████████ with writing the names of all my friends, but that was ridiculous: I had so many acquaintances that it would be impossible to include them in less than a big book. So I completed a list of my closest friends and a traditional resumé, using about 10 pages. For the first time I had some relatively good sleep that night.

Some time in the next couple of days ██████████████ ████████████ picked up the written materials and the empty papers as well. He counted the papers thoroughly.

"Is that all you have to write?"

"Yes, Sir!" ████████████████████████████ had been working day and night, and all he was doing was checking on detainees through the bin holes. Most of the time I didn't notice him. Once he caught me having a good time with a guard and he took me and interrogated me about what we were talking about. As to the guard, he disappeared and I never saw him again.

"Put your stuff together," a guard said, waking me in the morning. I grabbed my blanket, my Koran, and the one Library book I had. I was so happy because I thought I was being sent home.

The guard made me hold my stuff and blindfolded me. They didn't send me home; instead I found myself locked in the cellar, ████████████. The cell there was not clean. It seemed to have been abandoned for a long time. I still wanted to believe in good intentions, and I thought this was the transfer cell for detainees before their release. I was so tired and the cell was so cold that I went to sleep.

Around 4:30 p.m. Iftar was served, and I slowly came to life. I noticed an old paper on the door with the rules of the prison. The guards had clumsily forgotten to tear it off. I wasn't supposed to read the rules, but since nobody is perfect, I had the chance to discover something. The rules stated, among other things, (1) You are only allowed to smoke if you are cooperating; (2) Talking to the guards is forbidden; (3) the ICRC visits the prison every 14 days; (4) Do not talk to the ICRC about your political case.* I was happy, because I would at least be able to send letters to my family, but I missed a vital point: I had been taken temporarily to the cellar to hide me from the ICRC in a Cat-and-Mouse game that lasted eight months, my entire stay in Jordan.

Every fourteen days, the guards would consistently move me from my cell to the cellar, where I would spend a couple of days before they brought me back to my cell. When I discovered the trick, I explicitly asked my interrogator ███████████████ to see the ICRC.

"There is no ICRC here. This is a Military prison," he lied.

"I have seen the clauses of the Rules, and you're hiding me in the cellar every 14 days to prevent me from meeting the Red Cross."

████████████████████ looked at me firmly. "I am protecting you! And you are not going to see the ICRC." I knew then that there was no changing their minds, and ████████ ████████████ couldn't even decide the issue. It was way above him. The conspiracy between Mauritania, the U.S., and Jordan to commit the crime was perfect. If my involvement in terrorism were cemented, I would be executed and the party would be over, and who was to know what had happened?

---

* The ICRC is the International Committee of the Red Cross, which has a mandate under the Geneva Conventions to visit prisoners of war, civilians interned during conflicts, and others detained in situations of violence around the world. An internationally acknowledged purpose of these visits is to ensure humane treatment and deter and prevent abuse.

"I'd like to see the Mauritanian Ambassador," I asked the interrogator.

"Impossible."

"OK, what about Mauritanian Intel?" I asked.

"What do you want with them?"

"I would like to ask them about the reason for my incarceration in Jordan. At least you know that I have done nothing against your country."

"Look, your country is a good friend of ours, and they turned you over to us. We can do anything we like with you, kill you, arrest you indefinitely, or release you if you admit to your crime." ██████████████████████████ both lied and told the truth. Arab countries are not friends. On the contrary, they hate each other. They never cooperate; all they do is conspire against each other. To Mauritania, Jordan is worthless, and vice-versa. However, in my case the U.S. compelled them both to work together.

I tried so many times to contact my family but to no avail, and then I washed my hands of the evils and I prayed to God to take care of my family and make them know where I was. In time, I noticed that I was not the only hidden package: between one and three other detainees were subject to the cellar operation at any one time, and the numbers kept changing as time went by. My whole time in Jordan, I was always in isolation, of course. But I could tell whether there were detainees in the neighboring cells, based on the movements of the food chariot, the guards, and the movement of detainees.

For a while my neighbors were two courageous boys. Although talking was forbidden, those two boys were always shouting, "God's help is coming soon. Remember, God is on our side, and Satan is on theirs!" No matter what the guards did to them, they kept solacing the other detainees and reminding them of God's inevitable relief. You could tell from the accent that they were Jordanians, which made sense, since the locals are more likely to be protected by their families than foreigners. Nonetheless, I have no doubt those boys suffered for what they did.

████████████████████████████ I was the only constant in my neighborhood; the cells next to me kept changing owners.* At one point, my next-door neighbor happened to be a young Lebanese nitwit who kept crying and refusing to eat. His story, according to the guards, went like this: He came to Jordan from Lebanon to have some fun. When he bumped into a routine police patrol in downtown Amman, they found an AKM-47 in his trunk and arrested him. Now, having a gun on you in Lebanon is not a big deal, but in Jordan it is forbidden to carry weapons. Taken to jail, the young Lebanese suspect was losing his mind. He kept crying and refusing his food for at least two weeks until his release. Oh, what a relief for me, when they released him! I felt so bad for him. I am sure he learned his lesson, and will think twice about having a weapon in his trunk the next time he comes to Jordan.

████████████████████████████. He had been sentenced to one year, and at the end of the year he went crazy. He kept shouting, "I need to see my interrogator!" When I asked the guards why he was doing this, they answered, "Because his sentence is over, but they won't let him go." Sometimes he would start to sing loudly, and sometimes he shouted at the guards, asking for a cigarette. I don't blame him: unless you have nerves of steel, chances are you'll lose your mind in Jordanian custody.

---

* In this section of the manuscript, which MOS heads "My Detainee Neighbors," he is clearly profiling some of his fellow prisoners in Jordan. This redaction, which is preceded by the number 2, appears to introduce a second "neighbor," and the next two redactions seem to introduce two more.

██ kept
coughing the whole time. "He is very old," a guard told me.

"Why did they arrest him?" I wondered.

"Wrong place, wrong time," the guard answered. The older
man was always asking for more food and smokes. After a couple of weeks, he was released. I was happy for everybody released
from that crazy facility.

It is just amazing that the FBI trusts the Jordanians more than
the other American intelligence agencies. When I turned myself
in in the fall of 2001, the FBI confiscated my hard disk, and
when they sent me to Jordan, they sent the contents of my hard
disk to Jordan, too. The DoD has been trying for years to get
that disk. It doesn't make sense that the FBI would cooperate
more with foreign organizations than the domestic ones, but I
do believe that the Intel industry is like any other industry: you
buy the best product for the best price, regardless of the country
of origin. Do the Jordanians offer the best product in this case?
I'm not sure, but they understand the recipe of terrorism more
than Americans. Reportedly without the Jordanians in the field,
the Americans would never have achieved what they have.
However, the Americans over-estimate the capability of the
Jordanians by sending them people from all over the world, as
if the Jordanians were some super Intel Agency.

"I am going to show you some pictures, you tell me about
them," said ████████████████████████████. Lately, he and
████████████████████████████ Jordanian were appointed to
interrogate me; ████████████████████████ was the leader. In
Jordan, they have a technique in which two interrogators or
more interrogate you separately about the same thing, in order

to make sure that you don't change your statements. They rarely sat together and interrogated me.*

"Alright!" I said. ███████████████ started showing me pictures, and as soon as I saw the first one I knew it was from my computer, or more accurately the computer of the company I had been working for. My heart started to pound, and I felt my saliva getting extremely bitter. My face started to turn as red as an apple. My tongue got heavy and twisted. Not because I had done any crimes with my computer; there was really nothing on the hard drive but my business emails and other related data. I remember having over 1500 email messages, and a whole bunch of pictures. But there is more to it when somebody's freedom is violated.

The PC belonged to a company that trusted me, and the fact that a foreign country such as the U.S. was searching the disk and confiscating material was a big burden for the company. The PC held the financial secrets of a company, which the company wouldn't be willing to share with the rest of the world. Moreover, I worked for a family company and the family hardly drew a line between their company and their private lives, which meant that the computer also contained private familial data the family wouldn't share with the world. On top of that, in the office the PC was a shared station, and anybody in the company could and did use it, so there are a lot of data I didn't know of, though I was 100% sure there was no crime behind it, knowing my colleagues and their dedication to their work and life. I personally had emails with my friends in Germany, some of them aren't even Muslims. But I was more worried about my emails with the Muslim friends, especially any of the ones who had

---

* These might be the second and third of the Jordanian interrogators MOS mentioned at his 2005 ARB hearing and briefly profiles later in this chapter. ARB transcript, 21.

ever financially or spiritually helped the oppressed people in Bosnia or Afghanistan, because their messages would be interpreted evilly. Just put yourself in my shoes and imagine somebody storming your house and trying to mess with your whole private life! Would you welcome such an assault?

I started to answer him to the best of my knowledge, especially about my own pictures. He put the pictures I could identify on one side, and the rest on another side. I explained to him that the PC had been used by several colleagues, one of whom scanned all kinds of different pictures for the clients of the Internet café, including all kinds of private family pictures. I was so mad at myself, my government, the U.S., and the Jordanians because I saw how many people's private lives were being violated. I was also confronted in a later session with a couple emails I interchanged with ███████████████████████████. The funny thing was that Mehdi sent an email before I got arrested, and the Mauritanian government interrogated me about it and I explained to them with definite evidence that there was no evil in it.* As soon as I got back to my office I wrote ████████ the following email: "Dear Brother! Please stop sending emails, because the Intel are intercepting our emails and giving me a hard time." I openly didn't want any trouble, and so wanted to close any door that would lead in that direction.

"Why did you write ████████ this email?" asked ████████
████████████.

---

* The name "Mehdi" appears unredacted twice in this passage. This is likely Karim Mehdi. Born in Morocco, Mehdi lived in Germany and appears, from Judge Robertson's habeas opinion, to have traveled with MOS to Afghanistan in 1992. Mehdi was arrested in Paris in 2003 and sentenced to nine years in prison for plotting a bombing on Reunion Island. See https://www.aclu.org/files/assets/2010-4-9-Slahi-Order.pdf; http://articles.latimes.com/print/2003/jun/07/world/fg-terror7; and http://news.bbc.co.uk/2/hi/africa/6088540.stm.

I explained the message to him.

"No, it's because you are afraid that the government would learn about your mischiefs with your friend," he commented sillily.

"Well, this message was addressed to both Mehdi and the government. I know my emails are intercepted by the government, and I always assumed that the government got a copy of my email traffic," I said.

"You were using a code when you wrote ███████████ ████████████████████," he said.

"Well, I am sure you have dealt with coded messages in your career, or you have specialists who help you. Go to them first, before you make up your mind."

"No, I want you to explain the code to me."

"There is no code, what you understand is what I meant." But I had another issue with the Jordanian interrogators: my original emails were in German, and the Americans translated them into English and sent them to the Jordanians, who in their turn translated the English versions into Arabic. Under these circumstances, the original text suffered and the space for evil interpretations widened with every translation.

And there was no end to evil interpretations. In the summer 2001 I was tasked by my company to technologically assist the visit of the Mauritanian President to the city of Tidjikja. The family that employed me is from Tidjikja, so it made sense that their interest lay in the well-being of the city. We installed a small media consulting center that operated over the Internet to transmit the visit of the President in real time. The company took many pictures where my colleagues and I appeared close to the president. In the closest one, the President stood behind my neck wondering at me "magically playing with the computer."

"I can tell, you were plotting to kill the President," said
███████████████.

I couldn't help laughing. "So why didn't I kill him?"

"I don't know. You tell me," █████████████████ said.

"Look! If I tried to kill my president in my country, it's none
of your business, nor that of the Americans. Just turn me over
to my country and let them deal with me." I was both angry
and hopeful, angry because the U.S. wanted to pin any crime
on me, no matter what, and hopeful because they were going
to turn me over to my country to suffer the death penalty. The
Americans couldn't possibly have dreamt of a better option. But
the Jordanians were fishing on behalf of the Americans, and
whenever you notice your interrogator fishing, you can be sure
that he is bankrupt.

Though he was as evil as he could be, ██████████████████
was sort of a reasonable interrogator, and so he never asked me
again about the plot on my President, nor about the pictures in
my hard disk. And yet I regretted that I didn't act on the suspicion and make myself look guilty in order to get myself extradited back to Mauritania. It was a crazy and desperate idea, and
I don't think that the Mauritanians would have played along
because they knew for a fact I hadn't plotted against the president.
But when my situation worsened in the Jordanian prison, I
thought about confessing that I had an operation going on in
Mauritania, and had hidden explosives. The idea was that I
would try to be sent back to Mauritania.

"Don't do that! Just be patient and remember that Allah is
watching," one of my guards told me when I asked him for advice.
By then I had made a lot of friends among the guards; they brought
me the news and taught me about Jordanian culture, the torture
methods in the prison, and who's who among the interrogators.

It was categorically forbidden for the guards to interact with the detainees, but they always broke these rules. They recounted the latest jokes to me and offered me cigarettes, which I turned down because I don't smoke. They told me about the other detainees and their cases and also about their own private lives, marriage, children, and the social life in Jordan. I learned almost everything about life in Amman from speaking with them. They also brought me the best books from the library—even the Bible, which I requested because I wanted to study the book that must more or less have shaped the lives of the Americans. In Jordan they have a pretty respectable collection, though some of it is meant as propaganda for the King. The best part about the books was that detainees used them to pass messages back and forth, solacing each other by writing good things inside the book. I didn't know any detainees, but the first thing I always did was to sift through a book looking for messages. I memorized all of them.

The guards were picked mostly from the Bedouin tribes that are known for their historical loyalty to the King, and paid miserable wages, about $430 a month, give or take. Although this wage is among the best in Jordan, a guard can't start a family without another support of his own. But when a guard serves for fifteen years, he has the option of retiring with half of his current wage or continuing with that money plus his usual wage. The guards are part of Jordan's Elite Special Forces, and enjoy all kinds of training overseas. There are no females in the Special Forces.

████████████████████████ were responsible for moving detainees from one cell to another, to interrogations, to the shower, or to see their parents during the visits that took place on Fridays. I was so frustrated when I had to watch everybody seeing his family, while week after week I was deprived of that right. Lower ranking guards were responsible for the watch, and

▇▇▇▇▇▇▇▇ for the grocery that took place every Saturday. The responsible ▇▇▇▇▇▇ would go cell to cell with a list, writing down what each detainee wished to buy. You could buy juice, milk, candy, underwear, a towel, and that was about it; if you had enough money you would get what you ordered, and if not then not. I had about $87 on me when I was sent to Jordan, which seemed to have been enough for my modest groceries. One time, when the ▇▇▇▇▇▇▇ was going around with his list, I spotted my name and my accusation: "Participation in Terrorist attacks."

Every other day the guards offered you a five-minute recreation time. I hardly ever took advantage of it; the fact that I had to be shackled and blindfolded was just not worth it. Every once in a while detainees got their hair cut, and every Sunday the guards gave us cleaning materials to mop our cells, and they mopped the floor. The jail was not dirty.

The prison was run by three individuals: the director of the prison ▇▇▇▇▇▇▇▇▇▇▇▇▇▇▇ his two assistants, ▇▇▇▇▇▇▇▇▇▇▇▇▇▇▇▇▇▇▇▇▇▇▇▇▇▇▇▇▇▇▇ ▇▇▇. They played a role similar to the one ▇▇▇▇▇▇ in GTMO Bay. They are supposedly independent from the Intel community, but in practice both work together and collect Intels, each with its own methods. The director was a very big guy who dressed proudly in his Bedouin-civilian suits. He passed by every morning and asked every single detainee, "How are you doing? Need anything?" He always woke me up asking me the same question.

During my entire eight months in the Jordanian prison I asked him once for a water bottle, which he brought me. I wanted to put the ice-cold water I got from the faucet on the heater in order to warm it up so I could take care of my own hygiene. I do think that it was a good thing for him to check on detainees. However, the chances were really zero that detainees were going to fix any problems with the help of a director who also was actively taking part in torture. The Director made sure that everybody got three meals a day, breakfast around 7 a.m., lunch around 1 p.m., mostly chicken and rice, and dinner, a light meal with tea.

███

were continually patrolling through the corridor and checking on everybody, including whether the guards were following the rules. ████████████████████████ was responsible for what they call External Operations, such as capture and house searches.

Then there were the interrogators. Jordanian Interrogators have been working side-by-side with the Americans since the beginning of the operation baptized the "Global War Against Terrorism," interrogating people both inside and outside Jordan. They have agents in Afghanistan, where they profit from their average Middle Eastern looks. In the beginning the Jordanians were seen as a potential associate for doing the dirty work; the fact that Jordanians widely use torture as a means to facilitate interrogation seemed to impress the American authorities. But there was a problem: the Jordanians don't take anybody and torture him; they must have reason to practice heavy physical torture. As Americans grew hardened in their sins, they started to take the dirty job in their own hands. Nonetheless, being arrested in a Jordanian Jail is an irreparable torture already.

I had three interrogators in Jordan. ███████████████
███
███
█████████████████████████████. He has been leading the interrogators team in Jordan, and interrogating detainees himself in GTMO, and most likely in other secret places in Afghan-

istan and elsewhere, on behalf of the U.S. government. He seems to be widely-known in Jordan, as I learned from a Jordanian detainee in GTMO. ████████████████ seemed to be pretty well experienced: he saw my file once and decided it wasn't worth wasting his "precious" time on me, and so he never bothered to see me again.

██

██

███████████████████████.*

"You know, ███████████████, your only problem is your time in Canada. If you really haven't done nothing in Canada, you don't belong in jail," concluded ████████████████ after several sessions.

He was a specialist on Afghanistan; he himself had attended the training camps there as an undercover agent during the war against communism. When I was training in Al Farouq in '91, he was working undercover as a student in Khalden.† He questioned me thoroughly about my whole trip to Afghanistan and showed satisfaction with my answers. That was very much his whole job. In the winter of 2001 he was sent, maybe undercover, to Afghanistan and Turkey to help the U.S. capture Mujahideen, and I saw him when he came back in the summer of 2002 with a whole bunch of pictures. Part of his

---

* Preceded with a "2" in a passage subtitled "Interrogators," this redaction likely introduces the second Jordanian interrogator.

† Court documents indicate that MOS trained at the al-Farouq training camp near Khost, Afghanistan, for six months in late 1990 and early 1991. At the time, both the al-Farouq and Khalden camps were training al-Qaeda fighters for the conflict with the Soviet-backed government in Kabul. As the appellate court reviewing MOS's habeas case wrote, "When Salahi took his oath of allegiance in March 1991, al-Qaida and the United States shared a common objective: they both sought to topple Afghanistan's Communist government." See http://www.aclu.org/files/assets/2010-4-9-Slahi-Order. pdf; and http://caselaw.findlaw.com/us-dc-circuit/1543844.html.

mission was to gather Intels about me from other detainees in Afghanistan, but he didn't seem to have come up with anything. ████████████████████████████ showed me the pictures. I didn't recognize anybody, and felt bad for myself. Why did they show me more than 100 pictures, and I knew none of them? It didn't make sense. Usually, interrogators ask about people that are connected to you. So I decided to recognize at least one picture.

"This is Gamal Abdel Nasser," I said.

"You are making fun of me, aren't you?" said ████████████ ████████████████ angrily.

"No, no, I just thought it looks like him." ████████████ is a former Egyptian president who died before I was born.*

"These people are from the same gang as you are," ████ ████████████████ said.

"Maybe. But I don't know them," I said. He didn't say much after that; ██████████████████████ just spoke about his adventure in Afghanistan. "You're courageous," I remarked, to give him fuel for more talk.

"You know, the Americans are using smart weapons that follow their target based on temperature changes. Many brothers have been captured," ██████████████████████ recounted under the thick cloud of his cigarette smoke. I never saw ██████████████████████ after that session.

██████████████████████; I know his real first name.†

---

* Nasser, Egypt's second president, died in 1970. The redaction here seems especially absurd.

† Numbered "3," this redaction seems to introduce the third Jordanian interrogator, who appears to have been MOS's primary interrogator in Jordan. At his 2005 ARB hearing, MOS said that his main interrogator in Jordan was "young" and "a very bright guy." He testified that this particular interrogator "struck me twice in the face on different occasions and pushed me against concrete many times because I refused to talk to him," and

Boom! He slapped me across the face, and pushed my face against the wall. I was sobbing, maybe more because of frustration than pain.

"You are not a man! I am going to make you lick the dirty floor and tell me your story, beginning from the point when you got out of your mother's vagina," he continued. "You haven't seen nothing yet." He was correct, although he was the biggest liar I ever met. He lied so much that he contradicted himself because he would forget what he had said the last time about a specific topic. In order to give himself credibility, he kept swearing and taking the Lord's name in vain. I always wondered whether he thought I believed his garbage, though I always acted as if I did; he would have been angry if I called him a liar. He arrested big al Qaeda guys who talked about me being the bad guy, and he released them a thousand and one times from the prison when they told the truth. The funny thing was that he always forgot that he arrested and released them already.

"I arrested your cousin Abu Hafs and he told me the whole truth. As a matter of fact, he said 'Don't you put your hands on me, and I'm gonna tell you the truth,' and I didn't, and he did. He told me bad things about you. After that I bid him farewell and secretly sent him to Mauritania, where he was going to be interrogated for a couple of weeks and released. But you're different. You keep holding back Intels. I am going to send you to the secret political prison in the middle of the desert. Nobody is gonna give a shit about you." I had to keep listening to this same garbage over and over; the only thing he changed was the dates of arrest and release. In his dreams, he also arrested ████, ██████████████████████████████, and other individuals

---

"threatened me with a lot of torture and...took me to the one room where they torture and there was this guy who was beaten so much he was crying, crying like a child." ARB transcript, 21.

who had supposedly been providing information about me. Good for him; as long as he didn't beat me or attack me verbally I was cool, and would just listen carefully to his Thousand-and-One-Arabian-Nights tales.

"I've just arrived from the U.S., where I interrogated ███████████████████," he obviously lied.

"Well, that's good, because he must have told you that he doesn't know me."

"No, he said he does."

"Well, that's none of your business, right? According to you, I've done crimes against the U.S., so just send me to the U.S. or tell me what have I done against your country," I remarked sharply. I was growing tired of the futile conversation with him, and of trying to convince him that I had nothing to do with the Millennium Plot.

"I am not working for the Americans. Some of your friends are trying to hurt my country, and I'm asking you indirect questions as an interrogation technique," ██████████████ lied.

"Which friends of mine are trying to hurt your country?" I wondered.

"I cannot tell you!"

"Since I haven't tried to hurt your country, there's no blaming me. I am not my friends. Go and arrest them and release me." But if you are trying to make sense of things, the interrogation room is not for you. Whenever ███████████████ told me he had arrested somebody, I knew that the guy was still free.

Although he used physical violence against me only twice, he kept terrorizing me with other methods that were maybe worse than physical pain. He put a poor detainee next to my interrogation room, and his colleague started to beat him with a hard object until he burst out crying like a baby. How cheap! That was painful. I started to shake, my face got red, my saliva got as bitter as green persimmon, my tongue as heavy as metal. Those are the symptoms I always suffer when I get extremely scared, and the constant fear didn't seem to harden me. My depression reached its peak.

"Do you hear what's happening next door?"

"Yes."

"Do you want to suffer the same?" I almost said yes. It was so hard for me to helplessly listen to somebody suffering. It's not easy to make a grown-up cry like a baby.

"Why? I am talking to you!" I said, showing a fake composure. After all, the brother next door was also talking to his interrogator. ███████████████████ sardonically smiled and continued to smoke his cigarette as if nothing were happening. That night I was very cooperative and quiet; the logical and argumentative human being in me disappeared all of a sudden. ███████████████████ knew what he was doing, and he had apparently been doing it for a long time.

He would make me pass through the torture row so I would hear the cries and moans and the shouting of the torturers. I was blessed because the guards kept me blindfolded so I couldn't see the detainees. I was not supposed to see them, nor was I interested in seeing a brother, or actually anybody, suffering. The Prophet Mohamed (Peace be upon him) said, "God tortures whoever tortures human beings," and as far as I understand it, the person's religion doesn't matter.

"I am going to send you to the Shark Pool," ███████████ ███████ threatened me, when I refused to talk to him after he hit me.

"You don't know me. I swear by Almighty God I'll never talk to you. Go ahead and torture me. It will take my death to make me talk, and for your information I'm sorry for every bit of cooperation I have offered in the past," I said.

"First of all, your cooperation was achieved by force. You

didn't have a choice. Nor will you in the future: I am going to make you talk," ██████████████ said.

██████████████ started to push me against the wall and hit me on the sides of my face, but I didn't feel any pain. I don't think he hit me with his whole strength; the guy looks like a bull, and one real blow from him would have cost me 32 teeth. As he was hitting me, he started to ask me questions. I don't remember the questions, but I do remember my answers. There was only one answer.

"*Ana Bari'a*, I am innocent." I drove him crazy, but there was no making me talk.

"I have no time right now, but you're gonna suffer heavily tomorrow, son of a....." he said, and immediately left the room.

The escort took me back to my cell. It was around midnight; I sat on my prayer mat and started reading the Koran and praying until very late. I could hardly concentrate on what I was reading. I kept thinking, What will it be like in the Shark Pool? I had heard of an electrified pool, I knew they used one in Egypt, but "Shark Pool" sounded terrible.

But the rendezvous came and went without me being taken to the torture place, one day, two day, three days! Nothing happened to me, except for no food, not because they didn't give it to me but because I had no appetite, as always when I get depressed. I learned later from the Jordanian detainee in GTMO who spent fifty days in the same prison that there is no such thing as the Shark Pool, but that they do have other painful methods of torture, like hanging detainees from their hands and feet and beating them for hours, and depriving them from sleep for days until they lose their minds.

"In Jordan they don't torture unless they have evidence," ██████████████ said. "If they knew what I do, they wouldn't even bother arresting you. The Americans told them to," ███████████████ continued.

"The torture starts around midnight and finishes around dawn. Everybody takes part, the prison director, the interrogators, and the guards," ████████████████ said. ████████████████ information was consistent with what I saw. I personally heard beatings, but I don't know whether the detainees were hung up or not when the beating happened. And I witnessed sleep deprivation more than once.

Late one night when I was talking to some of my guard friends, I kept hearing sounds as if some people were performing harsh training with loud voices to get the whole energy out of their body, like in Kung-Fu. I heard heavy bodies hitting the floor. It was just too noisy, and too close to my ████████ ███████████.

"Are you guys training so late?" I asked one of the guards. Before he could say a word, another guy appeared dressed in a Ninja-like suit that covered him from head to toe. The guard looked at him and turned to me, smiling.

"Do you know this guy?" he asked. I forced an official smile.

"No." The new guy took his mask off, and he looked like the devil himself. Out of fear, my smile turned to laughter. "Oh, yes! We know each other," I said.

"████████████████ asks if you guys are training now?" my guard wryly asked the Ninja.

"Yes! Do you want to train with us? We have many detainees enjoying PT," he said sardonically. I knew right away that he meant torture. My laughter faded into a smile, and my smiled into fixed lips over my teeth. I didn't want to reveal my disappointment, fear, and confusion.

"No, I'm just fine," I said. The devil resumed his business, and I asked the guard, "Why do they put on the masks for this type of job?"

"They want to protect their identities. In Jordan, you can get killed for doing such things." He was right: most of the detainees were arrested because they know something, not because of crimes, and so they will be released sooner or later. I wished I hadn't known about that mischief; it was just impossible for me to sleep when I was listening to grown-ups crying like babies. I tried to put every object in my ears and around my head but nothing helped. As long as the torture lasted, I couldn't sleep. The good thing was that the torture wasn't every day, and the voices didn't always reach my cell.

In February 2002, the director of Jordan's Antiterrorism Department was the subject of an assassination plot.* He almost gave his soul back. Somebody planted a time bomb in the chassis of the car of the biggest target of the Islamic movement in Jordan. The bomb was supposed to explode on the way between his home and his office — and it did. But what happened seemed like a miracle. On his way to work, the Director felt like buying cigarettes. His driver stopped in front of a store and left to grab a pack of cigarettes. The director felt like going with his chauffeur. As soon as both left the car, the bomb exploded. Nobody was harmed, but the vehicle was history.

The investigation led to a suspect, but the secret police couldn't find him. But the King of the Fight against Terrorism cannot be messed with; suspects must be arrested and the guilty party must be found. Immediately. The Jordanian secret Agency had to have revenge for the big head. The peaceful brother of the

---

* Press reports document an assassination attempt like the one described here, aimed at General Ali Bourjaq, head of Jordan's antiterrorism unit, on February 20, 2002, in Amman. See, e.g., http://weekly.ahram.org.eg/2002/576/re72.htm.

suspect was to be taken as a pawn and tortured until his brother turned himself in. Special Forces were sent out, arrested the innocent boy in a crowded place, and beat him beyond belief. They wanted to show people the destiny of a family when one of its members tries to attack the government. The boy was taken to the prison and tortured every day by his interrogator.

"I don't care how long it takes, I am going to keep torturing you until your brother turns himself in," his interrogator said. The family of the boy was given the opportunity to visit the boy, not for humane reasons, but because the interrogator wanted the family to see the miserable situation of the boy so they would turn in the suspected son. The family was devastated, and soon the information leaked that the suspect was hiding in his family's house. Late that night, an operation stormed the house and arrested him. The next day his brother was released.

"What will you say if somebody asks you about the bruises and injuries I caused you?" the interrogator asked him.

"I'll say nothing!" answered the boy.

"Look, we usually keep people until they heal, but I'm releasing you. You go ahead and file anything you like against me. I did what I got to do to capture a terrorist, and you're free to go." As to his brother, he was taken care of by the director himself: he kept beating him for six straight hours. And that is not to mention what the other interrogators did to satisfy their chief. I learned all this from the guards when I noticed that the prison had become remarkably crowded. Not that I could see anybody, but the food supply shrunk decidedly; they kept moving detainees to and from their cells; whenever detainees were led past my cell the guards closed my bin hole; and I saw the different shifts of guards more frequently than usual. The situation started to improve in the summer of 2002.

By then, the Jordanians were basically done with me. When

██████████████████ finished my hearing, he handed me my statements. "Read the statements and sign them," he said.

"I don't need to read them, I trust you!" I lied. Why should I read something when I didn't have the option to sign or to refuse? No judge would take into consideration somebody's statements that were coerced in a prison facility such as the Jordanian Military prison.

After about a week ██████████████████ took me to interrogation in a nice room. "Your case is closed. You haven't lied. And I thank you for your cooperation. When it comes to me, I am done with you, but it's the decision of my boss when you'll go home. I hope soon."

I was happy with the news; I had expected it, but not that soon.

"Would you like to work for us?" he asked me.

"I'd like to, but I really am not qualified for this type of work," I said, partly lying and partly telling the truth. He tried in a friendly way to convince me, but I, with the most friendliness I could manage, told him that I was way too much of an idiot for Intel work.

But when the Jordanians shared the result of their investigation with the U.S. and sent them the file, the U.S. took the file and slapped the Jordanians in their faces. I felt the anger of Uncle Sam thousands of miles away, when ████████████ ██████ came back into his old skin during the last two months of my incarceration in Jordan. The interrogations resumed. I tried all I could to express myself. Sometimes I talked, sometimes I refused. I hunger-struck for days, but ██████████ ██████████████ made me eat under threat of torture. I wanted to compel the Jordanians to send me back home, but I failed. Maybe I wasn't hardcore enough.

GTMO

324

They had no reason to doubt me b/c I never lied to them
and ▓▓▓ made sure to get me the ▓▓▓▓▓ in GTMO.
I took

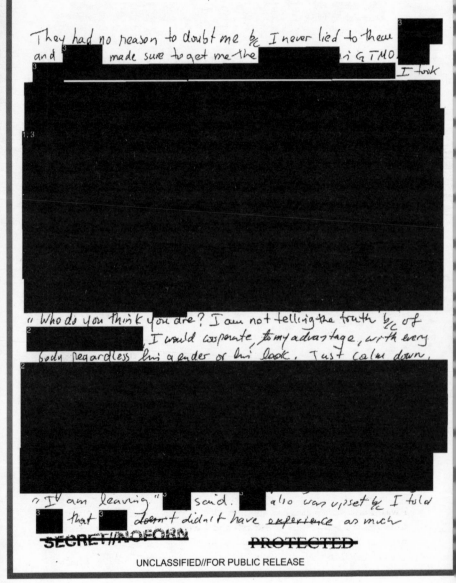

" Who do you think you are? I am not telling the truth b/c of
▓▓▓▓▓ I would cooperate, to my advantage, with every
body regardless his gender or his look. Just calm down,

" I am leaving " ▓▓▓ said. ▓▓▓ also was upset b/c I told
▓▓ that ▓▓ ~~doesn't~~ didn't have experience as much

FIVE

GTMO

February 2003–August 2003

First "Mail" and First "Evidence"...The Night of Terror...The DOD Takes Over...24 Hour Shift Interrogations...Abduction inside the Abduction...The Arabo-American Party

The rules have changed. What was no crime is now considered a crime."

"But I've done no crimes, and no matter how harsh you guys' laws are, I have done nothing."

"But what if I show you the evidence?"

"You won't. But if you do, I'll cooperate with you."

██████████ showed me the worst people in ██████████. There were fifteen, and I was number 1; number 2 was ██████████ ██████████.*

"You gotta be kidding me," I said.

---

* At his 2005 ARB hearing, MOS told the panel, "Then the FBI at GTMO Bay during the time era of General Miller, they released a list of the highest priority detainees here at GTMO. It was a list of 15 people and I was, guess which number, number ONE. Then they sent a special FBI team and the leader was [redacted] and I worked with him especially for my case....I thought he was just making fun of me when he said I was number ONE in the camp, but he was not lying; he was telling the truth,

"No, I'm not. Don't you understand the seriousness of your case?"

"So, you kidnapped me from my house, in my country, and sent me to Jordan for torture, and then took me from Jordan to Bagram, and I'm still worse than the people you captured with guns in their hands?"

"Yes, you are. You're very smart! To me, you meet all the criteria of a top terrorist. When I check the terrorist check list, you pass with a very high score."

I was so scared, but I always tried to suppress my fear. "And what is your ▓▓▓ check list?"

"You're Arab, you're young, you went to Jihad, you speak foreign languages, you've been in many countries, you're a graduate in a technical discipline."

"And what crime is that?" I said.

"Look at the hijackers: they were the same way."

"I am not here to defend anybody but myself. Don't even mention anybody else to me. I asked you about my crime, and not about x's or y's crimes. I don't give a damn!"

"But you are part of the big conspiracy against the U.S."

"You always say that. Tell me my part in this 'big conspiracy!'"

"I am going to tell you, just *sabr*, be patient."

My sessions continued with arguments of this nature. Then one day when I entered the interrogation room ▓▓▓▓▓▓ ▓▓▓▓▓▓▓▓▓▓▓▓▓▓, I saw video equipment already hooked up. To be honest, I was terrified that they were going to show me a video with me committing terrorist attacks. Not that I have done anything like that in my life. But a fellow detainee

---

as future events would prove. He stayed with me until May 22, 2003."
ARB transcript, 24.

called ███████████████████████████ told me that his
interrogators forged an American passport bearing his picture.
"Look: We now have definitive evidence that you forged this
passport and you were using it for terrorist purposes," they told
him. ████████████████ laughed wholeheartedly at the silliness
of his interrogators. "You missed that I'm a computer specialist,
and I know that the U.S. government would have no problem
forging a passport for me," he said. The interrogators quickly
took the passport back and never talked about it again.

Scenarios like that made me very paranoid about the government making up something about me. Coming from a third-
world country, I know how the police wrongly pin crimes on
political rivals of the government in order to neutralize them.
Smuggling weapons into somebody's house is common, in order
to make the court believe the victim is preparing for violence.

"Are you ready?" said ████████████.

"Y-e-e-s!" I said, trying to keep myself together, though my
blushing face said everything about me. ████████████ hit the
play button and we started to watch the movie. I was ready to
jump when I saw myself blowing up some U.S. facility in Tim-
buktu. But the tape was something completely different. It was
a tape of Usama bin Laden speaking to an associate I didn't
recognize about the attack of September 11. They were speaking in Arabic. I enjoyed the comfort of understanding the
talk, while the interrogators had to put up with the subtitles.

After a short conversation between UBL and the other guy,
a TV commentator spoke about how controversial the tape was.
The quality was bad; the tape was supposedly seized by U.S.
forces in a safehouse in Jalalabad.

But that was not the point. "What do I have to do with this
bullshit?" I asked angrily.

"You see Usama bin Laden is behind September 11," ▆▆▆▆
▆▆▆ said.

"You realize I am not Usama bin Laden, don't you? This is between you and Usama bin Laden; I don't care, I'm outside of this business."

"Do you think what he did was right?"

"I don't give a damn. Get Usama bin Laden and punish him."

"How do you feel about what happened?"

"I feel that I'm not a part of it. Anything else doesn't matter in this case!" When I came back to ▆▆▆▆▆▆ Block I was telling my friends about the masquerade of the "definitive evidence" against me. But nobody was surprised, since most of the detainees had been through such jokes.

During my conversations with ▆▆▆▆▆▆ and his associate, I brought up an issue that I believe to be basic.

"Why are you guys banning my incoming mails?"

"I checked, but you have none!"

"You're trying to say that my family is refusing to respond to me?"

The brothers in the block felt bad for me. I was dreaming almost every night that I had received mail from my family. I always passed on my dreams to my next door neighbors, and the dream interpreters always gave me hope, but no mails came. "I dreamt that you got a letter from your family," was a common phrase I used to hear. It was so hard for me to see other detainees having pictures of their families, and having nothing—zip—myself. Not that I wished they never got letters: on the contrary, I was happy for them, I read their correspondence as if it were from my own mom. It was customary to pass newly received mails throughout the block and let everybody read them, even the most intimate ones from lovers to the beloved.

▆▆▆▆▆▆ was dying to get me cooperating with him, and

he knew that I had brought my issue to the detainees. So he was working with the mail people to get me something. A recipe was prepared and cooked, and around 5 p.m. the postman showed up at my cell and handed me a letter, supposedly from my brother. Even before I read the letter, I shouted to the rest of the block, "I received a letter from my family. See, my dreams have come true, didn't I tell you?" From everywhere my fellow detainees shouted back, "Congratulations, pass me the letter when you're done!"

I hungrily started to read, but I soon got a shock: the letter was a cheap forgery. It was not from my family, it was the production of the Intel community.

"Dear brothers, I received no letter, I am sorry!"

"Bastards, they have done this with other detainees," said a neighbor. But the forgery was so clumsy and unprofessional that no fool would fall for it. First, I have no brother with that name. Second, my name was misspelled. Third, my family doesn't live where the correspondent mentioned, though it was close. Fourth, I know not only the handwriting of every single member of my family, but also the way each one phrases his ideas. The letter was kind of a sermon, "Be patient like your ancestors, and have faith that Allah is going to reward you." I was so mad at this attempt to defraud me and play with my emotions.

The next day, ▮▮▮▮▮▮▮▮ pulled me for interrogation.

"How's your family doing?"

"I hope they're doing well."

"I've been working to get you the letter!"

"Thank you very much, good effort, but if you guys want to forge mail, let me give you some advice."

"What are you talking about?"

I smiled. "If you don't really know, it's okay. But it was cheap to forge a message and make me believe I have contact with my dear family!" I said, handing the strange letter back.

"I don't shit like that," ▮▮▮▮▮▮▮ said.

"I don't know what to believe. But I believe in God, and if I don't see my family in this life, I hope to see them in the afterlife, so don't worry about it." I honestly don't have proof or disproof of whether ▮▮▮▮▮▮▮ was involved in that dirty business. But I do know that the whole matter is much bigger than ▮▮▮▮▮▮▮; there are a bunch of people working behind the scene.* ▮▮▮▮▮▮▮ was in charge of my case through ▮▮▮▮▮▮▮, but I was taken for interrogation a couple of times by other ▮▮▮▮▮▮▮▮▮▮▮ without his consent or even knowledge. As to letters from my family, I received my first letter, a Red Cross message, on February 14, 2004, 816 days after I was kidnapped from my house in Mauritania. The message was seven months old when it reached me.

"I am gonna show you the evidence bit by bit," said ▮▮▮▮▮▮▮ one day. "There is a big al Qaeda guy who told us that you are involved."

"I guess you shouldn't ask me questions then, since you have a witness. Just take me to court and roast me," I said. "What have I done, according to your witness?"

"He said you are a part of the conspiracy." I grew tired of the words Big Conspiracy against the U.S. ▮▮▮▮▮▮▮ could not give me anything to grab onto, no matter how much I argued with him.

As to ▮▮▮▮▮▮▮, he was not an argumentative guy. "If

---

* People were indeed "working behind the scene." Though the FBI was still leading MOS's interrogation, the DOJ IG found that through the spring of 2003, "Military Intelligence personnel observed many of Slahi's interviews by Poulson and Santiago from an observation booth," and that MI agents were complaining about the FBI's rapport-building approach. The Senate Armed Services Committee reported that military interrogators started circulating a draft "Special Interrogation Plan" for MOS in January 2003. DOJ IG, 298; SASC, 135.

the government believes that you're involved in bad things, they're gonna send you to Iraq or back to Afghanistan," ▆▆▆▆▆▆▆ said.*

"So if you guys torture me, I'm gonna tell you everything you want to hear?"

"No, look: if a mom asks her kid whether he's done something wrong, he might lie. But if she hits him, he's gonna admit it," replied ▆▆▆▆▆▆▆. I had no answer to this analogy. Anyway, the "big al Qaeda" guy who testified against me turned out to be ▆▆▆▆▆▆▆▆▆▆.† ▆▆▆▆▆▆▆▆▆▆▆▆ was said to have said that I helped him to go to Chechnya with two other guys who were among the hijackers, which I hadn't done. Though I had seen ▆▆▆▆▆▆▆ once or twice in Germany, I didn't even know his name. Even if I had helped them to go to Chechnya, that would be no crime at all, but I just hadn't.

By then I knew about the horrible torture that ▆▆▆▆▆▆▆ had suffered after his arrest ▆▆▆▆▆▆▆▆▆. Eyewitnesses who were captured with him in Karachi said, "We thought he was dead. We heard his cries and moans day and night until he was separated from us." We had even heard rumors in the camp that he died under torture. Overseas torture was obviously a

---

* This may be the agent the DOJ's Inspector General calls Santiago. The IG reported that MOS "identified Santiago as a 'nice guy,'" and recorded that MOS reported to investigators that "Santiago told Slahi he would be sent to Iraq or Afghanistan if the charges against him were proved." DOJ IG, 296.

† The passage likely refers to Ramzi bin al-Shibh. MOS explained at his ARB hearing, and indicates elsewhere in the manuscript as well, that he learned about bin al-Shibh's treatment in CIA black sites from detainees who were captured alongside bin al-Shibh and held with him in secret sites before being transferred to Guantánamo. MOS told the ARB panel that "a Yemeni guy who was captured with Ramiz [sic]" told him, "Ramiz was tortured. We would hear his cries every night, we would hear his moans every night." ARB transcript, 25; see also MOS manuscript, 83, 294.

common practice and professionally executed; I heard so many testimonies from detainees who didn't know each other that they couldn't be lies. And as you shall see, I was subject to torture in this base of GTMO, like many other fellow detainees. May Allah reward all of us.

"I don't believe in torture," said ███████. I didn't share with him my knowledge about Ramzi having been tortured. But because the government has sent detainees including me, ██████████████, and █████████████████████ overseas to facilitate our interrogation by torture, that meant that the government believes in torture; what ███████ believes in doesn't have much weight when it comes to the harsh justice of the U.S. during war.

███████████ finally came forth on his promise to deliver the reasons why his government was locking me up. But he didn't show me anything that was incriminating. In March 2002 CNN had broadcast a report about me claiming that I was the coordinator who facilitated the communication between the September 11 hijackers through the guestbook of my homepage. Now ████████████████ showed me the report.*

"I told you that you fucked up," ████████████ said.

"I didn't design my homepage for al Qaeda. I just made it a long time ago and never even checked on it since early 1997. Besides, if I decided to help al Qaeda, I wouldn't use my real

---

* This appears to refer to a story CNN aired on March 6, 2002, the transcript of which is titled "Al Qaeda Online for Terrorism." As MOS indicates here, the story suggested that he was "running a seemingly innocuous website" where al-Qaeda was secretly exchanging messages through the website's guestbook. The allegation that MOS ran a website that facilitated al-Qaeda communications does not appear in any of the summaries of evidence against MOS from Guantánamo. See http://transcripts.cnn.com/TRANSCRIPTS/0203/06/lt.15.html.

name. I could write a homepage in the name of John Smith."

▮▮▮▮▮▮ wanted to know everything about my homepage and why I even wrote one. I had to answer all that bullshit about a basic right of mine, writing a homepage with my real name and with some links to my favorite sites.

In one session, ▮▮▮▮▮▮ asked, "Why did you study microelectronics?"

"I study whatever the heck I want. I didn't know that I had to consult the U.S. government about what I should or should not study," I said wryly.

"I don't believe in the principle of black and white. I think everybody is somehow in between. Don't you think so?" ▮▮▮▮▮▮ asked.

"I've done nothing."

"It is not a crime to help somebody to join al Qaeda and he ended up a terrorist!" ▮▮▮▮▮▮▮▮▮▮▮▮▮▮▮▮▮▮. I understood exactly what ▮▮▮▮▮▮ meant: Just admit that you are a recruiter for al Qaeda.

"Might be. I'm not familiar with U.S. laws. But anyway, I didn't recruit anybody for al Qaeda, nor did they ask me to!" I said.

As a part of his "showing me the evidences against me," ▮▮▮▮▮▮ asked a colleague of his for help. ▮▮▮▮▮▮, a ▮▮▮▮▮▮▮▮▮▮▮▮ who interrogated me back in ▮▮▮▮▮▮▮▮▮▮▮▮▮.* ▮▮▮▮▮▮ is one of those guys, when they speak you think they're angry, and they might not be.

"I am happy that you showed up, because I would like to discuss some issues with you," I said.

---

* "Mauritania" appears unredacted a few sentences later; the agent is apparently one of the FBI agents who questioned MOS in Nouakchott in February 2000.

"Of course, ███████████ is here to answer your questions!" said ██████████.

"Remember when you guys came to interrogate me in Mauritania?" I began. "Remember how sure you were that I was not only involved in Millennium, but that I was the brain behind it? How do you feel now, knowing that I have nothing to do with it?"

"That's not the problem," ███████████████ answered. "The problem was that you weren't honest with us."

"I don't have to be honest to you. And here's a news flash for you: I'm not going to talk to you unless you tell me why I am here," I said.

"That's your problem," ████████████████ said. You could tell that ████████████ was used to humbled detainees who probably had to cooperate due to torture. He was by then interrogating ███████████████.* He spoke very arrogantly; he as much as told me, "You're gonna cooperate, even against your will, ha! ha!" I admit I was rude with him, but I was so angry since he had wrongly accused me of having been part of the Millennium Plot and now was dodging my requests to him to come clean and say he and his government were wrong.

███████████████ looked worn out from his trip; he was very tired that day. "I don't see why you don't cooperate," he said. "They share food with you, and speak to you in a civilized way," he said.

"Why should I cooperate with any of you? You're hurting me, locking me up for no reason."

"We didn't arrest you."

"Send me the guy who arrested me, I'd like to talk to him."

---

* Possibly Ramzi bin al-Shibh; see footnote on p. 203.

After that tense discussion, the interrogators left and sent me back to my cell.

"For these next sessions, I have asked for ███████████ to help me in laying out your case. I want you to be polite to him," ███████████ said at our next session.

I turned to his colleague. "Now you're convinced that I am not a part of Millennium. What's the next shit you're gonna pull on me?"

"You know, sometimes we arrest people for the wrong thing, but it turns out they are involved in something else!" ███████████ said.

"And when are you going to stop playing this game on me? Every time there is a new suspicion, and when that turns out to be incorrect, I get a new one, and so on and so forth. Is there a possibility in the world that I am involved in nothing?"

"Of course; therefore you have to cooperate and defend yourself. All I am asking is for you to explain some shit to me," said ███████████. When ███████████ arrived he had a bunch of small papers with notes, and he started to read them to me. "You called ███████████ and asked him to bring you some sugar. When you told him about ███████████ in Germany, he said, 'Don't say this over the phone.' I wouldn't say something like that to anybody I called."

"I don't care what ███████████ says over the phone. I am not here on behalf of ███████████; go and ask him. Remember, I'm asking you what *I* have done."

"I just want you to explain these conversations to me — and there's much more," said ███████████.

"No, I am not answering anything before you answer my question. What have I done?"

"I don't say you've done anything, but there are a lot of things that need to be clarified."

"I've answered those questions a thousand and one times; I told you I mean what I am saying and I'm not using any code. You're just so unjust and so paranoid. You're taking advantage of me being from a country with a dictatorship. If I were German or Canadian, you wouldn't even have the opportunity to talk to me, nor would you arrest me."

"In asking you to cooperate, we're giving you an opportunity. After we share the cause of your arrest with you, it will be too late for you!" ▮▮▮▮▮▮▮▮▮▮▮▮ said.

"I don't need any opportunities. Just tell me why you arrested me, and let it be too late." ▮▮▮▮▮▮▮▮ knew me better than ▮▮▮▮▮▮▮▮▮▮▮ did; thus, he tried to calm both of us down. ▮▮▮▮▮▮▮▮▮▮▮ was trying to scare me, but the more he scared me, the sharper and less cooperative I got.

The camp was locked down the whole day. Around 10 p.m. I was pulled out of my cell and taken to ▮▮▮▮▮▮▮▮ building. The room was extremely cold. I hate to be woken up for interrogation, and my heart was pounding: Why would they take me so late?

I don't know how long I'd been in the room, maybe two hours. I was just shaking. I made my mind up not to argue anymore with the interrogators. I'm just gonna sit there like a stone, and let them do the talking, I said to myself. Many detainees decided to do so. They were taken day after day to interrogation in order to break them. I am sure some got broken because nobody can bear agony the rest of his life.

After letting me sweat, or let's say "shake," for a couple hours, I was taken to another room ▮▮▮▮▮▮▮▮▮▮▮▮▮▮▮▮▮ ▮▮▮▮, where ▮▮▮▮▮▮▮▮▮▮▮▮▮▮▮▮▮ sat. This room was acceptably cold. The military people were watching and listening from another room as usual.

"We couldn't take you during the day because the camp was locked down," said ▇▇▇▇▇▇▇▇. "We had to take you now, because ▇▇▇▇▇▇▇▇ is leaving tomorrow."

I didn't open my mouth. ▇▇▇▇▇▇▇▇ sent his friends out. "What's wrong with you?" he said. "Are you OK? Did anything happen to you?" But no matter how he tried, there was no making me talk.

The team decided to take me back to the cold room. Maybe it wasn't so cold for somebody wearing regular shoes, underwear, and a jacket like the interrogators, but it was definitely cold for a detainee with flip-flops and no underwear whatsoever.

"Talk to us!" ▇▇▇▇▇▇▇▇ said. "Since you refuse to talk, ▇▇▇▇▇▇▇▇ is going to talk to you anyway."

▇▇▇▇▇▇▇▇ started his lecture, "We have been giving you an opportunity, but you don't seem to want to take advantage of it. Now it's too late, because I am going to share some information with you."

▇▇▇▇▇▇▇▇ put down three big pictures of four individuals who are believed to be involved in the September 11 attack. "This guy is ▇▇▇▇▇▇▇▇▇▇▇▇▇▇. He was captured ▇▇▇▇▇▇▇▇▇▇▇▇▇▇▇▇▇▇ and since then I've been interrogating him.* I know more about him than

---

* It appears that this interrogator has been, or claims to have been, questioning Ramzi bin al-Shibh in the CIA black sites. At his ARB hearing, naming bin al-Shibh, MOS described what could be the same exchange with an interrogator this way: "Okay, then his interrogator [redacted] from the FBI asked him to speculate who I was as a person. He said I think he is an operative of Usama bin Laden and without him I would have never been involved in September 11th. That was a big accusation. The interrogator could have lied because they lie all the time, but that is what they said." ARB transcript, 23–24.

he knows about himself. He was forthcoming and truthful with me. What he told me goes along with what we know about him. He said that he came to your house on advice of a guy named ████████████, whom he met on a train. ████████████ wanted somebody to help him getting to Chechnya."

"That was around Oct 1999," he continued. "He showed up at your house with these two guys," he said, pointing at ██ ████████████ and ████████████. "The other guy," he said, pointing at Atta, "was not able to see you because he had a test. You advised them to travel through Afghanistan instead of Georgia, because their Arab faces would give them away and they probably would have been turned back. Furthermore, you gave them a phone contact in Quetta of a guy named ████ ████████████. These guys traveled shortly after that meeting with you to Afghanistan, met Usama Bin Laden, and swore a pledge to him. Bin Laden assigned them to the attack of September 11, and sent them back to Germany."

He went on. "When I asked ████████████ what he thinks about you, he replied that he believes you to be a senior recruiter for Usama Bin Laden. That's his personal opinion. However, he said that without you, he would never have joined al Qaeda. In fact, I'd say without you September 11 would never have happened. These guys would have gone to Chechnya and died."

████████████ excused himself and left. I was kept the rest of the night with ████████████████████████ ████████████████. I was so scared. The guy made me believe I was the one behind September 11. How could that possibly have happened? I was like, Maybe he's right. And yet anybody who knew the basics about the attack, which were published and updated through time, can easily see what a swiss cheese ███████ was trying to sell me. The guys he mentioned were reportedly trained in 1998, and joined al Qaeda and were assigned to the attack then. How could I possibly have sent them in October 1999 to join al Qaeda, when they not only already were al Qaeda, but had already been assigned to the attack for more than a year?

I was kept up the rest of the night and forced to see pictures of dead body parts which were taken at the site of the Pentagon after the attack. It was a nasty sight. I almost broke down, but I managed to keep myself silent and together.

"See the result of the attack?" ███████ asked.

"I don't think he foresaw what these were going to do," said ███████. They were talking to each other, asking and answering each other. I kept myself as the present-absent. They kept sliding those nasty pictures in front of me the whole night. At the break of dawn, they sent me back to a cell in a new block, ███████. I prayed and tried to sleep, but I was kidding myself. I could not get the human body parts out of my head. My new neighbors, especially ███████ tried to help me.

"Don't worry! Just talk to them and everything is gonna be alright," he encouraged me. Maybe his advice was prudent, and anyway I felt that things were going to get nastier. So I decided to cooperate.

███████ pulled me to interrogation the next day. I was so worn out. I had no sleep last night, nor during the day.*

---

* A 1956 CIA study titled "Communist Control Techniques: An Analysis of the Methods Used by Communist State Police in the Arrest, Interrogation, and Indoctrination of Persons Regarded as 'Enemies of the State'" had this to say about the effects of sleep deprivation and temperature

"I am ready to cooperate unconditionally," I told him. "I don't need any proof whatsoever. You just ask me questions and I'm gonna answer you." And so our relationship seemed to enter a new era.

During his time with me, ██████████ made a couple of trips, one to ██████████████ and one to ████████████, in order to investigate my case and gather evidence against me. In February 2003, while he was on his trip to ██████████ an

---

manipulation as coercive interrogation methods: "The officer in charge has other simple and highly effective ways of applying pressure. Two of the most effective of these are fatigue and lack of sleep. The constant light in the cell and the necessity of maintaining a rigid position in bed compound the effects of anxiety and nightmares in producing sleep disturbances. If these are not enough, it is easy to have the guards awaken the prisoners at intervals. This is especially effective if the prisoner is always awakened as soon as he drops off to sleep. The guards can also shorten the hours available for sleep, or deny sleep altogether. Continued loss of sleep produces clouding of consciousness and a loss of alertness, both of which impair the victim's ability to sustain isolation. It also produces profound fatigue.

"Another simple and effective type of pressure is that of maintaining the temperature of the cell at a level which is either too hot or too cold for comfort. Continuous heat, at a level at which constant sweating is necessary in order to maintain body temperature, is enervating and fatigue producing. Sustained cold is uncomfortable and poorly tolerated. . . .

"The Communists do not look upon these methods as 'torture.' Undoubtedly, they use the methods which they do in order to conform, in a typical legalistic manner to overt Communist principles which demand that 'no force or torture be used in extracting information from prisoners.' But these methods do, of course, constitute torture and physical coercion. All of them lead to serious disturbances of many bodily processes."

Sleep deprivation has been used specifically in the service of conditioning prisoners to make false confessions. A study by the U.S. Air Force sociologist Albert Biderman of the means by which North Korean interrogators were able to coerce captured U.S. airmen into falsely confessing to war crimes found that sleep deprivation, as a form of induced debilitation, "weakens mental and physical ability to resist." See http://www.theblackvault.com/documents /mindcontrol/comcont.pdf; and http://www2.gwu.edu/~nsarchiv/torturing democracy/documents/19570900.pdf.

agent from the ███████████████████████████████ pulled me to interrogation.

"My name is ████████████, from ████████. I came here to ask you some questions about your time in ██████████," said ████████████ while flashing his badge. He was accompanied with one female and one male who were just taking notes.*

"Welcome! I'm glad that you have come because I want to clarify some reports you produced about me which are very inaccurate." I continued, "Especially since my case with the U.S. is spinning around my time in ████████████, and every time I argue with the Americans they refer to you. Now I want you guys to sit with the Americans and answer one question: Why are you arresting me? What crime have I done?"

"You have done nothing," ████████████ said.

"So I don't belong here, do I?"

"We didn't arrest you, the U.S. did."

"That's correct, but the U.S. claims that you pitted them on me."

"We just have some questions about some bad people, and we need your help."

"I'm not helping you unless you tell the Americans in front of me that one or the other of you lied."

The agents went out and brought ████████████ in, who was probably watching the session through the ████████████ ████████████.

"You are not honest, since you refuse to answer the ██████

---

* These might be agents of the Canadian Security Intelligence Service (CSIS). The *Toronto Star* has reported that CSIS agents interviewed detainees with ties to Canada in Guantánamo, including MOS, in February 2003. See Michelle Shephard, "CSIS Grilled Trio in Guantánamo," http://www.thestar.com/news/canada/2008/07/27/csis_grilled_trio_in_cuba.html.

questions. This is your opportunity to get help from them," ▆▆▆▆▆▆ said.

"▆▆▆▆▆▆, I know this game better than you do. Stop trying to talk nonsense to me," I said. "Look, you keep telling me the ▆▆▆▆▆▆ say such and such. Now it's you guys' opportunity to face me with my charges," I said.

"We don't accuse you of any crime," said ▆▆▆▆▆▆.

"Then release me!"

"That's not in my hands." ▆▆▆▆▆▆ tried to convince me but there was no convincing me. I was sent back to my cell and taken again the next day, but I just sat there like a stone. I didn't waste a word because I had told them clearly the conditions of my cooperation. The ▆▆▆▆▆▆ also interrogated a teenager ▆▆▆▆▆▆ called ▆▆▆▆▆▆ ▆▆▆▆▆▆ and made the Army take all his belongings. We detainees felt bad for him: he was just too young for this whole campaign.*

When ▆▆▆▆▆▆ came back, he was pissed off because the ▆▆▆▆▆▆ had ignored him and were exposing me to whomever they wanted. Now I knew the ▆▆▆▆▆▆ had no control over my

---

* The teenager is very likely Omar Khadr. In 2010 the Supreme Court of Canada found that Khadr's interrogations by Canadian Security Intelligence Service (CSIS) and the Foreign Intelligence Division of the Department of Foreign Affairs and International Trade (DFAIT) agents in Guantánamo in February and September 2003 and March 2004 violated the Canadian Charter of Rights and Freedoms. The Supreme Court held, "The deprivation of [Khadr]'s right to liberty and security of the person is not in accordance with the principles of fundamental justice. The interrogation of a youth detained without access to counsel, to elicit statements about serious criminal charges while knowing that the youth had been subjected to sleep deprivation and while knowing that the fruits of the interrogations would be shared with the prosecutors, offends the most basic Canadian standards about the treatment of detained youth suspects." The Supreme Court's opinion is available at http://scc-csc.lexum.com/decisia-scc-csc /scc-csc/scc-csc/en/item/7842/index.do.

fate; they didn't have the ability to deal with me, and henceforth I could not really trust them. I don't like to deal with somebody who cannot keep his word. I knew then for a fact that the ████████ was nothing but a step, and the real interrogation was going to be led by ████████. If you look at the situation, it makes sense: most of the detainees were captured by ████████ in a military operation, and they wanted to maintain the upper hand. ████████ are only guests in GTMO, no more, no less; the facility is run by ████████████████ ████████████████.

It happened again. When ████████ went to ████████ in May 2003, the ████████ reserved me for interrogation, and they were no luckier than their fellow citizens from ████████; ████ was completely overawed by his colleagues from the ████████ command.

████████ came back from ████████. "I was ordered to quit your case and go back to the U.S. My boss believes that I'm only wasting my time. The MI will take your case," ████████ told me. I wasn't happy that ████████ was leaving, but I wasn't really that upset. ████████ was the guy who understood the most about my case, but he had neither power nor people who backed him up.

The next day the team organized a pretty lunch party. They bought good food as a good-bye. "You should know that your next sessions will not be as friendly as these have been," ████████ said, smiling wryly. "You will not be brought food or drinks anymore." I understood the hint as rough treatment, but I still never thought that I was going to be tortured. Furthermore, I believed that ████████ and his associate ████████ would inform the proper authorities to stop a crime if they knew one was going to happen.

"I wish you good luck, and all I can tell you is to tell the truth," ▨▨▨▨▨▨▨ said. We hugged, and bid each other good-bye.*

When I entered the room a desk was prepared with several chairs on the other side of the table. As soon as the guards locked me up to the floor ▨▨▨▨▨▨▨▨▨▨▨▨▨

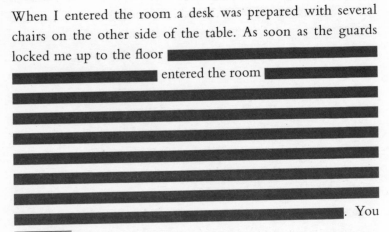 entered the room ▨▨▨▨▨▨▨▨▨▨▨▨▨. You

---

* MOS told the Administrative Review Board that his last interview with FBI interrogators took place on May 22, 2003; the DOJ IG report confirms that "in late May 2003 the FBI agents who were involved with Slahi left GTMO, and the military assumed control over Slahi's interrogation." ARB transcript, 25; DOJ IG, 122.

A few days after the military took over MOS's interrogation, an FBI agent circulated a report documenting FBI concerns about the military's interrogation methods in Guantánamo. According to the DOJ IG report, a month later, on July 1, 2003, the FBI's assistant general counsel, Spike Bowman, sent an e-mail to senior FBI officials, "alerting them that the military had been using techniques of 'aggressive interrogation,' including 'physically striking the detainees, stripping them and pouring cold water on them and leaving them exposed (one got hypothermia) and similar measures.' Bowman opined that: 'Beyond any doubt, what they are doing (and I don't know the extent of it) would be unlawful were these Enemy Prisoners of War (EPW). That they are not so designated cannot be license to do something that you cannot do to an EPW or criminal prisoner.' Bowman expressed concern that the FBI would be 'tarred by the same brush' and sought input on whether the FBI should refer the matter to the DOD Inspector General, stating that '[w]ere I still on active duty, there is no question in my mind that it would be a duty to do so.'" ARB transcript, 25; DOJ IG, 122, 121.

could tell they had a head start I didn't. ▆▆▆▆▆▆▆▆

▆▆▆▆▆▆▆▆ brought heavy binders with them, and were talking to each other.*

"When is the guy supposed to come?"

"Nine o'clock." Against interrogation customs, ▆▆▆▆▆▆▆

▆▆▆▆▆▆▆▆▆▆▆▆▆▆▆▆▆▆▆▆▆▆▆▆▆▆▆▆▆▆▆▆▆▆

▆▆▆▆. It was a technique used to scare and irritate the detainee.

The door opened. "I am sorry, I was thinking diplomatic time," the new arrival said. "You know, those of us from ▆▆▆▆▆▆▆▆▆ are on another time." The ▆▆▆▆▆▆▆ looking gentleman was dying to impress. I wasn't sure how much he succeeded. He was a ▆▆▆▆▆▆▆▆▆▆ ▆▆▆▆▆▆▆▆▆. He even brought his McDonald's with him, but offered nothing to anybody.

"I just arrived from Washington," he commenced. "Do you know how important you are to the U.S. government?"

"I know how important I am to my dear mom, but I'm not sure when it comes to the U.S. government." ▆▆▆▆▆▆▆ couldn't help smiling, although ▆▆▆▆ tried hard to keep ▆▆▆▆ frown. I was supposed to be shown harshness.

"Are you ready to work with us? Otherwise your situation is gonna be very bad," the man continued.

"You know that I know that you know that I have done

---

* MOS described this new DOD team at his ARB hearing, saying it was led by "a female interrogator" who was "a very beautiful lady and decent lady" whom he identified, apparently mistakenly, as an FBI agent. In fact, she may merely have been posing as an FBI agent. The DOJ Inspector General found that "the person who identified herself as 'Samantha' was actually an Army Sergeant." According to the IG, "On several occasions in early June 2003 an Army Sergeant on the DIA Special Projects Team at GTMO identified herself to Slahi as FBI SSA 'Samantha Martin' in an effort to persuade Slahi to cooperate with interrogators." At his ARB hearing, MOS said the team included "another weird guy, I think he was CIA or something but he was very young." ARB transcript, 25; DOJ IG, 296, 125.

nothing," I said. "You're holding me because your country is strong enough to be unjust. And it's not the first time you have kidnapped Africans and enslaved them."

"African tribes sold their people to us," he replied.

"I wouldn't defend slavery, if I were in your shoes." I said. I could tell ███████████████ was the one with the most power, even though the government let other agencies try their chances with detainees. It's very much like a dead camel in the desert, when all kinds of bugs start to eat it.

"If you don't cooperate with us we're gonna send you to a tribunal and you're gonna spend the rest of your life in prison," ████ said.

"Just do it!"

"You must admit to what you have done," ██████████████ said, gesturing to a big binder in front of ████.

"What have I done?"

"You know what you've done."

"You know what, I am not impressed, but if you have questions I can answer you," I said.

"I have been working along with ██████████████ ██████████████████ on your case. ████████████████ are gone. But I'm still here to give you an opportunity."

"Keep the opportunity for yourself, I need none." The purpose of this session was to scare the hell out of me, but it takes more than that to scare me. The ████████████████ disappeared for good, and I never saw him again; ████████████████ ████████████████ kept interrogating me for some time, but there was nothing new. Both ██████████████ were using dead-traditional methods and techniques I probably mastered better than they had.

"What is the name of your current wife?" ████████████ favorite question. When I arrived in Cuba on August ████, 2002

I was so hurt physically and mentally that I literally forgot the name of my wife and provided a wrong one. ▮▮▮▮▮▮▮▮ wanted to prove that I am a liar.

"Look, you won't provide us information we don't already know. But if you keep denying and lying, we'll assume the worst," said ▮▮▮▮▮▮▮▮. "I have interrogated some other detainees and found them innocent. I really have a problem sleeping in a comfortable room while they suffer in the block. But you're different. You're unique. There's nothing really incriminating, but there are a lot of things that make it impossible not to be involved."

"And what is the straw that broke the camel's back?"

"I don't know!" ▮▮▮▮▮▮▮ answered. ▮▮▮ was a respectable ▮▮▮▮ and I very much respected ▮▮▮ honesty. ▮▮▮ was appointed to torture me but ▮▮▮ ultimately failed, which led to ▮▮ separation from my case. To me ▮▮▮▮▮ ▮▮▮▮▮ was an evil person. ▮▮▮ always laughed sardonically.

"You're very rude," ▮▮ once said.

"So are you!" I replied. Our sessions were not fruitful. Both ▮▮▮▮▮▮▮▮▮▮▮▮▮▮▮▮▮▮▮ wanted to reach a breakthrough, but there was no breakthrough to be reached. Both wanted me to admit to being part of the Millennium Plot, which I wasn't. The only possible way to make me admit to something I haven't done is to torture me beyond my limit of pain.

"You're saying that I am lying about that? Well guess what, I have no reason not to keep lying. You don't seem any more impressive than the hundred interrogators I have had lately," I said. ▮▮▮▮▮▮▮ was playing the smart interrogator–bad guy.

"You're funny, you know that?"

"Whatever that means!"

"We're here to give you an opportunity. I've been in the

block for a while, and I am leaving soon, so if you don't cooperate..." ▇▇▇▇ continued.

"Bon Voyage!" I said. I felt good that ▇▇▇▇ was leaving because I didn't like ▇▇.

"You speak with a French accent."

"Oh, God, I thought I speak like Shakespeare," I said wryly.

"No you speak pretty well, I only mean the accent." ▇▇▇▇ ▇▇▇▇▇▇ was a polite and honest person. "Look, we have so many reports linking you to all kinds of stuff. There is nothing incriminating, really. But there are too many little things. We will not ignore anything and just release you."

"I'm not interested in your mercy. I only want to be released if my case is completely cleared. I really am tired of being released and captured in an endless Catch-22."

"You need your freedom, and we need information. You give us what we need and in return, you get what you need," ▇▇▇▇▇▇ said. The three of us argued this way for days without any success.

And then the guy I call "I-AM-THE-MAN" came into play. It was around noon when ▇▇▇▇▇▇▇▇ joined ▇▇▇ ▇▇▇▇▇▇ while they were interrogating me. ▇▇▇▇▇ ▇▇▇▇▇▇▇▇ said, gesturing to ▇▇▇▇ ▇▇.

"This ▇▇▇▇ is working for me. He is going to be seeing you often, among others who are working for me. But you're gonna see me also." ▇▇▇▇▇▇▇ sat there like a stone; he didn't greet me or anything. He was writing his notes and hardly looked at me, while the other ▇▇▇▇▇ were asking questions. "Don't make jokes, just answer ▇▇ questions," he said at one point. I was like, Oops. ▇▇▇▇▇▇▇ ▇▇▇▇▇▇▇▇▇▇▇▇▇▇▇▇▇▇▇▇▇▇ was chosen with some others to do the dirty work. He had experience in MI; he had interrogated Iraqis who were captured during operation Desert Storm. He speaks ████████████████████ ████████████████████████████. All he was able to hear was his own voice. I was always like, Is this guy listening to what I am saying? Or let's just say his ears were programmed to what he wanted to hear.*

"I'm an asshole," he said once. "That is the way people know me, and I have no problem with it."

For the next month I had to deal with ████████████ and his small gang. "We are not ██████████; we don't let lying detainees go unpunished. Just maybe not physical torture," he said. I had been witnessing for the last months how detainees were consistently being tortured under the orders of ████ ██████████████████.† ████████████████ was taken to interrogation every single night, exposed to loud music and scary pictures, and molested sexually. I would see ████████

---

* At his 2005 ARB hearing, MOS described a member of the military interrogation team who was as an army first sergeant, and said, "I don't hate him but he was a very hateful guy." MOS appears to have given the ARB panel this interrogator's real name. I believe this may be the same interrogator he refers to as "I-AM-THE-MAN" in this scene and also by the nickname Mr. Tough Guy, which appears unredacted on page 222. In all there appear to be four interrogators who play major roles in MOS's Special Projects Team. ARB transcript, 25.

† We do not know whom MOS specifically names here. It is a matter of record, however, that military interrogators in Guantánamo were under the command of the Joint Task Force Guantánamo (JTF-GTMO), which was led at this time by General Geoffrey Miller. Their interrogation methods were sanctioned first by the "Counter Resistance Techniques" memorandum that Defense Secretary Donald Rumsfeld signed on December 22, 2002; then by a March 13, 2003, legal opinion written by John Yoo of the Office of Legal Counsel; and finally by another authorization memo that Rumsfeld signed on April 16, 2003. The Senate Armed Services Committee found that General Miller sought official Pentagon approval for, and Rumsfeld personally signed off on, MOS's "Special Interrogation Plan." SASC, 135–38.

███ when the guards took him in the evening and brought him back in the morning. He was forbidden to pray during his interrogation. I remember asking the brothers what to do in that case. "You just pray in your heart since it's not your fault," said the Algerian Sheikh in the block. I profited from this fatwa since I would be exposed to the same situation for about a year. ██████████████ was not spared the cold room. ██ ████████████████ suffered the same; moreover his interrogator smashed the Koran against the floor to break him, and had the guards push his face down against the rough floor. ██████████████████ also suffered sexual molestation. I saw him taken back and forth almost every night as well. Not to speak of the poor young Yemenis and Saudis who were grossly tortured the same way.* But since I'm speaking in this book about my own experience, which reflects an example of the evil practices that took place in the name of the War Against Terrorism, I don't need to talk about every single case I witnessed. Maybe on another occasion, if God so wills.

When ████████████████ informed me about the intentions of his team, I was terrified. My mouth dried up, I started to sweat, my heart started to pound (a couple weeks later I developed hypertension) and I started to get nausea, a headache, a stomach-ache. I dropped into my chair. I knew that ████████████████ was not kidding, and I also knew that he

---

* The Schmidt-Furlow report, the DOJ IG report, the Senate Armed Services Committee report, and several other sources all document the sexual humiliation and sexual assault of Guantánamo prisoners, often carried out by female military interrogators. After the release of the Schmidt-Furlow report in 2005, a *New York Times* op-ed titled "The Women of GTMO" decried the "exploitation and debasement of women in the military," noting that the report "contained page after page of appalling descriptions of the use of women soldiers as sexual foils in interrogations." See http://www.nytimes.com/2005/07/15/opinion/15fri1.html.

was lying about physical pain-free torture. But I held myself together.

"I don't care," I said.

Things went more quickly than I thought. ███████████ ████ sent me back to the block, and I told my fellow detainees about being overtaken by the torture squad.

"You are not a kid. Those torturers are not worth thinking about. Have faith in Allah," said my next ███████████ ███████████. I really must have acted like a child all day long before the guards pried me from the cellblock later that day. You don't know how terrorizing it is for a human being to be threatened with torture. One literally becomes a child.

The Escort team showed up at my cell.

"You got to move."

"Where?"

"Not your problem," said the hateful ██████ guard. But he was not very smart, for he had my destination written on his glove.

"Brothers pray for me, I am being transferred ███████ ███████████████ was reserved by then for the worst detainees in the camp; if one got transferred ██████████████, many signatures must have been provided, maybe even the president of the U.S. The only people I know to have spent some time ███████████████ since it was designed for torture were a Kuwaiti detainee and another fellow detainee from ████████████*

---

* It is now likely around mid-June 2003. MOS told the Administrative Review Board, "Around June 18th, 2003, I was taken from Mike Block and put in India Block for total isolation." Former detainees who were held

When I entered the block, it was completely empty of any signs of life. I was put at the end of the block and the Yemeni fellow was at the beginning, so there was no interaction whatsoever between us. ████████████████████████ was put in the middle but with no contact either. Later on both were transferred somewhere else, and the whole block was reserved for me, only me, ALLAH, ████████████████████, and the guards who worked for them. I was completely exposed to the total mercy ██████████████████████, and there was little mercy.

In the block the recipe started. I was deprived of my comfort items, except for a thin iso-mat and a very thin, small, worn-out blanket. I was deprived of my books, which I owned, I was deprived of my Koran, I was deprived of my soap. I was deprived of my toothpaste and of the roll of toilet paper I had. The cell—better, the box—was cooled down to the point that I was shaking most of the time. I was forbidden from seeing the light of the day; every once in a while they gave me a rec-time at night to keep me from seeing or interacting with any detainees. I was living literally in terror. For the next seventy days I wouldn't know the sweetness of sleeping: interrogation 24 hours a day, three and sometimes four shifts a day. I rarely got a day off. I don't remember sleeping one night quietly. "If you start to cooperate you'll have some sleep and hot meals," ████ ████████████ used to tell me repeatedly.

Within a couple of days of my transfer, █████████████ from the International Committee of the Red Cross showed up

---

for a time in India Block describe windowless solitary confinement cells that were often kept at frigid temperatures. See, e.g., James Meek, "People the Law Forgot," *Guardian*, December 2, 2003. The second detainee being held in India Block when MOS arrives seems to be identified in the next paragraph as Yemeni. ARB transcript, 26; http://www.theguardian.com /world/2003/dec/03/guantanamo.usa1.

at my cell and asked me whether I wanted to write a letter. "Yes!" I said. ███████████████ handed me a paper and I wrote, "Mama, I love you, I just wanted to tell you that I love you!" After that visit I wouldn't see the ICRC for more than a year. They tried to see me, but in vain.*

"You're starting to torture me, but you don't know how much I can take. You might end up killing me," I said when ████████████ and ████████████ pulled me for interrogation.

"We do recommend things, but we don't have the final decision," ████████████ said.

"I just want to warn you: I'm suffering because of the harsh conditions you expose me to. I've already had a sciatic nerve attack. And torture will not make me more cooperative."

"According to my experience, you will cooperate. We are stronger than you, and have more resources," ████████████ ████ said. ████████████ never wanted me to know his name, but he got busted when one of his colleagues mistakenly called him by his name. He doesn't know that I know it, but, well, I do.

████████████ grew worse with every day passing by. He started to lay out my case. He began with the story of ████████████, and me having recruited him for the September 11 attack.†

---

* An October 9, 2003 JTF-GTMO Memorandum for the Record recounts a contentious meeting between a visiting delegation of the International Committee of the Red Cross and Guantánamo commander General Geoffrey Miller. During the meeting, General Miller "informed [ICRC team leader Vincent] Cassard that ISN 760, 558, and 990 were off limits during this visit due to military necessity." MOS is ISN 760. The minutes of the ICRC meeting are available at http://www.washingtonpost .com/wp-srv/nation/documents/GitmoMemo10-09-03.pdf.

† It seems likely from the context here that the interrogator is referring to Ramzi bin al-Shibh.

"Why should he lie to us," ████████████████ said.

"I don't know."

"All you have to say is, 'I don't remember, I don't know, I've done nothing.' You think you're going to impress an American jury with these words? In the eyes of the Americans, you're doomed. Just looking at you in an orange suit, chains, and being Muslim and Arabic is enough to convict you," ████████████████ said.

"That is unjust!"

"We know that you are a criminal."

"What have I done?"

"You tell me, and we'll reduce your sentence to thirty years, after which you'll have a chance to lead a life again. Otherwise you'll never see the light of day. If you don't cooperate, we're going to put you in a hole and wipe your name out of our detainee database." I was so terrified because I knew that even though he couldn't make such a decision on his own, he had the complete back-up of a high government level. He didn't speak from thin air.

"I don't care where you take me, just do it."

In another session when he was talking to me ████████████ ████████████████████████████. "What the fuck do you mean, tea or sugar?"

"I just meant what I said, I was not talking in code."

"Fuck you!" ████████████████ said. I figured I wouldn't degrade myself and lower myself to his level, so I didn't answer him. When I failed to give him the answer he wanted to hear, he made me stand up, with my back bent because my hands were shackled to my feet and waist and locked to the floor. ████████████████ turned the temperature control all the way down, and made sure that the guards maintained me in that situation until he decided otherwise. He used to start a fuss before going to lunch, so he could keep me hurt during his lunch, which took at least two to three hours. ▮▮▮▮▮▮▮▮▮ likes his food; he never missed his lunch. I always wondered how ▮▮▮▮▮▮▮▮▮ could possibly have passed the Army's fitness test. But I realized he was in the Army for a reason: he was good at being inhumane.

"Why are you in jail?" he asked me.

"Because your country is unjust, and my country isn't defending me?"

"Now you're saying that we Americans are just looking for skinny Arabs," he said. ▮▮▮▮▮▮▮ came with him occasionally, and it was kind of a blessing for me. I grew tired of dealing with a lifeless face like ▮▮▮▮▮▮▮▮. When ▮▮▮▮▮▮ came I felt like I was meeting with a human being. ▮▮▮ offered me the appropriate chair for my back pain, while ▮▮▮▮▮▮▮ always insisted on the metal chair or the dirty floor.*

"Do you know that ▮▮▮▮▮▮▮▮▮▮ is dealing such and such?" ▮▮▮ asked me, naming some kind of drug.

"What the hell do you mean?" I asked.

"You know what ▮▮▮ means," ▮▮▮▮▮▮▮▮ ▮▮▮▮▮▮▮ smiled because ▮▮▮ knew that I wasn't lying. I really could have been anything but a drug dealer, and ▮▮▮▮▮▮▮ was dying to link me to any crime no matter what.

"It's a type of narcotic," ▮▮▮▮▮▮▮▮ replied.

---

* MOS seems to be contrasting the approaches of two of his interrogators, possibly the female interrogator identified in government documents by the name of Samantha and the interrogator he called "I-AM-THE-MAN."

"I'm sorry, I am not familiar at all with that circle."

████████████ and his bosses realized that it took more ██████████████████████████████████. And so they decided to bring ██████ interrogator into play. Sometime ██████ ████████████ I was taken ████████████████████ to reservation. The escorting team was confused.

"They said ████████████████████? That's weird!" said one of the guards.

When we entered the building there were no monitoring guards. "Call the D.O.C.!" said the other.* After the radio call, the two guards were ordered to stay with me in the room until my interrogators showed up. "Something's wrong," said the ████████████ one. The escort team didn't realize that I understood what they were talking about; they always assume that detainees don't speak English, which they typically don't. The leadership in the camp always tried to warn the guards; signs like "DO NOT HELP THE ENEMY," and "CARELESS TALK GIVES SECRETS AWAY," were not rare, but the guards talked to each other anyway.

████████████████████████████ was at one point a regular interrogation booth, then a building for torture, then an administrative building. My heart was pounding; I was losing my mind. I hate torture so much. A slim, small ████████████ entered the room followed by Mr. Tough Guy.† ████████ ████████████ was a ████████████████████ ████████████████████████████ ████████████████████. Neither greeted me, nor released my hands ████████████████████.

---

* According to the 2003 Camp Delta Standard Operating Procedures, "DOC" is the acronym for the Detention Operations Center, which directs all movements within Guantánamo.

† "Mr. Tough Guy" appears here unredacted.

"What is this?" ▮▮▮▮▮▮ asked, showing me a plastic bag with a small welding stick inside.*

"It's Indian incense," I replied. That was the first thing that came to my mind. I thought ▮▮▮▮ wanted to give me a treat by burning the incense during the interrogation, which was a good idea.

"No, you're wrong!" ▮▮▮▮ almost stuck it in my face.

"I don't know," I said.

"Now we have found evidence against you; we don't need any more," said ▮▮▮▮. I was like, What the hell is going on, is that part of a bomb they want to pull on me?

"This is a welding stick you were hiding in your bathroom," ▮▮▮▮▮▮▮▮▮▮▮ said.

"How can I possibly have such a thing in my cell, unless you or my guards gave it to me? I have no contact whatsoever with any detainees."

"You're smart, you could have smuggled it," said ▮▮▮▮▮▮.

"How?"

"Take him to the bathroom," ▮▮▮ said. ▮▮▮▮▮▮▮▮▮▮ ▮▮▮▮▮▮▮▮▮▮▮▮▮▮▮▮▮▮▮▮▮▮▮ The guards grabbed me to the bathroom. I was thinking, "Are these people so desperate to pull shit on me, I mean any shit?" In the meantime, a ▮▮▮▮▮ guard was explaining to ▮▮▮▮▮▮▮▮▮▮▮▮ how these welding sticks end up in the cells; I caught his last words when the guards were leading me back from the restroom. "It's common. The contractors keep throwing them in the toilets

---

* It appears from the redacted pronouns here, and becomes clear from unredacted pronouns later in the scene, that this interrogator is female. In the ARB transcript, MOS indicates that a couple of days after the male first sergeant started interrogating him, a female interrogator joined the team. This seems to be the second of the four interrogators who will carry out the "Special Interrogation Plan." She will become a central character. ARB transcript, 25.

after finishing with them." As soon as I entered, everybody suddenly shut up. ██████ put the welding stick back in a yellow envelope. ██████ never introduced herself, nor did I expect ████ to do so. The worse an interrogator's intention is, the more ████████ covers his or ████ identity. But those people get busted the most, and so did ████████, when one of her colleagues mistakenly called ████████ by her name.

"How does your new situation look?" ████████ asked me.

"I'm just doing great!" I answered. I was really suffering, but I didn't want to give them the satisfaction of having reached their evil goal.

"I think he's too comfortable," ████████████ said.

"Get off the chair!" ████████ said, pulling the chair from beneath me. "I'd rather have a dirty farmer sitting on the chair than a smart ass like you," ████ continued, when my whole body dropped on the dirty floor. ██████████████████ ████████████████ killing me. Since June 20th I never got relief from them. ████████████████ obviously was getting tired of dealing with me, so his boss offered him fresh blood, manifesting in the person of ████████████████████████ spread the pictures of some September 11 suspects in front of me, namely ████████████████████████████████████ ████████████████████████.

"Look at these motherfuckers," said ████████.

"OK, now tell us what you know about those motherfuckers!" ██████ said.

"I swear to God, I will not tell you one word, no matter what."

"Stand up! *Guards!* If you don't stand up, it'll be ugly," ████████ said. And before the torture squad entered the room I stood up, with my back bent because ██████████████ ████████████████████████████ didn't allow me to stand up straight.* I had to suffer every-inch-of-my-body pain the rest of the day. I dealt with the pain silently; I kept praying until my assailants got tired and sent me back to my cell at the end of the day, after exhausting their resources of humiliations for that day. I didn't say a single word, as if I had not been there. You, Dear Reader, said more words to them than I did.

"If you want to go to the bathroom, ask politely to use the restroom, say 'Please, may I?'" Otherwise, do it in your pants," ▮▮▮▮▮▮ said.

Before lunch ▮▮▮▮▮▮▮▮▮▮▮▮▮▮ dedicated the time to speaking ill about my family, and describing my wife with the worst adjective you can imagine. For the sake of my family, I dismiss their degrading quotations. The whole time ▮▮▮▮▮ ▮▮▮▮▮▮▮▮▮▮▮▮▮ offered me just water and a cold meal; "You are not entitled to a warm meal unless you cooperate," ▮▮▮▮▮▮ said once. Whenever they started to torture me I refused to drink or eat. ▮▮▮▮▮▮ brought her lunch from outside to frustrate me.

"Yummy, ham is tasty," ▮▮▮▮ said, eating ▮▮▮ meal.

That afternoon was dedicated to sexual molestation. ▮▮▮▮▮
▮▮▮
▮▮▮
▮▮▮▮▮ blouse and was whispering in my ear, "You know how good I am in bed," and "American men like me to whisper in their ears," ▮▮▮▮▮▮▮▮▮▮▮▮▮▮▮▮▮▮▮▮▮▮▮▮▮▮▮▮▮▮
▮▮▮
▮▮▮

---

* Very likely because of shackling. Just a few pages before, MOS described how the interrogator "made me stand up, with my back bent because my hands were shackled to my feet and waist and locked to the floor." The Senate Armed Services Committee found that shackling MOS to the floor was prescribed in his "Special Interrogation Plan." SASC, 137.

███████████████████████████ "I have a great body." Every once in a while ████████ offered me the other side of the coin. "If you start to cooperate, I'm gonna stop harassing you. Otherwise I'll be doing the same with you and worse every day. I am ██████████████████████████ and that's why my government designated me to this job. I've always been successful. Having sex with somebody is not considered torture."*

████████ was leading the monologue █████████████ ██████████. Every now and then the ████████████ entered and tried to make me speak, "You cannot defeat us: we have too many people, and we'll keep humiliating you with American ██████████."

"I have a █████████████████████ friend I'm gonna bring tomorrow to help me," ███ said. "At least ██████████ cooperate," said ██████████ wryly. ██████████ didn't undress me, but ███ was touching my private parts with ███ body.

In the late afternoon, another torture squad started with another poor detainee. I could hear loud music playing. "Do you want me to send you to that team, or are you gonna cooperate?" ██████████ asked. I didn't answer. They guards used to call ██████████████████████████████████ because most of the torture took place in those buildings, and at night, when darkness started to cover the sorry camp.†

---

* This incident is well documented in the Schmidt-Furlow report, the DOJ IG's report, and elsewhere. Lt. Gen. Randall Schmidt and Lt. Gen. John Furlow, *Army Regulation 15-6: Final Report, Investigation into FBI Allegations of Detainee Abuse at Guantanamo Bay, Cuba Detention Facility* (hereinafter cited as Schmidt-Furlow). Schmidt-Furlow, 22–23; DOJ IG, 124. The Schmidt-Furlow Report is available at www.defense.gov/news/jul2005/d20050714 report.pdf.

† This might be "the Night Club." Elsewhere in the manuscript, MOS refers to a detainee who was "a member of the Night Club" and a guard who was "one of the Night Club attendants." MOS manuscript, 293.

███████████████████████ sent me back to my cell, warning me, "Today is just the beginning, what's coming is worse."

But in order ████████████████████████████ to know how much torture a detainee can take, they need medical assistance. I was sent to a doctor, an officer in the Navy. I would describe him as a decent and humane person.*

"████████████████████████████. I don't examine people with that shit on them," he said to the escorting ████████.

"The gentleman has a pretty serious case of sciatic nerve," he said.

"I cannot take the conditions I am in anymore," I told him. "I am being stopped from taking my pain medication and my Ensure, which were necessary to maintain my head above water," I said. The interrogators would organize the sessions so that they would cover the time when you are supposed to take your medication. I had two prescriptions, tabs for the sciatic nerve back pain and Ensure to compensate the loss of weight I had been suffering since my arrest. I usually got my meds between 4 and 5 p.m., and so the interrogators made sure that I was with them and missed my medication. But look at it, what sense does it make, if the interrogators work on hurting my back and then give me back pain medication, or to give me a bad diet and want me to gain weight?

---

* Court papers filed in MOS's habeas appeal reference records that may be from this exam: "The medical records document increased low back pain 'for the past 5 days while in isolation and under more intense interrogation'" and note that the pain medication prescribed for him could not be administered throughout July 2003 because he was at the "reservation." The June 9, 2010, Brief for Appellee is available at https://www.aclu.org/sites/default/files/assets /brief_for_appellee_-_july_8_2010.pdf.

"I don't have much power. I can write a recommendation, but it's the decision of other people. Your case is very serious!" he told me. I left the clinic with some hope, but my situation only worsened.

"Look, the doctor said I've developed high blood pressure. That's serious; you know that I was a hypotensive person before," I said the next time ████████ called me to interrogation

"You're alright, we spoke with the doctor," the interrogators replied. I knew then that my recipe was going to continue.

The torture was growing day by day. The guards on the block actively participated in the process. The ███████████████ tell them what to do with the detainees when they came back to the block. I had guards banging on my cell to prevent me from sleeping. They cursed me for no reason. They repeatedly woke me, unless my interrogators decided to give me a break. I never complained to my interrogators about the issue because I knew they planned everything with the guards.

As promised, ██████████ pulled me early in the day. Lonely in my cell, I was terrified when I heard the guards carrying the heavy chains and shouting at my door "Reservation!" My heart started to pound heavily because I always expected the worst. But the fact that I wasn't allowed to see the light made me "enjoy" the short trip between my freakin' cold cell and the interrogation room. It was just a blessing when the warm GTMO sun hit me. I felt life sneaking back into every inch of my body. I would always get this fake happiness, though only for a very short time. It's like taking narcotics.

"How you been?" said one of the Puerto Rican escorting guards in his weak English.

"I'm OK, thanks, and you?"

"No worry, you gonna back to your family," he said. When he said that I couldn't help breaking in ▮▮▮▮▮▮.* Lately, I'd become so vulnerable. What was wrong with me? Just one soothing word in this ocean of agony was enough to make me cry. ▮▮▮▮▮▮▮▮▮▮▮▮▮▮▮▮▮▮ we had a complete Puerto Rican division.† They were different than other Americans; they were not as vigilant and unfriendly. Sometimes, they took detainees to shower ▮▮▮▮▮▮▮▮▮▮▮▮▮▮▮▮. Everybody liked them. But they got in trouble with those responsible for the camps because of their friendly and humane approach to detainees. I can't objectively speak about the people from Puerto Rico because I haven't met enough; however, if you ask me, Have you ever seen a bad Puerto Rican guy? My answer would be no. But if you ask, Is there one? I just don't know. It's the same way with the Sudanese people.

"▮▮▮▮▮▮▮▮▮▮▮▮▮▮▮▮▮▮ and give him no chair," said the D.O.C. worker on the radio when the escort team dropped me in ▮▮▮▮▮▮▮▮▮▮▮▮▮▮▮▮▮▮ ▮▮▮▮▮▮▮▮▮▮▮▮▮▮▮▮▮▮ entered the room. They brought a picture of an American black man named ▮▮▮▮▮▮▮▮▮▮▮▮▮."We're gonna talk today about ▮▮▮▮▮▮▮▮▮▮▮▮▮▮▮▮ after bribing me with a weathered metal chair.‡

"I have told you what I know about ▮▮▮▮▮▮▮▮▮▮▮."

"No, that's bullshit. Are you gonna tell us more?"

---

* Is seems possible, if incredible, that the U.S. government may have here redacted the word "tears."

† MOS may be referring here to the particular cellblock in Camp Delta where he encountered the Puerto Rican division.

‡ It soon becomes clear that the lead interrogator is accompanied by another female interrogator, as his interrogator had threatened in the previous session.

"No, I have no more to tell."

The new ████████ pulled the metal chair away and left me on the floor. "Now, tell us about ███████████████ ████████!"

"No, that's passé," I said.

"Yes, you're right. So if it is passé, talk about it, it won't hurt," the new ████████ said.

"No."

"Then today, we're gonna teach you about great American sex. Get up!" said ████████. I stood up in the same painful position as I had every day for about seventy days.* I would rather follow the orders and reduce the pain that would be caused when the guards come to play; the guards used every contact opportunity to beat the hell out of the detainee. "Detainee tried to resist," was the "Gospel truth" they came up with, and guess who was going to be believed? "You're very smart, because if you don't stand up it's gonna be ugly," ████████████.

As soon as I stood up, the two ████████ took off their blouses, and started to talk all kind of dirty stuff you can imagine, which I minded less. What hurt me most was them forcing me to take part in a sexual threesome in the most degrading manner. What many ████████ don't realize is that men get hurt the same as women if they're forced to have sex, maybe more due to the traditional position of the man. Both ████████ stuck on me, literally one on the front and the other older ████████ stuck on my back rubbing ████ whole body on mine. At the same time they were talking dirty to me, and playing with my sexual parts. I am saving you here from quoting the disgusting and degrading talk I had to listen to from noon or before until

---

* That position is likely a forced stoop precipitated by the shackling of his wrists to the floor; see footnotes on pp. 225 and 227.

10 p.m. when they turned me over to ███████, the new character you'll soon meet.

To be fair and honest, the ███████ didn't deprive me from my clothes at any time; everything happened with my uniform on. The senior ███████████████ was watching everything ██.* I kept praying all the time.

"Stop the fuck praying! You're having sex with American ███████ and you're praying? What a hypocrite you are!" said ███████████████ angrily, entering the room. I refused to stop speaking my prayers, and after that, I was forbidden to perform my ritual prayers for about one year to come. I also was forbidden to fast during the sacred month of Ramadan October 2003, and fed by force. During this session I also refused to eat or to drink, although they offered me water every once in a while. "We must give you food and water; if you don't eat it's fine." They also offered me the nastiest MRE they had in the camp. We detainees knew that ███████████████ gathered Intels about what food a detainee likes or dislikes, when he prays, and many other things that are just ridiculous.

I was just wishing to pass out so I didn't have to suffer, and that was really the main reason for my hunger strike; I knew people like these don't get impressed by hunger strikes. Of course they didn't want me to die, but they understand there are many steps before one dies. "You're not gonna die, we're gonna feed you up your ass," said ███████████████.

I have never felt as violated in myself as I had since the DoD

---

* Like all interrogations, this session would likely be observed from a monitoring room. The 2003 Camp Delta Standard Operating Procedures mandated that during all interrogations "a JIIF monitor will be located either in a monitor room that is equipped with two-way mirrors and CCTV or in a CCTV only room." SOP, 14.2.

Team started to torture me to get me admit to things I haven't done. You, Dear Reader, could never understand the extent of the physical, and much more the psychological, pain people in my situation suffered, no matter how hard you try to put yourself in another's shoes. Had I done what they accused me of, I would have relieved myself on day one. But the problem is that you cannot just admit to something you haven't done; you need to deliver the details, which you can't when you hadn't done anything. It's not just, "Yes, I did!" No, it doesn't work that way: you have to make up a complete story that makes sense to the dumbest dummies. One of the hardest things to do is to tell an untruthful story and maintain it, and that is exactly where I was stuck. Of course I didn't want to involve myself in devastating crimes I hadn't done — especially under the present circumstances, where the U.S. government was jumping on every Muslim and trying to pin any crime on him.

"We are going to do this with you every single day, day in, day out, unless you speak about ▆▆▆▆▆ and admit to your crimes," said ▆▆▆▆▆.

"You have to provide us a smoking gun about another friend of yours. Something like that would really help you," ▆▆▆▆▆ said in a later session. "Why should you take all of this, if you can stop it?"

I decided to remain silent during torture and to speak whenever they relieved me. I realized that even asking my interrogators politely to use the bathroom, which was a dead basic right of mine, I gave my interrogators some kind of control they don't deserve. I knew it was not just about asking for bathroom: it was more about humiliating me and getting me to tell them what they wanted to hear. Ultimately an interrogator is interested in gathering Intels, and typically the end justifies the means in that regard. And that was another reason why I refused both to drink and to eat: so I didn't have to use the rest room. And it worked.

The extravagance of the moment gave me more strength. My statement was that I was going to fight to the last drop of my blood.

"We're stronger than you, we have more people, we have more resources, and we're going to defeat you. But if you start to cooperate with us, you'll start to have some sleep and hot meals," said ██████████ numerous times. "You cooperate not, you eat not, you get remedy not."

Humiliation, sexual harassment, fear, and starvation was the order of the day until around 10 p.m. Interrogators made sure that I had no clue about the time, but nobody is perfect; their watches always revealed it. I would be using this mistake later, when they put me in dark isolation.

"I'm gonna send you to your cell now, and tomorrow you'll experience even worse," said ████████ after consulting with ██████ colleagues. I was happy to be relieved; I just wanted to have a break and be left alone. I was so worn out, and only God knew how I looked. But ████████ lied to me; ██████ just organized a psychological trick to hurt me more. I was far from being relieved. The D.O.C., which was fully cooperating when it came to torture, sent another escort team. As soon as I reached the doorstep ████████████████████████████████ I fell face down, my legs refused to carry me, and every inch in my body was conspiring against me. The guards failed to make me stand up, so they had to drag me on the tips of my toes.

"Bring the motherfucker back!" shouted ████████, a celebrity among the torture squad.* He was about ████████████████,

---

* The third of the four interrogators who will carry out MOS's "Special Interrogation Plan," this masked interrogator is named "Mr. X" in the Schmidt-Furlow, DOJ IG, and Senate Armed Services Committee reports. (*cont'd*)

about six feet tall, athletically built, and ████████████
███
███
█████████████████████████████. ████████ was aware that
he was committing heavy war crimes, and so he was ordered
by his bosses to cover himself. But if there is any kind of basic
justice, he will get busted through his bosses; we know their
names and their ranks.

When I got to know ████████ more and heard him speaking
I wondered, How could a man as smart as he was possibly accept
such a degrading job, which surely is going to haunt him the
rest of his life? For the sake of fairness and honesty, I must say
that ████████ spoke convincingly to me, although he had no
information and was completely misled. Maybe he had few
choices, because many people in the Army come from poor
families, and that's why the Army sometimes gives them the
dirtiest job. I mean theoretically ████████ could have refused to
commit crimes of war, and he might even get away with it.
Later on I discussed with some of my guards why they executed
the order to stop me from praying, since it's an unlawful order.
"I could have refused, but my boss would have given me a shitty
job or transferred me to a bad place. I know I can go to hell for
what I have done to you," one of them told me. History repeats
itself: during World War II, German soldiers were not excused
when they argued that they received orders.

"You've been giving ██████████████████ a hard time," continued ████████, dragging me into a dark room with the help
of the guards. He dropped me on the dirty floor. The room was

---

At his 2005 Administrative Review Board hearing, with characteristic wit,
MOS said this interrogator was always covered "like in Saudi Arabia, how
the women are covered," with "openings for his eyes" and "O.J. Simpson
gloves on his hands." ARB transcript, 25–26.

as dark as ebony. ███████ started playing a track very loudly — I mean *very* loudly. The song was, "Let the bodies hit the floor." I might never forget that song. At the same time, ███████ turned on some colored blinkers that hurt the eyes. "If you fucking fall asleep, I'm gonna hurt you," he said. I had to listen to the song over and over until next morning. I started praying.*

"Stop the fuck praying," he said loudly. I was by this time both really tired and terrified, and so I decided to pray in my heart. Every once in a while ███████ gave me water. I drank the water because I was only scared of being hurt. I really had no real feeling for time.

To the best of my knowledge, ███████ sent me back to my cell around 5 a.m. in the morning.

"Welcome to hell," said the ████████████████ guard when I stepped inside the block. I didn't answer, and ███████ wasn't worth it. But I was like, "I think you deserve hell more than I do because you're working dutifully to get there!"

When ███████ joined the team, they organized a 24-hour shift regime. The morning shift with ████████████ started between 7 and 9 a.m. and ended between 3 and 4 p.m.; the dayshift with ███████ ran between 4:30 and 10 or 11 p.m.; and the nightshift was with ███████. He always took over when ███████ left; ███████ would literally hand me over to him. This

---

* The Senate Armed Services Committee, which reviewed JTF-GTMO interrogation records, dates what appears to be this interrogation session as July 8, 2003. On that day, the committee found, "Slahi was interrogated by Mr. X and was 'exposed to variable lighting patterns and rock music, to the tune of *Drowning Pool*'s 'Let the Bodies Hit [the] Floor.'" SASC, 139.

went on until August 24, 2003; I rarely got a break or relief from even one of the shifts.*

"Three shifts! Is it not too much for a human being to be interrogated 24 hours a day, day after day?" I asked ▮▮▮▮ ▮▮▮▮▮▮▮▮▮ was the least of many evils, so I just tried to talk to ▮▮▮ as a human being. You might be surprised if I tell you that ▮▮▮ possesses good qualities as a person. As much as I hated what ▮▮▮ was doing, I must be just, fair, and honest.†

"We could put on more personnel and make four shifts. We have more people," ▮▮▮▮▮▮ answered. And that's exactly what happened. The team was reinforced with another ▮▮▮▮ ▮▮▮▮▮▮▮▮▮▮▮▮▮▮▮, and instead of a three-shift team I had to deal with four fresh people during a 24-hour period.

"You fucked up!" said an escorting guard who by accident had to escort me twice in one day from one building to another. "What are you doing here? You've been in reservation already!"

"I get interrogated for 24 hours."

The guard laughed loudly and evilly repeated, "You fucked up!" I just looked at him and smiled.

On day three of the shifts the escorting team showed up at my door in the early morning, as soon as I fell asleep after a rough, 20-hour interrogation. You know, when you just fall asleep and the saliva starts to come out of your mouth?

"Reservation!" shouted one of the guards. My feet barely carried me. "Hurry up!" I quickly washed my face and my mouth. I tried to use every opportunity to keep myself clean,

---

* Based on MOS's descriptions of the interrogation sessions that follow, I believe the shifts may work like this: morning/early afternoon shift with the male first sergeant/"I-AM-THE-MAN"/Mr. Tough Guy interrogator; late afternoon/evening shift with the Special Projects Team's female interrogator; and overnight with the interrogator known as Mr. X.

† This paragraph could refer to the female member of the Special Projects Team; see footnote on p. 240.

although I was deprived from the right to take a shower like other detainees. The team wanted to humiliate me.

"What a smell!" ██████ used to say when he entered the room where he interrogated me.

"Man, you smell like shit!" said one of the guards more than once. I only got the opportunity to shower and change my clothes when his lowness ████████████ couldn't bear my smell anymore; "Take the guy, give him a shower, he smells like shit," he would say. Only then would I get a shower, for months to come.

"Hurry up!" the guards kept saying. ████████████████ ███████████████████████████████. I had a headache, nausea, and heartburn from the sleeplessness of the last several days. My eyes were playing games on me. I hated the place where I was going.

The guards dropped me in ████████████████. Nobody was in the room. I kept dozing off while waiting on ████████████. Oh, my neck really hurt. I badly wanted him to show up, because I hated to sleep like that: at least he would enjoy depriving me of sleeping. ████████████ is one of the laziest people I ever knew. He didn't take time to read reports, and so he always mistook me for other suspects. Most of the time he came late, but he reserved me early anyway, so I couldn't sleep.*

There really was not a lot of news: ████████████ and I facing each other with the same topics, like the movie *Groundhog Day*. But I had grown very nervous now that they were depriving me of the sweetness of sleep.

The order of the day always went as follows. ████████████

---

* Because it encompasses lunch, MOS seems to be describing the routine of his first shift/day shift interrogator.

▆▆ started to read some paper crap he brought with him and asked me questions.

"Why the fuck did you go to Canada?"

"I wanted to find a job and have a nice life."

"Fuck you! Stand up!"

"I'd rather stand up like this until death than talk to your ugly face!" When ▆▆▆▆▆▆ made me stand up, he made sure that the guards maintained his orders while ▆▆▆▆ was stuffing his big stomach during lunch; whenever I tried to change my inconvenient position, the guards surged from nowhere and forced me to stay as straight as I could. Every interrogator I knew missed a meal sometimes, for whatever reason. ▆▆▆▆▆ never missed his meal no matter what.

"If you stop denying what you've done, we'll start to give you hot meals and some sleep. We are stronger than you."

"I don't need what I don't have."

"We're gonna put you in a hole the rest of your life. You're already convicted. You will never see your family."

"It's not in your hands, but if it is, just do it, the sooner the better!"

Sometimes ▆▆▆▆▆▆ went through the propaganda posters of detainees who were supposedly released. "Look at this guy, he's a criminal but he admitted to everything, and now he's able to lead a normal life." I mean, all interrogators lie, but ▆▆▆▆▆▆ lies were more than obvious. Though if another interrogator lies, his appearance changes, but ▆▆▆▆▆ recounts a lie as well as the truth: his face always had the same hateful look.

When the pain became unbearable, I became smooth for negotiation, and he agreed to let me sit on the uncomfortable chair. But he soon got shocked when I didn't give him the answers he wanted to hear.

"I am going to do everything I am allowed to to break you!" ▬▬▬▬▬▬ said angrily. ▬▬▬▬▬▬▬▬ threatened me with all kind of horrible scenarios. "You're gonna spend the rest of your life in jail." "We will wipe you out of the database and put you in a hole where nobody knows about you." "You will never see your family again." My answer was always, "Do what you got to do! I have done nothing!" and as soon as I spit my words ▬▬▬▬▬▬ went wildly crazy, as if he wanted to devour me alive. So I avoided answering him and let him for the most part do the talking. As I say, ▬▬▬▬▬ likes to talk and hates to listen. I sometimes doubted that his ears functioned. He spoke as if he were reading some Gospels.

I was just wondering how he was so sure I was a criminal. "▬▬▬▬▬, what if you are wrong in what you're suspecting me of?" I asked him.

"I would be wasting my time," he answered.

"Fair enough."

"If you provide incriminating information about somebody, say ▬▬▬▬▬▬▬▬▬▬▬▬▬▬, that leads to his conviction, your life would change to a better one." I didn't answer him, because I didn't have what he was looking for. ▬▬▬▬▬▬▬ view of justice was very rough: even if I provided him everything he wanted, he would reduce my sentence from the electric chair to life, and then maybe thirty years in prison. I honestly was not interested in his offer.

During his shift, ▬▬▬▬ would be reporting to his boss during the breaks. I was not sure who his boss was at that point, probably ▬▬▬▬▬▬▬▬▬▬▬▬▬. But I'm sure that the highest authority in his chain of command in GTMO was ▬▬▬▬▬▬▬, and that he was briefed regularly about my case and always gave the orders for what to do next with "that bastard." According to ▬▬▬▬, President Bush

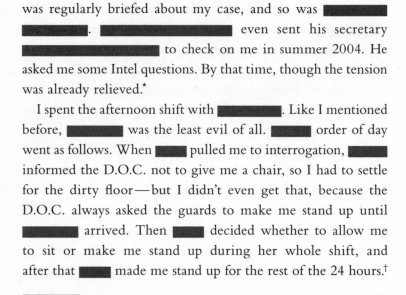

was regularly briefed about my case, and so was ███████

███████. ███████████████ even sent his secretary

███████████████ to check on me in summer 2004. He

asked me some Intel questions. By that time, though the tension

was already relieved.*

I spent the afternoon shift with ███████. Like I mentioned

before, ███████ was the least evil of all. ███████ order of day

went as follows. When ████ pulled me to interrogation, ████

informed the D.O.C. not to give me a chair, so I had to settle

for the dirty floor—but I didn't even get that, because the

D.O.C. always asked the guards to make me stand up until

███████ arrived. Then ████ decided whether to allow me

to sit or make me stand up during her whole shift, and

after that ████ made me stand up for the rest of the 24 hours.†

---

* As these July 2003 sessions were happening, General Miller was submitting Slahi's "Special Interrogation Plan" to SOUTHCOM commander
General James Hill for approval. On July 18, 2003, Hill forwarded the plan
to Secretary of Defense Donald Rumsfeld. The plan was approved by Dep-
uty Secretary of Defense Paul Wolfowitz on July 28, 2003, and signed by
Rumsfeld on August 13, 2003. For a detailed account of the development
and authorization of MOS's "Special Interrogation Plan," see SASC,
135–41.

† This "her" is unredacted, so it seems clear that the afternoon shift is
with the female member of the interrogation team. Described here as "the
least evil" of the evils he was facing, this is likely the same interrogator he
describes as "the least of many evils" a few pages earlier.

When Defense Secretary Rumsfeld issued his original authorization to
use interrogation techniques beyond those included in the Army Field
Manual, including forced standing, he famously appended the note "I stand
for 8–10 hours a day. Why is standing limited to four hours?" But as Albert
Biderman found in his study of coercive interrogation techniques employed
by North Korean interrogators during the Korean War, "Returnees who
underwent long periods of standing and sitting...report no other experience
could be more excruciating." Biderman explained, "Where the individual
is told to stand at attention for long periods an intervening factor is
introduced. The immediate source of pain is not the interrogator but the
victim himself. The contest becomes, in a way, one of the individual against

I started to recite the Koran quietly, for prayer was forbidden. Once ▮▮▮▮▮▮ said, "Why don't you pray? go ahead and pray!" I was like, How friendly! But as soon as I started to pray, ▮▮▮▮ started to make fun of my religion, and so I settled for praying in my heart so I didn't give ▮▮▮▮ the opportunity to commit blasphemy. Making fun of somebody else's religion is one of the most barbaric acts. President Bush described his holy war against the so-called terrorism as a war between the civilized and barbaric world. But his government committed more barbaric acts than the terrorists themselves. I can name tons of war crimes that Bush's government is involved in.

This particular day was one of the roughest days in my interrogation before the day around the end of August that was my "Birthday Party" as ▮▮▮▮▮▮ called it. ▮▮▮▮▮▮ brought someone who was apparently a Marine; he wore a ▮▮▮▮▮▮ ▮▮▮▮▮▮▮▮▮▮▮▮▮▮▮▮▮▮▮▮▮▮▮▮▮▮▮▮▮▮▮▮▮▮▮▮▮▮ ▮▮▮▮▮▮▮▮▮▮▮▮▮▮▮▮▮▮▮▮▮▮▮▮▮▮▮▮▮▮.

▮▮▮▮▮▮ offered me a metal chair. "I told you, I'm gonna bring some people to help me interrogate you," ▮▮▮▮▮▮ said, sitting inches away in front of me. The guest sat almost sticking on my knee. ▮▮▮▮▮▮ started to ask me some questions I don't remember.

"Yes or no?" the guest shouted, loud beyond belief, in a show to scare me, and maybe to impress ▮▮▮▮▮▮, who knows? I found his method very childish and silly.

---

himself. The motivational strength of the individual is likely to exhaust itself in this internal encounter. Bringing the subject to act 'against himself' in this manner has additional advantages for the interrogator. It leads the prisoner to exaggerate the power of the interrogator. As long as the subject remains standing, he is attributing to his captor the power to do something worse to him, but there is actually no showdown of the ability of the interrogator to do so." See http://www2.gwu.edu/~nsarchiv /torturingdemocracy/documents/19570900.pdf.

I looked at him, smiled, and said, "Neither!" The guest threw the chair from beneath me violently. I fell on the chains. Oh, it hurt.

"Stand up, motherfucker," they both shouted, almost synchronous. Then a session of torture and humiliation started. They started to ask me the questions again after they made me stand up, but it was too late, because I told them a million times, "Whenever you start to torture me, I'm not gonna say a single word." And that was always accurate; for the rest of the day, they exclusively talked.

████████ turned the air conditioner all the way down to bring me to freezing. This method had been practiced in the camp at least since August 2002. I had seen people who were exposed to the frozen room day after day; by then, the list was long. The consequences of the cold room are devastating, such as ████████tism, but they show up only at a later age because it takes time until they work their way through the bones. The torture squad was so well trained that they were performing almost perfect crimes, avoiding leaving any obvious evidence. Nothing was left to chance. They hit in predefined places. They practiced horrible methods, the aftermath of which would only manifest later. The interrogators turned the A/C all the way down trying to reach 0°, but obviously air conditioners are not designed to kill, so in the well insulated room the A/C fought its way to 49°F, which, if you are interested in math like me, is 9.4°C—in other words, very, very cold, especially for somebody who had to stay in it more than twelve hours, had no underwear and just a very thin uniform, and who comes from a hot country. Somebody from Saudi Arabia cannot take as much cold as somebody from Sweden; and vice versa, when it comes to hot weather. Interrogators took these factors in consideration and used them effectively.

You may ask, Where were the interrogators after installing the detainee in the frozen room? Actually, it's a good question. First, the interrogators didn't stay in the room; they would just come for the humiliation, degradation, discouragement, or other factor of torture, and after that they left the room and went to the monitoring room next door. Second, interrogators were adequately dressed; for instance ████████ was dressed like somebody entering a meat locker. In spite of that, they didn't stay long with the detainee. Third, there's a big psychological difference when you are exposed to a cold place for purpose of torture, and when you just go there for fun and a challenge. And lastly, the interrogators kept moving in the room, which meant blood circulation, which meant keeping themselves warm while the detainee was ████████████ the whole time to the floor, standing for the most part.* All I could do was move my feet and rub my hands. But the Marine guy stopped me from rubbing my hands by ordering a special chain that shackled my hands on my opposite hips. When I get nervous I always start to rub my hands together and write on my body, and that drove my interrogators crazy.

"What are you writing?" ████████████████ shouted. "Either you tell me or you stop the fuck doing that." But I couldn't stop; it was unintentional. The Marine guy started to throw chairs around, hit me with his forehead, and describe me with all kinds of adjectives I didn't deserve, for no reason.

"You joined the wrong team, boy. You fought for a lost cause," he said, alongside a bunch of trash talk degrading my family, my religion, and myself, not to mention all kinds of threats against my family to pay for "my crimes," which goes against any common sense. I knew that he had no power, but

---

* Again, likely shackled. See footnote on p. 225.

I knew that he was speaking on behalf of the most powerful country in the world, and obviously enjoyed the full support of his government. However, I would rather save you, Dear Reader, from quoting his garbage. The guy was nuts. He asked me about things I have no clue about, and names I never heard.

"I have been in ███████████," he said, "and do you know who was our host? The President! We had a good time in the palace." The Marine guy asked questions and answered them himself.*

When the man failed to impress me with all the talk and humiliation, and with the threat to arrest my family since the ████████████████████ was an obedient servant of the U.S., he started to hurt me more. He brought ice-cold water and soaked me all over my body, with my clothes still on me. It was so awful; I kept shaking like a Parkinson's patient. Technically I wasn't able to talk anymore. The guy was stupid: he was literally executing me but in a slow way. ██████ gestured to him to stop pouring water on me. Another detainee had told me a "good" interrogator suggested he eat in order to reduce the pain, but I refused to eat anything; I couldn't open my mouth anyway.

The guy was very hot when ████████ stopped him because ██████ was afraid of the paperwork that would result in case of my death. So he found another technique, namely he brought a CD player with a booster and started to play some rap music. I didn't really mind the music because it made me forget my pain. Actually, the music was a blessing in disguise; I was trying to make sense of the words. All I understood was that the music

---

* The interrogator may be referring to Mauritania, and to then-president Maaouya Ould Sid'Ahmed Taya. See footnotes on pp. 98 and 100.

was about love. Can you believe it? Love! All I had experienced lately was hatred, or the consequences thereof.

"Listen to that, Motherfucker!" said the guest, while closing the door violently behind him. "You're gonna get the same shit day after day, and guess what? It's getting worse. What you're seeing is only the beginning," said ▆▆▆▆▆. I kept praying and ignoring what they were doing.

"Oh, ALLAH help me . . . . . Oh Allah have mercy on me" ▆▆▆ kept mimicking my prayers, "ALLAH, ALLAH . . . . There is no Allah. He let you down!" I smiled at how ignorant ▆▆▆ was, talking about the Lord like that. But the Lord is very patient, and doesn't need to rush to punishment, because there is no escaping him.

Detainees knew the policy in the camp: if the MI believes that you're hiding crucial information, they torture you in Camp ▆▆▆▆▆▆▆▆▆▆▆▆▆▆, they kidnap you to a secret place and nobody knows what they're doing with you. During my time in ▆▆▆▆ Camp two individuals were kidnapped and disappeared for good, namely ▆▆▆▆ ▆▆▆▆▆▆▆▆▆▆▆▆▆▆▆▆▆▆▆▆ ▆▆. I started to get the feeling that I was going to be kidnapped because I really got stuck with my interrogators, and so I started to gather Intels.

"The camp out there is the worst one," said a young MP.

"They don't get food?" I wondered.

"Something like that," he replied.

Between 10 and 11 p.m., ▆▆▆▆▆ handed me over to ▆▆▆▆▆▆▆ gave orders to the guards to move me to his specially prepared room.* It was freezing cold and full of pictures showing the glories of the U.S.: weapons arsenals,

---

* This seems to be describing a night shift session with Mr. X. The scene is mentioned again in the final chapter.

planes, and pictures of George Bush. "Don't pray! You'll insult my country if you pray during my National anthem. We're the greatest country in the free world, and we have the smartest president in the world," he said. For the whole night I had to listen to the U.S. anthem. I hate anthems anyway. All I can remember was the beginning, "Oh say can you see..." over and over. I was happy that no ice-cold water was poured over me. I tried at the beginning to steal some prayers, but ▓▓▓▓▓ was watching closely by means of ▓▓▓▓▓▓▓▓▓▓▓▓▓▓▓▓▓▓▓▓ ▓▓▓▓. "Stop the fuck praying, you're insulting my country!" I was really tired and worn out, and I was anything but looking for trouble, and so I decided to pray in my heart. I was shaking all night long.

Between 4 and 5 a.m., ▓▓▓▓▓▓ released me, just to be taken a couple of hours later ▓▓▓▓▓▓▓▓▓▓▓▓▓▓ to start the same routine over. But the hardest step is the first step; the hardest days were the first days, and with every day going by I grew stronger. Meanwhile I was the main subject of talk in the camp. Although many other detainees were suffering similar fates, I was "Criminal Number One," and I was being treated that way. Sometimes when I was in the Rec yard, detainees shouted, "Be patient. Remember Allah tests the people he loves the most." Comments like that were my only solace beside my faith in the Lord.

Nothing really interesting changed in my routine: cold room, standing up for hours, interrogators repeating the same threats about me being kidnapped and locked up forever.* ▓▓▓▓▓▓

---

* Military, Department of Justice, and Senate investigators have described in more detail several of these threats. According to a footnote in the Schmidt-Furlow report, "On 17 Jul 03 the masked interrogator told that he had a dream about the subject of the second interrogation dying. Specifically he told the subject of the second special interrogation that in the dream he 'saw four detainees that were chained together at the feet. They dug a

made me write tons of pages about my life, but I never satisfied him. One night he undressed me with the help of ▮▮▮▮ ▮▮▮▮▮▮▮▮ a male guard. Expecting the cold room, I had put shorts on over my pants to reduce the cold that was penetrating through my bones, but he was extremely mad, which led him to make a ▮▮▮▮▮▮▮ guard undress me. I never felt so violated. I stood up all the night in the ice-cold room praying, ignoring all his barking and ordering me to stop praying. I couldn't have cared less about whatever he was going to do.*

---

hole that was six-feet long, six-feet deep, and four-feet wide. Then he observed the detainees throw a plain, pine casket with the detainee's identification number painted in orange lowered into the ground.' The masked interrogator told the detainee that his dream meant that he was never going to leave GTMO unless he started to talk, that he would indeed die here from old age and be buried on 'Christian...sovereign American soil.' On 20 Jul 03 the masked interrogator, 'Mr. X,' told the subject of the second Special Interrogation Plan that his family was 'incarcerated.'"

The report continues, "The MFR dated 02 Aug 03 indicates that the subject of the second special interrogation had a messenger that day there to 'deliver a message to him.' The MFR goes on to state: 'That message was simple: Interrogator's colleagues are sick of hearing the same lies over and over and over and are seriously considering washing their hands of him. Once they do so, he will disappear and never be heard from again. Interrogator assured detainee again to use his imagination to think of the worst possible scenario he could end up in. He told Detainee that beatings and physical pain are not the worst thing in the world. After all, after being beaten for a while, humans tend to disconnect the mind from the body and make it through. However, there are worse things than physical pain. Interrogator assured Detainee that, eventually, he will talk, because everyone does. But until then, he will very soon disappear down a very dark hole. His very existence will become erased. His electronic files will be deleted from the computer, his paper files will be packed up and filed away, and his existence will be forgotten by all. No one will know what happened to him, and eventually, no one will care.'" Schmidt-Furlow, 24–25.

* Context suggests there are two guards, one male and one female, and that the female guard undresses him. An incident in which MOS was "deprived of clothing by a female interrogator" is recorded in the DOJ IG report; the report suggests the date of that session was July 17, 2003. DOJ IG, 124.

███████████████████████████ crawled from behind the scene. ████████ told me a couple of times before ████ ██████████████ visit about a very high level government person who was going to visit me and talk to me about my family. I didn't take the information negatively; I thought he was going to bring me some messages from my family. But I was wrong, it was about hurting my family. █████████████████████████ was escalating the situation with me relentlessly.

██████████████████ came around 11 a.m., escorted by █████ and the new █████████████. He was brief and direct. "My name is █████████████████. I work for ███████████ ██████. My government is desperate to get information out of you. Do you understand?"*

"Yes."

---

* The date, according to the DOJ Inspector General, is now August 2, 2003. The IG reported, "On August 2, 2003, a different military interrogator posing as a Navy Captain from the White House" appeared to MOS. Both the Senate Armed Services Committee report and the DOJ IG report describe the letter he delivered. According to the Senate Armed Services Committee, the letter stated "that his mother had been detained, would be interrogated, and if she were uncooperative she might be transferred to GTMO." The DOJ IG reported that "the letter referred to 'the administrative and logistical difficulties her presence would present in this previously all-male environment,'" and "The interrogator told Slahi that his family was 'in danger if he (760) did not cooperate.'" The DOJ IG and SASC reports and the army's Schmidt-Furlow report all make clear that this interrogator was in fact the chief of MOS's "Special Projects Team," and the Schmidt-Furlow report indicates he presented himself to MOS as "Captain Collins." MOS describes him here as crawling from behind the scene; in his book *The Terror Courts: Rough Justice at Guantanamo Bay* (New Haven: Yale University Press, 2013), Jess Bravin, a reporter for the *Wall Street Journal*, writes that the Special Projects Team chief who carried out this ruse had taken over MOS's interrogation a month before, on July 1, 2003, which is the same day General Miller approved his "Special Interrogation Plan." DOJ IG, 123; SASC, 140; Schmidt-Furlow, 25; Bravin, *The Terror Courts*, 105.

"Can you read English?"

"Yes."

████████████████████ handed me a letter that he had obviously forged. The letter was from DoD, and it said, basically, "Ould Slahi is involved in the Millennium attack and recruited three of the September 11 hijackers. Since Slahi has refused to cooperate, the U.S. government is going to arrest his mother and put her in a special facility."

I read the letter. "Is that not harsh and unfair?" I said.

"I am not here to maintain justice. I'm here to stop people from crashing planes into buildings in my country."

"Then go and stop them. I've done nothing to your country," I said.

"You have two options: either being a defendant or a witness."

"I want neither."

"You have no choice, or your life is going to change decidedly," he said.

"Just do it, the sooner, the better!" I said. ████████████ ████ put the forged letter back in his bag, closed it angrily, and left the room. ████████████████ would lead the team working on my case until August or September 2004. He always tried to make me believe that his real name was ████████████ ████, but what he didn't know was that I knew his name even before I met him: ████████████.*

----

* The interrogator who posed as "Captain Collins" and led MOS's Special Projects Team has been identified by name in court documents filed in MOS's habeas corpus appeal, in footnotes to the Senate Armed Services Committee report, and in other published sources as Lt. Richard Zuley. In *The Terror Courts*, Jess Bravin describes Zuley as a Chicago police officer and navy reservist. SASC, 135, 136; Bravin, *The Terror Courts*, 100, 105; Brief for Appellee, 23.

*   *   *

After that meeting ██████████████████████████, he was just seeking the required formalities to kidnap me from the camp to an unknown place. "Your being here required many signatures. We've been trying for some time to get you here," one of my guards would tell me later. ██████████████ was also putting together a complete team which would execute the Abduction. All of this was carried out in secrecy; participants knew only as much as they needed to. I know for instance that ██████████ didn't know about the details of the plan.

On Monday August 25, 2003, around 4 p.m. ██████████ reserved me for interrogation ████████████████████████.* By then I had spent the weekend on ██████████████, which was entirely emptied of any other detainees, in order to keep me isolated from the rest of the community. But I saw it as a positive thing: the cell was warmer and I could see daylight, while in ████████████ I was locked in a frozen box.

"Now I have overall control. I can do anything I want with you; I can even move you to Camp ██████████████████.

"I know why you moved me to ██████████ Block," I said. "It's because you don't want me to see anybody." ██████████ didn't comment; ██████ just smiled. It was more of a friendly talk. Around 5:30 p.m., ██████████ brought me my cold MRE. I had gotten used to my cold portions; I didn't savor them, but I had been suffering weight loss like never before, and I knew in order to survive I had to eat.

I started to eat my meal. ██████████ was going in and out, but there was nothing suspicious about that, ██████ had always been that way. I barely finished my meal, when all of a sudden

---

* The time of day would make this the afternoon shift, and the redacted pronouns and later context suggest this is the team's female interrogator.

███████ and I heard a commotion, guards cursing loudly ("I told you motherfucker...!"), people banging the floor violently with heavy boots, dogs barking, doors closing loudly. I froze in my seat. ███████ went speechless. We were staring at each other, not knowing what was going on. My heart was pounding because I knew a detainee was going to be hurt. Yes, and that detainee was me.

Suddenly a commando team consisting of three soldiers and a German shepherd broke into our interrogation room. Everything happened quicker than you could think about it. ███████ punched me violently, which made me fall face down on the floor.

"Motherfucker, I told you, you're gone!" said ███████.* His partner kept punching me everywhere, mainly on my face and my ribs. He, too, was masked from head to toe; he punched me the whole time without saying a word, because he didn't want to be recognized. The third man was not masked; he stayed at the door holding the dog's collar, ready to release it on me.

"Who told you to do that? You're hurting the detainee!" screamed ███████, who was no less terrified than I was. ███████ was the leader of the assailing guards, and he was executing ███████████████ orders. As to me, I couldn't digest the situation. My first thought was, They mistook me for somebody else. My second thought was to try to recognize my environment by looking around while one of the guards was squeezing my face against the floor. I saw the dog fighting to get loose. I saw ███████ standing up, looking helplessly at the guards working on me.

"Blindfold the Motherfucker, if he tries to look—"

One of them hit me hard across the face, and quickly put the

---

* It will become clear, and explicit, that this is Mr. X.

goggles on my eyes, ear muffs on my ears, and a small bag over my head. I couldn't tell who did what. They tightened the chains around my ankles and my wrists; afterwards, I started to bleed. All I could hear was ████ cursing, "F-this and F-that!" I didn't say a word, I was overwhelmingly surprised, I thought they were going to execute me.

Thanks to the beating I wasn't able to stand, so ████ and the other guard dragged me out with my toes tracing the way and threw me in a truck, which immediately took off. The beating party would go on for the next three or four hours before they turned me over to another team that was going to use different torture techniques.

"Stop praying, Motherfucker, you're killing people," ████ said, and punched me hard on my mouth. My mouth and nose started to bleed, and my lips grew so big that I technically could not speak anymore. The colleague of ████ turned out to be one of my guards, ████████████████████████. ████ and ████████ each took a side and started to punch me and smash me against the metal of the truck. One of the guys hit me so hard that my breath stopped and I was choking; I felt like I was breathing through my ribs. I almost suffocated without their knowledge. I was having a hard time breathing due to the head cover anyway, plus they hit me so many times on my ribs that I stopped breathing for a moment.

Did I pass out? Maybe not; all I know is that I kept noticing ████ several times spraying Ammonia in my nose. The funny thing was that Mr. ██ was at the same time my "lifesaver," as were all the guards I would be dealing with for the next year, or most of them. All of them were allowed to give me medication and first aid.

After ten to fifteen minutes, the truck stopped at the beach, and my escorting team dragged me out of the truck and put me in a high-speed boat. ████████████████████ never gave me a break; they kept hitting me and ████████████ ████████ in order to make them stab me.* "You're killing people," said ██████. I believe he was thinking out loud: he knew his was the most cowardly crime in the world, torturing a helpless detainee who completely went to submission and turned himself in. What a brave operation! ██████ was trying to convince himself that he was doing the right thing.

Inside the boat, ██████ made me drink salt water, I believe it was directly from the ocean. It was so nasty I threw up. They would put any object in my mouth and shout, "Swallow, Mother-fucker!," but I decided inside not to swallow the organ-damaging salt water, which choked me when they kept pouring it in my mouth. "Swallow, you idiot!" I contemplated quickly, and decided for the nasty, damaging water rather than death.

██████ and ████████████ escorted me for about three hours in the high-speed boat. The goal of such a trip was, first, to torture the detainee and claim that "the detainee hurt himself during transport," and second, to make the detainee believe he was being transferred to some far, faraway secret prison. We detainees knew all of that; we had detainees reporting they had been flown around for four hours and found themselves in the same jail where they started. I knew from the beginning that I was going to be transferred to ████████████████████ about a five-minute ride. ████████████ had a very bad reputation: just hearing the name gave me nausea.† I knew the whole long trip

---

* It could be that MOS's escorts are pulling or manipulating his shackles to cause pain.

† The Senate Armed Services Committee found that the military's "Special Interrogation Plan" for MOS included a staged scene in which "military in full riot gear take him from his cell, place him on a watercraft, and drive him around to make him think he had been taken off the island." Afterward, the committee reported, "Slahi would be taken to Camp Echo,"

I was going to take was meant to terrorize me. But what difference does it make? I cared less about the place, and more about the people who were detaining me. No matter where I got transferred, I would still be a detainee of the U.S. Armed Forces; and as for rendition to a third country, I thought I was through with that because I was already sent to Jordan for eight months. The politics of the DoD toward me was to take care of me on their own; "September 11 didn't happen in Jordan; we don't expect other countries to pry Intels off detainees as we do," ████████████ said once. The Americans obviously were not satisfied with the results achieved by their "torture allies."

But I think when torture comes into play, things get out of

---

where his cell and interrogation room—self-contained in a single trailer-like isolation hut—had been "modified in such a way as to reduce as much outside stimuli as possible." The plan directed that "the doors will be sealed to a point that allows no light to enter the room. The walls may be covered with white paint or paper to further eliminate objects the detainee may concentrate on. The room will contain an eyebolt in the floor and speakers for sound." The SASC also recorded that an August 21, 2003, e-mail from a JTF-GTMO intelligence specialist to Lt. Richard Zuley reported on the final preparations to the Camp Echo hut: "The email described sealing Slahi's cell at Camp Echo to 'prevent light from shining' in and covering the entire exterior of his cell with [a] tarp to 'prevent him from making visual contact with guards.'"

According to the DOJ Inspector General, the original Special Interrogation Plan that General Miller signed on July 1, 2003, "stated that Slahi would be hooded and flown around Guantanamo Bay for one or two hours in a helicopter to persuade him that he had been moved out of GTMO to a location where 'the rules have changed.'" However, the IG reported, military interrogators told investigators that in the end "they did not use a helicopter because General Miller decided that it was too difficult logistically to pull off, and that too many people on the base would have to know about it to get this done." Instead, "on August 25, 2003, Slahi was removed from his cell in Camp Delta, fitted with blackout goggles, and taken on a disorienting boat ride during which he was permitted to hear pre-planned deceptive conversations among other passengers." SASC, 137–38, 140; DOJ IG 122–123, 127.

control. Torture doesn't guarantee that the detainee cooperates. In order to stop torture, the detainee has to please his assailant, even with untruthful, and sometimes misleading, Intels; sorting information out is time-consuming. And experience shows that torture doesn't stop or even reduce terrorist attacks: Egypt, Algeria, Turkey are good examples. On the other hand, discussion has brought tremendously good results. After the unsuccessful attack on the Egyptian president in Addis Ababa, the government reached a cease-fire with Al Gawaa al-Islamiyah, and the latter opted later on for a political fight. Nevertheless, the Americans had learned a lot from their torture-practicing allies, and they were working closely together.

When the boat reached the coast, ████ and his colleague dragged me out and made me sit, crossing my legs. I was moaning from the unbearable pain.

"Uh.... Uh... ALLAH... ALLAH.... I told you not to fuck with us, didn't I?" said Mr. X, mimicking me.* I hoped I could stop moaning, because the gentleman kept mimicking me and blaspheming the Lord. However, the moaning was necessary so I could breathe. My feet were numb, for the chains stopped the blood circulation to my hands and my feet; I was happy for every kick I got so I could alter my position. "Do not move Motherfucker!" said ████, but sometimes I couldn't help changing position; it was worth the kick.

"We appreciate everybody who works with us, thanks gentlemen," said ██████████.† I recognized his voice; although he was addressing his Arab guests, the message was addressed to me more than anybody. It was nighttime. My

---

* Mr. X appears here unredacted in the original.

† Based on court filings in MOS's habeas corpus appeal, this is likely to be Richard Zuley ("Captain Collins"), MOS's Special Projects Team chief. Brief for Appellee, 25.

blindfold didn't keep me from feeling the bright lighting from some kind of high-watt projectors.

"We happy for zat. Maybe we take him to Egypt, he say everything," said an Arab guy whose voice I had never heard, with a thick Egyptian accent. I could tell the guy was in his late twenties or early thirties based on his voice, his speech, and later on his actions. I could also tell that his English was both poor and decidedly mispronounced. Then I heard indistinct conversations here and there, after which the Egyptian and another guy approached. Now they're talking directly to me in Arabic:

"What a coward! You guys ask for civil rights? Guess you get none," said the Egyptian.

"Somebody like this coward takes us only one hour in Jordan to spit everything," said the Jordanian. Obviously, he didn't know that I had already spent eight months in Jordan and that no miracle took place.

"We take him to EEEgypt," said the Egyptian, addressing ▆▆▆▆▆▆▆▆▆▆▆.

"Maybe later," said ▆▆▆▆▆▆▆.

"How poor are these Americans! They really are spoiling these fuckers. But now we're working with them," said the Egyptian guy, now addressing me directly in Arabic. When I heard Egypt, and a new rendition, my heart was pounding. I hated the endless world tour I was forcibly taking. I seriously thought rendition to Egypt on the spot was possible, because I knew how irritated and desperate the Americans were when it came to my case. The government was and still is misled about my case.

"But you know we're working with Americans in the field," said the Egyptian. He was right: Yemeni detainees had told me that they were interrogated by ▆▆▆▆▆▆▆▆▆ and Americans at the same table when they were captured in Karachi and afterward transferred to a secret place on September 11, 2002.*

After all kinds of threats and degrading statements, I started to miss a lot of the trash talk between the Arabs and their American accomplices, and at one point I drowned in my thoughts. I felt ashamed that my people were being used for this horrible job by a government that claims to be the leader of the democratic free world, a government that preaches against dictatorship and "fights" for human rights and sends its children to die for that purpose: What a joke this government makes of its own people!

What would the dead average American think if he or she could see what his or her government is doing to someone who has done no crimes against anybody? As much as I was ashamed for the Arabic fellows, I knew that they definitely didn't represent the average Arab. Arabic people are among the greatest on the planet, sensitive, emotional, loving, generous, sacrificial, religious, charitable, and light-hearted. No one deserves to be used for such a dirty job, no matter how poor he is. No, we are better than that! If people in the Arab world knew what was happening in this place, the hatred against the U.S. would be heavily watered, and the accusation that the U.S. is helping and working together with dictators in our countries would be cemented. I had a feeling, or rather a hope, that these people would not go unpunished for their crimes. The situation didn't make me hate either Arabs or Americans; I just felt bad for the Arabs, and how poor we are!

---

* MOS may be referring here to detainees who were captured along with Ramzi bin al-Shibh on September 11, 2002, and also held for a time in CIA custody before being transferred to Guantánamo. See footnote on p. 197.

All these thoughts were sliding through my head, and distracted me from hearing the nonsense conversations. After about forty minutes, I couldn't really tell, ███████████ instructed the Arabic team to take over. The two guys grabbed me roughly, and since I couldn't walk on my own, they dragged me on the tips of my toes to the boat. I must have been very near the water, because the trip to the boat was short. I don't know, they either put me in another boat or in a different seat. This seat was both hard and straight.

"Move!"

"I can't move!"

"Move, Fucker!" They gave this order knowing that I was too hurt to be able to move. After all I was bleeding from my mouth, my ankles, my wrists, and maybe my nose, I couldn't tell for sure. But the team wanted to keep the factor of fear and terror maintained.

"Sit!" said the Egyptian guy, who did most of the talking while both were pulling me down until I hit the metal. The Egyptian sat on my right side, and the Jordanian on my left.

"What's your fucking name?" asked the Egyptian.

"M-O-O-H-H-M-M-EE-D-D-O-O-O-U!" I answered. Technically I couldn't speak because of the swollen lips and hurting mouth. You could tell I was completely scared. Usually I wouldn't talk if somebody starts to hurt me. In Jordan, when the interrogator smashed me in the face, I refused to talk, ignoring all his threats. This was a milestone in my interrogation history. You can tell I was hurt like never before; it wasn't me anymore, and I would never be the same as before. A thick line was drawn between my past and my future with the first hit ██████ delivered to me.

"He is like a kid!" said the Egyptian accurately, addressing his Jordanian colleague. I felt warm between them both, though not for long. With the cooperation of the Americans, a long torture trip was being prepared.

I couldn't sit straight in the chair. They put me in a kind of thick jacket which fastened me to the seat. It was a good feeling. However, there was a destroying drawback to it: my chest was so tightened that I couldn't breathe properly. Plus, the air circulation was worse than the first trip. I didn't know why, exactly, but something was definitely going wrong.

"I c....a...a...n't br...e...a...the!"

"Suck the air!" said the Egyptian wryly. I was literally suffocating inside the bag around my head. All my pleas and my begging for some free air ended in a cul-de-sac.

I heard indistinct conversations in English, I think it was ████████ and his colleague, and probably ██████████████████. Whoever it was, they were supplying the Arab team with torture materials during the 3 or 4 hour trip. The order went as follows: They stuffed the air between my clothes and me with ice-cubes from my neck to my ankles, and whenever the ice melted, they put in new, hard ice cubes. Moreover, every once in a while, one of the guards smashed me, most of the time in the face. The ice served both for the pain and for wiping out the bruises I had from that afternoon. Everything seemed to be perfectly prepared. People from cold regions might not understand the extent of the pain when ice-cubes get stuck on your body. Historically, kings during medieval and pre-medieval times used this method to let the victim slowly die. The other method, of hitting the victim while blindfolded in inconsistent intervals, was used by the Nazis during World War II. There is nothing more terrorizing than making somebody expect a smash every single heartbeat.

"I am from Hasi Matruh, where are you from?" said the Egyptian, addressing his Jordanian colleague. He was speaking as if nothing was happening. You could tell he was used to torturing people.

"I am from the south" answered the Jordanian. I tried to keep my prayers in my heart. I could hardly remember a prayer, but I did know I needed the Lord's help, as I always do, and in that direction went my prayers. Whenever I was conscious, I drowned in my thoughts. I finally had gotten used to the routine, ice-cubes until melted, smashing. But what would it be like if I landed in Egypt after about twenty-five hours of torture? What would the interrogation there look like? ███████ ████████████████████ an ██████████████████████████ described his unlucky trip from Pakistan to Egypt to me; so far everything I was experiencing, like the ice-cubes and smashing, was consistent with ██████████████████████ story. So I expected electric shocks in the pool. How much power can my body, especially my heart, handle? I know something about electricity and its devastating, irreversible damage: I saw ████████████ ████████████ collapsing in the blocks a couple of times every week with blood gushing out of his nose until it soaked his clothes. ██████████████████████ was a Martial art trainer and athletically built.

I was constructing the whole interrogation over and over, their questions, my answers. But what if they don't believe me? No, they would believe me, because they understand the recipe of terrorism more than the Americans, and have more experience. The cultural barrier between the Christian and the Muslim world still irritates the approach of Americans to the whole issue considerably; Americans tend to widen the circle of involvement to catch the largest possible numbers of Muslims. They always speak about the Big Conspiracy against the U.S. I personally had been interrogated about people who just practiced the basics of the religion and sympathized with Islamic movements; I was asked to provide every detail about Islamic movements, no matter how moderate. That's amazing in a country like the U.S., where Christian terrorist organizations such as Nazis and White Supremacists have the freedom to express themselves and recruit people openly and nobody can bother them. But as a Muslim, if you sympathize with the political views of an Islamic organization you're in big trouble. Even attending the same mosque as a suspect is big trouble. I mean this fact is clear for everybody who understands the ABCs of American policy toward so-called Islamic Terrorism.

The Arabo-American party was over, and the Arabs turned me over once more to the same U.S. Team. They dragged me out of the boat and threw me, I would say, in the same truck as the one that afternoon. We were obviously riding on a dirt road.

"Do not move!" said ████, but I didn't recognize any words anymore. I don't think that anybody beat me, but I was not conscious. When the truck stopped, ████ and his strong associate towed me from the truck, and dragged me over some steps. The cool air of the room hit me, and boom, they threw me face down on the metal floor of my new home.

"Do not move, I told you not to fuck with me, Motherfucker!" said ████, his voice trailing off. He was obviously tired. He left right away with a promise of more actions, and so did the Arab team.

A short time after my arrival, I felt somebody taking ████ ████████████████████████ off my head. Removing these things was both painful and relieving, painful because they had started to penetrate my skin and stick, leaving scars, and relieving because I started to breathe normally and the pressure around my head went away. When the blindfold was taken off I saw a ██ ███████████████████████████████████████. I figured he was a Doctor, but why the heck is he hiding behind a mask, and why is he U.S. Army, when the Navy is in charge of the medical care of detainees?

"If you fuckin' move, I'm gonna hurt you!" I was wondering how could I possibly move, and what possible damage I could do. I was in chains, and every inch in my body was hurting. That is not a Doctor, that is a human butcher!

When the young man checked on me, he realized he needed more stuff. He left and soon came back with some medical gear. I glimpsed his watch: it was about 1:30 a.m., which meant about eight hours since I was kidnapped from ██████████ Camp. The Doctor started to wash the blood off my face with a soaked bandage. After that, he put me on a mattress—the only item in the stark cell—with the help of the guards.

"Do not move," said the guard who was standing over me. The Doctor wrapped many elastic belts around my chest and ribs. After that, they made me sit. "If you try to bite me, I'm gonna fuckin' hurt you!" said the Doctor while stuffing me with a whole bunch of tablets. I didn't respond; they were moving me around like an object. Sometime later they took off the chains, and later still one of the guards threw a thin, small, worn-out blanket onto me through the bin hole, and that was everything I would have in the room. No soap, no toothbrush, no iso mat, no Koran, nothing.

I tried to sleep, but I was kidding myself; my body was conspiring against me. It took some time until the medications started to work, then I trailed off, and only woke up when one of the guards hit my cell violently with his boot.

"Get up, piece of shit!" The Doctor once more gave me a bunch of medication and checked on my ribs. "Done with the motherfucker," he said, showing me his back as he headed toward the door. I was so shocked seeing a Doctor act like that, because I knew that at least fifty percent of medical treatment is psychological. I was like, This is an evil place, since my only solace is this bastard Doctor.*

I soon was knocked out. To be honest I can report very little about the next couple of weeks because I was not in the right state of mind. I was lying on my bed the whole time, and I was not able to realize my surroundings. I tried to find out the *Kibla*, the direction of Mecca, but there was no clue.

---

* MOS's habeas appeal brief refers to medical records from what could be this exam, describing a corpsman "who treated his injuries while cursing him" and citing "medical records confirming the trauma to Salahi's chest and face, as '1) Fracture ?? 7–8 ribs, 2) Edema of the lower lip.'" Brief for Appellee, 26.

SIX

GTMO

September 2003–December 2003

First Visit in the Secret Place...My Conversation with My Interrogators, and How I Found a Way to Squinsh Their Thirst...Chain Reaction of Confessions...Goodness Comes Gradually...The Big Confession...A Big Milestone

B ack in ▮▮▮▮▮▮▮▮▮▮▮ the *Kibla* was indicated with an arrow in every cell. Even the call to prayer could be heard five times a day in ▮▮▮▮▮▮▮▮▮▮▮.* The U.S. has always repeated that the war is not against the Islamic religion — which is very prudent because it is strategically impossible to fight against a religion as big as Islam — and back there the U.S. was showing the rest of the world how religious freedom ought to be maintained.

---

* Defense Department publicity materials for Guantánamo indeed emphasize protections for religious expression in Guantánamo; see, e.g., "Ten Facts about Guantanamo," which states, "The Muslim call to prayer sounds five times a day. Arrows point detainees toward the holy city of Mecca." See http://www.defense.gov/home/dodupdate/For-the-record /documents/20060914.html. Here MOS seems to be contrasting the situation as he experienced it when he was held in Camp Delta with the situation in his Camp Echo cell.

But in the secret camps, the war against the Islamic religion was more than obvious. Not only was there no sign to Mecca, but the ritual prayers were also forbidden. Reciting the Koran was forbidden. Possessing the Koran was forbidden. Fasting was forbidden. Practically any Islamic-related ritual was strictly forbidden. I am not talking here about hearsay; I am talking about something I experienced myself. I don't believe that the average American is paying taxes to wage war against Islam, but I do believe that there are people in the government who have a big problem with the Islamic religion.

For the first couple of weeks after my "Birthday Party" I had no clue about time, whether it was day or night, let alone the time of day. I could only pray in my heart lying down, because I could not stand straight or bend. When I woke up from my semi-coma, I tried to make out the difference between day and night. In fact it was a relatively easy job: I used to look down the toilet, and when the drain was very bright to lightish dark, that was the daytime in my life. I succeeded in illegally stealing some prayers, but ▇▇▇▇▇▇▇▇▇▇▇▇▇▇▇▇▇▇▇▇ busted me.

"He's praying!" ▇▇▇▇▇▇▇▇▇▇▇▇▇▇▇▇▇▇▇▇▇▇. "Come on!" They put on their masks. "Stop praying." I don't recall whether I finished my prayer sitting, or if I finished at all. As a punishment ▇▇▇▇▇▇▇▇▇▇▇▇ forbade me to use the bathroom for some time.

As soon as the assessing doctor reported that I was relieved from my pain, it was time to hit again before the injuries healed, following the motto "Strike While the Iron's Hot." When I heard the melee behind the door, and recognized the voices of both ▇▇▇▇▇▇▇▇▇▇▇▇ and his Egyptian colleague, I drowned in sweat, got dizzy, and my feet failed to carry me.*

---

* MOS's habeas appeal brief describes what could be the same scene: "After Salahi had been in isolation for a few days, Zuley told him he had

My heart pounded so hard that I thought it was going to choke me and fly off through my mouth. Indistinct conversations involving ████████████ and the guards took place.

"████████████████████, let mee geet him," said the Egyptian guy in his stretched-out English to ████████████. "I wish ████████████████████ let me in to have a little conversation with you," said the Egyptian in Arabic, addressing me.

"Stand back now; let me see him alone," ████████████ said. I was shaking, listening to the bargaining between the Americans and the Egyptians about who was going to get me. I looked like somebody who was going through an autopsy while still alive and helpless.

"You are going to cooperate, whether you choose to or not. You can choose between the civilized way, which I personally prefer, or the other way," said ████████████████████ when the guards dragged me out of my cell to him. In the background the Egyptian guy was barking and threatening me with all kinds of painful revenge.

"I am cooperating," I said in a weak voice. It had been a while since I had talked the last time, and my mouth was not used to talking anymore. My muscles were very sore. I was scared beyond belief. The Halloween-masked ████████████ was literally stuck on me, moving around and ready to strike at an eye's wink.

"No, quit denying. We are not interested in your denials. Don't fuck with me," ████████████ said.

"I'm not."

"I am going to appoint some interrogators to question you. You know some of them, and some you don't."

---

to 'stop denying' the government's accusations. While Zuley was talking, the [redacted] man was behind the tarp, cursing and shouting for Zuley to let him in." Brief for Appellee, 26–27.

"OK!" I said. The conversation was closed. ▆▆▆▆▆▆ ▆▆▆▆▆▆▆▆▆ ordered the guards to put me back in my cell, and he disappeared.

Then nothing short of a "miracle" happened: ▆▆▆▆▆▆▆ ▆▆▆ made it to the "far faraway secret place."

"You've been causing me so much trouble—nah, well, in Paris it wasn't that bad but in Mauritania the weather was terrible. I sat at the table across from ▆▆▆▆▆▆▆, and when I asked him, 'Who recruited you for al Qaeda?' His answer was you. And the same with ▆▆▆▆▆▆▆▆▆▆▆. ▆▆▆▆▆▆▆ are working with us now. You know, you are a part of an organization which the free world wants to wipe out of the face of the earth," said ▆▆▆▆▆▆▆▆▆.

I was listening carefully, and wondering, Free world? I was saying to myself, Do I really have to listen to this crap? ▆▆▆▆▆▆▆▆ was accompanied by the same ▆▆▆▆▆▆ ▆▆▆▆▆▆▆▆▆ had brought about two months ago to molest me sexually.*

"You know, in jail the one who talks first wins. You lost and ▆▆▆▆▆▆▆▆▆▆ won. He said everything about you," ▆▆▆▆▆▆▆▆▆▆. "The good thing is, we don't have to dirty our hands with you; we have Israelis and Egyptians doing the job for us," ▆▆▆ continued, while taunting me sexually by touching me everywhere. I neither talked nor showed any resistance. I was sitting there like a stone.†

---

* The tone of this interrogation session suggests the lead interrogator may be the same "hateful" first sergeant whom MOS identified in his 2005 ARB hearing as a member of the Special Projects Team. The second interrogator in this scene appears to be the female interrogator who assisted in the earlier sexual assault.

† Threatening prisoners with the specter of abusive interrogations by Israeli or Egyptian agents apparently was commonplace. In 2010 a former Guantánamo military interrogator named Damien Corsetti testified at the

"Why is he shaking so much?" asked the ███████.

"I don't know," ███████████████ answered.

"But his hands are sweating like crazy!"

"If I were him, the same would be happening to me," said ███████. "You think this place is like ████████████ ██████, where you survived every attempt ████████████████, but you won't survive here if you keep playing games with us," he said.

"Like what?" I wondered.

"Like your trip to Slovenia. You only told me about it because you knew I knew about it. Now: are you going to cooperate with us?" he asked.

"I *was* cooperating," I said.

"No, you weren't, and guess what? I am going to write in my report that you're full of shit, and other people are going to take care of you. The Egyptian is very interested in you!"

Meanwhile the ████████ stopped molesting me since I showed no resistance. "What's wrong with him?" ██████ wondered once more.

"I don't know. But maybe he is too relaxed in this place. We should maybe take away some of his sleep," said ██████████ ██ ██ ███████. I've never seen a human being as emotionless as he was. He spoke about keeping me from sleeping without a single change in his voice, face, or composure. I mean, regardless of our religion or race, we human beings always feel more or less

---

military commissions trial of Omar Khadr that during his time at the Bagram air base, interrogations included threats of sending detainees to Israel and Egypt. See http://www.thestar.com/news/canada/omarkhadr /2010/05/05/interrogator_nicknamed_the_monster_remembers_omar _khadr_as_a_child.html.

bad for somebody who is suffering. I personally can never help breaking into tears when I read a sad story or watch a sad movie. I have no problem admitting this. Some people may say that I am a weak person; well, then, let me be!

"You should ask ███████████████ to forgive you the lies, and start everything over," said the ███████. I didn't say anything. "Start small. Give us a piece of information you never said before!" ██████ continued. I had no response to that malicious, nonsense suggestion either.

"Your mom is an old lady. I don't know how long she can withstand the conditions in the detention facility," ████████████ said. I knew that he was talking out of his tail. But I also knew that the government was ready to take any measures to pry information out of me, even if it would take injury to my family members, especially when you know that the ████████████ government is cooperating blindly with the U.S. I mean the U.S. government has more power over ███████████████ than over U.S. nationals, that's how far the cooperation goes. A U.S. citizen cannot be arrested without due process of law, but ███████████████ can—and by the U.S. government!* I always said to my interrogators, "Let's say I am criminal. Is an American criminal holier than a non–American?" And most of them had no answer. But I am sure that Americans are not much luckier. I've heard of many of them getting persecuted and wrongly arrested, especially Muslims and Arabs, in the name of the War Against Terror. Americans, non–Americans: it is as the German proverb puts it, Heute die! Morgen du! Today Them, Tomorrow You!

It was very hard to start a conversation with ███████████████

---

* The reference here might be to the Mauritanian government and its close cooperation with the U.S. government, and to MOS's own arrest in Mauritania at the behest of the United States.

███; even the guards hated him. Today I couldn't get anywhere with him; I just couldn't find a handrail in the train of
his speech. And as to the other ███████████ was only sent to
harass me sexually, but I was at a stage where I had no feeling
███████████████████████. Thus, ███ mission was dead
before it was born.

"You know how it looks when you feel our wrath," ██████
███████████████ said, and left me with many other threats
including sleep deprivation and starvation, which I believed to
be true and serious. The guards put me roughly back in my cell.

Over the next several days, I almost lost my mind. Their
recipe for me went like this: I must be kidnapped from ███████
███████████ and put in a secret place. I must be made to
believe I was on a far, faraway island. I must be informed by
███████████████ that my mom was captured and put in a special facility.

In the secret place, the physical and psychological suffering
must be at their highest extremes. I must not know the difference between day and night. I couldn't tell a thing about days
going by or time passing; my time consisted of a crazy darkness
all the time. My diet times were deliberately messed up. I was
starved for long periods and then given food but not given time
to eat.

"You have three minutes: Eat!" a guard would yell at me,
and then after about half a minute he would grab the plate.
"You're done!" And then it was the opposite extreme: I was
given too much food and a guard came into my cell and forced
me to eat all of it. When I said "I need water" because the food
got stuck in my throat, he punished me by making me drink
two 25-ounce water bottles.

"I can't drink," I said when my abdomen felt as if it was going
to explode. But ███████████ screamed and threatened me,

pushing me against the wall and raising his hand to hit me. I figured drinking would be better, and drank until I vomited.

All the guards were masked with Halloween-like masks, and so were the Medics, and the guards were briefed that I was a high-level, smart-beyond-belief terrorist.

"You know who you are?" said ▆▆▆▆▆▆▆▆ friend. "You're a terrorist who helped kill 3,000 people!"

"Indeed I am!" I answered. I realized it was futile to discuss my case with a guard, especially when he knew nothing about me. The guards were all very hostile. They cursed, shouted, and constantly put me through rough Military-like basic training. "Get up," "Walk to the bin hole." "Stop!" "Grab the shit!" "Eat." "You got two minutes!" "You're done!" "Give the shit back!" "Drink!" "You better drink the whole water bottle!" "Hurry up!" "Sit down!" "Don't sit down unless I say it!" "Search the piece of shit!" Most of the guards rarely attacked me physically, but ▆▆▆▆▆▆ hit me once until I fell face-down on the floor, and whenever he and his associate grabbed me they held me very tight and made me run in the heavy chains: "Move!"

No sleep was allowed. In order to enforce this, I was given 25-ounce water bottles in intervals of one to two hours, depending on the mood of the guards, 24 hours a day. The consequences were devastating. I couldn't close my eyes for ten minutes because I was sitting most of the time on the bathroom. Later on, after the tension was relieved, I asked one of the guards, "Why the water diet? Why don't you just make me stay awake by standing up, like in ▆▆▆▆▆▆▆▆?"

"Psychologically it's devastating to make somebody stay awake on his own, without ordering him," said ▆▆▆▆▆▆▆▆ ▆▆. "Believe me, you haven't seen anything. We have put detainees naked under the shower for days, eating, pissing, and shitting in the shower!" he continued. Other guards told me about other torture methods that I wasn't really eager to know about.

I was allowed to say three sentences: "Yes, sir!" "Need my interrogator!" and "Need the medics." Every once in a while the whole guard team stormed my cell, dragged me out, put me facing the wall, and threw out whatever was in my cell, shouting and cursing in order to humiliate me. It wasn't much: I was deprived from all comfort items that a detainee needs except for a mattress and a small, thin, worn-out blanket. For the first weeks I also had no shower, no laundry, no brushing. I almost developed bugs. I hated my smell.

No sleep. Water diet. Every move behind my door made me stand up in a military-like position with my heart pounding like boiling water. My appetite was non-existent. I was waiting every minute on the next session of torture. I hoped I would die and go to heaven; no matter how sinful I am, these people can never be more merciful than God. Ultimately we all are going to face the Lord and beg for his mercy, admitting our weaknesses and our sinfulness. I could hardly remember any prayers, all I could say was, "Please, God, relieve my pain..."

I started to hallucinate and hear voices as clear as crystal. I heard my family in a casual familial conversation that I couldn't join. I heard Koran readings in a heavenly voice.* I

---

* This is corroborated chillingly in government documents. According to the Senate Armed Services Committee, on October 17, 2003, a JTF-GTMO interrogator sent an e-mail to a GTMO Behavioral Science Consultation Team (BSCT) psychologist that read, "Slahi told me he is 'hearing voices' now....He is worried as he knows this is not normal....By the way...is this something that happens to people who have little external stimulus such as daylight, human interaction, etc???? seems a little creepy." The psychologist responded, "Sensory deprivation can cause hallucinations, usually visual rather than auditory, but you never know....In the dark you create things out of what little you have." SASC, 140–41.

heard music from my country. Later on the guards used these hallucinations and started talking with funny voices through the plumbing, encouraging me to hurt the guards and plot an escape. But I wasn't misled by them, even though I played along.

"We heard somebody—maybe a genie!" they used to say.

"Yeah, but I ain't listening to him," I responded. I just realized I was on the edge of losing my mind. I started to talk to myself. Although I tried as hard as I could to convince myself that I was not in Mauritania, I was not near my family, so I could not possibly hear them speaking, I kept hearing the voices constantly, day and night. Psychological assistance was out of the question, or really any medical assistance, beside the asshole I didn't want to see.

I couldn't find a way on my own. At that moment I didn't know if it was day or night, but I assumed it was night because the toilet drain was rather dark. I gathered my strength, guessed the *Kibla*, kneeled, and started to pray to God. "Please guide me. I know not what to do. I am surrounded by merciless wolves, who fear not thee." When I was praying I burst into tears, though I suppressed my voice lest the guards hear me. You know there are always serious prayers and lazy prayers. My experience has taught me that God always responds to your serious prayers.

"Sir," I said, when I finished my prayers. One of the guards showed up in his Halloween mask.

"What?" asked the guard with a dry, cold emotion.

"I want to see ██████████████. Not ████████████ ████; I want the guy ████████████████████," I said.

"You mean ████████████████████?" Oops, the guard just made a big mistake by revealing the real name of ████ ████████████. In fact I was already familiar with the name, because I saw it a long time before on a file ████████████

carried, and if you can put two and two together the puzzle is solved.*

"Yes, ███████████████████████████, not the ████████ ███████." I really wanted to speak to somebody who was likely to understand me, rather than ███████████████, who hardly had an understanding for anything. But ████████ ████████████ didn't show up, ███████████████ did.

"You asked for ████████████████████?"

"I did."

"And you asked not to see me?"

"I did."

"Well, I work for ███████████████████, and he sent me!" said ███████████████ dryly.

"OK, I have no problem with cooperating with you just as I would with ████████████████████. However, I would also like Mr. █████████████████ to take part in the interviews," I said.

"I am not the one who decides about that, but I guess it would be no problem," he said.

"I am starving, I want you to tell the guards to give me some food."

"If you start to cooperate, you'll get more food. I am going to come later today to interview you. I just want to tell you that you made the right decision."

---

* The Schmidt-Furlow report places the date of this session as September 8, 2003, noting that interrogation records show that on that date "the subject of the second special interrogation wanted to see 'Captain Collins' " and that the interrogation team "understood that detainee had made an important decision and that the interrogator was anxious to hear what Detainee had to say." It appears that another member of the Special Projects Team continued to lead the interrogation instead. Schmidt-Furlow, 25.

*   *   *

Confessions are like the beads of a necklace: if the first bead falls, the rest follow.

To be honest and truthful, I am telling many things here that I had been holding back merely because of fear. I just couldn't find any common ground to discuss my case comfortably in a relaxed environment. I had no crimes to confess to, and that is exactly where I got stuck with my interrogators, who were not looking for innocent undertakings. They were looking for evil enterprises. But through my conversations with the FBI and the DoD, I had a good idea as to what wild theories the government had about me.

"We know you came to Canada to plot to harm the U.S.," said ██████████████████.

"And what was my evil plan?"

"Maybe not exactly to harm the U.S., but to attack the CN Tower in Toronto?" he said. I was thinking, Is the guy crazy? I've never heard of such a tower.

"You realize if I admit to such a thing I have to involve other people! What if turns out I was lying?" I said.

"So what? We know your friends are bad, so if they get arrested, even if you lie about ████████ it doesn't matter, because they're bad." I thought, "What an asshole! he wants to lock up innocent people just because they're Muslim Arabs! That's Nuts!" So ████████████████ very much told me a precise crime I could admit to which would comply with the Intel theory.

"Back in the states, if I recommend somebody to a good school and he ended up shooting and killing people, is that my fault?" ████████ asked me once.

"No!"

"So, if you have recruited people for al Qaeda, it's not your fault if they become terrorists!" said ███████.

"The only problem is that I haven't, regardless of the consequences."

███████ was clearer. "We don't give a shit if you helped ████████████ and two other hijackers go to Chechnya. We only give a shit if you sent them to your ████████████ ████████." So, according to ███████, I could stop the torture if I said I recruited ████████████ and two hijackers. To be honest with you, they made me believe I recruited ███████ ███████; I thought, God, I might have recruited the guy before I was born!

"Looks like a dog, walks like a dog, smells like a dog, barks like a dog, must be a dog," ███████ used to say repeatedly during his sessions with me. It sounded awful, I know I am not a dog, and yet I must be one. The whole police theory of doing every trick to keep people in jail by pinning things on them doesn't make sense to me. I believe simply that an innocent suspect should be released. As the just, legendary Arabic King Omar put it, "I would rather release a criminal than imprison an innocent man."

████████████████ explained the ████████████ the most: ███████ said that you helped him go to Chechnya by suggesting that he and his friends transit through Afghanistan, because Georgia was sending Mujahideen back. Furthermore, when I asked ████████████ what he thinks you do for al Qaeda, he said that you're an al Qaeda recruiter."

"I believe that without you September 11 would never have happened," ████████████████ concluded. According to his theory I was the guy; all I needed to do was to admit it.

Many interrogators asked me, "What do you know about al Qaeda cells in Germany and Canada?" To be honest with you, I'd never heard of such a thing; I know al Qaeda organizations, but I don't know about al Qaeda cells in other countries, though that doesn't necessarily mean there aren't.

██████████████ pushed the issue even more into the light. "You are a leader, people like you, respect you, and follow you," he said to me multiple times. As you can see, my recipe was already cooked for me. I am not only a part of an al Qaeda cell in both Germany and Canada, but I am the leader.

I argued the case of ████████ with ██████████ many times. "According to you, I recruited ████████ and his two friends for al Qaeda," I said.

"Yes."

"Okay, but that allegation requires many other things and coincidences."

"Like what?" he said.

First, I explained, I supposedly knew ████████ and ██████████ himself said he has seen me only once, and that is not enough for knowing somebody, let alone recruiting him. Second, I must have recruited ████████ without his knowledge, because all he claims is that I told him how to get to Chechnya. "According to you," I told him, "And maybe to him, too, I told him to travel through Afghanistan, so what guaranteed that he was going to stay in Afghanistan? And if he miraculously stayed in Afghanistan, what guaranteed that he was going to train? And if he decided to train, what guaranteed that he was going to meet al Qaeda's criteria? And if by chance he met al Qaeda's criteria, what told me that he was ready to be a suicide bomber, and was ready to learn how to fly? This is just ridiculous!"

"But you are very smart," ██████████ said.

"Under these circumstances, I agree with you that I'm beyond smart: I am a psychic! But what makes you guys think that I'm so evil?"

"We just don't know, but smart people don't leave any traces. For instance, we had an ███████████████████ who had been working for Russia for 20 years without being noticed," said ███████████.*

"We have people who still believe that you conspired with ███████████████████ said ███████████████ when I told her not to ask me about ███████████████████████ because the FBI had settled his case since he had started cooperating.†

"Obviously there is no way out with you guys," I addressed ███████████.

"I'm telling you how!" ██████ responded.

Now, thanks to the unbearable pain I was suffering, I had nothing to lose, and I allowed myself to say anything to satisfy my assailants. Session followed session since I called ██████ ███████████████.

"People are very happy with what you're saying," said ██████ ███████████████ after the first session. I answered all the questions he asked me with incriminating answers. I tried my best to make myself look as bad as I could, which is exactly the way you can make your interrogator happy. I made my mind up to spend the rest of my life in jail. You see most people can put up with being imprisoned unjustly, but nobody can bear agony day in and day out for the rest of his life.

---

* The reference here might be to Robert Hanssen, an FBI agent who spied for Soviet and then Russian intelligence services from 1979 until his arrest and conviction in 2001.

† This may refer to Ahmed Ressam and his cooperation with U.S. authorities. See footnote on p. 66.

▓▓▓▓▓▓▓▓▓▓▓▓▓▓▓▓ started to take the shape of a human being, though a bad one. "I write my report like newspaper articles, and the members of the community submit their comments. They're really happy," ▓▓▓▓▓▓▓▓▓ said.

"So am I," I said. I was wondering about the new, half-happy face of ▓▓▓▓▓▓▓▓▓▓▓▓▓▓▓▓▓▓▓ is an angry person; if he talks to you he always looks at the roof, he hardly ever looks anybody in the eyes. He can barely lead a dialogue, but he's very good when it comes to monologues. "I divorced my wife because she was just so annoying," he once said to me.

"Your request to see ▓▓▓▓▓▓▓▓▓▓▓▓▓▓ is not approved, in the meantime I am working on your case," he said.

"Alright!" I knew that ▓▓▓▓▓▓▓▓▓▓▓▓ was a trial, and that the DoD still wanted me to deal with the "bad guy."

"▓▓▓▓▓▓▓▓▓▓▓▓▓▓▓▓▓▓▓▓▓▓▓▓▓▓," he said.

"But since you don't know my limit, you drove me beyond it," I responded. When I started to talk generously to ▓▓▓▓▓▓▓▓▓▓▓, ▓▓▓▓▓▓▓▓▓▓▓ brought ▓▓▓▓▓▓▓ back into the picture; for some reason the team wanted ▓▓▓ back, too.

"Thank you very much for getting the ▓▓▓▓▓▓ back," I said.

▓▓▓▓▓▓▓ looked both sad and happy. "I enjoy talking to you, you're easy to talk to, and you have pretty teeth," ▓▓▓ told me before I was kidnapped from ▓▓▓▓▓▓▓▓▓▓▓▓▓. ▓▓▓▓▓▓▓ was the closest person to me; ▓▓▓▓ was the only one I could relate to.*

"I can never do what ▓▓▓▓▓▓▓▓▓▓▓▓ is doing; all he's

---

* The redacted pronouns and the descriptions "the person closest to me" and "the only one I could relate to" suggest that this may be the female member of the Special Projects Team who previously led the second-shift interrogations. See footnote on p. 240.

worried about is getting his job done," said ▇▇▇▇▇▇ commenting ▇▇▇▇▇▇▇▇▇▇▇ methods when ▇▇▇▇▇▇▇▇▇▇ was absent. ▇▇▇▇▇▇▇▇▇▇▇▇▇▇▇▇▇▇ were now interrogating me in turn. They dedicated the whole time until around November 10, 2003, to questioning me about Canada and September 11; they didn't ask me a single question about Germany, where I really had the center of gravity of my life. Whenever they asked me about somebody in Canada I had some incriminating information about that person, even if I didn't know him. Whenever I thought about the words, "I don't know," I got nauseous, because I remembered the words of ▇▇▇▇▇▇▇▇▇▇▇▇, "All you have to say is, "I don't know, I don't remember, and we'll fuck you!" Or ▇▇▇▇▇▇▇▇▇ "We don't want to hear your denials anymore!" And so I erased these words from my dictionary.

"We would like you to write your answers on paper; it's too much work to keep up with your talk, and you might forget things when you talk to us," said ▇▇▇▇▇▇▇▇▇▇▇.

"Of course!" I was really happy with the idea because I would rather talk to a paper than talk to him; at least the paper wouldn't shout in my face or threaten me. ▇▇▇▇▇▇▇▇▇▇▇ drowned me in a pile of papers, which I duly filled with writings. It was a good outlet for my frustration and my depression.

"You're very generous in your written answers; you even wrote a whole bunch about ▇▇▇▇▇▇▇▇▇▇▇▇▇, whom you really don't know," ▇▇▇▇▇▇▇▇▇▇ accurately said, forgetting that he forbade me to use the words "I don't know."

"▇▇▇▇▇▇▇▇▇▇▇▇▇▇ reads your writing with a lot of interest," said ▇▇▇▇▇▇▇▇▇▇▇. I was extremely frightened, because this statement was ambiguous. "We're gonna give you an assignment about ▇▇▇▇▇▇▇▇▇. He is detained in Florida and they cannot make him talk; he keeps denying everything. You better provide us a Smoking Gun against him," said ██████████████. I was so sad: how rude was this guy, to ask me to provide a smoking gun about somebody I hardly know?

"All I can say is that Ahmed L. is a criminal and should be locked up the rest of his life.* I'm ready to testify against him in court," I said, though I was not ready to lie in court to burn an innocent soul.

"██████████████ is facing the death penalty if we can make him guilty of drug smuggling," ██████████████ said once, showing me his picture. I burst out laughing as soon as I saw the expression on his face and the Bob Barker–Calvin Klein prison uniform.†

"What are you laughing at?" ██████████████ asked me.

"It's just funny!"

"How can you laugh at your friend?" I felt guilty right away, even though I knew I was not laughing at him. After all, my situation was worse than his. I was laughing at the situation: I could read everything that was going on in his head just from the expression on his face. I'd been made to take that same picture many times, in Senegal, in Mauritania, in Germany, in Jordan, in Bagram, and in GTMO. I hate the pose, I hate the look, I hate the height measure. Let me tell you something, whenever you see that bleak-looking face in a jail uniform,

---

★ "Ahmed L." appears in the manuscript unredacted. This could refer to Ahmed Laabidi, a Tunisian national who lived in Montreal in 2000 and was later detained in the United States on an immigration violation. Laabidi was held in U.S. immigration custody and then deported to Tunisia in September 2003. See footnote on p. 294 for more on Laabidi.

† Bob Barker Company, Incorporated, which identifies itself as "America's Leading Detention Supplier," is a major supplier of prison uniforms for the U.S. Department of Defense. See http://news.google.com/newspapers?nid= 1454&dat=20020112&id=6gJPAAAAIBAJ&sjid=Ux8EAAAAIBAJ &pg=5765,3098702.

posing in front of a height measure scaled on a wall, you can be sure that is not a happy person.

In fact, I really felt bad for that poor guy. He had sought asylum in Canada for a certain time but the Canadians refused his petition, partly because they considered him as Islamist. ▆▆▆▆▆▆▆▆▆▆ was willing to try his chances in the U.S., where he faced the harsh reality of the highly electrified environment against Muslims and Arabs, and where the U.S. gave him asylum in a high-level security prison and now was trying to link him to any crime. When I saw his face, I knew he was like, "Screw these Americans. How much I hate them! What do they want from me? How did I end up in jail when I came here seeking protection?"

"I talked today with the Canadians and they told me they don't believe your story about ▆▆▆▆▆▆▆▆▆▆ being involved in drug smuggling into the U.S., but we know he is," he told me once.

"I can only tell you what I know," I said.

"But we want you to give an evidence linking ▆▆▆▆▆▆▆▆ ▆▆▆▆ to the Millennium Plot. Things like, he supports the Mujs or believes in Jihad are good, but not good enough to lock him up the rest of his life," he told me.

"Oh, yes, I will," I said. He handed me a bunch of papers and I went back in my cell. Oh, my God, I am being so unjust to myself and my brothers, I kept thinking, and then repeating "Nothing's gonna happen to us....*They'll* go to hell....Nothing's gonna happen to us....*They'll*...." I kept praying in my heart, and repeating my prayers. I took the pen and paper and wrote all kinds of incriminating lies about a poor person who was just seeking refuge in Canada and trying to make some money so he could start a family. Moreover, he is handicapped. I felt so bad, and kept praying silently, "Nothing's gonna happen to you dear brother..." and blowing on the papers as I finished. Of course it was out of the question to tell them what I knew about him truthfully, because ▒▒▒▒▒▒▒▒ already gave me the guidelines: "▒▒▒▒▒▒▒▒▒▒▒ is awaiting your testimony against ▒▒▒▒▒▒▒▒▒ with extreme interest!" I gave the assignment to ▒▒▒▒▒▒▒▒▒▒▒, and after evaluation, I saw ▒▒▒▒▒▒▒▒▒ smiling for the first time.

"Your writing about Ahmed was very interesting, but we want you to provide more detailed information," he said. I thought, What information does the idiot want from me? I don't even remember what I've just written.

"Yes, no problem," I said. I was very happy that God answered my prayers for ▒▒▒▒▒▒▒▒▒ when I learned in 2005 that he was unconditionally released from custody and sent back to his country. "He's facing the death penalty," ▒▒▒▒▒ used to tell me! I was really in no better situation.

"Since I am cooperating, what are you going to do with me?" I asked ▒▒▒▒▒▒.

"It depends. If you provide us a great deal of information we didn't know, it's going to be weighed against your sentence. For instance, the death penalty could be reduced to life, and life to thirty years," he responded. Lord have mercy on me! What harsh justice!

"Oh, that's great," I replied. I felt bad for everybody I hurt with my false testimonies. My only solaces were, one, that I didn't hurt anybody as much as I did myself; two, that I had no choice; and three, I was confident that injustice will be defeated, it's only a matter of time. Moreover, I would not blame anybody for lying about me when he gets tortured. Ahmed was just an example. During this period I wrote more than a thousand pages about my friends with false information. I had to wear the suit the U.S. Intel tailored for me, and that is exactly what I did.

At the beginning of this phase of cooperation the pressure hardly relieved. I was interrogated ████████████████████ ████████████████████. It was so rude to question a human being like that, especially somebody who is cooperating. They made me write names and places ████████████ ████████████████████. I was shown thousands of pictures. I knew them all by heart because I had seen them so many times; everything was deja-vu. I was like, What ruthless people!

The whole time, the guards were driven madly against me.

"Show him no mercy. Increase the pressure. Drive the hell out of him crazy," said ████████████████████. And that was exactly what the guards did. Banging on my cell to keep me awake and scared. Taking me violently out of my cell at least twice a day for cell search. Taking me outside in the middle of the night and making me do PT I couldn't due to my health situation. Putting me facing the wall several times a day and threatening me directly and indirectly. Sometimes they even interrogated me, but I never said a word to my interrogators because I knew the interrogators were behind everything.

"You know who you are?" said ████████████████.

"Uh..."

"You are a terrorist," he continued.

"Yes, Sir!"

"If we kill you once it wouldn't do. We must kill you three thousand times. But instead we feed you!"

"Yes, Sir."

The water diet kept working on me harshly. "You haven't seen nothing yet," they kept telling me.

"I am not looking forward to seeing that. I'm just fine without further measures."

The guards were working in a two-shift routine, day shift and night shift. Whenever the new shift showed up, they made their presence known by banging heavily on the door of my cell to scare me. Whenever the new shift appeared my heart started to pound because they always came up with new ideas to make my life a living hell, like giving me very little food by allowing me about 30 seconds to one minute to eat it, or forcing me to eat every bit of food I got in a very short time. "You better be done!" they would shout. Or they made me clean the shower excessively, or made me fold my towels and my blanket in an impossible way again and again until they were satisfied. To forbidding me any kind of comfort items, they added new rules. One: I should never be lying down; whenever a guard showed up at my bin hole, I always had to be awake, or wake up as soon as a guard walked into my area. There was no sleeping in the terms that we know. Two: My toilet should always be dry! And how, if I am always urinating and flushing? In order to meet the order, I had to use my only uniform to dry the toilet up and stay soaked in shit. Three: My cell should be in a predefined order, including having a folded blanket, so I could never use my blanket.

That was the guards' recipe. I always showed more fear than I felt as a self-defense technique. Not that I would like to play the hero; I'm not, but I wasn't scared of the guards because I just knew they had orders from above. If they reported back that "detainee wasn't scared!" the doses would have been increased.

Meanwhile, I had my own recipe. First of all, I knew that I was really just a stone's throw away from ███████████

██████.* The Interrogators and the guards always hinted at the "God-forsaken nowhere" I was in, but I ignored them completely, and when the guards asked me "Where do you think you are?" I just responded, "I'm not sure, but I am not worried about it; since I am far from my family, it doesn't really matter to me where I am." And so I always closed the door whenever they referred to the place. I was afraid that I would be tortured if they knew I knew where I was, but it was kind of solacing, knowing that you are not far from your fellow detainees.

Once I figured out how to tell day from night, I kept count of the days by reciting 10 pages of the Koran every day. In 60 days I would finish and start over, and so I could keep track of the days. "Shut the fuck up! There is nothing to sing about," said ████████████ when he heard me reciting the Koran. After that I recited quietly so nobody could hear me. But my days of the week were still messed up; I failed to keep track of them until I glimpsed ████████████████ watch when he pulled it out of his pocket to check the time. He was very vigilant and careful but it was too late, I saw MO████████████████, but he didn't notice. Friday is a very important Muslim holiday, and that was the reason I wanted to keep track of the weekdays. Besides, I just hated the fact that they deprived me of one of my basic freedoms.

I tried to find out everybody's name who was involved in my torture—not for retaliation or anything like that; I just didn't want those people to have the upper hand over any of my brothers, or anybody, no matter who he is. I believe they should not only be deprived of their powers, but they should also be locked up. I succeeded in knowing the names of the ████████████

---

* MOS may be referring to the distance between the isolation cell where he is being held and the main detention blocks of Camp Delta, where he was held previously.

████████████████████████ two of my interrogators, two of the guards, and other interrogators who weren't involved directly in my torture but could serve as witnesses.

When I first met Americans I hated their language because of the pain they made me suffer without a single reason; I didn't want to learn it. But that was emotion; the call of wisdom was stronger, and so I decided to learn the language. Even though I already knew how to conjugate "to be" and "to have," my luggage of English was very light. Since I wasn't allowed to have books, I had to pick up the language mostly from the guards and sometimes my interrogators, and after a short time I could speak like common folk: "He don't care, she don't care, I ain't done nothin', me and my friend did so and so, F—this and F—that, damn x and damn y..."

I also studied the people around me. My observations resulted in knowing that only white Americans were appointed to deal with me, both guards and interrogators. There was only one black guard, but he had no say. His associate was a younger, white ████████████████ but the latter was always in charge. You might say, "How do you know the ranks of the guards, when they were covered?" I wasn't supposed to know who was in charge, nor should they have given me a hint as to who the boss was, but in America it's very easy to notice who the boss is: there's just no mistaking him.

My suspicion of me being near ██████████████████████ was cemented when one day I got some of the diet I was used to back in ████████████████. "Why did they give me a hot meal?" I asked the sarcastic head guard. "Doctor said we had to." I really looked like a ghost, just bones, no meat. In a matter of weeks I had developed grey hair on the lower half of the sides of my head, a phenomenon people in my culture refer to as the extreme result of depression. Keeping up the pressure was vital in the process of my interrogation. The plan worked: the more pressure, the more stories I produced and the better my interrogators felt toward me.

And then, slowly but surely, the guards were advised to give me the opportunity to brush my teeth, to give me more warm meals, and to give me more showers. The interrogators started to interrogate me ████████████████████████████ ████████████████████████ was the one who took the first steps, but I am sure there had been a meeting about it. Everybody in the team realized that I was about to lose my mind due to my psychological and physical situation. I had been so long in segregation.

"Please, get me out of this living hell!" I said.

"You will not go back to the population anytime soon." ████████ told me. Her answer was harsh but true: there was no plan to get me back.* The focus was on holding me segregated as long as they could and gathering information from me.

I still had nothing in my cell. Most of the time I recited the Koran silently. The rest of the time I was talking to myself and thinking over and over about my life and the worst-case scenarios that could happen to me. I kept counting the holes of the cage I was in. There are about four thousand one hundred holes.

Maybe because of this, ████████ happily started to give me some puzzles that I could spend my time solving. "If we discover that you lied to us, you're gonna feel our wrath, and we're gonna take everything back. This can all go back to the old days, you know that," ████████ used to tell me whenever he gave me a puzzle. My heart would pound, but I was like,

---

* "Her" appears here unredacted.

What a jackass! Why can't he let me enjoy my "reward" for the time being? Tomorrow is another day.

I started to enrich my vocabulary. I took a paper and started to write words I didn't understand, and ████████████ explained them to me. If there is anything positive about ████████████ is his rich vocabulary. I don't remember asking him about a word he couldn't explain to me. English was his only real language, though he claimed to be able to speak Farsi. "I wanted to learn French, but I hated the way they speak and I quit," he said.

████████████████████ wants to see you in a couple of days," ████████████ said. I was so terrified; at this point I was just fine without his visit.

"He is welcome," I said. I started to go to the toilet relentlessly. My blood pressure went crazily high. I was wondering what the visit would be like. But thank God the visit was much easier than what I thought. ████████████ came, escorted by ██████████. He was, as always, practical and brief.

"I am very happy with your cooperation. Remember when I told you that I preferred civilized conversations? I think you have provided 85% of what you know, but I am sure you're gonna provide the rest," he said, opening an ice bag with some juice.

"Oh, yeah, I'm also happy!" I said, forcing myself to drink the juice just to act as if I were normal. But I wasn't: I was like, 85% is a big step coming out of his mouth. ████████████ advised me to keep cooperating.

"I brought you this present," he said, handing me a pillow. Yes, a pillow. I received the present with a fake overwhelming happiness, and not because I was dying to get a pillow. No, I took the pillow as a sign of the end of the physical torture. We have a joke back home about a man who stood bare naked on the street. When someone asked him, "How can I help you?" He replied, "Give me shoes." And that was exactly what happened to me. All I needed was a pillow! But it was something: alone in my cell, I kept reading the tag over and over.

"Remember when ████████████ told you about the 15% you're holding back," said ████████ a couple of days after ███████████████ visit. "I believe that your story about Canada doesn't make sense. You know what we have against you, and you know what the FBI has against you," he continued.

"So what would make sense?" I asked.

"You know exactly what makes sense," he said sardonically.

"You're right, I was wrong about Canada. What I did exactly was...."

"I want you to write down what you've just said. It made perfect sense and I understood, but I want it on paper."

"My pleasure, Sir!" I said.

I came to Canada with a plan to blow up the CN Tower in Toronto. My accomplices were ██████████████████████████ ██████████ *and* ████████████. ████████████ *went to Russia to get us the supply of explosives.* ████████████ *wrote an explosives simulation software that I picked up, tested myself, and handed in a data medium to* ████████████. *The latter was supposed to send it with the whole plan to* ████████████ *in London so we could get the final fatwa from the Sheikh.* ████████ *was supposed to buy a lot of sugar to mix with the explosives in order to increase the damage.* ████████████ *provided the financing. Thanks to Canadian Intel, the plan was discovered and sentenced to failure. I admit that I am as guilty as any other participants and am so sorry and ashamed for what I have done. Signed, M.O. Slahi*

When I handed the paper to ████████████████████ read it happily.

"This statement makes perfect sense."

"If you're ready to buy, I am selling," I said. ████████████████ could hardly hold himself on the chair; he wanted to leave immediately. I guess the prey was big, and ████████████████ was overwhelmed because he reached a breakthrough where no other interrogators had, in spite of almost four years of uninterrupted interrogation from all kinds of agencies from more than six countries. What a success! ██████████████████ almost had a heart attack from happiness.

"I'll go see him!"

I think the only unhappy person in the team was ████████, because ███ doubted the truthfulness of the story.

Indeed the next day ██████████████████ came to see me, escorted as always by his ██████████████████. "Remember when I told you about the 15% you were holding back?"

"Yes, I do."

"I think this confession covered that 15%!" I was like, Hell, yes!

"I am happy that it did," I said.

"Who provided the money?"

"████████████ did.

"And you, too?" ██████████████ asked.

"No, I took care of the electrical part." I don't really know why I denied the financial part. Did it really make a difference? Maybe I just wanted to maintain the consistency.

"What if we tell you that we found your signature on a fake credit card?" said ██████████████████. I knew he was bullshitting me because I knew I never dealt with such dubious things. But I was not going to argue with him.

"Just tell me the right answer. Is it good to say yes or to say no?" I asked. At that point I hoped I was involved in something so I could admit to it and relieve myself of writing about every practicing Muslim I ever met, and every Islamic organization I ever heard of. It would have been much easier to admit to a true crime and say that's that. "This confession is consistent with the Intels we and other agencies possess," ████████ ████████ said.

"I am happy."

"Is the story true?" asked ████████████.

"Look, these people I was involved with are bad people anyway, and should be put under lock and key. And as to myself, I don't care as long as you are pleased. So if you want to buy, I am selling."

"But we have to check with the other agencies, and if the story is incorrect, they're gonna find out," ████████████████

"If you want the truth, this story didn't happen," I said sadly. ████████████████ had brought some drinks and candies that I forced myself to swallow. They tasted like dirt because I was so nervous. ████████████ took his ████████ outside and pitted him on me. ████████████████ came back harassing me and threatening me with all kinds of suffering and agony. ████████

██

██

████████████████████.

"You know how it feels when you experience our wrath," ████████████████ said. I was like, what the heck does this asshole want from me? If he wants a confession, I already provided one. Does he want me to resurrect the dead? Does he want me to heal his blindness? I am not a prophet, nor does he believe in them. "The Bible is just the history of the Jewish people, nothing more," he used to say. If he wants the truth, I told him I

have done nothing! I couldn't see a way out. "Yes!…Yes!…Yes!"
After 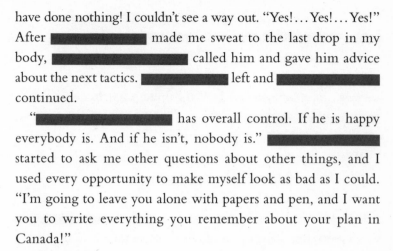 made me sweat to the last drop in my
body, ███████████████ called him and gave him advice
about the next tactics. ██████████ left and ██████████
continued.

"██████████████ has overall control. If he is happy
everybody is. And if he isn't, nobody is." ████████████
started to ask me other questions about other things, and I
used every opportunity to make myself look as bad as I could.
"I'm going to leave you alone with papers and pen, and I want
you to write everything you remember about your plan in
Canada!"

"Yes, Sir."

Two days later they were back at my door.

"Get up! Get your hands through the bin hole!" said an
unfriendly-sounding guard. I didn't welcome the visit: I hadn't
missed my interrogators' faces over the weekend, and they
scared the hell out of me. The guards shackled me and took me
outside the building where ██████████████████████ were
waiting for me. It was my first time seeing the daylight. Many
people take daylight for granted, but if you are forbidden to see
it, you'll appreciate it. The brightness of the sun made my eyes
squint until they adjusted. The sun hit me mercifully with its
warmth. I was terrified and shaking.

"What's wrong with you?" one of the guards asked me.

"I am not used to this place."

"We brought you outside so you can see the sun. We will
have more rewards like this."

"Thank you very much," I managed to say, though my mouth
was dry and my tongue was heavy as steel. "Nothing is gonna
happen to you if you tell us about the bad things. I know you're

afraid that we will change our opinion toward you," said
████████████████████████ while ████████████████ was taking
notes.

"I know."

"Let's talk hypothetically. You understand hypothetical?"
████████████████████ said.

"Yes, I do."

"Let's assume you've done what you confessed to."

"But I haven't."

"Just let's assume."

"Okay," I said. As high-ranking as ██████████████████████
was, he was the worst interrogator I've ever met. I mean professionally. He just jumps back and forth without focusing on any specific thing. If I had to guess, I would say his job was anything but interrogating people.

"Between you and ████████████████, who was in charge?"

"It depends: in the mosque I was in charge, and outside he was in charge," I answered. The questions assumed that Hannachi and I are members of a gang, but I didn't even know Mr. ████████████████, let alone conspire with him as part of a corps that never existed.* But anyway I could not tell some-

---

* "Hannachi" might refer to Raouf Hannachi, a Tunisian-born Canadian citizen who also lived in Montreal in 2000. It appears from MOS's 2008 Detainee Assessment and from MOS's habeas corpus decision that confessions like those MOS is describing here became part of the government's allegations against him. Both Hannachi and Ahmed Laabidi appear in both the 2008 Detainee Assessment and Judge James Robertson's 2010 habeas memorandum order; in both the government portrays MOS, Hannachi, and Laabidi as members of a Montreal cell of al-Qaeda, with Hannachi as the cell's leader and Laabidi as the cell's financier. A footnote to Judge Robertson's opinion specifically notes that MOS's statement under interrogation that "Laabidi [is] a terrorist who supported use of suicide bombers" came in an interrogation session dated September 16, 2003— right around the time of the scene MOS describes here. The 2008 Detainee Assessment is available at http://projects.nytimes.com/guantanamo

thing like that to ███████████████; I had to tell him something that made me look bad.

"Have or haven't you conspired with those individuals as you admitted?"

"You want the truth?"

"Yes!"

"No, I haven't," I said. ████████████████ and ██████ ██████████ tried to play all kinds of tricks on me, but first of all I knew all the tricks, and second I had already told them the truth. So it was futile to play tricks on me. But they drove me into the infamous Catch-22: if I lie to them, "You'll feel our wrath." And if I tell the truth, it will make me look good, which would make them believe I am withholding information because in their eyes I AM A CRIMINAL and I wasn't yet able to change that opinion.

████████████████████████ handed me a printed version of the so-called Witness Protection Program. He obviously forgot to disable the date printout footnote, so I could read it. I wasn't supposed to know the date, but nobody is perfect.

"Oh, thank you very much," I said.

"If you help us, you'll see how generous our government is," ██████████████████ said.

"I'll read it."

"I think this is something for you."

"Sure." ██████████████████ gestured to the guards to take me back in my cell. They were still holding me all this time ██████████████████████.*

/detainees/760-mohamedou-ould-slahi. Detainee Assessment, 10; Memorandum Order, 26–28.

* MOS indicates later in the manuscript that he remained in the same cell he was delivered into at the end of his staged abduction through the time of the manuscript's creation. There are no indications that he has been moved since. A 2010 *Washington Post* report described a "little fenced-in

As soon as the interrogation team left, one of the guards was opening my cell and shouting, "Get up Motherfucker." I was like, Oh my God, again? ███████████████████████████
████████ took me out of the cell and made me face the wall.

"You fucking pussy. Why don't you admit?"

"I've been telling the truth."

"You ain't. Interrogators never ask if they don't have proof. They just wanted to test you. And guess what? You failed. You blew your chance," he continued. I was sweating and shaking, and I showed even more fear than I really felt. "It's so easy: we just want you to tell us what you've done, how you've done it, and who else was involved with you. We use this information to stop other attacks. Is that not easy?"

"Yeah, it is."

"So why do you keep being a pussy?"

"Because he's gay!" said ████████████████████████.

"You think the ██████████████ just gave you the Witness Protection information for fun? Hell, we should kill you, but we don't; instead, we're gonna give you money, a house, and a nice car, how frustrating is that? In the end, you are a terrorist," he continued. "You better tell them everything the next time they come. Take a pen and paper and write everything down."

The Interrogators and guards believed the Witness Protection Program is a U.S. specialty, but it isn't. It's practiced all over the world; even in the darkest dictatorship countries, criminals can profit from such a program. ██████████████████████ provided me stories about other criminals who became friends of the U.S.

---

compound at the military prison" that matches the description of his living situation at the time the manuscript was written. See Peter Finn, "For Two Detainees Who Told What They Knew, Guantanamo Becomes a Gilded Cage," *Washington Post*, March 24, 2010, http://www.washingtonpost .com/wp-dyn/content/article/2010/03/24/AR2010032403135.html. MOS manuscript, 233.

government, such as ████████████████████████████ and another communist who fled the Soviets during the Cold War. I was really not enlightened by any of this, but I took the papers anyway: something to read beside the pillow tag. I kept reading and reading and reading it again because I just like to read and I had nothing to read.

"You remember what you told ████████████████████, when he told you you're hiding 15%," ████████████ said in our next session.

"Yeah, but you see I can't argue with ████████████████████. Otherwise he gets mad." ████████████ took a printed version of my confession and started to read it, smiling.

"But you're not only hurting yourself. You're hurting other innocent people."

"That's correct. But what else should I do?"

"You said you guys wanted to mix sugar with explosives?"

"Yes, I did." ████████████ smiled.

"But that's not we wanted to hear when we asked you what you meant by 'sugar.' As a matter of fact, ████████████████ ██."

"████████ I really don't know that," I said.

"You cannot possibly lie about something as big as that," ████████ said. "We have a highly qualified expert who could come and question you. What do you think about ████████████ ████████?"

"████████████████ I'm dying to take one!" I said, though my heart was pounding because I knew I might fail the test even if was telling the truth.

"I'm gonna organize a ████████████ for you as soon as possible."*

---

* Context, including the unredacted word "poly" a bit farther into this passage, suggests that the subject of this conversation and the long redaction

"I know you want to make yourself look good," I said.

"No, I care about you. I would like to see you out of jail, leading a normal life. There are some detainees I want to see stay here the rest of their lives. But you, no!" ▆▆▆▆▆▆ genuinely.

"Thank you very much." ▆▆▆▆▆▆ left with that promise and I retreated back to my cell, completely depressed.

"Remember that the ▆▆▆▆▆▆ is decidedly important in your life," said ▆▆▆▆▆▆▆ shortly before he left one of his sessions, trying with the help of his executioner ▆▆▆▆▆▆▆▆ to pry nonexistent information out of my mouth. He scared the hell out of me, because my whole life was now hanging on a ▆▆▆▆▆▆.

"Yes, Sir, I know."

"Who would you like to have with you during the ▆▆▆▆▆," asked ▆▆▆▆▆▆ a couple of days before the ▆▆▆▆.

"I think ▆▆▆▆▆▆▆▆ wouldn't be a good idea, but I would be just fine if you would be here!"

"Or the other ▆▆▆▆," ▆▆▆▆▆▆▆.

"Yeah," I said reluctantly. "But why don't you just come?"

"I'll try, but if not me, it will be the ▆▆▆▆▆."

"I am very scared because of what ▆▆▆▆▆▆▆▆ said," I told ▆▆▆▆▆ the day before the test.

---

that follows could be the polygraph exam MOS describes toward the end of his ARB testimony. After recounting the boat trip and its aftermath, MOS stated, "Because they said to me either I am going to talk or they will continue to do this, I said I am going to tell them everything they wanted....I told them I was on my own trying to do things and they said write it down and I wrote it and I signed it. I brought a lot of people, innocent people with me because I got to make a story that makes sense. They thought my story was wrong so they put me on [a] polygraph." ARB transcript, 27.

"Look, I've taken the test several times and passed. All you need to do is clear your mind and be honest and truthful," ██████████ answered.

"I will."

██████████████████████ "Guess what?" said ███████████, looking at me through the cage of my cell. I quickly stood up at the bin hole.

"Yes, Sir!" I thought ████ was one of the guards. ██████████ startled, and █████ looked at me, smiling.

"Oh, it's you! I am sorry, I thought you were one of the guards. You came for the ██████████, didn't you?"

"Yes, in a couple of hours I'll be back with the guy with the ██████████. I just want you to be prepared."

"OK, thank you very much." █████ left. I performed a ritual wash and managed to steal a prayer off the guards, I don't remember whether I performed it formally or informally. "Oh, God! I need your help more than ever. Please show them that I am telling the truth. Please give not these merciless people any reason to hurt me. Please. Please!" After the prayer I exercised a kind of yoga. I never really practiced that meditation technique before, but now I sat on my bed, put my hands on my thighs, and imagined my body connected to the poly.*

"Have you done any crimes against the U.S.?" I asked myself.

"No." Would I really pass? Screw them! I've done no crimes; why should I be worried? They're evil! And then I thought, No, they're not evil: it's their right to defend their own country. They're good people. They really are! And then again, Screw them, I don't owe them anything. They tortured me, they owe me! I did the █████ with all the possible questions.

"Did you tell the truth about ████████████████.

---

* "Poly" appears here unredacted.

"No." Oh, that's a big problem, because ██████████ said, "When we catch you lying you're gonna feel our wrath." Screw ████████████; I'm not gonna lie to please him and destroy my own life. No way. I'm gonna tell the truth no matter what. But what if I fail the test, even after answering truthfully? OK! No problem, I'm gonna lie. But what if the ████████ shows my new lies? Then I'm really gonna be stuck in a cul-de-sac. Only God can help me: my situation is serious and the Americans are crazy. Don't worry about that, just take the ████████ and you're gonna be alright. I was going to the bathroom so often that I thought I was going to urinate my kidneys.

The doorbell rang and ████████████ surged through with the ██ ██ ████████████.

"My name is ████████████████████. Nice to meet you."

"Nice to meet you," I said, shaking his hand. I knew he was dishonest about his name. He unluckily chose the wrong name, ████████████████████, which I knew to be a generic name. But I really didn't care. After all, what interrogator is honest about anything? He could as well have introduced himself as ████████████████████ with the same effect. "You will be working with me today. How are you?"

"I am very nervous," I answered.

"Perfect. That is the way you should be. I don't like relaxed detainees. Give me a minute, I am going to install the ████████ ████████." In fact ████████ and I helped him ████████████████ ████████████████████████████.

"Now, I want you to sit and look at me the whole time while I am speaking to you." ████████████████ was not exactly the evil-looking interrogator. He was, I think, skeptical but fair.

"Have you taken ████████████████████████ before?"

"Yes, I have!"

"So you understand the ▮▮▮▮▮▮▮▮▮▮▮▮▮▮▮▮▮▮▮▮▮▮▮

▮▮▮▮▮▮▮▮▮▮."

"I guess I do."

But anyway, ▮▮▮▮▮▮▮▮▮▮▮▮▮▮▮▮▮▮▮▮▮▮▮▮▮▮

▮▮▮▮▮▮▮▮▮▮▮▮▮▮▮▮▮▮▮▮▮▮▮▮▮▮▮▮▮▮▮▮▮▮▮

▮▮▮▮▮▮▮▮▮▮▮▮▮▮▮▮▮▮▮▮▮▮▮▮▮▮▮▮▮▮▮▮▮▮▮

▮▮▮▮▮▮▮▮▮▮▮▮▮▮▮▮▮▮▮▮▮▮▮▮▮▮▮▮▮▮▮▮▮▮▮

▮▮▮▮▮▮▮▮▮▮▮▮▮▮▮▮▮▮▮▮▮▮▮▮▮▮▮▮▮▮▮▮▮▮▮

▮▮▮▮▮▮▮▮▮▮▮▮▮▮▮▮▮▮▮▮▮▮▮▮▮▮▮▮▮▮▮▮▮▮▮

▮▮▮▮▮▮▮▮▮▮▮▮▮▮▮▮▮▮▮▮▮▮▮▮▮▮▮▮▮▮▮▮▮▮▮

▮▮▮▮▮▮▮▮▮▮▮▮▮▮▮▮▮▮▮▮▮▮▮▮▮▮▮▮▮▮▮▮▮▮▮

▮▮▮▮▮▮▮▮▮▮▮▮▮▮▮▮▮▮▮▮▮▮▮▮▮▮▮▮▮▮▮▮▮▮▮

▮▮▮▮▮▮▮▮▮▮▮▮▮▮▮▮▮▮▮▮▮▮▮▮▮▮▮▮▮▮▮▮▮▮▮

▮▮▮▮▮▮▮▮▮▮▮▮▮▮▮▮▮▮▮▮▮▮▮▮▮▮▮▮▮▮▮▮▮▮▮

▮▮▮▮▮▮▮▮▮▮▮▮▮▮▮▮▮▮▮▮▮▮▮▮▮▮▮▮▮▮▮▮▮▮▮

▮▮▮▮▮▮▮▮▮▮▮▮▮▮▮▮▮▮▮▮▮▮▮▮▮▮▮▮▮▮▮▮▮▮▮

▮▮▮▮▮▮▮▮▮▮▮▮▮▮▮▮▮▮▮▮▮▮▮▮▮▮▮▮▮▮▮▮▮▮▮

▮▮▮▮▮▮▮▮▮▮▮▮▮▮▮▮▮▮▮▮▮▮▮▮▮▮▮▮▮▮▮▮▮▮▮

▮▮▮▮▮▮▮▮▮▮▮▮▮▮▮▮▮▮▮▮▮▮▮▮▮▮▮▮▮▮▮▮▮▮▮

▮▮▮▮▮▮▮▮▮▮▮▮▮▮▮▮▮▮▮▮▮▮▮▮▮▮▮▮▮▮▮▮▮▮▮

▮▮▮▮▮▮▮▮▮▮▮▮▮▮▮▮▮▮▮▮▮▮▮▮▮▮▮▮▮▮▮▮▮▮▮

▮▮▮▮▮▮▮▮▮▮▮▮▮▮▮▮▮▮▮▮▮▮▮▮▮▮▮▮▮▮▮▮▮▮▮

▮▮▮▮▮▮▮▮▮▮▮▮▮▮▮▮▮▮▮▮▮▮▮▮▮▮▮▮▮▮▮▮▮▮▮

▮▮▮▮▮▮▮▮▮▮▮▮▮▮▮▮▮▮▮▮▮▮▮▮▮▮▮▮▮▮▮▮▮▮▮

▮▮▮▮▮▮▮▮▮▮▮▮▮▮▮▮▮▮▮▮▮▮▮▮▮▮▮▮▮▮▮▮▮▮▮

▮▮▮▮▮▮▮▮▮▮▮▮▮▮▮▮▮▮▮▮▮▮▮▮▮▮▮▮▮▮▮▮▮▮▮

▮▮▮▮▮▮▮▮▮▮▮▮▮▮▮▮▮▮▮▮▮▮▮▮▮▮▮▮▮▮▮▮▮▮▮

▮▮▮▮▮▮▮▮▮▮▮▮▮▮▮▮▮▮▮▮▮▮▮▮▮▮▮▮▮▮▮▮▮▮▮

SEVEN

GTMO

2004-2005

The Good News...Goodbye Like Family Members...
The TV and the Laptop...The First Unofficial Laugh-
ter in the Ocean of Tears...The Present Situation...
The Dilemma of the Cuban Detainees

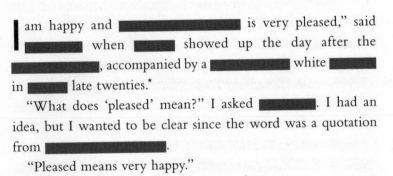

I am happy and ▆▆▆▆▆▆▆▆▆ is very pleased," said
▆▆▆▆▆▆▆ when ▆▆▆▆ showed up the day after the
▆▆▆▆▆▆▆▆▆▆, accompanied by a ▆▆▆▆▆▆▆ white ▆▆▆▆▆▆
in ▆▆▆▆ late twenties.*

"What does 'pleased' mean?" I asked ▆▆▆▆▆▆▆. I had an
idea, but I wanted to be clear since the word was a quotation
from ▆▆▆▆▆▆▆▆▆▆.

"Pleased means very happy."

---

* In *The Terror Courts*, Jess Bravin published details of a polygraph examination of MOS that he dates to October 31, 2004. Bravin reported that
MOS answered "No" to five questions about whether he knew about or
participated in the Millennium and 9/11 plots, and whether he was concealing any information about other al-Qaeda members or plots. The results,
according to Bravin, were either "No Deception Indicated" or "No Opinion"—results that Lt. Col. Stuart Couch, the Military Commissions prosecutor assigned to MOS's case, considered potentially exculpatory
information that would need to be shared with defense attorneys if MOS
was ever charged and prosecuted. Bravin, *The Terror Courts*, 110–11.

"Ah, OK. Didn't I tell you that I wasn't lying?"

"Yes, I'm glad," said ▮▮▮▮▮▮ smiling. ▮▮▮▮▮▮ happiness was obvious and honest. I was hardly happier about my success than ▮▮▮▮▮▮.* Now I could tell that the resented torture was heading the other direction, slowly but surely. And yet I was extremely skeptical, since I was still surrounded by the same people as I had been since day one.

"Look at your uniform and ours. You are not one of us. You are our enemy!" ▮▮▮▮▮▮ used to say.

"I know."

"I don't want you to forget. If I speak to you, I speak to my enemy."

"I know!"

"Don't forget."

"I won't!" Such talk left no doubt that the animosity of the guards had been driven to its extreme. Most of the time I had the feeling that they were trained to devour me alive.

▮▮▮▮▮▮ introduced ▮▮▮ company to me. "This is another interrogator you can ▮▮▮▮▮▮▮▮▮▮ like me."

The new interrogator ▮▮▮▮▮▮▮▮▮▮ was quiet and polite. I can't really say anything negative about ▮▮▮▮▮▮▮▮▮▮ was a workaholic, and not really open to other people. ▮▮▮▮▮▮▮▮ literally followed the orders of ▮▮▮ boss ▮▮▮▮▮▮▮▮▮▮, and sometimes even worked like a computer.

"Do you know about ▮▮▮▮▮▮ travel to Iraq in 2003?" ▮▮▮ asked me once.

---

* The redacted pronouns and tone of this conversation suggest that the lead interrogator might be the female member from the special interrogation team. In this scene she seems to be introducing a new interrogator who will be working with MOS as well; redactions hint that this interrogator, too, might be female.

"Come on, ▇▇▇▇ you know that I turned myself in in 2001. How am I supposed to know what went on in 2003? It doesn't make sense, does it?" I said.

▇▇▇▇▇ smiled. "I have the question in my request."

"But you know that I've been in detention since 2001!" I said. ▇▇▇▇▇▇ was very careful, too careful: ▇▇▇▇▇ used to cover ▇▇▇ rank and ▇▇▇ name all the time, and ▇▇▇ never made any reference to ▇▇▇ beliefs. I personally was content with that, as long as ▇▇▇ didn't give me a hard time.

"I like the way you make connections," ▇▇▇▇▇▇▇ said, smiling at me in that session. Interrogators have a tendency to enter the house through the window and not the door; instead of asking a direct question, they ask all kinds of questions around it. I took it as a challenge, and for the most part I would search out the direct question and answer that. "Your question is whether or not…," I would say. And ▇▇▇▇▇▇ seemed to like that shortcut.

But has there ever, in all of recorded human history, been an interrogation that has gone on, day in and day out, for more than six years? There is nothing an interrogator could say to me that would be new; I've heard every variation. Each new interrogator would come up with the most ridiculous theories and lies, but you could tell they were all graduates of the same school: before an interrogator's mouth opened I knew what he ▇▇▇▇▇▇ was going to say and why he ▇▇▇▇▇▇ was saying it.[*]

"I am your new interrogator. I have very long experience doing this job. I was sent especially from Washington D.C. to assess your case."

---

[*] Context suggests that the redactions in this sentence may be "or she." If so, this would be a particularly absurd example of the effort to conceal the fact that the U.S. deployed female interrogators.

"You are the most important detainee in this camp. If you cooperate with me, I am personally going to escort you to the airport. If you don't cooperate, you're gonna spend the rest of your life on this island."

"You're very smart. We don't want to keep you in jail. We would rather capture the big fish and release the small fish, such as yourself."

"You haven't driven a plane into a building; your involvement can be forgiven with just a five-minute talk. The U.S. is the greatest country in the world; we would rather forgive than punish."

"Many detainees have talked about you being the bad person. I personally don't believe them; however, I would like to hear your side of the story, so I can defend you appropriately."

"I have nothing against Islam, I even have many Muslim friends."

"I have helped many detainees to get out of this place; just by writing a positive report stating that you told you the whole truth . . . . ."

And so on, in an endless recitation that all the interrogators recited when they met with their detainees. Most detainees couldn't help laughing when they had to hear this *Groundhog Day* nonsense; in fact, it was the only entertainment we got in the interrogation booth. When his interrogator told him, "I know you are innocent," one of my fellow detainees laughed hard and responded, "I'd rather be a criminal and sitting home with my kids." I believe anything loses its influence the more we repeat it. If you hear an expression like, "You are the worst criminal on the face of the earth" for the first time, you'll most likely get the hell scared out of you. But the fear diminishes the more times you hear it, and at some point it will have no effect at all. It may even sound like a daily compliment.

And yet let's look at it from the interrogator's perspective. They were literally taught to hate us detainees. "Those people are the most evil creatures on earth...Do not help the enemy... Keep in mind they are enemies...Look out, the Arabs are the worst, especially the Saudis and the Yemenis. They're hardcore, they're savages....Watch out, don't ███████████████████ unless you secure everything..." In GTMO, interrogators are taught more about the potential behavior of detainees than about their actual Intelligence value, and so the U.S. Interrogators consistently succeeded in missing the most trivial information about their own detainees. I'm not speaking about second hand information; I'm speaking about my own experience.

"████████ spoke about you!" ████████ said to me once.

"████████ doesn't know me, how could he possibly have spoken about me? Just read my file again."

"I am sure that he did. I'm gonna show you!" ████ said. But ████ never did because ████ was wrong. I had ████████ of such and worse examples depicting the ignorance of interrogators about their detainees. The government would hold back basic information from its interrogators for tactical reasons, and then tell them, "The detainee you are assigned to is deeply involved in terrorism and has vital information about coming and already performed attacks. Your job is to get everything he knows." In fact, I hardly met a detainee who was involved in a crime against the United States.

So you have interrogators who are prepared, schooled, trained, and pitted to meet their worst enemies. And you have detainees who typically were captured and turned over to U.S. forces without any proper judicial process. After that, they experienced heavy mistreatment and found themselves incarcerated in another hemisphere, in GTMO Bay, by a country that claims to safeguard human rights all over the world—but a country that many Muslims suspect is conspiring with other evil forces to wipe the Islamic religion off the face of the earth. All in all, the environment is not likely to be a place of love and reconciliation. The hatred here is heavily watered.

But believe it or not, I have seen guards crying because they had to leave their duties in GTMO.

"I am your friend, I don't care what anybody says," said one guard to me before he left.

"I was taught bad things about you, but my judgment tells me something else. I like you very much, and I like speaking with you. You are a great person," said another.

"I hope you get released," said ▬▬▬▬ genuinely.

"You guys are my brothers, all of you," another whispered to me.

"I love you!" said a ▬▬▬▬ corpsman once to my neighbor, a funny young guy I personally enjoyed talking to. He was shocked.

"What...Here no love...I am Mouslim!" I just laughed about that "forbidden" love.

But I couldn't help crying myself one day when I saw a German-descendent ▬▬▬▬ guard crying because ▬▬▬▬ got just a little bit hurt. The funny thing was I hid my feelings because I didn't want them to be misinterpreted by my brethren, or understood as a weakness or a betrayal. At one point I hated myself and confused the hell out of myself. I started to ask myself questions about the humane emotions I was having toward my enemies. How could you cry for somebody who caused you so much pain and destroyed your life? How could you possibly like somebody who ignorantly hates your religion? How could you put up with these evil people who keep hurting your brothers? How could you like somebody who works day and night to pull shit on you? I was in a worse situation than a slave: at least a slave is not always shackled in chains, has some limited freedom, and doesn't have to listen to some interrogator's bullshit every day.

I often compared myself with a slave. Slaves were taken forcibly from Africa, and so was I. Slaves were sold a couple of times on their way to their final destination, and so was I. Slaves suddenly were assigned to somebody they didn't choose, and so was I. And when I looked at the history of slaves, I noticed that slaves sometimes ended up an integral part of the master's house.

I have been through several phases during my captivity. The first phase was the worst: I almost lost my mind fighting to get back to my family and the life I was used to. My torture was in my rest; as soon as I closed my eyes, I found myself complaining to them about what has happened to me.

"Am I with you for real, or is it a mere dream?"

"No, you're really at home!"

"Please hold me, don't let me go back!" But the reality always hit me as soon as I woke up to the dark bleak cell, looking around just long enough to fall asleep and experience it all again. It was several weeks before I realized that I'm in jail and not going home anytime soon. As harsh as it was, this step was necessary to make me realize my situation and work objectively to avoid the worst, instead of wasting my time with my mind playing games on me. Many people don't pass this step; they lose their minds. I saw many detainees who ended up going crazy.

Phase two is when you realize for real that you're in jail and you possess nothing but all the time in the world to think about your life—although in GTMO detainees also have to worry about daily interrogations. You realize you have control over nothing, you don't decide when you eat, when you sleep, when you take a shower, when you wake up, when you see the doctor, when you see the interrogator. You have no privacy; you cannot even squeeze a drop of urine without being watched. In the beginning it is a horrible thing to lose all those privileges in the blink of an eye, but believe me, people get used to it. I personally did.

Phase three is discovering your new home and family.

Your family comprises the guards and your interrogators. True, you didn't choose this family, nor did you grow up with it, but it's a family all the same, whether you like it or not, with all the advantages and disadvantages. I personally love my family and wouldn't trade it for the world, but I have developed a family in jail that I also care about. Every time a good member of my present family leaves it feels as if a piece of my heart is being chopped off. But I am so happy if a bad member has to leave.*

"I'm going to leave soon," ▓▓▓▓▓ said a couple of days before ▓▓▓ left.

"Really? Why?"

"It's about time. But the other ▓▓▓▓▓▓▓▓ is going to stay with you." That was not exactly comforting, but it would have been futile to argue: the transfer of MI agents is not a subject of discussion. "We're gonna watch a movie together before I leave," ▓▓▓▓▓ added.

"Oh, good!" I said. I hadn't digested the news yet.

▓▓▓▓▓▓ most likely studied psychology, and came from the west coast, maybe California ▓▓▓▓▓▓▓▓▓▓▓▓ ▓▓▓▓▓▓▓▓▓▓▓▓ early twenties ▓▓▓▓▓▓▓▓▓▓ ▓▓▓▓▓▓▓▓▓▓. I think that ▓▓▓▓▓▓ comes from

---

* MOS adds a note here in the margin of the handwritten original: "Phase four: getting used to the prison, and being afraid of the outside world."

a rather poor family. The ███████████████ provides a great deal of opportunity for people from the lower classes, and most of the █████████████ people I've seen are from the lower class. █████████████████████████ and has a rather shaky relation ███████ ██████████████████ has a very strong personality, ████ looks at ███████████████ and ██████ ideas very highly. At the same time ████████████ likes █████ job, and might have been forced to step over the red line of █████ principles sometimes. "I know what we are doing is not healthy for our country," ██████ used to tell me.

███████████████ was my first real encounter with an American ████████████████████████████████ you are so foul-mouthed! I feel ashamed for you," I wondered once. ██████ smiled.

"It's because I've been most of the time ███████████████████ ████." At first I had a problem starting a conversation with a foul-mouthed ██████████████, but later I learned that there was no way to speak colloquial English without F—ing this and F—ing that. English accepts more curses than any other language, and I soon learned to curse with the commoners. Sometimes guards would ask me to translate certain words into Arabic, German, or French, but the translation spun around in my head and I could not spit it out; it just sounded so gross. On the other hand, when I curse in English I really have no bad feeling whatsoever, because that's the way I learned the language from day one. I had a problem when it comes to blasphemy, but everything else was tolerable. The curses are just so much more harmless when everybody uses them recklessly.

███████████████ was one of my main teachers of the dictionary of curse words, alongside ████████████████████████████████████ █████████████████████ has been through some bad relationships; ████████ had been cheated on and some bad things like that.

"Did you cry when you knew?" I asked ████████.

"No, I didn't want to ████████████████████████ ████████████████████████. I have a problem when it comes to crying."

"I see." But I personally don't see the problem: I cry whenever I feel like it and it makes me stronger to admit my weakness.

████████████ was misused by ████████████ and his colleague ████████████████████████████ and some other behind-the-scenes guys. I know that I am looking for excuses to acquit ████████████████ was old enough to know that what ████ was doing was wrong, and ████ could have both saved ████ job and had the other higher-ranking officers fired. ████████████ certainly contributed to the pressure to which I had been subjected. But I do also know that ████████████ doesn't believe in torture.

I used to make fun of the signs they put up for the interrogators and the guards to raise their morale, "Honor bound to defend freedom." I once cited that big sign to ████████████.

"I hate that sign," ████ said.

"How could you possibly be defending freedom, if you're taking it away?" I would say.

The bosses had noticed the close relationship developing between ████████ and me, and so they separated ████ from me when I was kidnapped. The last words I heard were, "You're hurting him! Who gave you the orders?" ████ shouts fading away as ████████ and ████████████████████████ dragged me out of the room in ████████████████. And when they decided to give me a chance at a halfway humane interrogation, ████████████ appeared in the picture again. But this time ████ was somewhat unfriendly to me, and used any opportunity to make my statements look stupid. I couldn't understand ████ behavior. Was it in my favor, or was ████ just pissed off at everybody?

I'm not going to judge anybody; I'm leaving that part to Allah. I am just providing the facts as I have seen and experienced them, and I don't leave anything out to make somebody look good or bad. I understand that nobody is perfect, and everybody does both good and bad things. The only question is, How much of each?

"Do you hate my government?" ██████████ asked me once while sifting through a map.

"No, I hate nobody."

"I would hate the U.S. if I were you!" █████ said. "You know, nobody really knows what we're doing here. Only a few people in the government know about it."

"Really?"

"Yes. The President reads the files of some detainees. He reads your case."

"Really?"

██████████ enjoyed rewarding rather than punishing detainees. I can say without a doubt that █████████ didn't enjoy harassing me, although █████ tried to keep █████ "professional" face; on the other hand, █████ very much enjoyed giving some stuff back. █████ was even the one who came with most of the ideas related to literature that I was given to read.

"This book is from ██████████████ said one day, handing me a thick novel that was called something like *Life in the Forest.*★ It was historical fiction, written by a British writer, and it covered a great deal of the medieval European history and the Norman invasion. I received the book gratefully and read it hungrily, at least three times. Later on, █████ brought me several

---

★ The description suggests the book might be Edward Rutherfurd's historical novel *The Forest*, which was published in 2000.

Star Wars books. Whenever I finished one, ▬▬▬ traded it for a new one.

"Oh, thank you very much!"

"Did you like the Star Wars?"

"I sure do!" In truth, I didn't really like the Star Wars books and their language, but I had to settle for any books they gave to me. In prison you have nothing but all the time in world to think about your life and the goal thereof. I think prison is one of the oldest and greatest schools in the world: you learn about God and you learn patience. A few years in prison are equivalent to decades of experience outside it. Of course there is the devastating side of the prison, especially for innocent prisoners who, besides dealing with the daily hardship of prison, have to deal with the psychological damages that result from confinement without a crime. Many innocent people in prison contemplate suicide.

Just imagine yourself going to bed, putting all your worries aside, enjoying your favorite magazine to put you to sleep, you've put the kids to bed, your family is already sleeping. You are not afraid of being dragged out of your bed in the middle of the night to a place you've never seen before, deprived of sleep, and terrorized all the time. Now imagine that you have no say at all in your life—when you sleep, when you wake up, when you eat, and sometimes when you go to the toilet. Imagine that your whole world comprises, at most, a 6 by 8 foot cell. If you imagine all of that, you still won't understand what prison really means unless you experience it yourself.

▬▬▬▬▬▬ showed up as promised a few days later with a laptop and two movies, and told me. "You can decide which one you'd like to watch!" I picked the movie *Black Hawk Down*; I don't remember the other choice.

The movie was both bloody and sad. I paid more attention to the emotions of ███████ and the guards than to the movie itself. ███████ was rather calm; ███████████████ every once in a while paused the movie to explain the historical background of certain scenes to me. The guards almost went crazy emotionally because they saw many Americans getting shot to death. But they missed that the number of U.S. casualties is negligible compared to the Somalis who were attacked in their own homes. I was just wondering at how narrow-minded human beings can be. When people look at one thing from one perspective, they certainly fail to get the whole picture, and that is the main reason for the majority of misunderstandings that sometimes lead to bloody confrontations.

After we finished watching the movie, ███████ packed ████ computer and got ready to leave.

"Eh, by the way, you didn't tell me when you're going to leave!"

"I am done, you won't see me anymore!" I froze as if my feet were stuck on the floor. ███████ didn't tell me that ████ was leaving *that* soon; I thought maybe in a month, three weeks, something like that—but today? In my world that was impossible. Imagine if death were devouring some friend of yours and you just were helplessly watching him fading away.

"Oh, really, that soon? I'm surprised! You didn't tell me. Good-bye," I said. "I wish everything good for you."

"I have to follow my orders, but I leave you in good hands." And off ████ went. I reluctantly went back to my cell and silently burst in tears, as if I'd lost ███████████, and not somebody whose job was to hurt me and extract information in an end-justifies-the-means way. I both hated and felt sorry for myself for what was happening to me.

"May I see my interrogator please?" I asked the guards, hoping they could catch ███████ before they reached the main gate.

"We'll try," said ███████. I retreated back in my cell, but soon ███████ showed up at the door of my cell.

"That is not fair. You know that I suffered torture and am not ready for another round."

"You haven't been tortured. You must trust my government. As long as you're telling the truth, nothing bad is gonna happen to you!" Of course ████ meant The Truth as it's officially defined. But I didn't want to argue with ████ about anything.

"I just don't want to start everything over with new interrogators," I said.

"It's not gonna happen," ███████ said. "Besides, you can write me. I promise I'll answer every email of yours," ████ continued.

"No, I will not write you," I said.

"OK." ███████ said. "Are you alright?" ████ asked.

"I'm not, but you may surely leave."

"I am not leaving until you assure me everything's alright," ████ said.

"I said what I had to say. Have a good trip. May Allah guide you. I'll be just fine."

"I am sure you will. It will take at most a week and you'll forget me." I didn't speak after that. Instead I went back and lay myself down. ███████ stayed a couple of minutes repeating ███████ "I am not leaving until you assure me everything is alright."

After ████ left, I never saw ████ again or tried to get in contact with ████. And so the chapter of ███████ time with me was sealed.

"I heard yesterday's goodbye was very emotional. I never

thought of you this way. Would you describe yourself as a criminal?" ▮▮▮▮▮▮▮▮▮ said the next day.

I prudently answered, "To an extent." I didn't want to fall in
any possible trap, even though I felt that he was honestly and
innocently asking the question, now that he realized that his
evil theories about me were null. "All the evil questions are
gone," ▮▮▮▮▮▮▮▮▮▮ said.

"I won't miss them," I said.

▮▮▮▮▮▮▮▮▮▮▮▮▮▮▮▮ had come to give me a haircut.
It was about time! One of the measures of my punishment was
to deprive me of any hygienic shaves, toothbrushing, or hair-
cuts, so today was a big day. They brought a masked barber; the
guy was scary looking, but he did the job. ▮▮▮▮▮▮▮▮▮▮
also brought me a book he promised me a long time ago, *Fermat's Last Theorem*, which I really enjoyed—so much so that I
hungrily read it more than twice. The book is written by a
British journalist and speaks about the famous De Fermat theorem that says the equation $A^n + B^n = C^n$ has no solution when
n is greater than two. For more than three hundred years, math-
ematicians from all around the world were boxing against this
harmless-looking theorem without succeeding in tackling it,
until a British Mathematician in 1993 came up with a very
complicated proof, which was surely not the one De Fermat
meant when he wrote, "I have a neat proof but I have no space
on my paper."

I got a haircut, and later on a decent shower. ▮▮▮▮▮▮▮▮▮
was not a very talkative person; ▮▮▮▮▮ asked me just one question about computers.

"Are you going to cooperate with the new ▮▮▮▮▮?"
"Yes."

"Or anybody who's going to work with ▮▮▮?"
"Yes."

*   *   *

The guards wanted to be baptized with the names of characters in the *Star Wars* movies. "From now on we are the ████████ and that's what you call us. Your name is Pillow," ████████████ said. I eventually learned from the books that ████████████ are sort of Good Guys who fight against the Forces of Evil. So for the time being I was forced to represent the Forces of Evil, and the guards the Good Guys.

"████████████████, that's what you call me," he said. I also called him ████████████████████████████████████ ██ ██ was in his early forties, married with children, small but athletically built. He spent some time working in the ████████████ ████████████████, and then ended up doing "special missions" for the ████████████ "████████████████████████████ ████████. I've been working ████████████████████████," he told me.

"Your job is done. I am broken," I answered.

"Don't ask me anything. If you want to ask for something, ask your interrogator."

"I got you," I said. It sounds confusing or even contradictory, but although ████████████ was a rough guy, he was humane. That is to say his bark was worse than his bite. ████████████ understood what many guards don't understand: if you talk and tell your interrogators what they want to hear, you should be relieved. Many of the other nitwits kept doubling the pressure on me, just for the sake of it.

████████████ was in charge of all the other guards. "My job is to make you see the light," said ████████████, addressing me for the first time when he was watching me eating my meal.

Guards were not allowed to talk to me or to each other, and I couldn't talk to them. But ▆▆▆▆▆▆▆ was not a by-the-book guy. He thought more than any other guard, and his goal was to make his country victorious: the means didn't matter.

"Yes sir," I answered, without even understanding what he meant. I thought about the literal sense of the light I hadn't seen in a long time, and I believed he wanted to get me cooperating so I could see the daylight. But ▆▆▆▆▆ meant the figurative sense. ▆▆▆▆▆ always yelled at me and scared me, but he never hit me. He illegally interrogated me several times, which is why I called him ▆▆▆▆▆▆▆▆▆▆▆▆▆▆▆▆▆▆▆▆▆▆ wanted me to confess to many wild theories he heard the interrogators talking about. Furthermore, he wanted to gather knowledge about terrorism and extremism. I think his dream in life was to become an interrogator. What a hell of a dream!

▆▆▆▆▆▆▆▆▆▆ is an admitted Republican, and hates the Democrats, especially Bill Clinton. He doesn't believe that the U.S. should interfere in other countries' business, and instead should focus more on internal issues—but if any country or group attacks the U.S., it should be destroyed ruthlessly.

"Fair enough," I said. I just wanted him to stop talking. He is the kind of guy who never stops when he gets started. Gosh, he gave me an earache! When ▆▆▆▆▆ first started talking to me I refused to answer, because all I was allowed to say was, "Yes, sir, No Sir, Need Medics, Need Interrogators." But he wanted a conversation with me.

"You are my enemy," ▆▆▆▆ said.

"Yes, Sir."

"So let's talk as enemy to enemy," ▆▆▆▆ said. He opened my cell and offered me a chair. ▆▆▆▆▆ did the talking for the most part. He was talking about how great the U.S. is, and how powerful; "America is this, American is that, We Americans are so and so..." I was just wondering and nodding slightly. Every once in a while I confirmed that I was paying attention, "Yes, sir...Really?...Oh, I didn't know...You're right...I know..." During our conversations, he sneakily tried to make me admit to things I hadn't really done.

"What was your role in September 11?"

"I didn't participate in September 11."

"Bullshit!" he screamed madly. I realized it would be no good for my life to look innocent, at least for the time being. So I said, "I was working for al Qaeda in Radio Telecom."

He seemed to be happier with a lie. "What was your rank?" he kept digging.

"I would be a Lieutenant."

"I know you've been in the U.S.," he tricked me. This is a big one and I couldn't possibly lie about it. I could vaguely swallow having done a lot of things in Afghanistan, because Americans cannot confirm or disconfirm it. But the Americans could check right away whether or not I had been in their own country.

"I really haven't been in the U.S.," I answered, though I was ready to change my answer when I had no options.

"You've been in Detroit," he sardonically smiled.

I smiled back. "I really haven't." Though ▇▇▇▇ didn't believe me, he didn't push the matter further; ▇▇▇▇ was interested in a long-term dialogue with me. In return for my confessions ▇▇▇▇ gave me extra food and stopped yelling at me. Meanwhile, in order to maintain the terror, the other guards kept yelling at me and banging the metal door to my cell. Every time they did, my heart started to pound, though the more they did such things, the less effect it had.

"Why are you shaking?" ▇▇▇▇ asked me once when he took me out for conversation. I both hated and liked when he was on duty: I hated him interrogating me, but I liked him giving me more food and new uniforms.

"I don't know," I answered.

"I am not gonna hurt you."

"OK." It took some time until I accepted talking to ███████. He started to give me lessons and made me practice them the hard way. The lessons were proverbs and made up of phrases he wanted me to memorize and practice in my life. I still do remember the following lessons: 1) Think before you act. 2) Do not mistake kindness for weakness. 3) ████████ questions always in mind when you are asked about somebody. Whenever ████████ judged me to have broken one of the lessons, he took me out of my cell and strew my belongings all over the place, and then ████████ asked me to put everything back in no time. I always failed to organize my stuff, but he would make me do it several times, after which I miraculously put all my stuff back in time.

My relationship with ████████████ developed positively with every day that went by, and so with the rest of the guards, too, because they regarded him highly.

"Fuck it! If I look at Pillow I don't think he is a terrorist, I think he's an old friend of mine, and I enjoy playing games with him," he said to the other guards. I relaxed somewhat and gained some self-confidence. Now the guards discovered the humorous guy in me, and used their time with me for entertainment. They started to make me repair their DVD players and PC's, and in return I was allowed to watch a movie. ████████ didn't exactly have the most recent PC model, and when ██████ ████████████ asked me whether I had seen ████████ PC, I answered, "You mean that museum piece?"

████████████████ laughed hard. "Better hope he doesn't hear what you said."

"Don't tell him!"

We slowly but surely became a society and started to gossip about the interrogators and call them names. In the mean time, ▆▆▆▆ taught me the Rules of chess. Before prison, I didn't know the difference between a pawn and the rear end of a knight, nor was I really a big gamer. But I found in chess a very interesting game, especially the fact that a prisoner has total control over his pieces, which gives him some confidence back. When I started playing, I played very aggressively in order to let out my frustration, which was really not very good chess playing; ▆▆▆ was my first mentor and ▆▆▆ beat me in my first game ever. But the next game was mine, and so were all the other games that followed. Chess is a game of strategy, art, and mathematics. It takes deep thinking, and there is no luck involved. You get rewarded or punished for your actions.

▆▆▆▆▆▆▆▆▆▆▆▆▆▆▆▆▆▆ brought me a chessboard so I could play against myself. When the guards noticed my chessboard, they all wanted to play me, and when they started to play me, they always won. The strongest among the guards was ▆▆▆▆▆▆. He taught me how to control the center. Moreover, ▆▆▆▆▆ brought me some literature, which helped decidedly in honing my skills. After that the guards had no chance to defeat me.

"That is not the way I taught you to play chess," ▆▆▆▆ commented angrily when I won a game.

"What should I do?"

"You should build a strategy, and organize your attack! That's why the fucking Arabs never succeed."

"Why don't you just play the board?" I wondered.

"Chess is not just a game," he said.

"Just imagine you're playing against a computer!"

"Do I look like a computer to you?"

"No." The next game I tried to build a strategy in order to let ▓▓▓▓▓ win.

"Now you understand how chess must be played," he commented. I knew ▓▓▓▓▓▓ had issues dealing with defeat, and so I didn't enjoy playing him because I didn't feel comfortable practicing my newly acquired knowledge. ▓▓▓▓▓ believes there are two kinds of people: white Americans and the rest of the world. White Americans are smart and better than anybody. I always tried to explain things to him by saying, for instance, "If I were you," or "If you were me," but he got angry and said, "Don't you ever dare to compare me with you, or compare any American with you!" I was shocked, but I did as he said. After all, I didn't have to compare myself with anybody. ▓▓▓▓▓ hated the rest of the world, especially the Arabs, Jews, French, Cubans, and others. The only other country he mentioned positively was England.

After one game of chess with him, he flipped the board. "Fuck your Nigger chess, this is Jewish chess," he said.

"Do you have something against Black people?" I asked.

"Nigger is not black, Nigger means stupid," he argued. We had many discussions like that. At the time we had only one Black guard who had no say, and when he worked with ▓▓▓▓▓ they never interacted. ▓▓▓▓▓ resented him. ▓▓▓▓▓ had a very strong personality, dominant, authoritarian, patriarchal, and arrogant.

"My wife calls me asshole," he proudly told me. ▓▓▓▓▓▓ listened mostly to Rock-n-Roll music and some type of country. His favorite songs were "Die Terrorist Die," "The Taliban Song," and "Let the Bodies Hit the Floor."

▓▓▓▓▓▓▓▓▓▓▓▓▓▓▓▓▓▓▓▓▓▓▓▓▓▓▓▓▓▓▓▓▓▓▓

▓▓▓▓▓▓▓▓▓▓▓▓▓▓▓▓▓▓▓▓▓▓▓▓▓▓▓▓▓▓▓▓▓▓▓

▓▓▓▓▓▓▓▓▓▓▓▓▓▓▓▓▓▓▓▓▓▓▓▓▓▓▓▓▓▓▓▓▓▓▓

██

██

██

██

████████ I never had the chance to see his face because he left

██

████████. But that was OK with me; I really wasn't interested in seeing anybody's face at that point. In the beginning, he was rough with me: he used to pull me hard and make me run in the shackles, screaming loudly "Move!"*

"You know who you are?" he asked me.

"Yes, Sir!"

"You are a terrorist!"

"Yes, Sir!"

"So let's do some math: if you killed five thousand people by your association with al Qaeda, we should kill you five thousand times. But no, because we are Americans we feed you and are ready to give you money if you give us information."

"That's right, Sir!" But after ████████████████ ordered the guards to be friendly with me, ██████████████ started to treat me like a human being. I enjoyed discussing things with him because his English was decent, although he was always "right" in his position.

"Our job is to accommodate you!" he used to tell me sarcastically. "You need a house maid." Since guards copy each other,

---

* In this section, which MOS headed "Guards," he introduces several characters. Everything from the opening of the section to this multiline redaction appears to refer to guard number one, clearly a leader on the guard team. Redactions make it difficult to distinguish among the several guards that follow, though this redaction likely marks the introduction of guard number two, whose tour apparently ended before the Special Projects Team interrogators permitted MOS's guards to remove their masks in his presence.

███████████████████ tended to copy ████████████.
████████████████ was the Inspector: he liked to inspect my
room and make sure everything was put where it belongs,
the sheet was wrapped around the edge of the mattress in a
45° angle, and things like that. He also constantly inspected
the shower and if he found a tiny hair left in it, he and
████████████████████ made me clean everything again. It
didn't matter how often I cleaned; everything had to be perfect.

████████████████████ was especially interested in how I
could keep a calendar in my head and know the days and nights
in spite of the techniques the guards used to mess up my head.
They once tried to make me believe Christmas was Thanksgiv-
ing, but I didn't buy it.

"It doesn't really matter, but I do believe it's Christmas," I
told them.

"We want you to explain to us what mistakes we made so
we can avoid them when we get our next detainee." I explained
as much as necessary, but I am sure they will make plenty of
mistakes with the next detainee because nobody is perfect.

████████████████████████ explained to me how my
recipe could get worse. "You haven't seen nothing."

"And I assure you I am not eager to see more," I would say.
He was probably right, though he missed the fact that none
of the guards had witnessed everything that happened to me.
The only guard who participated in the transport party was
███████████████, and he used every opportunity to hit me in
the new place. You could tell he found no problem in beating
me, since he did it with the blessing of the highest authority in
GTMO.

████████████████ was the only guard who didn't sleep
during his watch. He would drive me crazy pacing around all
the time, and liked to surprise me in the middle of the night

by banging the metal door to my cell and making me take a shower and clean everything perfectly. I should not feel rested in my cell for more than an hour: that is one of the most important methods in breaking somebody in detention, because you must hate your life, your guards, your cell, your interrogators, and even yourself. And that is exactly what ███████████ ██████ did until ███████████████ and ███████████████ ordered otherwise.

███████████████ was a white man in his twenties, very tall, lazy, non-athletic looking.*

"███████████ is my best friend," he told me once.

"How do you know ███████████?" He didn't answer me, he just smiled, but he kept mentioning ███████████ and how he had abused me. I always changed the subject because I didn't want the other guards to know that beating me was something normal. I was glad my guards didn't know everything that happened to me; I didn't need the gang to be encouraged to do crimes.

███████████████ was the most violent guard. In Building ███████████ the guards performed regular assaults on me in order to maintain the terror. They came in a big masked team, screaming and giving contradictory orders so I wouldn't know what to do. They would drag me out of my cell and throw my belongings all over the place.

"Get up...Face the wall...You've been resting lately too much...You have a Pillow...Ha Ha!...Look inside his cell... The piece of shit might be hiding something...We found two kernels of rice hidden beneath his mattress...You have twenty seconds to put everything where it belongs!" The game was over when they made me sweat. I knew the guards didn't have

---

* This redaction may introduce the third guard that MOS is profiling.

the order to beat me, but this guard used every opportunity to hit me and claw me deeply. I don't think that he is the smartest guy, but he was well trained in how to beat somebody without leaving irreparable injuries. "Hitting in the ribs is painful and doesn't leave permanent scars, especially when treated right away with ice-cubes," one of the guards told me. ███████████ ████ was both violent and loud, but thank God, he was very lazy; he only barked at the beginning of the shift and after a short time he disappeared from the stage to watch a movie or go to sleep.

███████████████████ didn't have any bad feelings about his job; on the contrary, he was rather proud of what he was doing, and he was mad at the fact that he was taking care of the dirty part of the job and he wanted to be rewarded adequately. "Fuck the interrogators: we do the work and they take the credit," ████████████ told me once.

He also didn't get along with ████████████████, the only guy that outranked him. "████████ is a pussy!" he described him once. But ████████████████ was not a social person anyway. He could not lead a normal conversation like everybody else. He rarely spoke, and when he did, it was about his wild sex experiences. One common thing among the guards is that most of them never understood the fact that some people don't have sex outside marriage.

"You're gay," was the usual response.

"That is OK with me, but I cannot have sex outside marriage. You may consider me an idiot, but that's OK!"

"How can you buy a car without test-driving it?"

"First of all, a woman is not a car. And I am doing it because of my religion." Even ████████████ interrogator ████████ shocked me once when ████ said, "I wouldn't marry anybody before test driving him." But I still do believe that some Americans don't believe in premarital sex.

███

███

███

██████ about himself.* He told me he had been tasked to gather Intels about me before my kidnapping from ████████████████████, and gave evidence of this by accurately recounting details of my special situation. I had never noticed him in the blocks of ██████████████████ nor was I supposed to. ██████████████████ was mostly partnered with ████████████████████; at the beginning, and in the decisive period, ████████████ was in charge. ████████████████████ was in good physical shape, unlike his friend ████████████████████

████████████████████ moderately and dutifully followed the rules he was given by ████████████████████ and the rest of the ████████████████████ and his associate delivered my water diet, gave me PTs, forbade me to pray or fast, and kept giving me a "Party-shower." ████████████████████ was even the one who came up with that annoying ██ ██████ every piece in a defined place, toilet and sink always dry, so I ended up having to use my uniform because I had no towel. ██ ██ Nonetheless, I can tell you truthfully that ████████████ didn't enjoy bothering me or torturing me.

"Why did you forbid me to pray when you knew it's an illegal order?" I asked him when we became friends.

"I could have but they would have given me some shitty job."

---

* This redaction appears to introduce the fourth guard that MOS profiles in this section.

He also told me that ███████████████ gave him the order preventing me from practicing any religious activities. ████████████ said, "I'm going to hell because I forbade you to pray."

████████████ was so happy when he was ordered to treat me nicely. "I really enjoyed being here with you more than being at home," he genuinely said. He was a very generous guy; he used to give me muffins, movies, and PS2 games. Before he left he asked me to choose between two games, Madden 2004 and Nascar 2004. I chose Nascar 2004, which I still have. Above all, ████████████ was a hell of an entertainer. He tended to stretch the truth, and he would tell me all kinds of stuff. Sometimes he gave me too much information, things I didn't want to know, nor was I supposed to know.

████████████ was a big gamer. He used to play video games all the time. I'm terrible when it comes to video games; it's just not for me. I always told the guards, "Americans are just big babies. In my country it's not appropriate for somebody my age to sit in front of a console and waste his time playing games." Indeed, one of the punishments of their civilization is that Americans are addicted to video games.

And Americans worship their bodies. They eat well. When I was delivered to Bagram Air Base, I was like, What the heck is going on, these soldiers never stop chewing on something. And yet, though God blessed Americans with a huge amount of healthy food, they are the biggest food wasters I ever knew: if every country lived as Americans do, our planet could not absorb the amount of waste we produce.

They also work out. I have a big variety of friends who come from all backgrounds, and I really had never heard any other group of mortals speaking about the next workout plan.

"Is that a homosexual magazine?" I asked one of the guards

who was holding a man fitness magazine with those oversized guys. You know, those guys who keep working out until their necks disappear, and their heads barely fit between their overgrown shoulders.

"What the fuck are you talking about? This is a workout magazine," he responded. American men are more intolerant toward male homosexuals compared to German men, and they work out as if they're preparing for a fight.

"When I hug my wife, she feels secure," ████████████ ████ told me once.

"My wife always feels secure; she doesn't need a hug to be calmed," I answered.

████████████████ was like anybody else: he bought more food than he needed, worked out even during duty, planned to enlarge his member, played video and computer games, and was very confused when it comes to his religion.

"Pillow, I am telling you, I really don't know. But I am Christian and my parents celebrate Christmas every year," he told me, adding, "My girlfriend wants to convert to Islam but I said no."

"Come on, ████████████, you should let her choose. Don't you guys believe in freedom of religion?" I replied. ████████████ had all the qualities of a human being; I liked conversing with him because he always had something to say. He liked to impress the females on the island. And he especially resented ████████████████; I really can't blame him!

Everyone resented him.* He was lazy and on the slower side. Nobody wanted to work with him, and they talked ill about him all the time. ████████████████ didn't have any initiative or personality of his own, and he used to copy every

---

* The passage from here to the section break seems to refer to a fifth guard.

other guard. When he started working on the team he was quiet; he just served me my food and dutifully made me drink water every hour. And that was cool. But he quickly learned that I could be yelled at, have food taken from, and made to do harsh PTs I didn't want to do. He couldn't believe that he was entitled to so much power. He almost went wild making me stand up for hours during the night, even though he knew I suffered from sciatic nerve. He made me clean my cell over and over. He made me clean the shower over and over.

"I wish you'd make a mistake, any mistake, so I can strike," he used to say while performing some corny fake martial arts he must have learned for purposes of his mission. Even after ▇▇▇▇▇▇▇▇▇▇▇▇▇▇ ordered the guards to be nice to me, he became worse, as if trying to catch up on something he missed.

"You call me Master, OK?" he said.

"Oh, yes," I answered, thinking, Who the heck does he think he is? When he saw the other guards playing chess with me, he wanted to play, too, but I soon discovered how weak a person can be in chess. Moreover, he had his own rules, which he always enforced, him being the Master, and me the detainee. In his chess world the king belonged to his own color, breaking the basic rule in chess that states that the king sits on the opposite color when the game begins. I knew he was wrong, but there was no correcting him, so with him I had to play his version of chess.

Around March ▇▇ ▇▇▇▇▇▇▇▇▇▇▇▇ gave me a TV with an integrated VCR to watch the movies they would give me. ▇▇▇▇▇▇▇▇▇▇▇▇ himself gave me the movie *Gladiator* from his personal collection. I like that movie because it vividly depicts how the forces of evil get defeated at the end, no matter how strong they seem. On advice and approval, ███████████████ and ███ colleague got me many interesting movies.*

In my real life I was not a big fan of movies; I don't remember watching a single movie all the way through since I turned eighteen. I do like documentaries and movies based on true stories, but I have a problem giving up my mind and going with the flow of the acting when I know that everything that happens in the movie is fake. But in prison, I'm different: I appreciate everything that shows regular human beings wearing casual clothes and talking about something besides terrorism and interrogation. I just want to see some mammals I can relate to.

The Americans I met watch movies a lot. In America it's like, "Tell me how many movies you've seen, and I'll tell you who you are." But if Americans can be proud of something, they have the right to be proud of their motion picture industry.

Of course, the TV had no receiver, because I was not allowed to watch TV or know anything that happened outside my cell; all I was allowed to watch were the movies that had been approved ███████████████████. It is so evidently unjust to cut off a person from the rest of the world and forbid him to know what's going on in the outside world, regardless of whether or not he is involved in criminal activities. I noticed that the TV/VCR combo had an FM Radio receiver that could receive local broadcasts, but I never touched it: although it is my basic right to listen to whatever radio I wish, I find it so

---

* This would likely be March 2004—more than seven months after MOS was dragged into the isolation cell in Camp Echo. The paragraph may refer to "Captain Collins," who appears from later passages to have remained in control of Slahi's interrogation until he was transferred to Iraq in the summer of 2004, and the new female interrogator. See footnote on p. 347.

dishonest to stab the hand that reaches out to help you. And regardless of what ███████████████████████ have done to me, I found it positive that they offered me this entertainment tool, and I would not use it against them. Moreover, ████████████████ got me a laptop, which I mightily enjoyed. Of course one of the main reasons for the laptop was to make me type my answers during interrogations to save both time and manpower ███████████████████████. But I had no problem with that idea; after all, I wanted to deliver my words and not their interpretation thereof.

"Look, I got some Arabic Music," said █████████████ handing me an Audio CD.

"Oh, fine!" But the CD was not even close to the Arabic language: it was Bosnian. I laughed wholeheartedly. "Close enough. It's Bosnian music," I said when the CD started to play.

"Is it not the same, Bosnian and Arabic?" asked ███████████ ██████. That is just one example of how little Americans know about Arabs and Islam. ███████████████ is a member of ████████ and not just anybody; ██████████ is supposedly armed with basic knowledge about Arabs and Islam. But ████████████████ and the other interrogators always addressed me, "You guys from the middle east...," which is so completely wrong. For many Americans, the world comprises three places: The U.S., Europe, and the rest of the world, the Middle East. Unfortunately, the world, geographically speaking, is a little bit more than that. In my job in my country, I had to make some calls to the U.S. for professional purposes. I remember the following conversation:

"Hello, we are dealing with office materials. We are interested in representing your company."

"Where are you calling from?" asked the lady at the other end.

"Mauritania."

"What state?" asked the lady, seeking more precise information. I was negatively surprised at how small her world was.

The confusion ██████████████████ was as obvious as his ignorance about the whole terrorism issue. The man was completely terrified, as if he were drowning and looking for any straw to grasp. I guess I was one of the straws he bumped into in his flailing, and he grasped me really hard.

"I don't understand why people hate us. We help everybody in the world!" he stated once, seeking my opinion.

"Neither do I," I replied. I knew it was futile to enlighten him about the historical and objective reasons that led to where we're at, and so I opted to ignore his comment; besides, it was not exactly easy to change the opinion of a man as old as he was.

Many young men and women join the U.S. forces under the misleading propaganda of the U.S. government, which makes people believe that the Armed Forces are nothing but a big Battle of Honor: if you join the Army, you are a living martyr; you're defending not only your family, your country, and American democracy but also freedom and oppressed people all around the world. Great, there is nothing wrong with that; it may even be the dream of every young man or woman. But the reality of the U.S. forces is a little tiny bit different. To go directly to the bottom line: the rest of the world thinks of Americans as a bunch of revengeful barbarians. That may be harsh, and I don't believe the dead average American is a revengeful barbarian. But the U.S. government bets its last penny on violence as the magic solution for every problem, and so the country is losing friends every day and doesn't seem to give a damn about it.

"Look, ██████████, everybody hates you guys, even your

traditional friends. The Germans hate you, the French hate you," I said once to ████████████████.*

"Fuck all of them. We would rather have them hate us, and we'll whup their asses," ██████ replied. I just smiled at how easy a solution can be made.

"That's one way to look at it," I answered.

"Fuck them Terrorists."

"OK," I would say. "But you should find the terrorists first. You can't just go wild and hurt everybody in the name of terrorism." He believed that every Arab is a terrorist until proven innocent.

"We need you to help us lock up ████████████ for the rest of his life," he said.

"I am. I've been providing enough Intels to convict him."

"But he keeps denying. He is dealing with other agencies that have different rules than we do. I wish I could get my hands on him: things would be different then!"

I was like, "I hope you never get your hands on anybody."

"All he says is that he did the operation on his own, and that's it," ████████ said.

"Oh, that's very convenient!" I said wryly. Lately I had started to copy ████████████, using the exact same phrases as ████████████. He used to tell me "All you can say is I don't know, I don't remember. That's very convenient! You think you are going to impress an American jury with your charisma?" He always liked to quote the U.S. President, saying "We will not send you guys to court and let you use our justice system, since you're planning to destroy it."

"Is that part of the Big Conspiracy?" I wryly wondered.

"Al Qaeda is using our liberal justice system," he continued.

---

* Here and for the next several paragraphs, MOS appears to be recalling a previous conversation or conversations with one of his interrogators.

I really don't know what liberal justice system he was talking about: the U.S. broke the world record for the number of people it has in prison. Its prison population is over two million, more than any other country in the world, and its rehabilitation programs are a complete failure. The United States is the "democratic" country with the most draconian punishment system; in fact, it is a good example of how draconian punishments do not help in stopping crimes. Europe is by far more just and humane, and the rehab programs there work, so the crime rate in Europe is decisively lower than the U.S. But the American proverb has it, "When the going gets rough, the rough get going." Violence naturally produces violence; the only loan you can make with a guarantee of payback is violence. It might take some time, but you will always get your loan back.

As things improved, I asked ████████████████████ to transfer me to another place because I wanted to forget the bad memories I experienced where I was. ████████████████ tried to meet my request; he promised me the transfer many times, but he failed to keep his promises. I don't doubt his seriousness, but I could tell there was some kind of power struggle in the small island of GTMO. Everybody wanted the biggest portion of the pie, and the most credit for the work of ████████ ████. He genuinely promised me many other things, but couldn't hold those promises either.

One amazing thing about ████████████████████ was that he never brought up the story of my torture. I always expected him to open the topic, but nothing like that happened: Taboo! Personally I was scared to talk about it; I didn't feel secure enough. Even if he had brought the topic up, I would have dodged talking about it.

But at least he finally told me where I was.

"I have to inform you, against the will of many members in

our team, that you are in GTMO," he said. "You've been honest with us and we owe you the same." Although the rest of the world didn't have a clue as to where the U.S. government was incarcerating me, I had known since day one thanks to God and the clumsiness of the ███████████. But I acted as if this was new information, and I was happy because it meant many things to me to be told where I am. As I write these lines, I am still sitting in that same cell, but at least now I don't have to act ignorant about where I am, and that is a good thing.

███████████████████████ the U.S. Army released the first letter from my family.* It was sent through the International Committee of the Red Cross. My family wrote it months before, in July 2003. It had been 815 days since I was kidnapped from my house and had all contacts with my family forcibly broken. I had been sending many letters to my family since I arrived in Cuba, but to no avail. In Jordan I was forbidden even to send a letter.

█████████████████████ was the one who handed me that historical piece of paper, which read:

Nouakchott, ██████████████████
  In the Name of God the most Merciful.
  Peace be with you and God's mercy.
  From your mom ███████████████████
  After my greeting I inform you of my wellbeing and that of the rest of your family. We hope you are the same way. My health situation is OK. I still keep up with my schedule with the Doctors. I feel I am getting better. And the family is OK.

---

* Earlier in the manuscript, MOS indicates that he received the first letter from his family on February 14, 2004.

As I mentioned everybody sends his greeting to you. Beloved son! As of now we have received three letters from you. And this is our second reply. The neighbors are well and they send their greetings. At the end of this letter I renew my greeting. Peace be with you.

Your Mom ███████████

I couldn't believe that after all I had been through I was holding a letter from my mom. I smelled the odor of a letter that had touched the hand of my mom and other members of my beloved family. The emotions in my heart were mixed: I didn't know what to do, laugh or cry. I ultimately ended up doing both. I kept reading the short message over and over. I knew it was for real, not like the fake one I got one year ago. But I couldn't respond to the letter because I was still not allowed to see the ICRC.

Meanwhile, I kept getting books in English that I enjoyed reading, most of them Western literature. I still remember one book called *The Catcher in the Rye* that made me laugh until my stomach hurt. It was such a funny book. I tried to keep my laughter as low as possible, pushing it down, but the guards felt something.

"Are you crying?" one of them asked.

"No, I'm alright," I responded. It was my first unofficial laughter in the ocean of tears. Since interrogators are not professional comedians, most of the humor they came up with was a bunch of lame jokes that really didn't make me laugh, but I would always force an official smile.

██

████████████████████████████ came one Sunday morning and waited outside the building. ████████████ appeared before my cell ███████████████. I didn't recognize him, of course; I thought he was a new interrogator.* But when he spoke I knew it was him.

"Are ███████████████?"

"Don't worry. Your interrogator is waiting on you outside." I was overwhelmed and terrified at the same time; it was too much for me. ███████████████ led me outside the building; I saw ███████████████ looking away from me, shy that I see his face. If you deal with somebody for so long behind a face cover, that is how you know him ████████. But now if he ██████ takes off the face cover you have to deal with his features, and that is a completely different story for both sides. I could tell the guards were uncomfortable to show me their faces.

███████████████████ put it bluntly. "If I catch you looking at me, I'm gonna hurt you."

"Don't you worry, I'm not dying to see your face." Through time I had built a perception about the way everybody looked, but imagination was far from the reality.

██████████ prepared a small table with a modest breakfast. I was scared as hell; for one, ██████████ never took me outside the building, and for two, I was not used to my guards' "new" faces. I tried to act casually but my shaking gave me away.

"What's wrong with you," ██████████ asked.

"I am very nervous. I am not used to this environment."

"But I meant it for your good," █████ said. ███████████ was a very official person; if █████ interrogates you, she does it officially, and if █████ eats with you, █████ does it as part of █████ job, and that was cool.† I was just waiting for the breakfast

---

* This could be one of MOS's guards, appearing unmasked for the first time.

† "She" appears unredacted; this might be the businesslike female interrogator introduced at the beginning of the chapter.

to be done so I could go back to my cell, because ████████ had brought me the movie *King Henry V* by Shakespeare.

"████████, may I watch the movie more than once?" I asked. "I am afraid I am not going to understand it right away."

"Yes, you can watch it as many times as you wish."

When ████████████████ brought the TV ████████ briefed the guards to let me watch a movie only once, and then the party is over. "You're allowed to watch your movie only once, but as far as we're concerned you can watch it as many times as you wish, as long as you don't tell your interrogator about it. We really don't care," ████████████ told me later.

"No, if ████████ said so, I am going to stick with it. I am not gonna cheat," I told him. I really didn't want to mess with a comfort item I had just gotten, so I chose to treat everything carefully. But I did ask for one thing.

"████████, can I keep my water bottle in my cell, and drink whenever I choose?" I was just tired of the lack of sleep; as soon as I closed my eyes, the heavy metal door opened and I had to drink another bottle of water. I knew ████████████ was not the right person to ask to take the initiative; ████████████ had literally been following the orders of ████████████████. But to my surprise, ████████████ came the next day and briefed the guards that the water bottle now belonged in my cell. You cannot imagine how happy I was to be able to decide the time and the amount of water I could drink. People who never have been in such a situation cannot really appreciate the freedom of drinking water whenever they want, however much they want.

Then, in July 2004, I found a copy of The Holy Koran in my box of laundry. When I saw the Holy Koran beneath the clothes I felt bad, thinking I had to steal it in order to save it. But I took the Koran to my cell, and nobody ever asked me why I did so. Nor did I bring it up on my own. I had been forbidden all kinds of religious rituals, so I figured a copy of the Koran in my cell would not have made my interrogators too happy. More than that, lately the religious issue had become very delicate. The Muslim chaplain of GTMO was arrested and another Muslim soldier was charged with treason—oh, yes, *treason*.* Many Arabic and religious books were banned, and books teaching the English language were also banned. I sort of understood religious books being banned. "But why English learning books?" I asked ███████████.

"Because Detainees pick up the language quickly and understand the guards."

"That's so communist, ███████████" I said. To this date I have never received any Islamic books, though I keep asking for them; all I can get are novels and animal books. ███████
███████████ my prayers started to be tolerated. I had been gauging the tolerance toward the practice of my religion; every once in a while I put the tolerance of the ███████████ to the test, and they kept stopping me from praying. So I would pray secretly. But on this day at the very end of July 2004, I performed my prayer under the surveillance of some new guards

---

* Three Guantánamo-based personnel who were practicing Muslims were arrested in September 2003 and accused of carrying classified information out of the prison. MOS may be referring here specifically to army chaplain Captain James Yee, who was charged with five offenses including sedition and espionage, and Senior Airman Ahmad al-Halabi, an Arabic-language translator who was charged with thirty-two counts ranging from espionage and aiding the enemy to delivering unauthorized food, including the dessert baklava, to detainees. The sedition and spying cases collapsed. All charges against Yee were eventually dropped, and he received an honorable discharge; al-Halabi pled guilty to four counts, including lying to investigators and disobeying orders, and received a "bad conduct" discharge. See, e.g., http://usatoday30.usatoday.com/news/nation/2004-05-16 -yee-cover_x.htm; and http://usatoday30.usatoday.com/news/washington /2004-09-23-gitmo-airman_x.htm.

and nobody made a comment. A new era in my detention had emerged.

██████████████████████ turned the leadership of the team over to a ████████████████████████████, I don't know his real name. Many people in the ███████████ tried to make me think ████████████████████ was still in charge, in order to maintain the fear factor; in fact, ████████████████ was sent to Iraq ████████████████. ████████████████ came back from there once in ████████████ ██████ and paid me a visit, assuring me he was still in charge.*

"You see, I have a lot of work to do in D.C. and overseas. You might not see me as often as you used to. But you know what makes me happy, and what makes me mad," he said.

"I sure do!" ████████████████ fixed some differences I had with the new team in my favor, and he gave me a desert camouflage hat as a souvenir. I still have the hat. I never saw him again after that session.

Finally, in September 2004, the ICRC was allowed to visit after a long fight with the government. It was very odd to the ICRC that I had all of sudden disappeared from the camp, as if the earth had swallowed me. All attempts by ICRC representatives to see me or just to know where I was were thoroughly flushed down the tube.

The ICRC had been very worried about my situation, but they couldn't come to me when I needed them the most. I cannot blame them; they certainly tried. In GTMO, the ████████████████ is integrally responsible for both detainees' happiness and their agony, in order to have total control

---

* This might be referring to the Special Projects Team chief, "Captain Collins." In April 2004, General Miller left Guantánamo to assume command of prison and interrogation operations in Iraq; it appears from this passage that the chief of MOS's Special Projects Team was also reassigned to Iraq.

over the detainees. 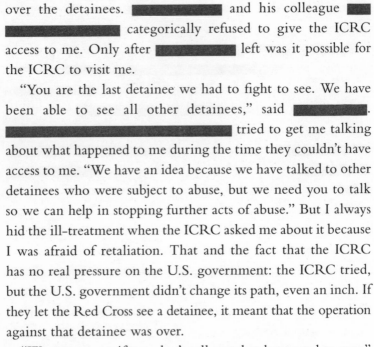 and his colleague ▆▆▆
▆▆▆▆▆▆▆▆▆▆▆▆ categorically refused to give the ICRC
access to me. Only after ▆▆▆▆▆▆▆▆ left was it possible for
the ICRC to visit me.

"You are the last detainee we had to fight to see. We have
been able to see all other detainees," said ▆▆▆▆▆▆▆.
▆▆▆▆▆▆▆▆▆▆▆▆▆▆▆▆▆▆▆ tried to get me talking
about what happened to me during the time they couldn't have
access to me. "We have an idea because we have talked to other
detainees who were subject to abuse, but we need you to talk
so we can help in stopping further acts of abuse." But I always
hid the ill-treatment when the ICRC asked me about it because
I was afraid of retaliation. That and the fact that the ICRC
has no real pressure on the U.S. government: the ICRC tried,
but the U.S. government didn't change its path, even an inch. If
they let the Red Cross see a detainee, it meant that the operation
against that detainee was over.

"We cannot act if you don't tell us what happened to you,"
they would urge me.

"I am sorry! I am only interested in sending and receiving
mail, and I am grateful that you're helping me to do so."
▆▆▆▆▆▆ brought a very high level ICRC ▆▆▆▆▆▆
from Switzerland who has been working on my case; ▆▆▆▆▆
tried to get me talking, but to no avail.

"We understand your worries. All we're worried about is
your well-being, and we respect your decision."

Although sessions with the ICRC are supposedly private, I
was interrogated about the conversations I had during that first
session, and I truthfully told the interrogators what we had said.
Later on I told the ICRC about this practice, and after that
nobody asked me what happened in our sessions. We detainees
knew that the meetings with ICRC were monitored; some

detainees had been confronted with statements they made to the ICRC and there was no way for the ███████████████ to know them unless the meeting was monitored. Many detainees refused to talk to the ICRC, and suspected them to be interrogators disguised in ICRC clothes. I even know some interrogators who presented themselves as private journalists. But to me that was very naïve: for a detainee to mistake an interrogator for a journalist he would have to be an idiot, and there are better methods to get an idiot talking. Such mischievous practices led to tensions between detainees and the ICRC. Some ICRC people were even cursed and spit on.

Around this same time, I was asked to talk to a real journalist. ████████████████████ time had been a hard time for everybody; he was a very violent person, and he decidedly hurt the already damaged image of the U.S. government.* Now many people in the government were trying to polish the reputation it had earned from its mischief toward detainees. "You know many people are lying about this place and claiming that detainees get tortured. We'd like you to talk to a moderate journalist from *The Wall Street Journal* and refute the wrong things we're suspected of."

"Well, I got tortured, and I am going to tell the journalist the truth, the naked truth, without exaggeration or understatement. I'm not polishing anybody's reputation," I said. After that the interview was completely canceled, which was good because I didn't want to talk to anybody anyway.

Gradually I was introduced to the "secret" new boss. I don't exactly know why the team kept him secret from me and tried to make me believe the ████████████████████ was still in charge, but most likely they thought that I would be less cooperative

---

* Possibly referring to General Miller's era, which encompassed his "special interrogation."

when somebody other than ▇▇▇▇▇▇▇ took over. But they were wrong: I was interested more than anybody in the Intel community in bringing my case into the light. ▇▇▇▇▇▇▇ had been counseled to work on my case from behind the scenes, which he did for a certain time, and then he came and introduced himself. I don't know his real name, but he introduced himself as a ▇▇▇▇▇ is ▇▇▇▇▇▇▇▇▇▇▇▇▇▇ ▇▇▇▇▇▇▇▇▇▇▇▇▇▇▇▇▇▇▇▇▇▇▇▇▇▇▇▇▇▇▇ ▇▇▇▇▇▇▇▇▇▇▇▇▇▇▇▇▇▇▇▇▇▇▇▇▇▇▇▇▇▇▇ ▇▇▇▇▇▇▇▇▇▇▇▇▇▇▇▇▇▇▇▇▇▇▇▇▇▇▇▇▇▇▇ rather humble. He tried everything in the realm of his power to make my life in custody as easy as possible.

I asked him to end my segregation and let me see other detainees, and he successfully organized several meetings between me and ▇▇▇▇▇▇▇▇▇▇▇▇▇▇▇▇▇▇▇▇▇▇, mainly to eat together and play chess. ▇▇▇▇▇▇▇ was not my first choice, but it was not up to me who I could meet, and in any case, I was just dying to see some other detainee I could relate to.

In early summer ▇▇▇▇ they moved ▇▇▇▇▇▇▇▇ next to my hut, and we were allowed to see each other during recreation.* ▇▇▇▇▇▇▇▇▇▇▇ is on the older side, about

---

* Press reports have identified a detainee who became neighbors with MOS as Tariq al-Sawah. A 2010 *Washington Post* article indicated that MOS and al-Sawah occupied "a little fenced-in compound at the military prison, where they live a life of relative privilege—gardening, writing and painting." In a 2013 interview with *Slate*, Col. Morris Davis, who served as chief prosecutor of the Guantánamo military commissions in 2005 and 2006, described meetings with both MOS and Sawah in the summer of 2006. "They're in a unique environment: They're inside the detention perimeter, there's a big fence around the facility, and then they're inside what they call the wire, which is another layer within that, so it's a manpower-intensive effort to deal with two guys," he said. Davis suggested in that interview that this living arrangement has remained unchanged. See http://

████████████████ old. ███████████████ did not seem to have passed detention's shock sanely; He suffered from paranoia, amnesia, depression, and other mental problems. Some interrogators claimed that he was playing a game, but to me he was completely out of his mind. I really didn't know what to believe, but I didn't care too much; I was dying to have company, and he was sort of company.

There is a drawback to detainees being together, though, especially if you know the detainee only from the camp: We detainees tend to be skeptical about each other. But I was very relaxed in that regard because I really didn't have anything to hide.

"Did they tell you to gather Intels from me?" he asked me once. I wasn't shocked, because I assumed the same about him. "████████, relax and just assume that I am only here to spy on you. Just keep your mouth shut and don't speak about anything you're not comfortable speaking about," I told him.

"You have no secrets?" he wondered.

"No, I don't, and I allow you to provide anything you may learn about me," I said.

I do remember the first day in August when ███████ surged through the door smiling and greeted me, "Salamu Alaikum."

"Waalaikum As-Salam! Tetkallami Arabi?" I answered her greeting, asking if ███ spoke Arabic.*

---

www.washingtonpost.com/wp-dyn/content/article/2010/03/24/AR2010 032403135_pf.html; and http://www.slate.com/articles/news_and_politics /foreigners/2013/04/mohamedou_ould_slahi_s_guant_namo_memoirs _an_interview_with_colonel_morris.html.

* The "her" appears unredacted. This section seems to introduce, and center on, a new female lead interrogator. See footnote on p. 362, citing records indicating that MOS had a female interrogator in late 2004.

"I don't." In fact ▮▮▮▮▮ had already used all the Arabic ▮▮▮ knew, namely the Greeting, Peace be upon you. ▮▮▮▮▮ and I started to talk as if we had known each other for years. ▮▮▮▮▮▮▮ studied Biology and joined ▮▮▮▮▮▮▮ recently as an enlisted person, most likely to pay her college tuition. Many Americans do; college education in the U.S. is sinfully high.

"I am going to help you start your garden," ▮▮▮▮▮ said. A long time before, I had asked the interrogators to get me some seeds in order to experiment around, and maybe succeed in growing something in the aggressive soil of GTMO. "I have experience in gardening," ▮▮▮ continued. And indeed ▮▮▮ seemed to have experience: ▮▮▮ helped me to grow sunflowers, basil, sage, parsley, cilantro, and things of that nature. But as helpful as ▮▮▮ was, I kept giving ▮▮▮ a hard time about one single bad experience ▮▮▮ made me do.

"I have a problem with crickets that keep destroying my garden," I complained.

"Take some soap and put it in water and keep spraying it lightly on the plants every day," ▮▮▮▮▮ suggested. And I blindly followed ▮▮▮ advice. However, I noticed that my plants were growing unhappy and sort of sick. So I decided to spray only the half of the plants with the diluted soap and watch the results. It didn't take long to see the soap was responsible for the bad effects, and so I completely stopped the story of soap.

After that I kept telling ▮▮▮▮▮, "I know what you studied: You studied how to kill plants with diluted soap!"

"Shut up! You just didn't do it right."

"Whatever."

▮▮▮▮▮▮▮ had introduced ▮▮▮▮▮ to me, and

from then on ▓▓▓ took my case in hand entirely. For some reason the ▓▓▓▓▓▓▓▓▓▓▓ thought that I would disrespect ▓▓▓, and were skeptical as to whether ▓▓▓ was the right choice. But they had no reason to worry: ▓▓▓▓▓▓ treated me as if I were ▓▓▓ brother, and I as if ▓▓▓ were my sister. Of course some might say that all that interrogators' stuff is a trick to lure detainees to provide them information; they can be friendly, sociable, humane, generous, and sensitive but still they are evil and ungenuine about everything. I mean, there is a good reason to doubt the integrity of interrogators, if only due to the nature of the interrogators' job. The ultimate goal of an interrogator is to get Intel from his target, the nastier the better. But interrogators are human beings, with feelings and emotions; I have been uninterruptedly interrogated since January 2000, and I have seen all kinds of interrogators, good, bad, and in between. Besides, here in GTMO Bay everything is different. In GTMO, the U.S. government assigns a team of interrogators who stick with you almost on a daily basis for some time, after which they leave and get replaced with a new team, in a never ending routine. So whether you like it or not, you have to live with your interrogators and try to make the best out of your life. Furthermore, I deal with everybody according to what he shows me, and not what he could be hiding. With this motto I approach everybody, including my interrogators.

Since I have not had a formal education in the English language, I needed and still do a lot of help honing my language skills. ▓▓▓▓▓▓▓ worked hard on that, especially on my pronunciation and spelling. When it comes to spelling, English is a terrible language: I don't know any other language that writes *Colonel* and pronounces it *Kernel*. Even natives of the language have a tremendous problem with the inconsistency of the sounds and the corresponding letter combinations.

On top of that, prepositions in English don't make any sense; you just have to memorize them. I remember I kept saying "I am afraid from...," and ▮▮▮▮▮▮ jumping and correcting me: "afraid *of.*" I am sure I was driving ▮▮▮ crazy. My problem is that I had been picking the language from the "wrong" people—namely, U.S. Forces recruits who speak grammatically incorrectly. So I needed somebody to take away the incorrect language from me and replace it with the correct one. Maybe you *can* teach an old dog new tricks, and that is exactly what ▮▮▮▮▮▮ duly tried to do with me. I think ▮▮▮ was successful, even though I gave ▮▮▮ a hard time sometimes. ▮▮▮ once forgot that ▮▮▮ was around me and said something like, "Amana use the bathroom," and I went, "Oh, is 'Amana' one of the words I missed?"

"Don't even go there!" ▮▮▮ would say.

▮▮▮▮▮▮ taught me the way Americans speak English. "But British people say so and so," I would say.

"You're not British," ▮▮▮▮▮ would say.

"I am just saying that there are different ways to pronounce it," I would answer. But ▮▮▮ failed to give me the Grammar Rules to follow, which is the only way I can really learn. Being a native speaker, ▮▮▮▮▮ has a feel for the language, which I don't. Besides ▮▮▮ mother-tongue, ▮▮▮▮▮ also spoke Russian and proposed to teach me; I was eager but ▮▮▮▮▮ didn't have enough time, and with time I lost the passion. A person as lazy as me won't learn a new language unless he has to. ▮▮▮▮ was dying to learn Arabic but ▮▮▮ didn't have time for that either. ▮▮▮ job kept ▮▮▮ busy day and night.

By this time, my health situation was way better than in Jordan, but I was still underweight, vulnerable, and sick most of the time, and as days went by, my situation decidedly worsened. Sometimes when the escorting team led me past the wall mirror I would get terrorized when I saw my face. It was a very pitiful sight. Although the diet kept getting better and better in the camp, I couldn't profit from it.

"Why don't you eat?" the guards always asked.

"I am not hungry," I used to reply. Then one day my interrogator ███████ just happened to witness one time when I got my lunch served.

"May I check your meal?"

"Yeah, sure."

"What the hell do they serve you? That is garbage!" said ███████.

"No, it's okay. I don't like speaking about food," I said. And I really don't.

"Look it may be OK for you, but it's not OK by my standards. We've got to change your diet," ███ said. And nothing short of a miracle, ███████ managed in a relatively short time to organize an adequate diet, which decidedly improved my health situation.

███████ also turned out to be a religious person when measured at American standards. I was very excited to have somebody I could learn from.

"███████, can you get me a Bible?"

"I'll see if I can," ███ said, and indeed, ███████ brought me ███ own Bible, a Special Edition.

"According to your religion, what is the way to heaven?" I asked ███████.

"You take Christ as your Savior, and believe that he died for your sins."

"I do believe Christ was one of the greatest prophets, but I don't believe that he died for my sins. It doesn't make sense to

me. I should save my tail on my own, by doing the right things,"
I replied.

"That is not enough to be saved."

"So where am I going after death?" I wondered.

"According to my religion, you go to hell." I laughed wholeheartedly. I told ███████████, "That is very sad. I pray every day
and ask God for forgiveness. Honestly, I worship God much
more than you do. As a matter of fact, as you see, I am not very
successful in this worldly life, so my only hope is in the
afterlife."

███████████ was both angry and ashamed—angry because I
laughed at ████ statement, and ashamed because ████ couldn't
find a way to save me. "I am not gonna lie to you: that's what
my religion says," ████ said.

"No, I really don't have any problem with that. You can cook
your soup as you please. I am not angry that you sent me to
hell."

"What about the Islamic belief? Do I go to heaven?"

"That's a completely different story. In Islam, in order to go
to heaven, you have to accept Mohamed, the natural successor
of Christ, and be a good Muslim. And since you reject Mohamed
you don't go to Heaven," I honestly answered.

███████████ was relieved because I also sent ████ to hell. "So,
let's both of us go to Hell and meet over there!" ███████████
said.

"I'm not willing to go to Hell. Although I am an admitted
sinner, I ask God for forgiveness." Whenever we had time, we
discussed religion and took out the Bible and the Koran to show
each other what the Books say.

"Would you marry a Muslim?"

"Never," ████ replied.

I smiled. "I personally wouldn't have a problem marrying a

Christian woman as long as she doesn't have anything against my religion."

"Are you trying to convert me?" ▆▆▆▆▆▆ asked emotionally.

"Yes, I am."

"I will never, never, never be a Muslim."

I laughed. "What are you so offended about? You're sort of trying to convert me, and I don't feel offended, since that's what you believe in."

I continued. "Would you marry a Catholic, ▆▆▆▆▆▆?"

"Yes, I would."

"But I don't understand. It says in the Bible that you cannot marry after a divorce. So you are a potential sinner." ▆▆▆▆▆▆ was completely offended when I showed ▆▆▆ the verses in the Bible.

"Don't even go there, and if you don't mind, let's change the topic." I was shocked, and smiled a dry smile.

"Oh, OK! I'm sorry about talking about that." We stopped discussing religion for the day and took a break for the next few days, and then we resumed the dialogue.

"▆▆▆▆▆▆, I really don't understand the Trinity doctrine. The more I look into it, the more I get confused."

"We have the Father, the Son, and the Holy Spirit, three things that represent the Being God."

"Hold on! Break it down for me. God is the father of Christ, isn't he?"

"Yes!"

"Biological Father?" I asked.

"No."

"Then why do you call him Father? I mean if you're saying that God is our father in the sense that he takes care of us, I have no problem with that," I commented.

"Yes, that's correct," ▇▇▇ said.

"So there is no point in calling Jesus 'the Son of God.'"

"But he said so in the Bible," ▇▇▇▇▇▇ said.

"But ▇▇▇▇▇▇, I don't believe in the 100 percent accuracy of the Bible."

"Anyway, Jesus is God," ▇▇▇ said.

"Oh, is Jesus God, or Son of God?"

"Both!"

"You don't make any sense, ▇▇▇▇▇▇▇, do you?"

"Look, I really don't understand the Trinity. I have to research and ask an expert."

"Fair enough," I said. "But how can you believe in something you don't understand?" I continued.

"I understand but I cannot explain it," ▇▇▇▇▇▇▇ replied.

"Let's move on and hit another topic." I suggested. "According to your religion I seem to be doomed anyway. But what about the bushmen in Africa who never got the chance to know Jesus Christ?" I asked.

"They are not saved."

"But what did they do wrong?"

"I don't agree that they should suffer, but that's what my religion says."

"Fair enough."

"But how about Islam?" ▇▇▇▇▇▇ asked.

"In the Koran it says that God doesn't punish unless he sends a messenger to teach the people."

▇▇▇▇▇▇▇▇▇▇▇▇▇▇▇▇▇▇▇▇▇▇▇▇▇▇▇▇▇▇▇▇

▇▇▇▇▇▇ was one of those guys who you like the first time you meet.* ▇▇▇▇▇▇▇▇▇▇▇▇▇▇▇▇▇▇▇▇▇▇▇

▇▇▇▇▇▇▇▇▇▇▇▇▇▇▇▇▇▇▇▇▇▇▇▇▇▇▇▇▇▇▇▇

---

* It appears that the interrogator enlists a colleague to help with the theological discussion.

▐▉▊▉▉▉▉▉▉▉▉▉▉▉▉▉▉▉▉▉▉▉▉▉▉▉▉▉▉▉

▐▉▊▉▉▉▉▉▉▉▉▉▉▉▉▉▉▉▉▉▉▉▉▉▉▉▉▉▉▉

▐▉▊▉▉▉▉▉▉▉▉▉▉▉▉▉▉▉▉▉▉▉▉▉▉▉▉▉▉▉

██████████████ He is more of a lover than a hater. ██████████████████████ are good friends, and he was fighting for the betterment of our condition.

████████████ introduced him to me as a friend and someone to help ████████ my thirst for information about Christianity. Although I enjoyed getting to know ██████████████, he didn't help me understand the Trinity. He confused me even more, and my lot with him was no better: he, too, sent me to hell. ████████████████ ended up arguing with ██████████ because they had some difference in their beliefs, although both were Protestant. I realized that they could not help me understand, and so I dismissed the topic for good, and we started to talk about other issues.

It's very funny how false the picture is that western people have about Arabs: savage, violent, insensitive, and cold-hearted. I can tell you with confidence is that Arabs are peaceful, sensitive, civilized, and big lovers, among other qualities.

"██████████, you guys claim that we are violent, but if you listen to the Arabic music or read Arabic poetry, it is all about love. On the other hand, American music is about violence and hatred, for the most part." During my time with ████████████, many poems went across the table. I haven't kept any copies; ██████ has all the poems. ██████ also gave me a small Divan. ██████ is very surrealistic, and I am terrible when it comes to surrealism. I hardly understood any of her poems.

One of my poems went

▐▉▊▉▉▉▉▉▉▉▉▉▉▉▉▉▉▉▉▉▉▉▉▉▉▉▉▉▉▉

▐▉▊▉▉▉▉▉▉▉▉▉▉▉▉▉▉▉▉▉▉▉▉▉▉▉▉▉▉▉

▐▉▊▉▉▉▉▉▉▉▉▉▉▉▉▉▉▉▉▉▉▉▉▉▉▉▉▉▉▉

▬▬
▬▬
▬▬

—by Salahi, GTMO

All this time I kept refusing to talk about the way I had been treated, which ███████████ understood and respected. I didn't want to talk, first, because I was afraid of retaliation, and second, because I was skeptical about the readiness of the government to deal with things appropriately, and third, because the Islamic religion suggests that it is better to bring your complaints to God rather than disclosing them to human beings. But ███████████ kept patiently trying to persuade me; furthermore, ███████████ explained to me that ████ must report any misbehavior by ████ colleagues to ████ superiors.

After thoroughly contemplating the options, I decided to talk to ███████████. When ████ heard my account, ███████

brought ██████████████████████████ who interrogated me about the issue after having sent the guards away. ██████████████████████ prudently wanted to avoid any possible leak and spread of the story. I have no idea what happened after that, but I think there is sort of an internal DOD investigation, because I was asked some questions about my story in a later time.*

"You are a very courageous guy!" ████████████ used to tell me in relation with my story.

"I don't think so! I just enjoy peace. But I certainly know that people who torture helpless detainees are cowards." ██████

██
██
██
██
██
██

---

* The Schmidt-Furlow report records that on December 11, 2004, "after months of cooperation with interrogators," "the subject of the second special interrogation notified his interrogator that he had been 'subject to torture' by past interrogators during the months of July to October 2003." A footnote elaborates: "He reported these allegations to an interrogator. The interrogator was a member of the interrogation team at the time of the report. The interrogator reported the allegations to her supervisor. Shortly after being advised of the alleged abuse, the supervisor interviewed the subject of the second special interrogation, with the interrogator present, regarding the allegations. Based on this interview, and notes taken by the interrogator, the supervisor prepared an 11 Dec 04 MFR addressed to JTF-GTMO JIG and ICE. The supervisor forwarded his MFT to the JTF-GTMO JIG. The JIG then forwarded the complaint to the JAG for processing IAW normal GTMO procedures for investigating allegations of abuse. The JAG by email on 22 Dec 04 tasked the JDOG, the JIG, and the JMG with a review of the complaint summarized in the Dec 04 MFR and directed them to provide any relevant information. The internal GTMO investigation was never completed." Schmidt-Furlow, 22.

██████████████████████████████████████

██████████████████████████████████████

███████████████████████████

Not long after that, ██████████ took a leave for three weeks. "I'm going to Montreal with a ██████████ friend of mine. Tell me about Montreal." I provided █████ with everything I remembered about Montreal, which wasn't much.

When ██████████ came back, █████ hardly changed out of █████ travel clothes before █████ came to see me; █████ was genuinely excited to see me again, and so was I. ██████████ said that █████ enjoyed █████ time in Canada and that everything was alright, but █████ was probably happier to be in GTMO. ██████████ was tired from the trip, so █████ stayed only for short time to check on me, and off █████ went.

I went back to my cell and wrote ██████████ the following letter.

"Hi, ██████████ I know you were in Canada ██████████

██████████████████████████████████████

██████████████████████████████████████

██████████████████████████████████████

██████████████████████████████████████

██████████████████████████ I haven't asked you about it, but I don't appreciate somebody lying to me and taking me for an idiot. I really don't know what you were thinking when you made up that story to mislead me. I don't deserve to be treated like that. I chose to write and not talk to you, just to give you the opportunity to think about everything, instead of making you come up with inaccurate answers. Furthermore, you don't have to give me any answer or comment. Just destroy this letter and consider it non-existent. Yours truly Salahi."

I read the letter to the guards before I handed the sealed envelope to ▇▇▇▇▇▇ and asked ▇▇▇ not to read it in my presence.

"Wha' the? How the hell do you know that ▇▇▇▇▇▇ was with ▇▇▇▇▇▇▇▇▇▇▇?" the guard on duty asked me.

"Something in my heart that never lies to me!"

"You don't make any sense. Besides, why the fuck should you care?"

"If you cannot tell whether ▇▇▇▇▇▇▇▇ had some intimacy with a man, you ain't no man," I said. "I don't care, but I don't appreciate when ▇▇▇▇▇▇ uses my manhood and plays games on me, especially in my situation. ▇▇▇▇▇ might think I am vulnerable but I am strong."

"You're right! That's fucked up."

▇▇▇▇▇ came the next day and confessed everything to me.

"I am sorry! I just figured we had a close relationship, and I thought it would hurt you ▇▇▇▇▇▇▇▇▇▇▇▇ ▇▇▇▇▇▇▇▇

"First I thank you very much for being forthcoming. I'm just confused! Do you think I'm looking forward ▇▇▇ ▇▇▇▇▇▇▇▇? I'm not! For Pete's sake, you are a Christian ▇▇▇▇▇▇ who is engaged in a war against my religion and my people! Besides, I am ▇▇▇▇▇▇▇▇ ▇▇▇▇▇▇ inside this prison."

▇▇▇▇▇ always tried after that to tell me that ▇▇▇ didn't think that ▇▇▇ would continue ▇▇▇▇▇▇▇▇ ▇▇▇▇▇. But I didn't make any comment about the issue. All I did was I handcrafted a bracelet and sent it to him as the ▇▇▇▇▇▇▇▇▇▇▇▇▇▇ who I liked and who had helped me in many issues.

*　　*　　*

"We are desperate to get information from you," said ▮▮▮▮ ▮▮▮▮▮▮▮▮▮▮▮▮▮▮▮▮ when he first met with me.

It was true: when I arrived in the camp in August 2002, the majority of detainees were refusing to cooperate with their interrogators.

"Look, I told you my story over and over a million times. Now either you send me to court or let me be," they were saying.

"But we have discrepancies in your story," the interrogators would say, as a gentle way of saying, "You're lying."

Like me, every detainee I know thought when he arrived in Cuba it would be a typical interrogation, and after interrogation he would be charged and sent to court, and the court would decide whether he is guilty or not. If he was found not guilty, or if the U.S. government pressed no charges, he would be sent home. It made sense to everybody: the interrogators told us this is how it would go, and we said, "Let's do it." But it turned out either the interrogators deliberately lied to encourage detainees to cooperate with them, or the government lied to the interrogators about the procedure as a tactic to coerce information from the detainees.

Weeks went by, months went by, and the interrogators' thirst for information didn't seem close to being satisfied. The more information a detainee provided, the more interrogators complicated the case and asked for more questions. All detainees had, at some point, one thing in common: they were tired of uninterrupted interrogation. As a newcomer, I first was part of a small minority that was still cooperating, but I soon joined the other group. "Just tell me why you arrested me, and I'll answer every question you have," I would say.

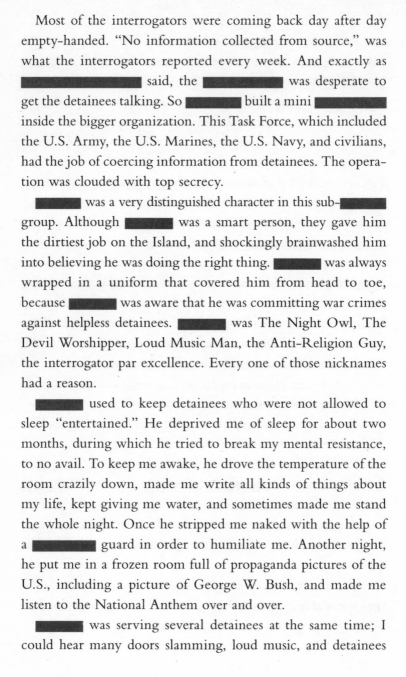

Most of the interrogators were coming back day after day empty-handed. "No information collected from source," was what the interrogators reported every week. And exactly as ███████████████████ said, the ██████████████ was desperate to get the detainees talking. So ██████████ built a mini ██████████████ inside the bigger organization. This Task Force, which included the U.S. Army, the U.S. Marines, the U.S. Navy, and civilians, had the job of coercing information from detainees. The operation was clouded with top secrecy.

██████████ was a very distinguished character in this sub-██████████ group. Although ██████████ was a smart person, they gave him the dirtiest job on the Island, and shockingly brainwashed him into believing he was doing the right thing. ██████████ was always wrapped in a uniform that covered him from head to toe, because ██████████ was aware that he was committing war crimes against helpless detainees. ██████████ was The Night Owl, The Devil Worshipper, Loud Music Man, the Anti-Religion Guy, the interrogator par excellence. Every one of those nicknames had a reason.

██████████ used to keep detainees who were not allowed to sleep "entertained." He deprived me of sleep for about two months, during which he tried to break my mental resistance, to no avail. To keep me awake, he drove the temperature of the room crazily down, made me write all kinds of things about my life, kept giving me water, and sometimes made me stand the whole night. Once he stripped me naked with the help of a ██████████ guard in order to humiliate me. Another night, he put me in a frozen room full of propaganda pictures of the U.S., including a picture of George W. Bush, and made me listen to the National Anthem over and over.

██████████ was serving several detainees at the same time; I could hear many doors slamming, loud music, and detainees coming and leaving, the sound of their heavy metal chains giving them away. ████████ used to put detainees in a dark room with pictures that were supposed to represent devils. He made detainees listen to the music of hatred and madness, and to the song "Let the Bodies hit the Floor" over and over for the whole night in the dark room. He was very open about his hatred toward Islam, and he categorically forbade any Islamic practices, including prayers and mumbling the Koran.

Even with all that, on around ████████████████ the special team realized that I was not going to cooperate with them as they wished, and so the next level of torture was approved. ██████████████████████ and another guy with a German shepherd pried open the door of the interrogation room where ██████████ and I were sitting. It was in ████████ Building. ██████████ and his colleague kept hitting me, mostly on my ribs and my face, and made me drink salt water for about three hours before giving me over to an Arabic team with an Egyptian and a Jordanian interrogator. Those interrogators continued to beat me while covering me in ice cubes, one, to torture me, and two, to make the new, fresh bruises disappear.

Then, after about three hours, Mr. X and his friend took me back and threw me in my present cell.* "I told you not to fuck with me, Motherfucker!" was the last thing I heard from ████████. Later on, ██████████████████████ told me that ████████ wanted to visit me for friendly purposes, but I didn't show any eagerness, and so the visit was cancelled. I am still in that same cell, although I no longer have to pretend I don't know where I am.

They finally allowed doctors to see me around March 2004, and I was able to get psychological assistance for the first time

---

★ "Mr. X" appears here unredacted.

that April. Since then I have been taking the anti-depressant Paxil and Klonopin to help me sleep. The doctors also pre-scribed a multi-vitamin for a condition that was due to a lack of exposure to the sun. I also got some sessions with some psy-chologists who were assessing me; they really helped me, though I couldn't tell them the real reason for my sickness because I was afraid of retaliation.

"My job is to help your rehabilitation," one of my guards told me in the summer of 2004. The government realized that I was deeply injured and needed some real rehab. From the moment he started to work as my guard in July 2004, ▮▮▮▮▮▮▮▮ related to me right; in fact, he hardly talked to anybody beside me. He used to put his mattress right in front of my cell door, and we started to talk about all kinds of topics like old friends. We talked about history, culture, politics, religion, women, everything but current events. The guards were taught that I was a detainee who would try to outsmart them and learn cur-rent events from them, but the guards are my witnesses, I didn't try to outsmart anybody, nor was I interested in current events at the time because they only made me sick.

Before ▮▮▮▮▮▮▮▮ left he brought me a couple of souvenirs, and with ▮▮▮▮▮▮▮▮ and ▮▮▮▮▮▮▮▮ dedicated a copy of Steve Martin's *The Pleasure of My Company* to me.

▮▮▮▮▮▮▮▮ wrote, "Pill, over the past 10 months I have gotten to know you and we have become friends. I wish you good luck, and I am sure I will think of you often. Take good care of yourself. ▮▮▮▮▮▮▮▮"

▮▮▮▮▮▮▮▮ wrote, "Pillow, good luck with your situation. Just remember Allah always has a plan. I hope you think of us as more than just guards. I think we all became friends.

▮▮▮▮▮▮▮▮ wrote, "19 April 2005. Pillow: For the past 10 months I have done my damnedest to maintain a

Detainee–Guard relationship. At times I have failed: it is almost impossible not to like a character like yourself. Keep your faith. I'm sure it will guide you in the right direction."

I used to debate faith with one of the new guards. ▓▓▓▓▓▓▓▓ was raised as a conservative Catholic. He was not really religious, but I could tell he was his family's boy. I kept trying to convince him that the existence of God is a logical necessity.

"I don't believe in anything unless I see it," he told me.

"After you've seen something, you don't need to believe it," I responded. "For instance, if I tell you I have a cold Pepsi in my fridge, either you believe it or you don't. But after seeing it, you know, and you don't need to believe me." Personally, I do have faith. And I picture him, and these other guards, as good friends if we would meet under different circumstances. May God guide them and help them make the right choices in life.

Crisis always brings out the best and worst in people — and in countries, too. Did the Leader of the Free World, the United States, really torture detainees? Or are stories of torture part of a conspiracy to present the U.S. in a horrible way, so the rest of the world will hate it?

I don't even know how to treat this subject. I have only written what I experienced, what I saw, and what I learned firsthand. I have tried not to exaggerate, nor to understate. I have tried to be as fair as possible, to the U.S. government, to my brothers, and to myself. I don't expect people who don't know me to believe me, but I expect them, at least, to give me the benefit of the doubt. And if Americans are willing to stand for what they believe in, I also expect public opinion to compel the U.S. government to open a torture and war crimes investigation. I am more than confident that I can prove every single thing I have written in this book if I am ever given the opportunity to call witnesses in a proper judicial procedure, and if military personnel are not given the advantage of straightening their lies and destroying evidence against them.

Human beings naturally hate to torture other human beings, and Americans are no different. Many of the soldiers were doing the job reluctantly, and were very happy when they were ordered to stop. Of course there are sick people everywhere in the world who enjoy seeing other people suffering, but generally human beings make use of torture when they get chaotic and confused. And Americans certainly got chaotic, vengeful, and confused, after the September 11, 2001 terrorist attacks.

At the direction of President Bush, the U.S. began a campaign against the Taliban government in Afghanistan. On September 18, 2001, a joint resolution of Congress authorized President Bush to use force against the "nations, organizations, or persons" that "planned, authorized, committed, or aided the terrorist attacks on September 11, 2001, or harbored such organizations or persons." Then the U.S. government started a secret operation aimed at kidnapping, detaining, torturing, or killing terrorist suspects, an operation that has no legal basis.

I was the victim of such an operation, though I had done no such thing and have never been part of any such crimes. On September 29, 2001, I got a call on my cellphone and was asked to turn myself in, and I immediately did, sure I would be cleared. Instead, Americans interrogated me in my home country, and then the U.S. reached a joint agreement with the Mauritanian government to send me to Jordan to squeeze the last bits of information out of me. I was incarcerated and interrogated under horrible conditions in Jordan for eight months, and then the Americans flew me to Bagram Air Base for two weeks of interrogation, and finally on to the Guantánamo Navy Base ████████████████████████████, where I still am today.

So has the American democracy passed the test it was subjected to with the 2001 terrorist attacks? I leave this judgment to the reader. As I am writing this, though, the United States and its people are still facing the dilemma of the Cuban detainees.

In the beginning, the U.S. government was happy with its secret operations, since it thought it had managed to gather all the evils of the world in GTMO, and had circumvented U.S. law and international treaties so that it could perform its revenge. But then it realized, after a lot of painful work, that it had gathered a bunch of non-combatants. Now the U.S. government is stuck with the problem, but it is not willing to be forthcoming and disclose the truth about the whole operation.

Everybody makes mistakes. I believe the U.S. government owes it to the American people to tell them the truth about what is happening in Guantánamo. So far, I have personally cost American taxpayers at least one million dollars, and the counter is ticking higher every day. The other detainees are costing more or less the same. Under these circumstances, Americans need and have the right to know what the hell is going on.

Many of my brothers here are losing their minds, especially the younger detainees, because of the conditions of detention. As I write these words, many brothers are hunger-striking and are determined to carry on, no matter what.* I am very worried about these brothers I am helplessly watching, who are practically dying and who are sure to suffer irreparable damage even

---

* MOS completed this manuscript in the fall of 2005; the last page is signed and dated September 28, 2005. One of the largest Guantánamo hunger strikes started in August 2005 and extended through the end of the year. See, e.g., http://www.nytimes.com/2005/09/18/politics/18gitmo.html?pagewanted=1&_r=0; and http://america.aljazeera.com/articles/multimedia/guantanamo-hungerstriketimeline.html.

if they eventually decide to eat. It is not the first time we have had a hunger strike; I personally participated in the hunger strike in September 2002, but the government did not seem to be impressed. And so the brothers keep striking, for the same old, and new, reasons. And there seems to be no solution in the air. The government expects the U.S. forces in GTMO to pull magic solutions out of their sleeves. But the U.S. forces in GTMO understand the situation here more than any bureaucrat in Washington, DC, and they know that the only solution is for the government to be forthcoming and release people.

What do the American people think? I am eager to know. I would like to believe the majority of Americans want to see Justice done, and they are not interested in financing the detention of innocent people. I know there is a small extremist minority that believes that everybody in this Cuban prison is evil, and that we are treated better than we deserve. But this opinion has no basis but ignorance. I am amazed that somebody can build such an incriminating opinion about people he or she doesn't even know.

Author's Note

In a recent conversation with one of his lawyers, Mohamedou said that he holds no grudge against any of the people he mentions in this book, that he appeals to them to read it and correct it if they think it contains any errors, and that he dreams to one day sit with all of them around a cup of tea, after having learned so much from one another.

~~UNCLASSIFIED~~   ~~PROTECTED~~

331

personality, very confident, knows what he is supped to do, and doesn't respect his less comptent superiors. Before █ left he ~~so~~ bought me a couple of souvenirs, and dedicated to me The Pleasure of My Company by Steve Martin, with █ and █ wrotes " PILL, over the past 10 months I have gotten to know you and we have become friends. I wish you good luck and I am sure I will think of you often. take good care of yourself. ███ ". ████ wrote: " Pillow, Good Luck with your situation. Just remember Allah always has a plan. I hope you think of us as more than just guards. I think we all became friends. ██ ". ████ wrote: " Pillow 19 APRIL, 2005 For the past 10 months I have done my damnest to Detainee Guard relationship. At time I have ~~failed~~. It is almost impossible not to like a charachter like yourself. Keep your ~~fevith~~ faith + I'm sure it will guide you in the right direction. ███ " That was not exactly a bad time. ②████

██████████████████████

Religions, Islam, Christianity, and Judaism as the Middle Eastern culture as well. He ~~found~~ found in me the ~~bi~~ right address as I did in him. We had been discussing all the time, without any prejudices or any taboos. We had been even hitting some tins, Racism in the U.S when the ~~other~~ his other black colleague █████ worked with him, █████ is proud on his █████ all he reads, watches is mostly █████ and that why █████ and I always started a friendly discussion with him. █████ suspected me of having some times, instigated the discussion, and

Editor's Acknowledgments

That we are able to read this book at all is thanks to the efforts of Mohamedou Ould Slahi's pro-bono lawyers, who fought for more than six years to have the manuscript cleared for public release. They did this quietly and respectfully, but also tenaciously, believing—and ultimately proving—that the truth is not incompatible with security. Time will only underscore what an accomplishment this has been, and how much readers everywhere owe a debt of gratitude to Nancy Hollander and Theresa M. Duncan, his lead attorneys; to their private co-counsel Linda Moreno, Sylvia Royce, and Jonathan Hafetz; and to their co-counsel Hina Shamsi, Brett Kaufman, Jonathan Manes, and Melissa Goodman of the National Security Project of the American Civil Liberties Union and Art Spitzer of the ACLU of the National Capital Area.

I owe my own profound thanks to Nancy Hollander and the rest of Mohamedou Ould Slahi's legal team, and above all to Mohamedou Ould Slahi himself, for offering me the opportunity to help bring these words to print. Every day I have spent reading, thinking about, and working with Mohamedou's manuscript has illuminated in some new way what a gift their trust and confidence has been.

Publishing material that remains subject to severe censorship restrictions is not for the faint of heart, and so I am especially grateful to all those who have championed the publication of Mohamedou's work: to Will Dobson and *Slate* for the chance to present excerpts from the manuscript and the space to put those excerpts in context; to Rachel Vogel, my literary agent, to Geoff Shandler, Michael Sand, and Allie Sommer at Little, Brown, and to Jamie Byng and Katy Follain at Canongate for their vision and patient navigation of a variety of publication challenges; and to everyone at Little, Brown/Hachette, Canongate, and all the foreign language publishers of *The Guantánamo Diary* for making it possible for this once-suppressed but irrepressible work to be read around the world.

Anyone who has written about what has happened in Guantánamo owes a debt to the ACLU's National Security Project, whose Freedom of Information Act litigation unearthed the trove of secret documents that stands as the stark historical record of the United States' abusive post-9/11 detention and interrogation practices. I am grateful for that record, without which the cross-referencing, corroboration, and annotation of Mohamedou's account would not have been possible, and even more grateful for the opportunities the ACLU has given me over the last five years to explore, absorb, and write about that indispensible record.

I am indebted to many who shared their time, insights, experiences, and ideas with me as I was working with this manuscript. I cannot mention them all, but I cannot fail to mention Hahdih Ould Slahi, for helping me understand Mohamedou's experience from his family's perspective, and Jameel Jaffer, Hina Shamsi, Lara Tobin, and Eli Davis Siems, for their constant support, thoughtful counsel, and careful readings of edited versions of this book.

Finally, I am forever indebted to Mohamedou Ould Slahi, for the courage to write his manuscript, for the integrity, wit, and humanity of his writing, and for the faith he has shown in all of us, the reading public, in committing his experiences to print. May he at least, and at last, receive the same honest judgment he has afforded us.

Notes to Introduction

1 Transcript, Administrative Review Board Hearing for Mohamedou Ould Slahi, December 15, 2005, 18. The ARB transcript is available at http://www.dod.mil/pubs/foi/operation_and_plans/Detainee/csrt_arb /ARB_Transcript_Set_8_20751-21016.pdf, 184–216.

EDITOR'S NOTE ON THE INTRODUCTION: None of Mohamedou Ould Slahi's attorneys holding security clearances has reviewed this introduction, contributed to it in any way, or confirmed or denied anything in it. Nor has anyone else with access to the unredacted manuscript reviewed this introduction, contributed to it in any way, or confirmed or denied anything in it.

2 Letter to attorney Sylvia Royce, November 9, 2006, http://online .wsj.com/public/resources/documents/couch-slahiletter-03312007.pdf.

3 Transcript, Combatant Status Review Tribunal Hearing for Mohamedou Ould Slahi, December 8, 2004, 7–8. The CSRT transcript is available at http://online.wsj.com/public/resources/documents/couch -slahihearing-03312007.pdf.

4 ARB transcript, 14, 18–19, 25–26.

5 ARB transcript, 26–27.

6 Department of Defense News Briefing, Secretary Rumsfeld and Gen. Myers, January 11, 2002, http://www.defense.gov/transcripts/transcript .aspx?transcriptid=2031.

7 Department of Defense Press Release, April 3, 2006, http://www .defense.gov/news/newsarticle.aspx?id=15573.

8 John Goetz, Marcel Rosenbach, Britta Sandberg, and Holger Stark, "From Germany to Guantanamo: The Career of Prisoner No. 760," *Der Spiegel*, October 9, 2008, http://www.spiegel.de/international/world/from -germany-to-guantanamo-the-career-of-prisoner-no-760-a-583193.html.

9 CSRT transcript, 3–4.

10 ARB transcript, 15–16.

11 Memorandum Order, *Mohammedou Ould Salahi v. Barack H. Obama*, No. 1:05-cv-00569-JR, 13–14. The Memorandum Order is available at https://www.aclu.org/files/assets/2010-4-9-Slahi-Order.pdf.

12 ARB transcript, 19.

13 Goetz et al., "From Germany to Guantanamo."

14 "Keep the Cell Door Shut: Appeal a Judge's Outrageous Ruling to Free 9/11 Thug," Editorial, *New York Daily News*, March 23, 2010, http://www .nydailynews.com/opinion/cell-door-shut-appeal-judge-outrageous-ruling -free-9-11-thug-article-1.172231.

15 Memorandum Order, 4.

16 The Reminiscences of V. Stuart Couch, March 1–2, 2012, Columbia Center for Oral History Collection (hereafter cited as CCOHC), 94, 117, http://www.columbia.edu/cu/libraries/inside/ccoh_assets/ccoh_10100507 _transcript.pdf.

17 CIA Office of the Inspector General, "Counterterrorism Detention and Interrogation Activities, September 2001–October 2003," May 7, 2004, 96. The CIA OIG report is available at http://media.luxmedia.com/aclu /IG_Report.pdf.

18 Bob Drogin, "No Leaders of Al Qaeda Found at Guantanamo," *Los Angeles Times*, August 18, 2002, http://articles.latimes.com/2002/aug/18 /nation/na-gitmo18.

19 ARB transcript, 23–24.

20 The National Commission on Terrorist Attacks upon the United States, *The 9/11 Commission Report* 165–166. The 9/11 Commission report is available at http://govinfo.library.unt.edu/911/report/911Report.pdf.

21 CCOHC interview with V. Stuart Couch, 90.

22 Memorandum Order, 19.

23 Jess Bravin, "The Conscience of the Colonel," *Wall Street Journal*, March 31, 2007, http://online.wsj.com/news/articles/SB117529704337355155.

24 U.S. Senate Committee on Armed Services, "Inquiry into the Treatment of Detainees in U.S. Custody," November 20, 2008, 140–41. The committee's report is available at http://www.armed-services.senate .gov/imo/media/doc/Detainee-Report-Final_April-22-2009.pdf.

25 Transcript of interview with Lt. Col. Stuart Couch for *Torturing Democracy*, http://www2.gwu.edu/~nsarchiv/torturingdemocracy/interviews /stuart_couch.html.

26 Bravin, "The Conscience of the Colonel."

27 CCOHC interview with V. Stuart Couch, 95.

28 Colonel Morris Davis, interview by Larry Siems, *Slate*, May 1, 2013, http://www.slate.com/articles/news_and_politics/foreigners/2013/04 /mohamedou_ould_slahi_s_guant_namo_memoirs_an_interview_with _colonel_morris.html.

29 Order, *Salahi v. Obama*, 625 F.3d 745, 746 (D.C. Cir. 2010). The decision is available at http://caselaw.findlaw.com/us-dc-circuit/1543844 .html.

30 Ibid., 750, 753.

372

responded the detainee in broken Arabic with his obvious Turkish accent. I right away knew the setup. This interrogation ~~was meant~~ for me in the first place. "Liar!" shouted ███ "I ain't lying" responded the guy in Arabic, although ███ kept speaking his loose English. "I don't care if you have a German or American passport you're going to tell me the truth!" said ███ Now, I knew that the ███ The setup fitted perfectly, and meant to terrorize me even more. Although I knew right away it was a setup but the scaring effect was not affected. "Hi ███ said ███ "Hi" I responded feeling his breath right in front of my face. I was so terrorized that I couldn't realize what he was saying. "~~Do you~~ so your name is ███ he concluded "No!" "But you responded when I called you ███ he argued. I didn't really realize that he had called me ███ but I found it idiot to tell him that I was so terrorized that I couldn't realize what name he call me "If you look at it we all are ███ I correctly answered. ███ means in Arabic God's servant. However, I knew ~~where Abu Ter~~ How ███ came up with the name of ███ The Story of the Name ███ : When I arrived in Montreal / Canada on 26 Nov 1999 my friend ███ introduced me to his roommate ███ with my ~~name~~ Civilian name. When I later on met with another ███ who happened to see a year before with me, he called me ███ and I responded b/ I found it impolite to correct him. Since then ███ called me ███